MAKE A Gliste

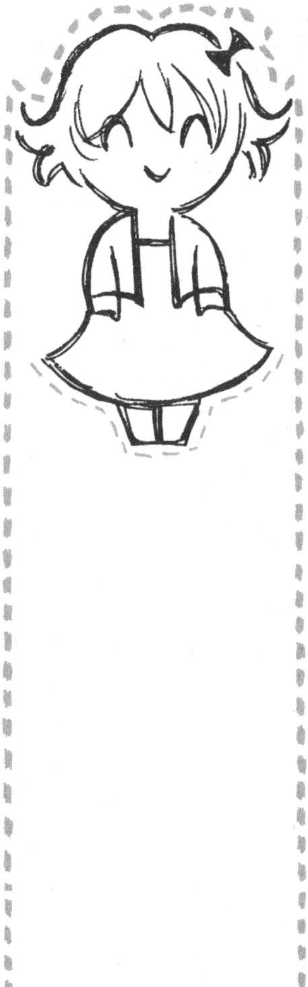

cut along dotted line

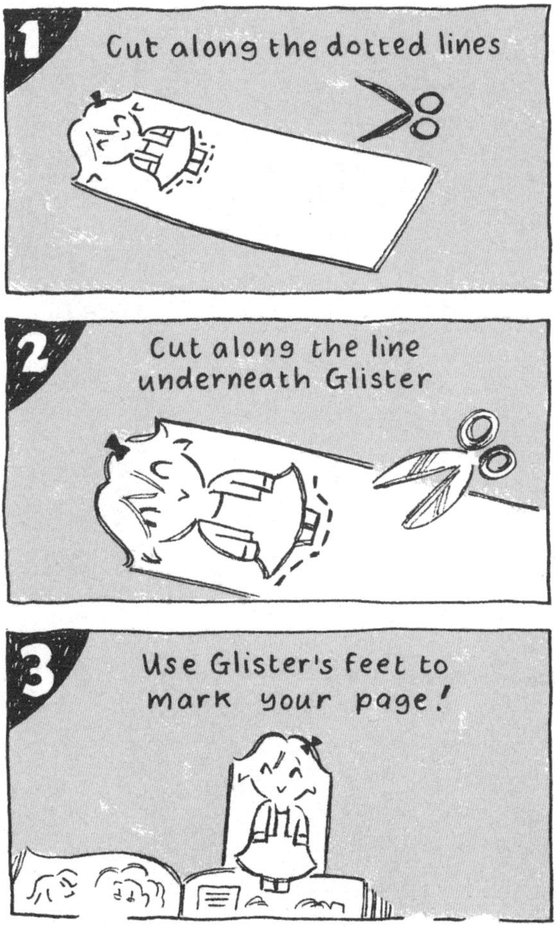
1
Cut along the dotted lines
2
Cut along the line underneath Glister
3
Use Glister's feet to mark your page!

Trace the bookmark design and follow the instructions!
Make sure there is an adult nearby to help you out!

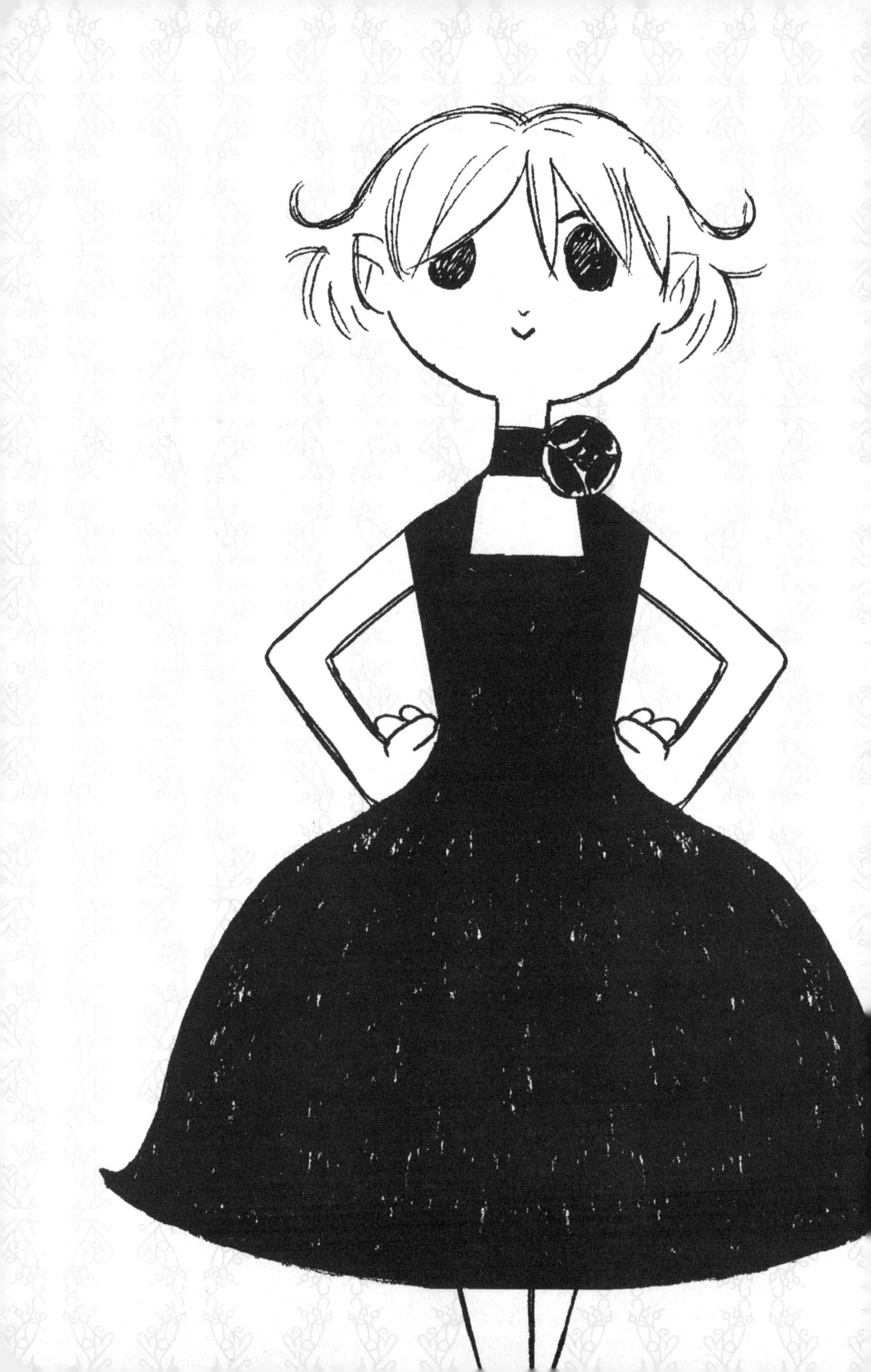

Written and illustrated by

ANDI WATSON

DARK HORSE BOOKS

President & Publisher
MIKE RICHARDSON

Collection Editor
SHANTEL LaROCQUE

Collection Assistant Editor
KATII O'BRIEN

Collection Designer
CINDY CACEREZ-SPRAGUE

Digital Art Technician
CHRISTINA McKENZIE

NEIL HANKERSON Executive Vice President **TOM WEDDLE** Chief Financial Officer **RANDY STRADLEY**
Vice President of Publishing **MATT PARKINSON** Vice President of Marketing **DAVID SCROGGY** Vice President
of Product Development **DALE LAFOUNTAIN** Vice President of Information Technology **CARA NIECE** Vice
President of Production and Scheduling **NICK McWHORTER** Vice President of Media Licensing **MARK
BERNARDI** Vice President of Book Trade and Digital Sales **KEN LIZZI** General Counsel **DAVE MARSHALL** Editor
in Chief **DAVEY ESTRADA** Editorial Director **SCOTT ALLIE** Executive Senior Editor **CHRIS WARNER** Senior Books
Editor **CARY GRAZZINI** Director of Specialty Projects **LIA RIBACCHI** Art Director **VANESSA TODD** Director of
Print Purchasing **MATT DRYER** Director of Digital Art and Prepress **SARAH ROBERTSON** Director of Product
Sales **MICHAEL GOMBOS** Director of International Publishing and Licensing

Published by Dark Horse Books
A division of Dark Horse Comics, Inc.
10956 SE Main Street
Milwaukie, OR 97222

DarkHorse.com
International Licensing: 503-905-2377

To find a comics shop in your area, call the Comic Shop Locator Service toll-free at (888) 266-4226.

First edition: July 2017
ISBN 978-1-50670-319-0

1 3 5 7 9 10 8 6 4 2
Printed in China

This book collects *Glister: The Haunted Teapot*, *Glister: The House Hunt*, *Glister: The Faerie Host*, and *Glister:
The Family Tree*, all previously published by Walker Books.

Library of Congress Cataloging in Publication data is on file.

TABLE OF CONTENTS

CC

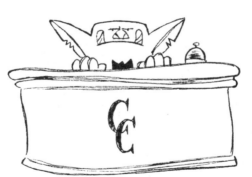

for
Philippa & Clara

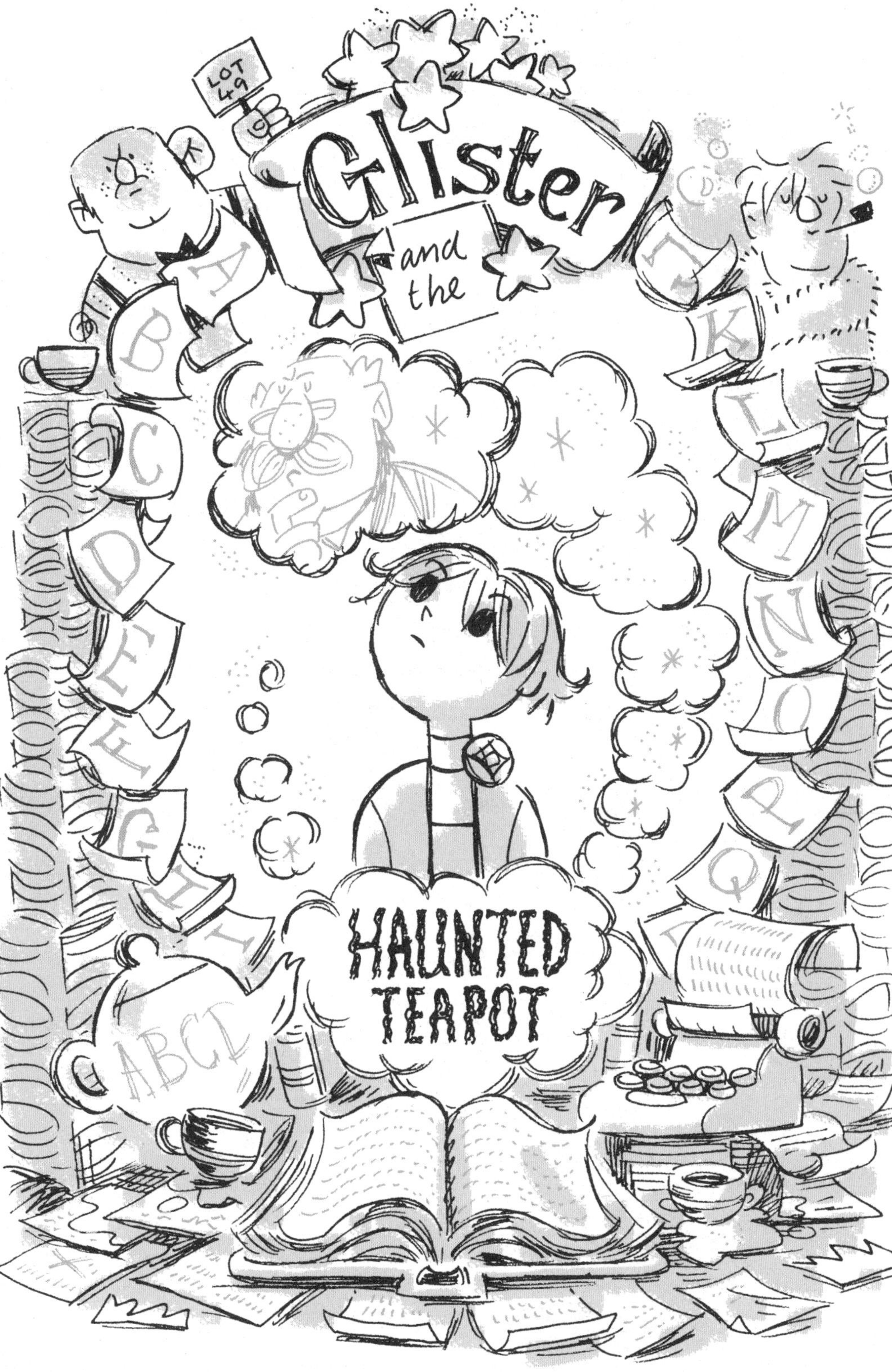
LOT 49
Glister
and the
HAUNTED
TEAPOT

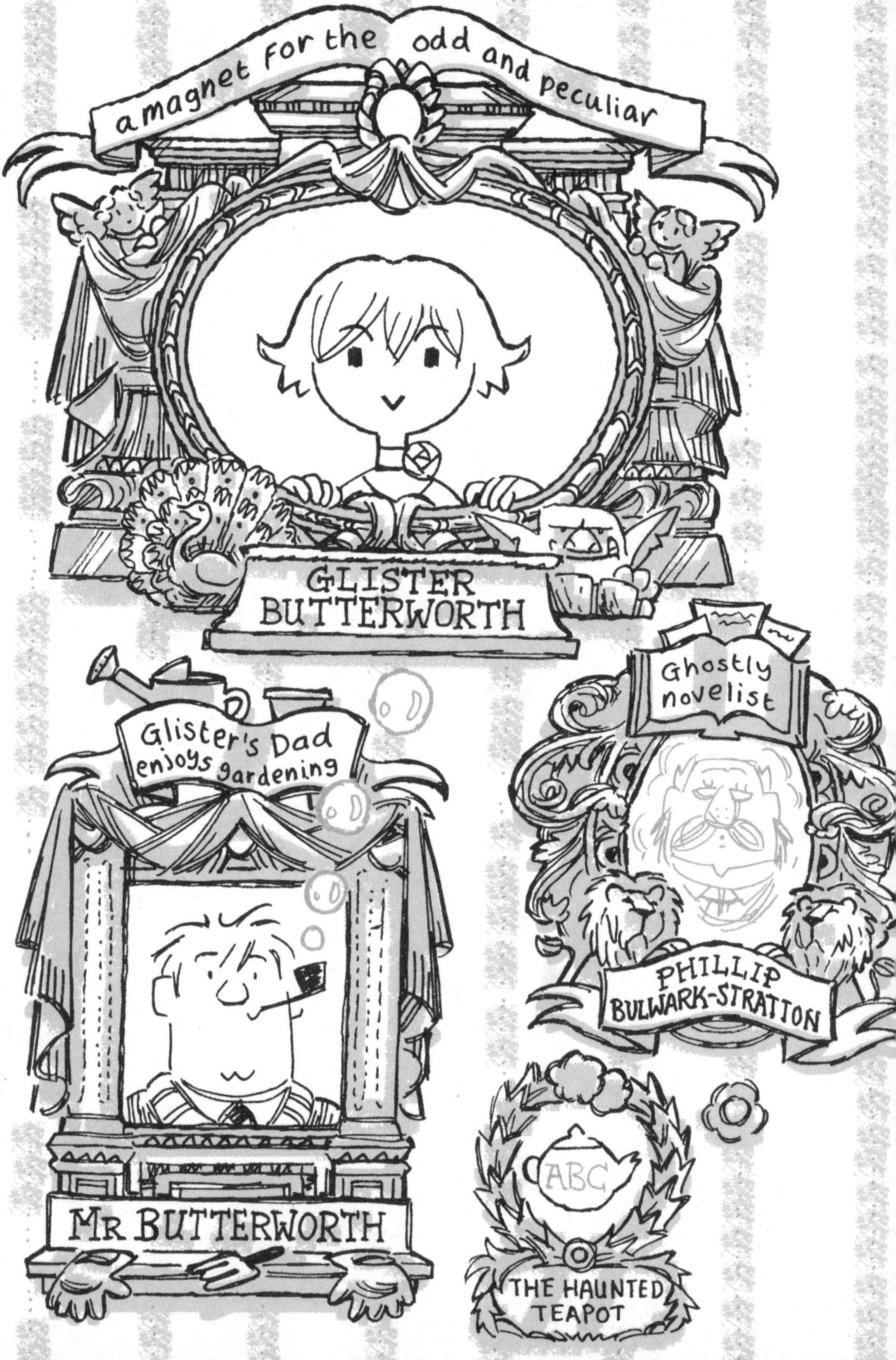
a magnet for the odd and peculiar
GLISTER BUTTERWORTH
Ghostly novelist
PHILLIP BULWARK-STRATTON
Glister's Dad enjoys gardening
MR BUTTERWORTH
ABC
THE HAUNTED TEAPOT

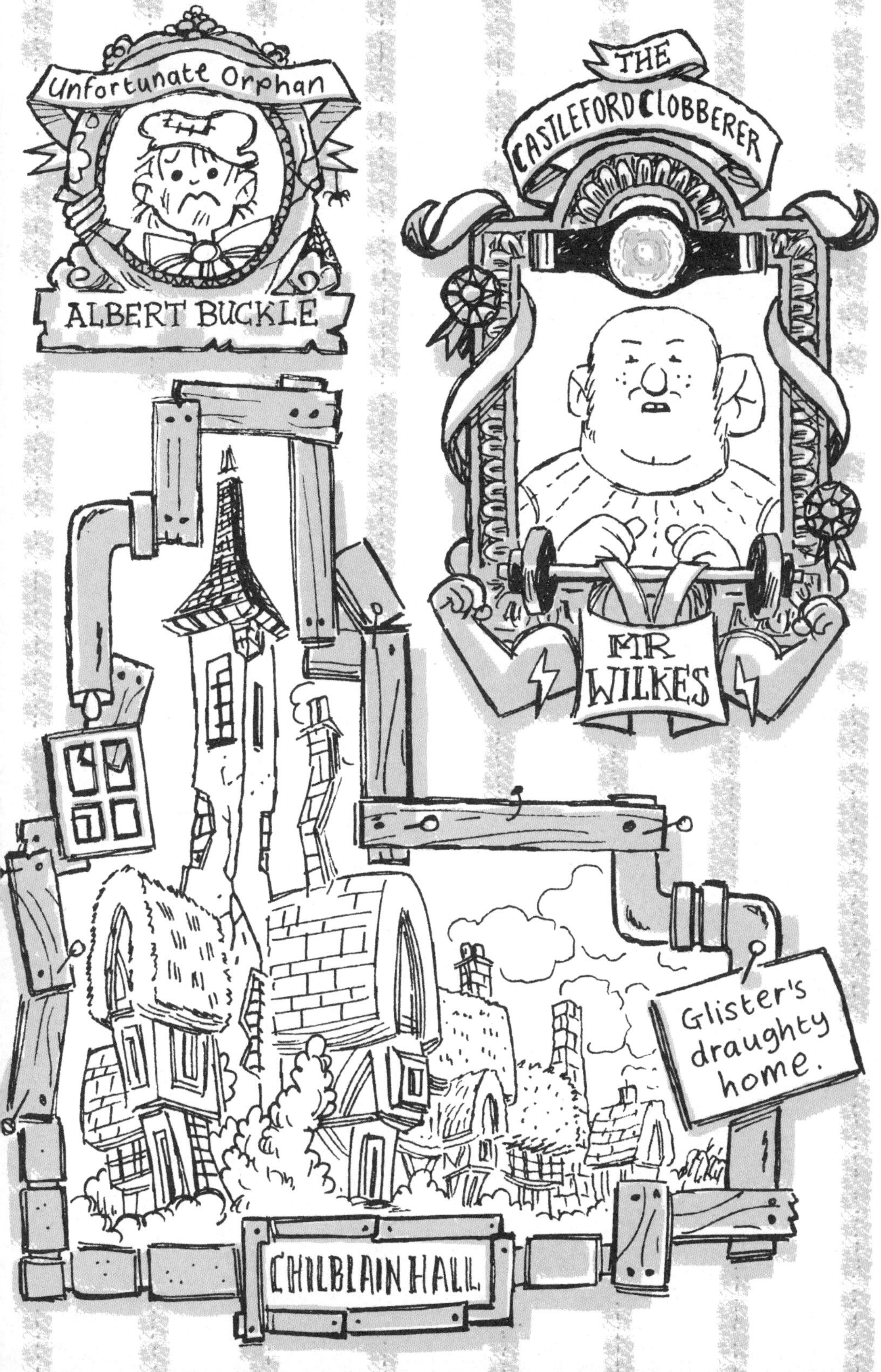
Unfortunate Orphan
ALBERT BUCKLE
THE
CASTLEFORD CLOBBERER
MR WILKES
Glister's draughty home.
CHILBLAIN HALL

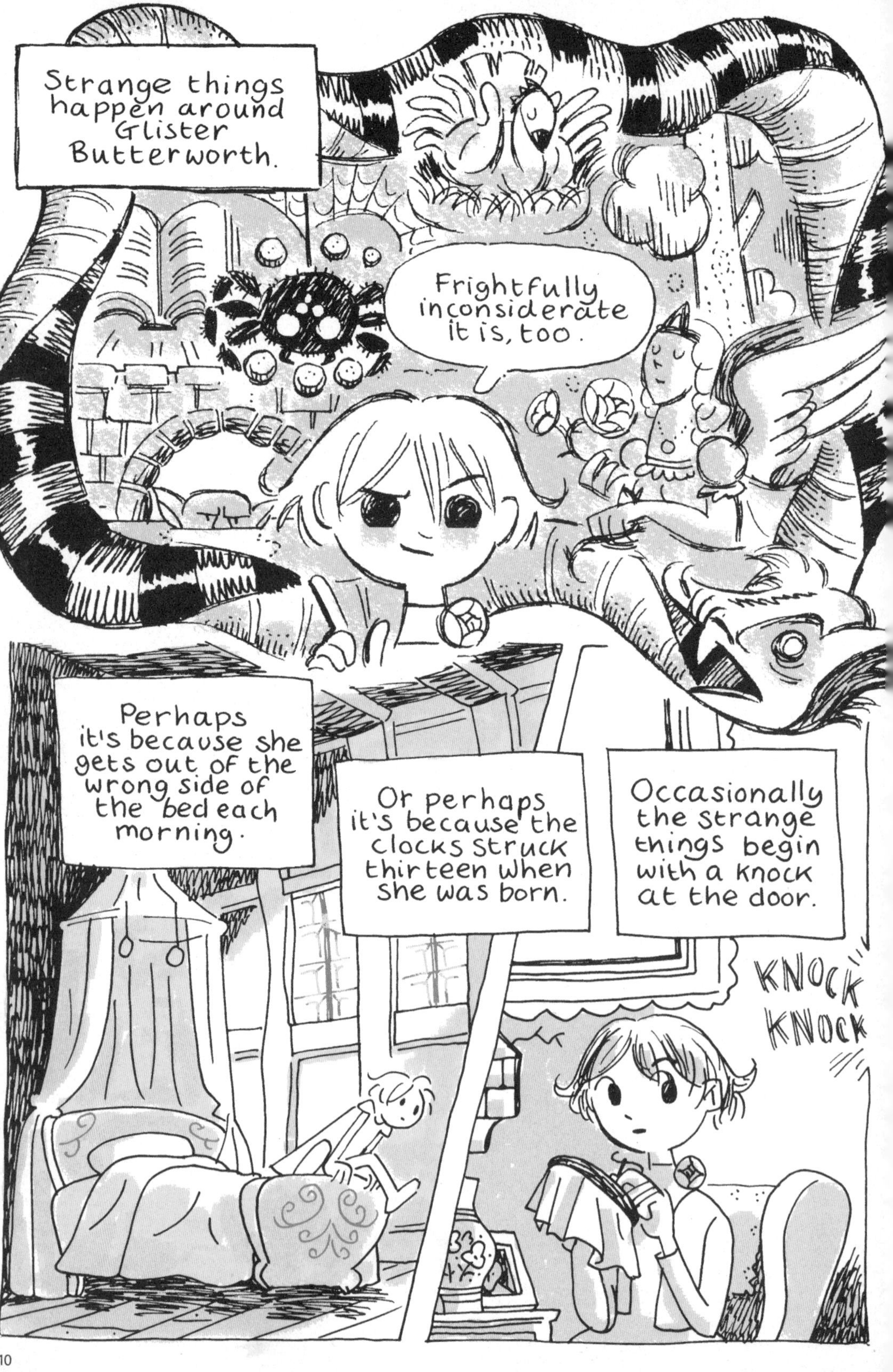
Strange things happen around Glister Butterworth.
Frightfully inconsiderate it is, too.
Perhaps it's because she gets out of the wrong side of the bed each morning.
Or perhaps it's because the clocks struck thirteen when she was born.
Occasionally the strange things begin with a knock at the door.
KNOCK KNOCK

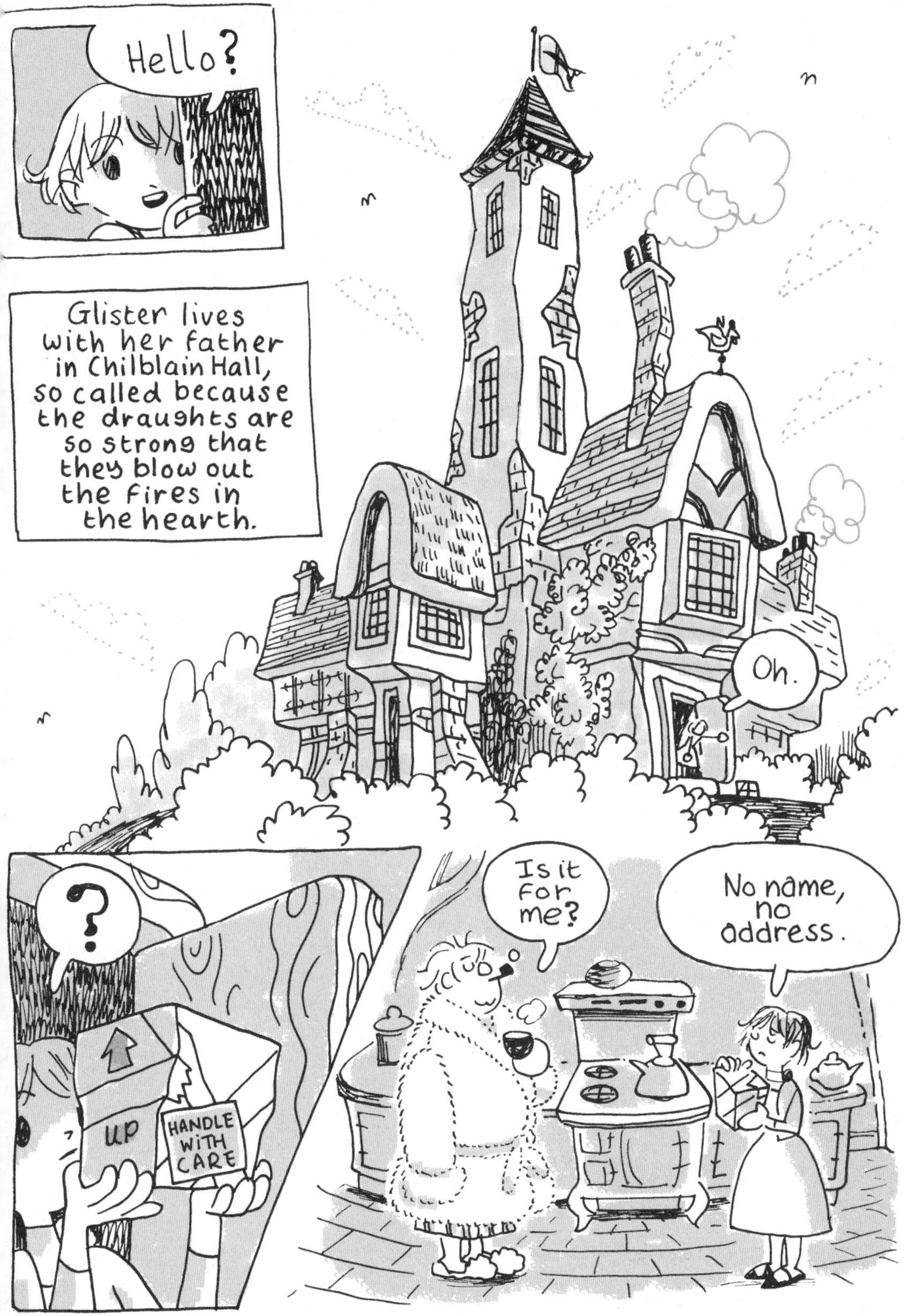
Hello?
Glister lives with her father in Chilblain Hall, so called because the draughts are so strong that they blow out the fires in the hearth.
Oh.
?
UP
HANDLE WITH CARE
Is it for me?
No name, no address.

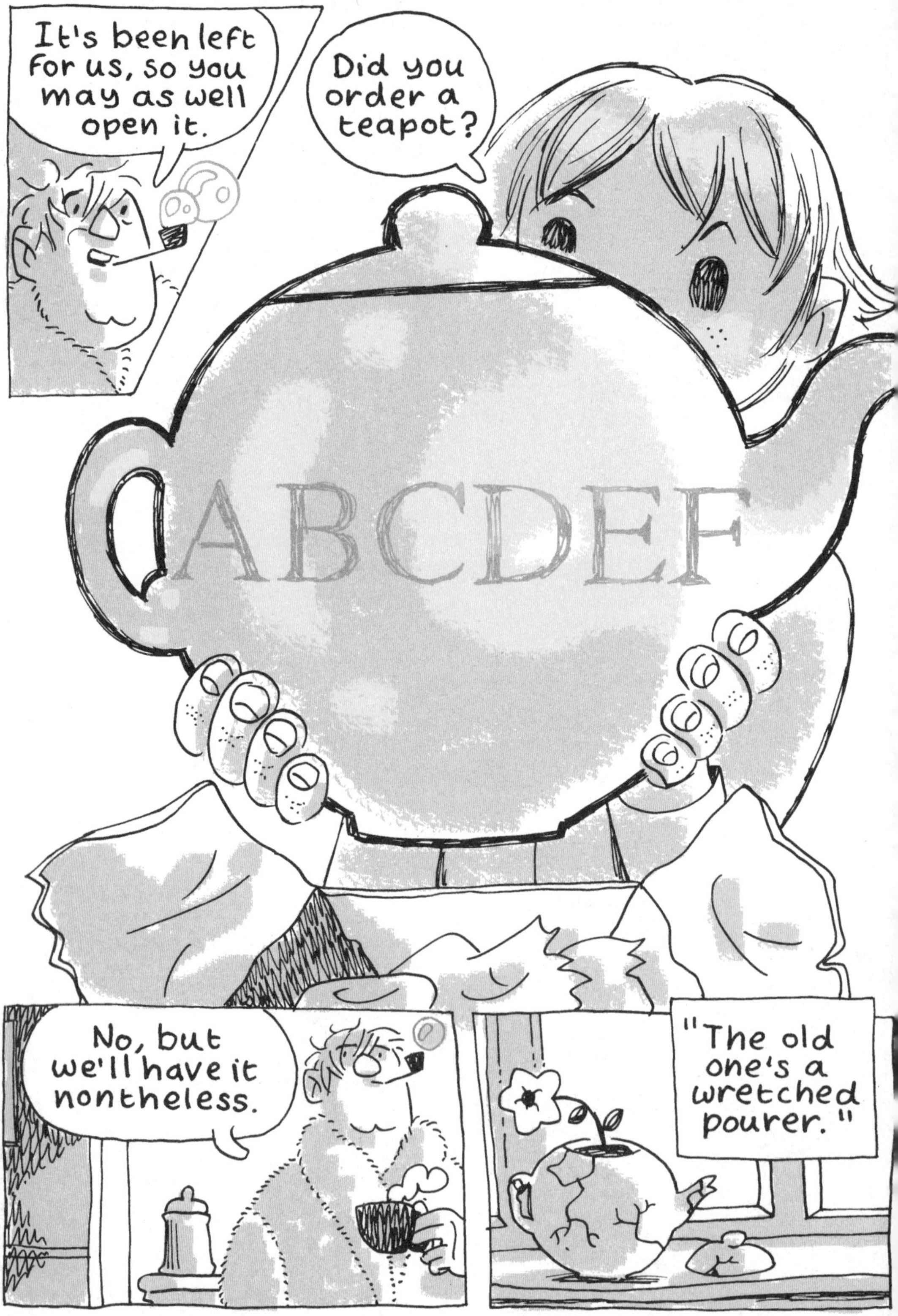
It's been left for us, so you may as well open it.
Did you order a teapot?
ABCDEF
No, but we'll have it nontheless.
"The old one's a wretched pourer."

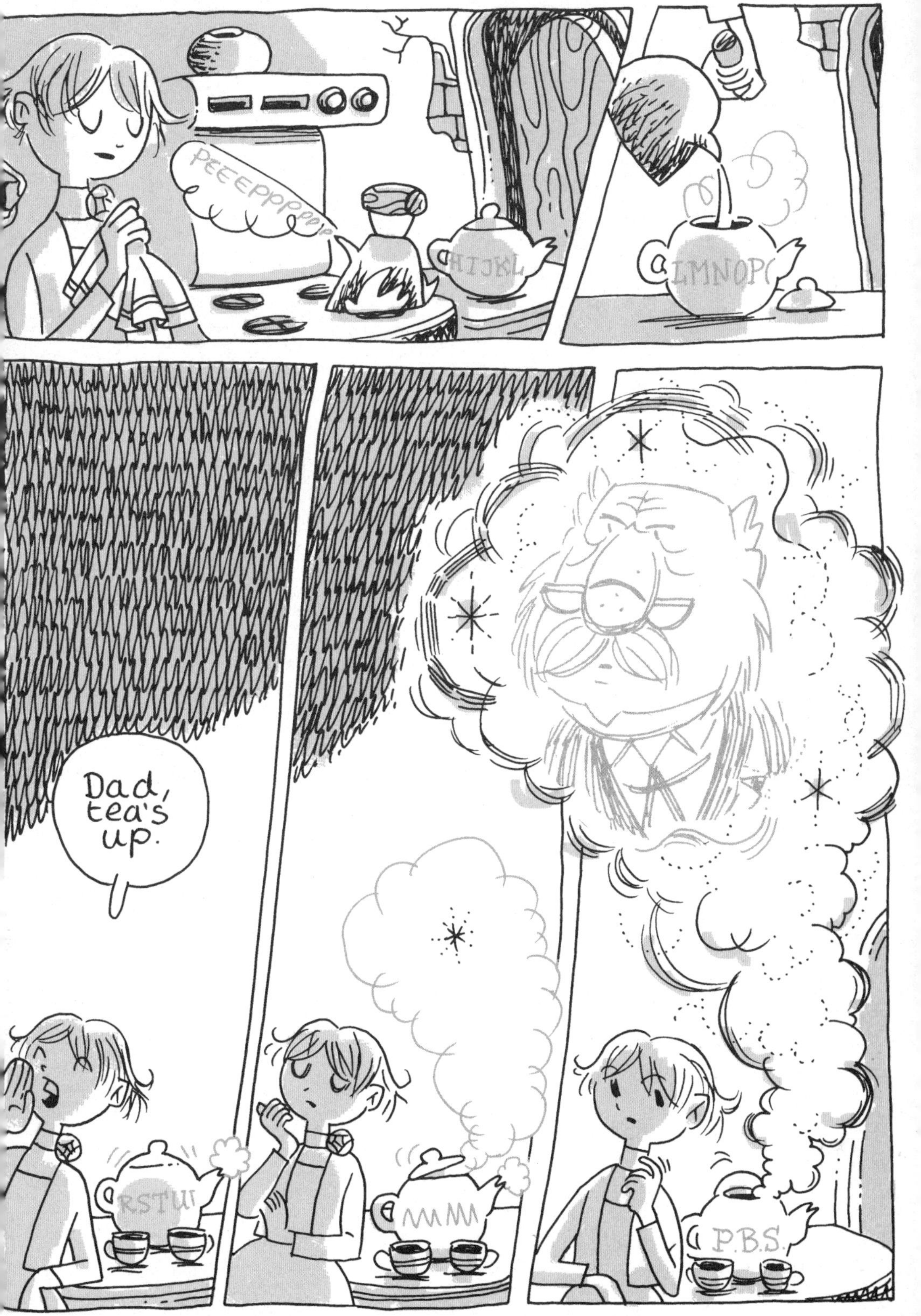
PEEEPPPPPPP
HIJKL
LMNOP
Dad, tea's up.
RSTU
MMM
P.B.S.

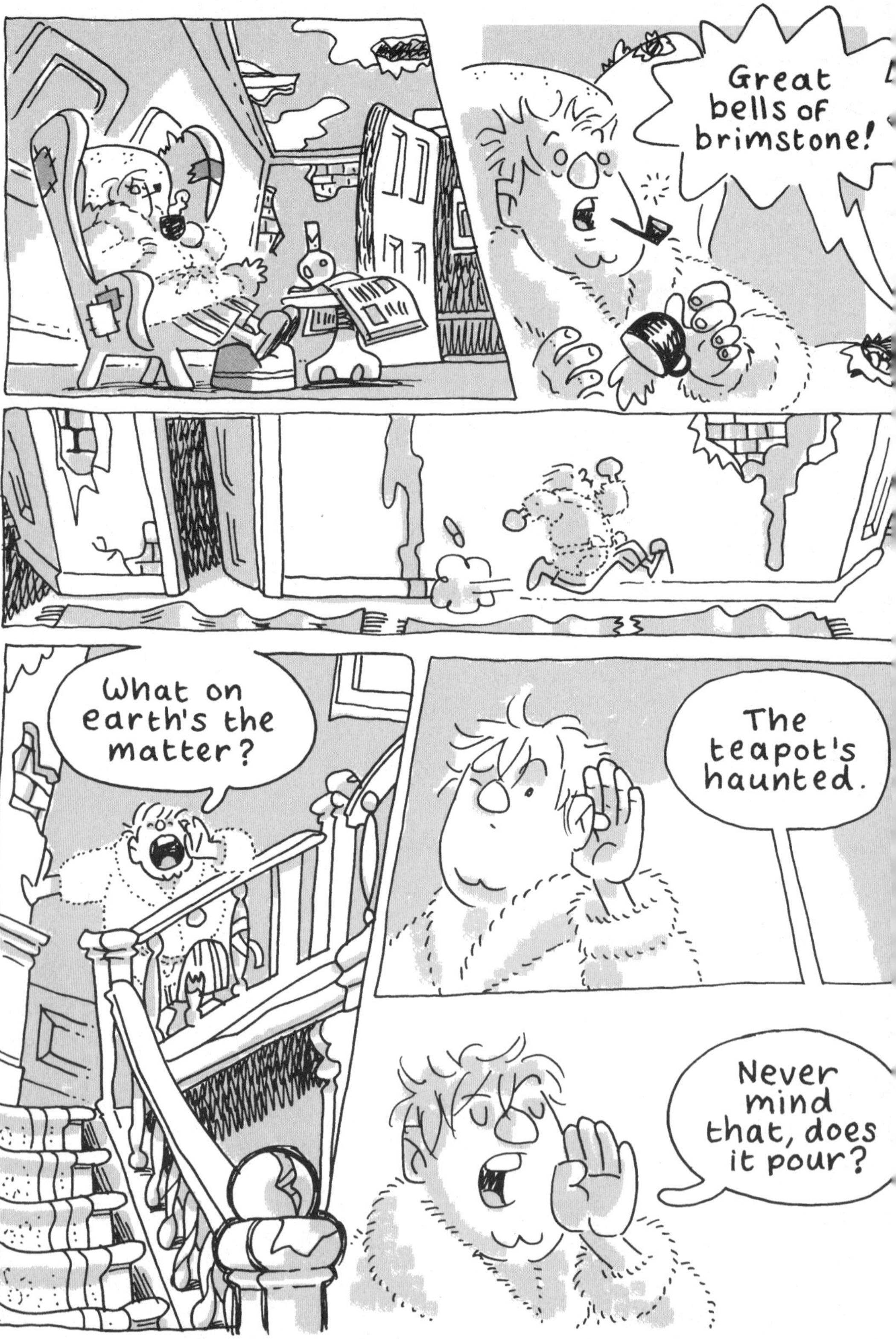
Great bells of brimstone!
What on earth's the matter?
The teapot's haunted.
Never mind that, does it pour?

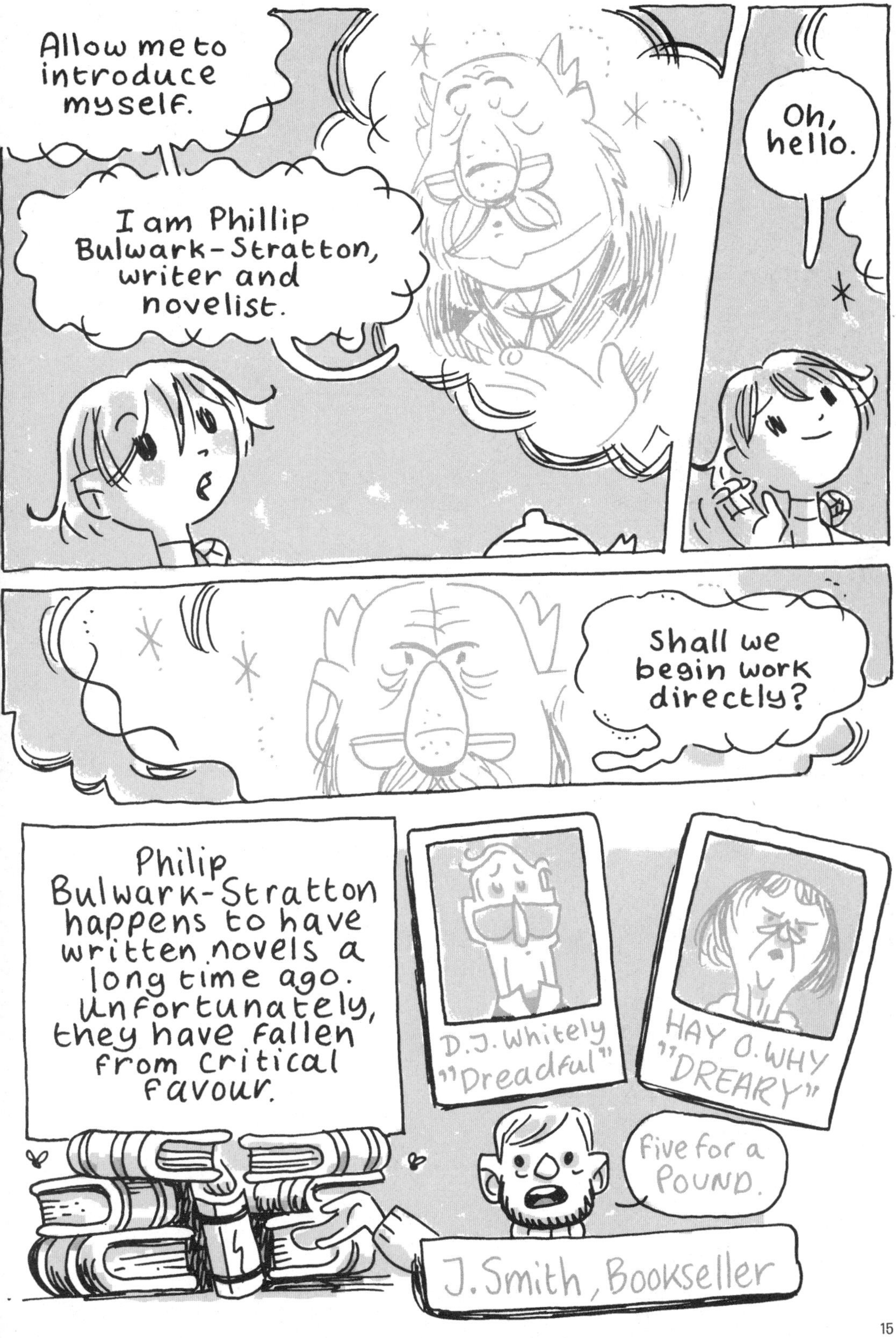
Allow me to introduce myself.
I am Phillip Bulwark-Stratton, writer and novelist.
Oh, hello.
Shall we begin work directly?
Philip Bulwark-Stratton happens to have written novels a long time ago. Unfortunately, they have fallen from critical favour.
D.J. Whitely "Dreadful"
HAY O. WHY "DREARY"
Five for a POUND.
J. Smith, Bookseller

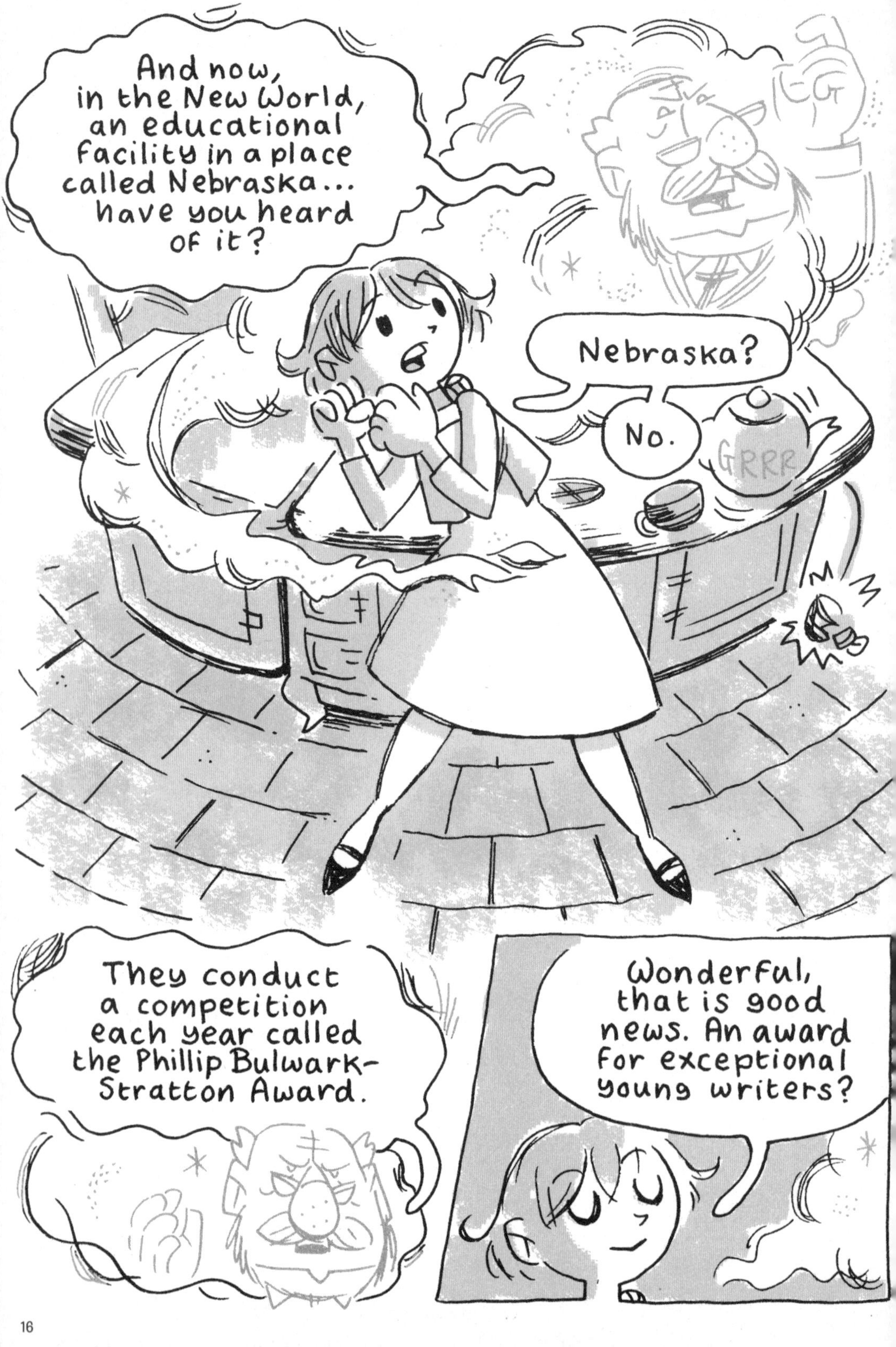
And now, in the New World, an educational facility in a place called Nebraska... have you heard of it?
Nebraska?
No.
GRRR
They conduct a competition each year called the Phillip Bulwark-Stratton Award.
Wonderful, that is good news. An award for exceptional young writers?

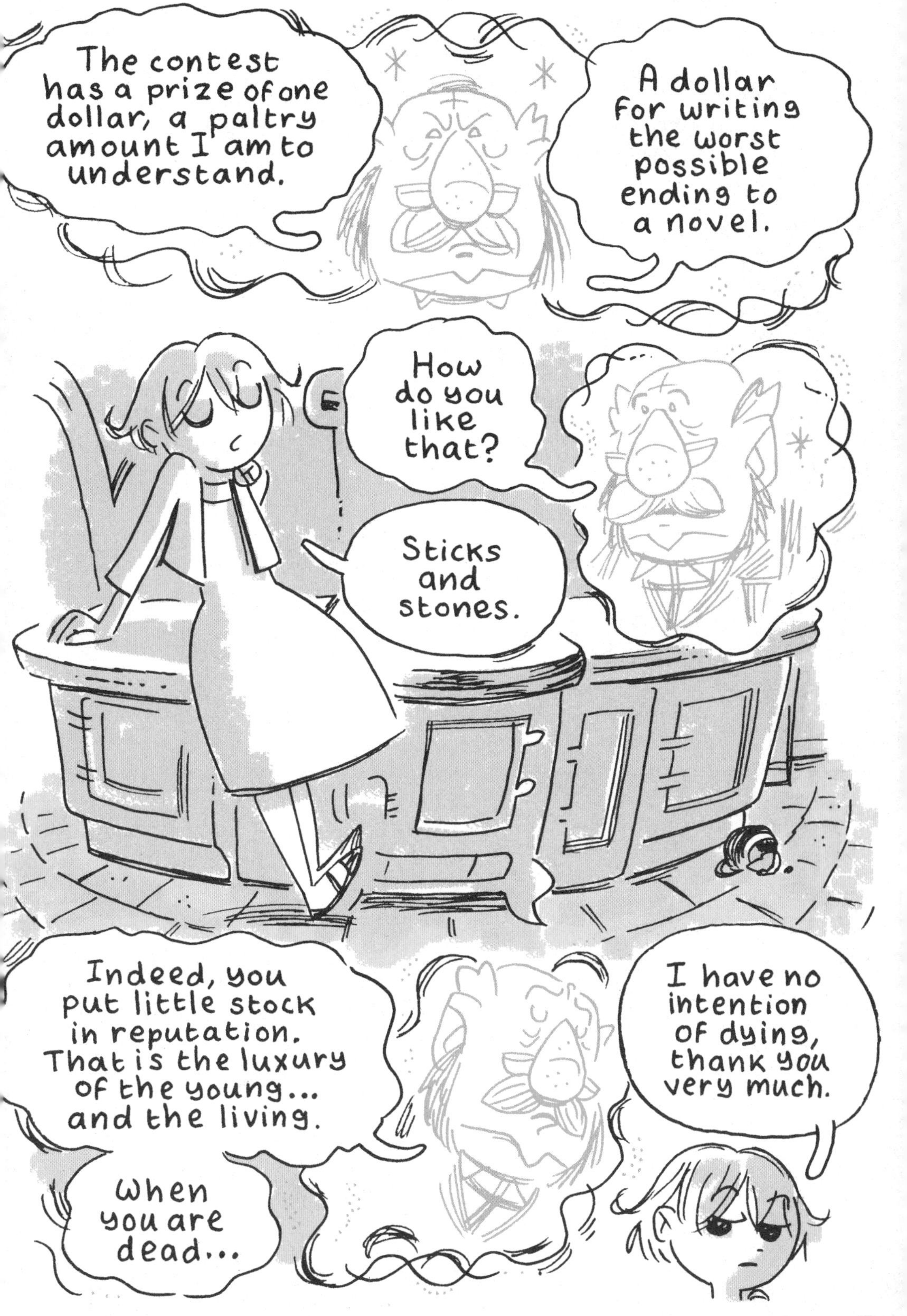

The contest has a prize of one dollar, a paltry amount I am to understand.
A dollar for writing the worst possible ending to a novel.
How do you like that?
Sticks and stones.
Indeed, you put little stock in reputation. That is the luxury of the young... and the living.
When you are dead...
I have no intention of dying, thank you very much.

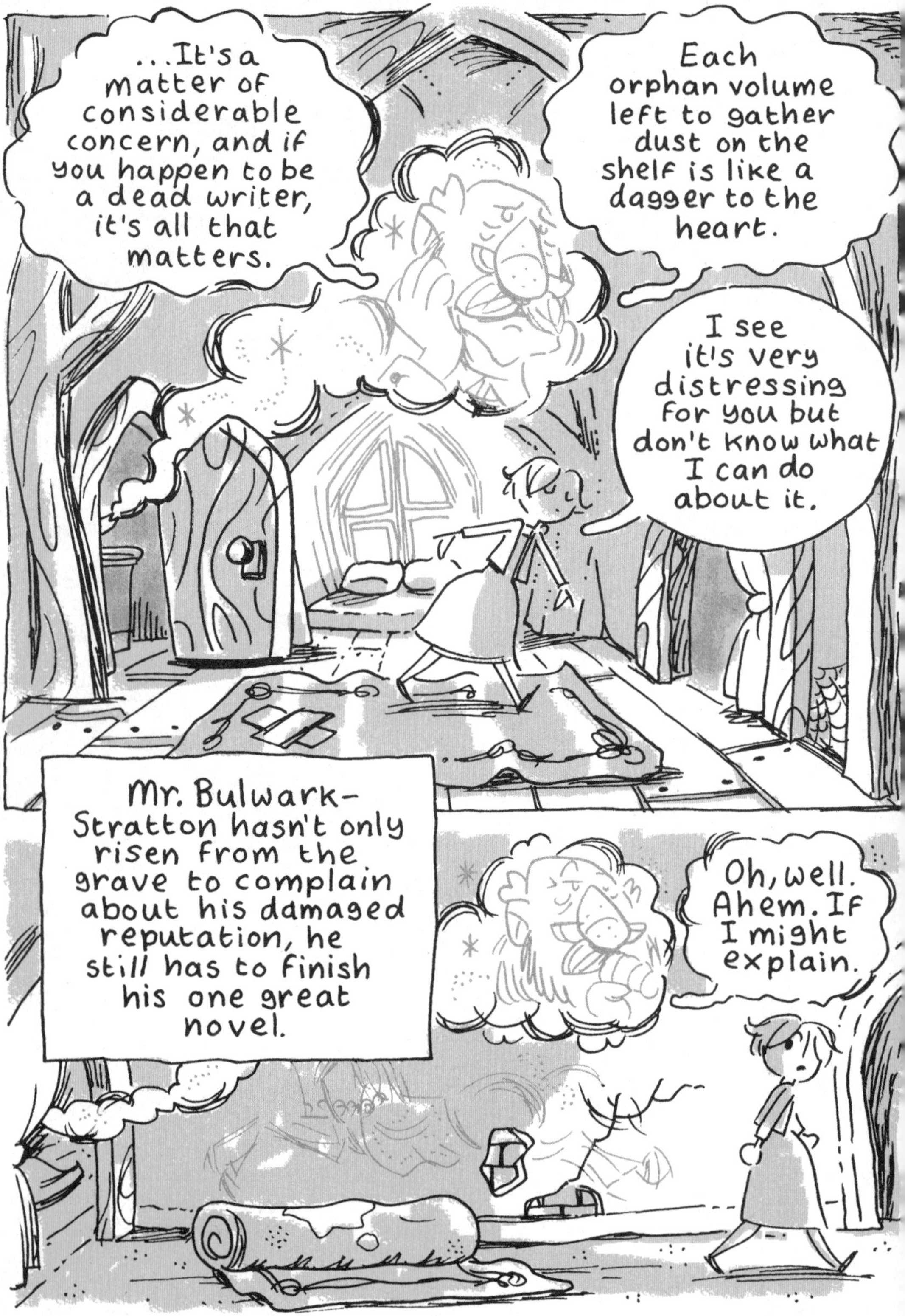
...It's a matter of considerable concern, and if you happen to be a dead writer, it's all that matters.
Each orphan volume left to gather dust on the shelf is like a dagger to the heart.
I see it's very distressing for you but don't know what I can do about it.
Mr. Bulwark-Stratton hasn't only risen from the grave to complain about his damaged reputation, he still has to finish his one great novel.
Oh, well. Ahem. If I might explain.

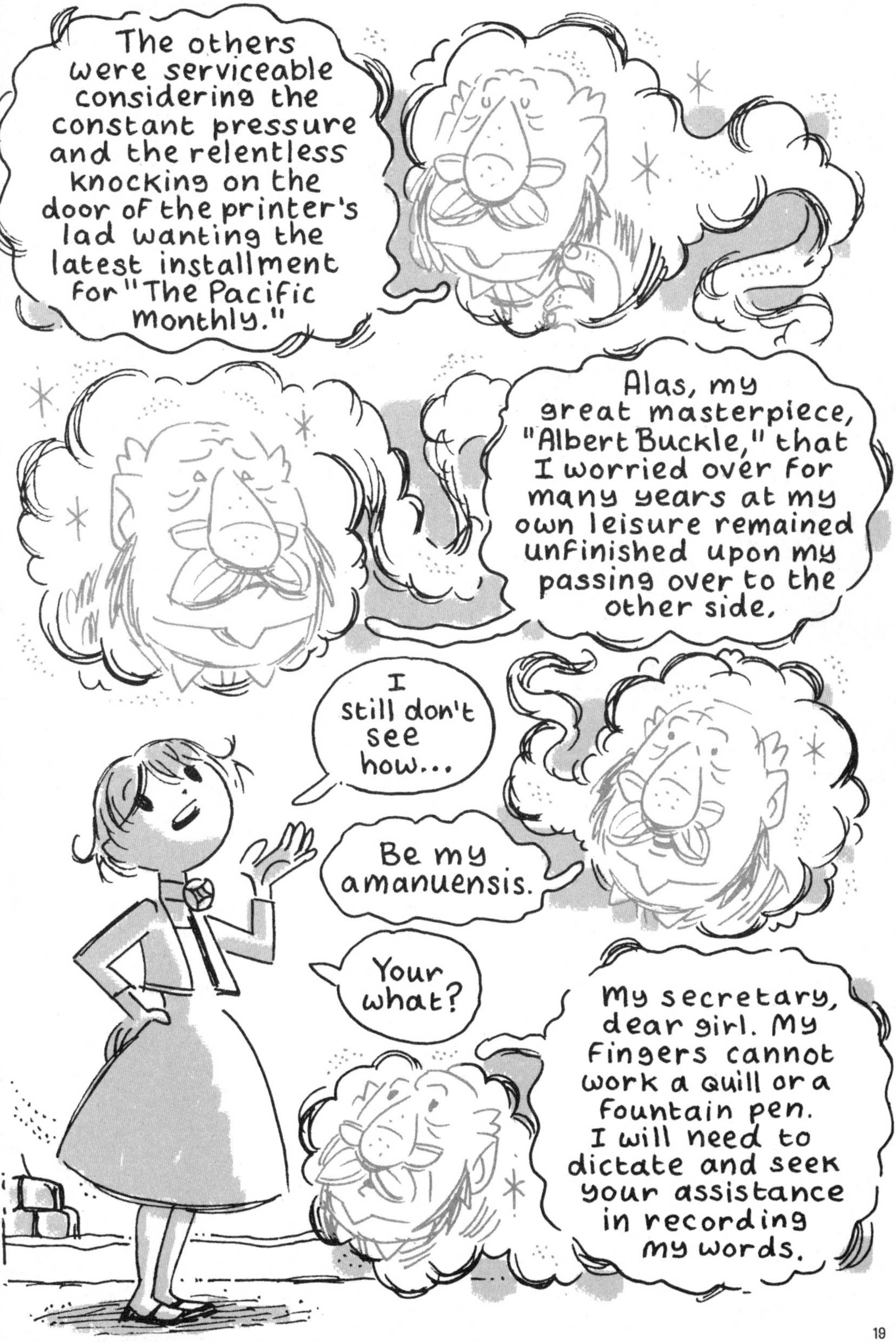
The others were serviceable considering the constant pressure and the relentless knocking on the door of the printer's lad wanting the latest installment for "The Pacific Monthly."
Alas, my great masterpiece, "Albert Buckle," that I worried over for many years at my own leisure remained unfinished upon my passing over to the other side.
I still don't see how...
Be my amanuensis.
Your what?
My secretary, dear girl. My fingers cannot work a quill or a fountain pen. I will need to dictate and seek your assistance in recording my words.

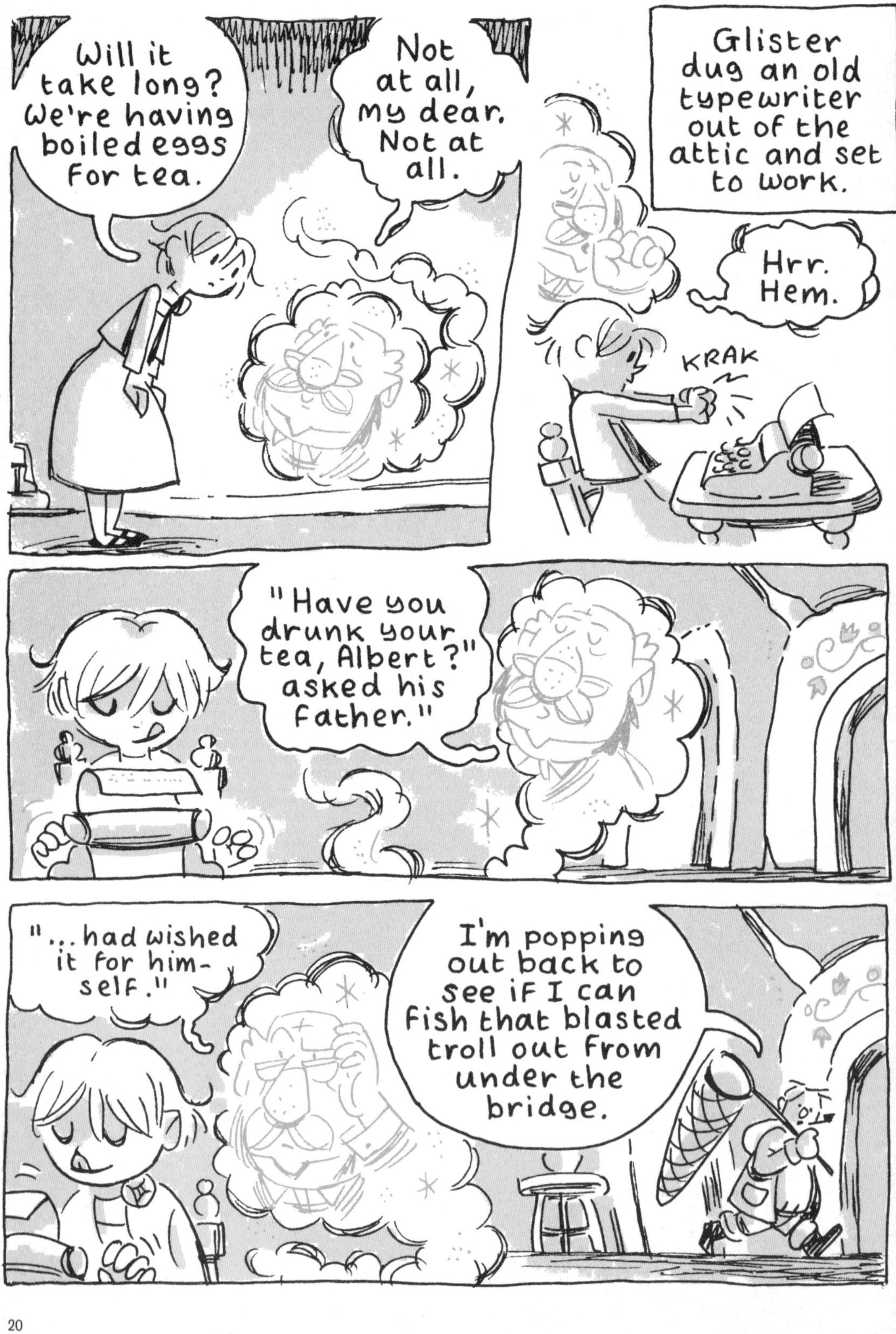
Will it take long? We're having boiled eggs for tea.
Not at all, my dear. Not at all.
Glister dug an old typewriter out of the attic and set to work.
Hrr. Hem.
KRAK
"Have you drunk your tea, Albert?" asked his father."
"...had wished it for him-self."
I'm popping out back to see if I can fish that blasted troll out from under the bridge.

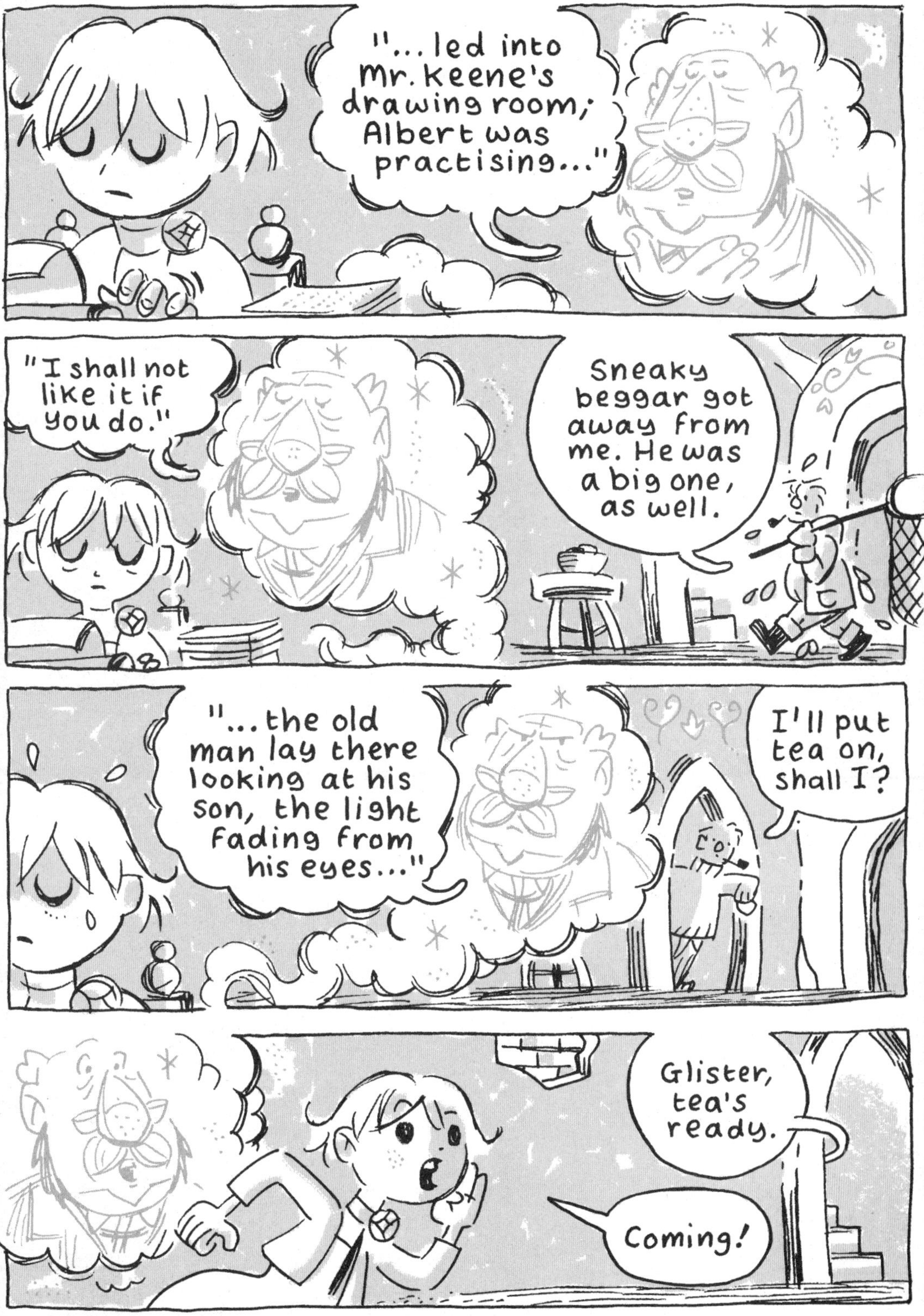
"...led into Mr. keene's drawing room; Albert was practising..."
"I shall not like it if you do."
Sneaky beggar got away from me. He was a big one, as well.
"...the old man lay there looking at his son, the light fading from his eyes..."
I'll put tea on, shall I?
Glister, tea's ready.
Coming!

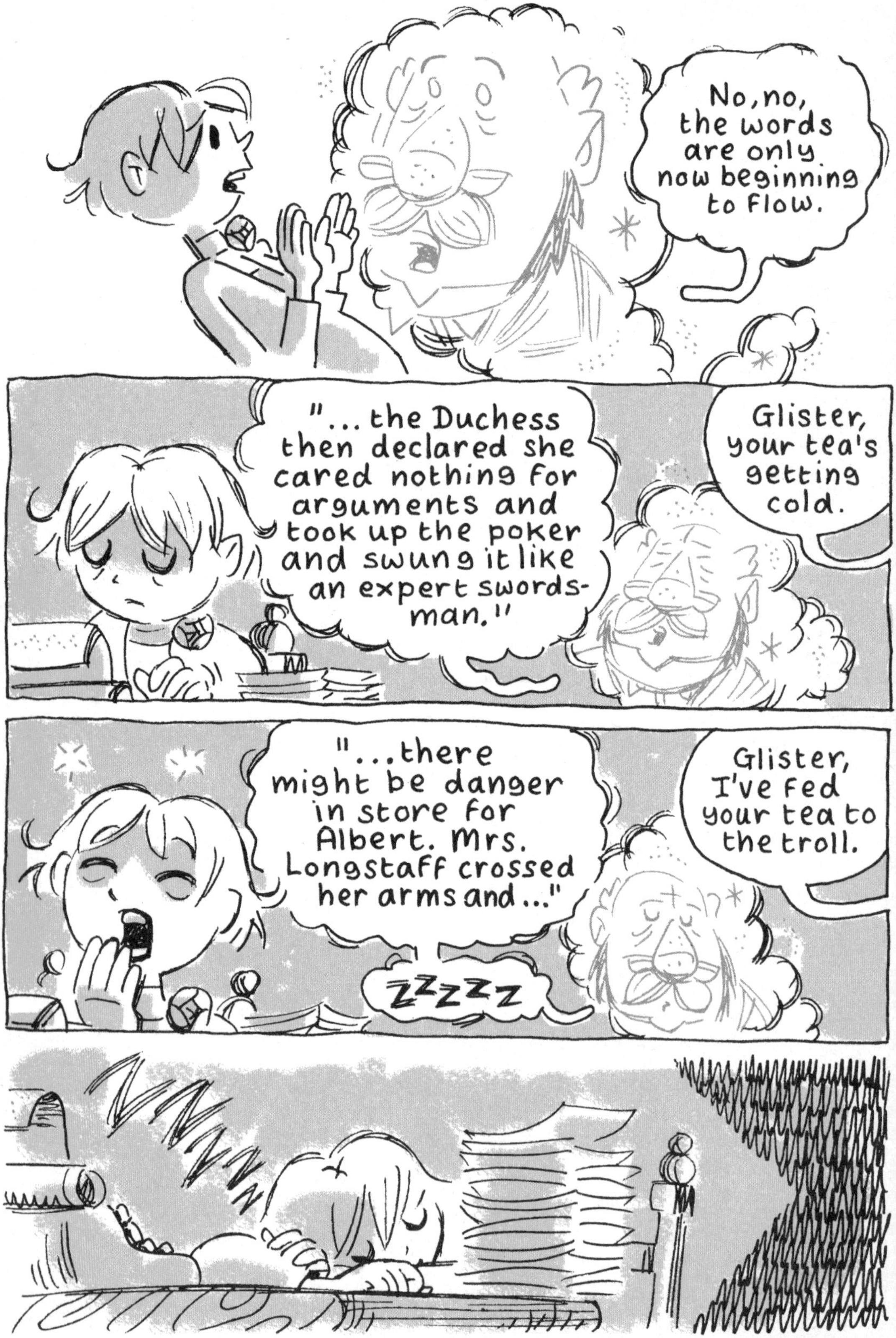

No, no, the words are only now beginning to flow.
"... the Duchess then declared she cared nothing for arguments and took up the poker and swung it like an expert swords-man."
Glister, your tea's getting cold.
"...there might be danger in store for Albert. Mrs. Longstaff crossed her arms and ..."
ZZZZZ
Glister, I've fed your tea to the troll.

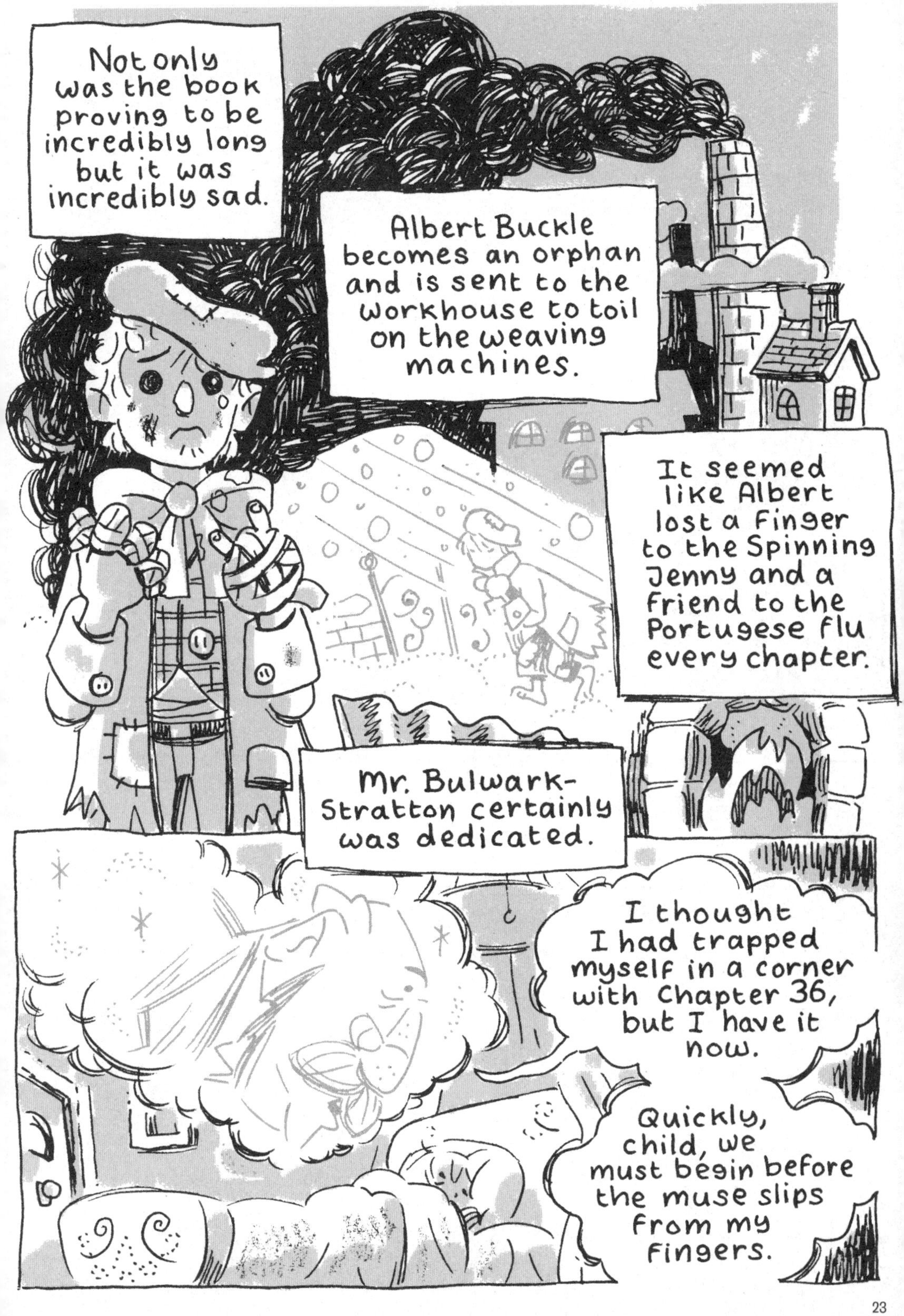
Not only was the book proving to be incredibly long but it was incredibly sad.
Albert Buckle becomes an orphan and is sent to the workhouse to toil on the weaving machines.
It seemed like Albert lost a finger to the Spinning Jenny and a friend to the Portugese flu every chapter.
Mr. Bulwark-Stratton certainly was dedicated.
I thought I had trapped myself in a corner with Chapter 36, but I have it now.
Quickly, child, we must begin before the muse slips from my fingers.

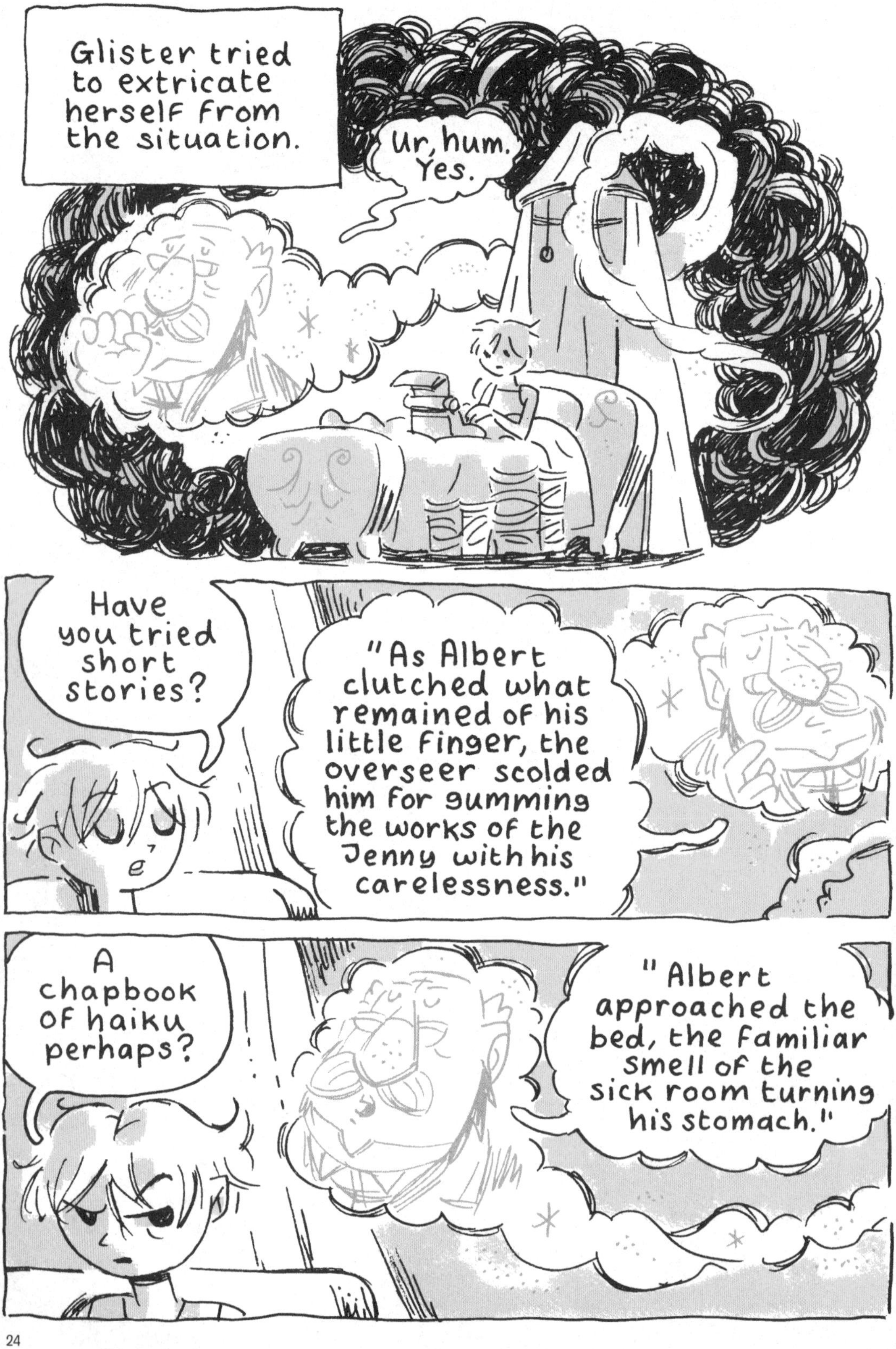
Glister tried to extricate herself from the situation.
Ur, hum. Yes.
Have you tried short stories?
"As Albert clutched what remained of his little finger, the overseer scolded him for gumming the works of the Jenny with his carelessness."
A chapbook of haiku perhaps?
"Albert approached the bed, the familiar smell of the sick room turning his stomach."

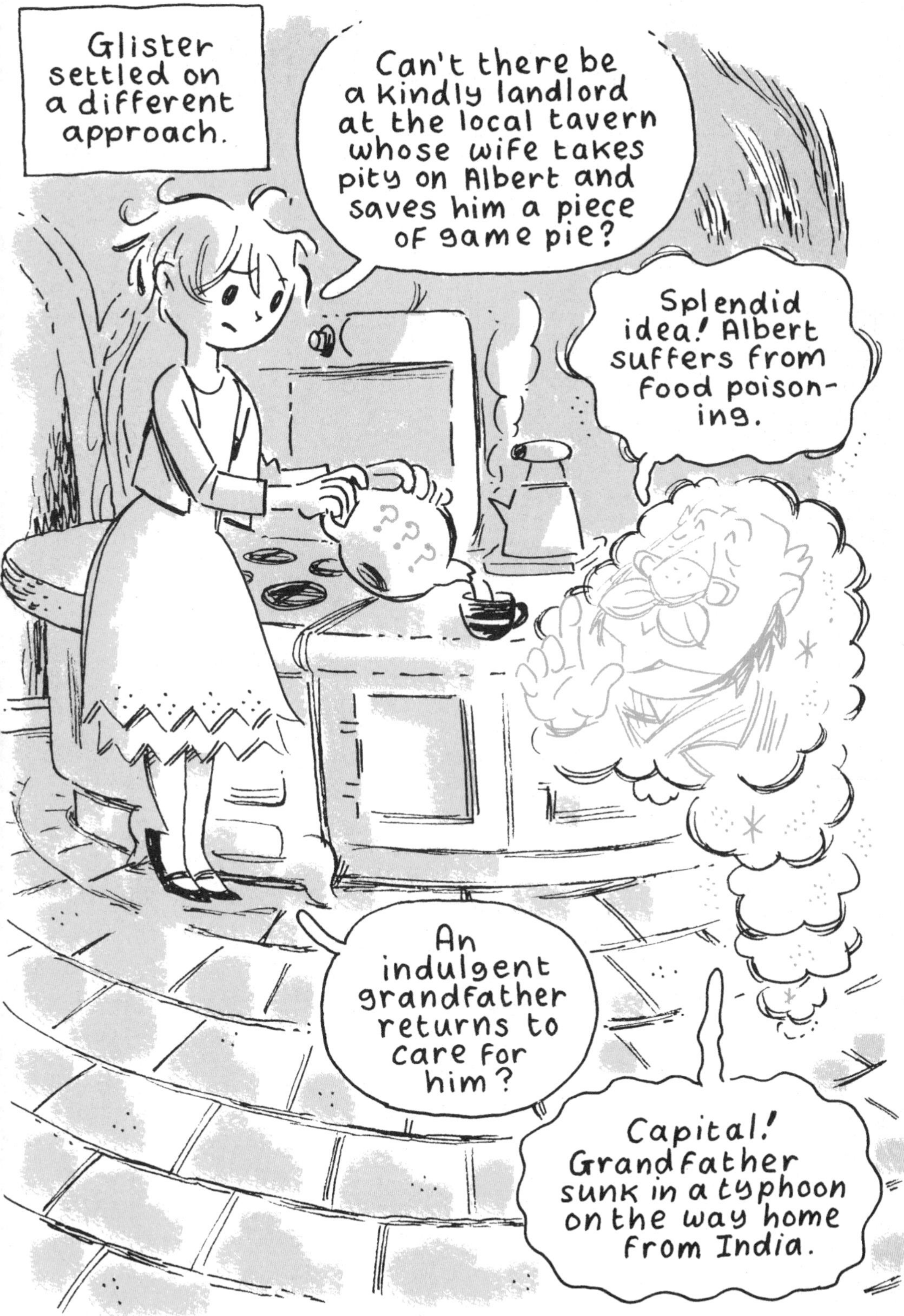
Glister settled on a different approach.
Can't there be a kindly landlord at the local tavern whose wife takes pity on Albert and saves him a piece of game pie?
Splendid idea! Albert suffers from food poisoning.
An indulgent grandfather returns to care for him?
Capital! Grandfather sunk in a typhoon on the way home from India.

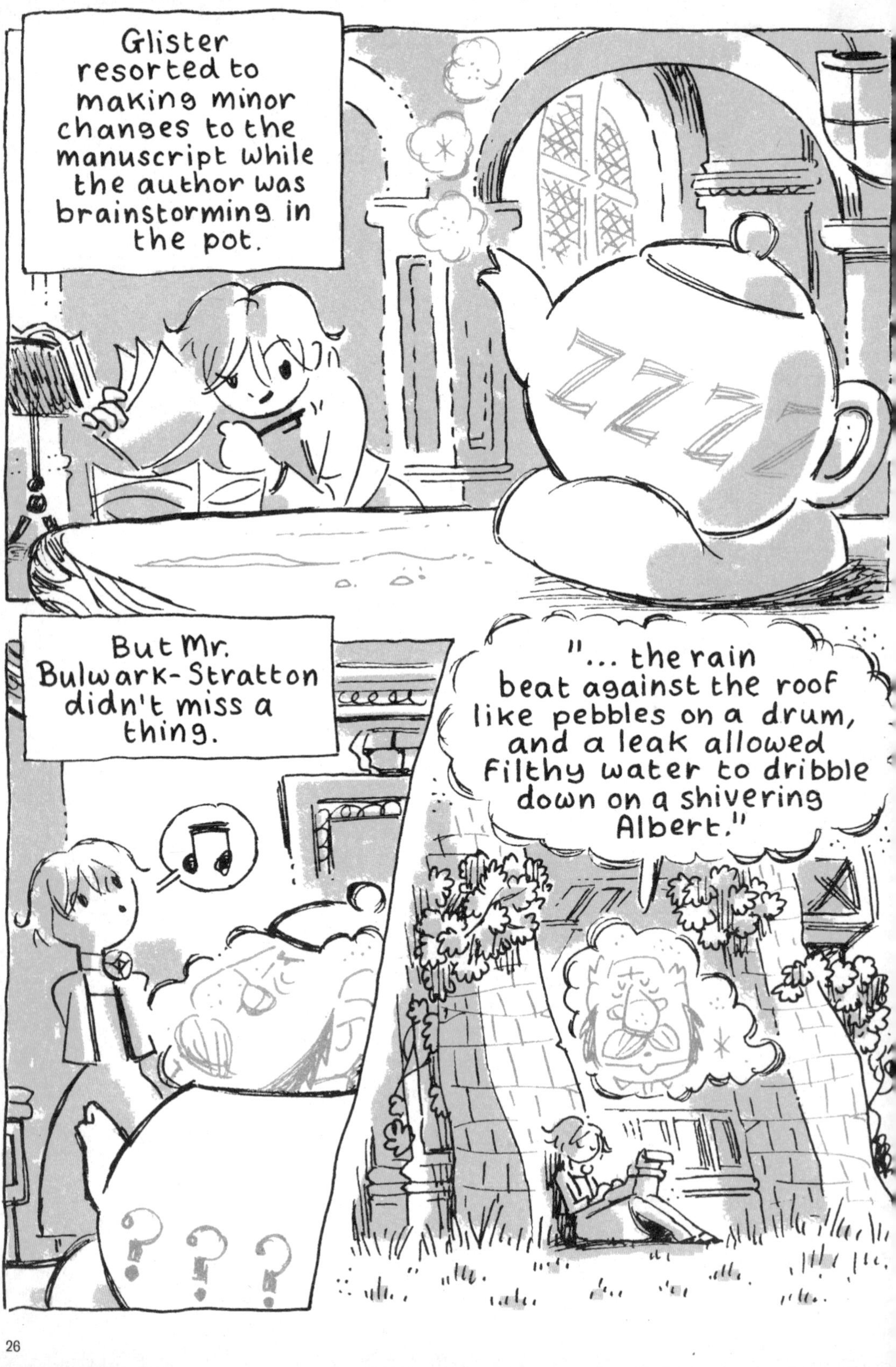
Glister resorted to making minor changes to the manuscript while the author was brainstorming in the pot.
But Mr. Bulwark-Stratton didn't miss a thing.
"... the rain beat against the roof like pebbles on a drum, and a leak allowed filthy water to dribble down on a shivering Albert."

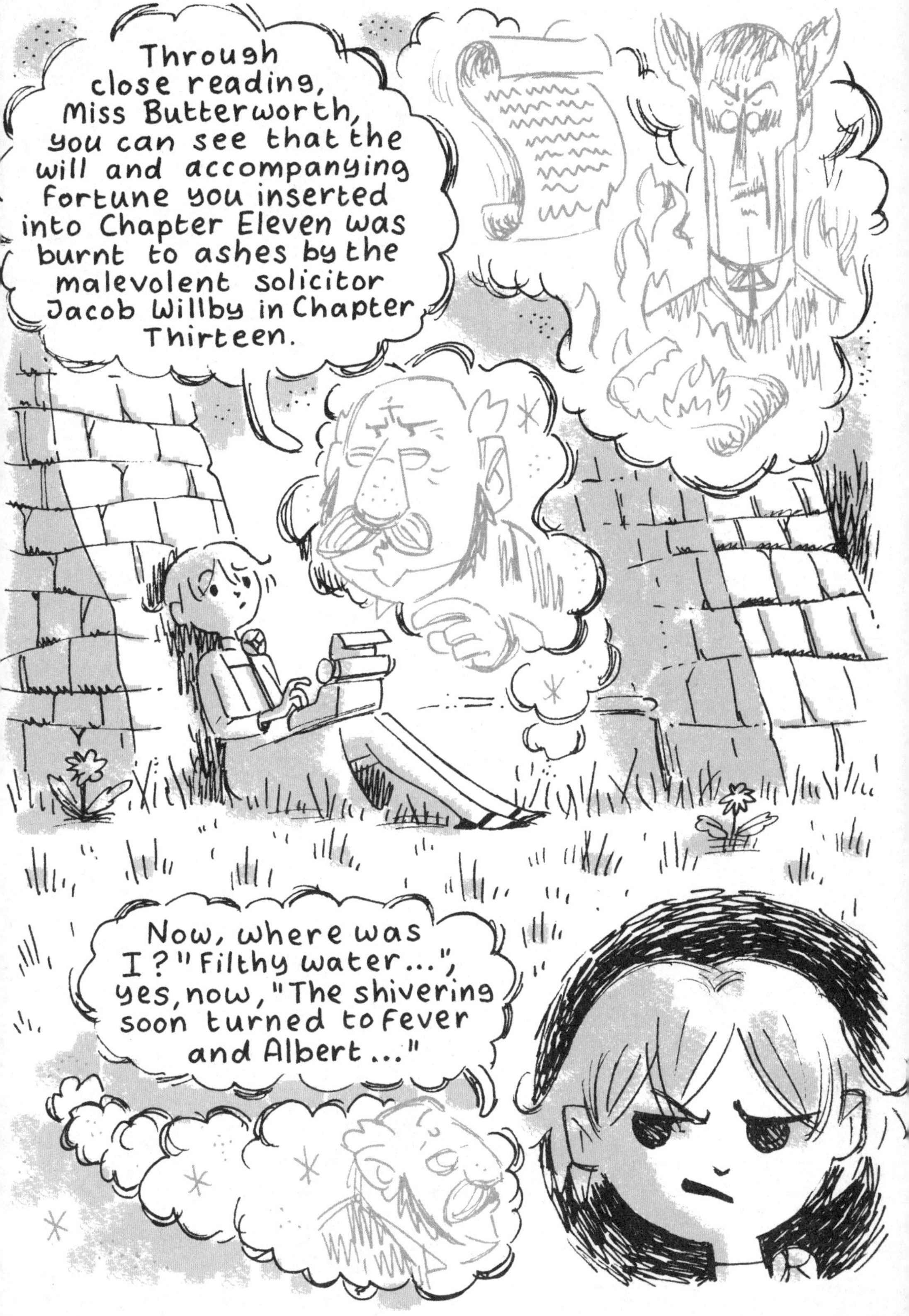
Through close reading, Miss Butterworth, you can see that the will and accompanying fortune you inserted into Chapter Eleven was burnt to ashes by the malevolent solicitor Jacob Willby in Chapter Thirteen.
Now, where was I? "Filthy water...", yes, now, "The shivering soon turned to fever and Albert..."

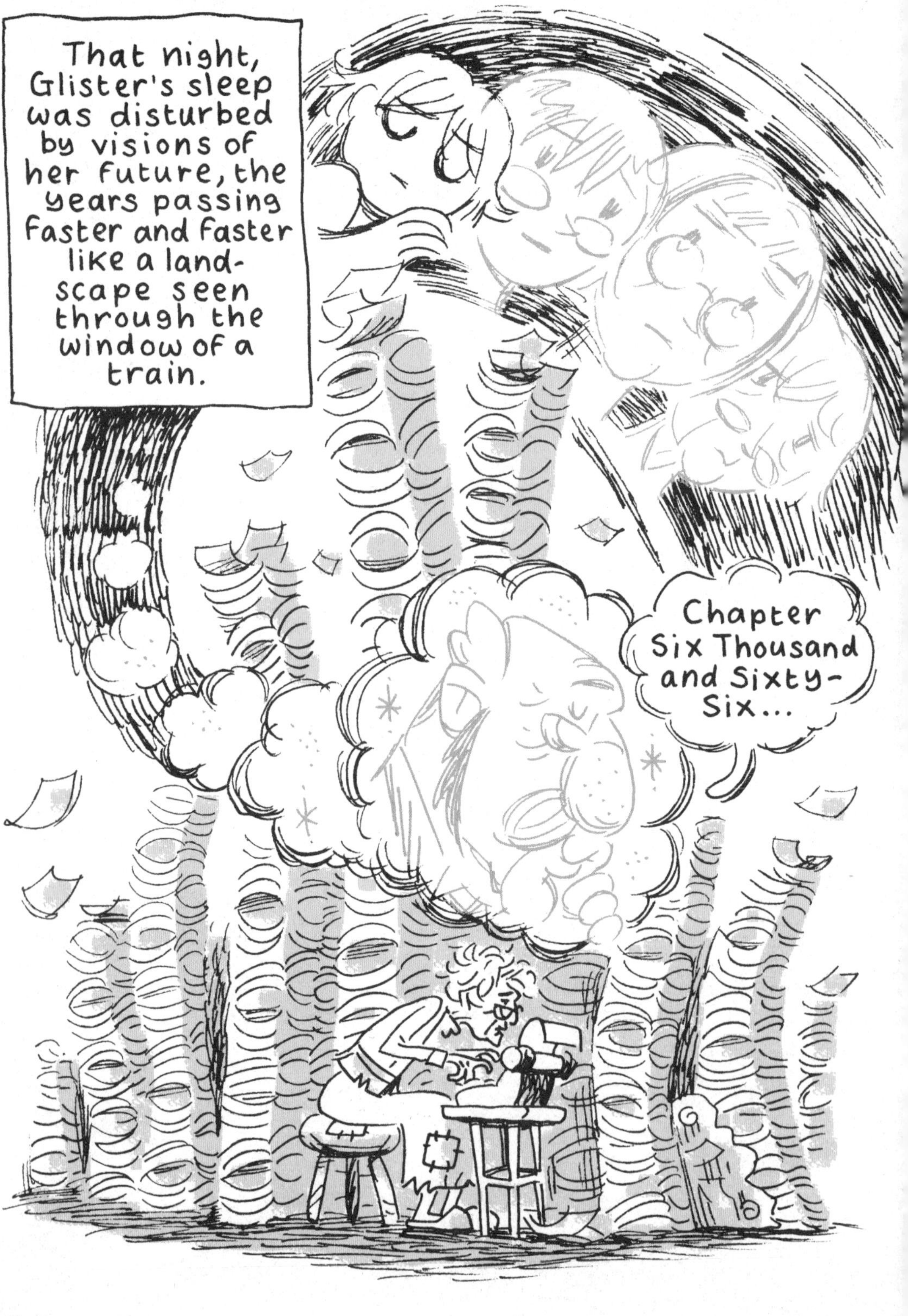
That night, Glister's sleep was disturbed by visions of her future, the years passing faster and faster like a landscape seen through the window of a train.
Chapter Six Thousand and Sixty-Six...

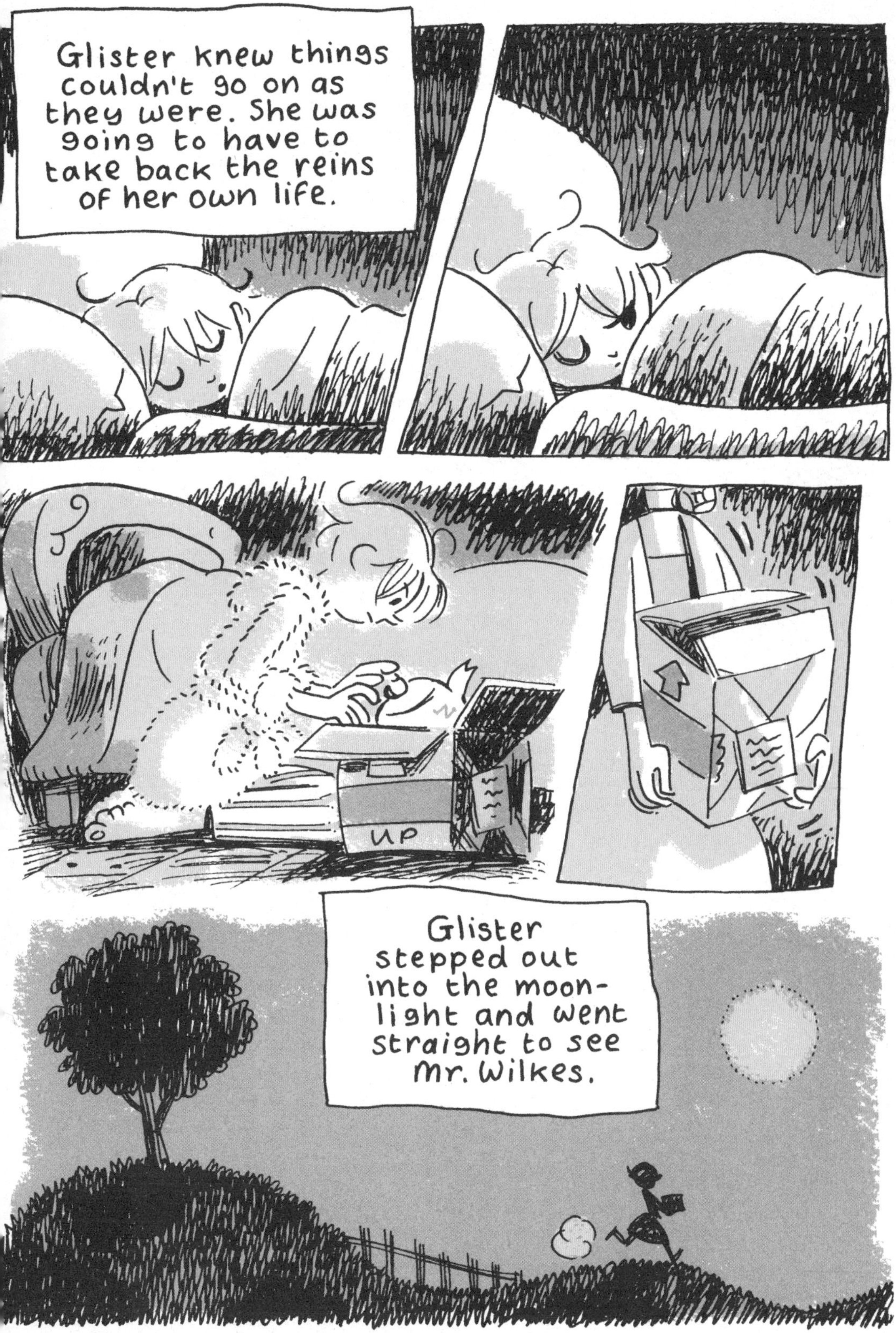
Glister knew things couldn't go on as they were. She was going to have to take back the reins of her own life.
UP
Glister stepped out into the moon-light and went straight to see Mr. Wilkes.

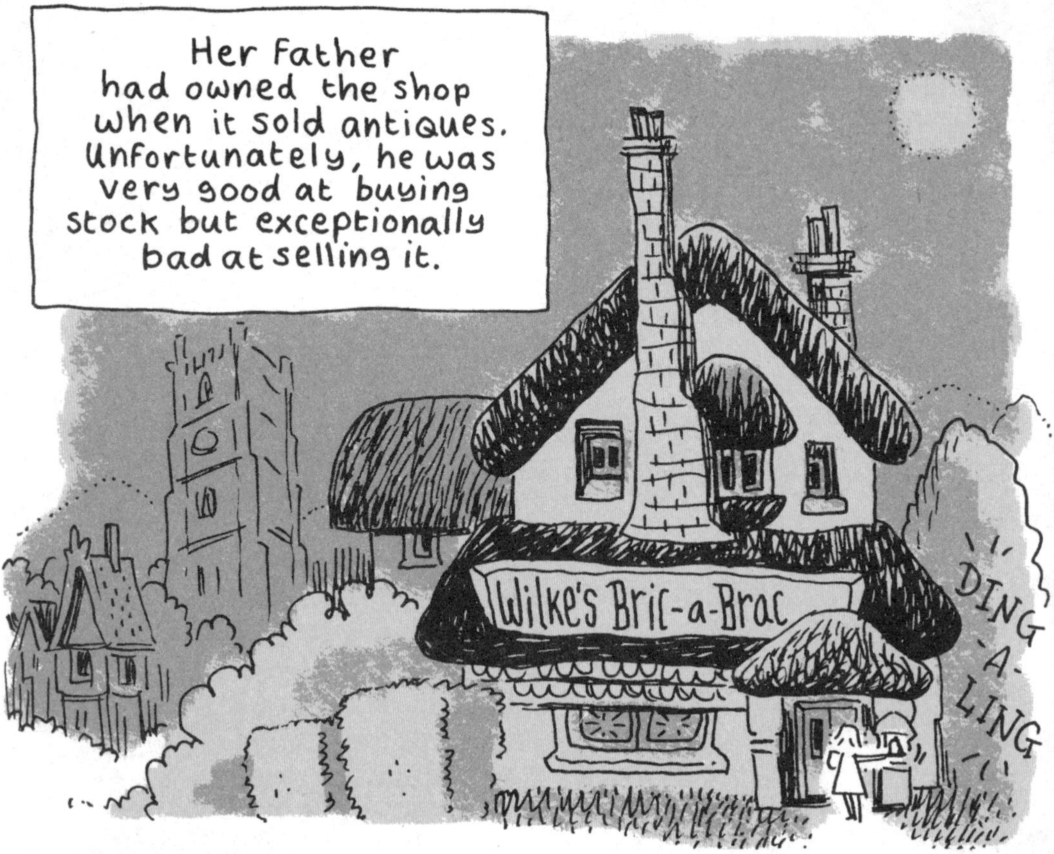
Her Father had owned the shop when it sold antiques. Unfortunately, he was very good at buying stock but exceptionally bad at selling it.
Wilke's Bric-a-Brac
DING-A-LING

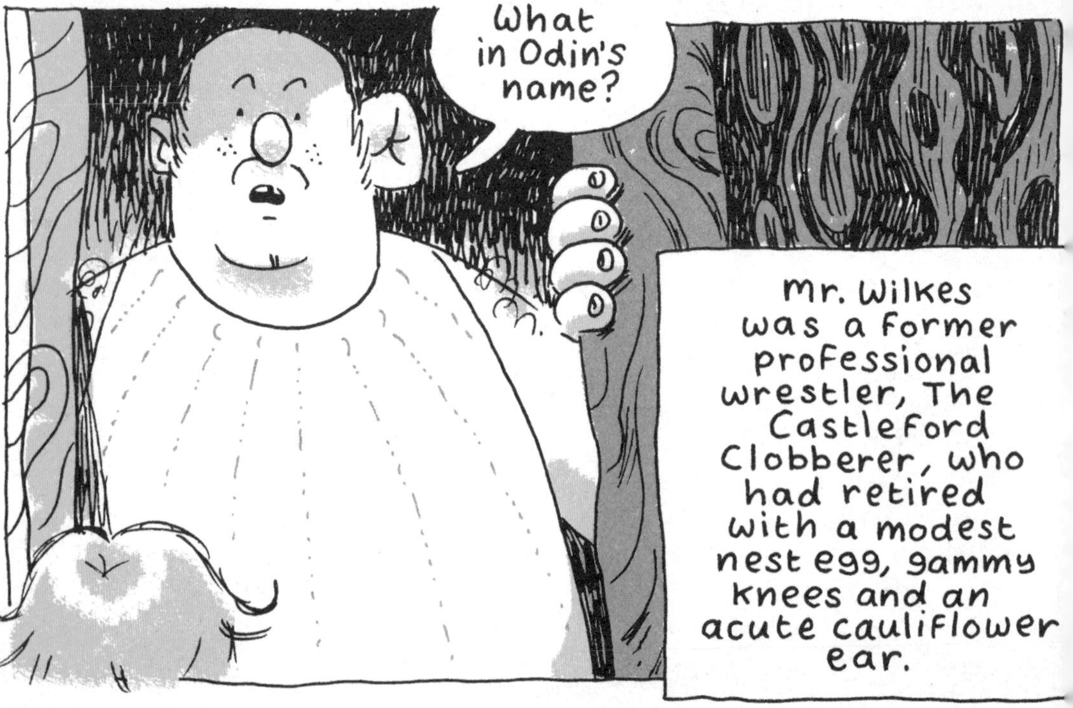
What in Odin's name?
Mr. Wilkes was a former professional wrestler, The Castleford Clobberer, who had retired with a modest nest egg, gammy knees and an acute cauliflower ear.

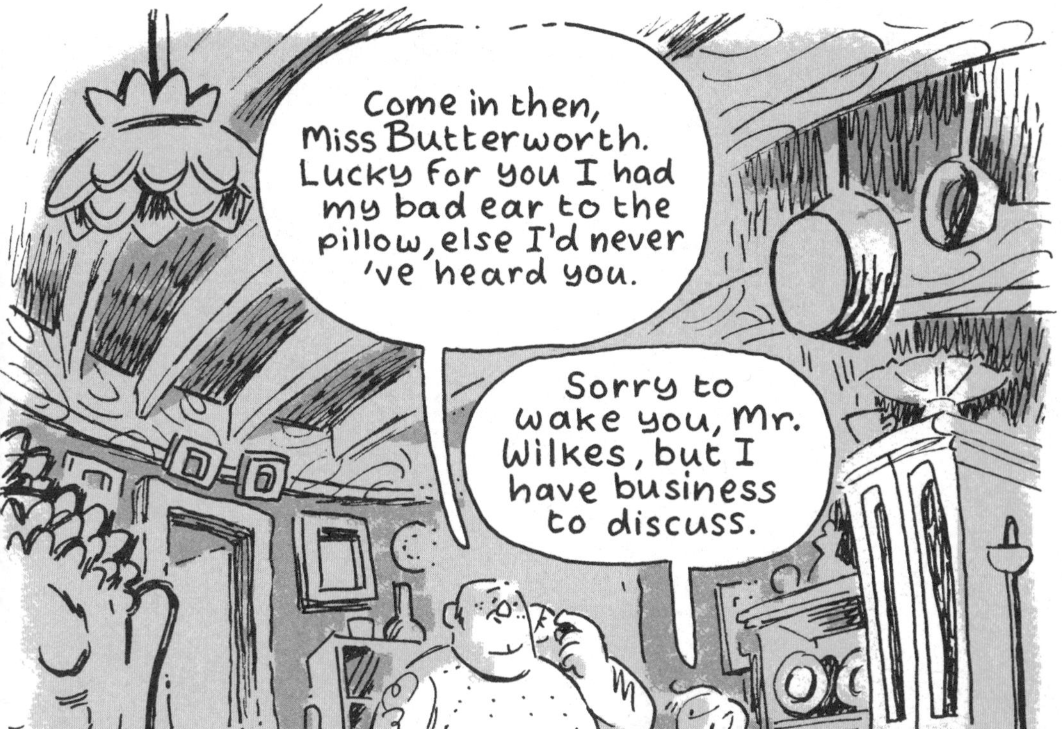
Come in then, Miss Butterworth. Lucky for you I had my bad ear to the pillow, else I'd never 've heard you.
Sorry to wake you, Mr. Wilkes, but I have business to discuss.

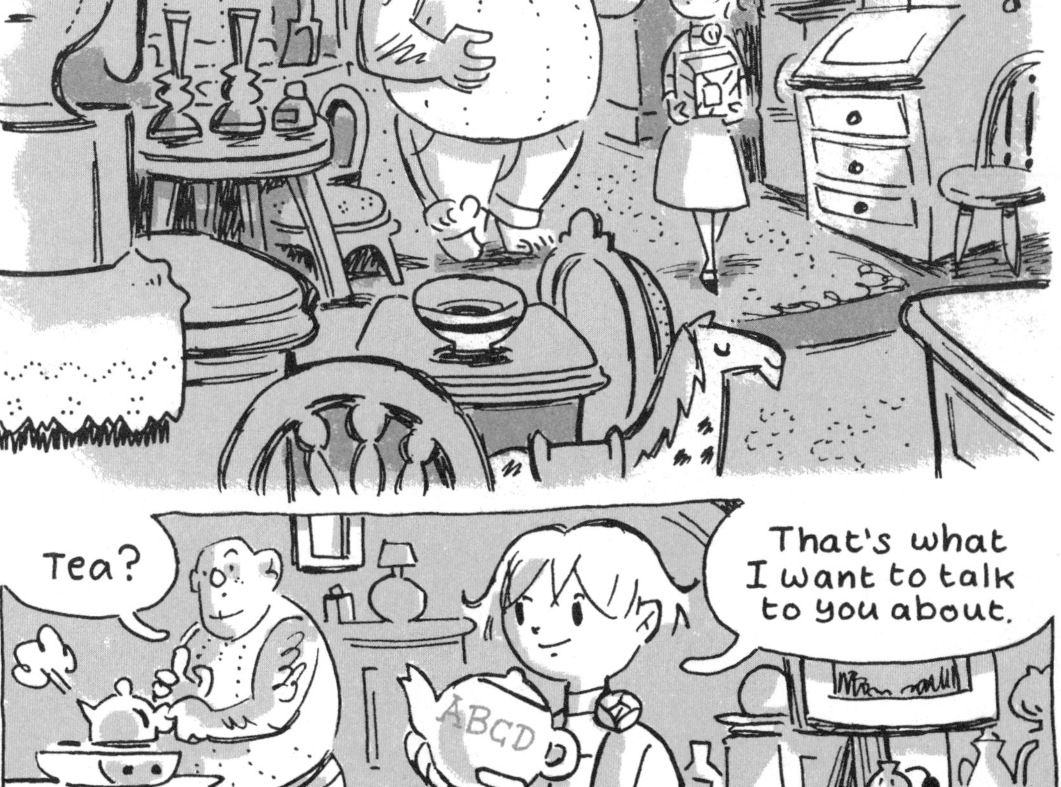
Tea?
That's what I want to talk to you about.
ABCD

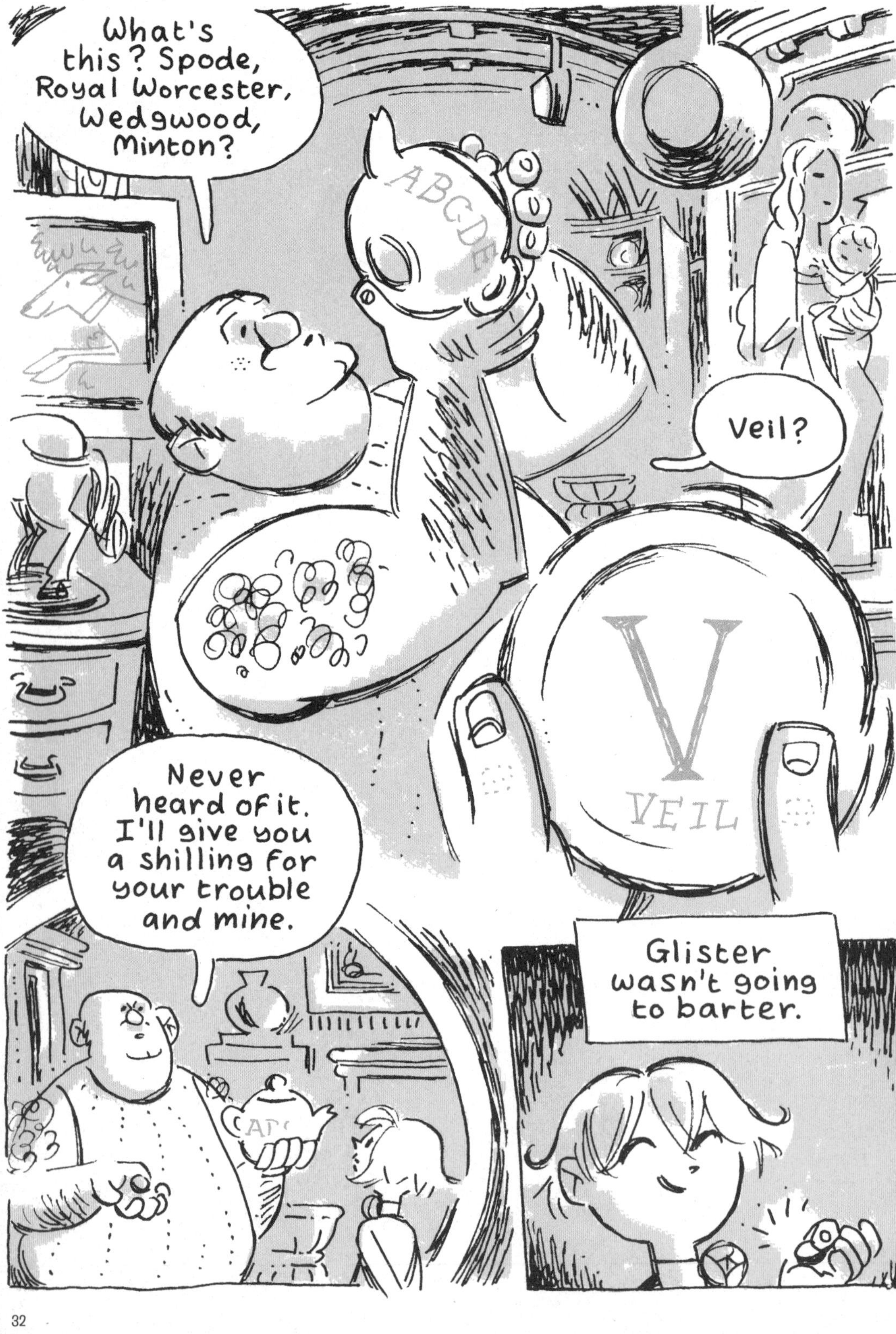
What's this? Spode, Royal Worcester, Wedgwood, Minton?
ABCDE
Veil?
V
VEIL
Never heard of it. I'll give you a shilling for your trouble and mine.
Glister wasn't going to barter.

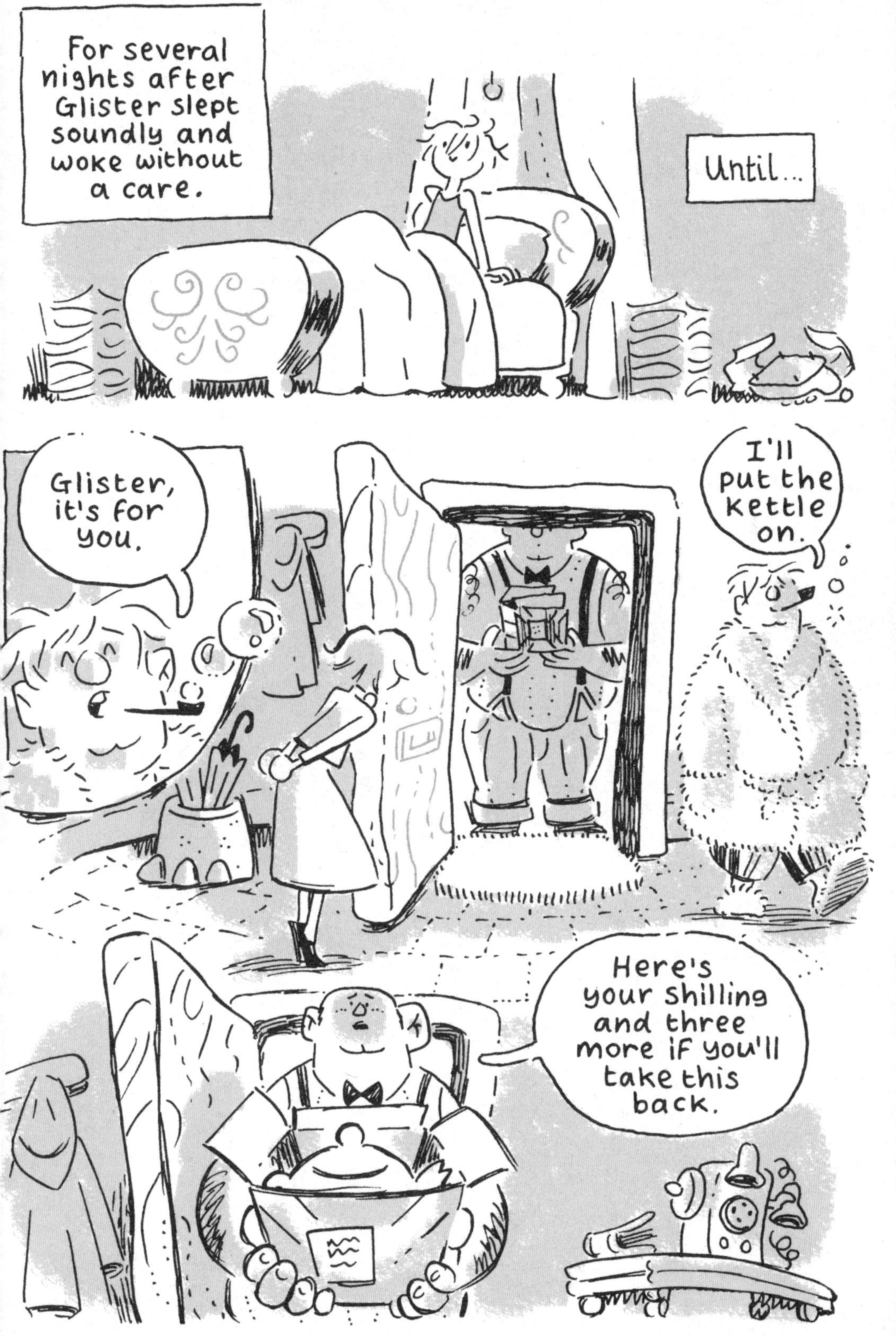

For several nights after Glister slept soundly and woke without a care.
Until...
Glister, it's for you.
I'll put the kettle on.
Here's your shilling and three more if you'll take this back.

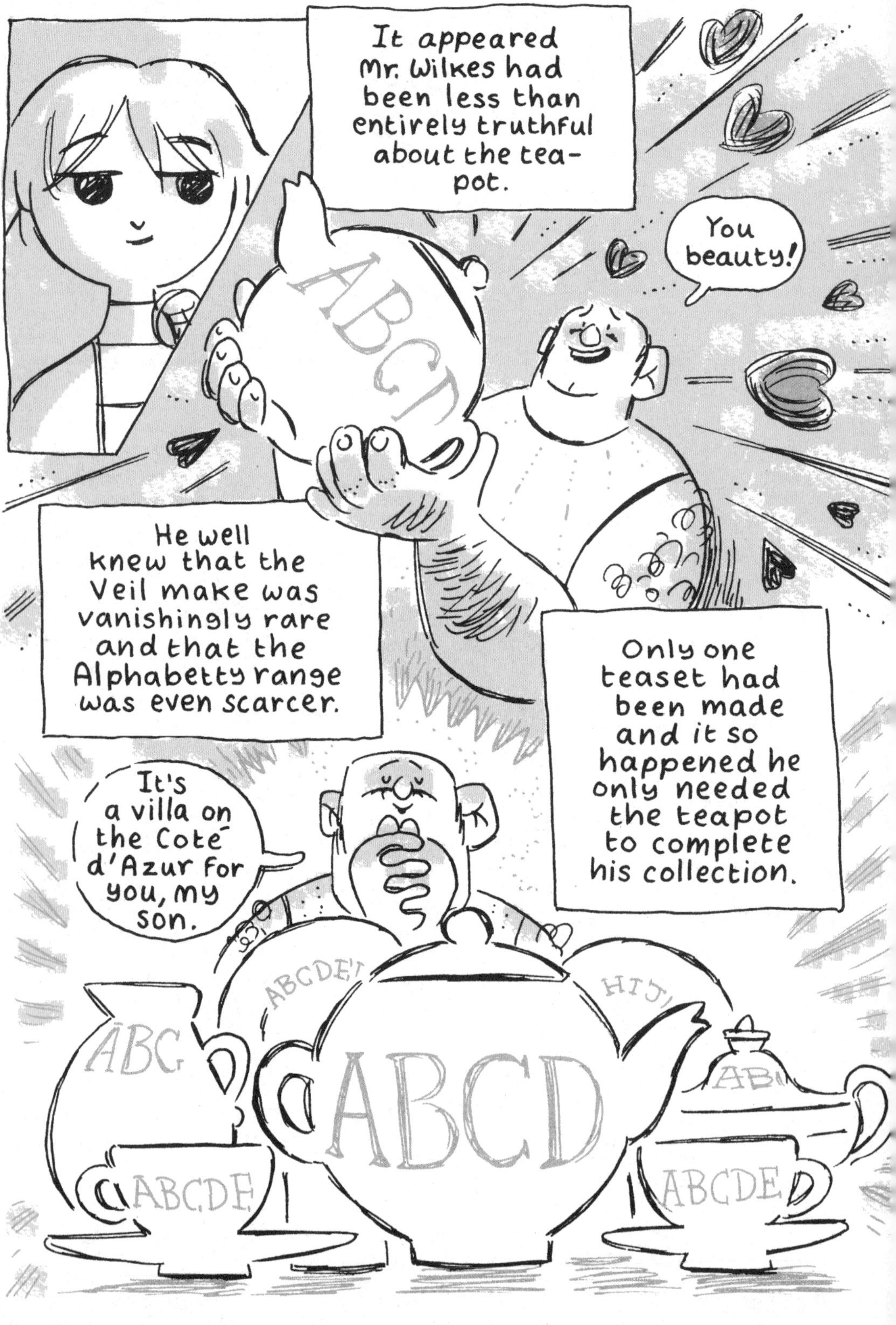
It appeared Mr. Wilkes had been less than entirely truthful about the tea-pot.
You beauty!
He well knew that the Veil make was vanishingly rare and that the Alphabetty range was even scarcer.
Only one teaset had been made and it so happened he only needed the teapot to complete his collection.
It's a villa on the Coté d'Azur for you, my son.
ABCD
ABC
ABCDE
ABCD
ABCDE
ABCDE

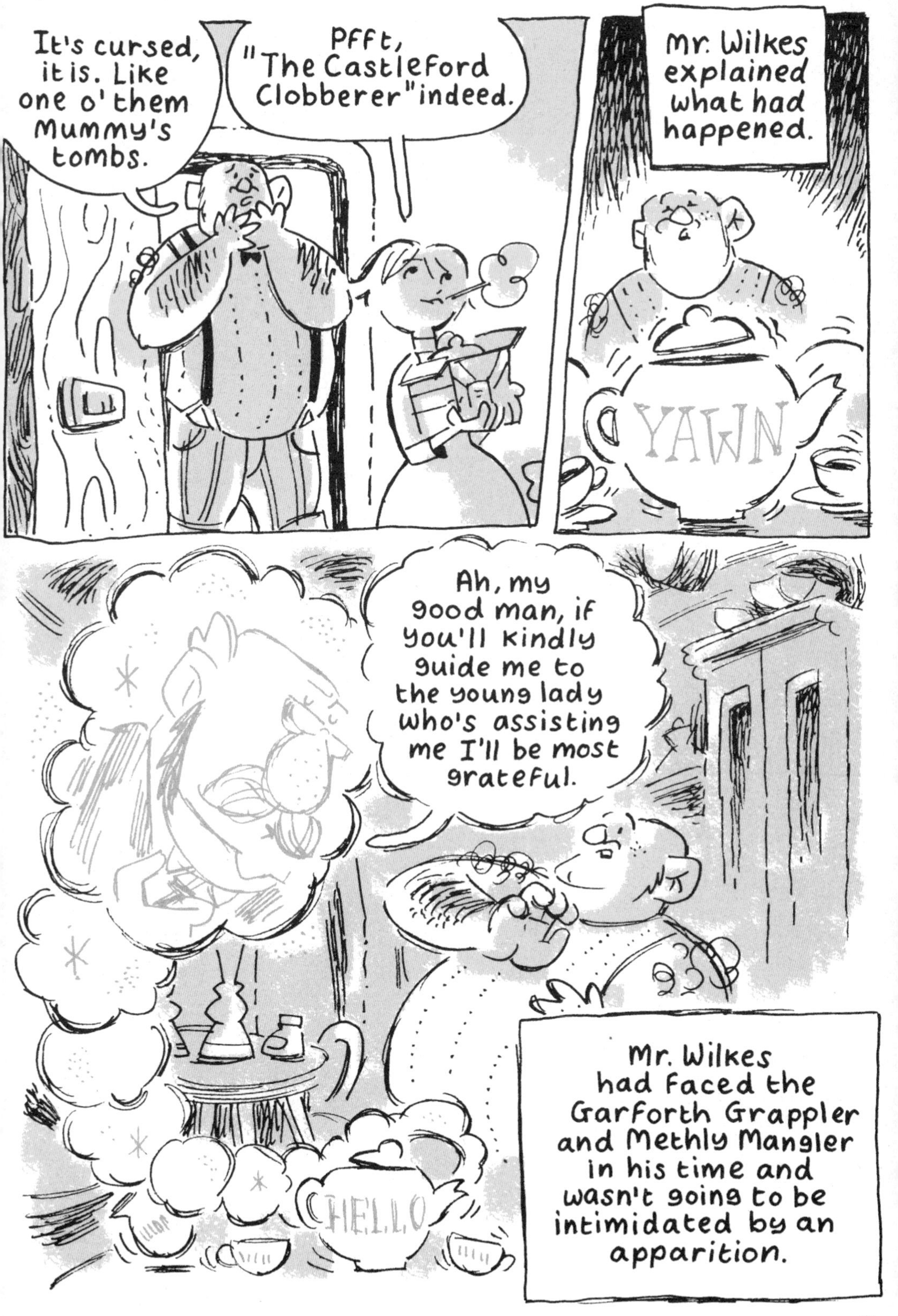
It's cursed, it is. Like one o' them Mummy's tombs.
Pfft, "The Castleford Clobberer" indeed.
Mr. Wilkes explained what had happened.
YAWN
Ah, my good man, if you'll kindly guide me to the young lady who's assisting me I'll be most grateful.
HELLO
Mr. Wilkes had faced the Garforth Grappler and Methly Mangler in his time and wasn't going to be intimidated by an apparition.

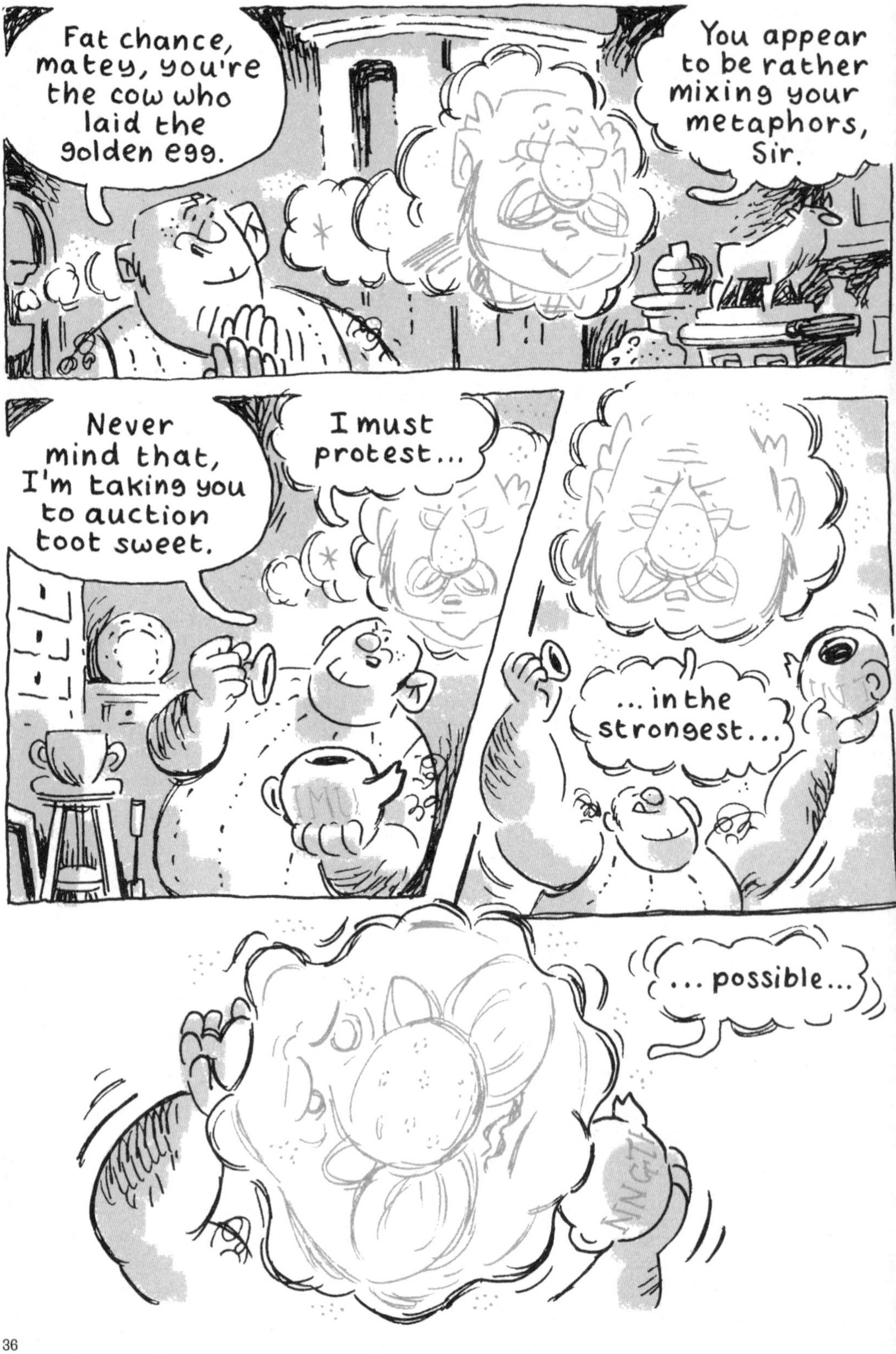

Fat chance, matey, you're the cow who laid the golden egg.
You appear to be rather mixing your metaphors, Sir.
Never mind that, I'm taking you to auction toot sweet.
I must protest...
... in the strongest...
... possible...

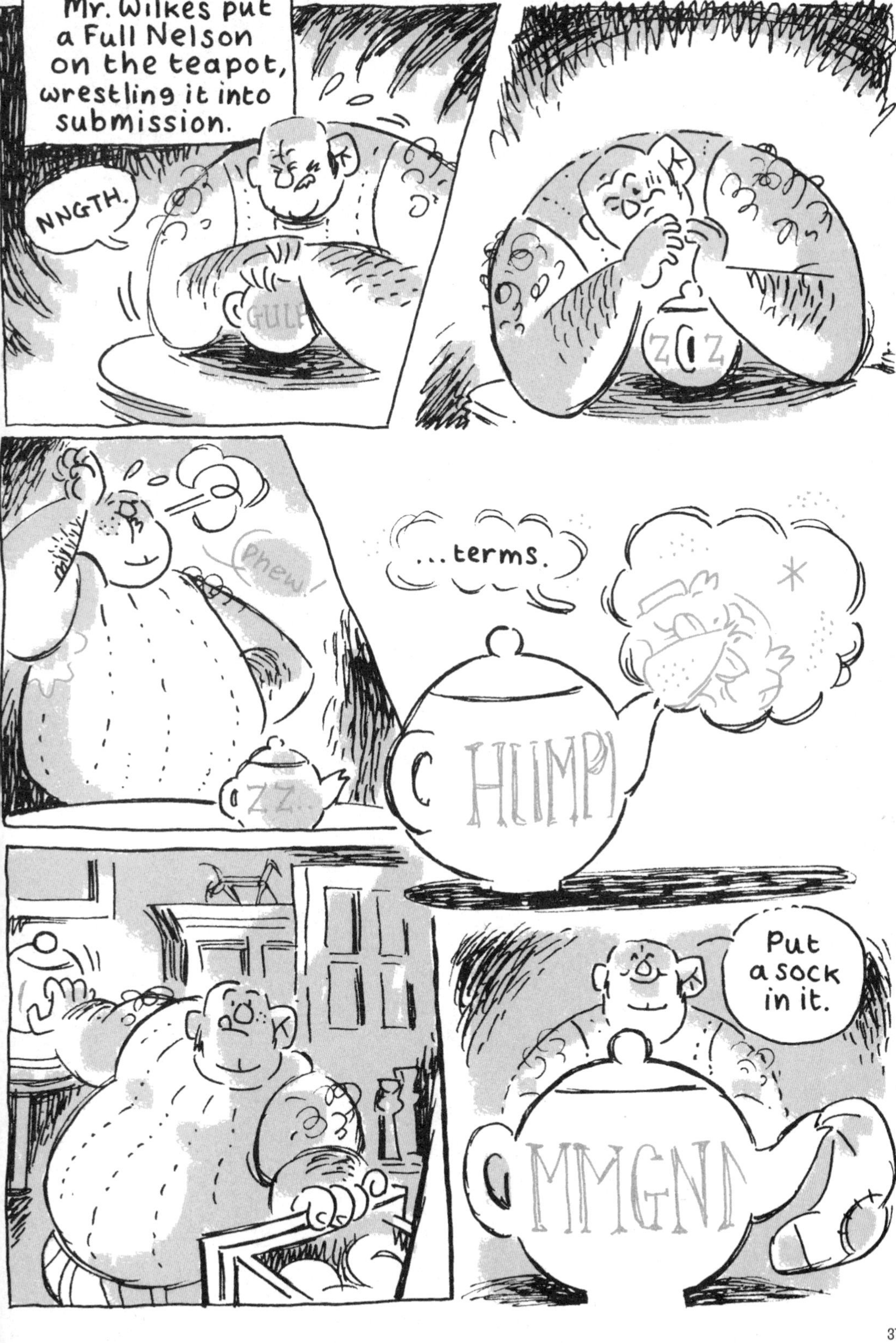
Mr. Wilkes put a Full Nelson on the teapot, wrestling it into submission.
NNGTH.
GULP
ZZ
phew
ZZ..
...terms.
HUMPH
Put a sock in it.
MMGNM

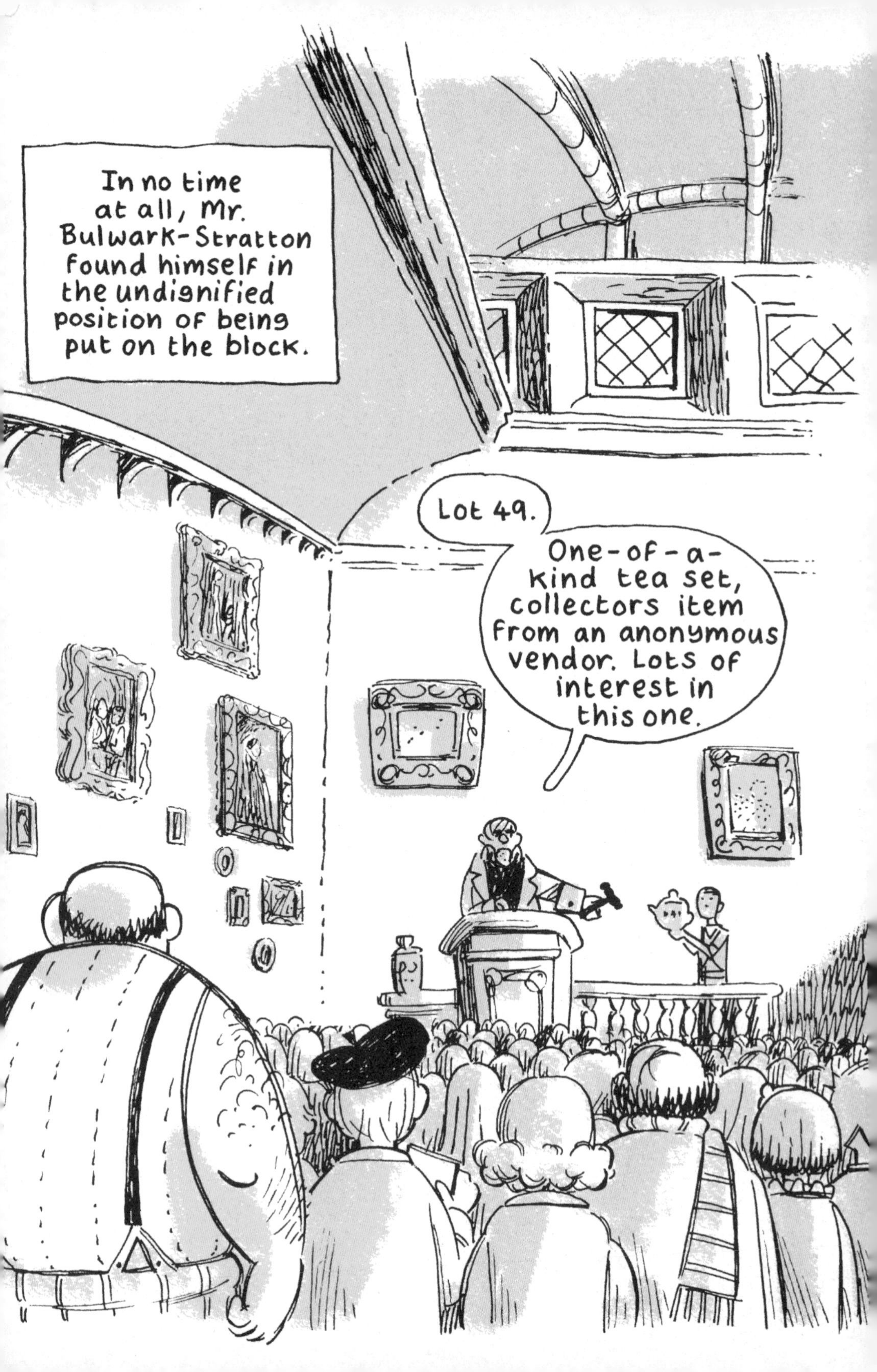
In no time at all, Mr. Bulwark-Stratton found himself in the undignified position of being put on the block.
Lot 49.
One-of-a-kind tea set, collectors item from an anonymous vendor. Lots of interest in this one.

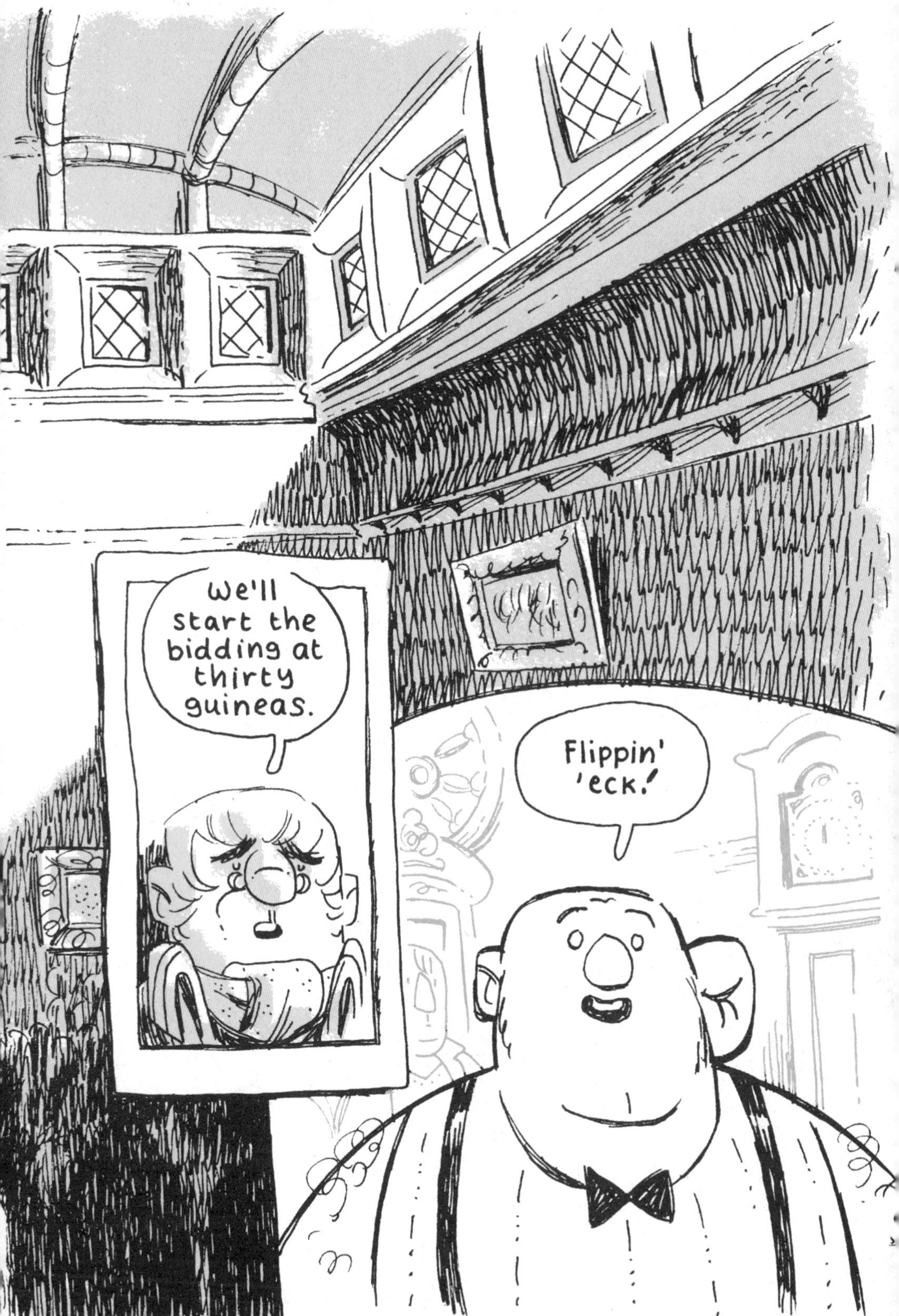
We'll start the bidding at thirty guineas.
Flippin' 'eck!

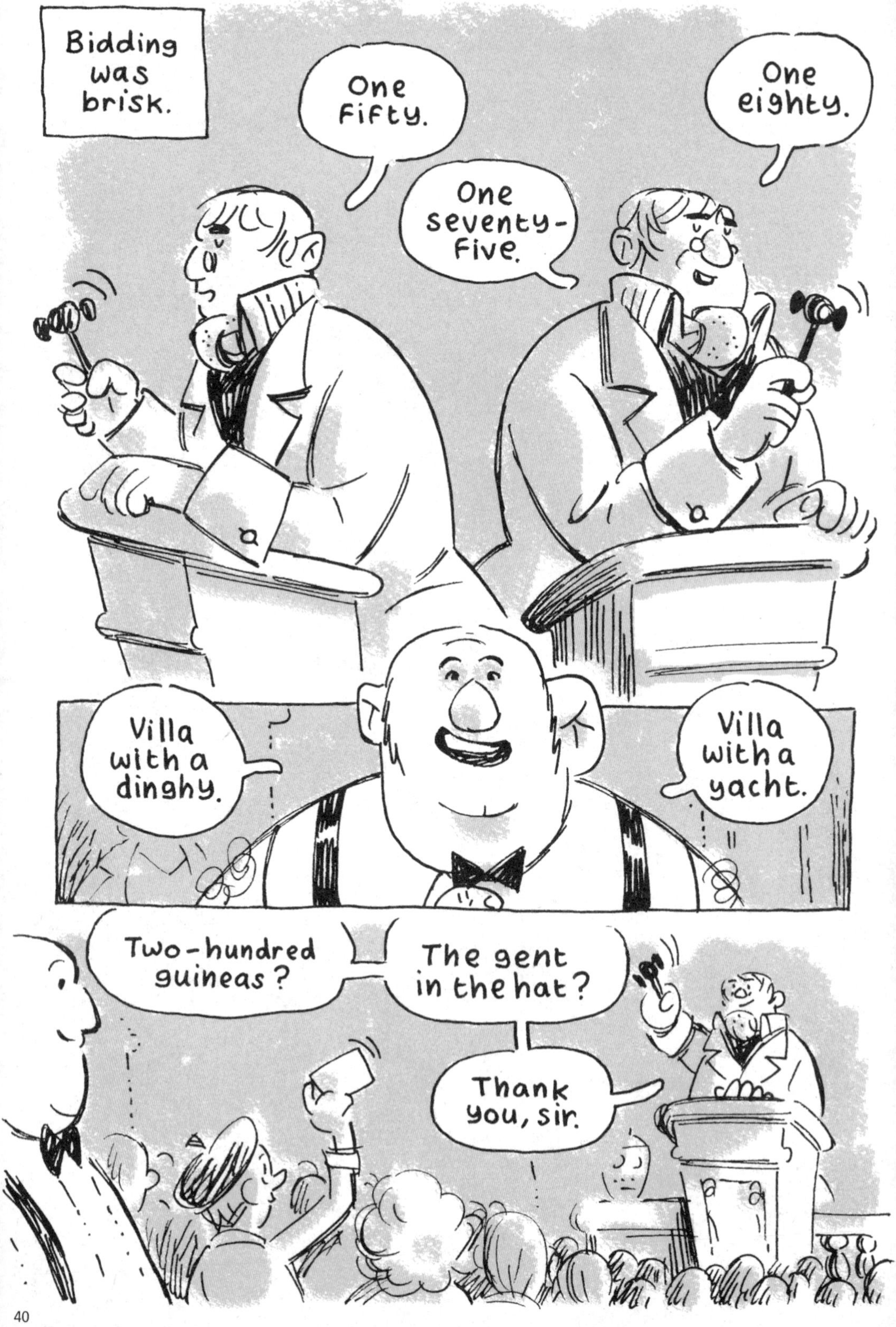
Bidding was brisk.
One fifty.
One seventy-five.
One eighty.
Villa with a dinghy.
Villa with a yacht.
Two-hundred guineas?
The gent in the hat?
Thank you, sir.

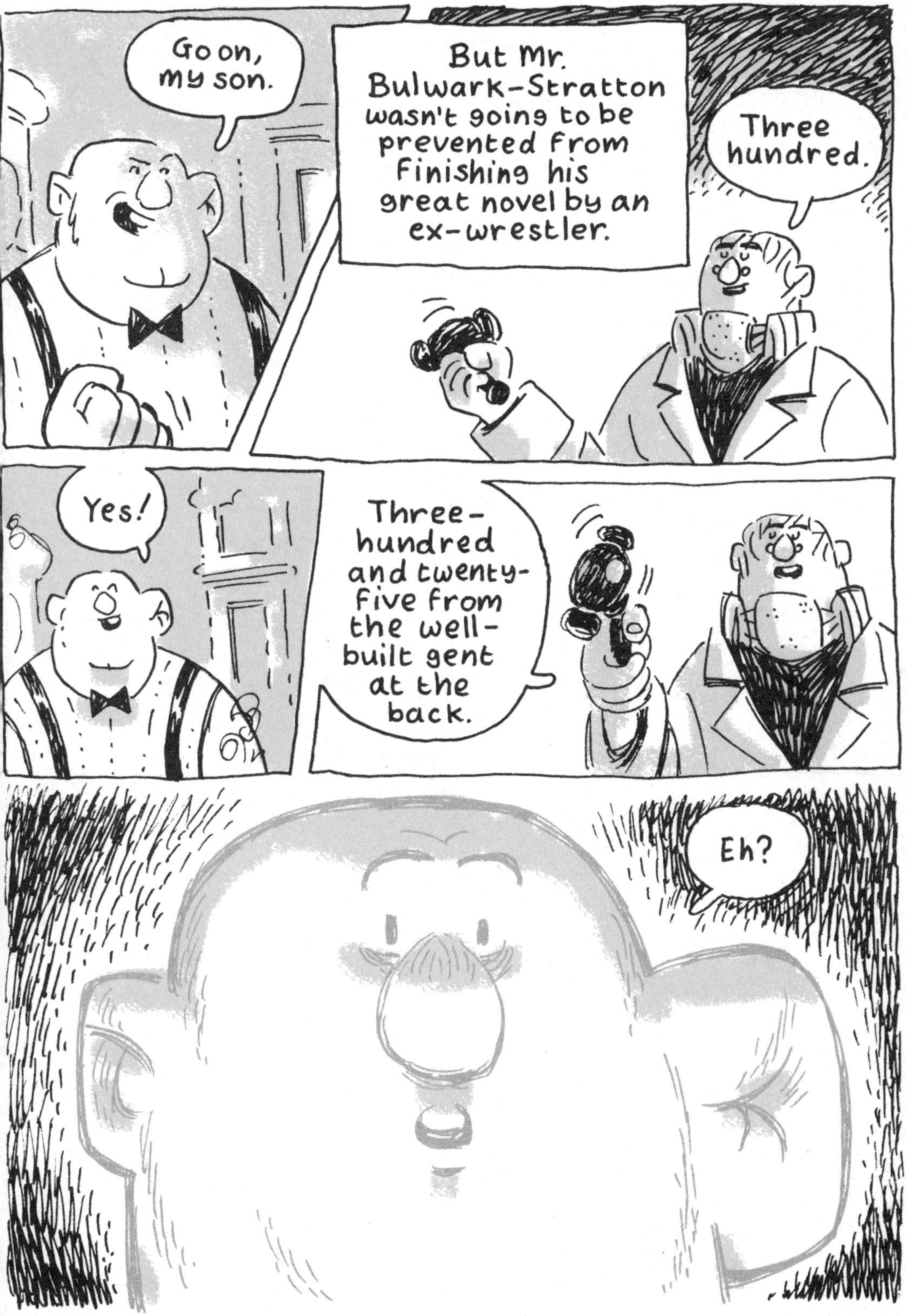
Go on, my son.
But Mr. Bulwark-Stratton wasn't going to be prevented from finishing his great novel by an ex-wrestler.
Three hundred.
Yes!
Three-hundred and twenty-five from the well-built gent at the back.
Eh?

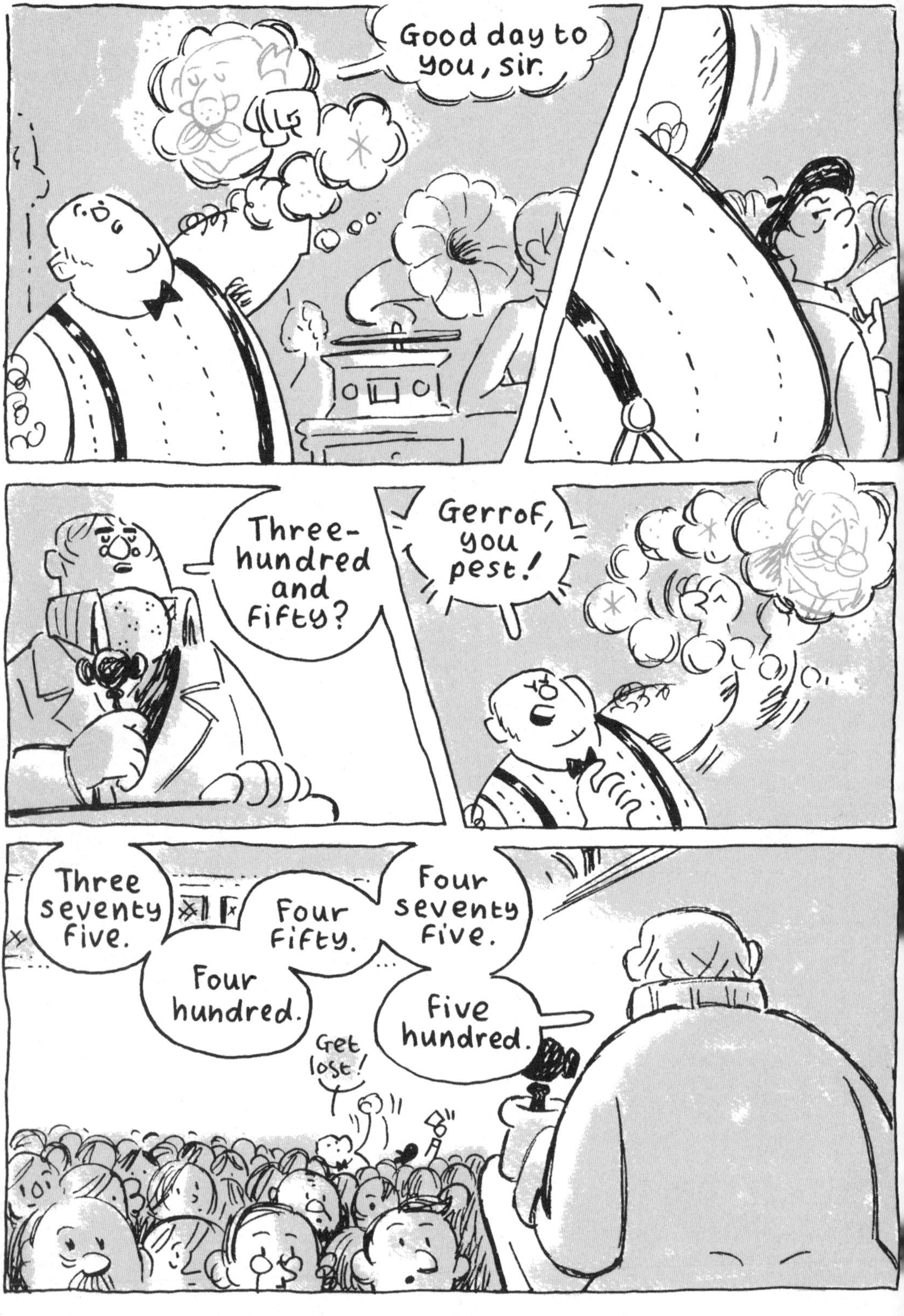
Good day to you, sir.
Three-hundred and Fifty?
Gerrof, you pest!
Three seventy five.
Four hundred.
Four Fifty.
Four seventy five.
Five hundred.
Get lost!

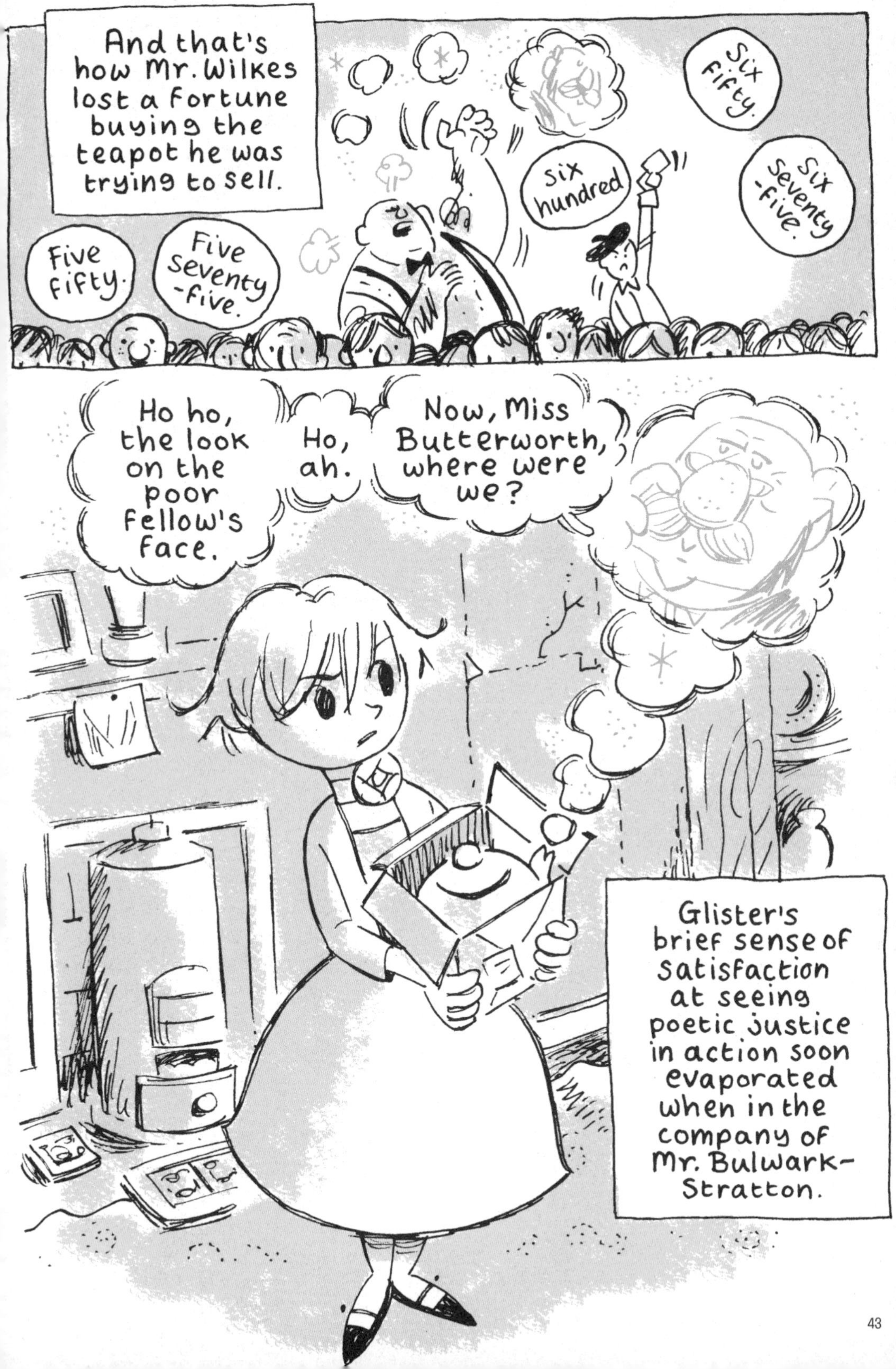
And that's how Mr. Wilkes lost a fortune buying the teapot he was trying to sell.
Five fifty.
Five seventy -five.
six hundred
Six fifty.
Six seventy -five.
Ho ho, the look on the poor fellow's face.
Ho, ah.
Now, Miss Butterworth, where were we?
Glister's brief sense of satisfaction at seeing poetic justice in action soon evaporated when in the company of Mr. Bulwark-Stratton.

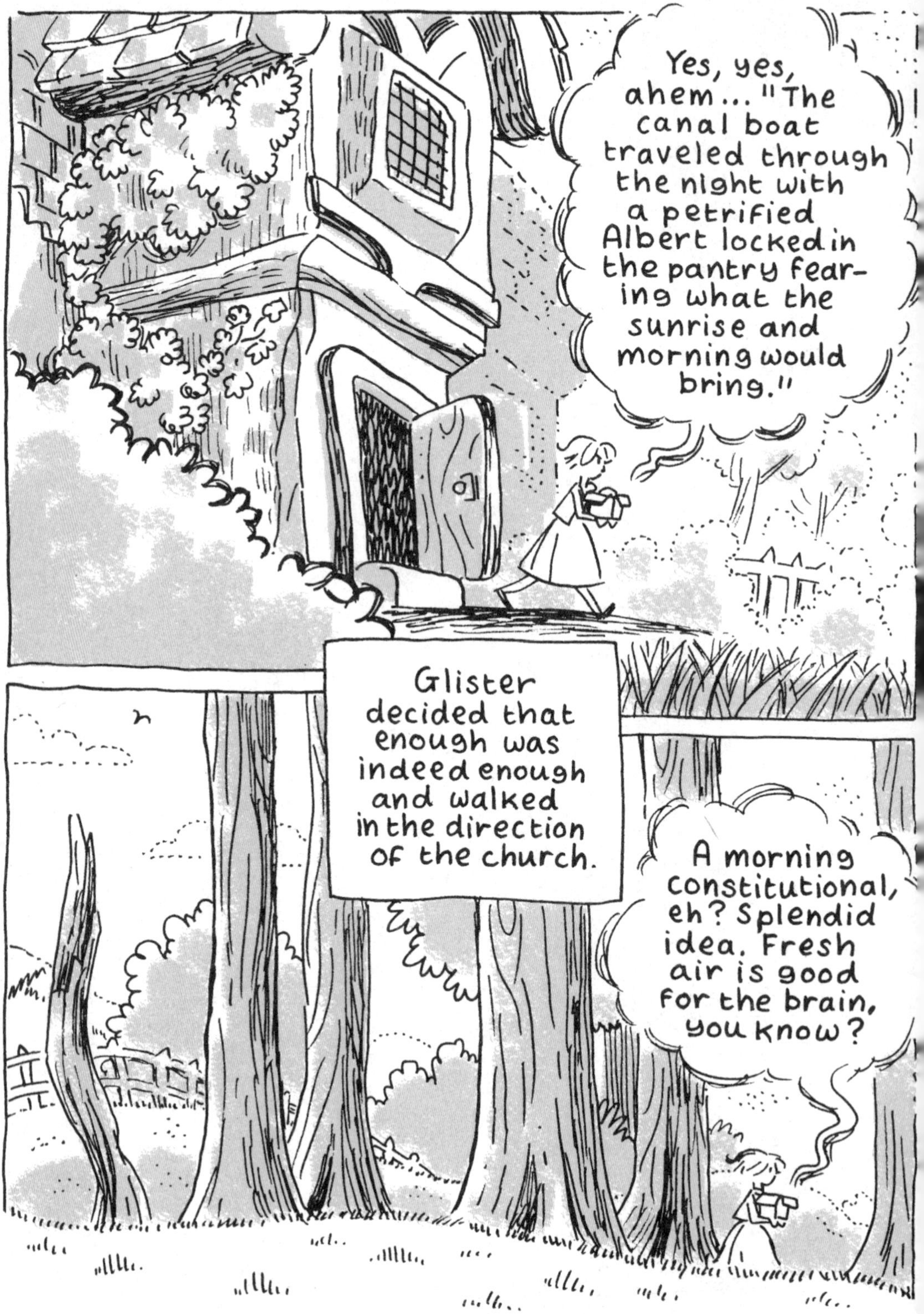
Yes, yes, ahem... "The canal boat traveled through the night with a petrified Albert locked in the pantry fearing what the sunrise and morning would bring."
Glister decided that enough was indeed enough and walked in the direction of the church.
A morning constitutional, eh? Splendid idea. Fresh air is good for the brain, you know?

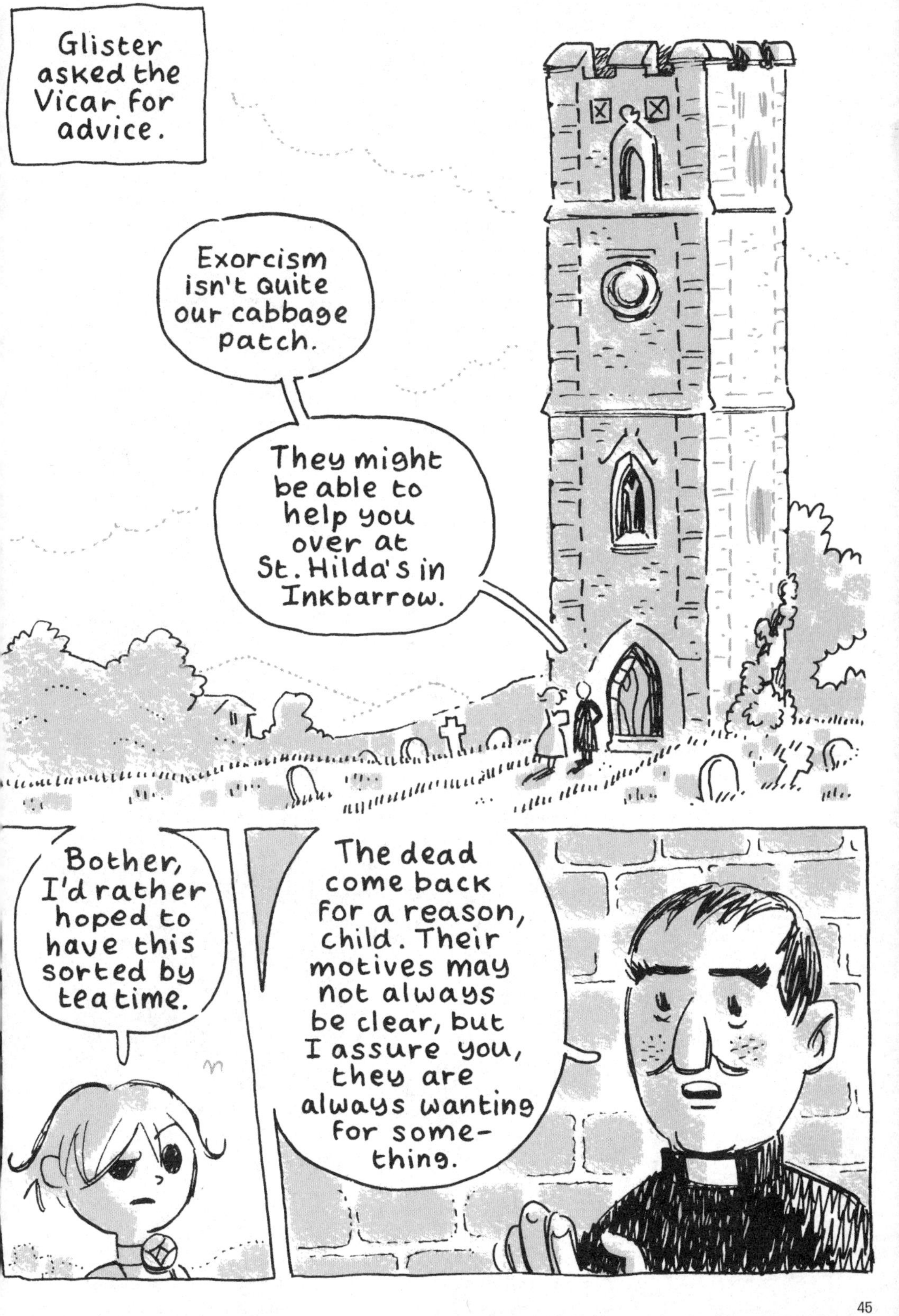
Glister asked the Vicar for advice.
Exorcism isn't quite our cabbage patch.
They might be able to help you over at St. Hilda's in Inkbarrow.
Bother, I'd rather hoped to have this sorted by teatime.
The dead come back for a reason, child. Their motives may not always be clear, but I assure you, they are always wanting for some-thing.

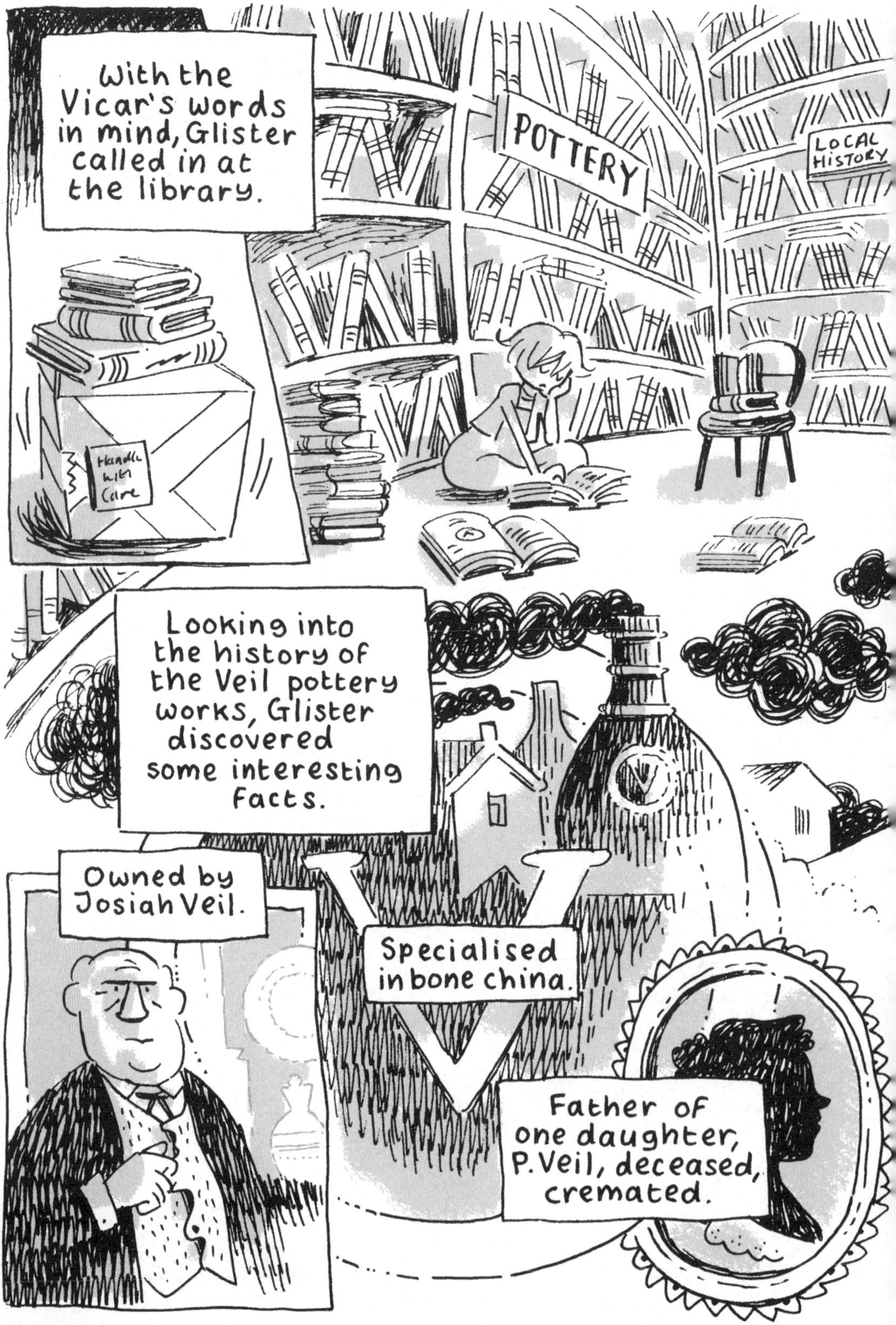

With the Vicar's words in mind, Glister called in at the library.
POTTERY
LOCAL HISTORY
Handle with Care
Looking into the history of the Veil pottery works, Glister discovered some interesting facts.
Owned by Josiah Veil.
Specialised in bone china.
Father of one daughter, P. Veil, deceased, cremated.

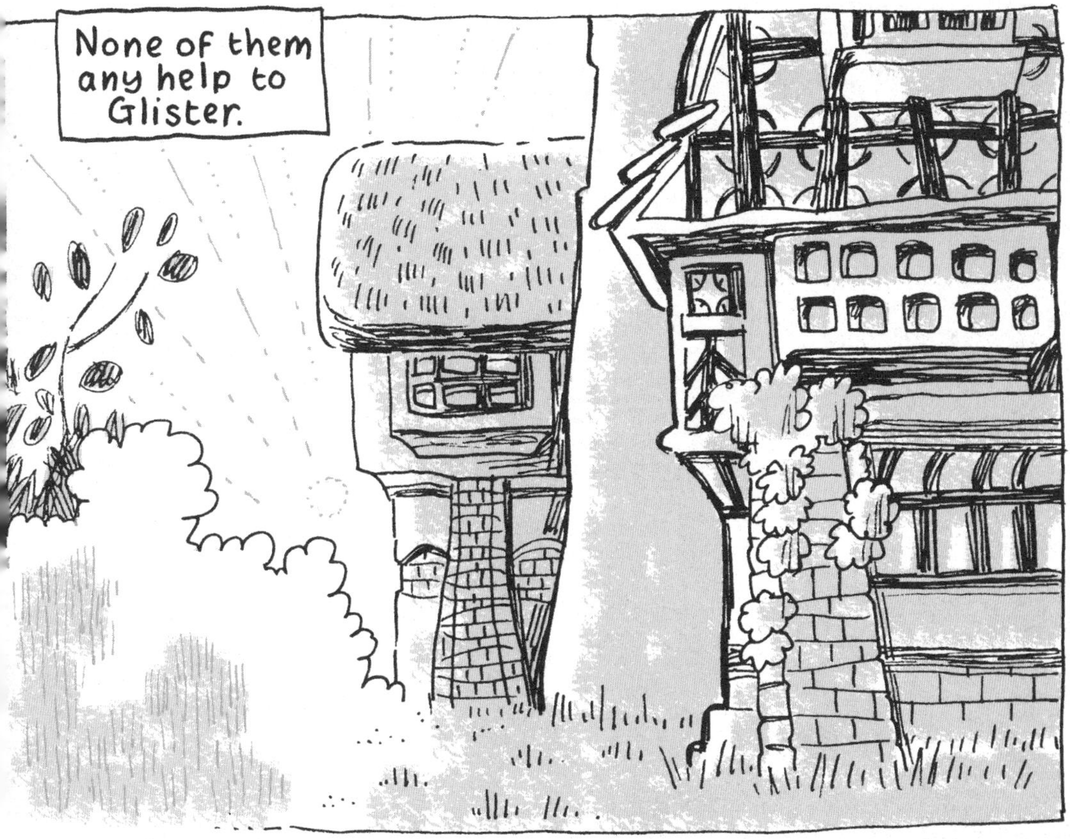
None of them any help to Glister.

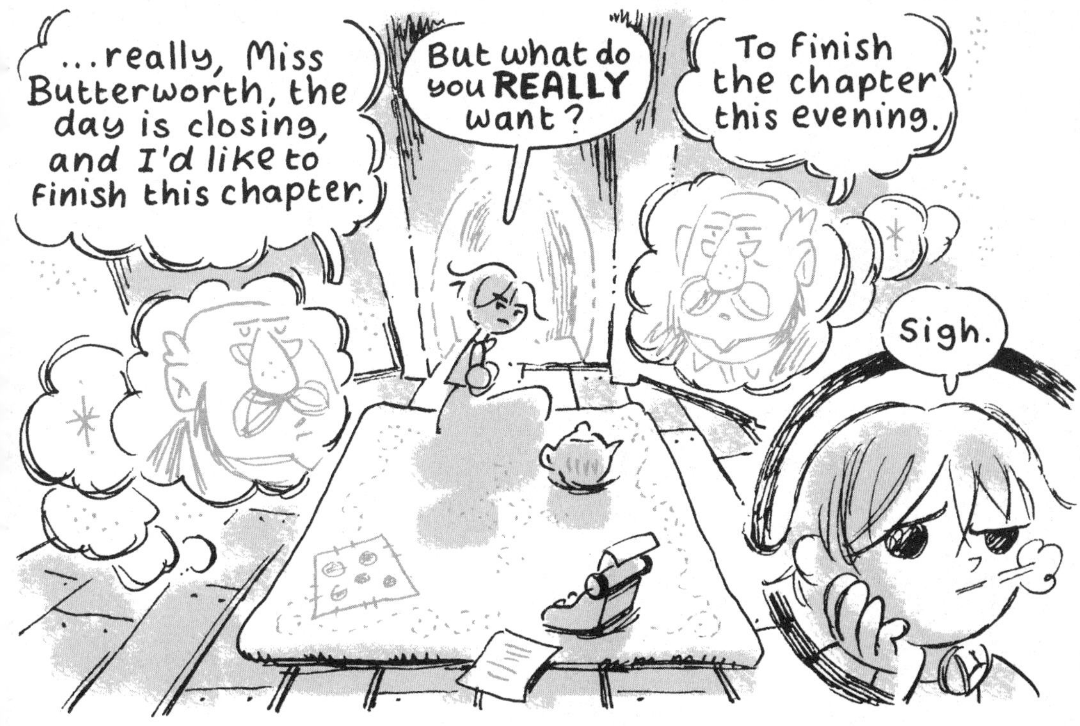
...really, Miss Butterworth, the day is closing, and I'd like to finish this chapter.
But what do you **REALLY** want?
To finish the chapter this evening.
Sigh.

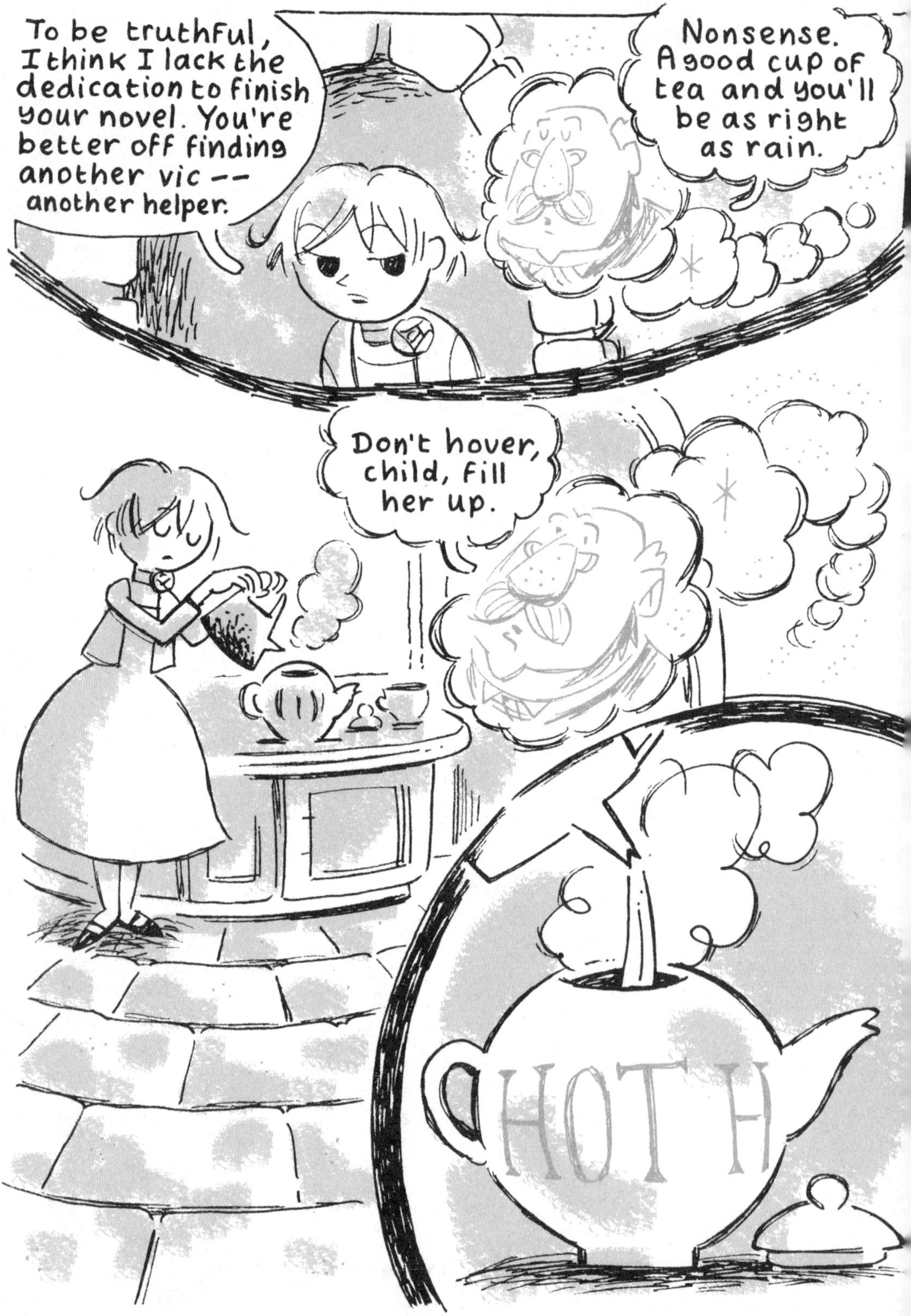
To be truthful, I think I lack the dedication to finish your novel. You're better off finding another vic -- another helper.
Nonsense. A good cup of tea and you'll be as right as rain.
Don't hover, child, fill her up.
HOT H

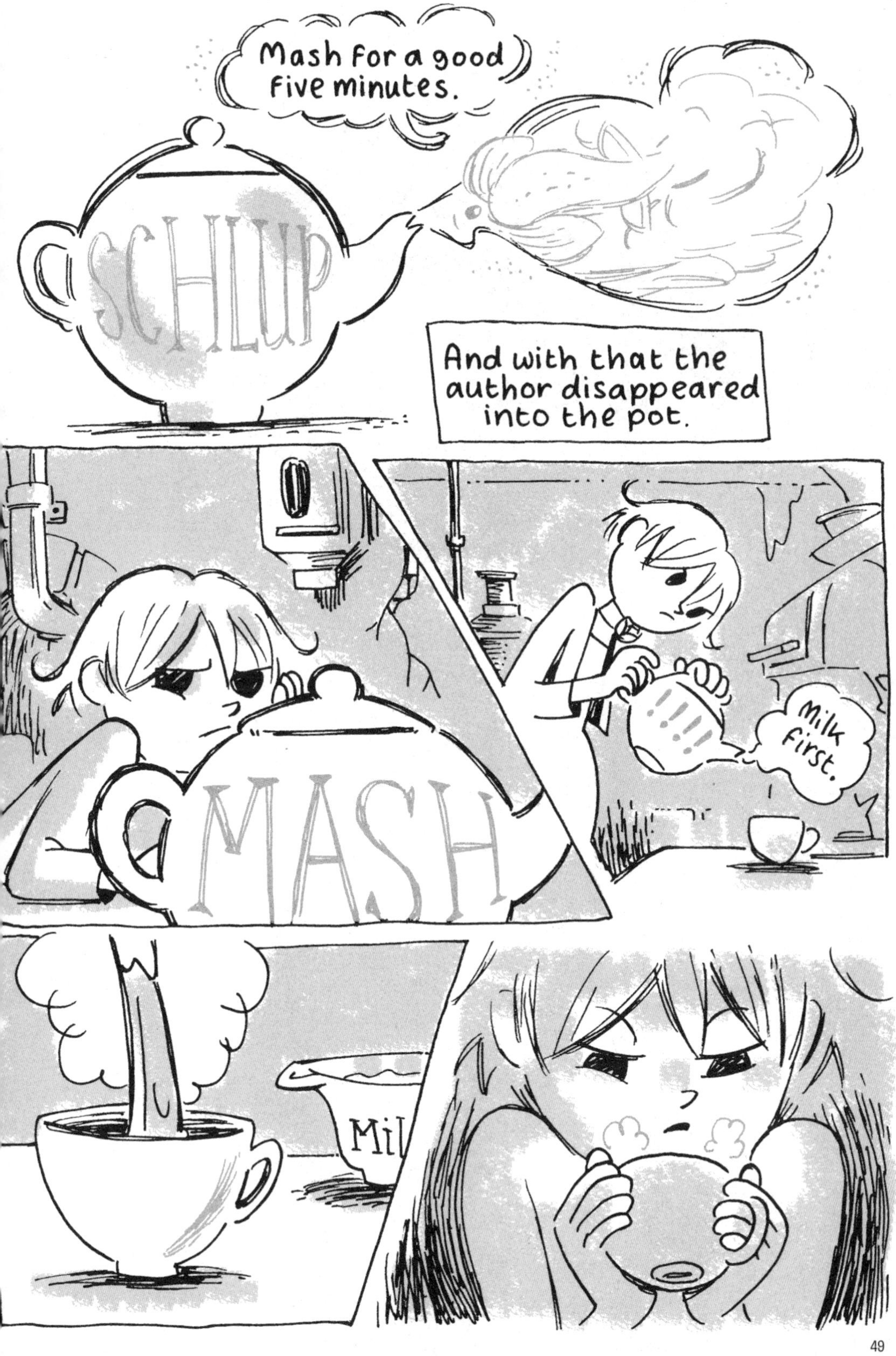

Mash for a good five minutes.
SCHLUP
And with that the author disappeared into the pot.
MASH
Milk first.
Mil

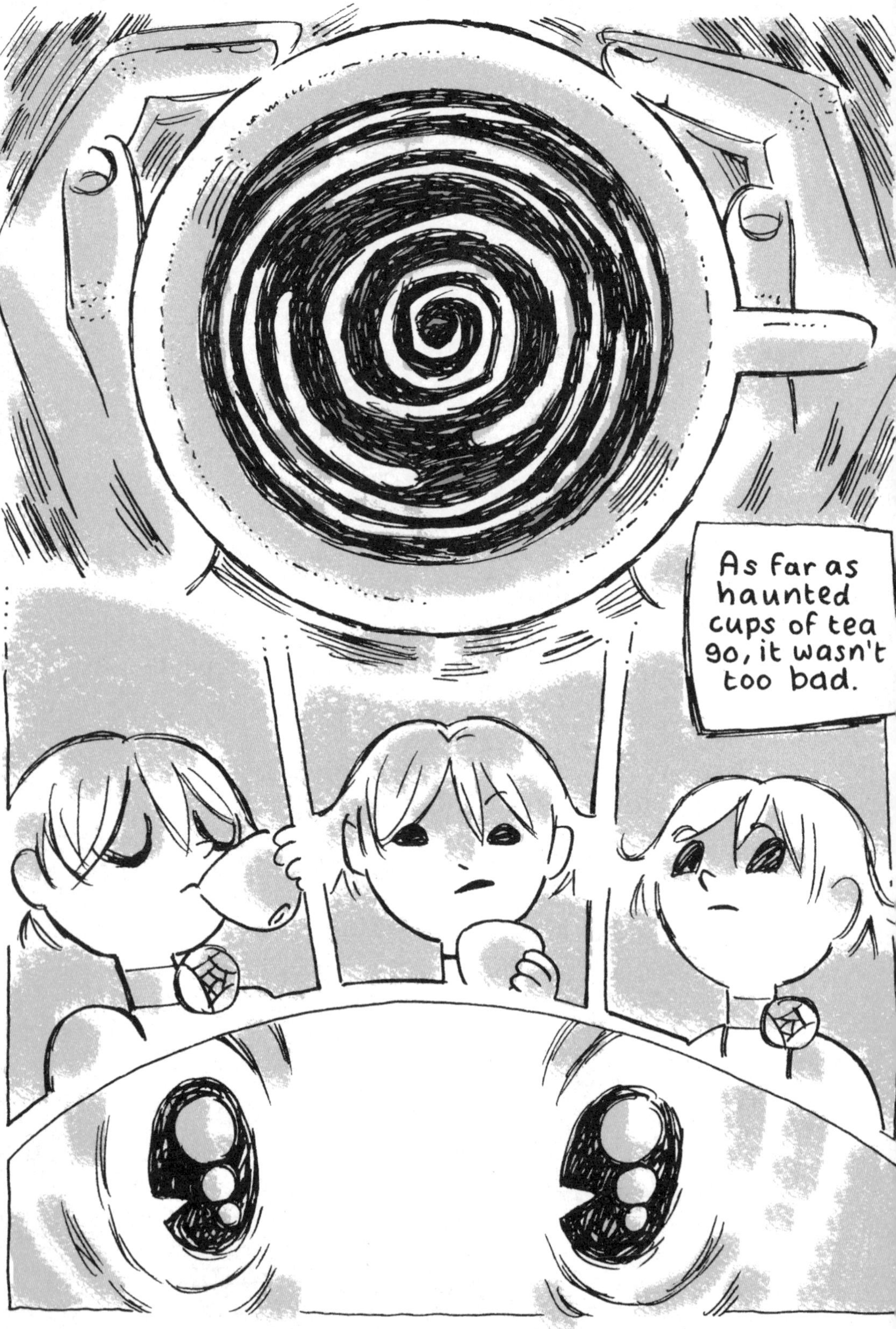
As far as haunted cups of tea go, it wasn't too bad.

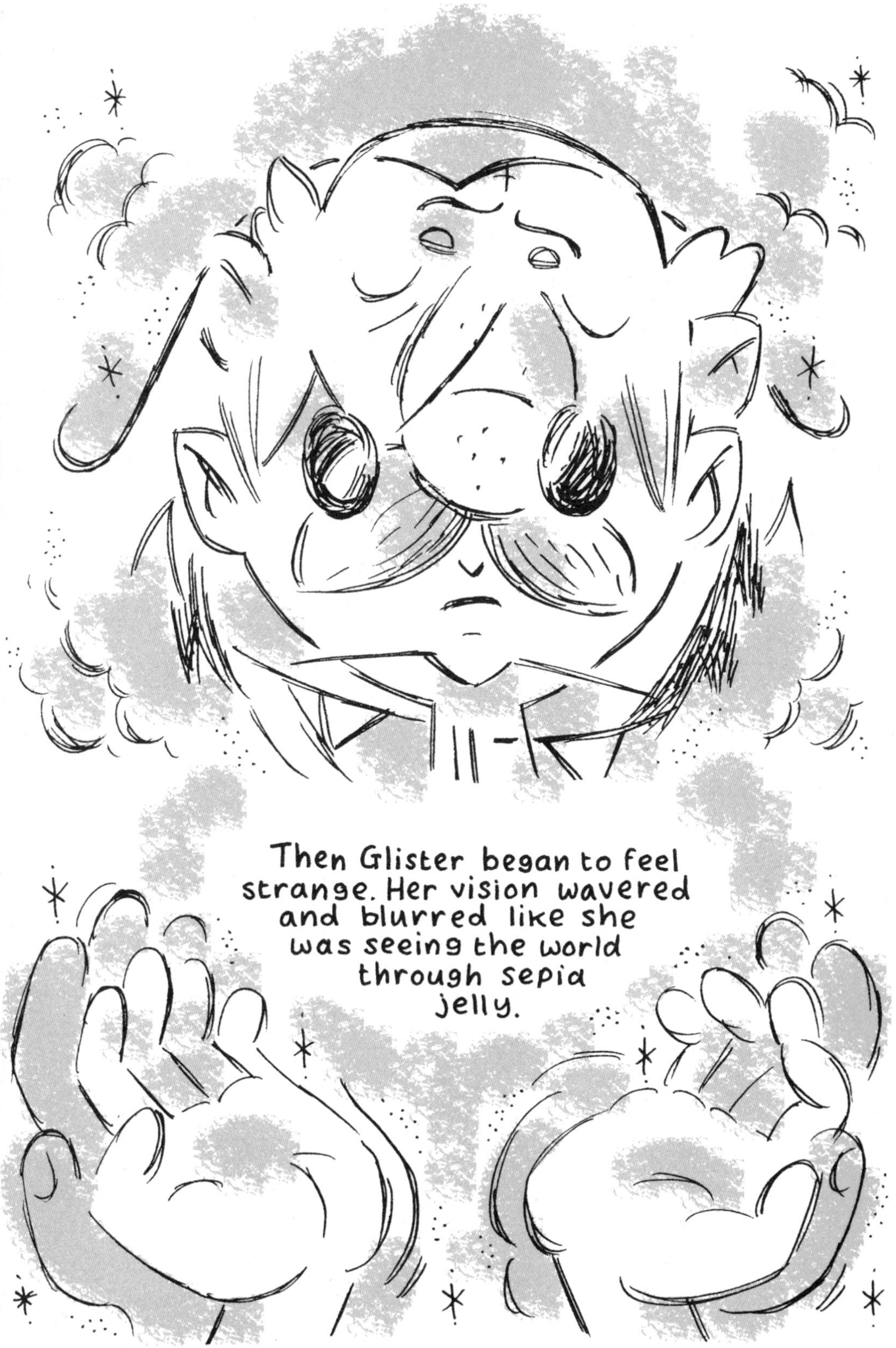
Then Glister began to feel strange. Her vision wavered and blurred like she was seeing the world through sepia jelly.

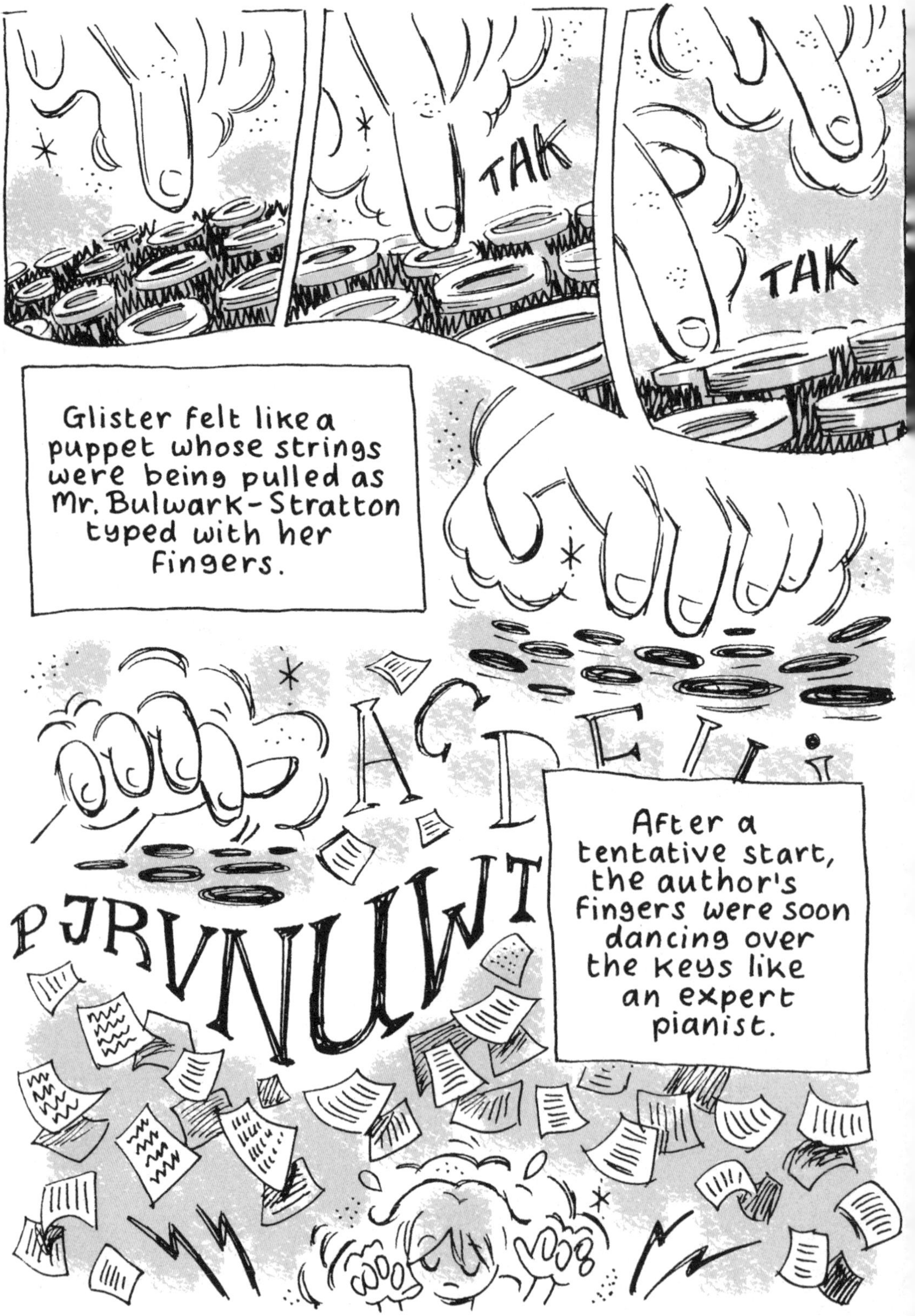
TAK
TAK
Glister felt like a puppet whose strings were being pulled as Mr. Bulwark-Stratton typed with her fingers.
After a tentative start, the author's fingers were soon dancing over the keys like an expert pianist.

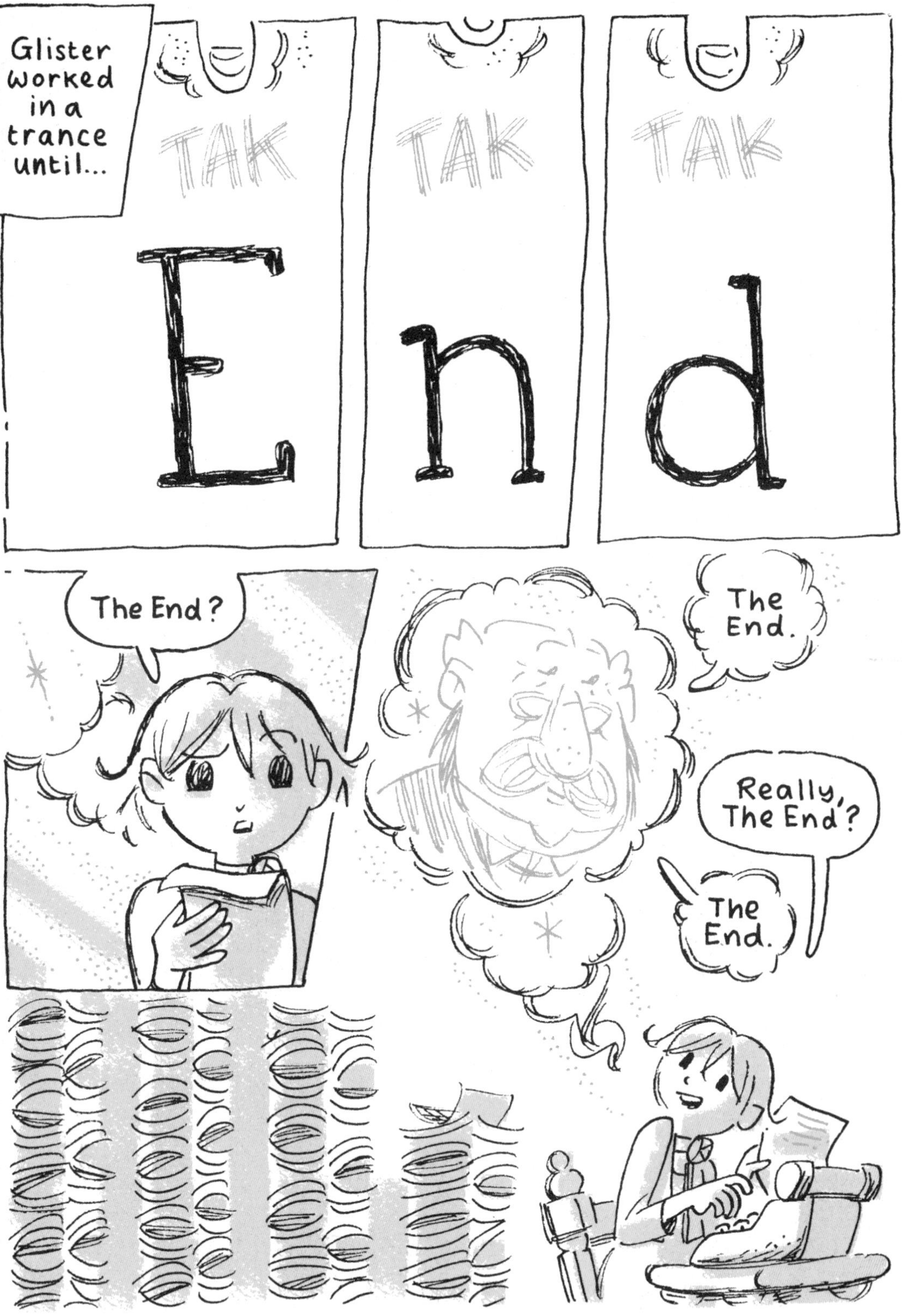

Glister worked in a trance until...
TAK
TAK
TAK
End
The End?
The End.
Really, The End?
The End.

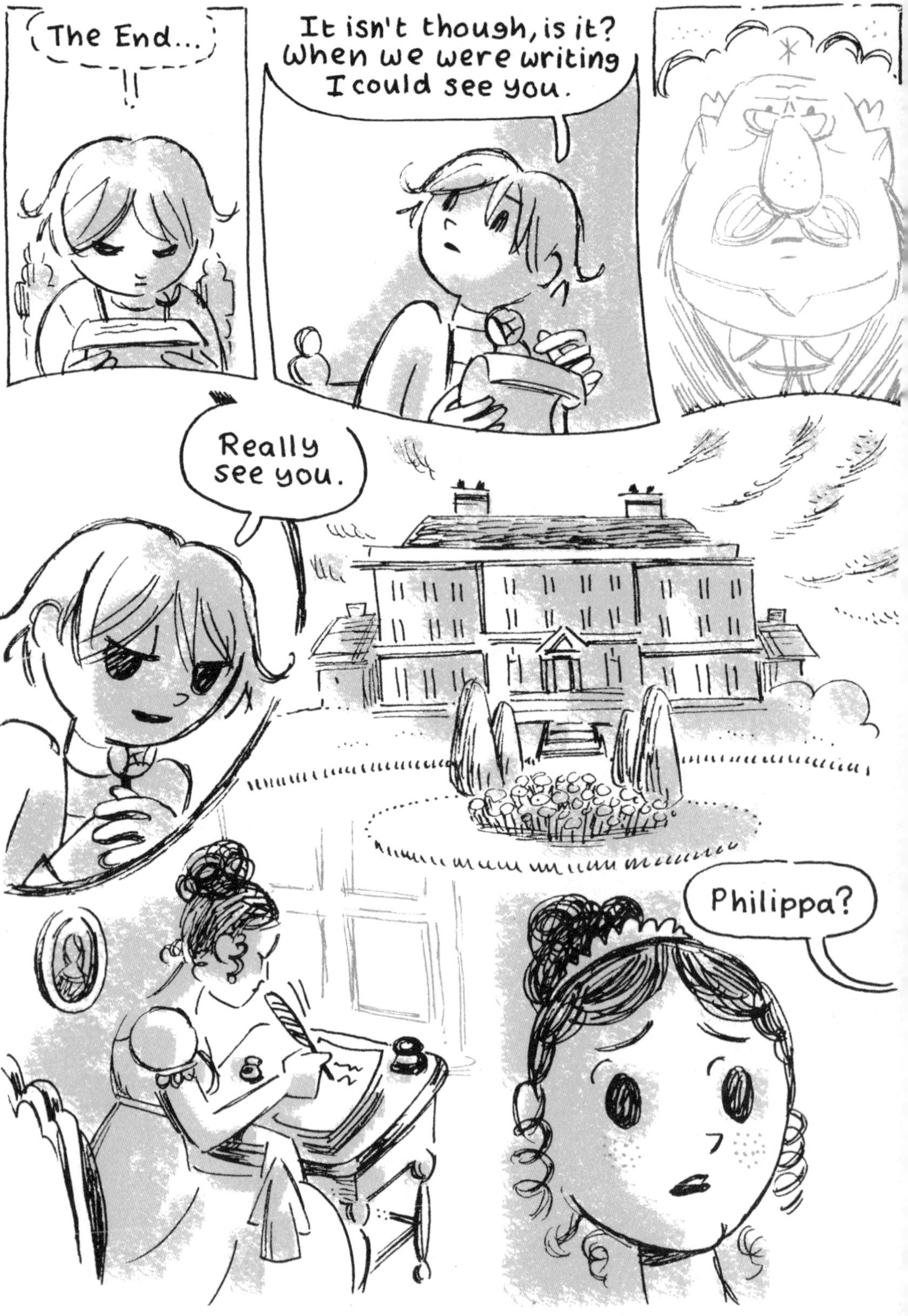
The End...
!!
It isn't though, is it? When we were writing I could see you.
Really see you.
Philippa?

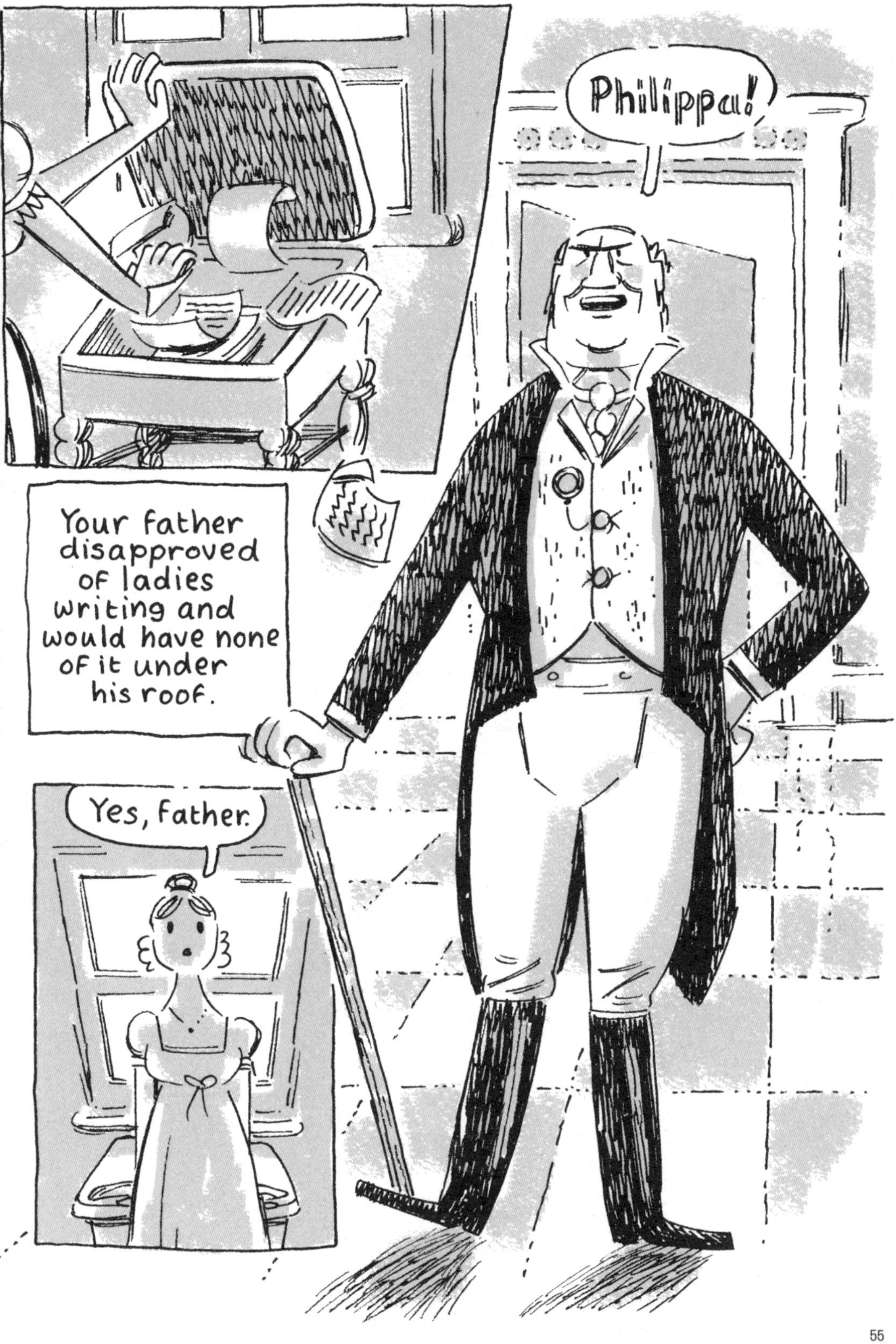
Philippa!
Your father disapproved of ladies writing and would have none of it under his roof.
Yes, father.

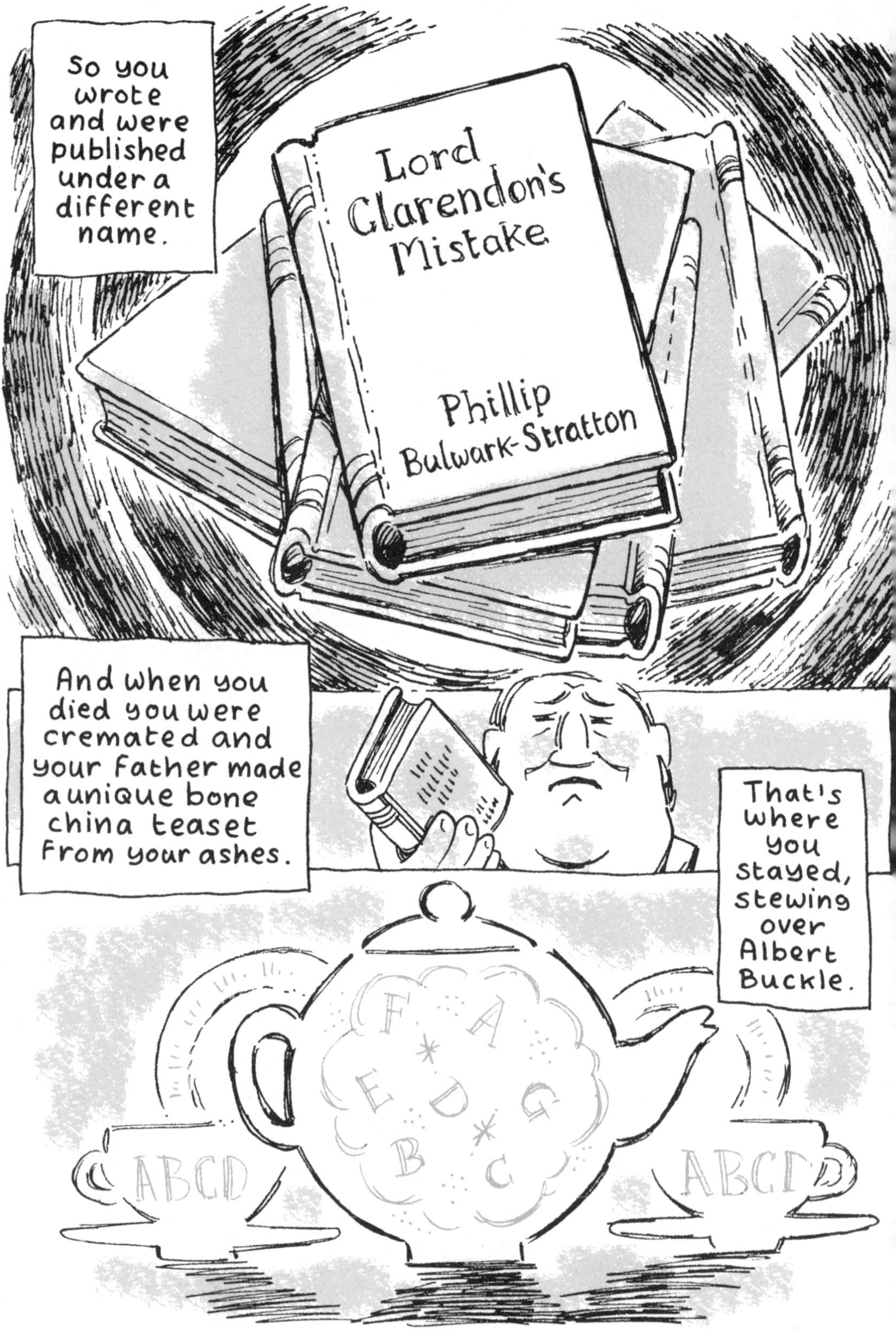
So you wrote and were published under a different name.
Lord Clarendon's Mistake
Phillip Bulwark-Stratton
And when you died you were cremated and your father made a unique bone china teaset from your ashes.
That's where you stayed, stewing over Albert Buckle.
F A E D G B C
ABCD
ABCD

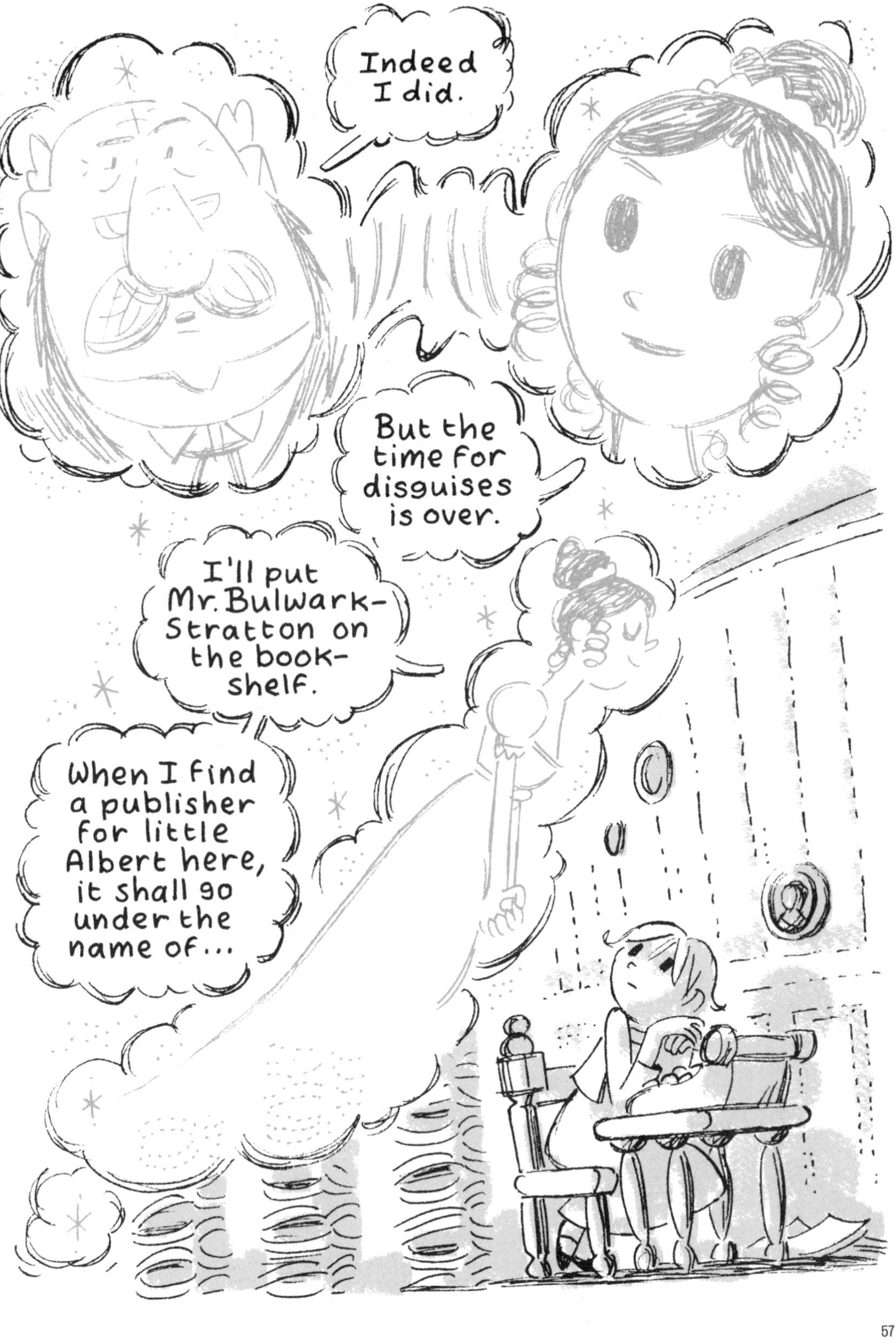
Indeed I did.
But the time for disguises is over.
I'll put Mr. Bulwark-Stratton on the book-shelf.
When I find a publisher for little Albert here, it shall go under the name of...

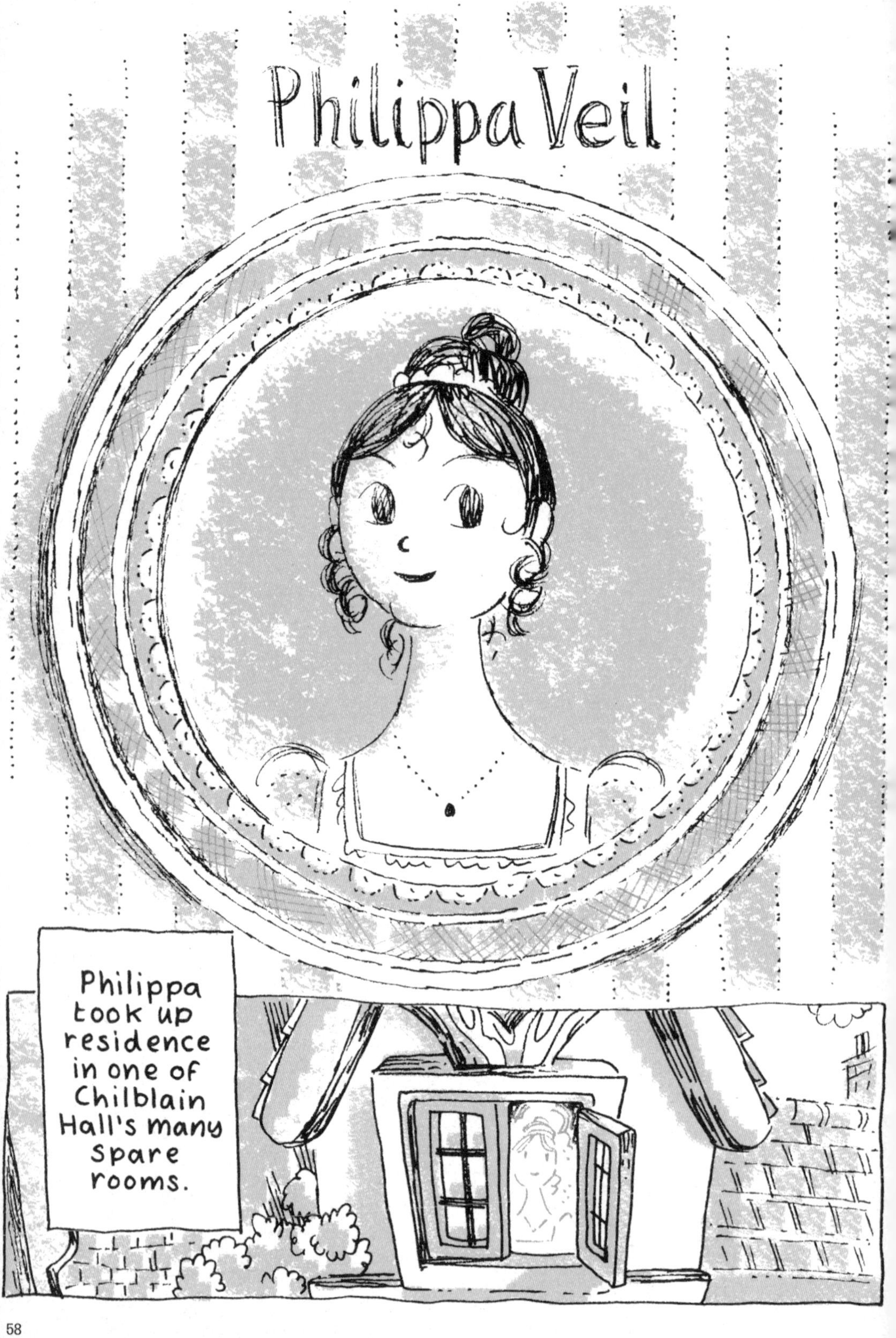
Philippa Veil
Philippa took up residence in one of Chilblain Hall's many spare rooms.

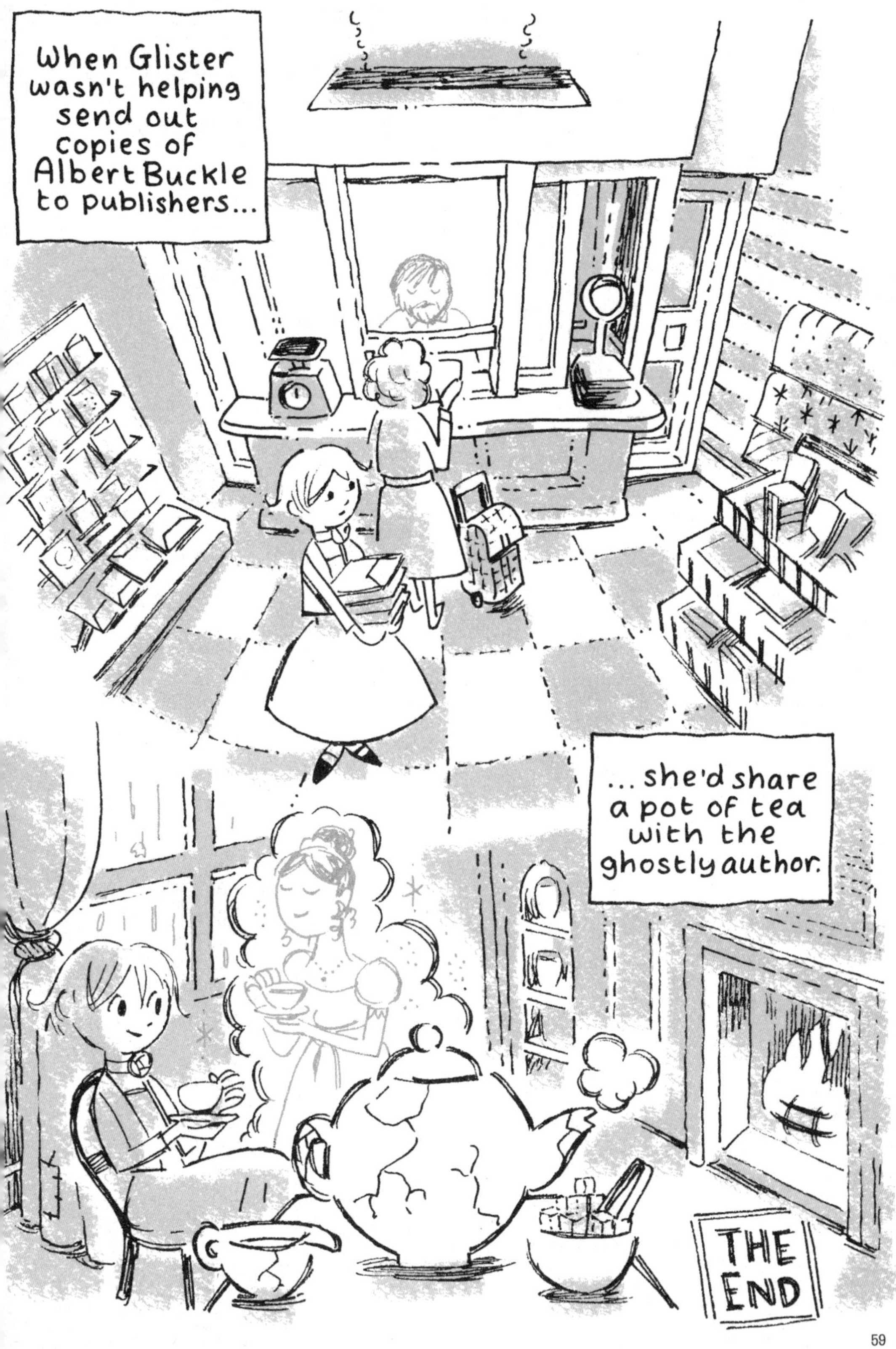
When Glister wasn't helping send out copies of Albert Buckle to publishers...
...she'd share a pot of tea with the ghostly author.
THE END

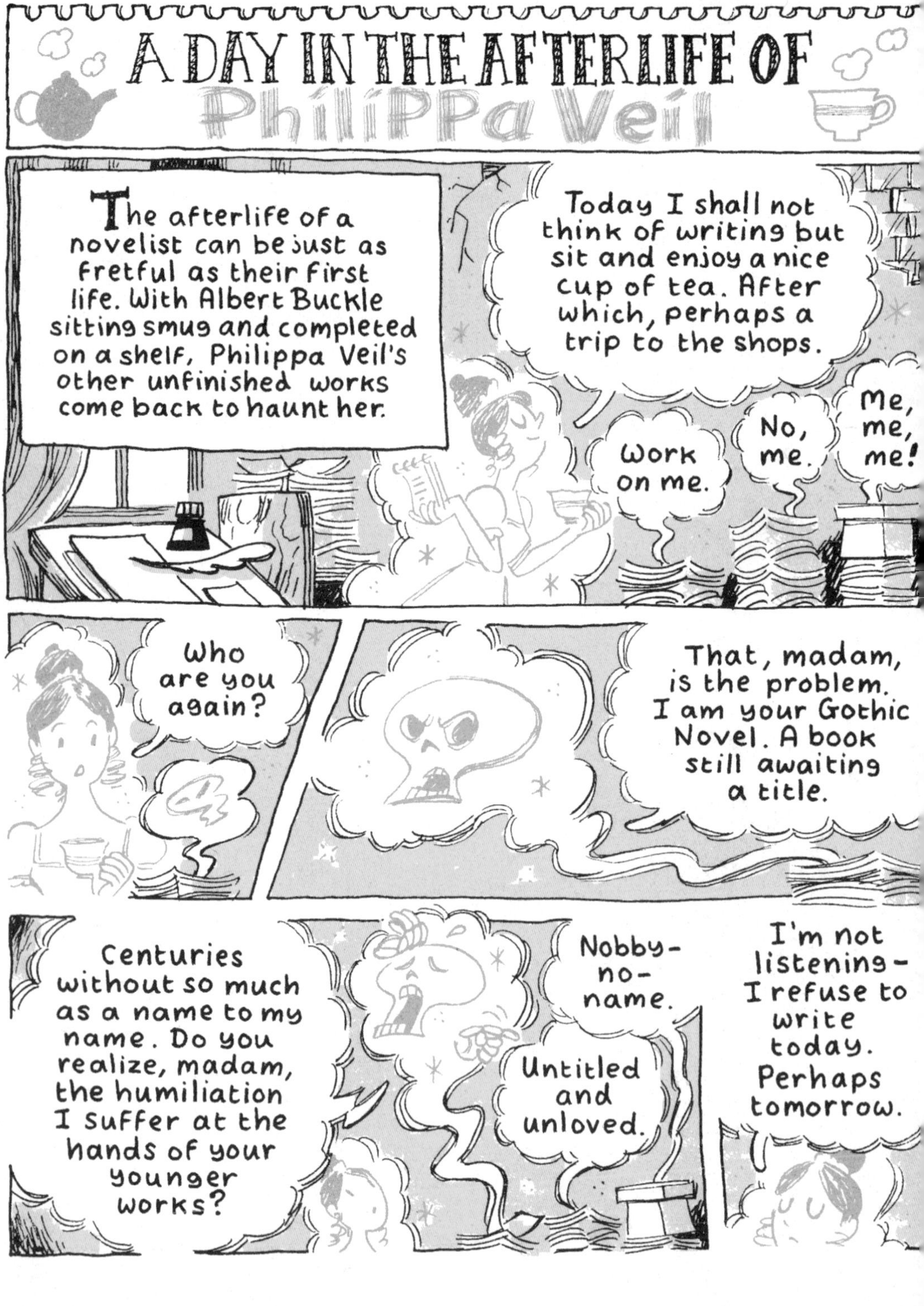
A DAY IN THE AFTERLIFE OF
Philippa Veil
The afterlife of a novelist can be just as fretful as their first life. With Albert Buckle sitting smug and completed on a shelf, Philippa Veil's other unfinished works come back to haunt her.
Today I shall not think of writing but sit and enjoy a nice cup of tea. After which, perhaps a trip to the shops.
Work on me.
No, me.
Me, me, me!
Who are you again?
That, madam, is the problem. I am your Gothic Novel. A book still awaiting a title.
Centuries without so much as a name to my name. Do you realize, madam, the humiliation I suffer at the hands of your younger works?
Nobby-no-name.
Untitled and unloved.
I'm not listening - I refuse to write today. Perhaps tomorrow.

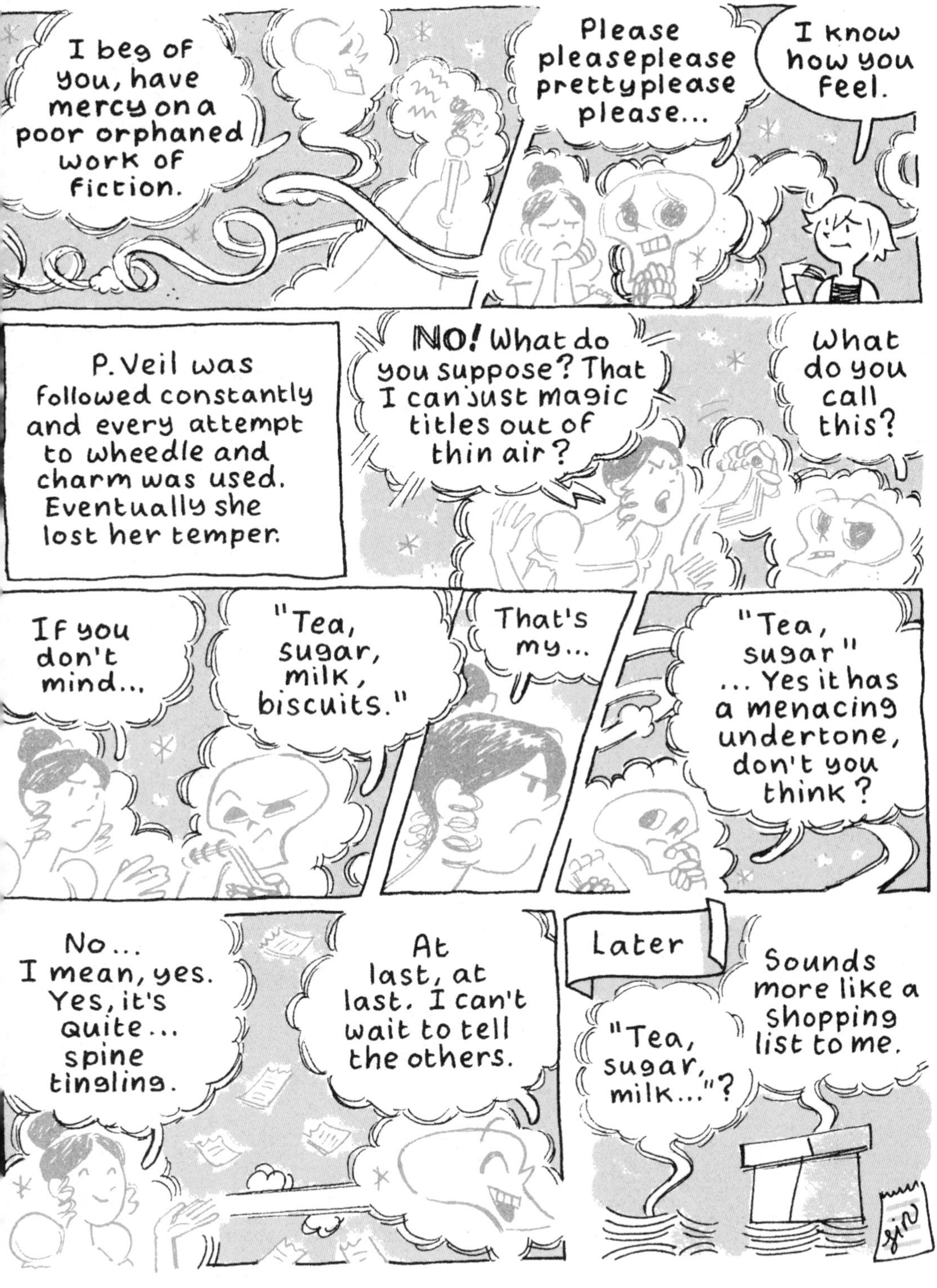
I beg of you, have mercy on a poor orphaned work of fiction.
Please pleaseplease prettyplease please...
I know how you feel.
P. Veil was followed constantly and every attempt to wheedle and charm was used. Eventually she lost her temper.
NO! What do you suppose? That I can just magic titles out of thin air?
What do you call this?
If you don't mind...
"Tea, sugar, milk, biscuits."
That's my...
"Tea, sugar" ... Yes it has a menacing undertone, don't you think?
No... I mean, yes. Yes, it's quite... spine tingling.
At last, at last. I can't wait to tell the others.
Later
"Tea, sugar, milk..."?
Sounds more like a shopping list to me.

WHAT Mr. Wilkes DID NEXT?

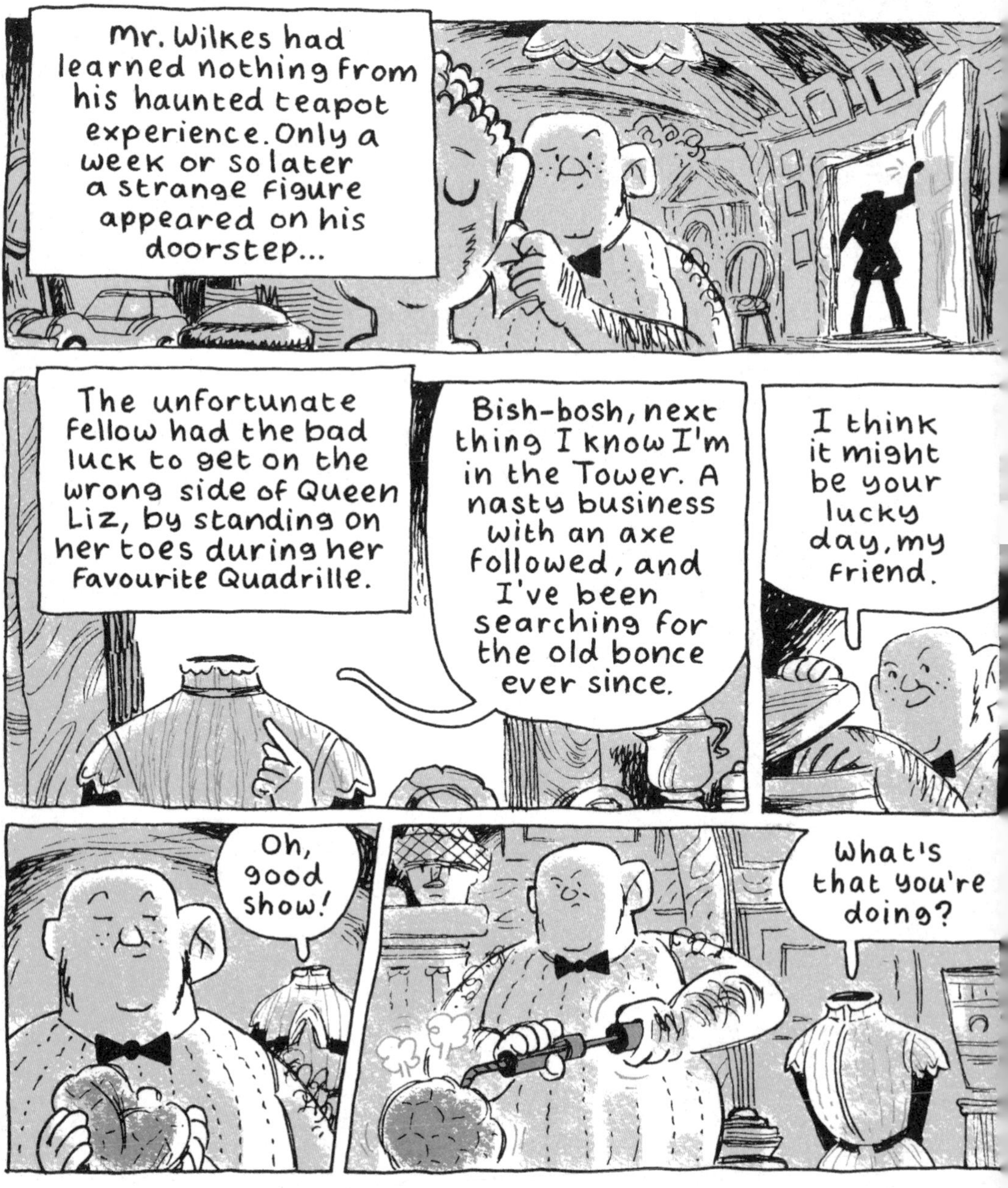
Mr. Wilkes had learned nothing from his haunted teapot experience. Only a week or so later a strange figure appeared on his doorstep...
The unfortunate fellow had the bad luck to get on the wrong side of Queen Liz, by standing on her toes during her favourite Quadrille.
Bish-bosh, next thing I know I'm in the Tower. A nasty business with an axe followed, and I've been searching for the old bonce ever since.
I think it might be your lucky day, my friend.
Oh, good show!
What's that you're doing?

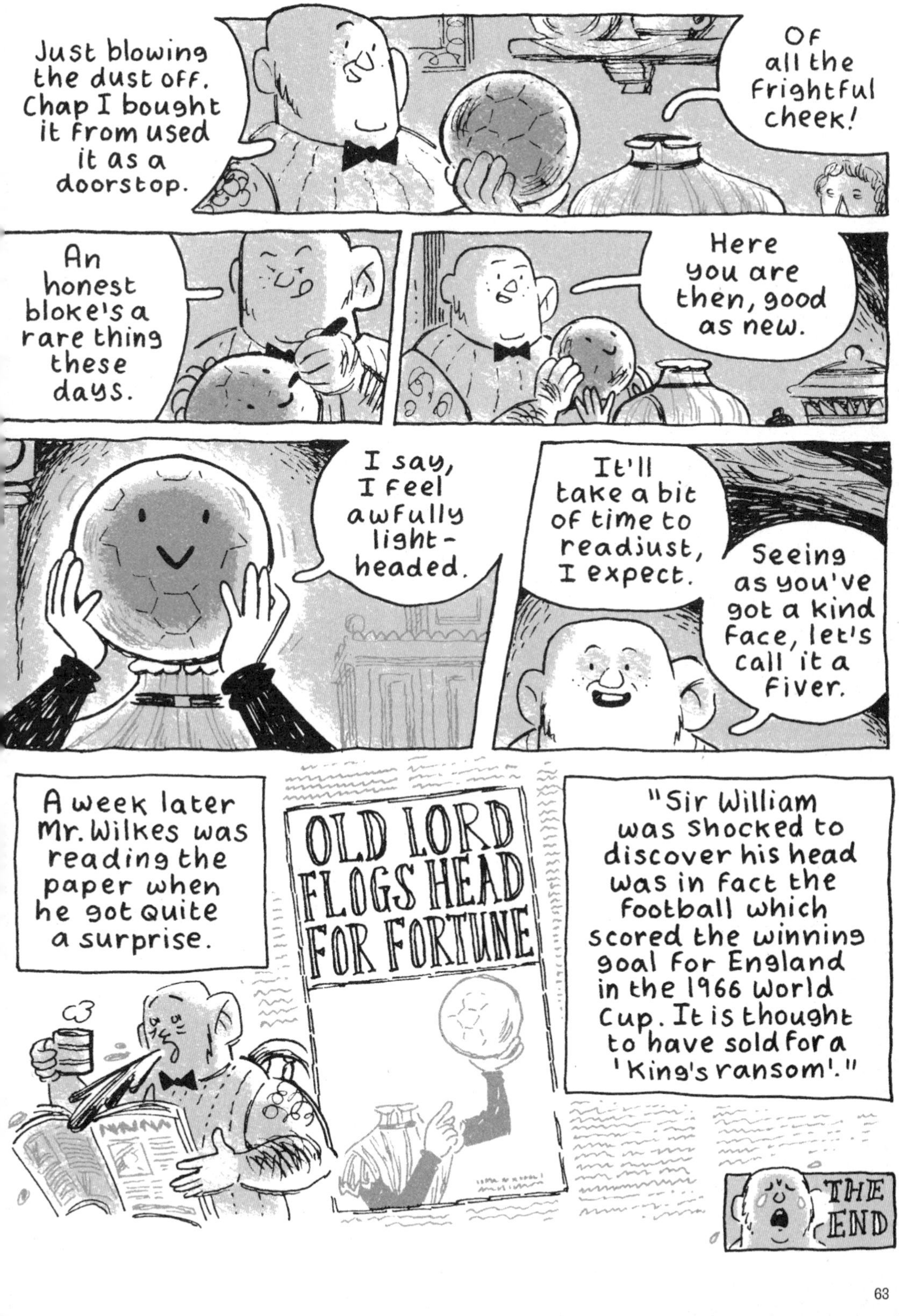

Just blowing the dust off. Chap I bought it from used it as a doorstop.
Of all the frightful cheek!
An honest bloke's a rare thing these days.
Here you are then, good as new.
I say, I feel awfully light-headed.
It'll take a bit of time to readjust, I expect.
Seeing as you've got a kind face, let's call it a fiver.
A week later Mr. Wilkes was reading the paper when he got quite a surprise.
OLD LORD FLOGS HEAD FOR FORTUNE
"Sir William was shocked to discover his head was in fact the football which scored the winning goal for England in the 1966 World Cup. It is thought to have sold for a 'King's ransom'."
THE END

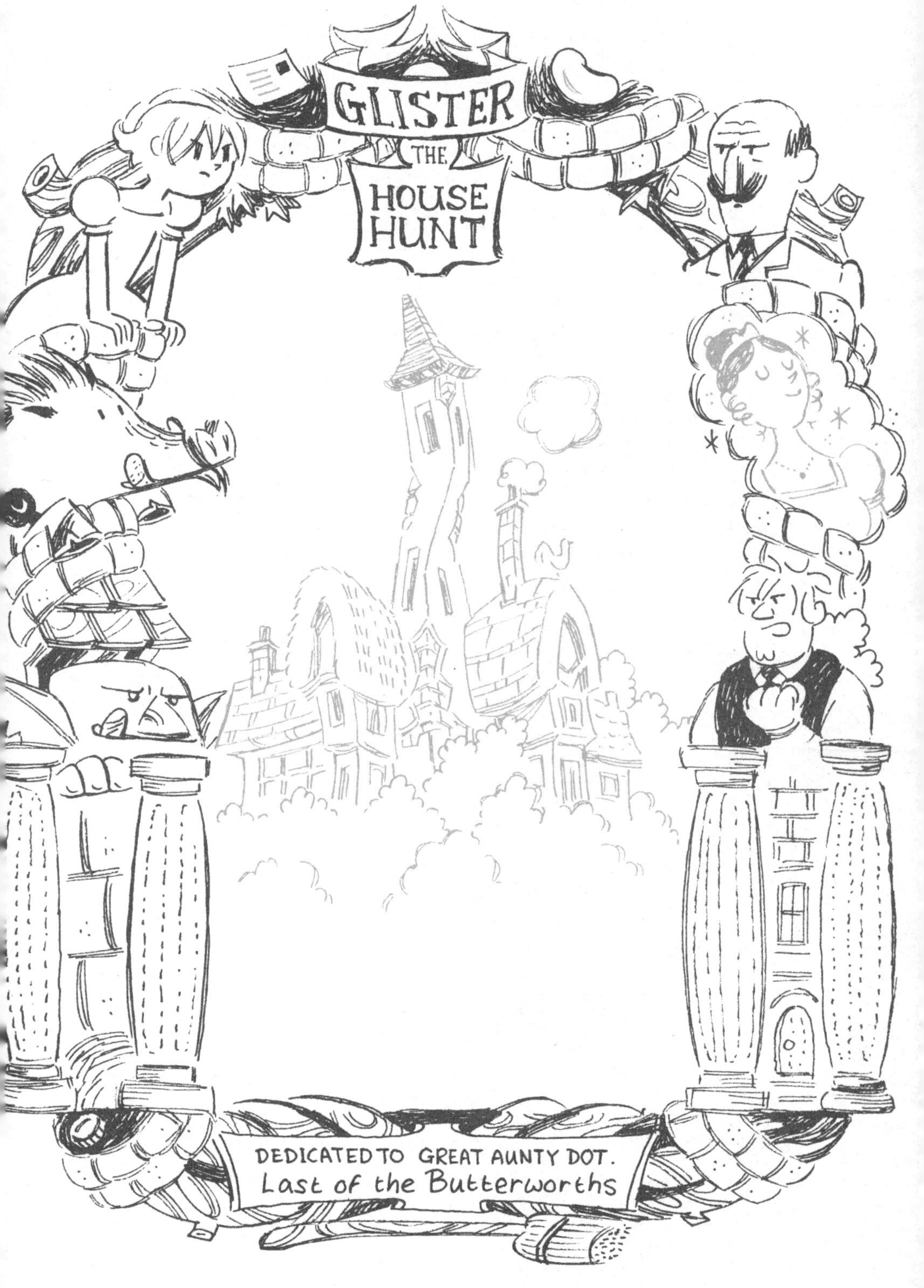

GLISTER
THE
HOUSE HUNT
DEDICATED TO GREAT AUNTY DOT.
Last of the Butterworths

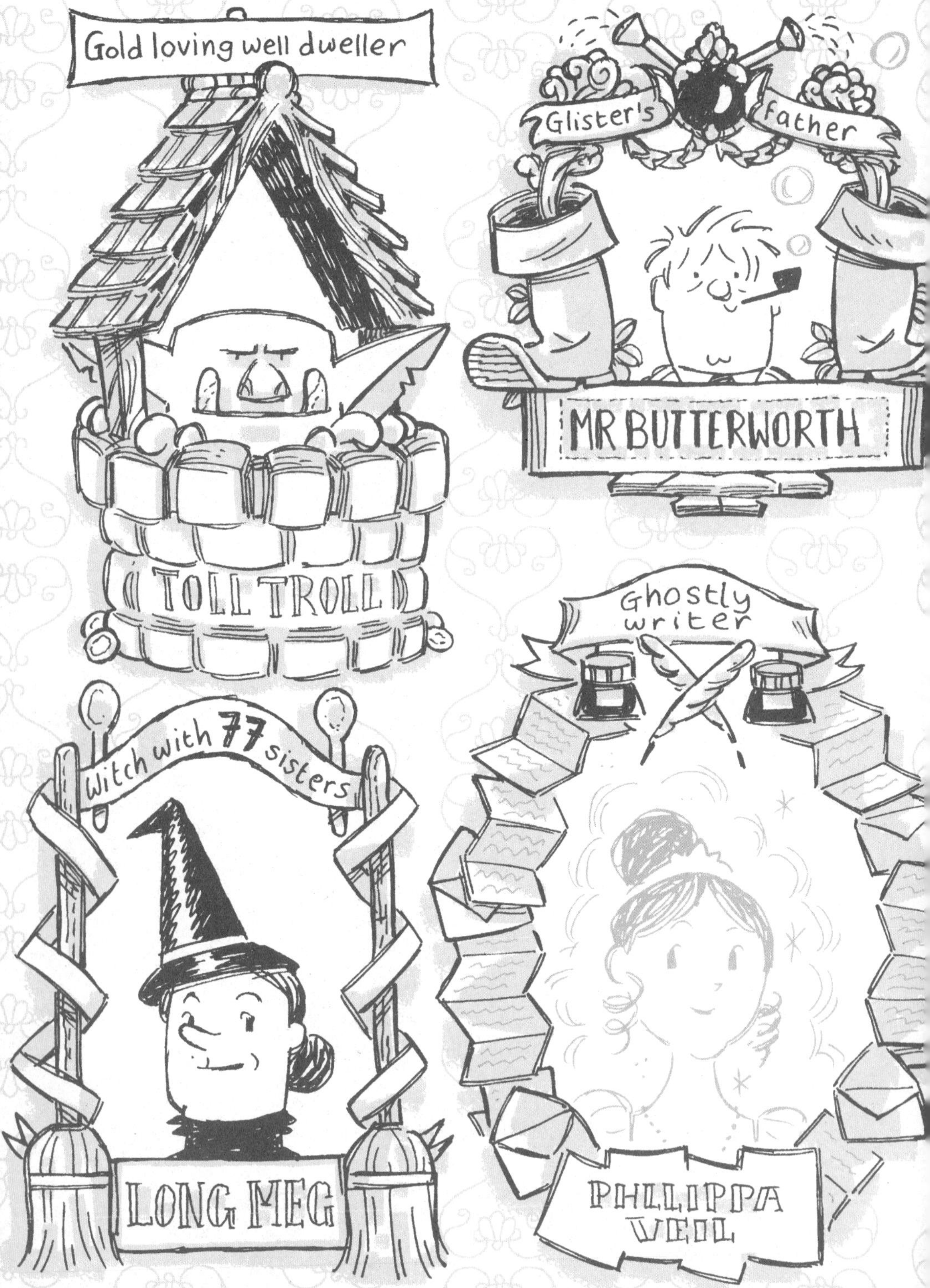
Gold loving well dweller
TOLL TROLL
Glister's father
MR BUTTERWORTH
Witch with 77 sisters
LONG MEG
Ghostly writer
PHILLIPPA VEIL

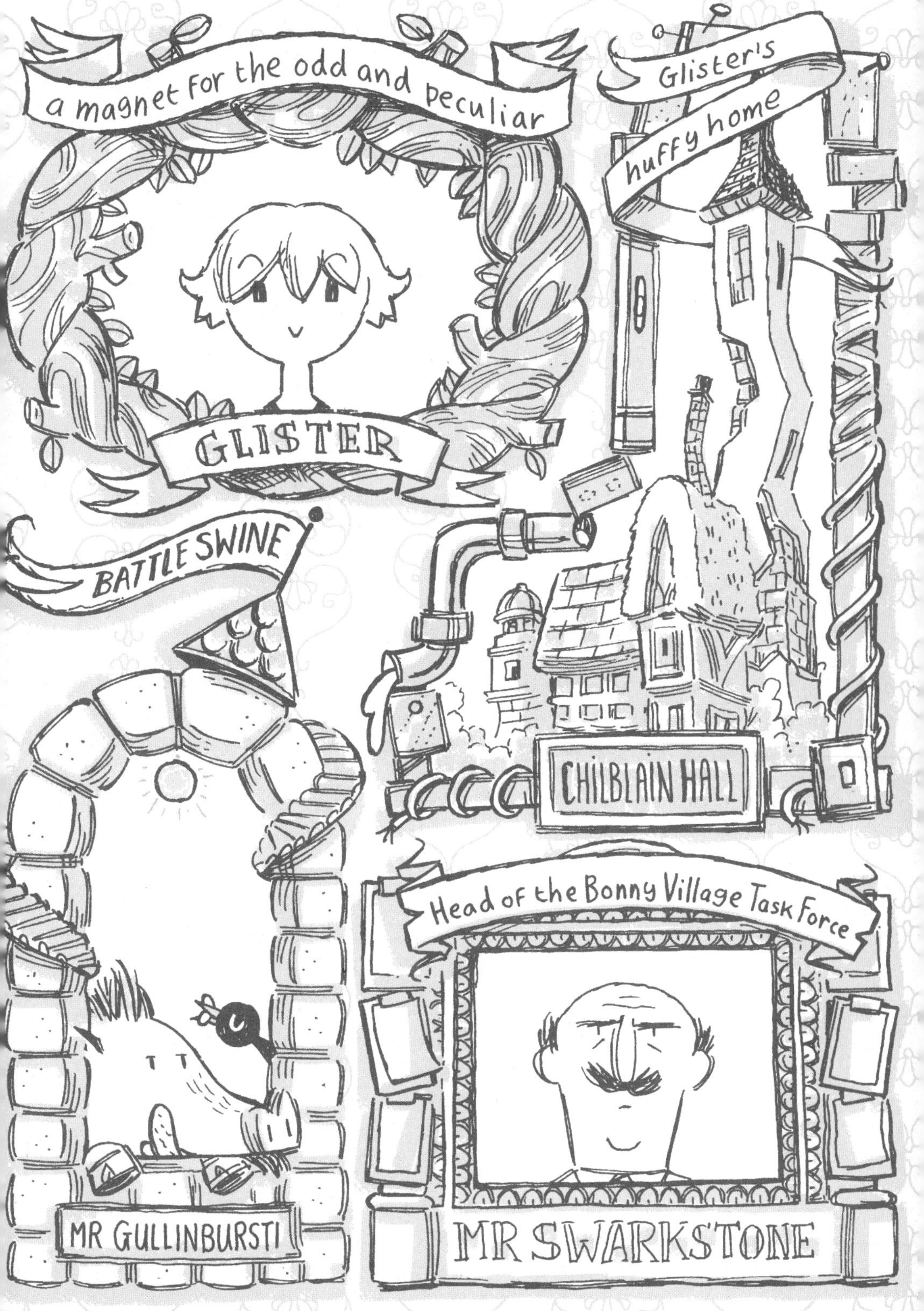
a magnet for the odd and peculiar
GLISTER
Glister's huffy home
CHILBLAIN HALL
BATTLE SWINE
MR GULLINBURSTI
Head of the Bonny Village Task Force
MR SWARKSTONE

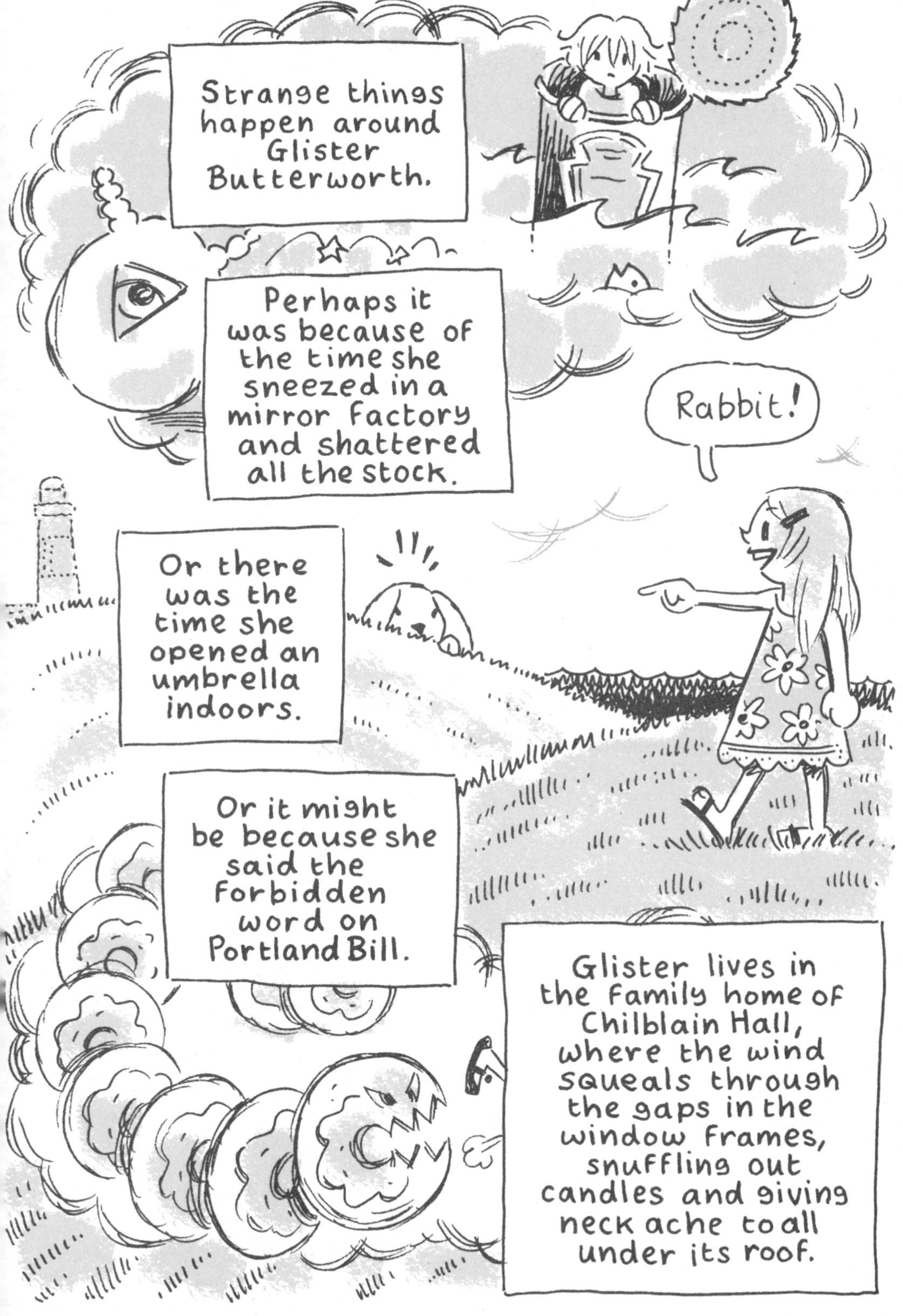

Strange things happen around Glister Butterworth.
Perhaps it was because of the time she sneezed in a mirror factory and shattered all the stock.
Rabbit!
Or there was the time she opened an umbrella indoors.
Or it might be because she said the forbidden word on Portland Bill.
Glister lives in the family home of Chilblain Hall, where the wind squeals through the gaps in the window frames, snuffling out candles and giving neck ache to all under its roof.

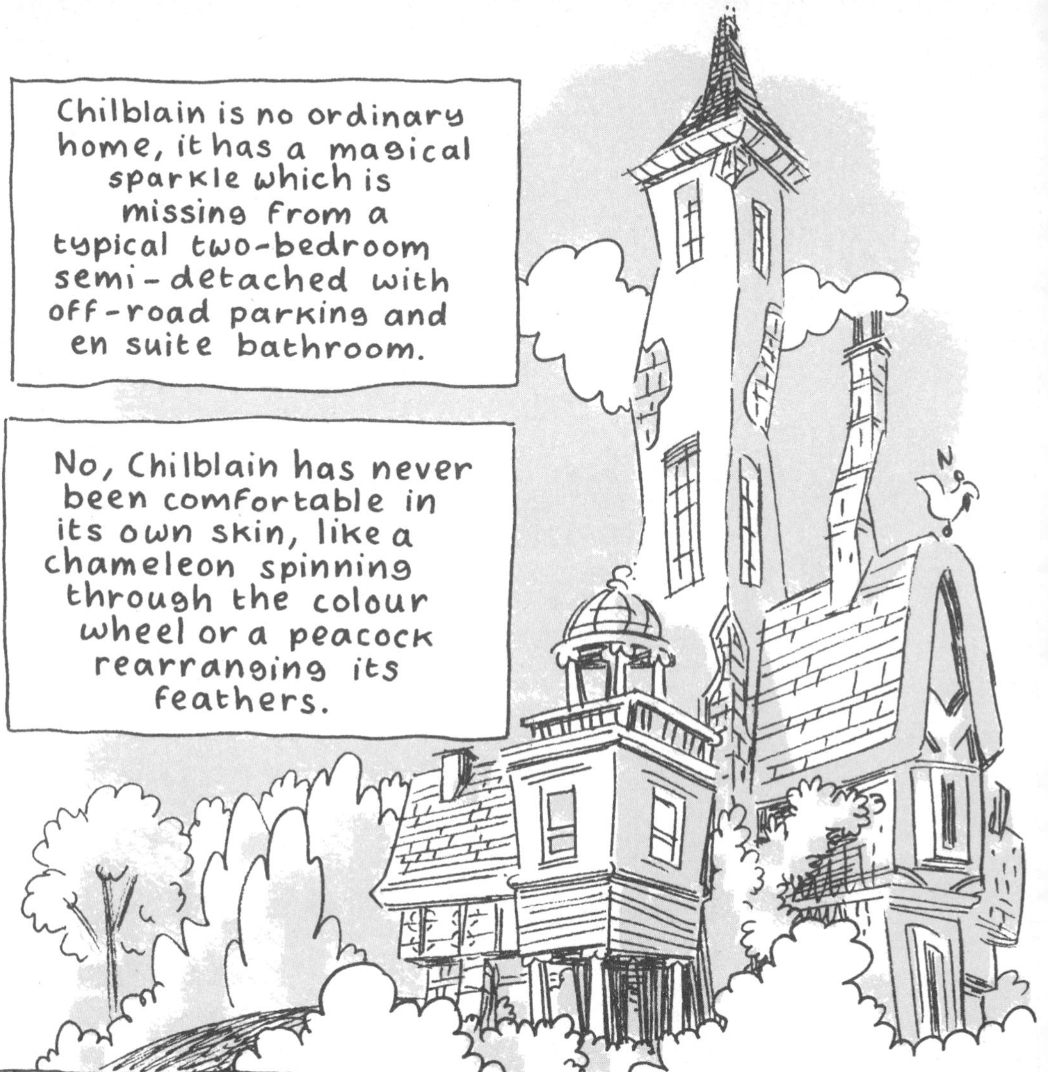
Chilblain is no ordinary home, it has a magical sparkle which is missing from a typical two-bedroom semi-detached with off-road parking and en suite bathroom.
No, Chilblain has never been comfortable in its own skin, like a chameleon spinning through the colour wheel or a peacock rearranging its feathers.

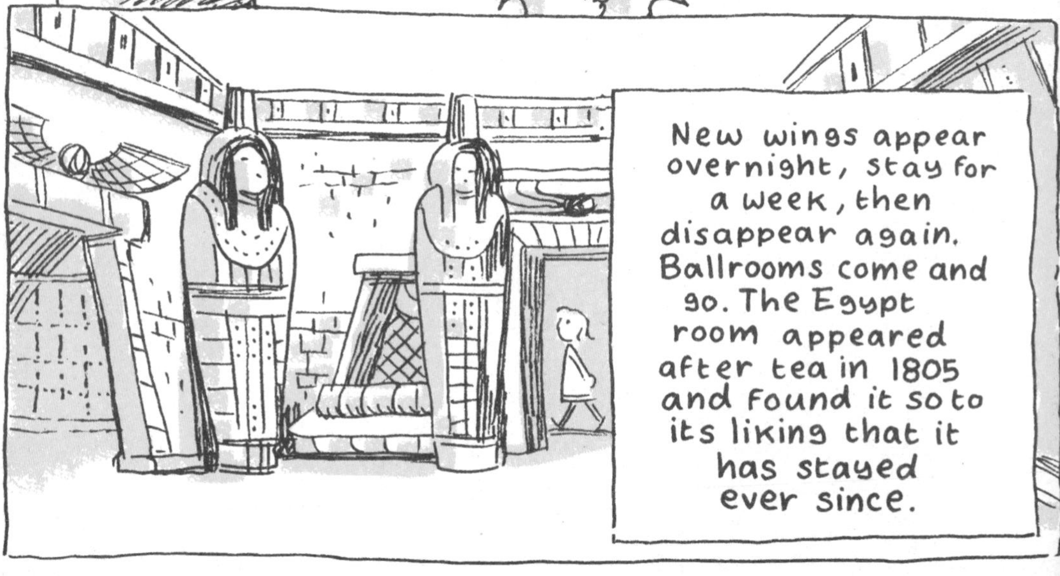
New wings appear overnight, stay for a week, then disappear again. Ballrooms come and go. The Egypt room appeared after tea in 1805 and found it so to its liking that it has stayed ever since.

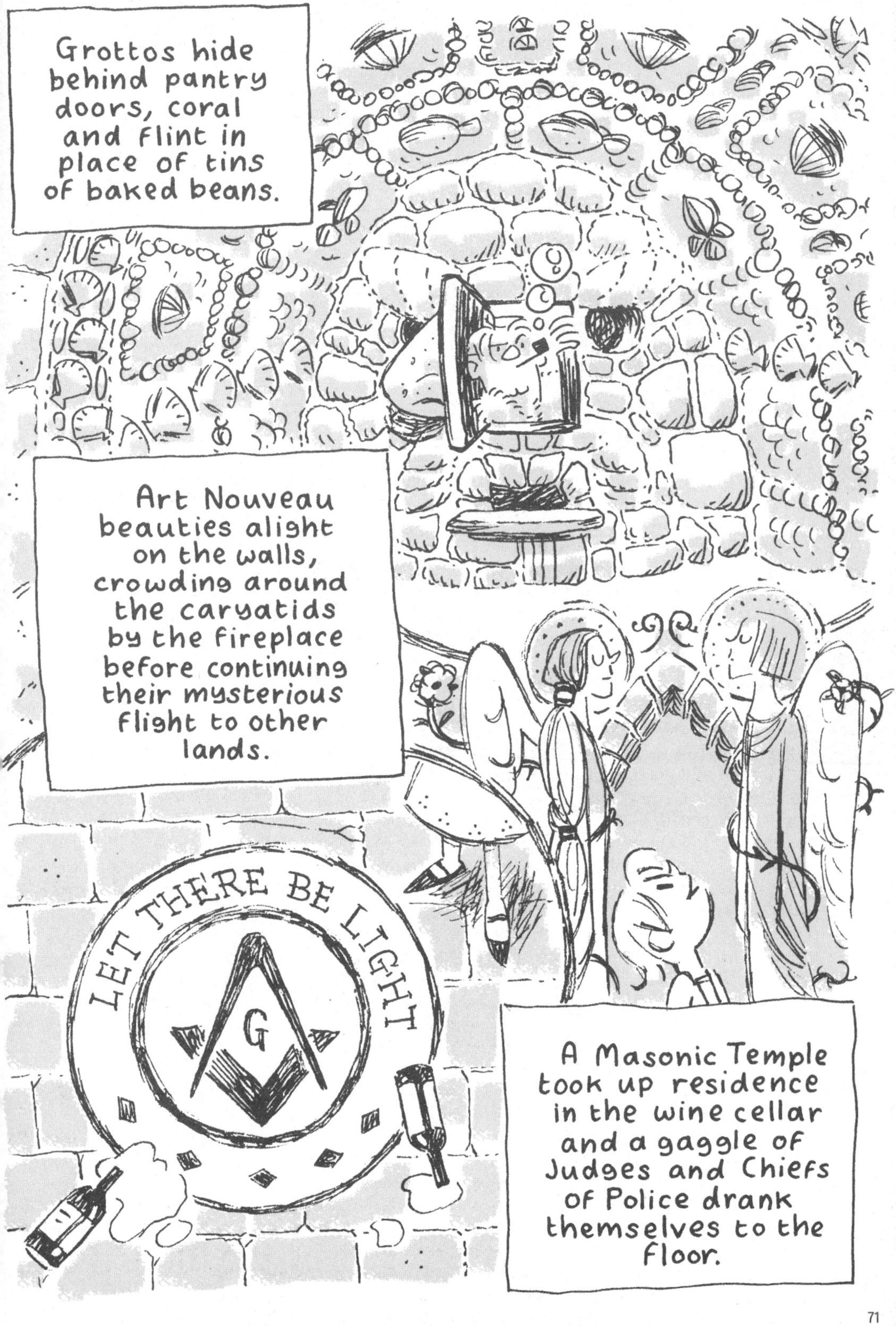

Grottos hide behind pantry doors, coral and flint in place of tins of baked beans.
Art Nouveau beauties alight on the walls, crowding around the caryatids by the fireplace before continuing their mysterious flight to other lands.
LET THERE BE LIGHT
G
A Masonic Temple took up residence in the wine cellar and a gaggle of Judges and Chiefs of Police drank themselves to the floor.

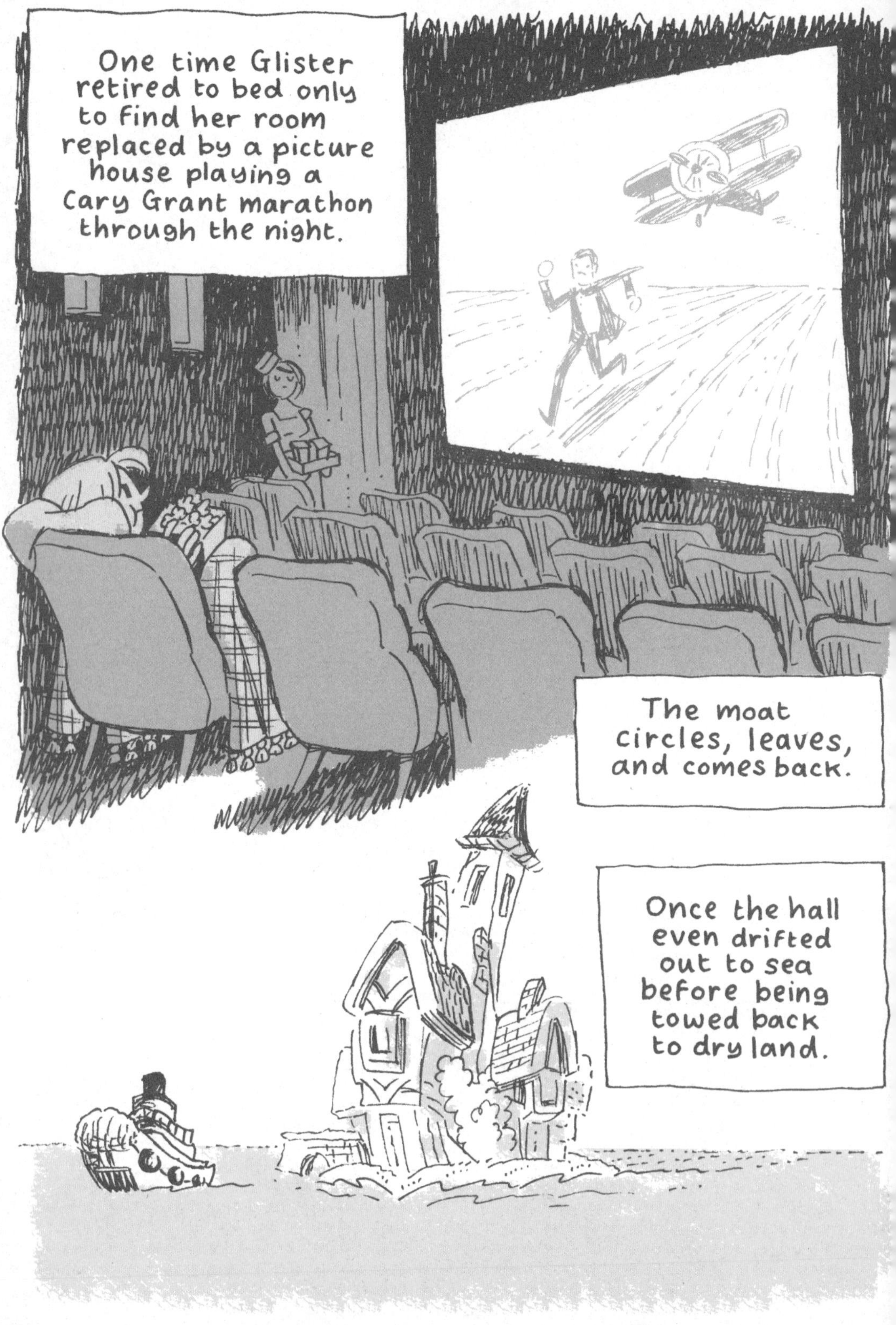
One time Glister retired to bed only to find her room replaced by a picture house playing a Cary Grant marathon through the night.
The moat circles, leaves, and comes back.
Once the hall even drifted out to sea before being towed back to dry land.

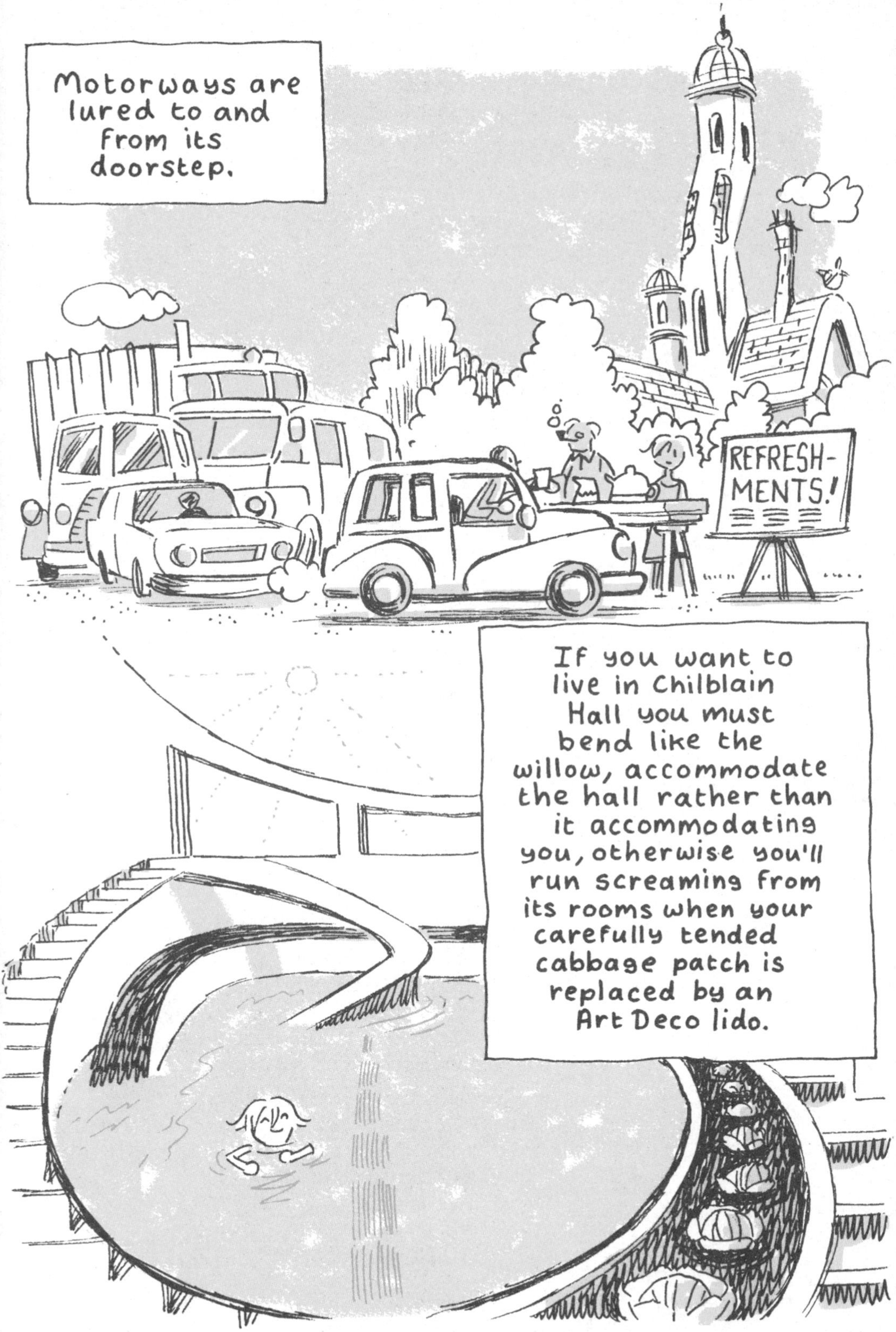

Motorways are lured to and from its doorstep.
REFRESH-MENTS!
If you want to live in Chilblain Hall you must bend like the willow, accommodate the hall rather than it accommodating you, otherwise you'll run screaming from its rooms when your carefully tended cabbage patch is replaced by an Art Deco lido.

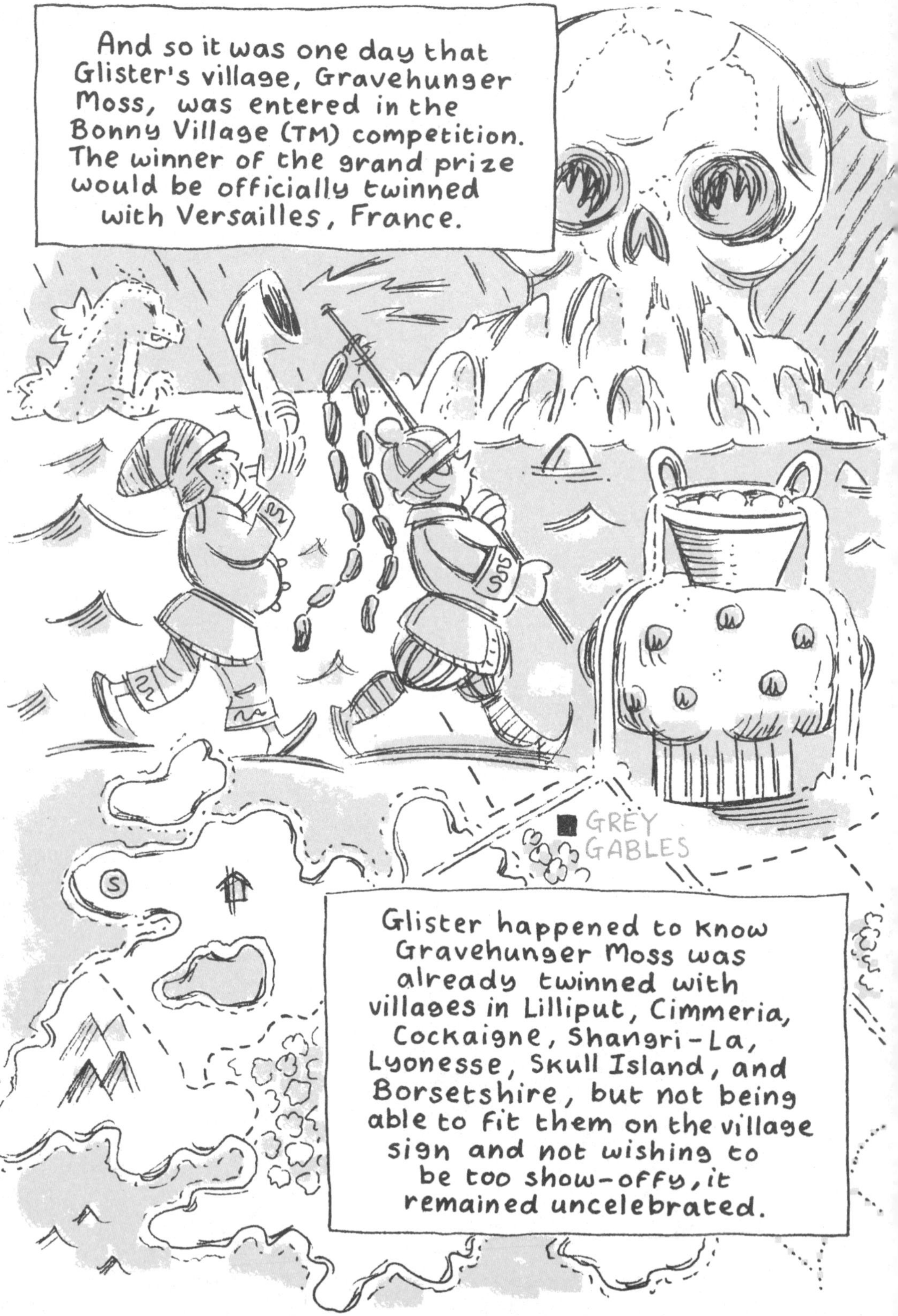
And so it was one day that Glister's village, Gravehunger Moss, was entered in the Bonny Village (TM) competition. The winner of the grand prize would be officially twinned with Versailles, France.
GREY GABLES
Glister happened to know Gravehunger Moss was already twinned with villages in Lilliput, Cimmeria, Cockaigne, Shangri-La, Lyonesse, Skull Island, and Borsetshire, but not being able to fit them on the village sign and not wishing to be too show-offy, it remained uncelebrated.

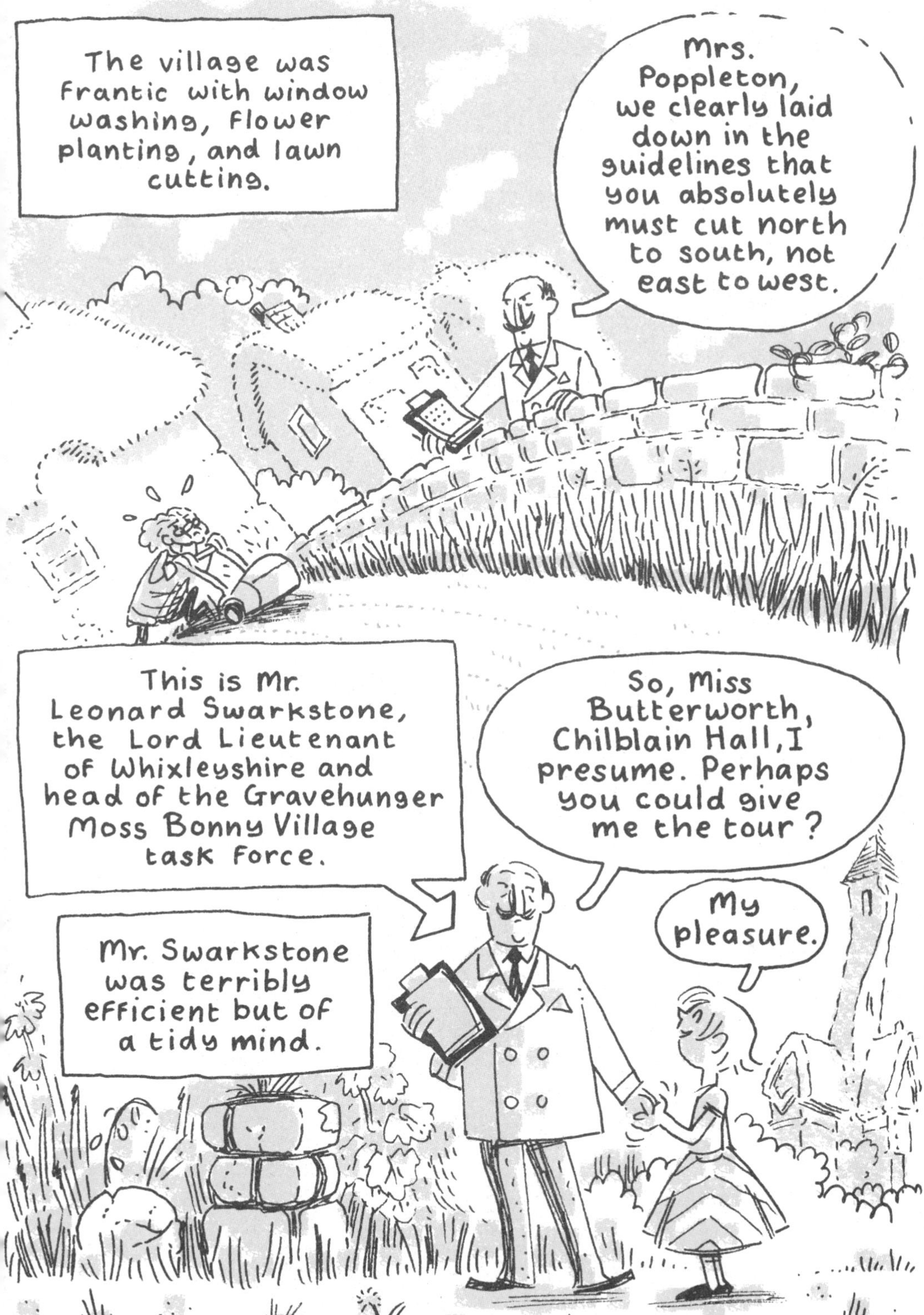
The village was frantic with window washing, flower planting, and lawn cutting.
Mrs. Poppleton, we clearly laid down in the guidelines that you absolutely must cut north to south, not east to west.
This is Mr. Leonard Swarkstone, the Lord Lieutenant of Whixleyshire and head of the Gravehunger Moss Bonny Village task force.
So, Miss Butterworth, Chilblain Hall, I presume. Perhaps you could give me the tour?
My pleasure.
Mr. Swarkstone was terribly efficient but of a tidy mind.

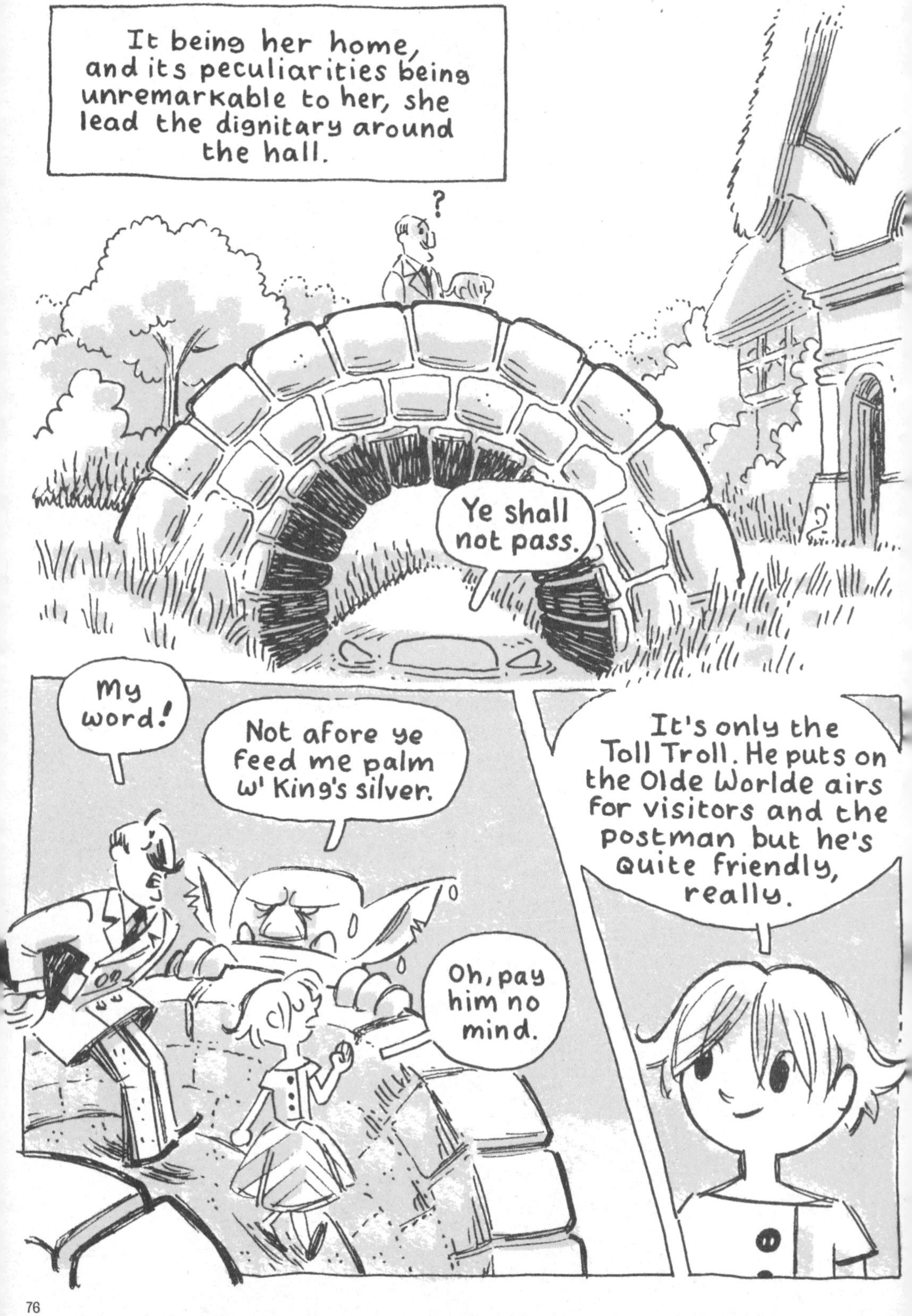
It being her home, and its peculiarities being unremarkable to her, she lead the dignitary around the hall.
?
Ye shall not pass.
My word!
Not afore ye feed me palm w' King's silver.
Oh, pay him no mind.
It's only the Toll Troll. He puts on the Olde Worlde airs for visitors and the postman but he's quite friendly, really.

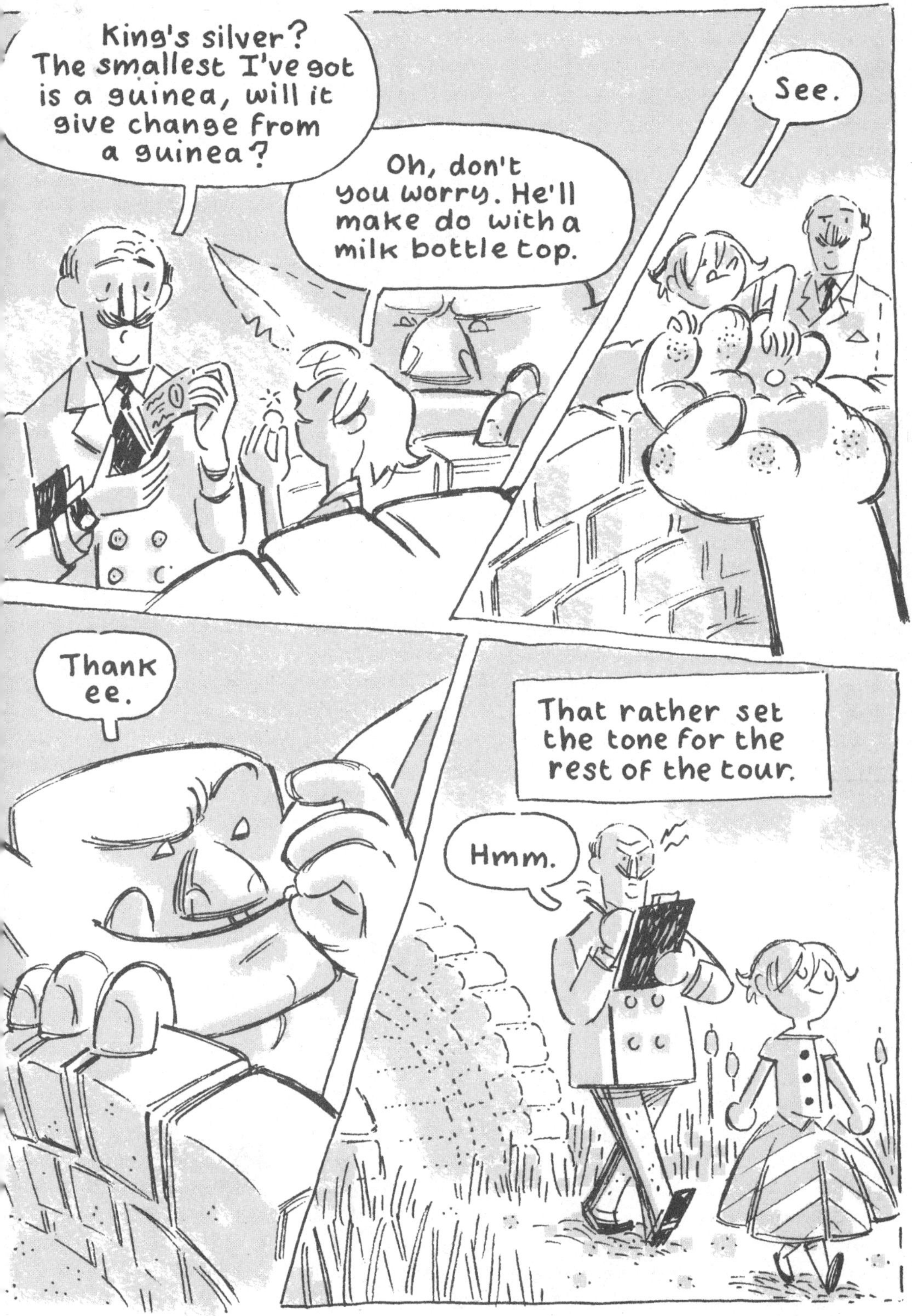

King's silver? The smallest I've got is a guinea, will it give change from a guinea?
Oh, don't you worry. He'll make do with a milk bottle top.
See.
Thank ee.
That rather set the tone for the rest of the tour.
Hmm.

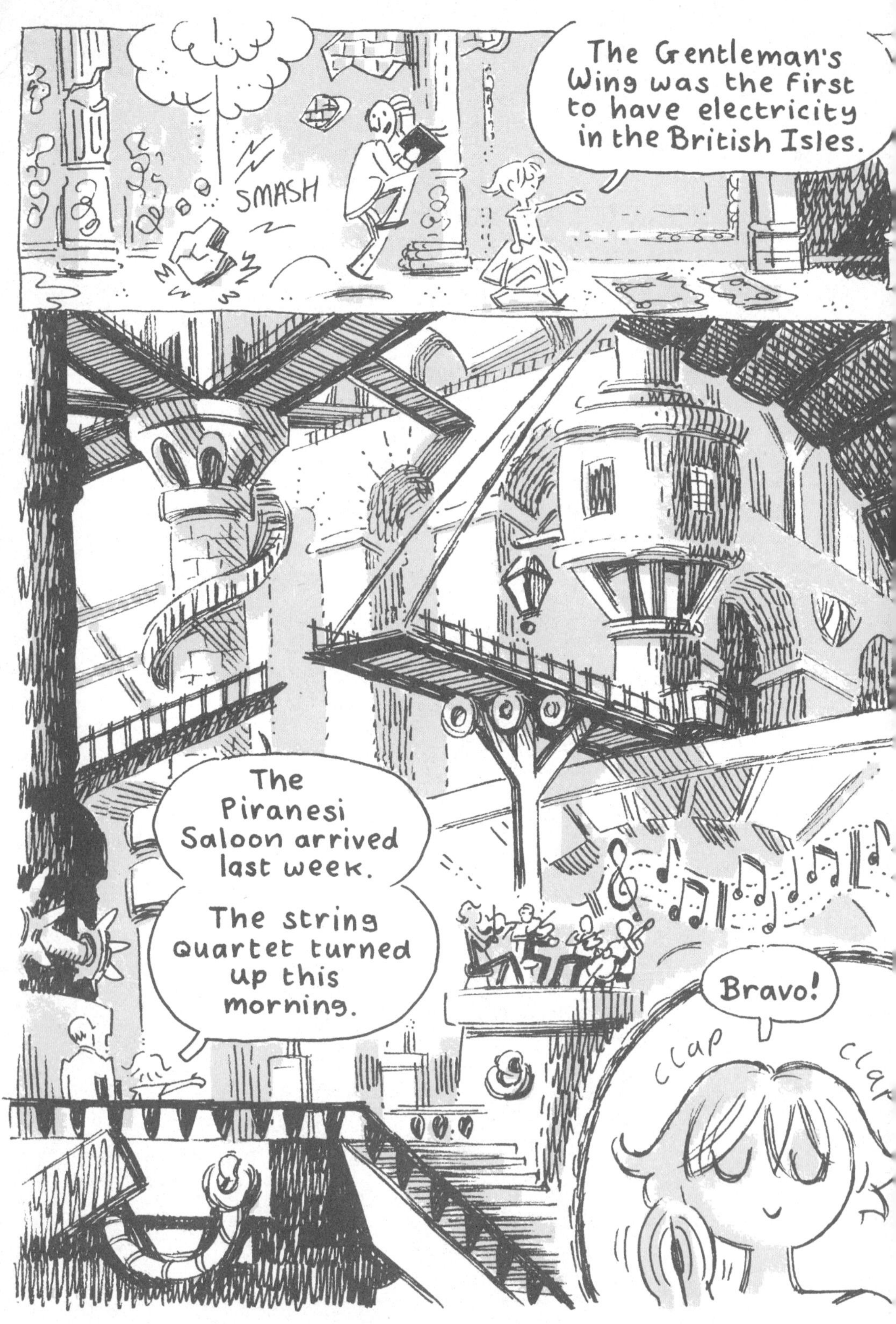
SMASH
The Gentleman's Wing was the first to have electricity in the British Isles.
The Piranesi Saloon arrived last week.
The string quartet turned up this morning.
Bravo!
clap
clap

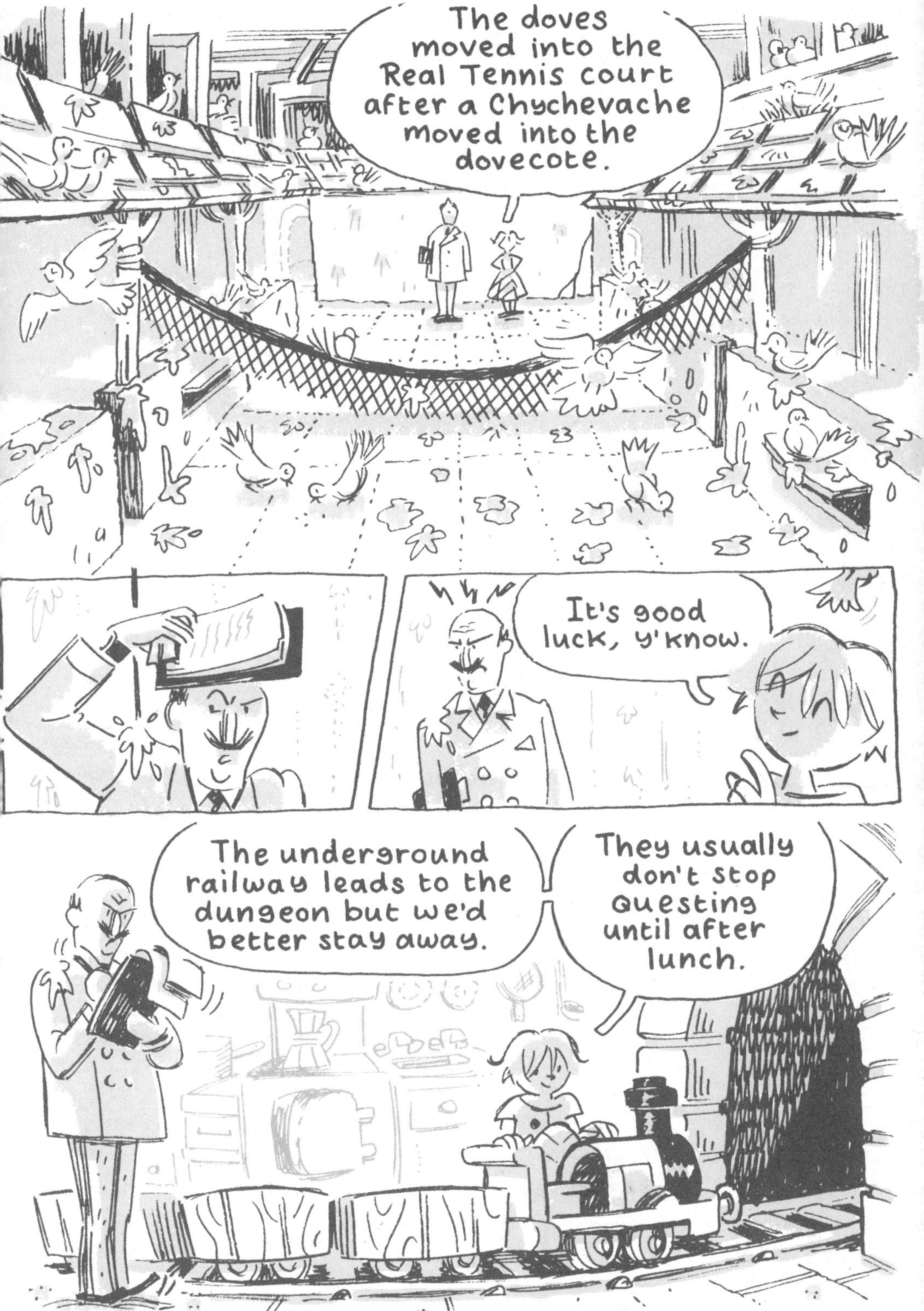
The doves moved into the Real Tennis court after a Chychevache moved into the dovecote.
It's good luck, y'know.
The underground railway leads to the dungeon but we'd better stay away.
They usually don't stop questing until after lunch.

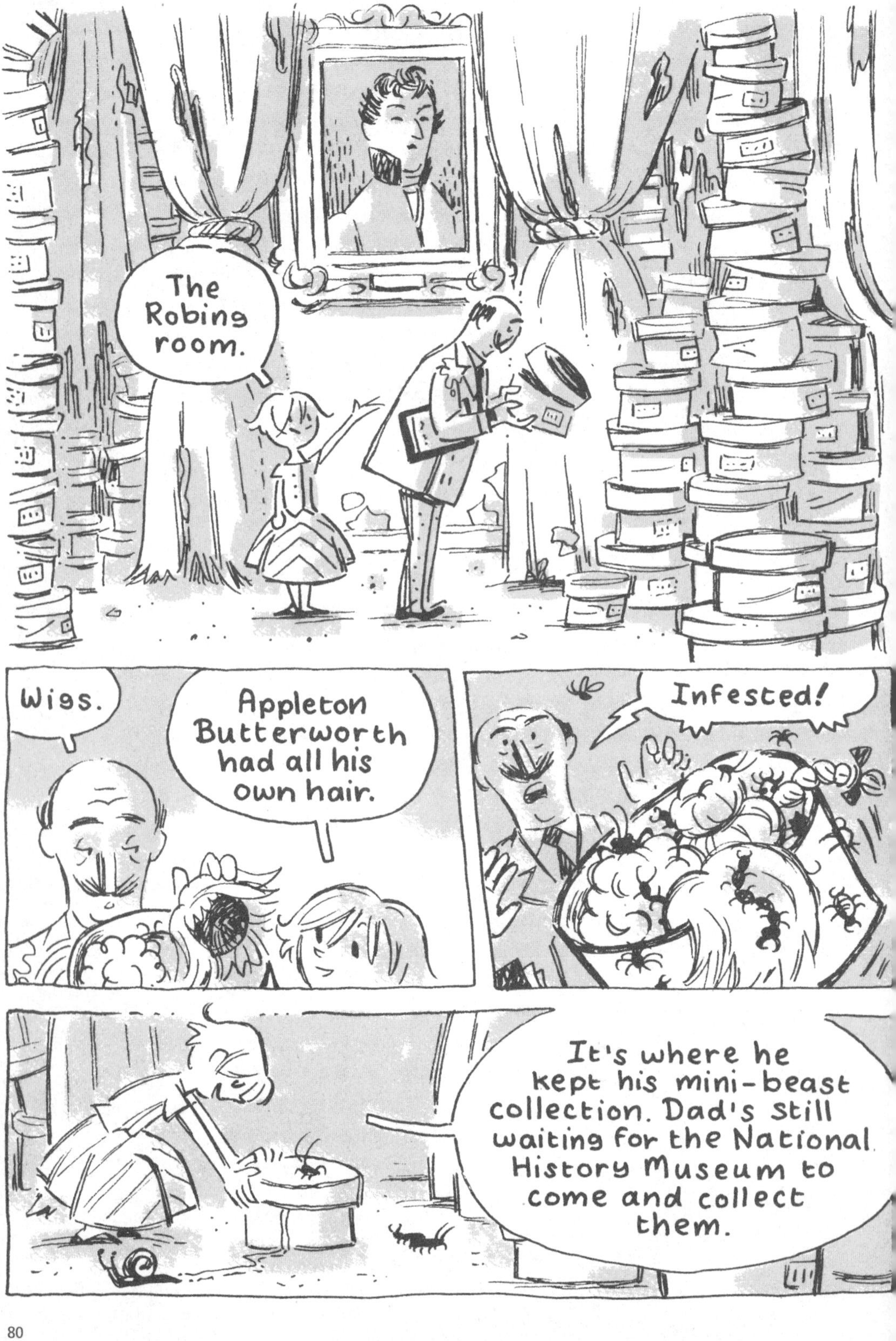
The Robing room.
Wigs.
Appleton Butterworth had all his own hair.
Infested!
It's where he kept his mini-beast collection. Dad's still waiting for the National History Museum to come and collect them.

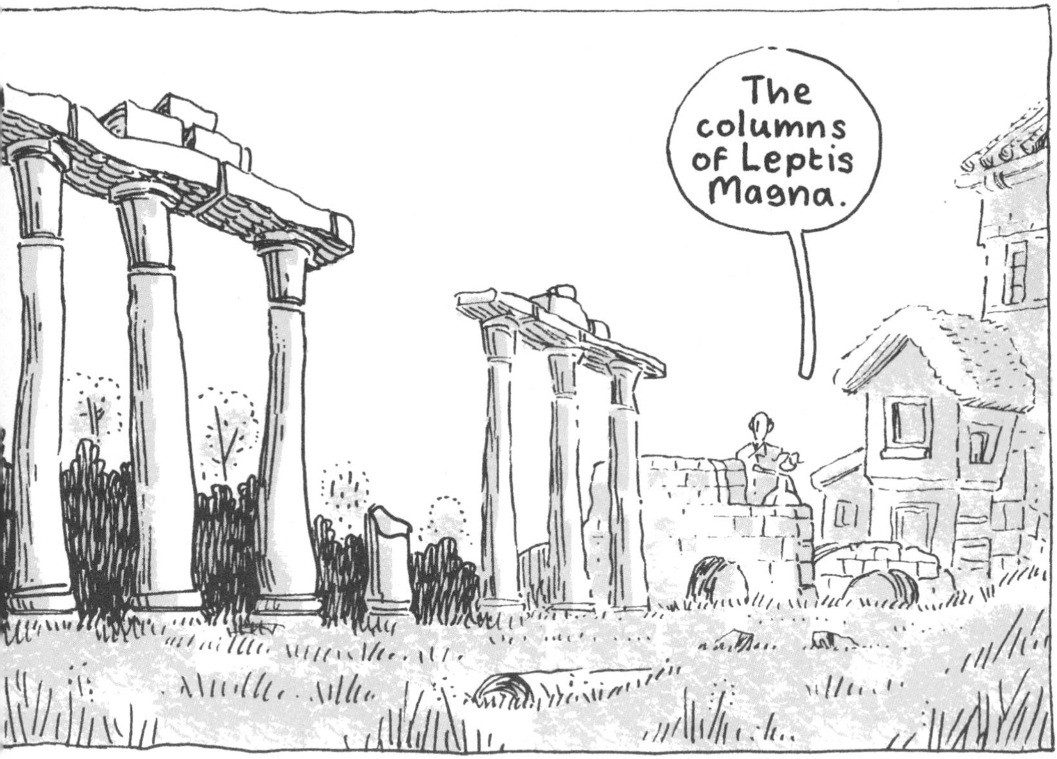
The columns of Leptis Magna.

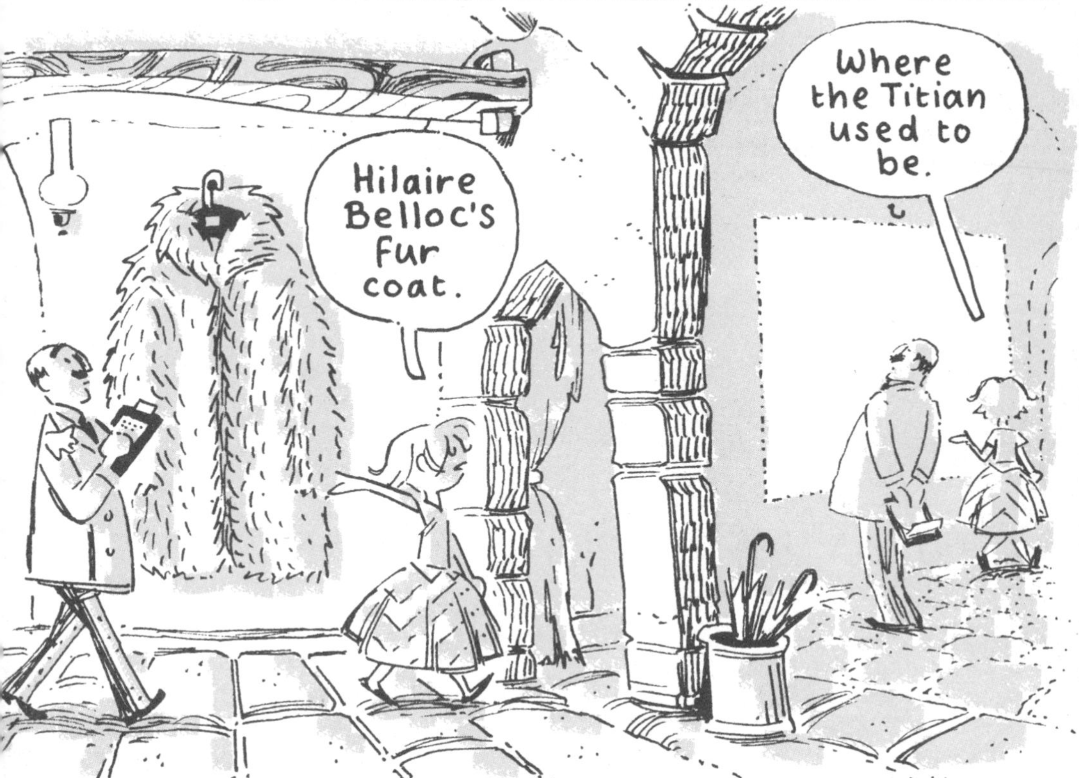
Hilaire Belloc's fur coat.
Where the Titian used to be.

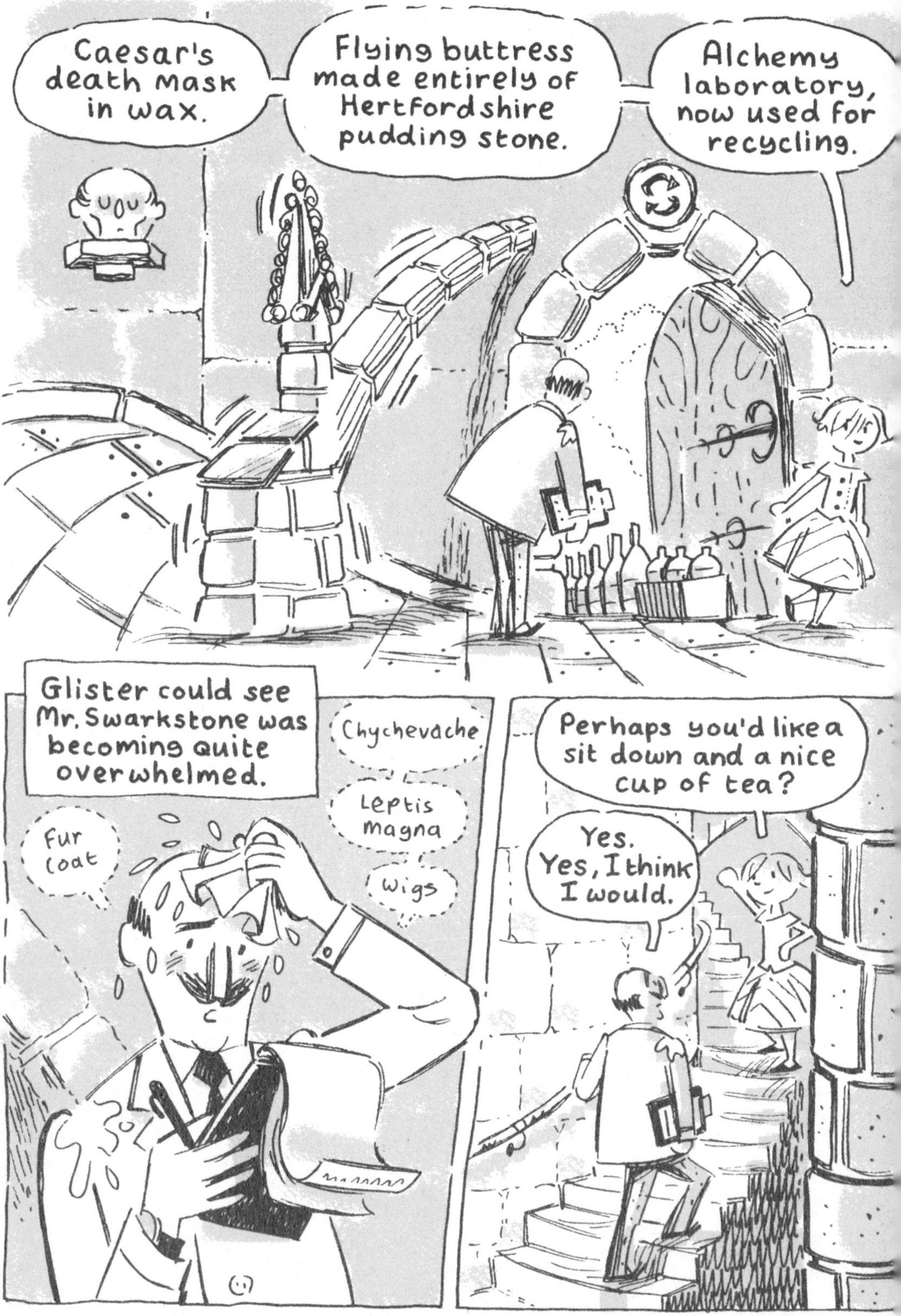
Caesar's death mask in wax.
Flying buttress made entirely of Hertfordshire pudding stone.
Alchemy laboratory, now used for recycling.
Glister could see Mr. Swarkstone was becoming quite overwhelmed.
Fur coat
Chychevache
Leptis magna
Wigs
Perhaps you'd like a sit down and a nice cup of tea?
Yes. Yes, I think I would.

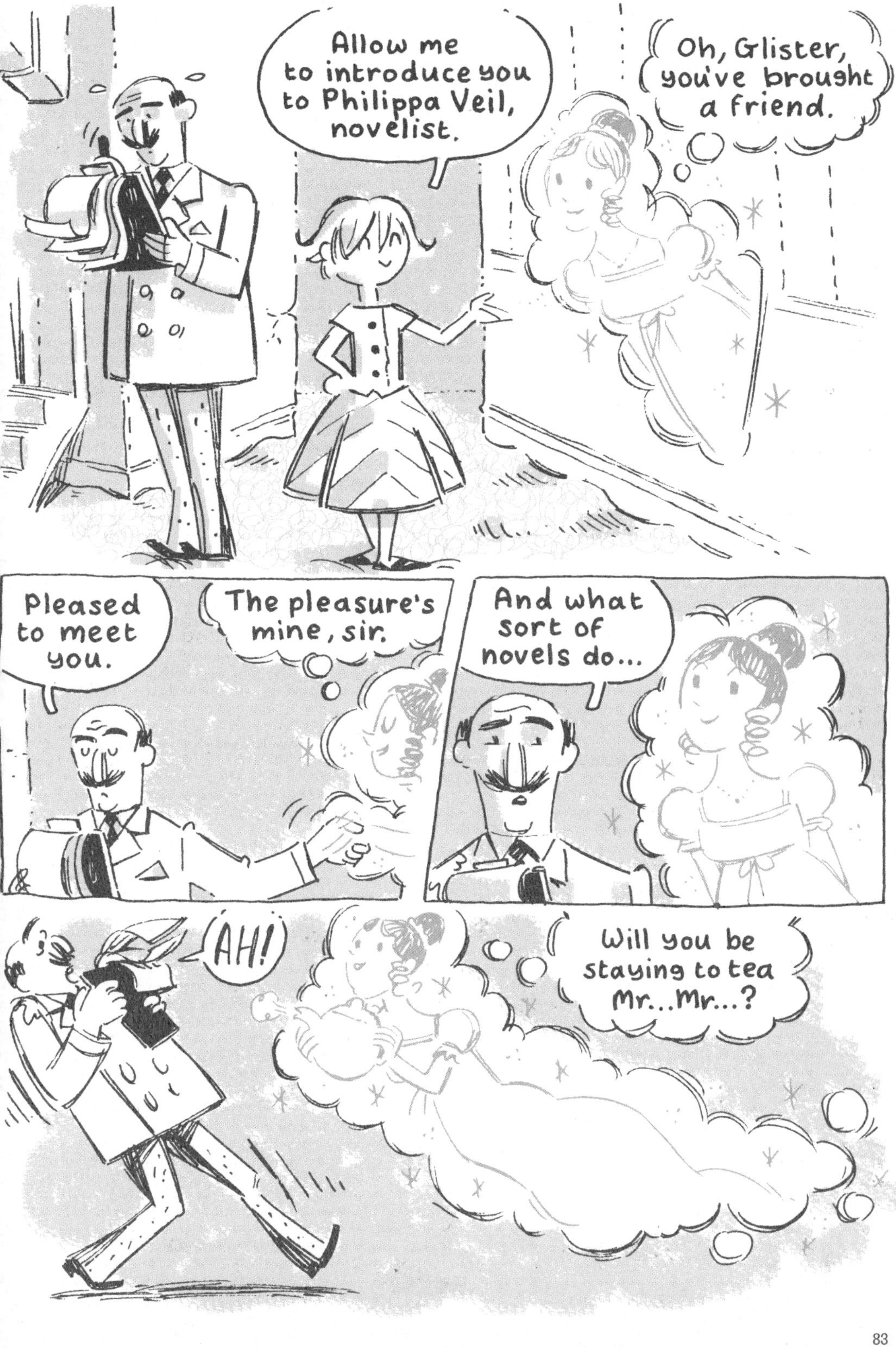
Allow me to introduce you to Philippa Veil, novelist.
Oh, Glister, you've brought a friend.
Pleased to meet you.
The pleasure's mine, sir.
And what sort of novels do...
AH!
Will you be staying to tea Mr...Mr...?

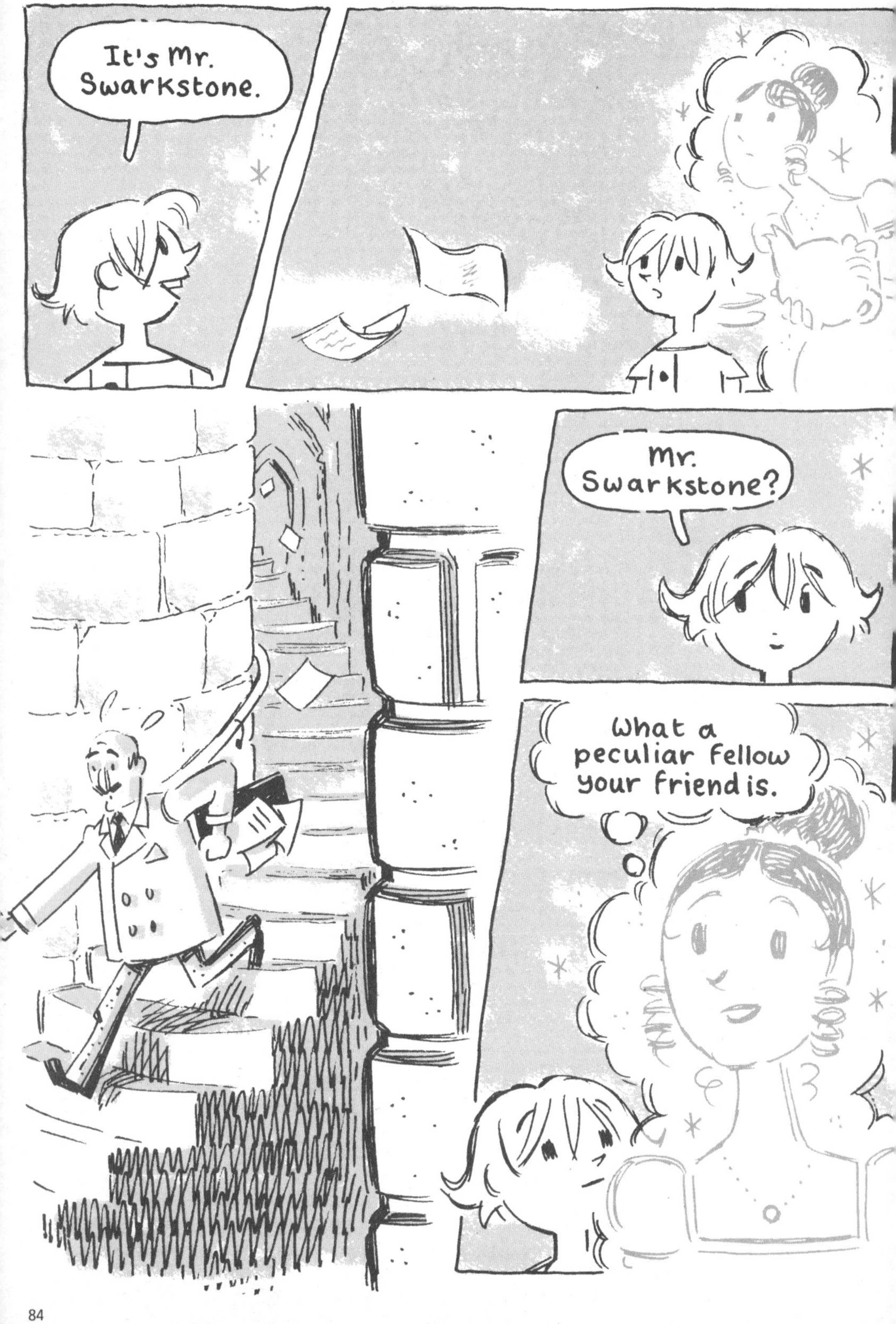
It's Mr. Swarkstone.
Mr. Swarkstone?
What a peculiar fellow your friend is.

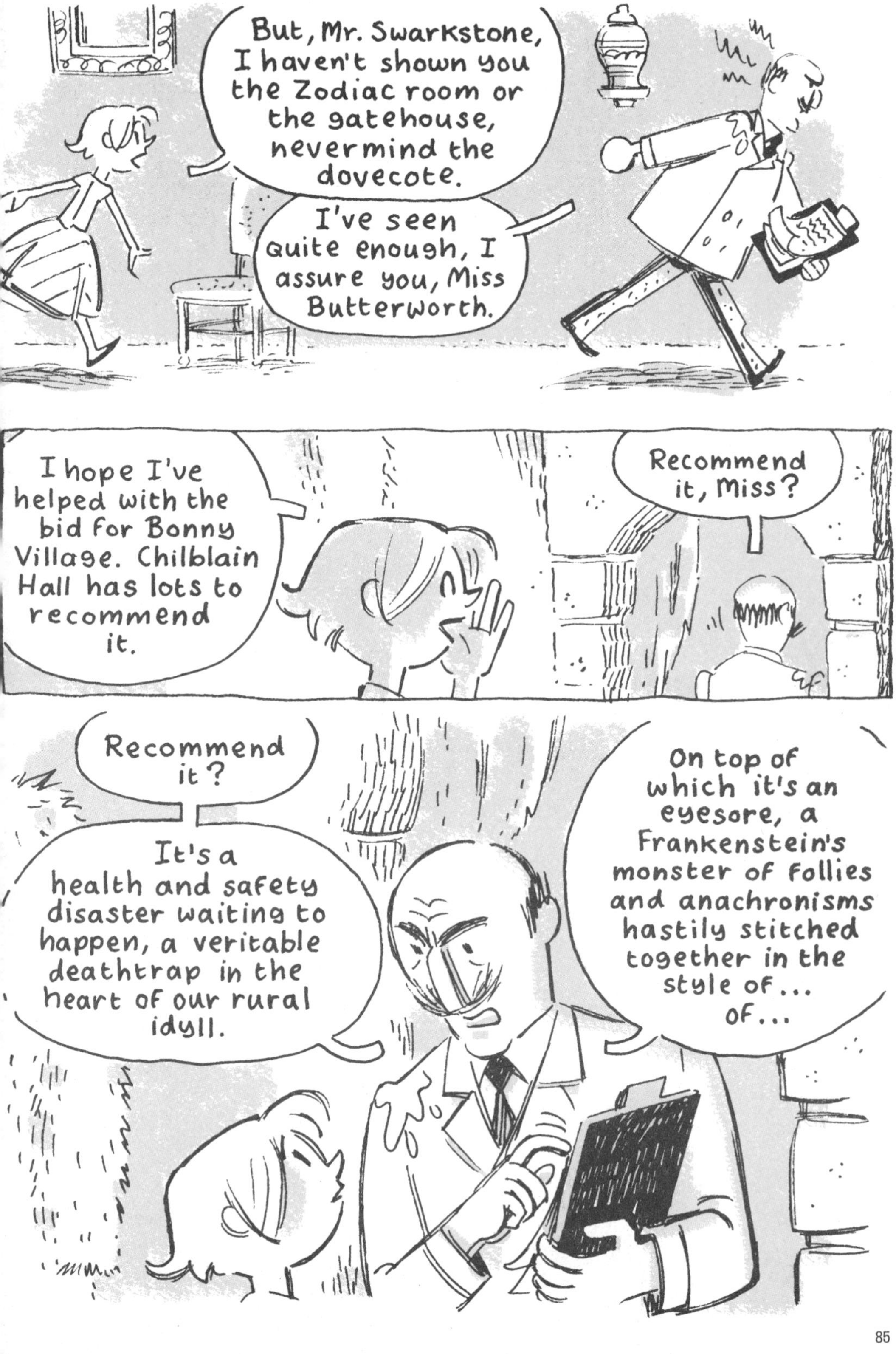
But, Mr. Swarkstone, I haven't shown you the Zodiac room or the gatehouse, nevermind the dovecote.
I've seen quite enough, I assure you, Miss Butterworth.
I hope I've helped with the bid for Bonny Village. Chilblain Hall has lots to recommend it.
Recommend it, Miss?
Recommend it?
It's a health and safety disaster waiting to happen, a veritable deathtrap in the heart of our rural idyll.
On top of which it's an eyesore, a Frankenstein's monster of follies and anachronisms hastily stitched together in the style of... of...

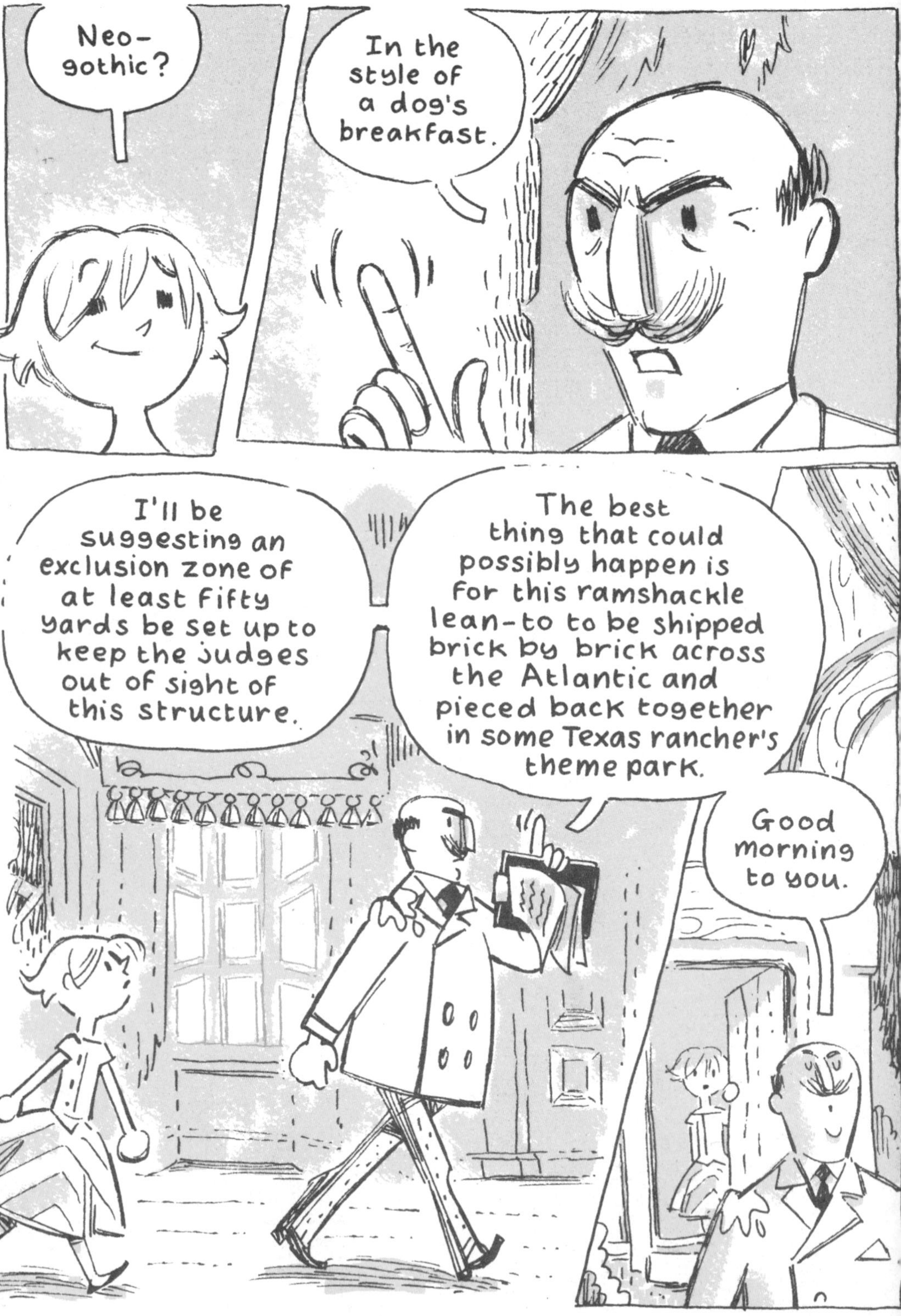
Neo-gothic?
In the style of a dog's breakfast.
I'll be suggesting an exclusion zone of at least fifty yards be set up to keep the judges out of sight of this structure.
The best thing that could possibly happen is for this ramshackle lean-to to be shipped brick by brick across the Atlantic and pieced back together in some Texas rancher's theme park.
Good morning to you.

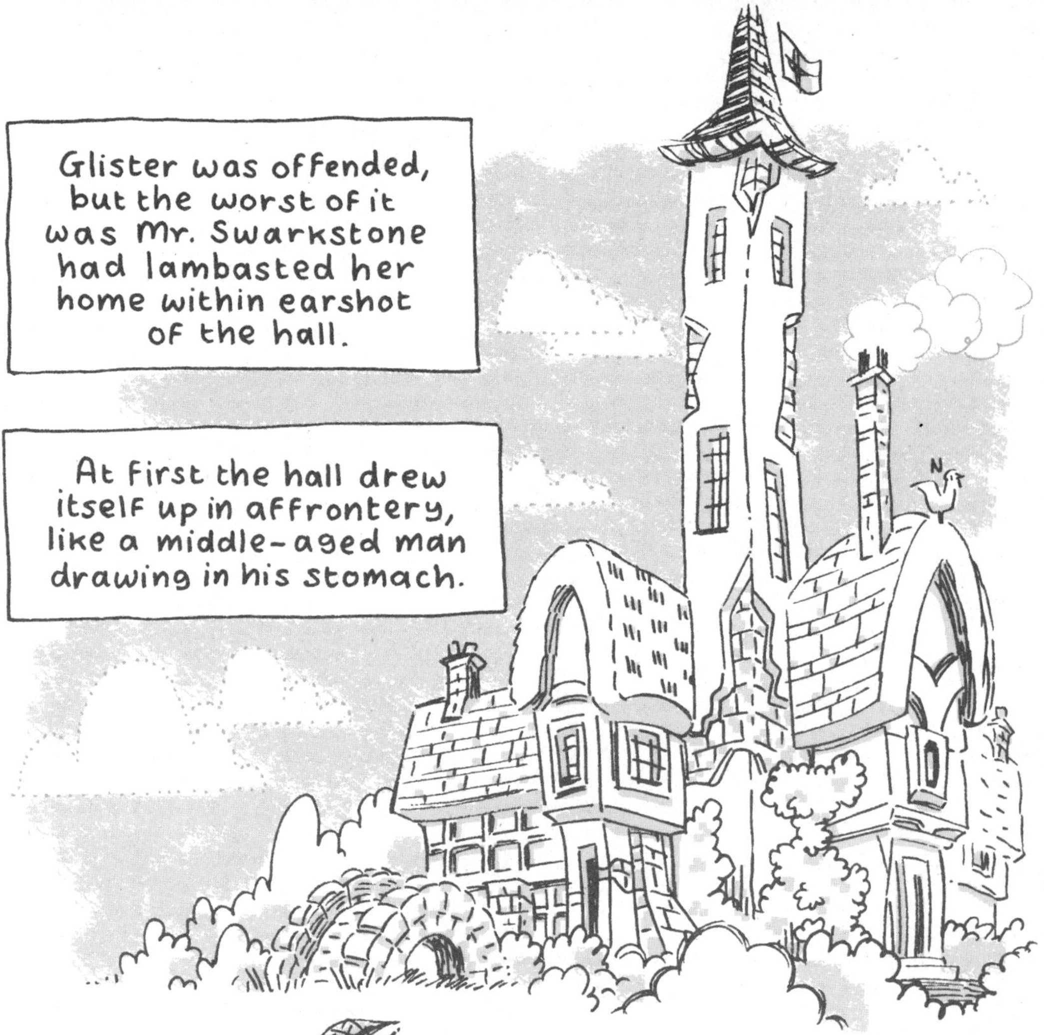
Glister was offended, but the worst of it was Mr. Swarkstone had lambasted her home within earshot of the hall.
At first the hall drew itself up in affrontery, like a middle-aged man drawing in his stomach.

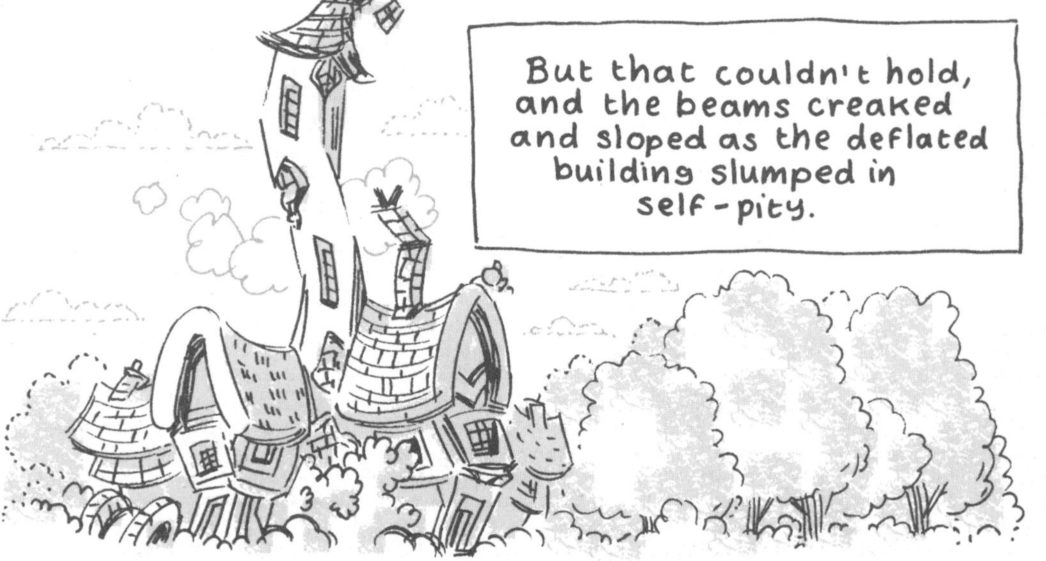
But that couldn't hold, and the beams creaked and sloped as the deflated building slumped in self-pity.

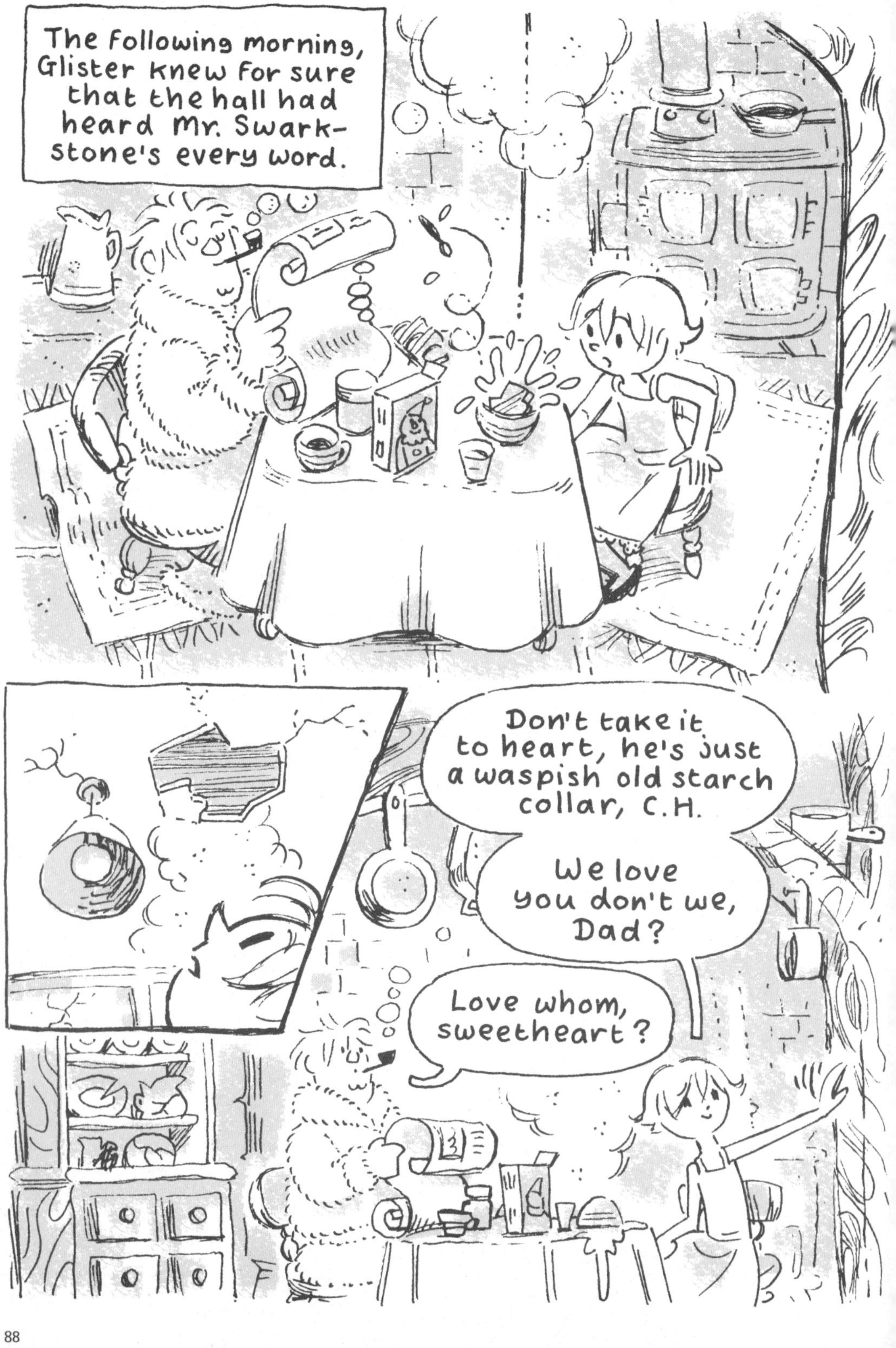
The following morning, Glister knew for sure that the hall had heard Mr. Swark-stone's every word.
Don't take it to heart, he's just a waspish old starch collar, C.H.
We love you don't we, Dad?
Love whom, sweetheart?

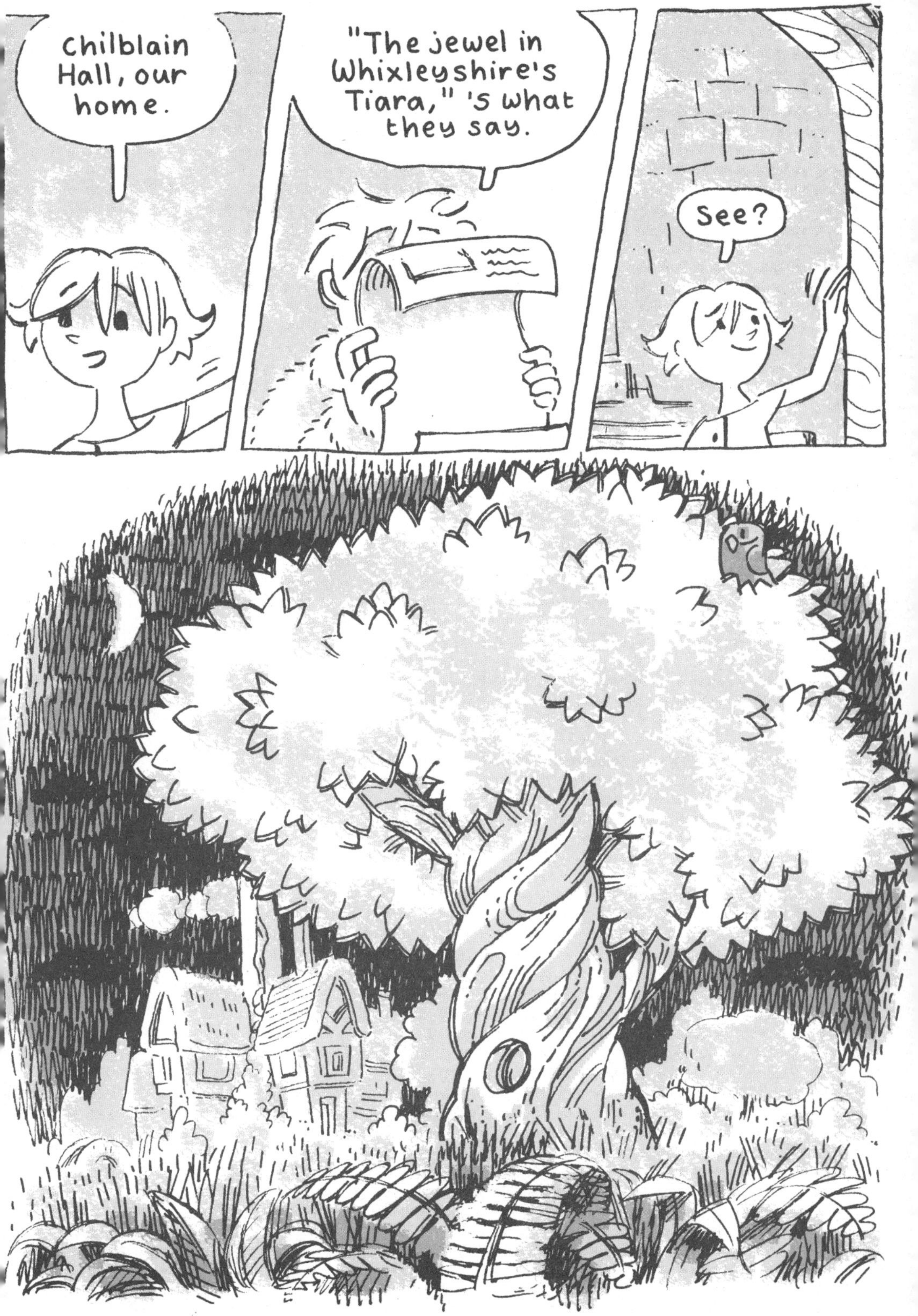
Chilblain Hall, our home.
"The jewel in Whixleyshire's Tiara," 's what they say.
See?

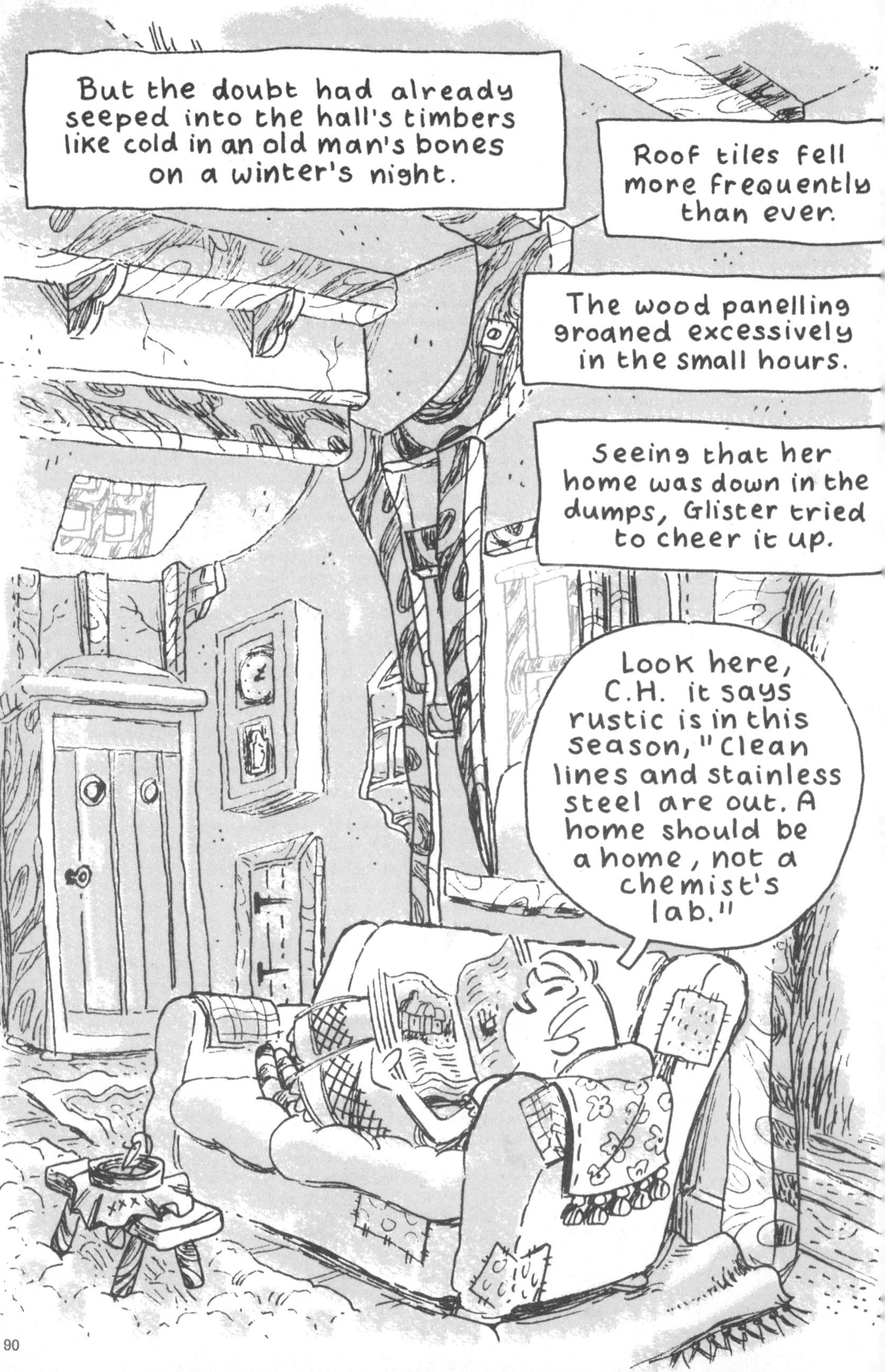
But the doubt had already seeped into the hall's timbers like cold in an old man's bones on a winter's night.
Roof tiles fell more frequently than ever.
The wood panelling groaned excessively in the small hours.
Seeing that her home was down in the dumps, Glister tried to cheer it up.
Look here, C.H. it says rustic is in this season, "Clean lines and stainless steel are out. A home should be a home, not a chemist's lab."

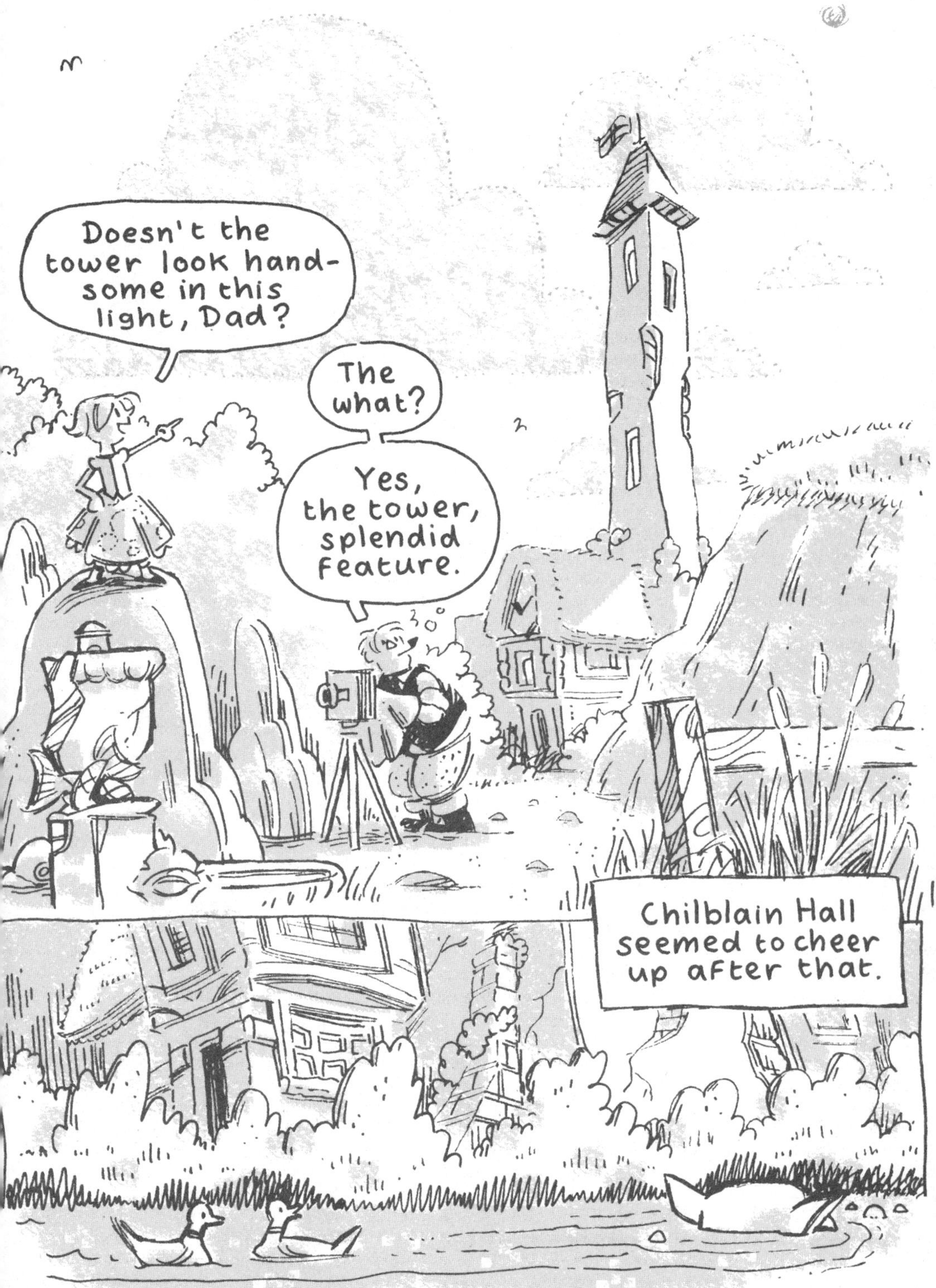
Doesn't the tower look handsome in this light, Dad?
The what?
Yes, the tower, splendid feature.
Chilblain Hall seemed to cheer up after that.

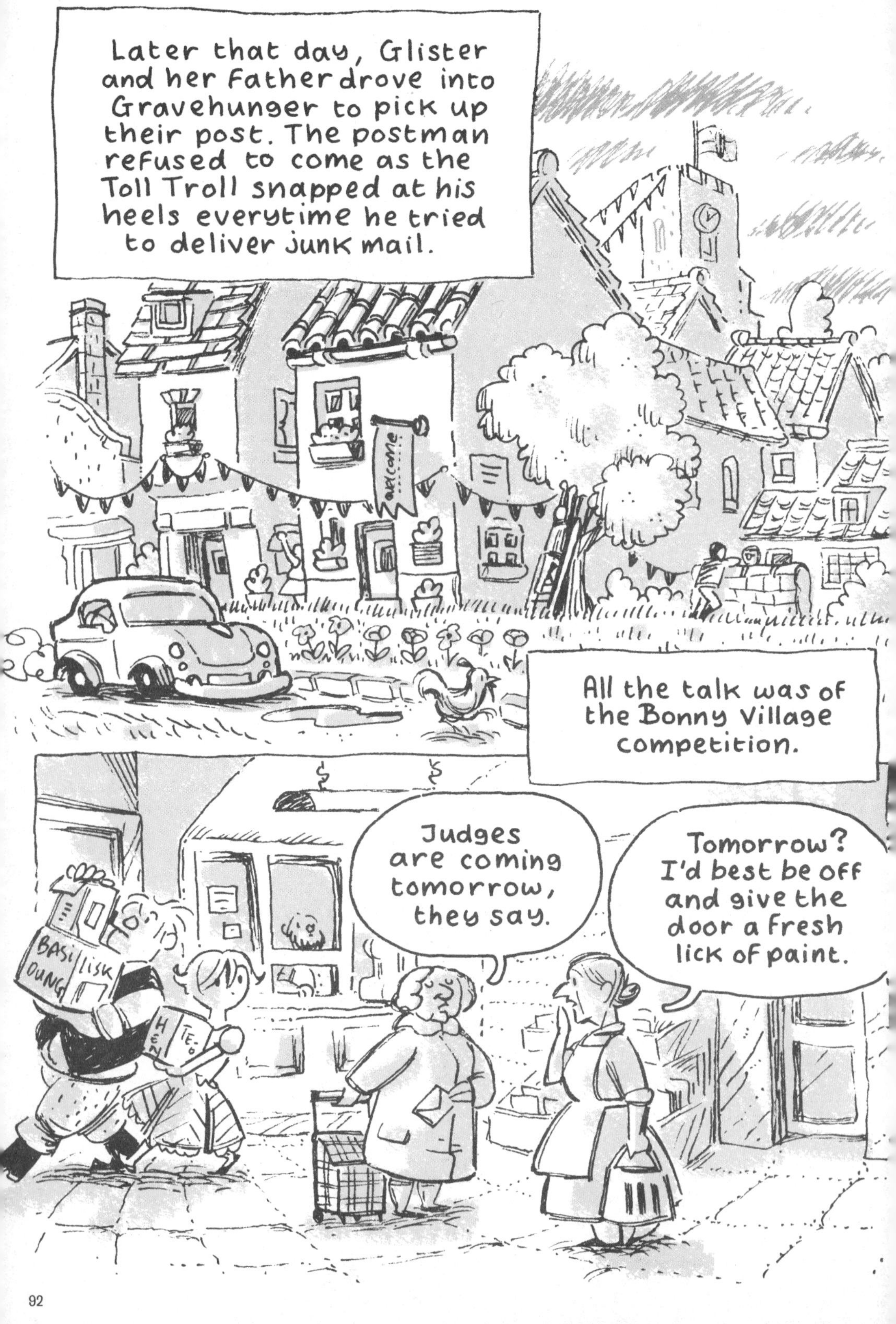
Later that day, Glister and her father drove into Gravehunger to pick up their post. The postman refused to come as the Toll Troll snapped at his heels everytime he tried to deliver junk mail.
Welcome
All the talk was of the Bonny Village competition.
Judges are coming tomorrow, they say.
Tomorrow? I'd best be off and give the door a fresh lick of paint.

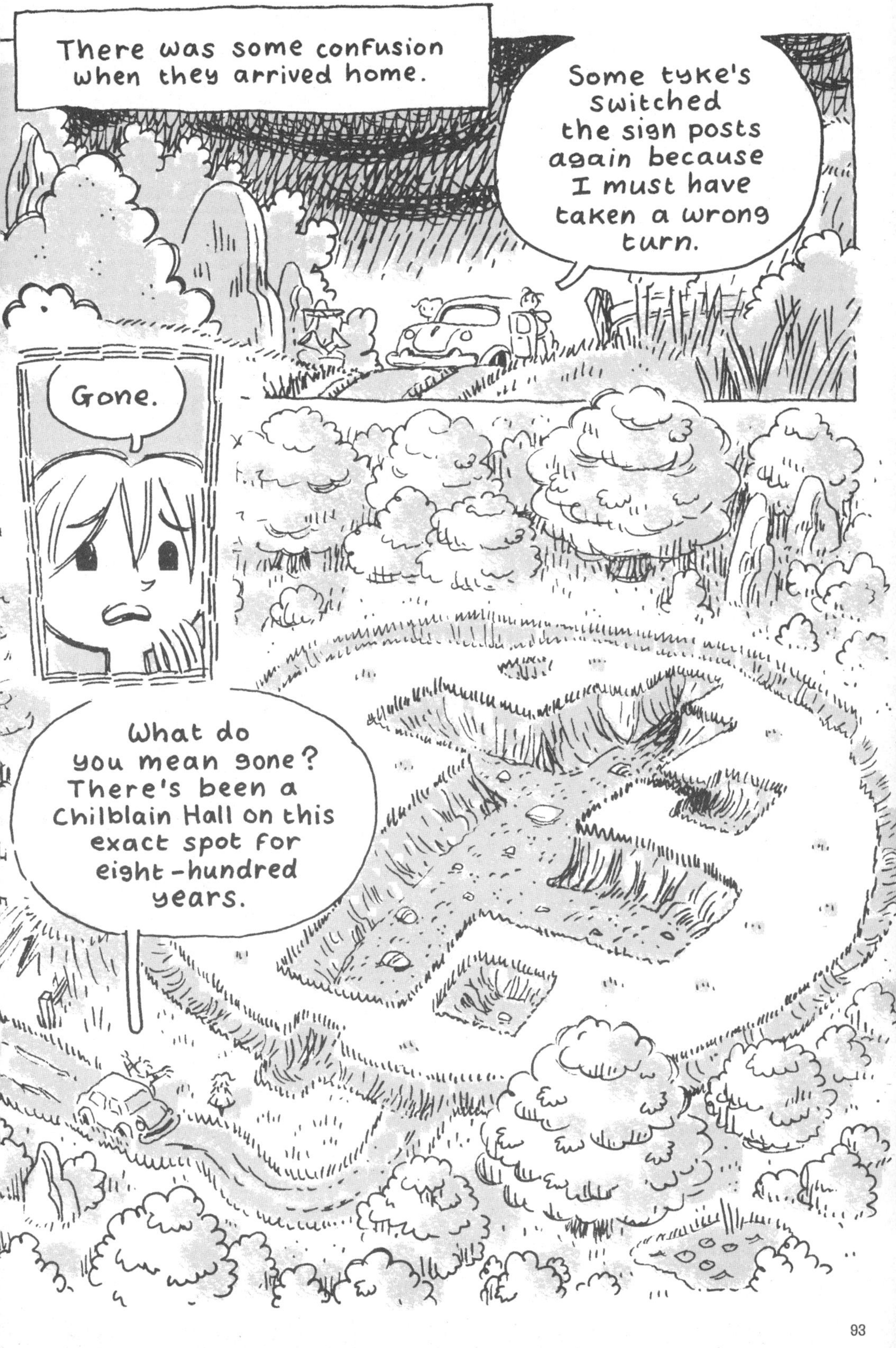

There was some confusion when they arrived home.
Some tyke's switched the sign posts again because I must have taken a wrong turn.
Gone.
What do you mean gone? There's been a Chilblain Hall on this exact spot for eight-hundred years.

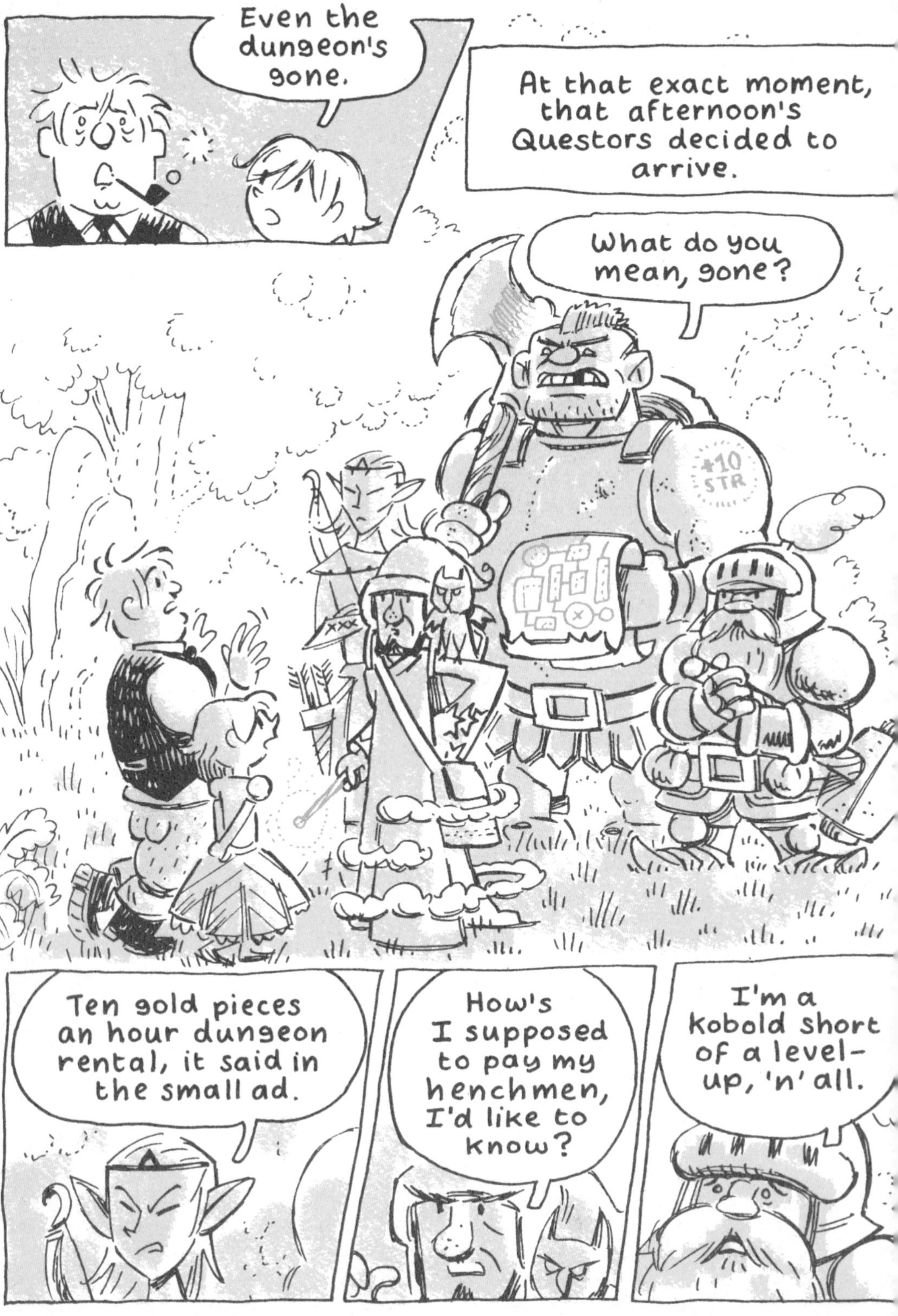
Even the dungeon's gone.
At that exact moment, that afternoon's Questors decided to arrive.
What do you mean, gone?
+10 STR
Ten gold pieces an hour dungeon rental, it said in the small ad.
How's I supposed to pay my henchmen, I'd like to know?
I'm a kobold short of a level-up, 'n' all.

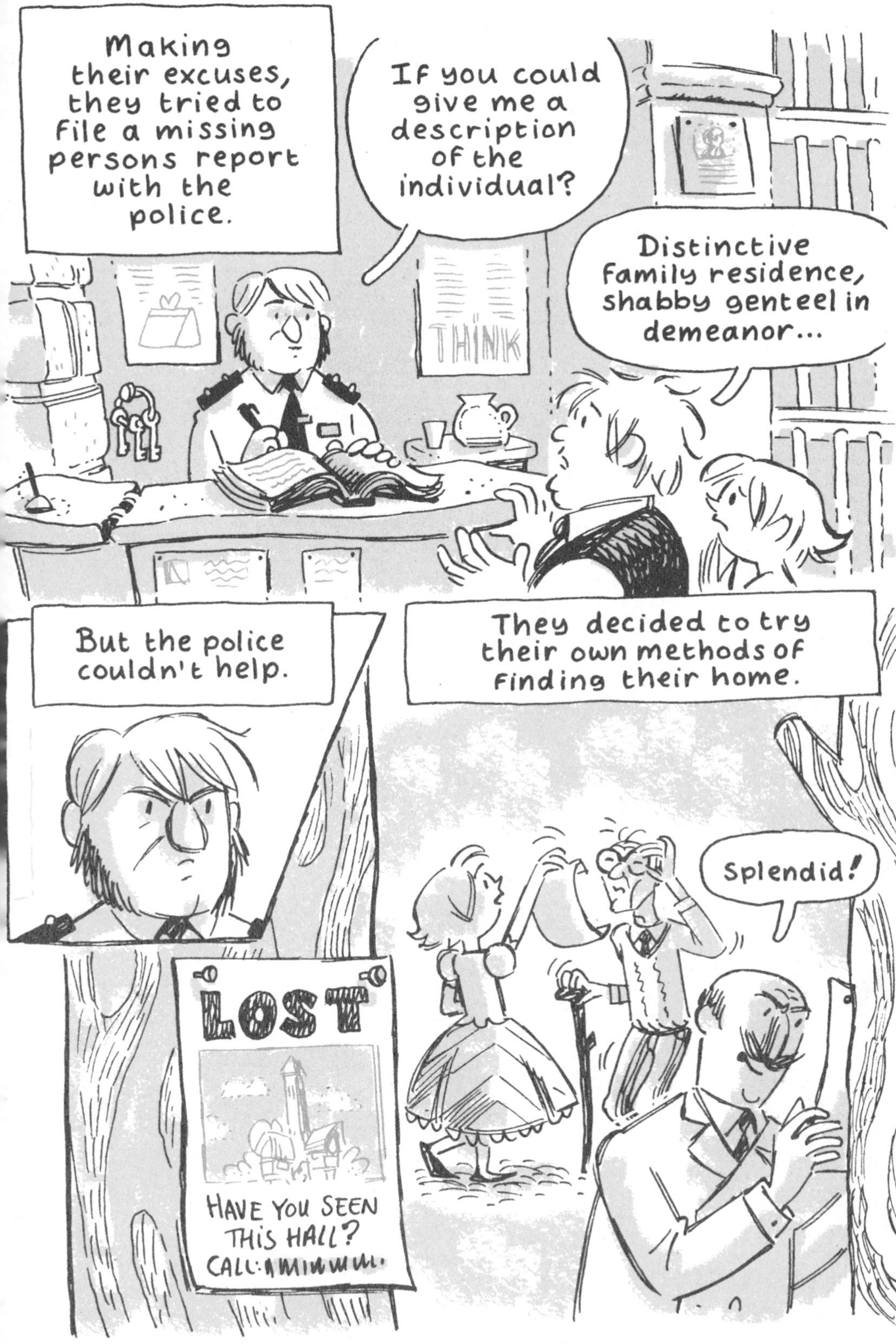
Making their excuses, they tried to file a missing persons report with the police.
If you could give me a description of the individual?
THINK
Distinctive family residence, shabby genteel in demeanor...
But the police couldn't help.
They decided to try their own methods of finding their home.
Splendid!
LOST
HAVE YOU SEEN THIS HALL?
CALL:

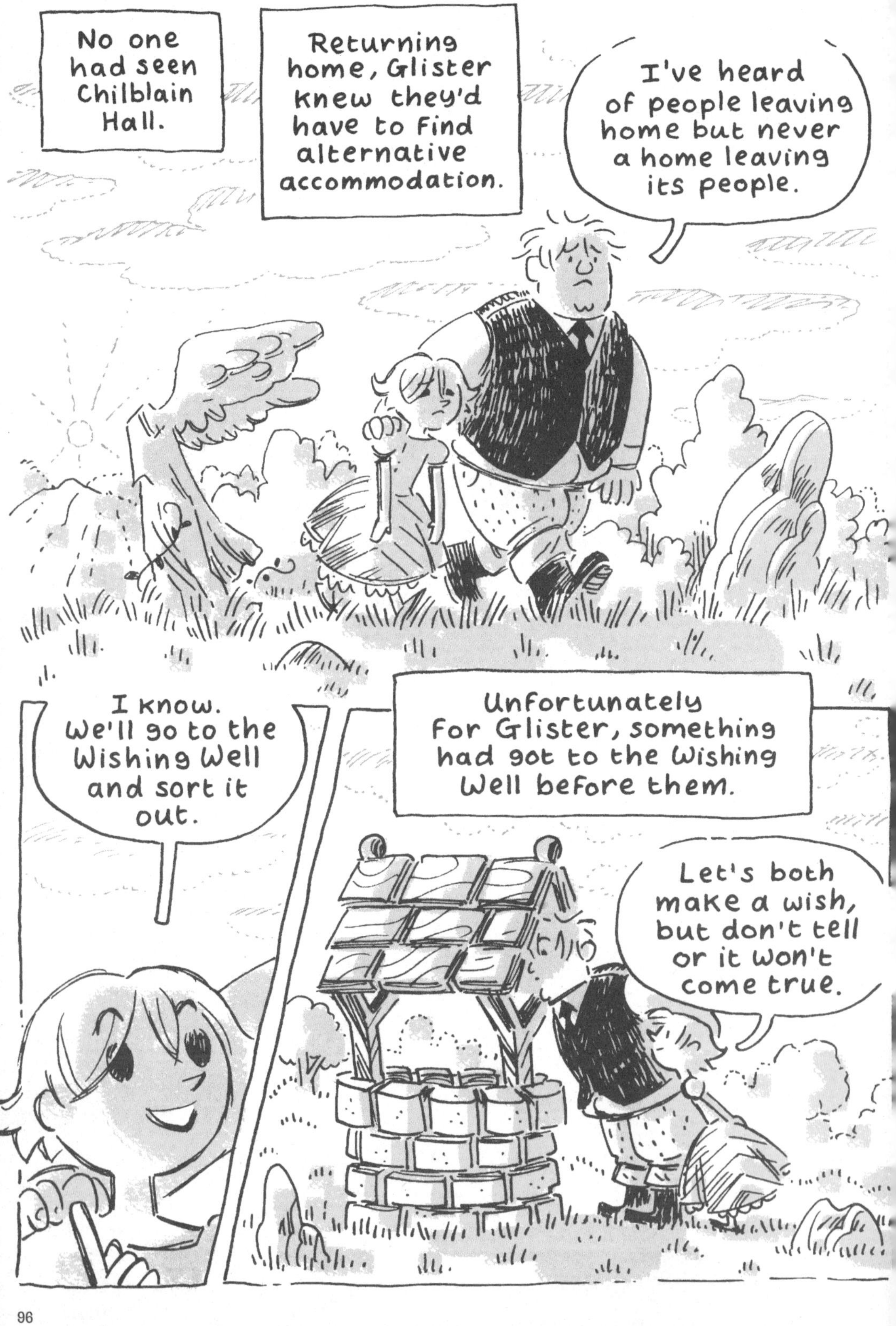
No one had seen Chilblain Hall.
Returning home, Glister knew they'd have to find alternative accommodation.
I've heard of people leaving home but never a home leaving its people.
I know. We'll go to the Wishing Well and sort it out.
Unfortunately for Glister, something had got to the Wishing Well before them.
Let's both make a wish, but don't tell or it won't come true.

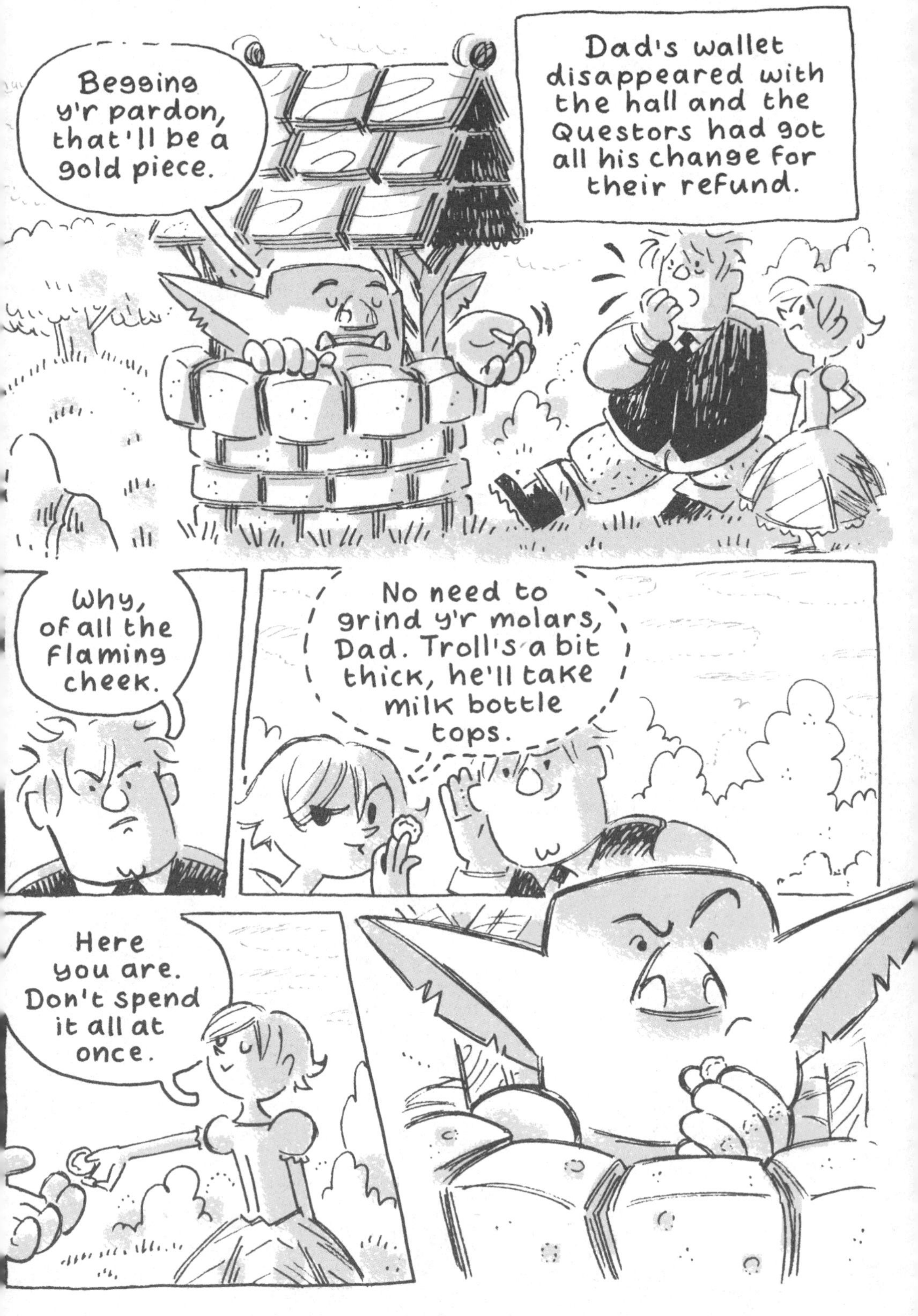
Begging y'r pardon, that'll be a gold piece.
Dad's wallet disappeared with the hall and the Questors had got all his change for their refund.
Why, of all the flaming cheek.
No need to grind y'r molars, Dad. Troll's a bit thick, he'll take milk bottle tops.
Here you are. Don't spend it all at once.

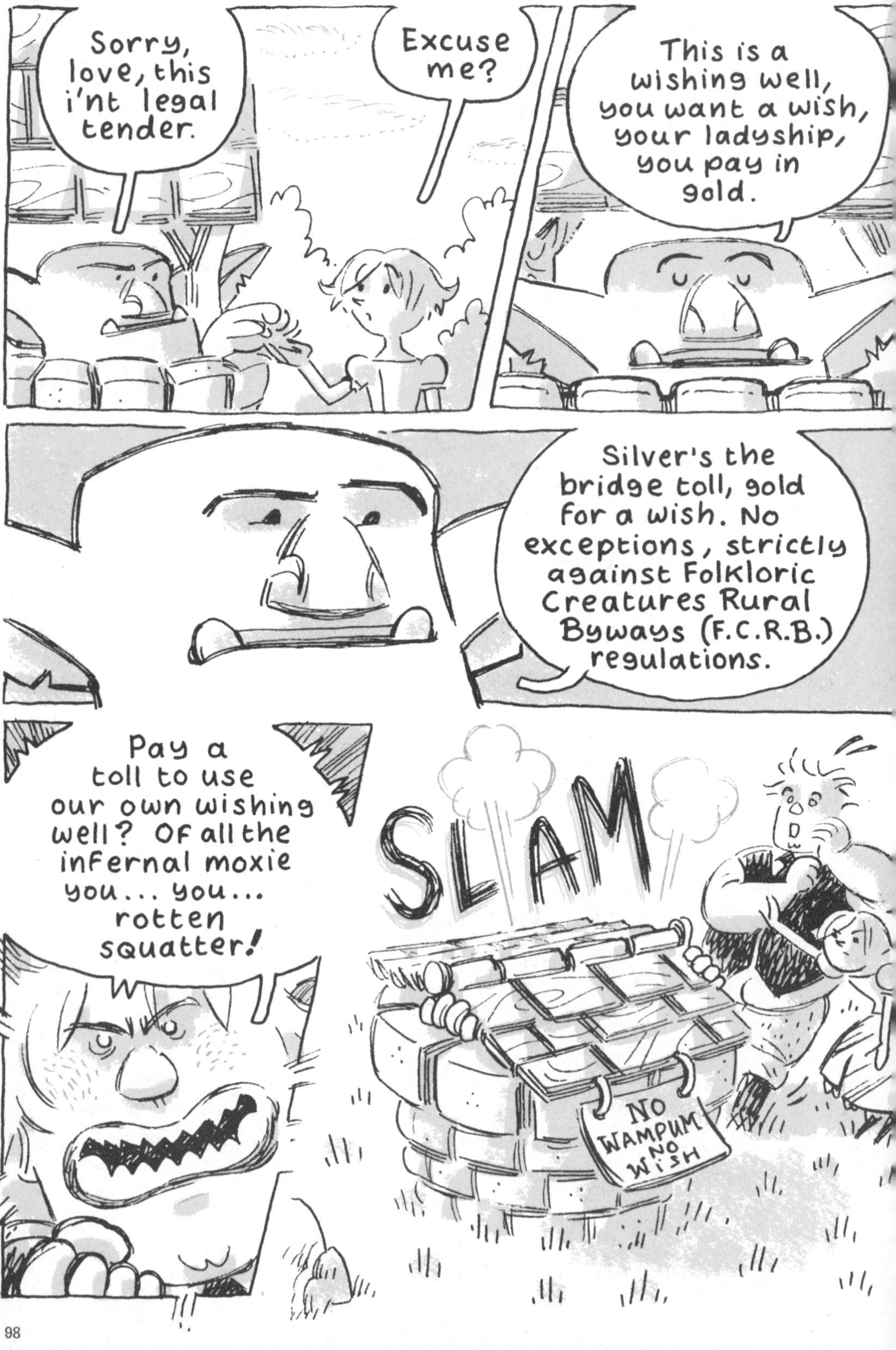

Sorry, love, this i'nt legal tender.
Excuse me?
This is a wishing well, you want a wish, your ladyship, you pay in gold.
Silver's the bridge toll, gold for a wish. No exceptions, strictly against Folkloric Creatures Rural Byways (F.C.R.B.) regulations.
Pay a toll to use our own wishing well? Of all the infernal moxie you... you... rotten squatter!
SLAM
NO WAMPUM NO WISH

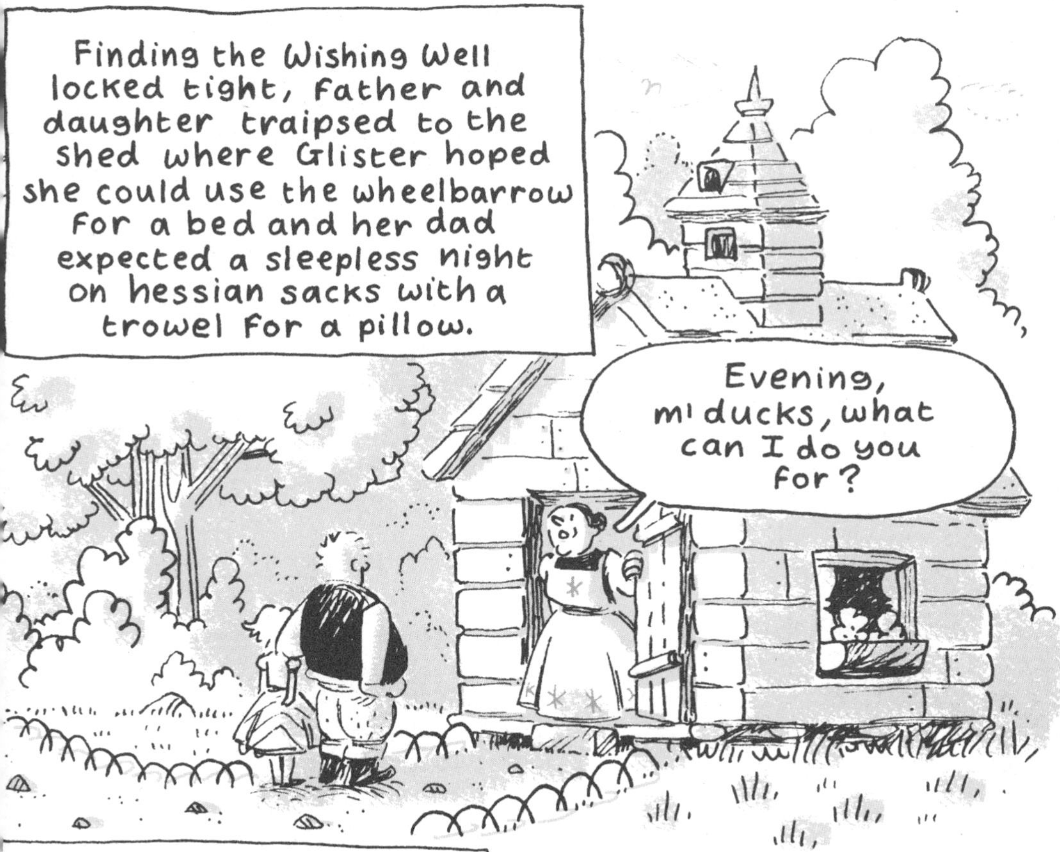
Finding the Wishing Well locked tight, father and daughter traipsed to the shed where Glister hoped she could use the wheelbarrow for a bed and her dad expected a sleepless night on hessian sacks with a trowel for a pillow.
Evening, m' ducks, what can I do you for?

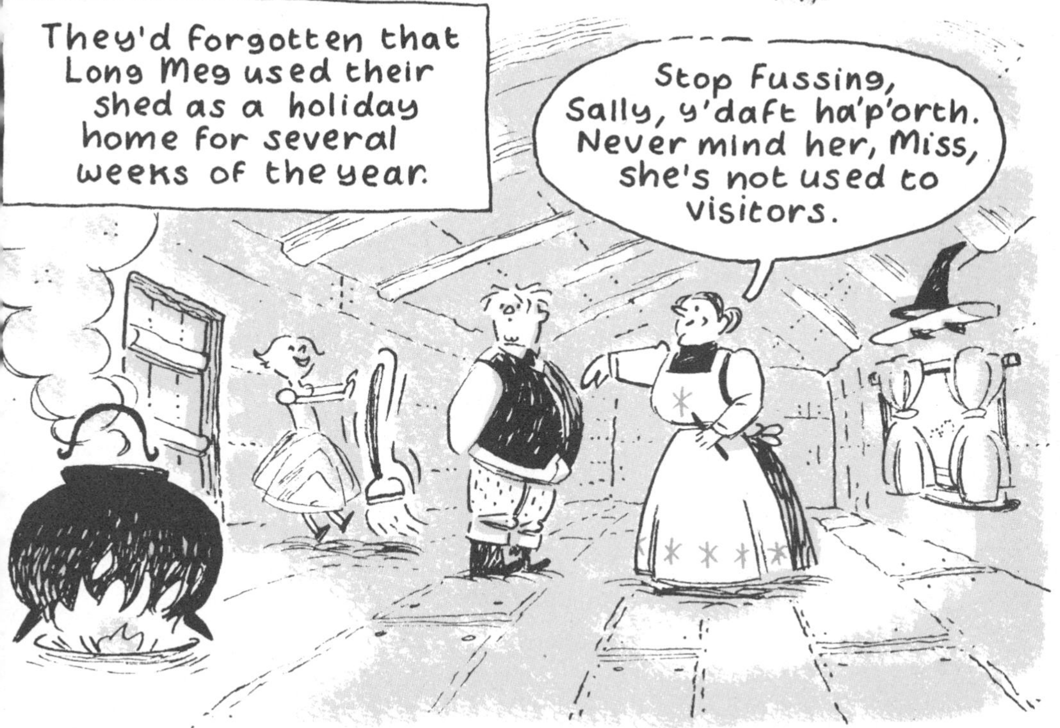
They'd forgotten that Long Meg used their shed as a holiday home for several weeks of the year.
Stop fussing, Sally, y'daft ha'p'orth. Never mind her, Miss, she's not used to visitors.

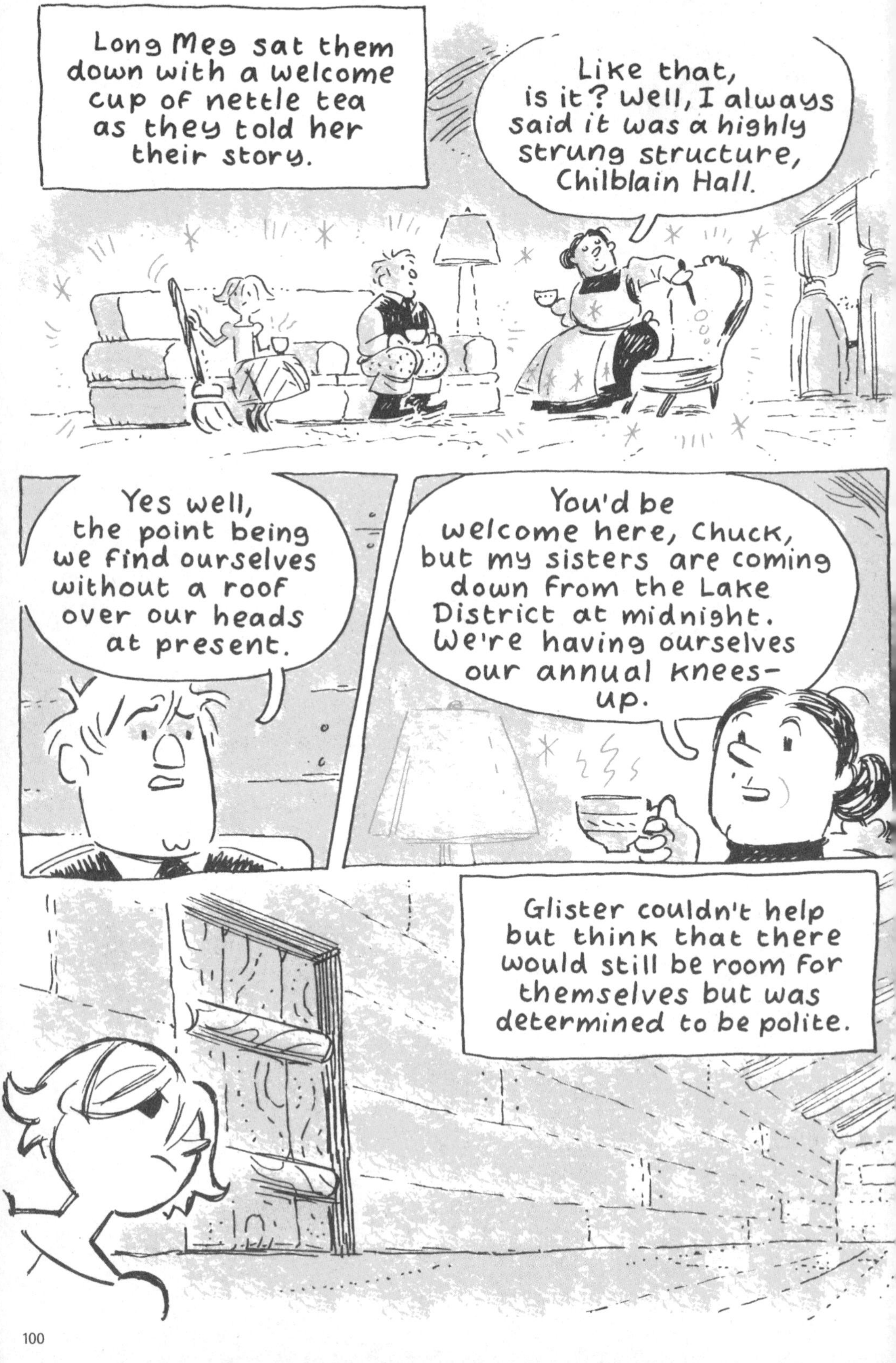

Long Meg sat them down with a welcome cup of nettle tea as they told her their story.
Like that, is it? Well, I always said it was a highly strung structure, Chilblain Hall.
Yes well, the point being we find ourselves without a roof over our heads at present.
You'd be welcome here, Chuck, but my sisters are coming down from the Lake District at midnight. We're having ourselves our annual knees-up.
Glister couldn't help but think that there would still be room for themselves but was determined to be polite.

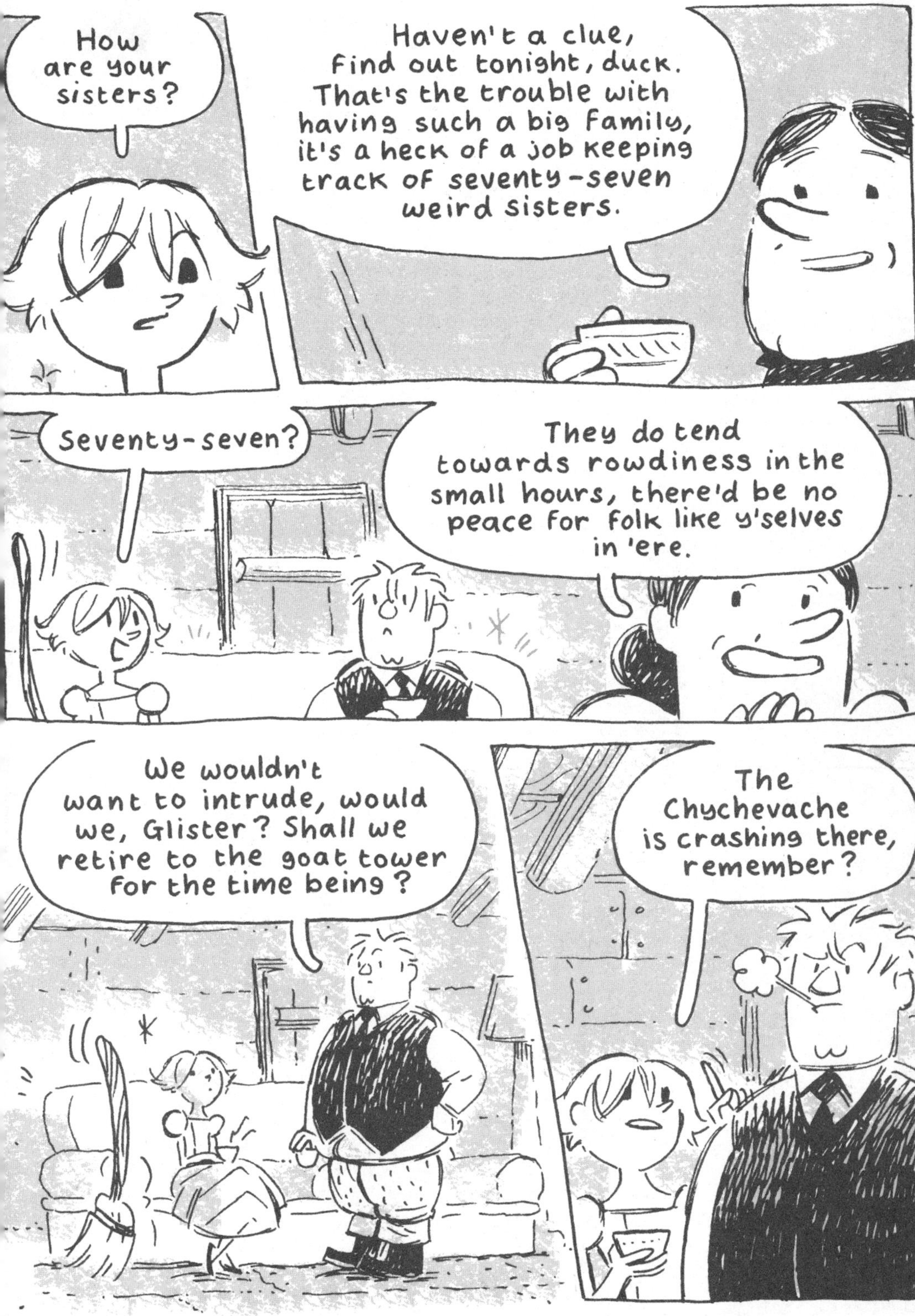
How are your sisters?
Haven't a clue, find out tonight, duck. That's the trouble with having such a big family, it's a heck of a job keeping track of seventy-seven weird sisters.
Seventy-seven?
They do tend towards rowdiness in the small hours, there'd be no peace for folk like y'selves in 'ere.
We wouldn't want to intrude, would we, Glister? Shall we retire to the goat tower for the time being?
The Chychevache is crashing there, remember?

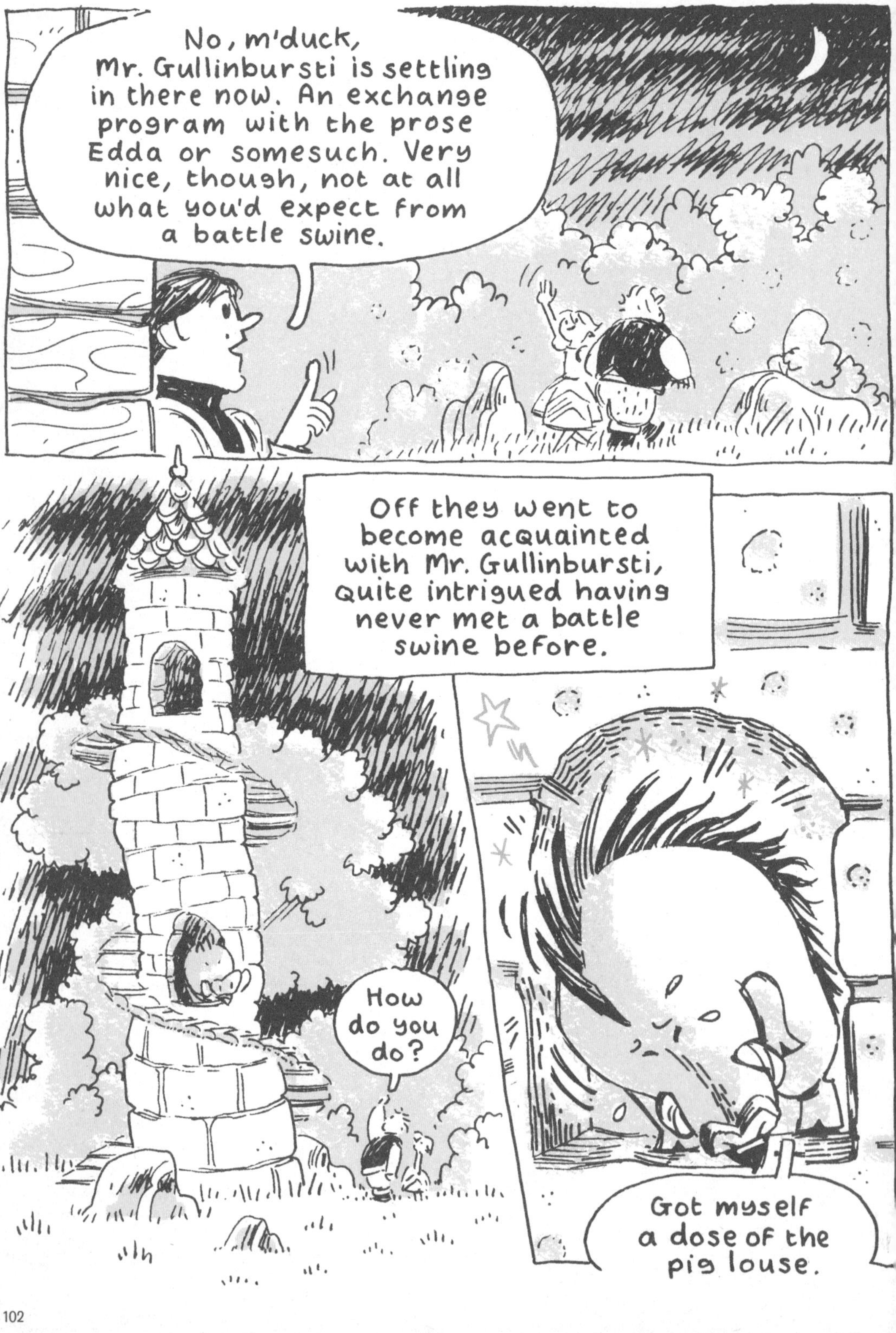
No, m'duck, Mr. Gullinbursti is settling in there now. An exchange program with the prose Edda or somesuch. Very nice, though, not at all what you'd expect from a battle swine.
Off they went to become acquainted with Mr. Gullinbursti, quite intrigued having never met a battle swine before.
How do you do?
Got myself a dose of the pig louse.

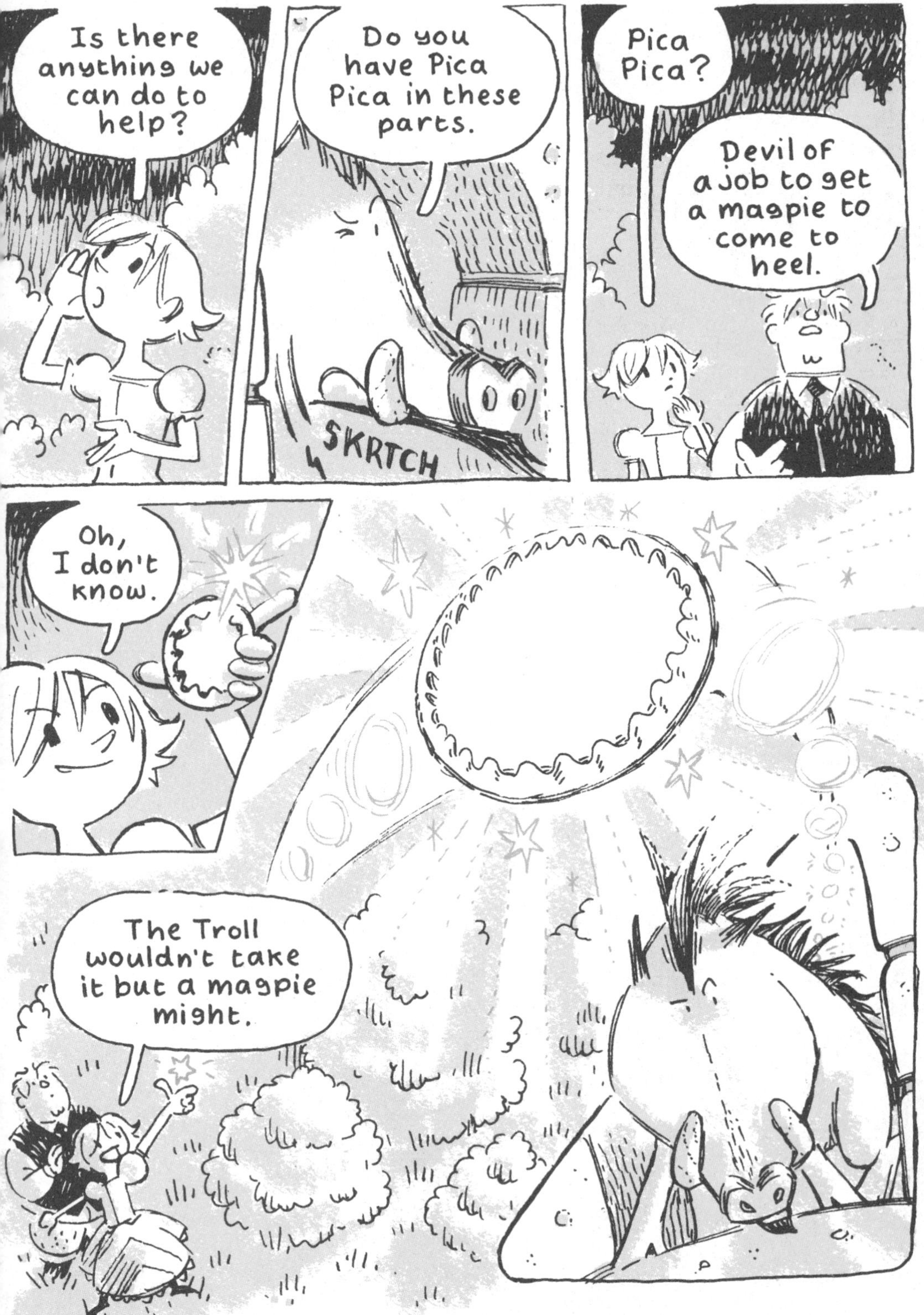
Is there anything we can do to help?
Do you have Pica Pica in these parts.
SKRTCH
Pica Pica?
Devil of a job to get a magpie to come to heel.
Oh, I don't know.
The Troll wouldn't take it but a magpie might.

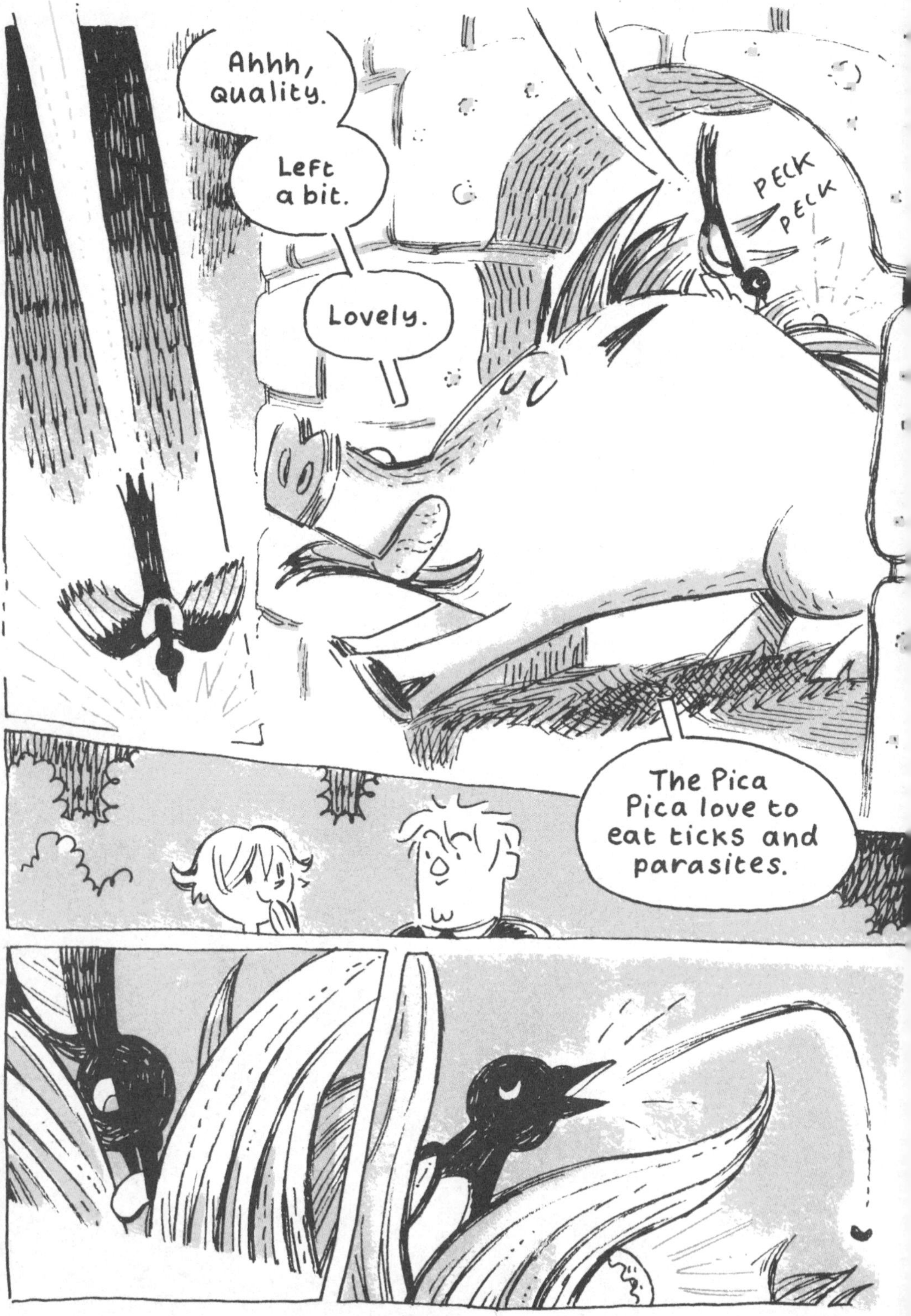
Ahhh, quality.
Left a bit.
Lovely.
PECK
PECK
The Pica Pica love to eat ticks and parasites.

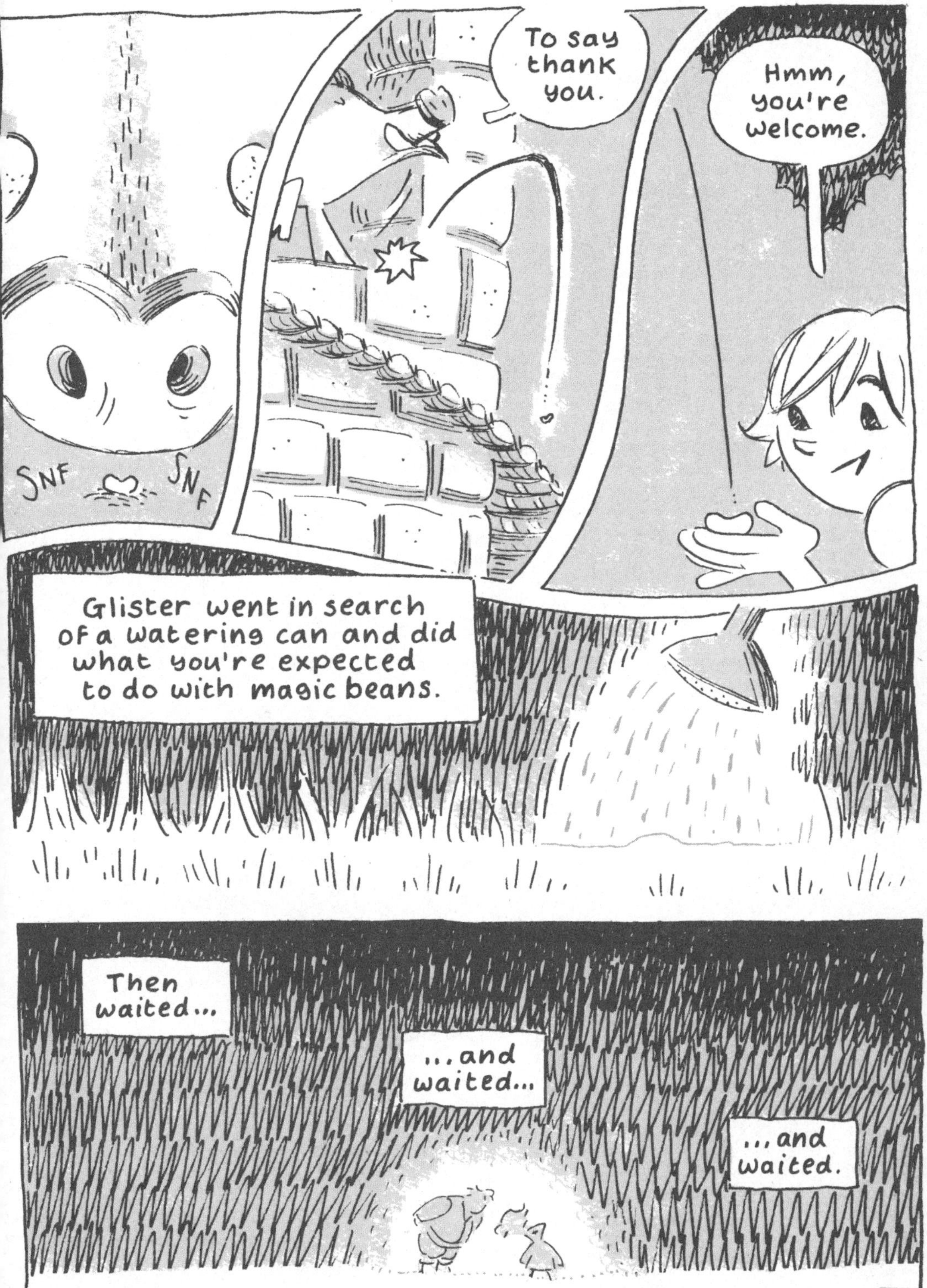
To say thank you.
Hmm, you're welcome.
SNF SNF
Glister went in search of a watering can and did what you're expected to do with magic beans.
Then waited...
...and waited...
...and waited.

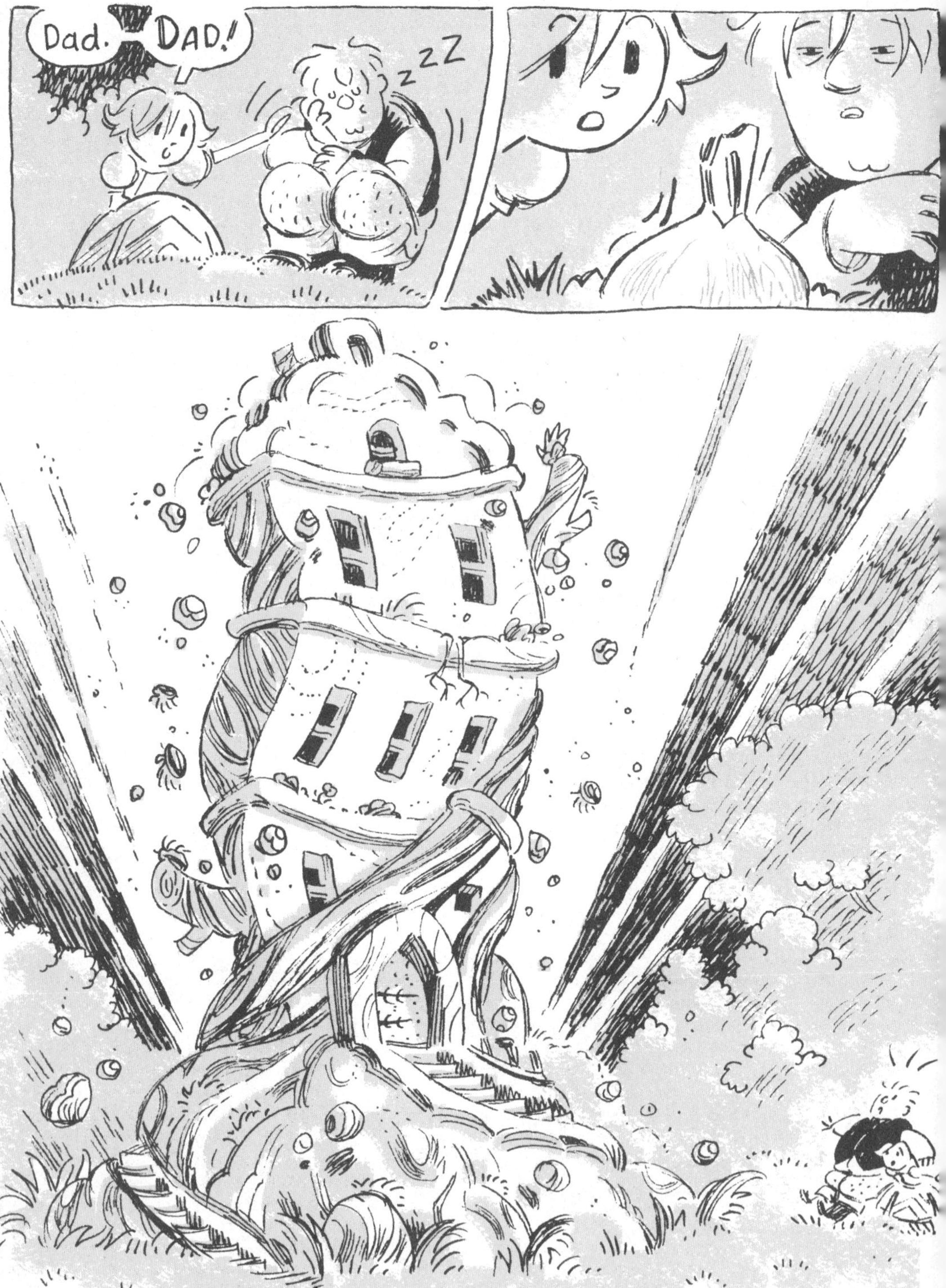
Dad.
DAD!
zZZ

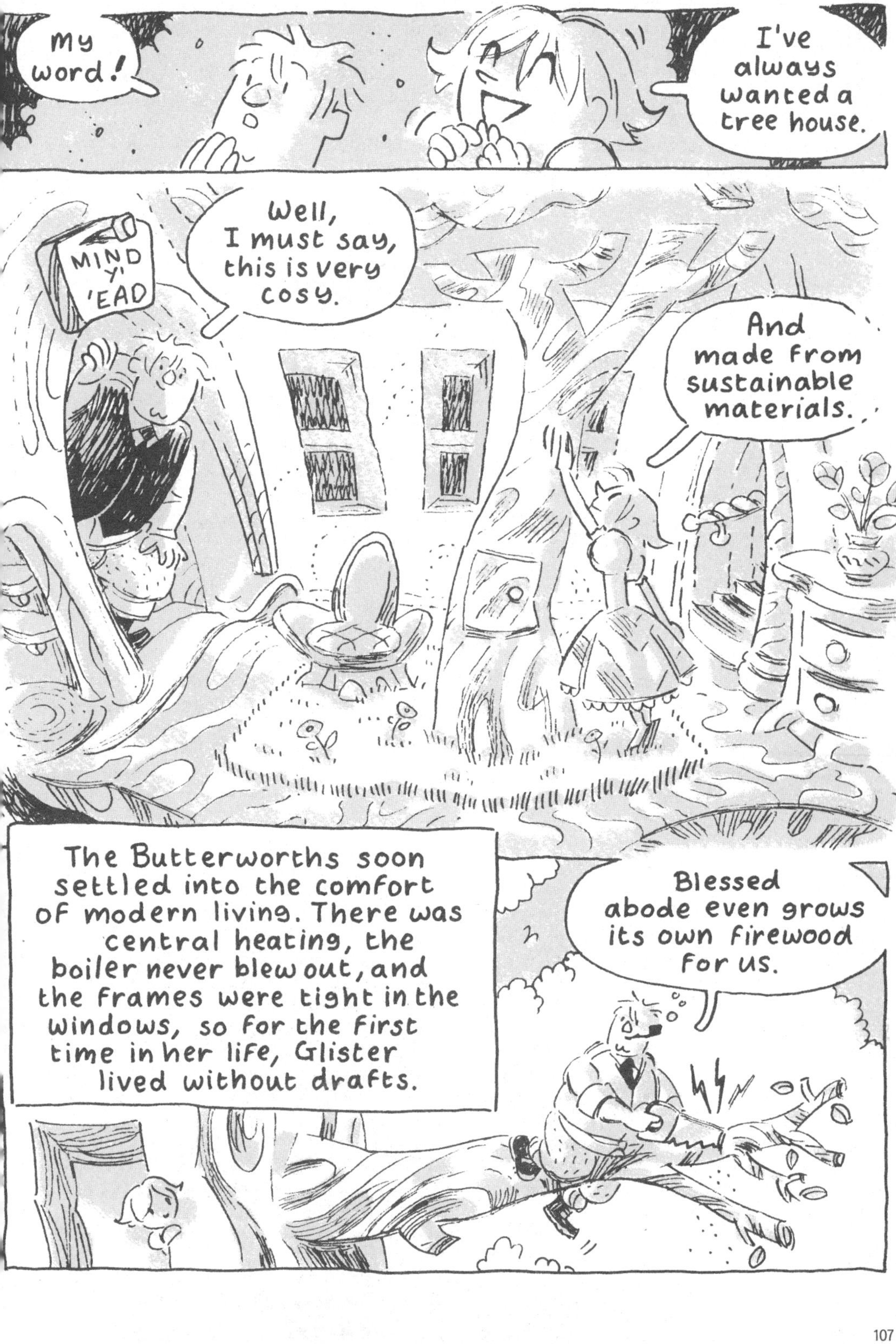
My word!
I've always wanted a tree house.
MIND YI 'EAD
Well, I must say, this is very cosy.
And made from sustainable materials.
The Butterworths soon settled into the comfort of modern living. There was central heating, the boiler never blew out, and the frames were tight in the windows, so for the first time in her life, Glister lived without drafts.
Blessed abode even grows its own firewood for us.

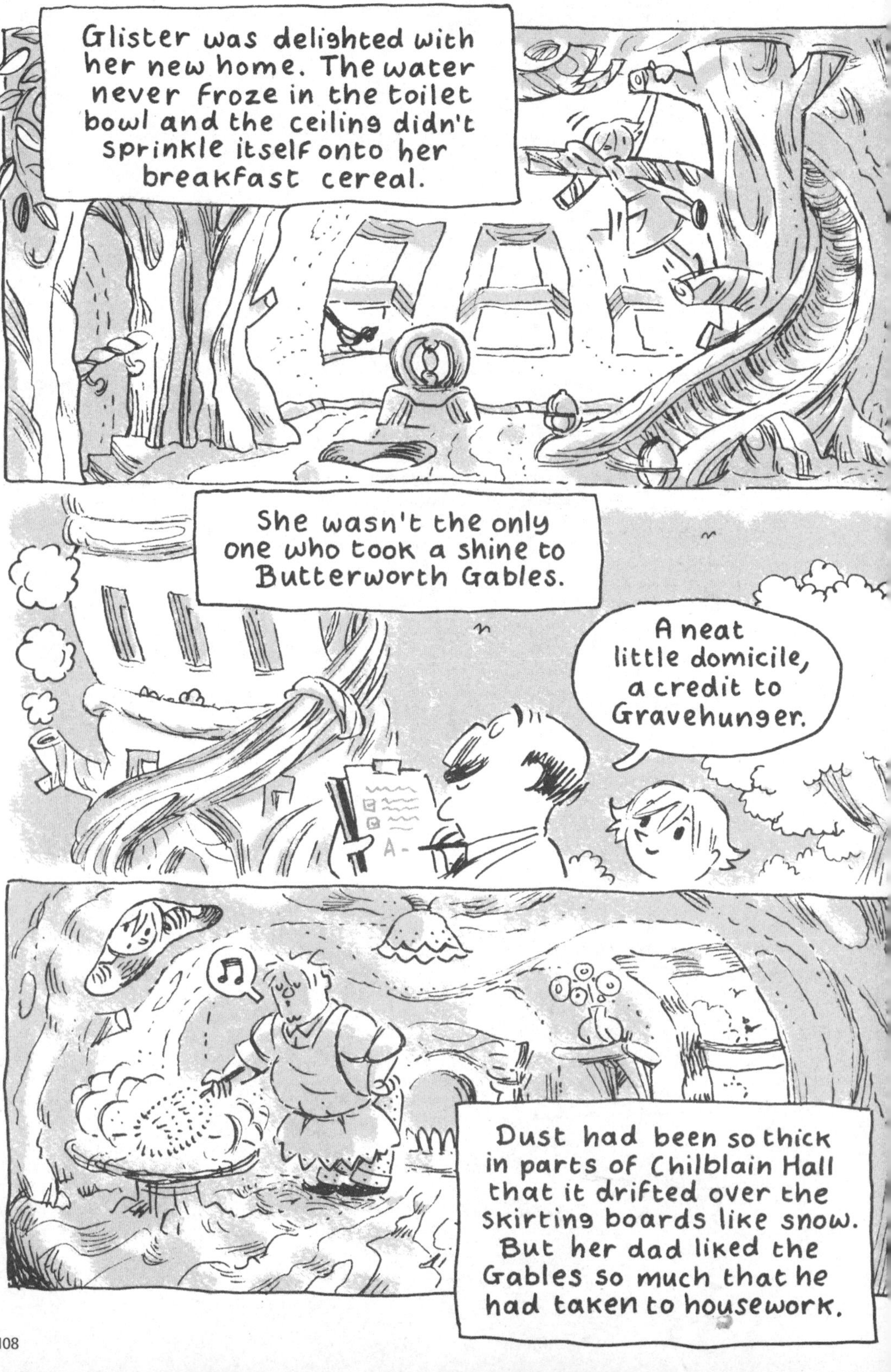
Glister was delighted with her new home. The water never froze in the toilet bowl and the ceiling didn't sprinkle itself onto her breakfast cereal.
She wasn't the only one who took a shine to Butterworth Gables.
A neat little domicile, a credit to Gravehunger.
Dust had been so thick in parts of Chilblain Hall that it drifted over the skirting boards like snow. But her dad liked the Gables so much that he had taken to housework.

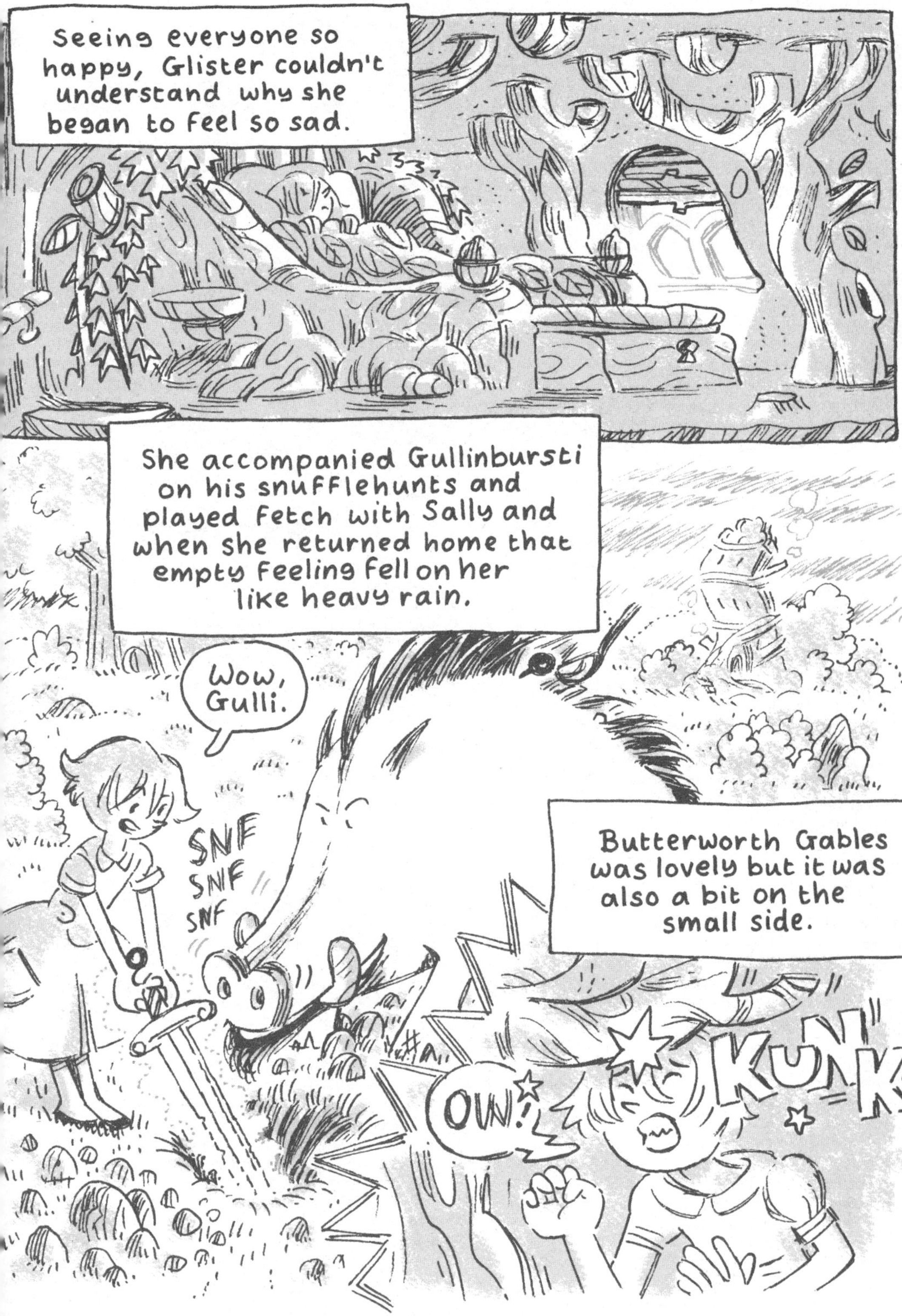
Seeing everyone so happy, Glister couldn't understand why she began to feel so sad.
She accompanied Gullinbursti on his snufflehunts and played fetch with Sally and when she returned home that empty feeling fell on her like heavy rain.
Wow, Gulli.
SNF
SNF
SNF
Butterworth Gables was lovely but it was also a bit on the small side.
OW!
KUNK

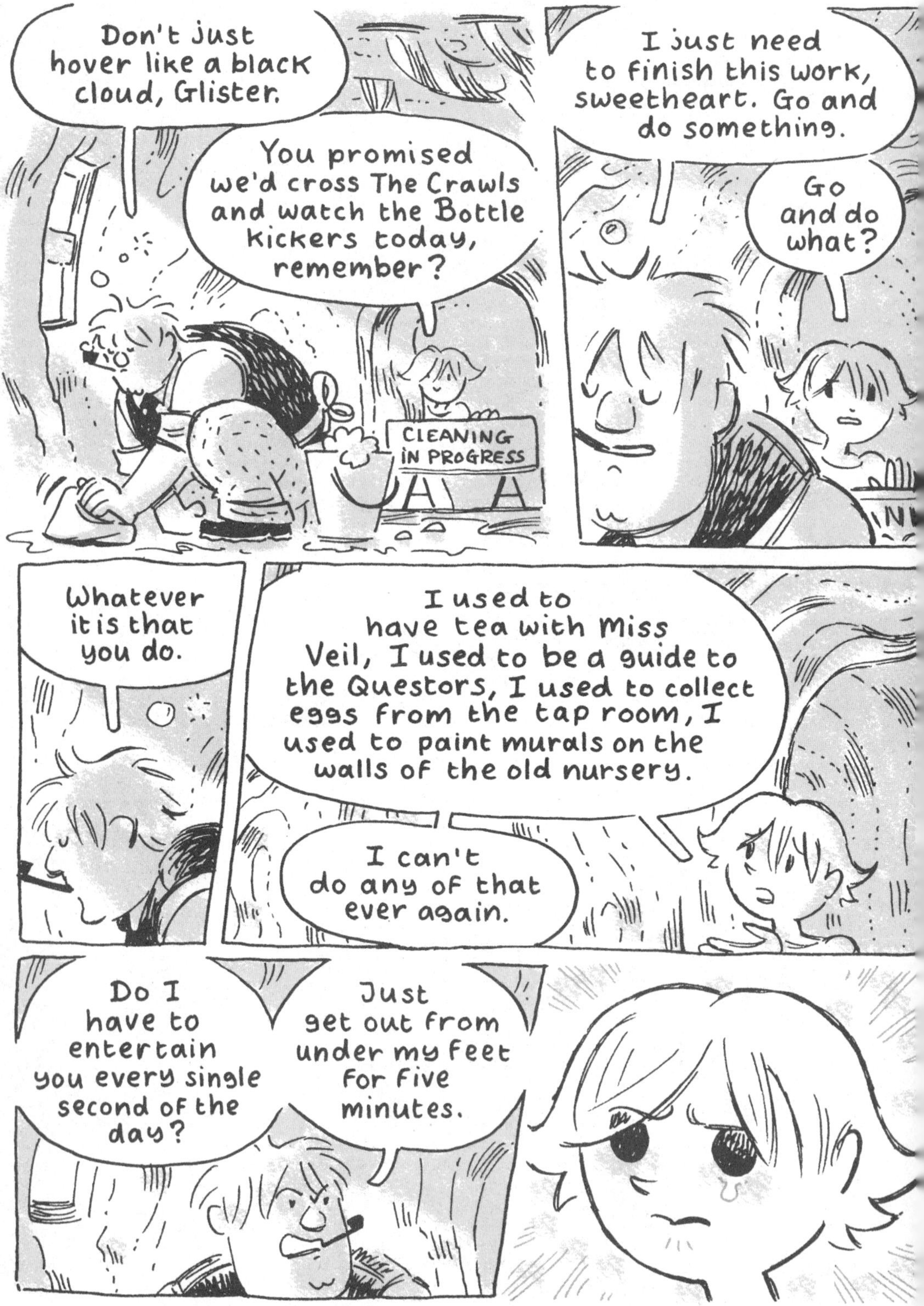
Don't just hover like a black cloud, Glister.
You promised we'd cross The Crawls and watch the Bottle kickers today, remember?
CLEANING IN PROGRESS
I just need to finish this work, sweetheart. Go and do something.
Go and do what?
Whatever it is that you do.
I used to have tea with Miss Veil, I used to be a guide to the Questors, I used to collect eggs from the tap room, I used to paint murals on the walls of the old nursery.
I can't do any of that ever again.
Do I have to entertain you every single second of the day?
Just get out from under my feet for five minutes.

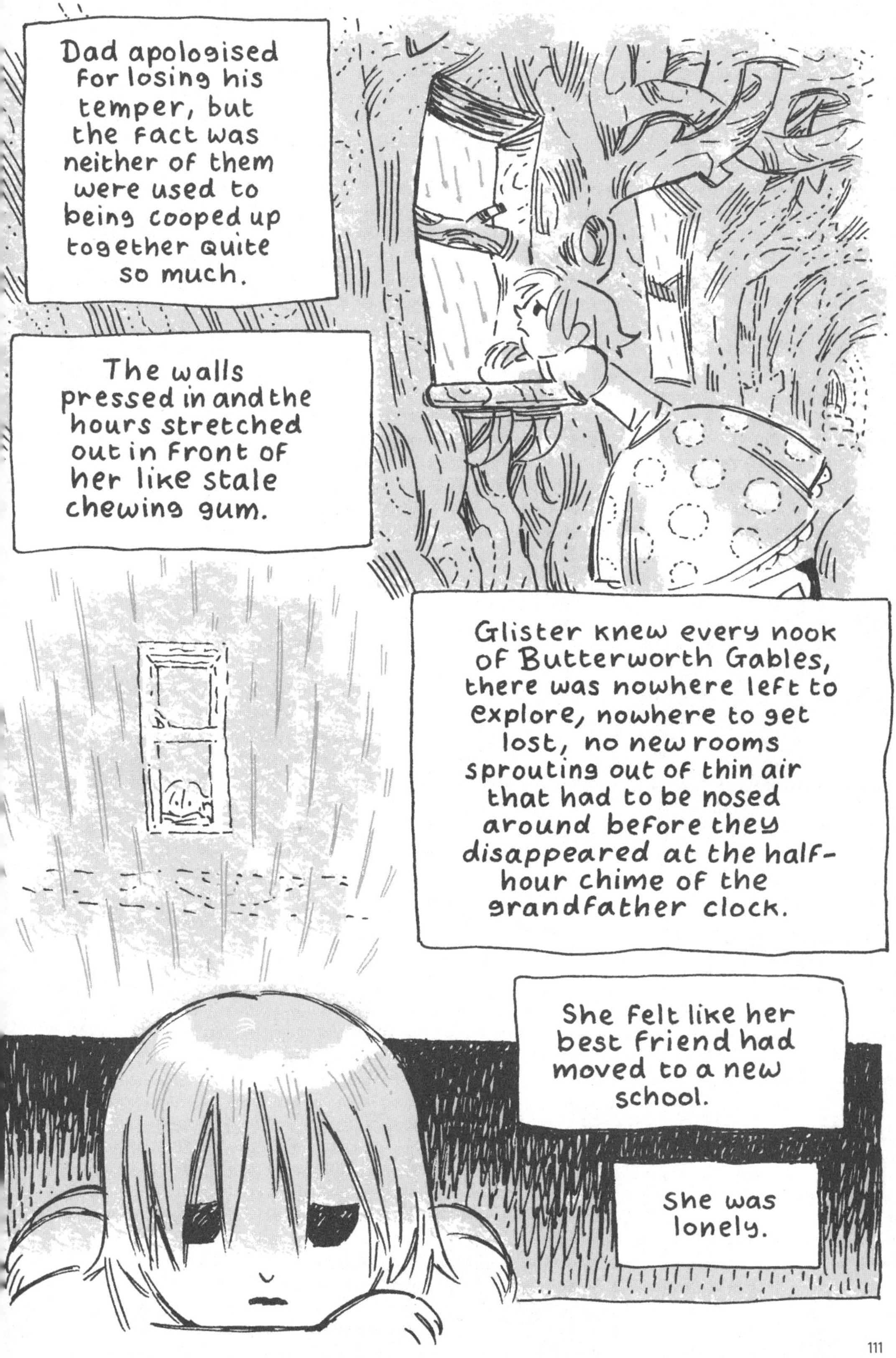
Dad apologised for losing his temper, but the fact was neither of them were used to being cooped up together quite so much.
The walls pressed in and the hours stretched out in front of her like stale chewing gum.
Glister knew every nook of Butterworth Gables, there was nowhere left to explore, nowhere to get lost, no new rooms sprouting out of thin air that had to be nosed around before they disappeared at the half-hour chime of the grandfather clock.
She felt like her best friend had moved to a new school.
She was lonely.

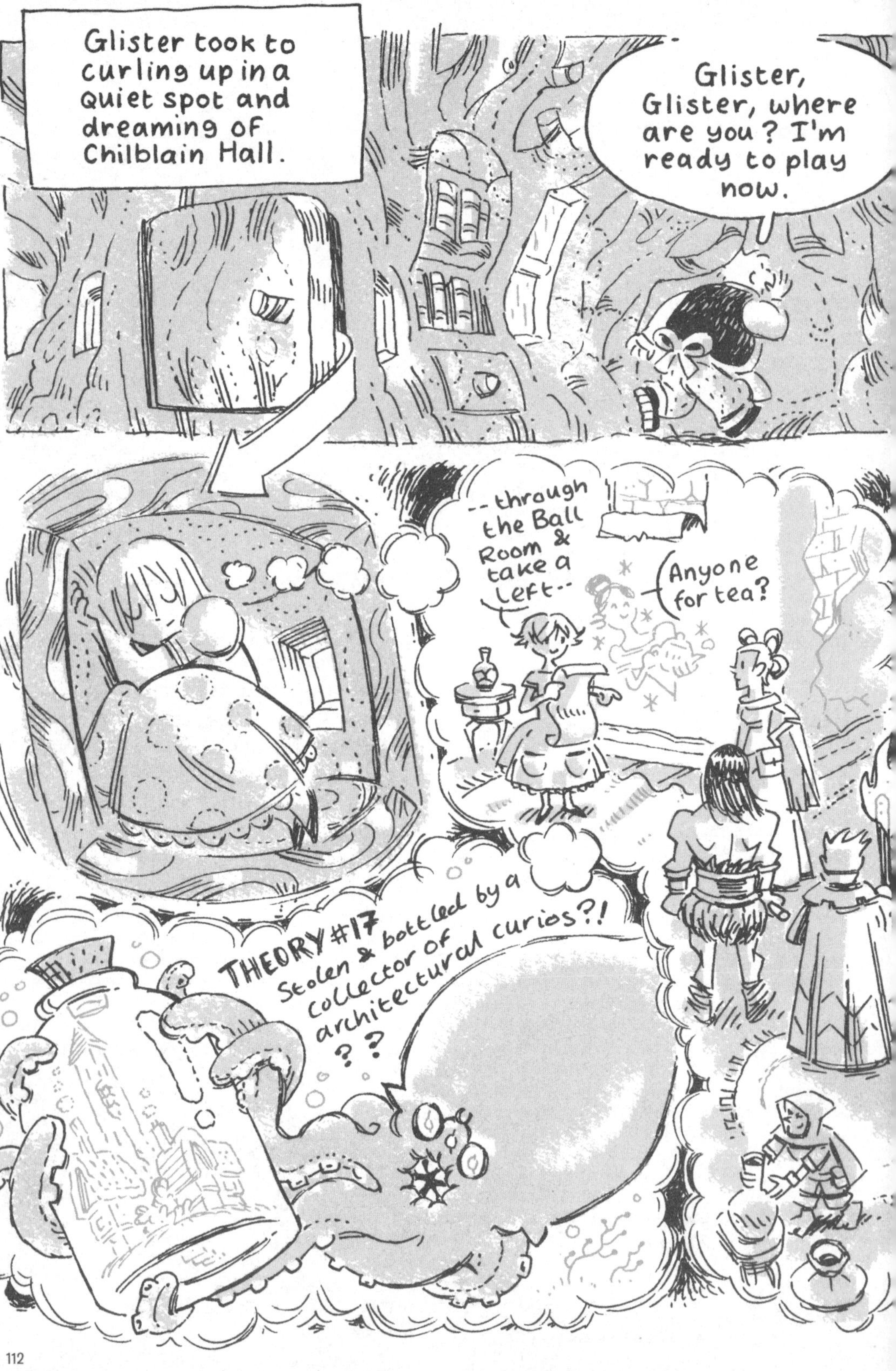
Glister took to curling up in a quiet spot and dreaming of Chilblain Hall.
Glister, Glister, where are you? I'm ready to play now.
--through the Ball Room & take a left--
Anyone for tea?
THEORY #17 Stolen & bottled by a collector of architectural curios?! ??

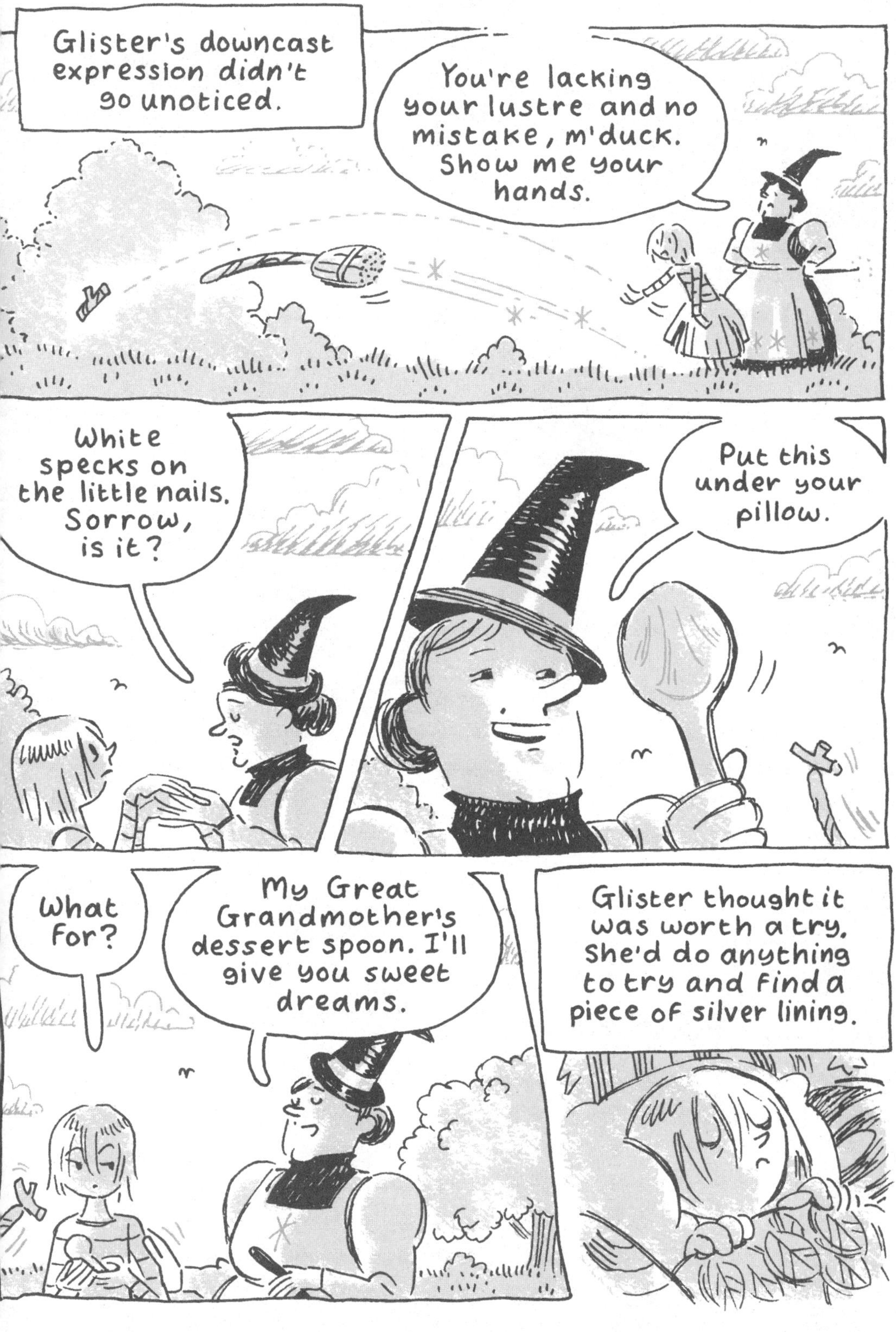

Glister's downcast expression didn't go unoticed.
You're lacking your lustre and no mistake, m'duck. Show me your hands.
White specks on the little nails. Sorrow, is it?
Put this under your pillow.
What for?
My Great Grandmother's dessert spoon. I'll give you sweet dreams.
Glister thought it was worth a try. She'd do anything to try and find a piece of silver lining.

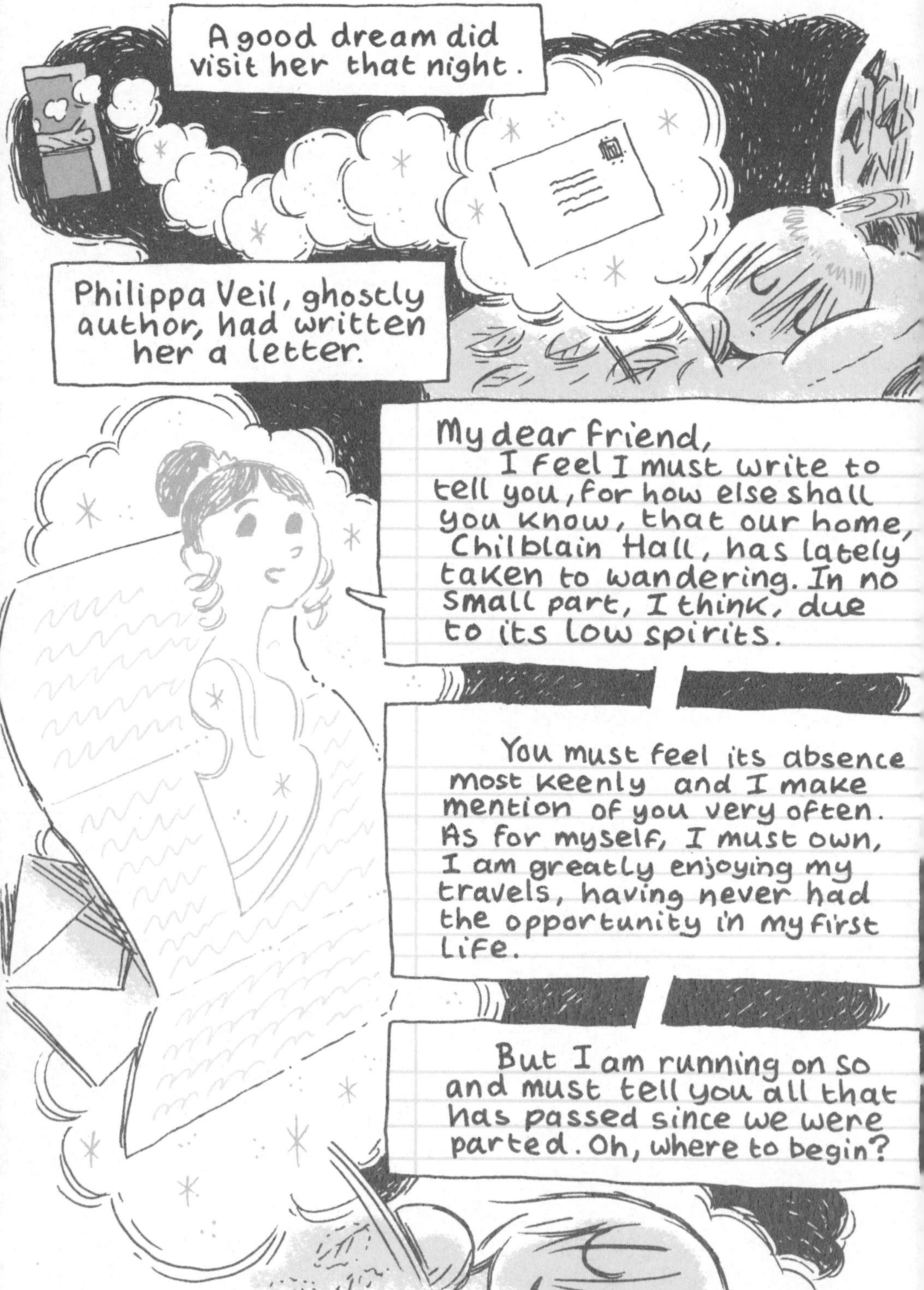
A good dream did visit her that night.
Philippa Veil, ghostly author, had written her a letter.
My dear friend,
I feel I must write to tell you, for how else shall you know, that our home, Chilblain Hall, has lately taken to wandering. In no small part, I think, due to its low spirits.
You must feel its absence most keenly and I make mention of you very often. As for myself, I must own, I am greatly enjoying my travels, having never had the opportunity in my first life.
But I am running on so and must tell you all that has passed since we were parted. Oh, where to begin?

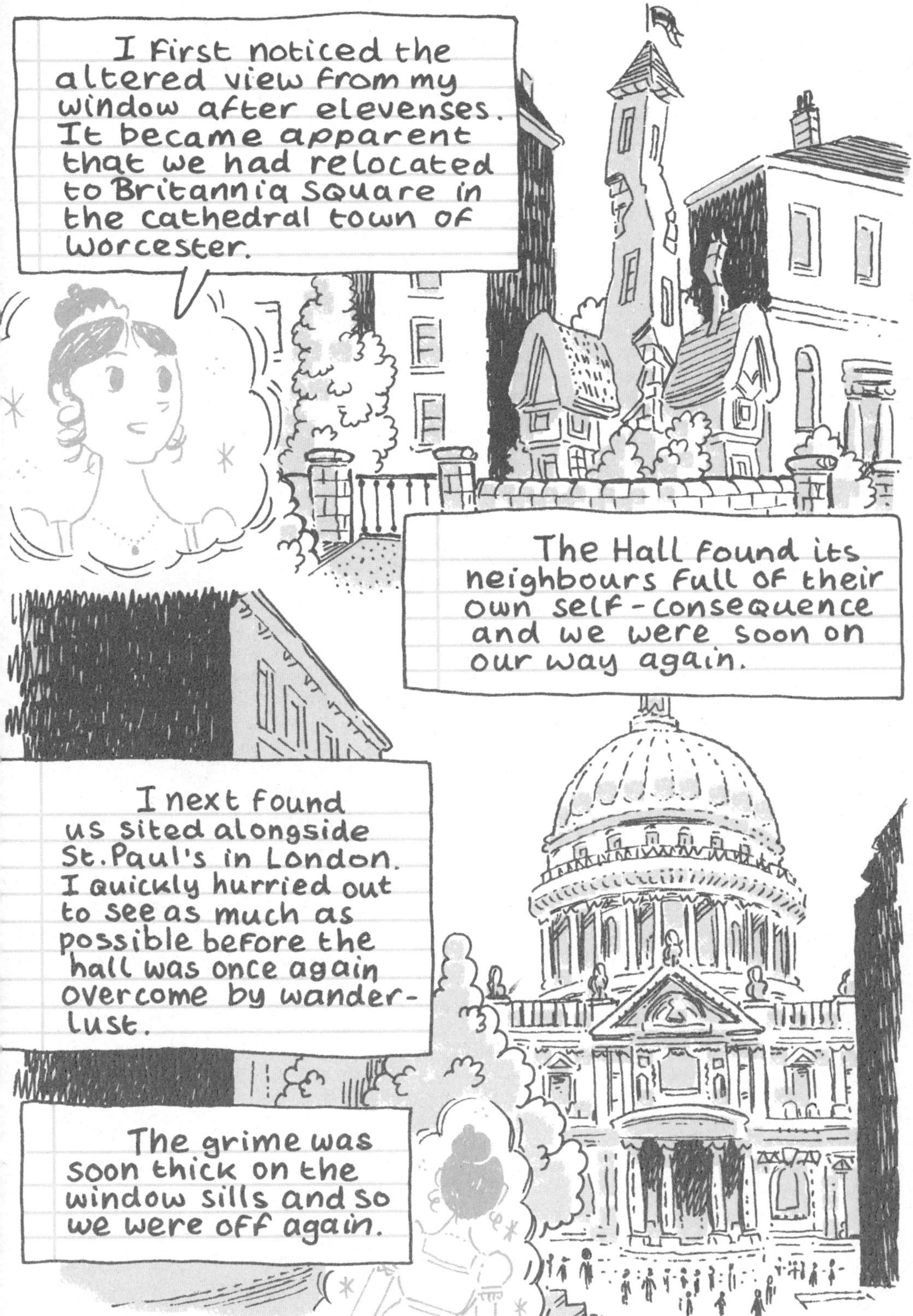
I first noticed the altered view from my window after elevenses. It became apparent that we had relocated to Britannia Square in the cathedral town of Worcester.
The Hall found its neighbours full of their own self-consequence and we were soon on our way again.
I next found us sited alongside St. Paul's in London. I quickly hurried out to see as much as possible before the hall was once again overcome by wander-lust.
The grime was soon thick on the window sills and so we were off again.

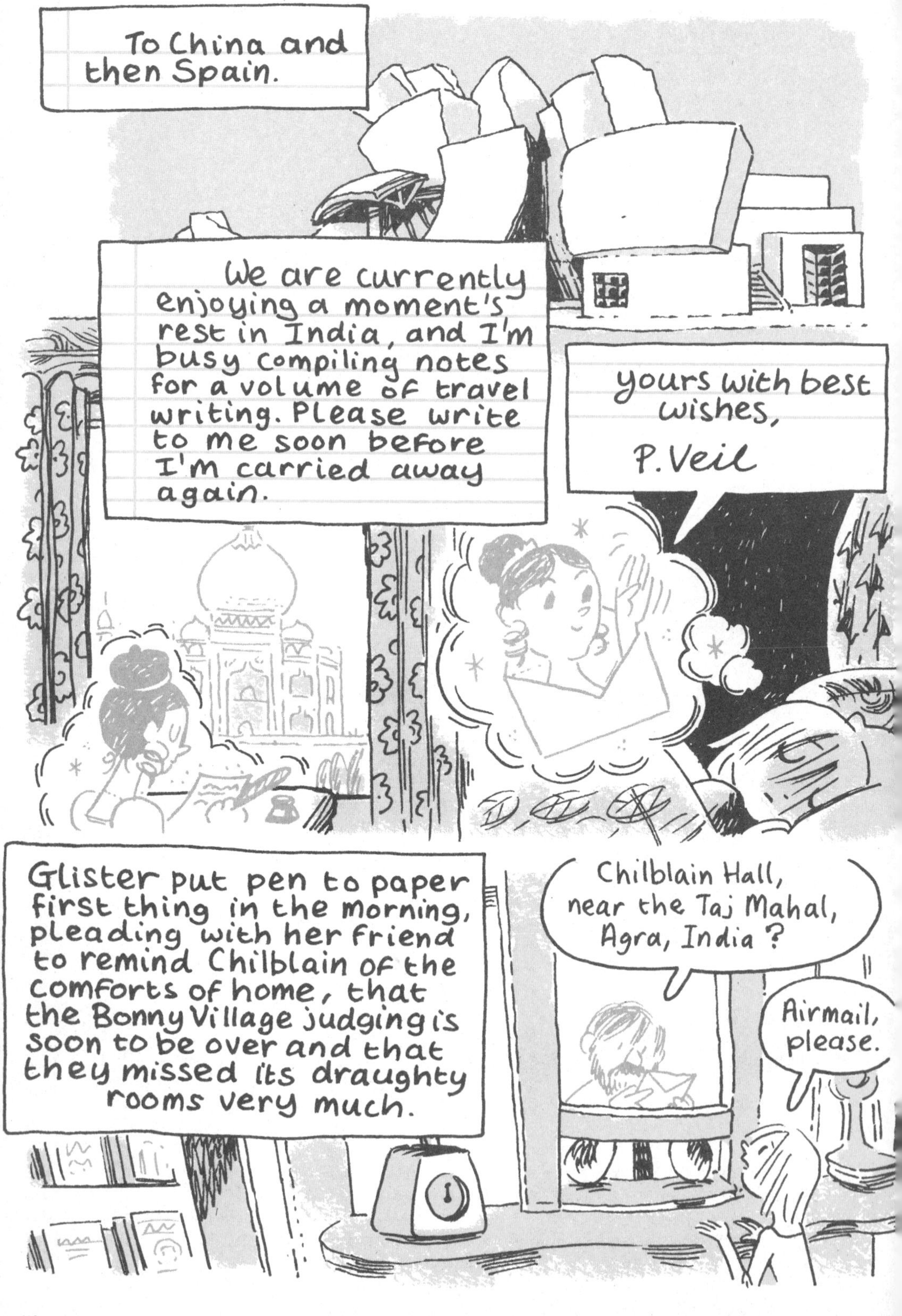

To China and then Spain.
We are currently enjoying a moment's rest in India, and I'm busy compiling notes for a volume of travel writing. Please write to me soon before I'm carried away again.
yours with best wishes,
P. Veil
Glister put pen to paper first thing in the morning, pleading with her friend to remind Chilblain of the comforts of home, that the Bonny Village judging is soon to be over and that they missed its draughty rooms very much.
Chilblain Hall, near the Taj Mahal, Agra, India?
Airmail, please.

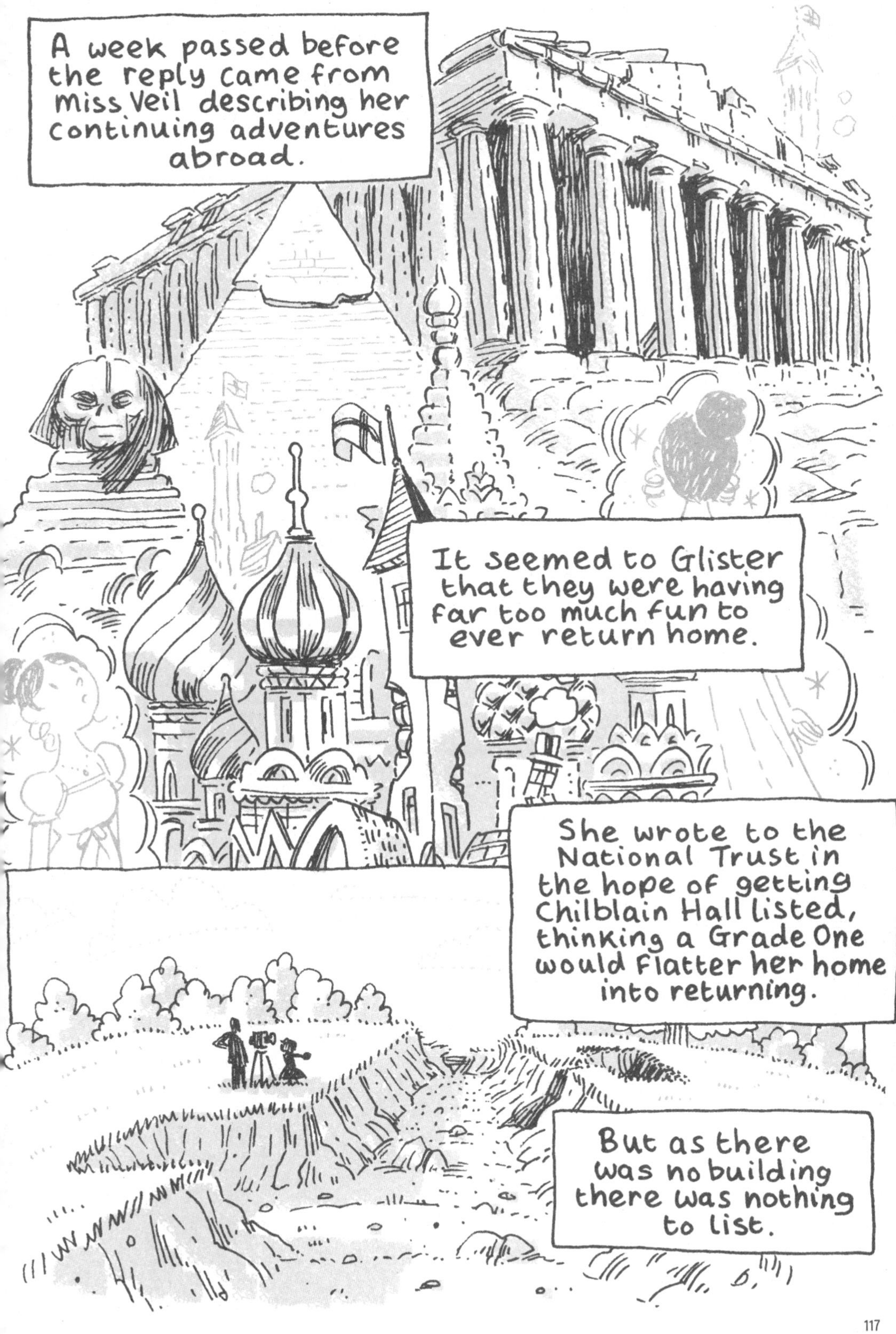
A week passed before the reply came from Miss Veil describing her continuing adventures abroad.
It seemed to Glister that they were having far too much fun to ever return home.
She wrote to the National Trust in the hope of getting Chilblain Hall listed, thinking a Grade One would flatter her home into returning.
But as there was no building there was nothing to list.

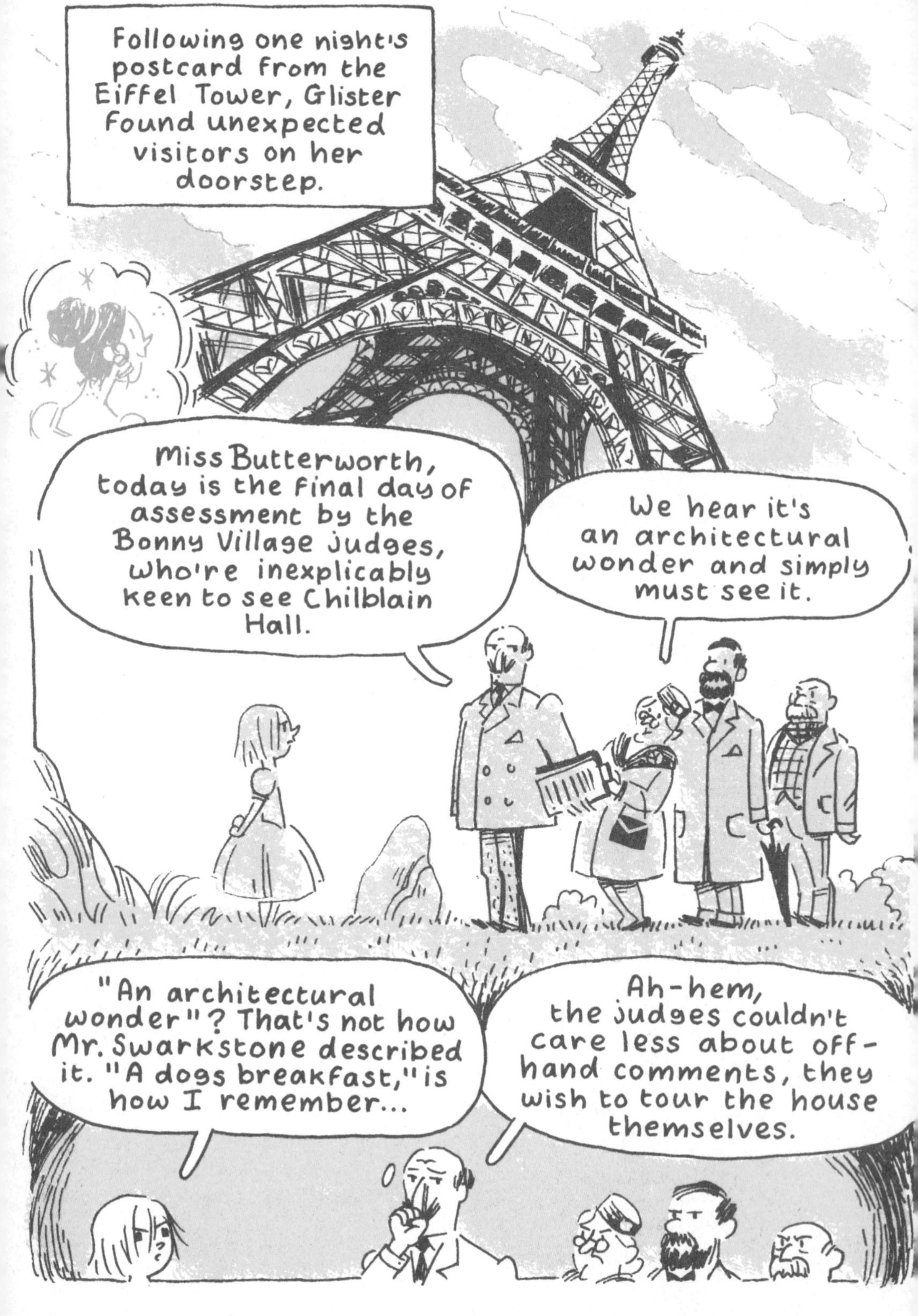
Following one night's postcard from the Eiffel Tower, Glister found unexpected visitors on her doorstep.
Miss Butterworth, today is the final day of assessment by the Bonny Village judges, who're inexplicably keen to see Chilblain Hall.
We hear it's an architectural wonder and simply must see it.
"An architectural wonder"? That's not how Mr. Swarkstone described it. "A dogs breakfast," is how I remember...
Ah-hem, the judges couldn't care less about off-hand comments, they wish to tour the house themselves.

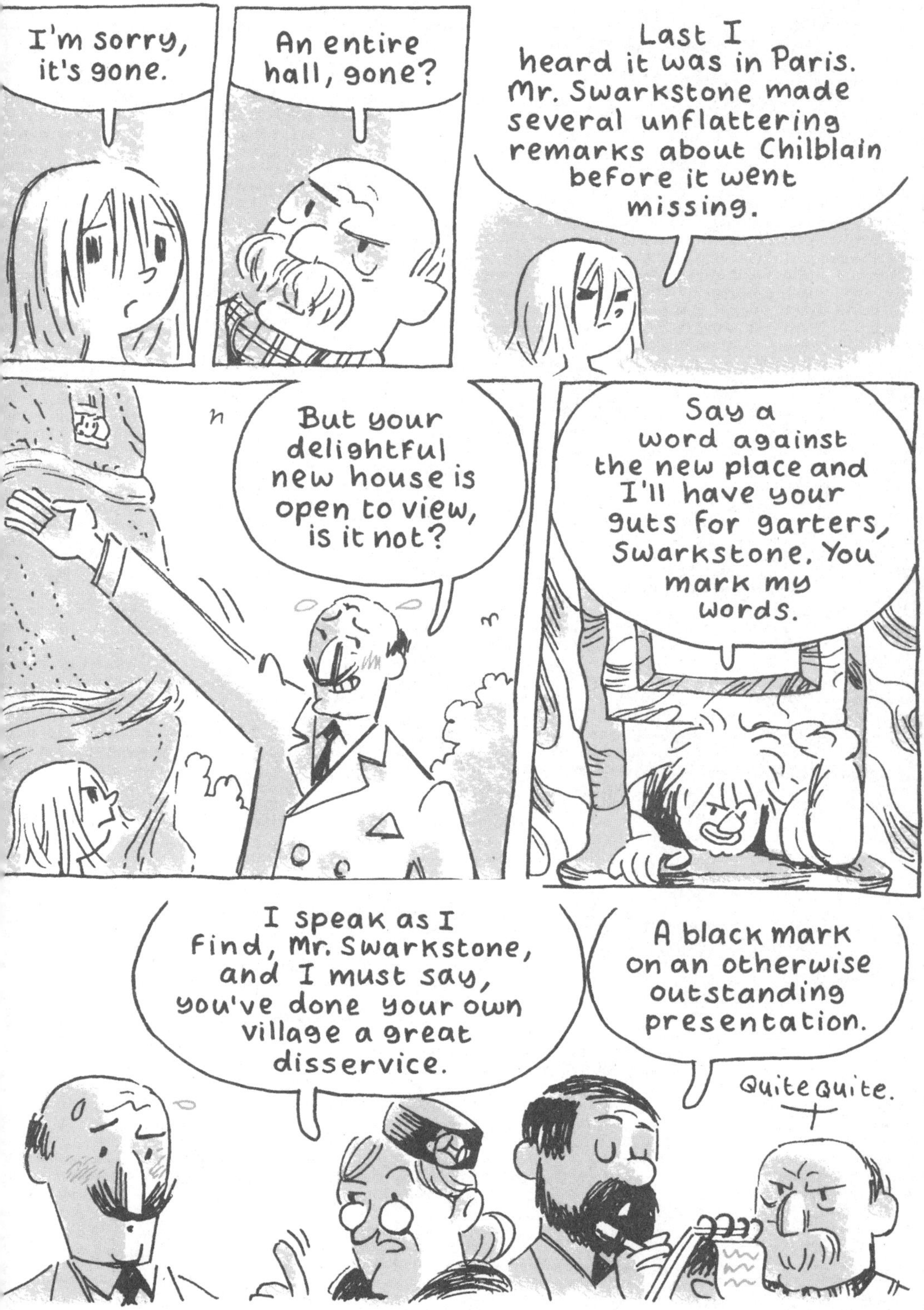
I'm sorry, it's gone.
An entire hall, gone?
Last I heard it was in Paris. Mr. Swarkstone made several unflattering remarks about Chilblain before it went missing.
But your delightful new house is open to view, is it not?
Say a word against the new place and I'll have your guts for garters, Swarkstone. You mark my words.
I speak as I find, Mr. Swarkstone, and I must say, you've done your own village a great disservice.
A black mark on an otherwise outstanding presentation.
Quite quite.

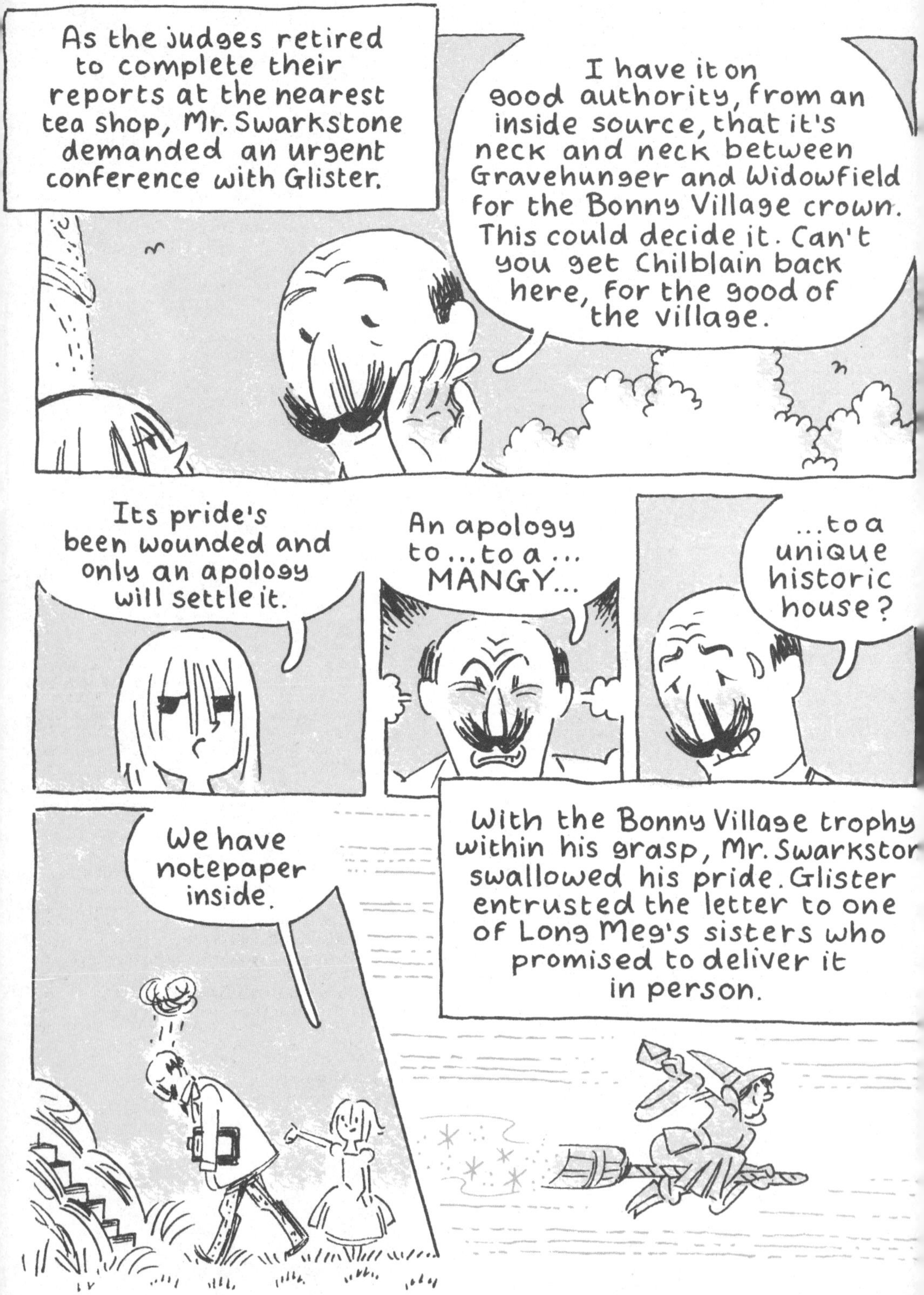

As the judges retired to complete their reports at the nearest tea shop, Mr. Swarkstone demanded an urgent conference with Glister.
I have it on good authority, from an inside source, that it's neck and neck between Gravehunger and Widowfield for the Bonny Village crown. This could decide it. Can't you get Chilblain back here, for the good of the village.
Its pride's been wounded and only an apology will settle it.
An apology to...to a... MANGY...
...to a unique historic house?
We have notepaper inside.
With the Bonny Village trophy within his grasp, Mr. Swarkstone swallowed his pride. Glister entrusted the letter to one of Long Meg's sisters who promised to deliver it in person.

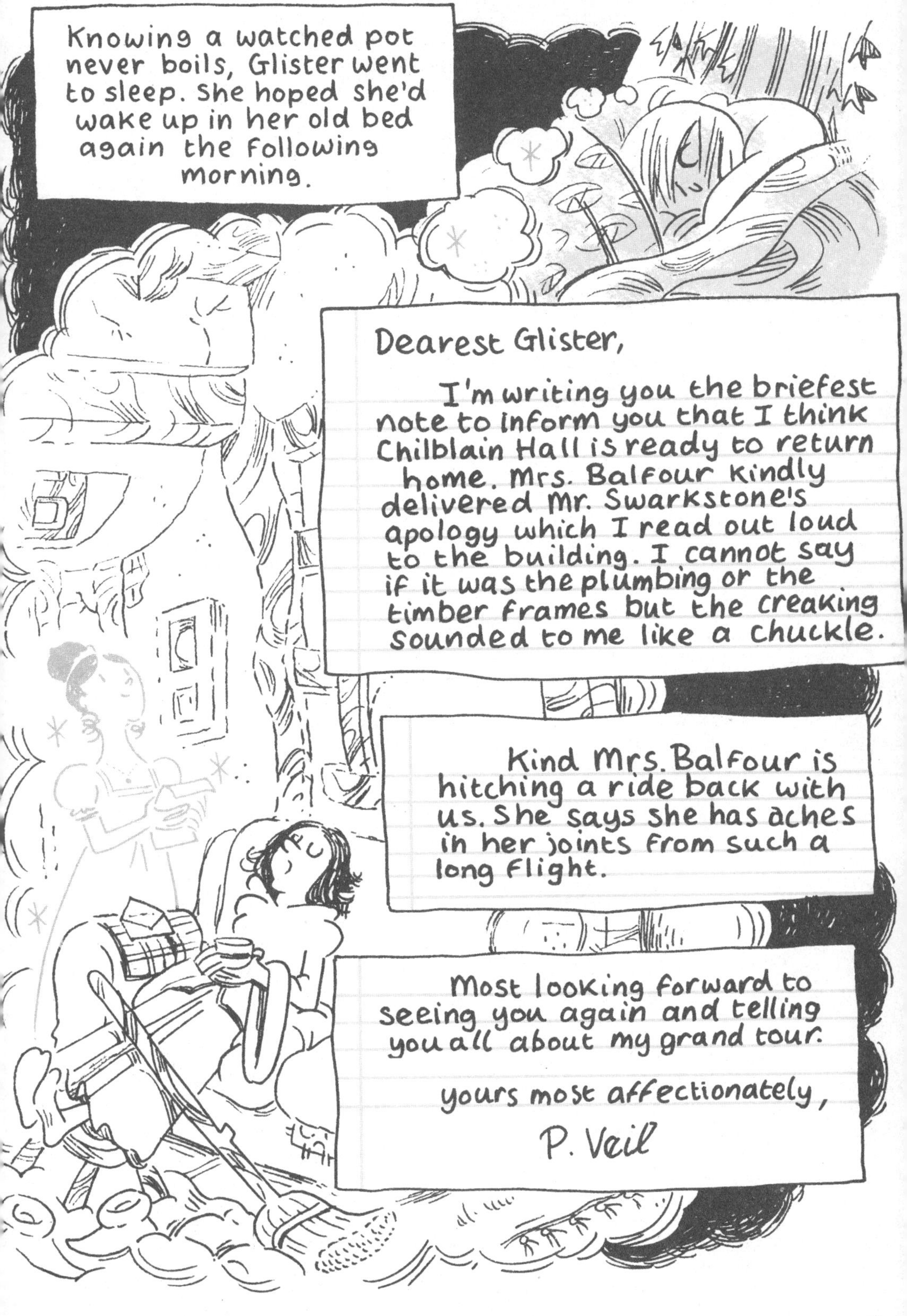
Knowing a watched pot never boils, Glister went to sleep. She hoped she'd wake up in her old bed again the following morning.
Dearest Glister,
I'm writing you the briefest note to inform you that I think Chilblain Hall is ready to return home. Mrs. Balfour kindly delivered Mr. Swarkstone's apology which I read out loud to the building. I cannot say if it was the plumbing or the timber frames but the creaking sounded to me like a chuckle.
Kind Mrs. Balfour is hitching a ride back with us. She says she has aches in her joints from such a long flight.
Most looking forward to seeing you again and telling you all about my grand tour.
yours most affectionately,
P. Veil

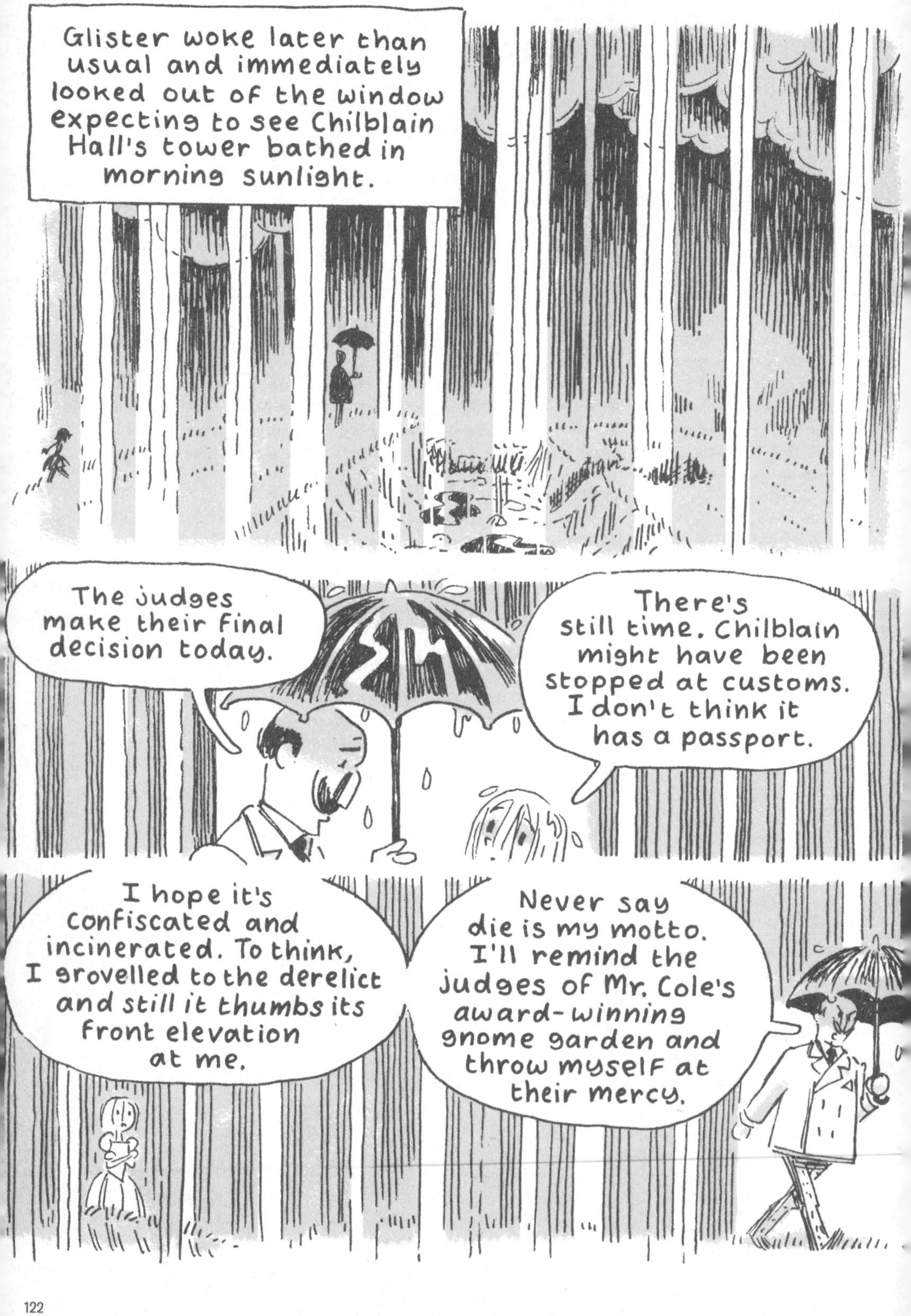
Glister woke later than usual and immediately looked out of the window expecting to see Chilblain Hall's tower bathed in morning sunlight.
The judges make their final decision today.
There's still time. Chilblain might have been stopped at customs. I don't think it has a passport.
I hope it's confiscated and incinerated. To think, I grovelled to the derelict and still it thumbs its front elevation at me.
Never say die is my motto. I'll remind the judges of Mr. Cole's award-winning gnome garden and throw myself at their mercy.

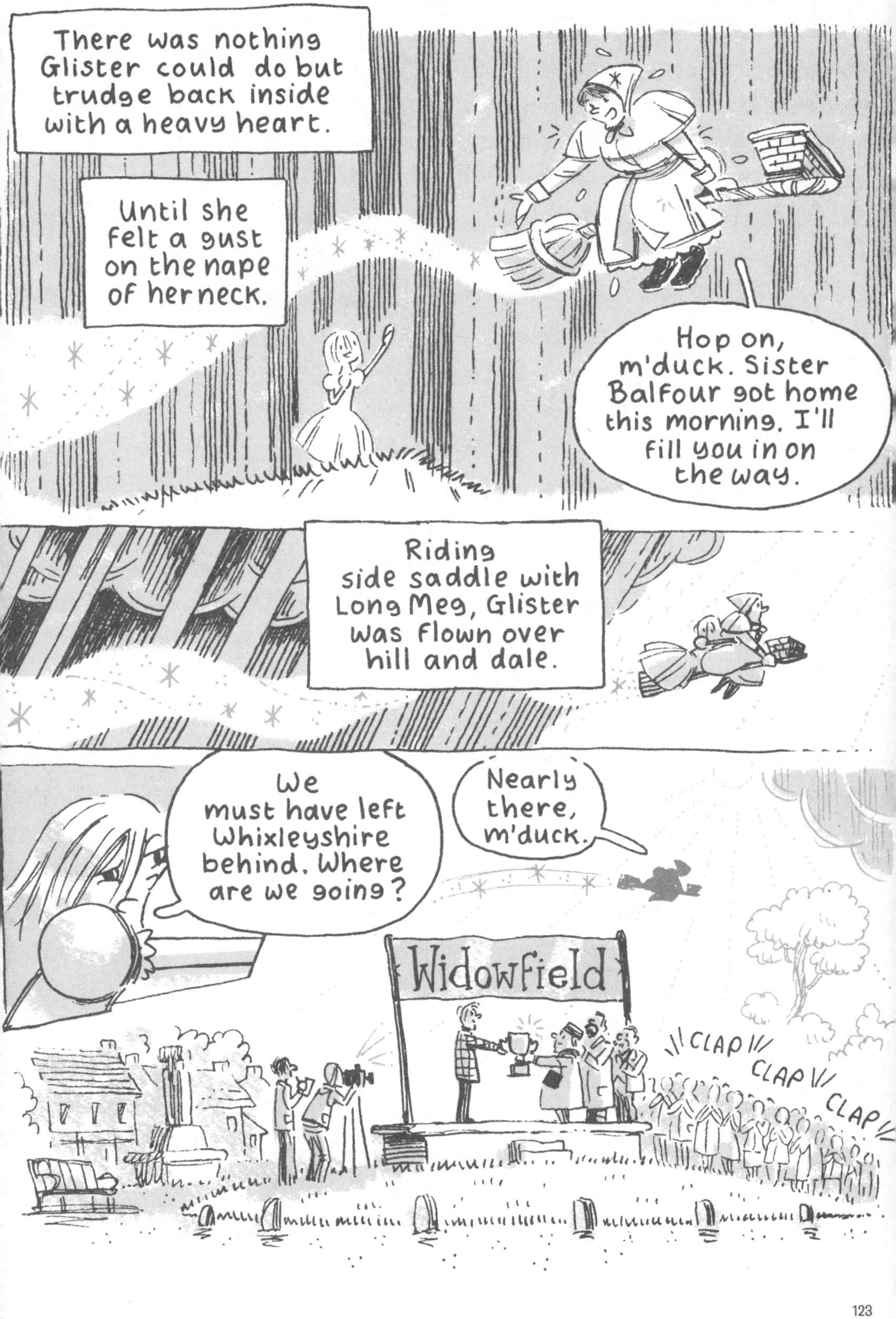
There was nothing Glister could do but trudge back inside with a heavy heart.
Until she felt a gust on the nape of her neck.
Hop on, m'duck. Sister Balfour got home this morning. I'll fill you in on the way.
Riding side saddle with Long Meg, Glister was flown over hill and dale.
We must have left Whixleyshire behind. Where are we going?
Nearly there, m'duck.
Widowfield
CLAP
CLAP
CLAP

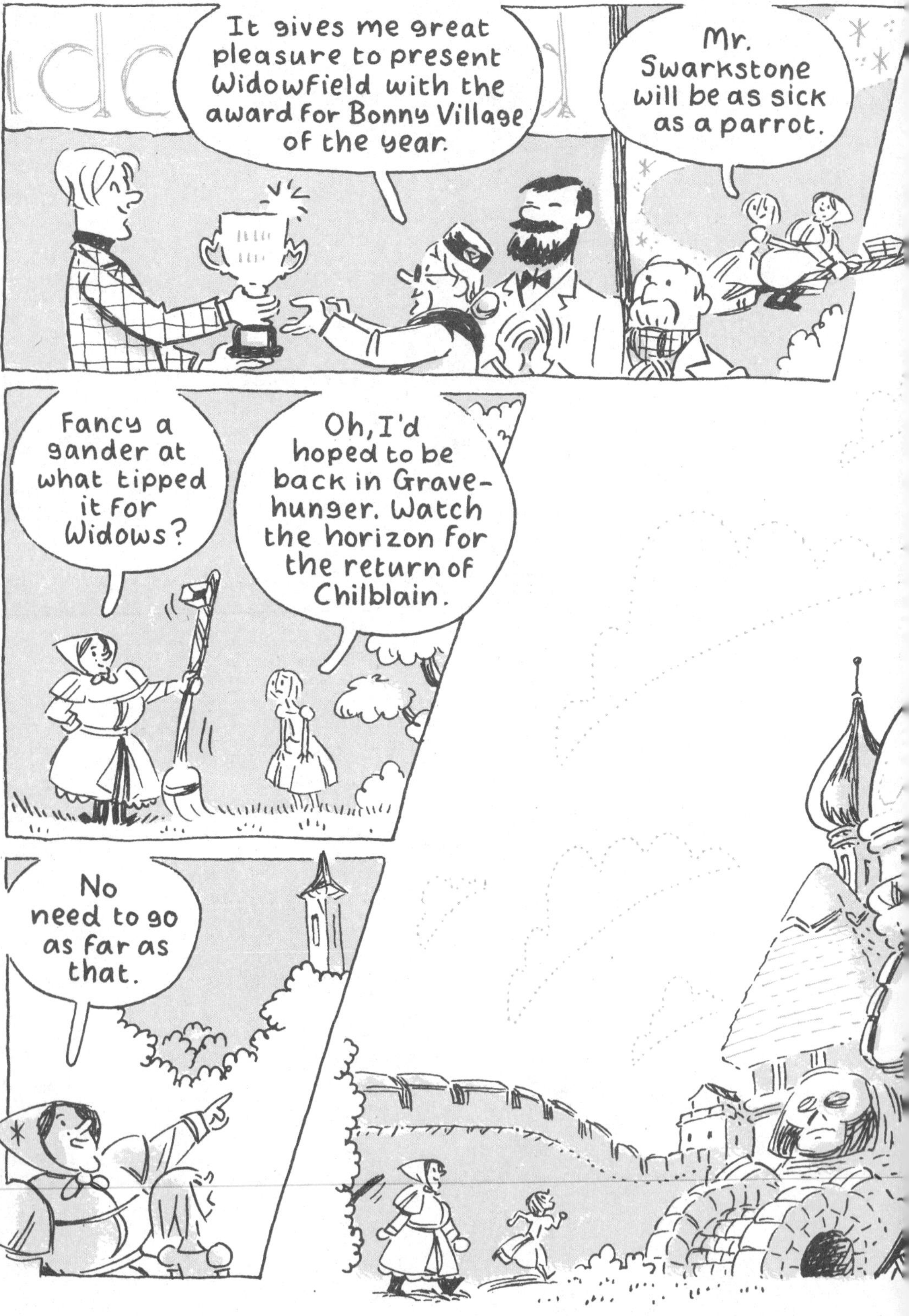
It gives me great pleasure to present Widowfield with the award for Bonny Village of the year.
Mr. Swarkstone will be as sick as a parrot.
Fancy a gander at what tipped it for Widows?
Oh, I'd hoped to be back in Grave-hunger. Watch the horizon for the return of Chilblain.
No need to go as far as that.

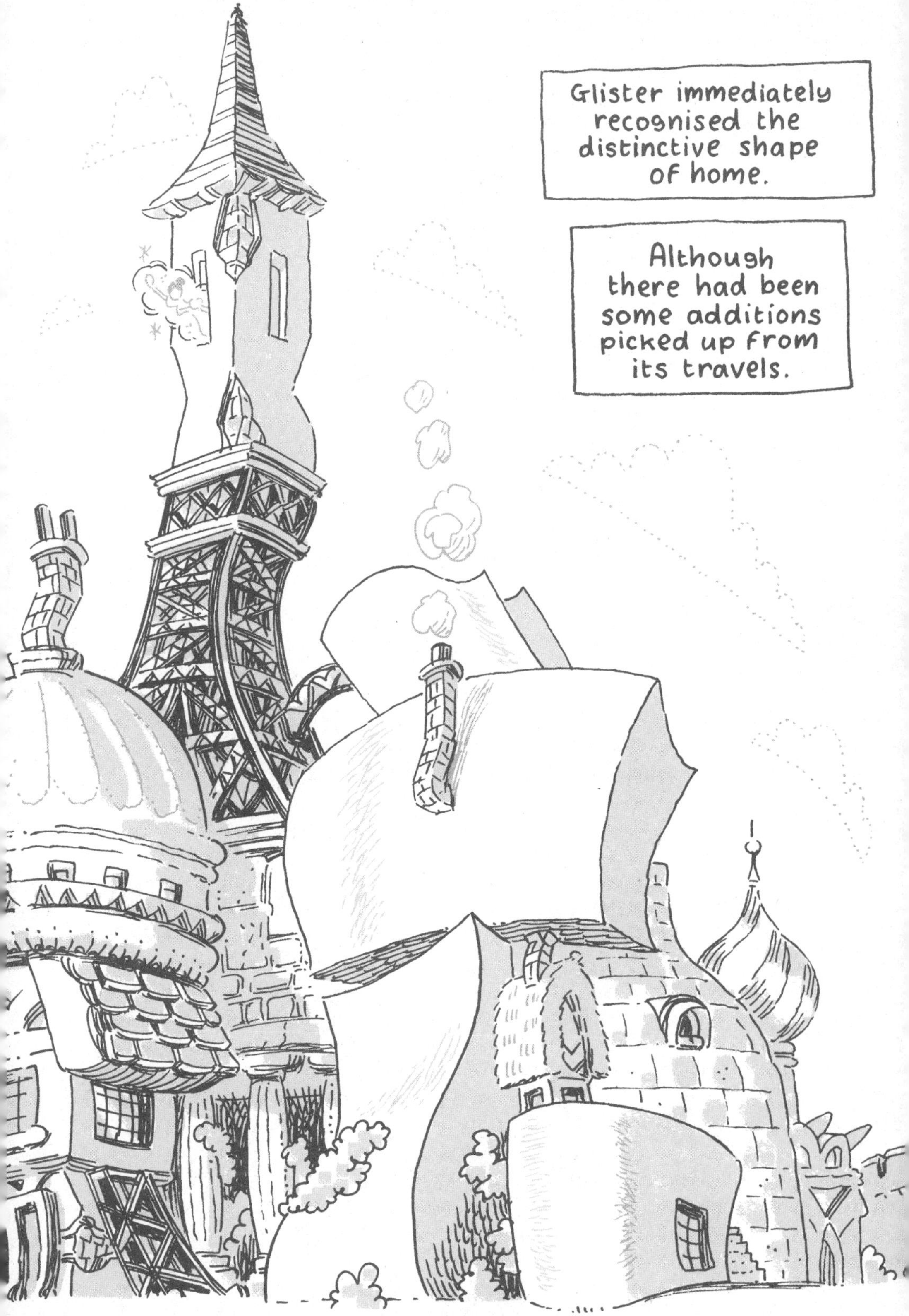
Glister immediately recognised the distinctive shape of home.
Although there had been some additions picked up from its travels.

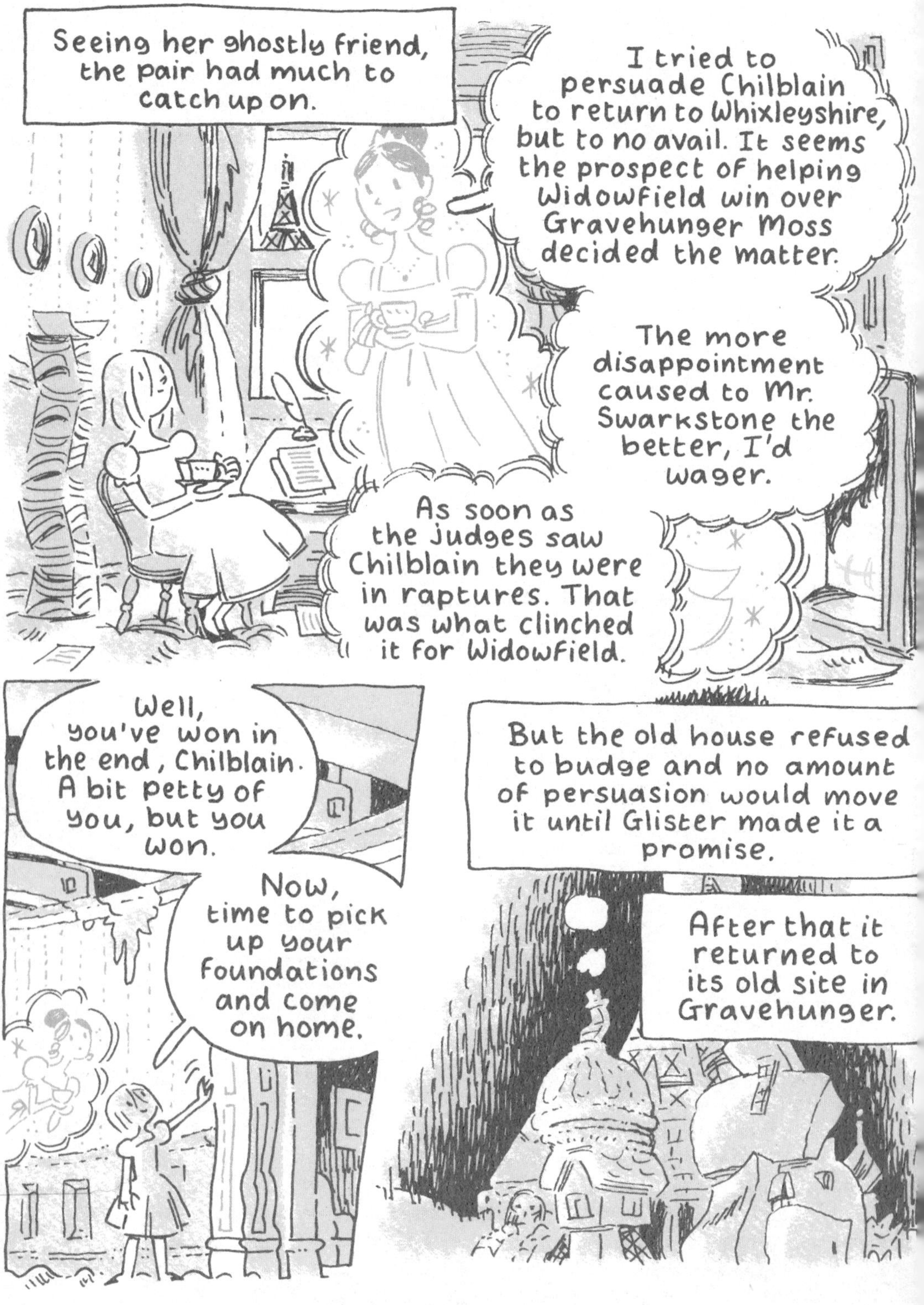
Seeing her ghostly friend, the pair had much to catch up on.
I tried to persuade Chilblain to return to Whixleyshire, but to no avail. It seems the prospect of helping Widowfield win over Gravehunger Moss decided the matter.
The more disappointment caused to Mr. Swarkstone the better, I'd wager.
As soon as the judges saw Chilblain they were in raptures. That was what clinched it for Widowfield.
Well, you've won in the end, Chilblain. A bit petty of you, but you won.
Now, time to pick up your foundations and come on home.
But the old house refused to budge and no amount of persuasion would move it until Glister made it a promise.
After that it returned to its old site in Gravehunger.

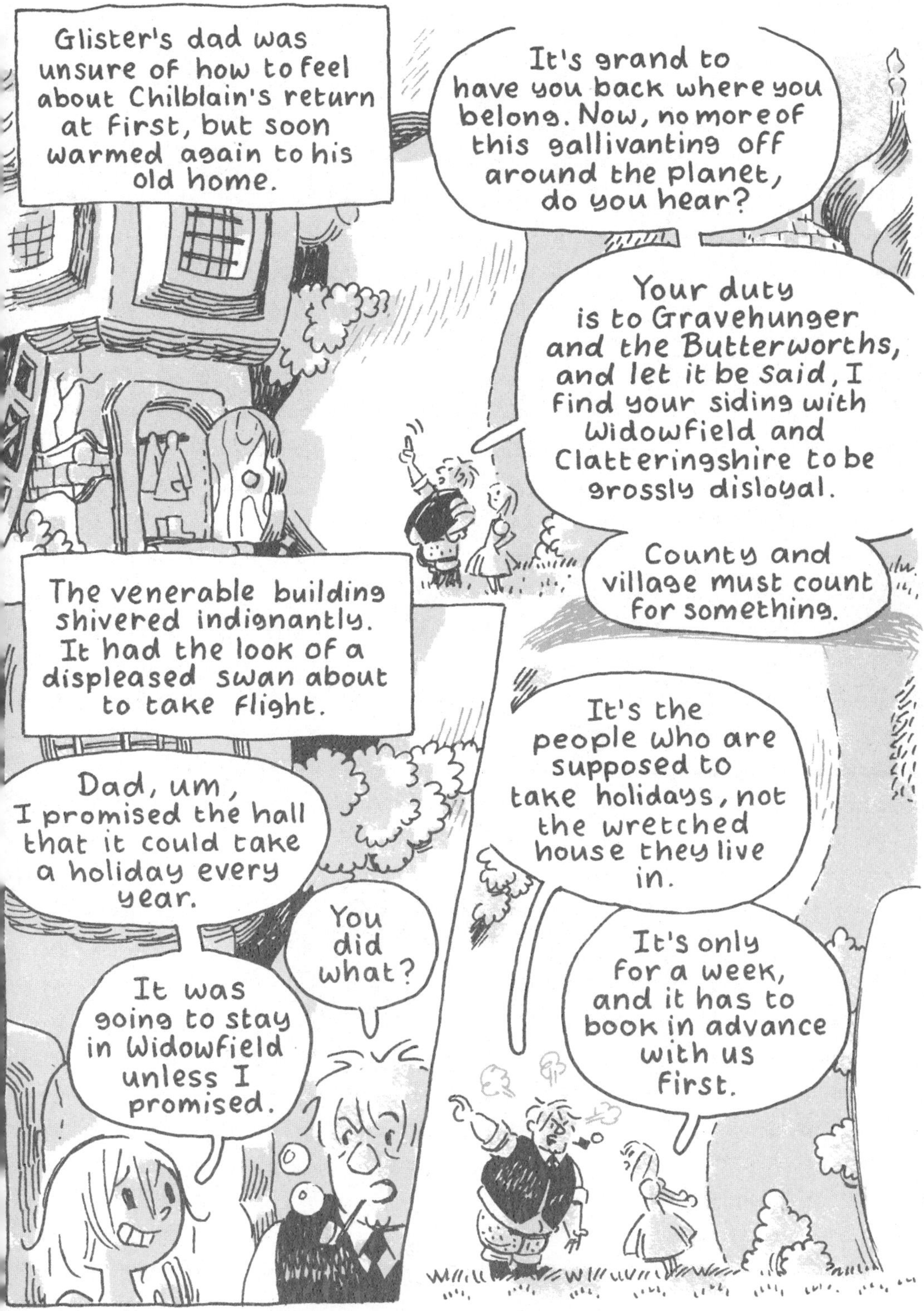
Glister's dad was unsure of how to feel about Chilblain's return at first, but soon warmed again to his old home.
It's grand to have you back where you belong. Now, no more of this gallivanting off around the planet, do you hear?
Your duty is to Gravehunger and the Butterworths, and let it be said, I find your siding with Widowfield and Clatteringshire to be grossly disloyal.
County and village must count for something.
The venerable building shivered indignantly. It had the look of a displeased swan about to take flight.
Dad, um, I promised the hall that it could take a holiday every year.
You did what?
It was going to stay in Widowfield unless I promised.
It's the people who are supposed to take holidays, not the wretched house they live in.
It's only for a week, and it has to book in advance with us first.

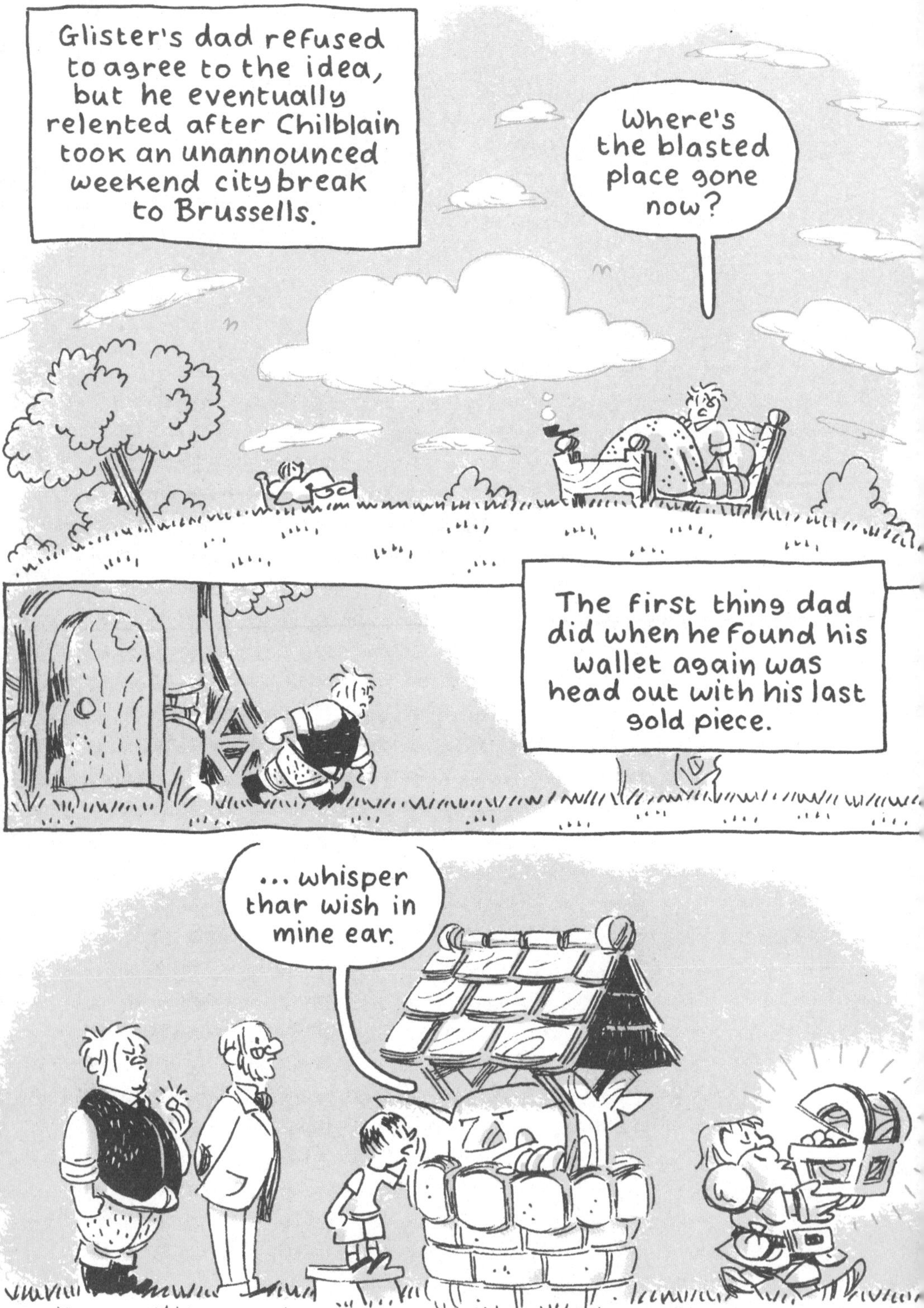
Glister's dad refused to agree to the idea, but he eventually relented after Chilblain took an unannounced weekend city break to Brussells.
Where's the blasted place gone now?
The first thing dad did when he found his wallet again was head out with his last gold piece.
... whisper thar wish in mine ear.

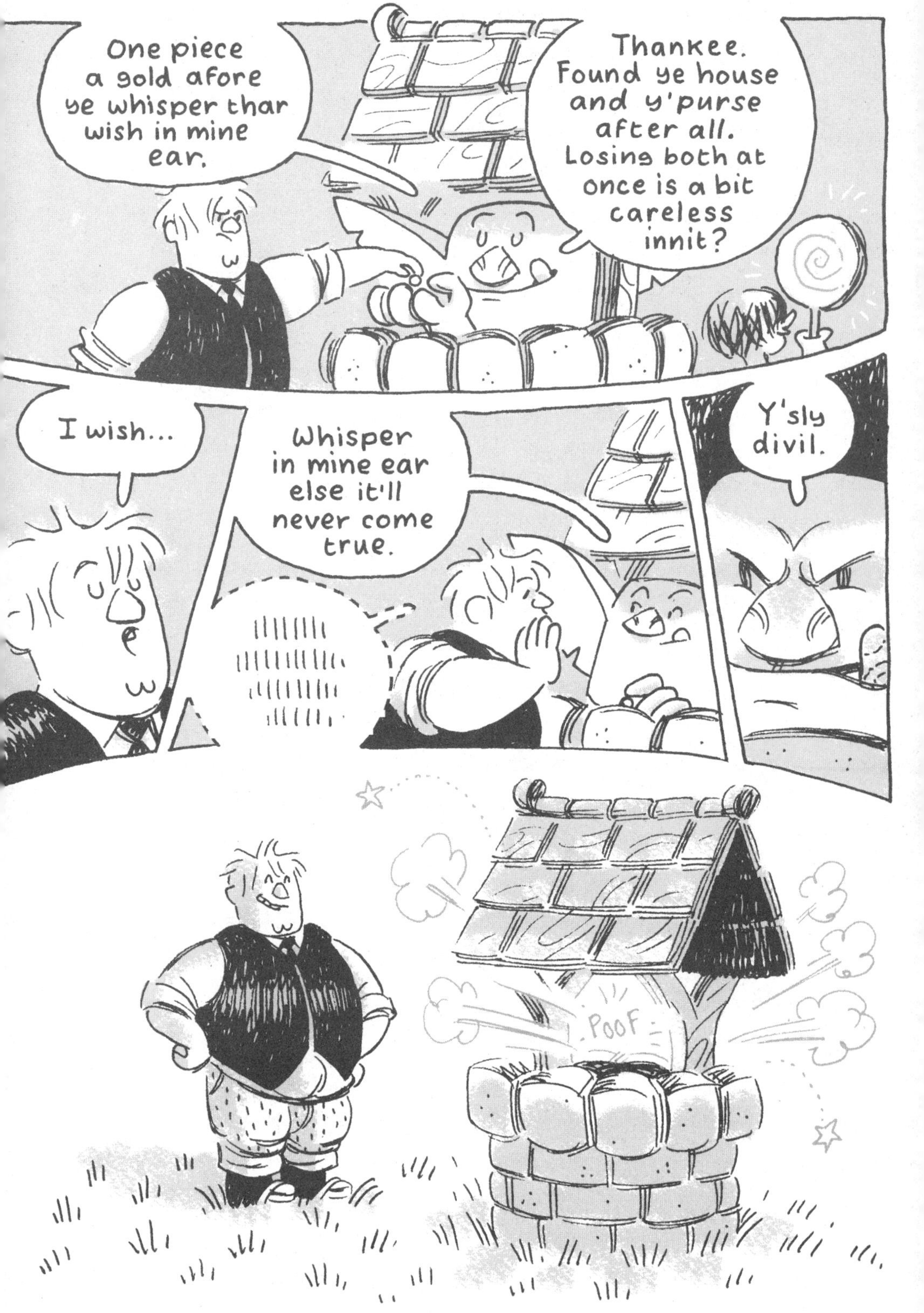
One piece a gold afore ye whisper thar wish in mine ear.
Thankee. Found ye house and y'purse after all. Losing both at once is a bit careless innit?
I wish...
Whisper in mine ear else it'll never come true.
Y'sly divil.
POOF

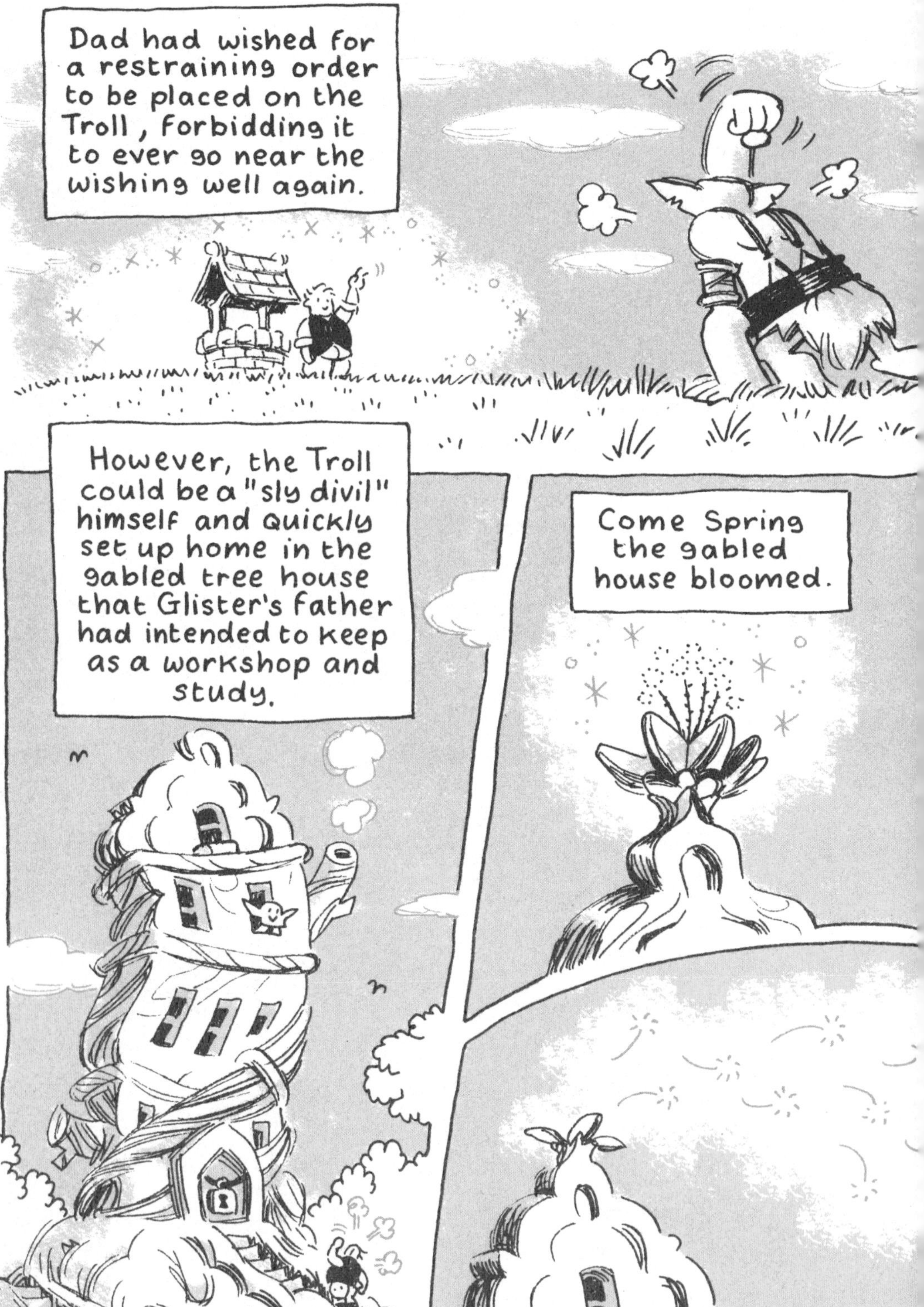
Dad had wished for a restraining order to be placed on the Troll, forbidding it to ever go near the wishing well again.
However, the Troll could be a "sly divil" himself and quickly set up home in the gabled tree house that Glister's father had intended to keep as a workshop and study.
Come Spring the gabled house bloomed.

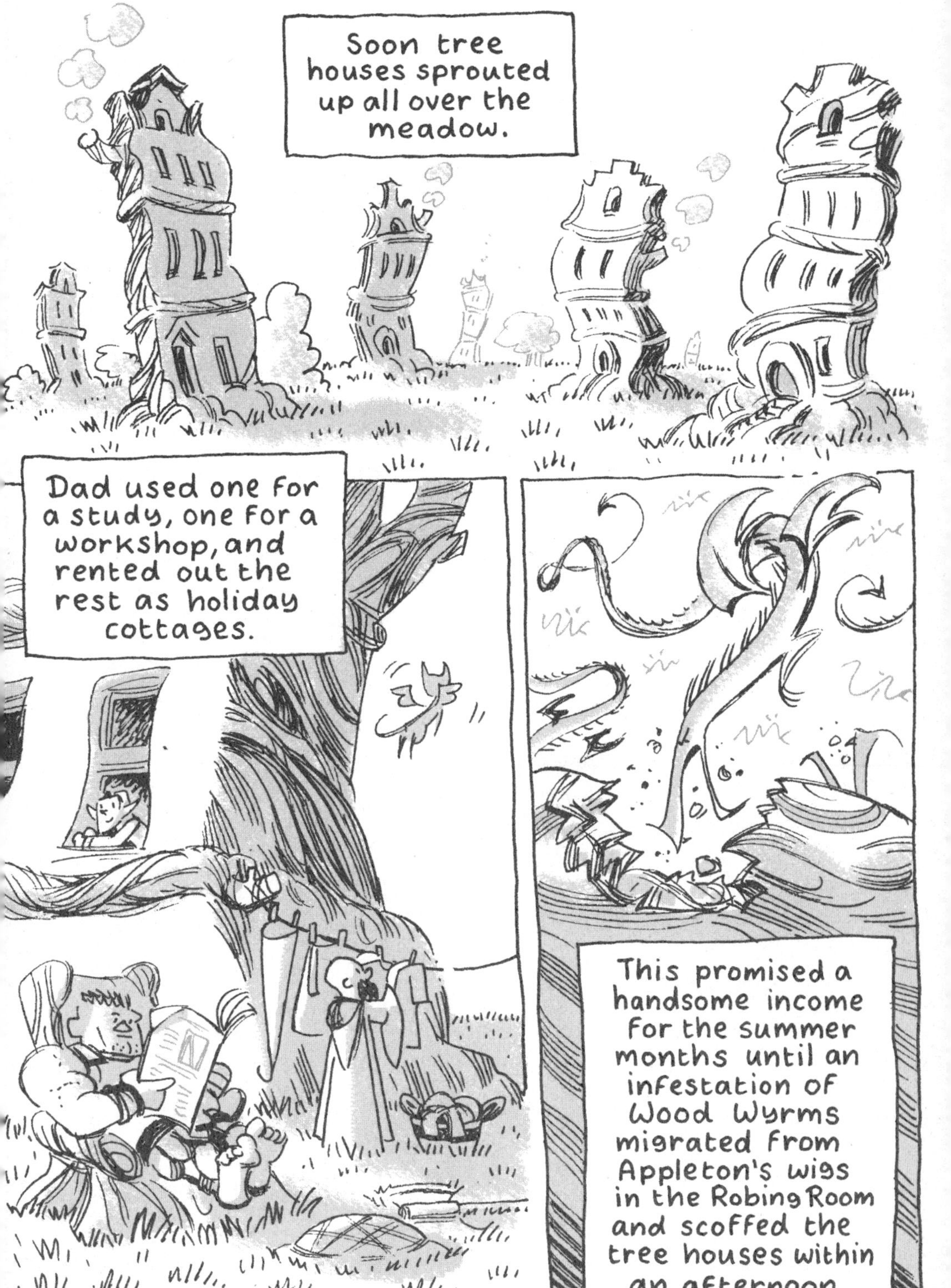
Soon tree houses sprouted up all over the meadow.
Dad used one for a study, one for a workshop, and rented out the rest as holiday cottages.
This promised a handsome income for the summer months until an infestation of Wood Wyrms migrated from Appleton's wigs in the Robing Room and scoffed the tree houses within an afternoon.

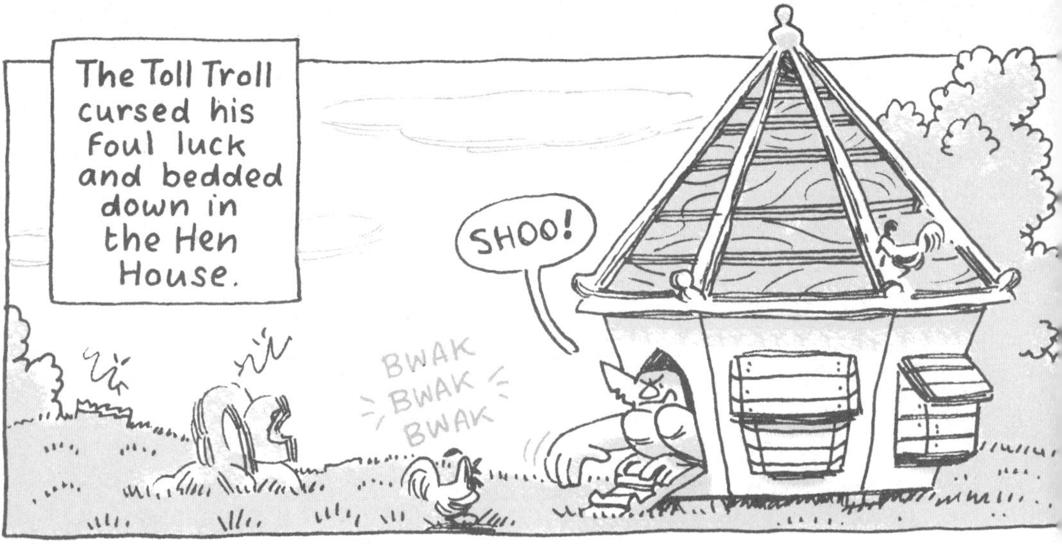
The Toll Troll cursed his foul luck and bedded down in the Hen House.
SHOO!
BWAK BWAK BWAK

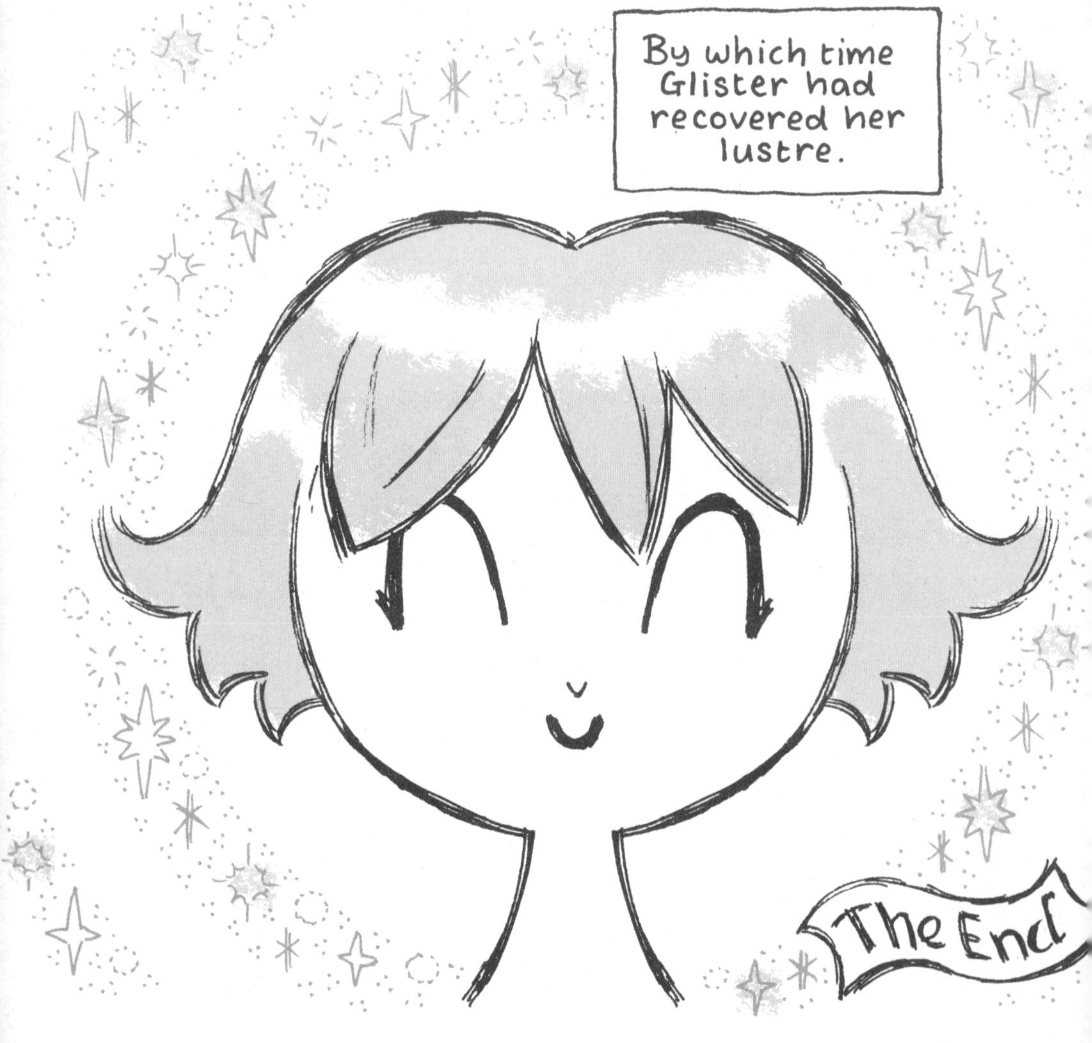
By which time Glister had recovered her lustre.
The End

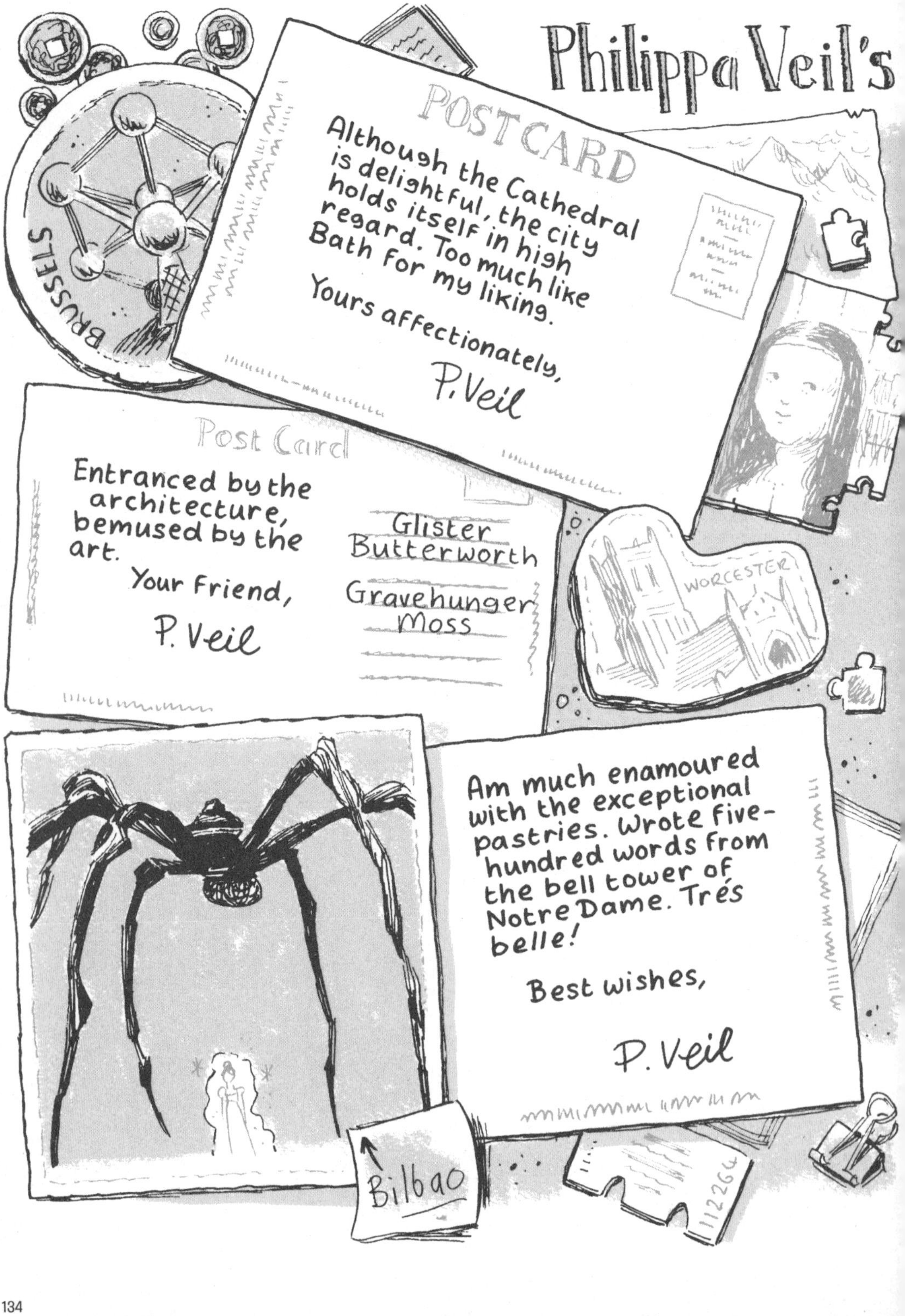
Philippa Veil's
BRUSSELS
POSTCARD
Although the Cathedral is delightful, the city holds itself in high regard. Too much like Bath for my liking.
Yours affectionately,
P. Veil
Post Card
Entranced by the architecture, bemused by the art.
Your friend,
P. Veil
Glister Butterworth
Gravehunger Moss
WORCESTER
Am much enamoured with the exceptional pastries. Wrote five-hundred words from the bell tower of Notre Dame. Trés belle!
Best wishes,
P. Veil
Bilbao
112264

Postcards

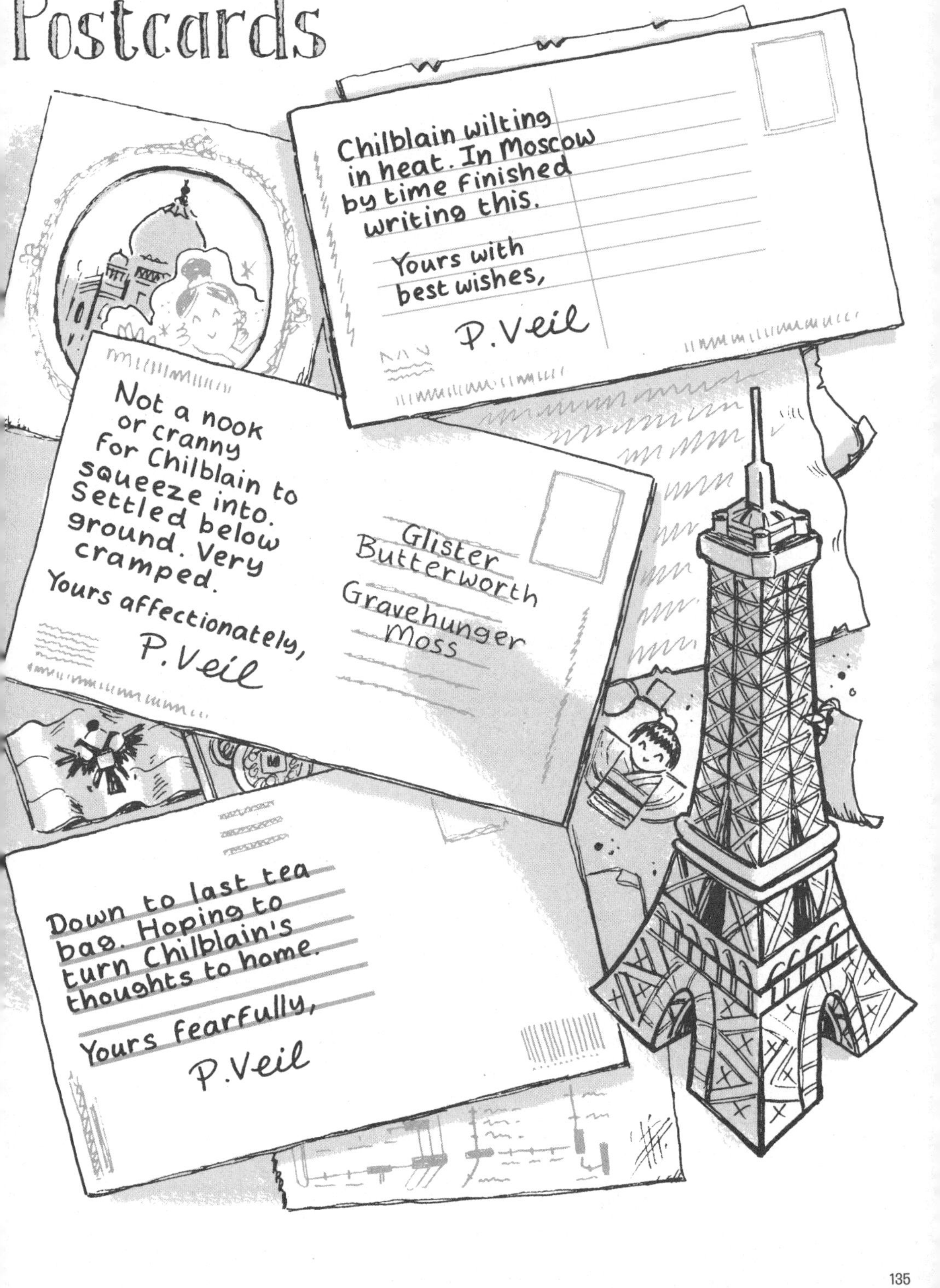
Chilblain wilting in heat. In Moscow by time finished writing this.
Yours with best wishes,
P. Veil
Not a nook or cranny for Chilblain to squeeze into. Settled below ground. Very cramped.
Yours affectionately,
P. Veil
Glister Butterworth
Gravehunger Moss
Down to last tea bag. Hoping to turn Chilblain's thoughts to home.
Yours fearfully,
P. Veil

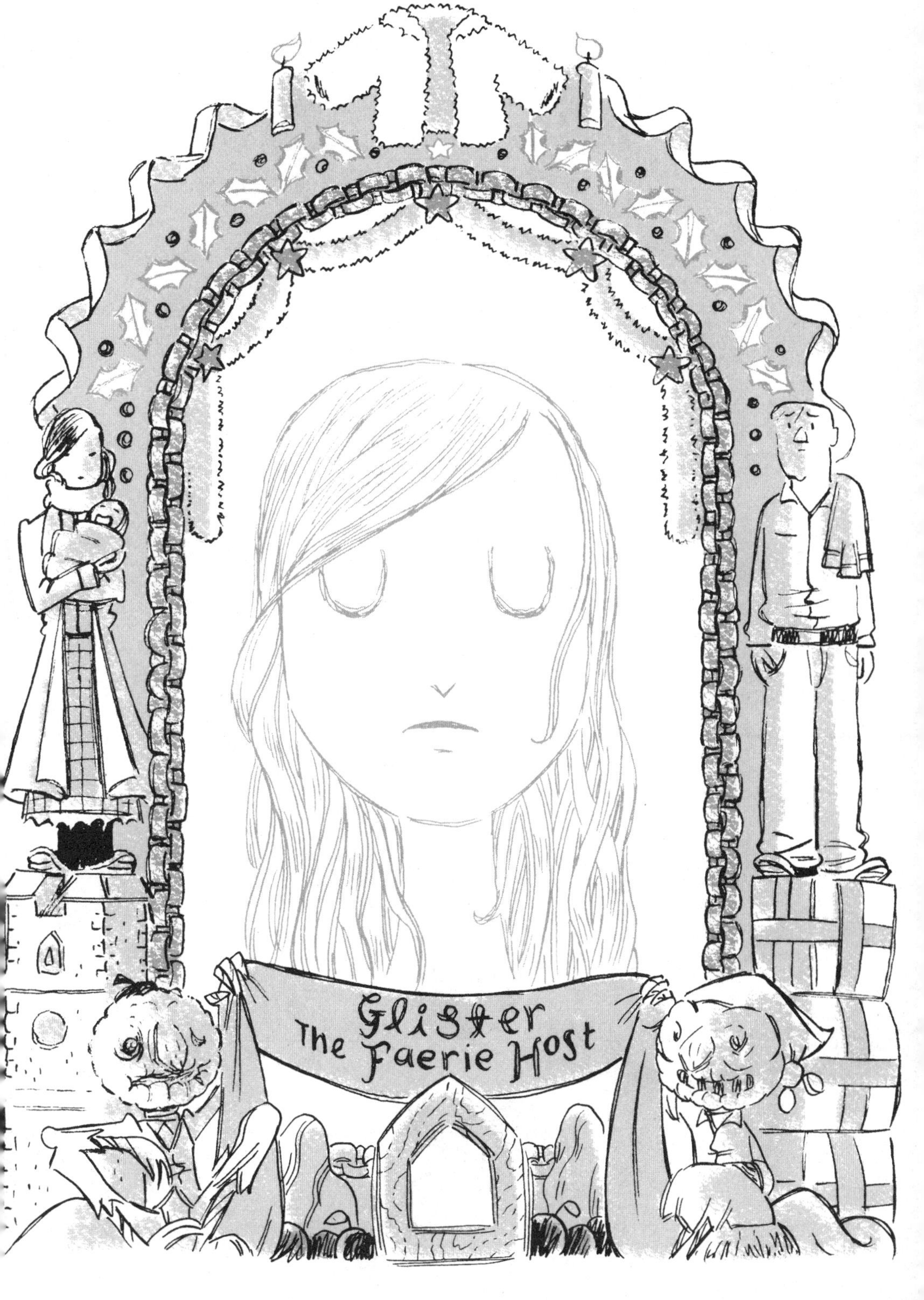
Glister
The Faerie Host

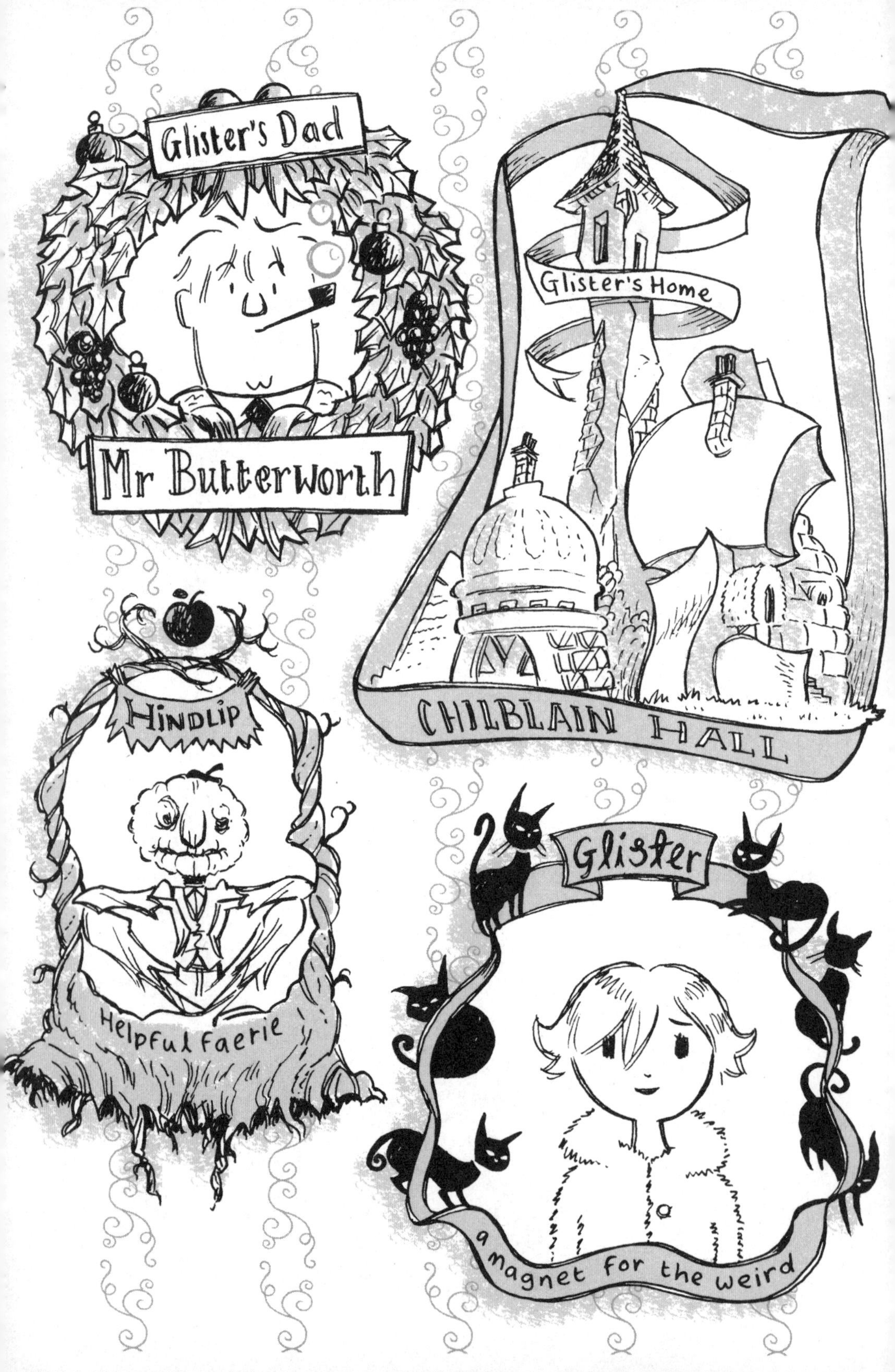
Glister's Dad
Mr Butterworth
Glister's Home
CHILBLAIN HALL
HINDLIP
Helpful Faerie
Glister
a magnet for the weird

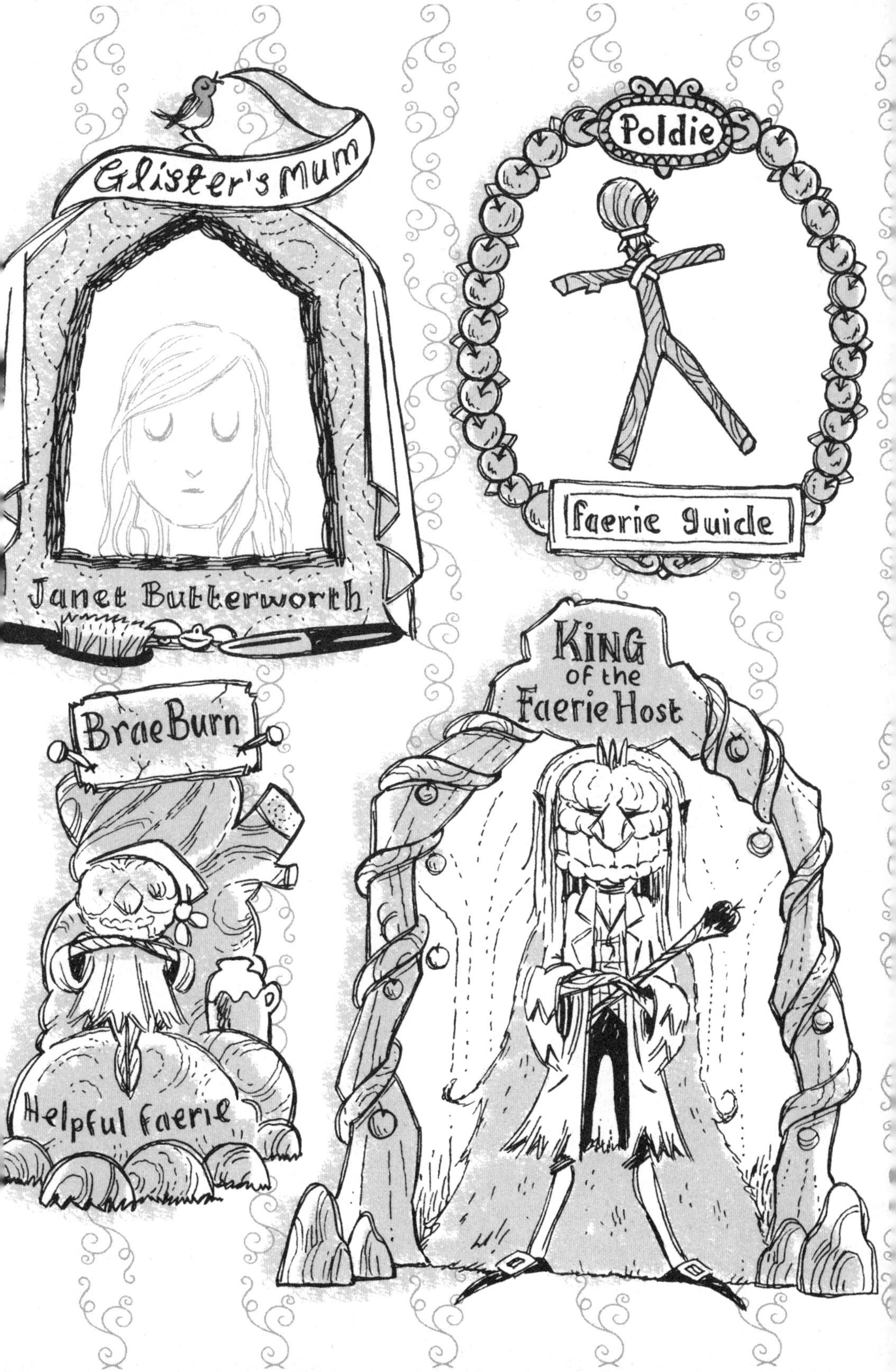
Glister's Mum
Janet Butterworth
Poldie
faerie guide
BraeBurn
Helpful faerie
KING
of the
Faerie Host

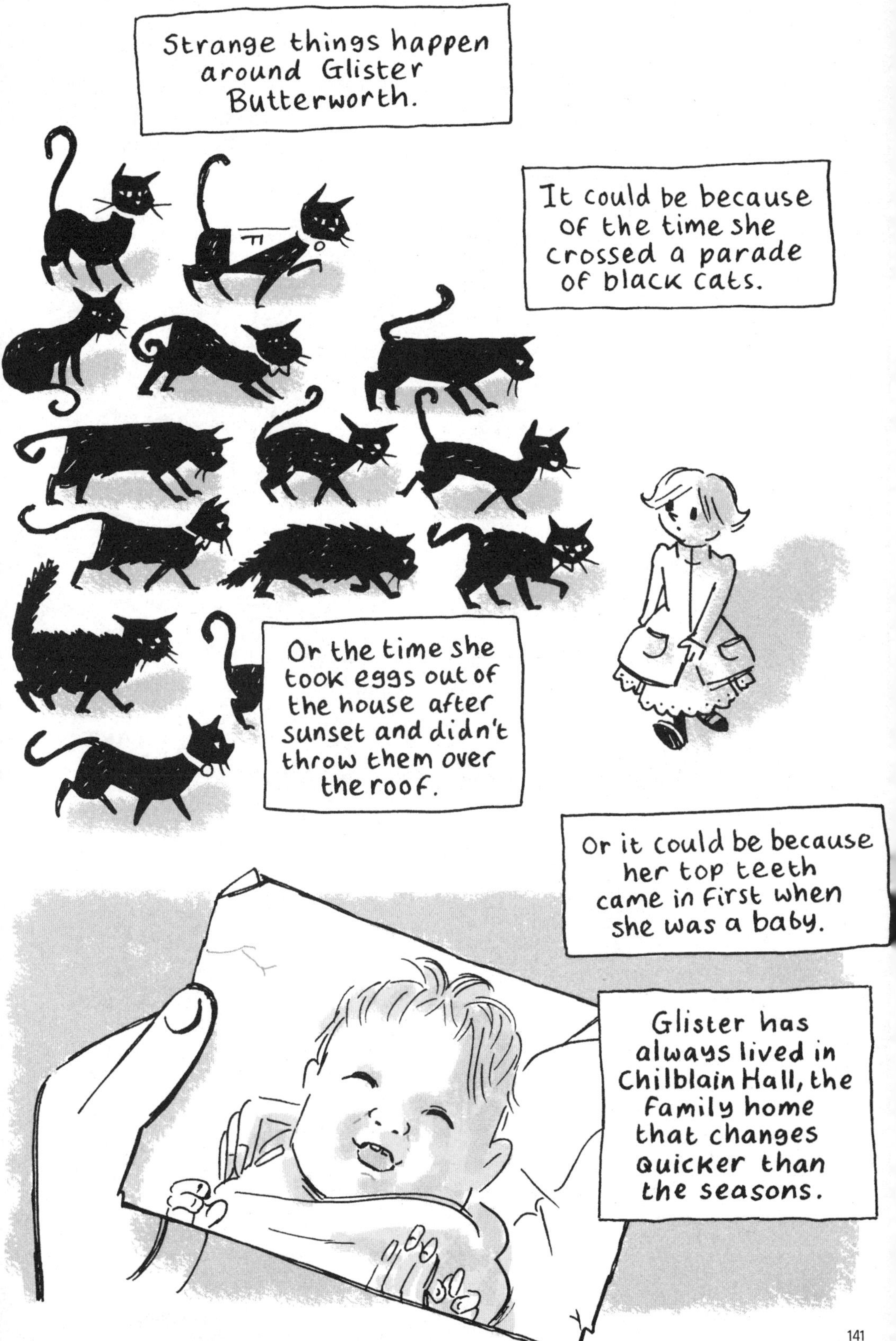
Strange things happen around Glister Butterworth.
It could be because of the time she crossed a parade of black cats.
Or the time she took eggs out of the house after sunset and didn't throw them over the roof.
Or it could be because her top teeth came in first when she was a baby.
Glister has always lived in Chilblain Hall, the family home that changes quicker than the seasons.

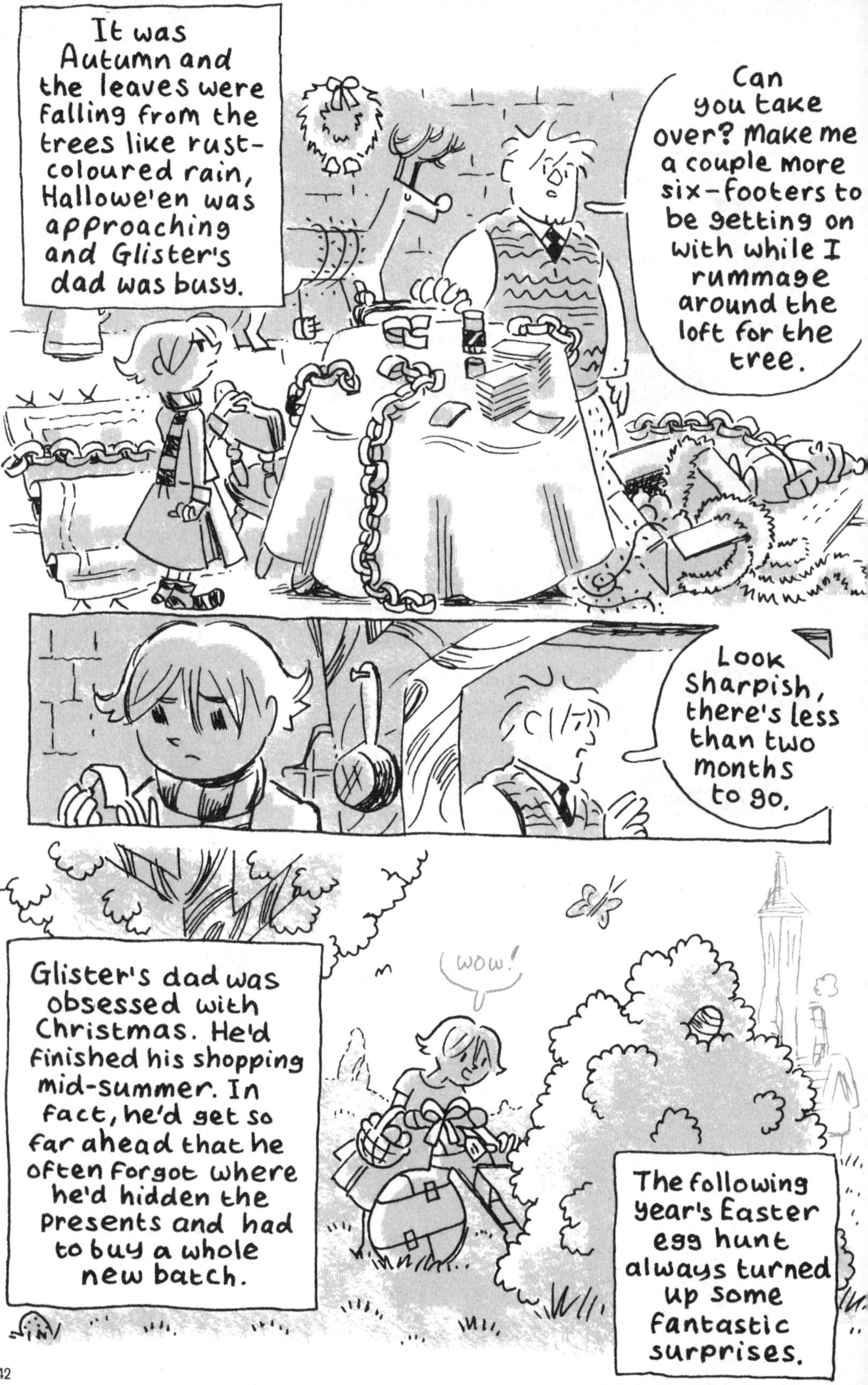
It was Autumn and the leaves were falling from the trees like rust-coloured rain, Hallowe'en was approaching and Glister's dad was busy.
Can you take over? Make me a couple more six-footers to be getting on with while I rummage around the loft for the tree.
Look sharpish, there's less than two months to go.
Glister's dad was obsessed with Christmas. He'd finished his shopping mid-summer. In fact, he'd get so far ahead that he often forgot where he'd hidden the presents and had to buy a whole new batch.
WOW!
The following year's Easter egg hunt always turned up some fantastic surprises.

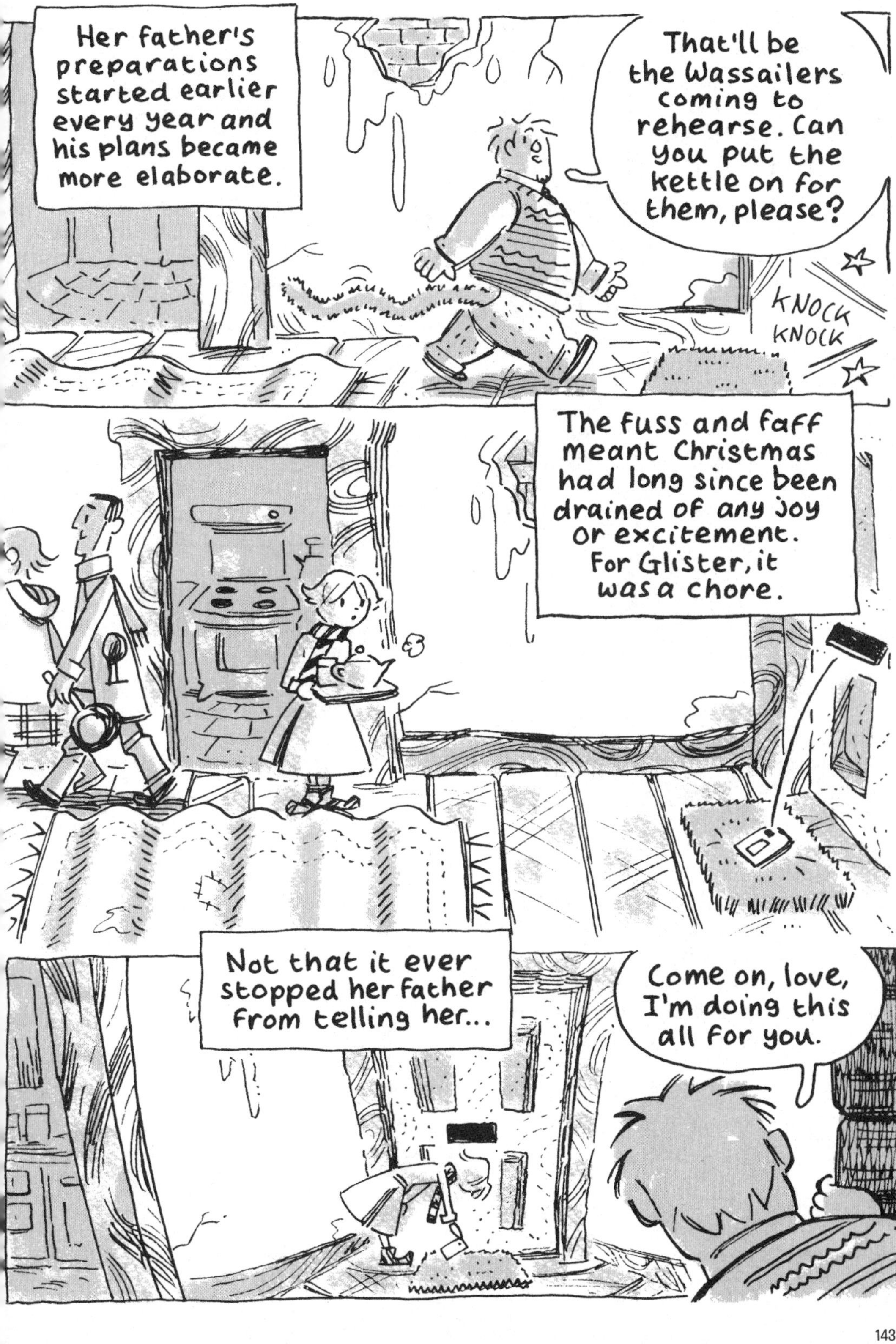
Her father's preparations started earlier every year and his plans became more elaborate.
That'll be the Wassailers coming to rehearse. Can you put the kettle on for them, please?
KNOCK KNOCK
The fuss and faff meant Christmas had long since been drained of any joy or excitement. For Glister, it was a chore.
Not that it ever stopped her father from telling her...
Come on, love, I'm doing this all for you.

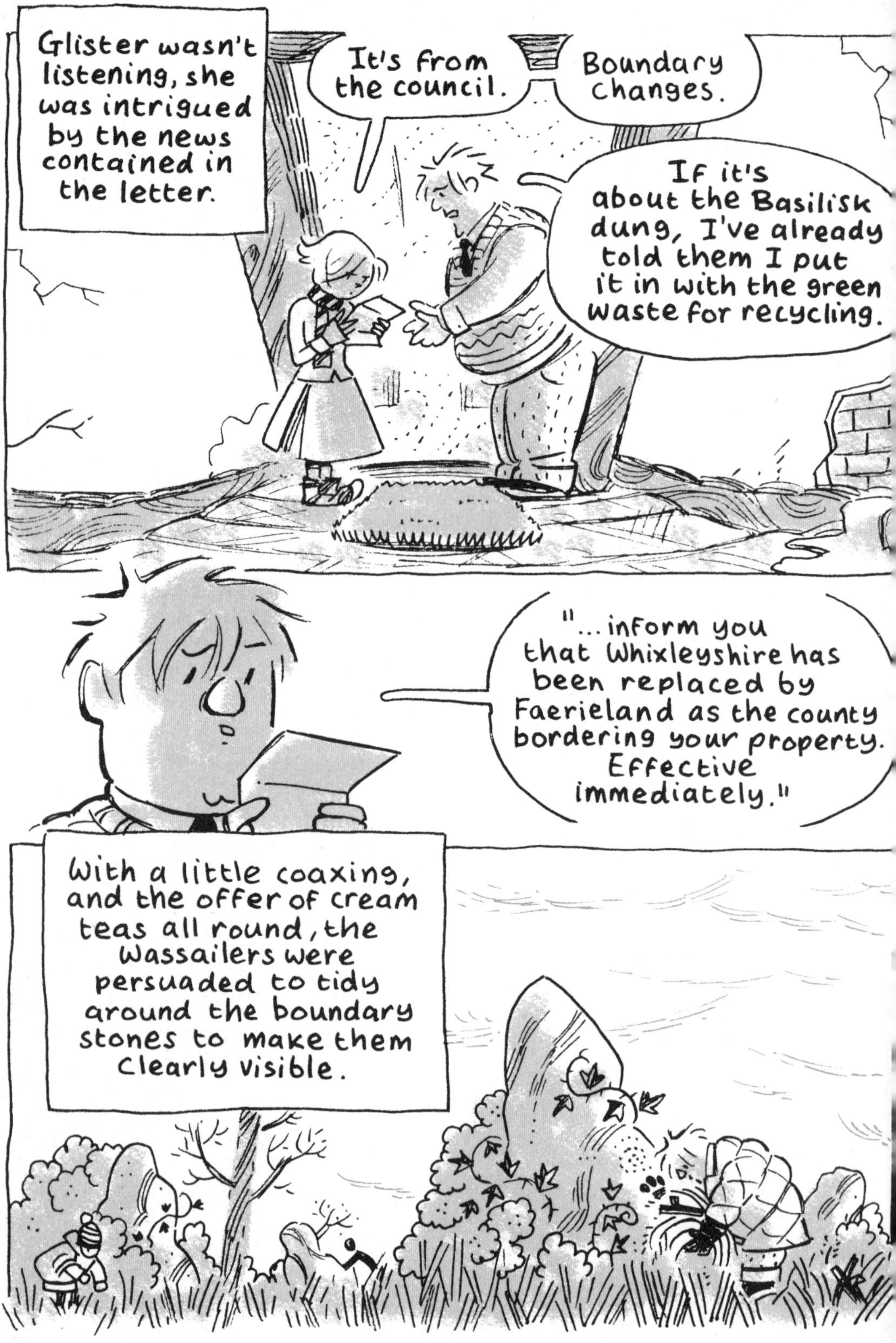
Glister wasn't listening, she was intrigued by the news contained in the letter.
It's from the council.
Boundary changes.
If it's about the Basilisk dung, I've already told them I put it in with the green waste for recycling.
"...inform you that Whixleyshire has been replaced by Faerieland as the county bordering your property. Effective immediately."
With a little coaxing, and the offer of cream teas all round, the Wassailers were persuaded to tidy around the boundary stones to make them clearly visible.

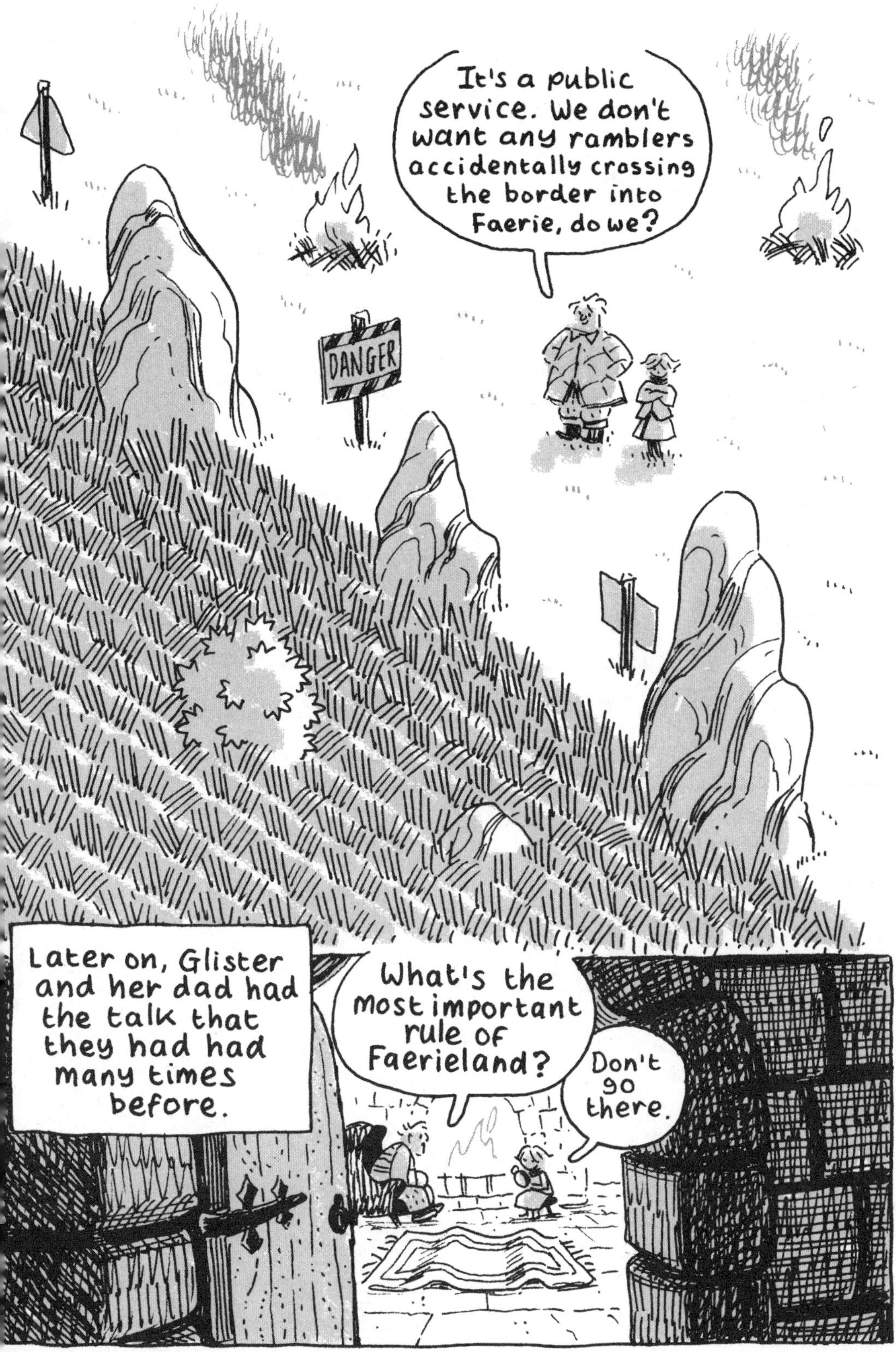
It's a public service. We don't want any ramblers accidentally crossing the border into Faerie, do we?
DANGER
Later on, Glister and her dad had the talk that they had had many times before.
What's the most important rule of Faerieland?
Don't go there.

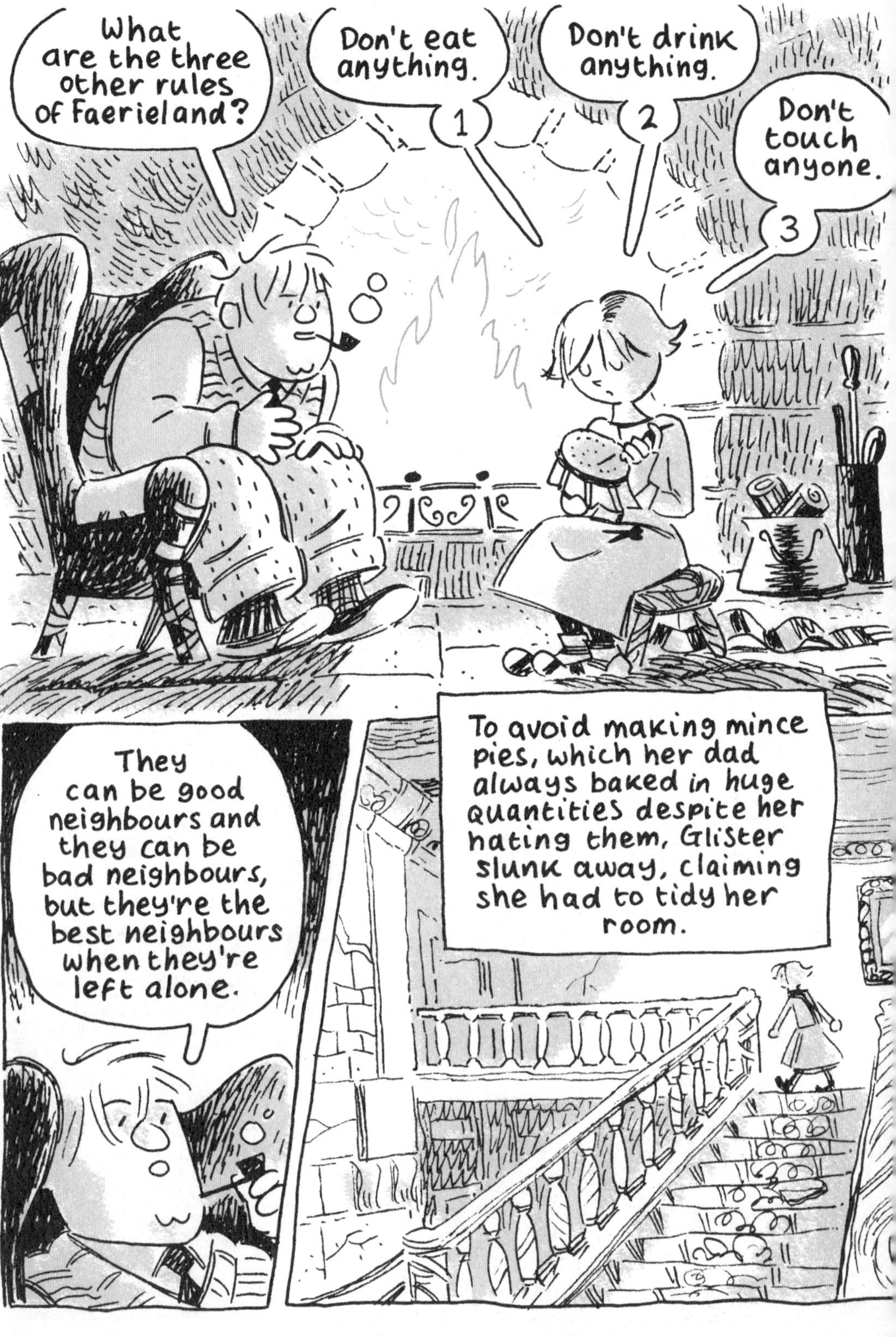
What are the three other rules of Faerieland?
Don't eat anything.
1
Don't drink anything.
2
Don't touch anyone.
3
They can be good neighbours and they can be bad neighbours, but they're the best neighbours when they're left alone.
To avoid making mince pies, which her dad always baked in huge quantities despite her hating them, Glister slunk away, claiming she had to tidy her room.

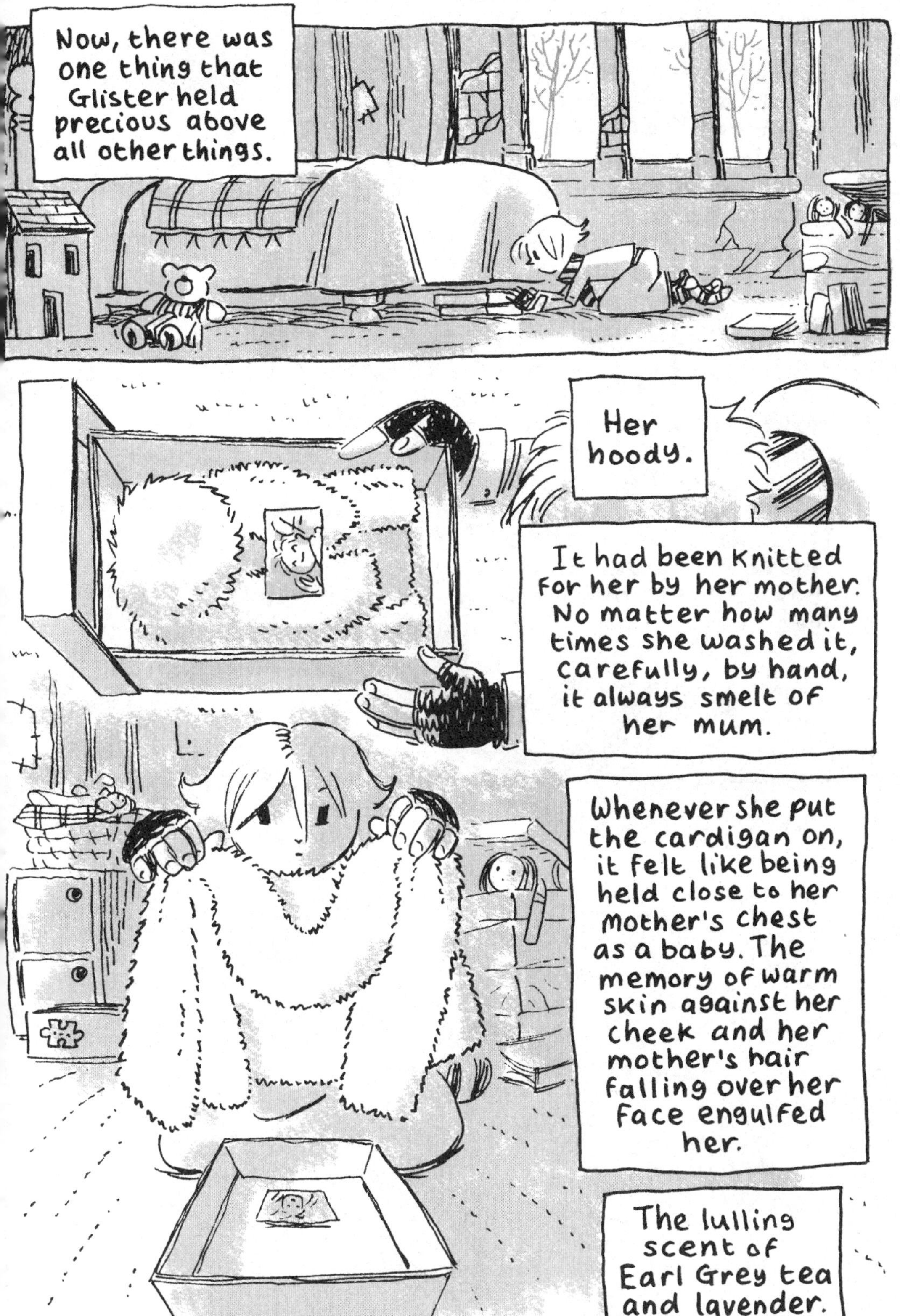
Now, there was one thing that Glister held precious above all other things.
Her hoody.
It had been knitted for her by her mother. No matter how many times she washed it, carefully, by hand, it always smelt of her mum.
Whenever she put the cardigan on, it felt like being held close to her mother's chest as a baby. The memory of warm skin against her cheek and her mother's hair falling over her face engulfed her.
The lulling scent of Earl Grey tea and lavender.

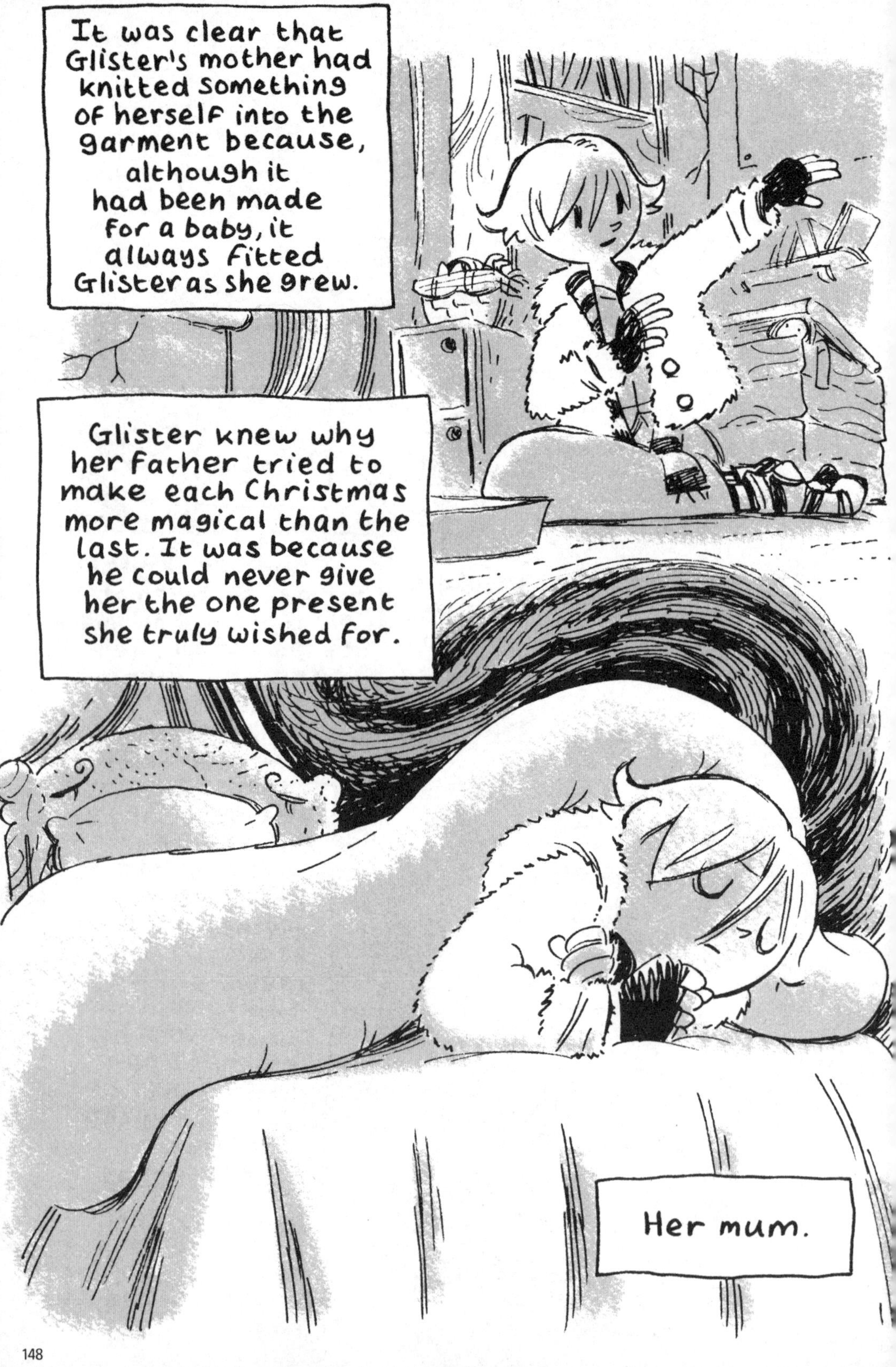
It was clear that Glister's mother had knitted something of herself into the garment because, although it had been made for a baby, it always fitted Glister as she grew.
Glister knew why her father tried to make each Christmas more magical than the last. It was because he could never give her the one present she truly wished for.
Her mum.

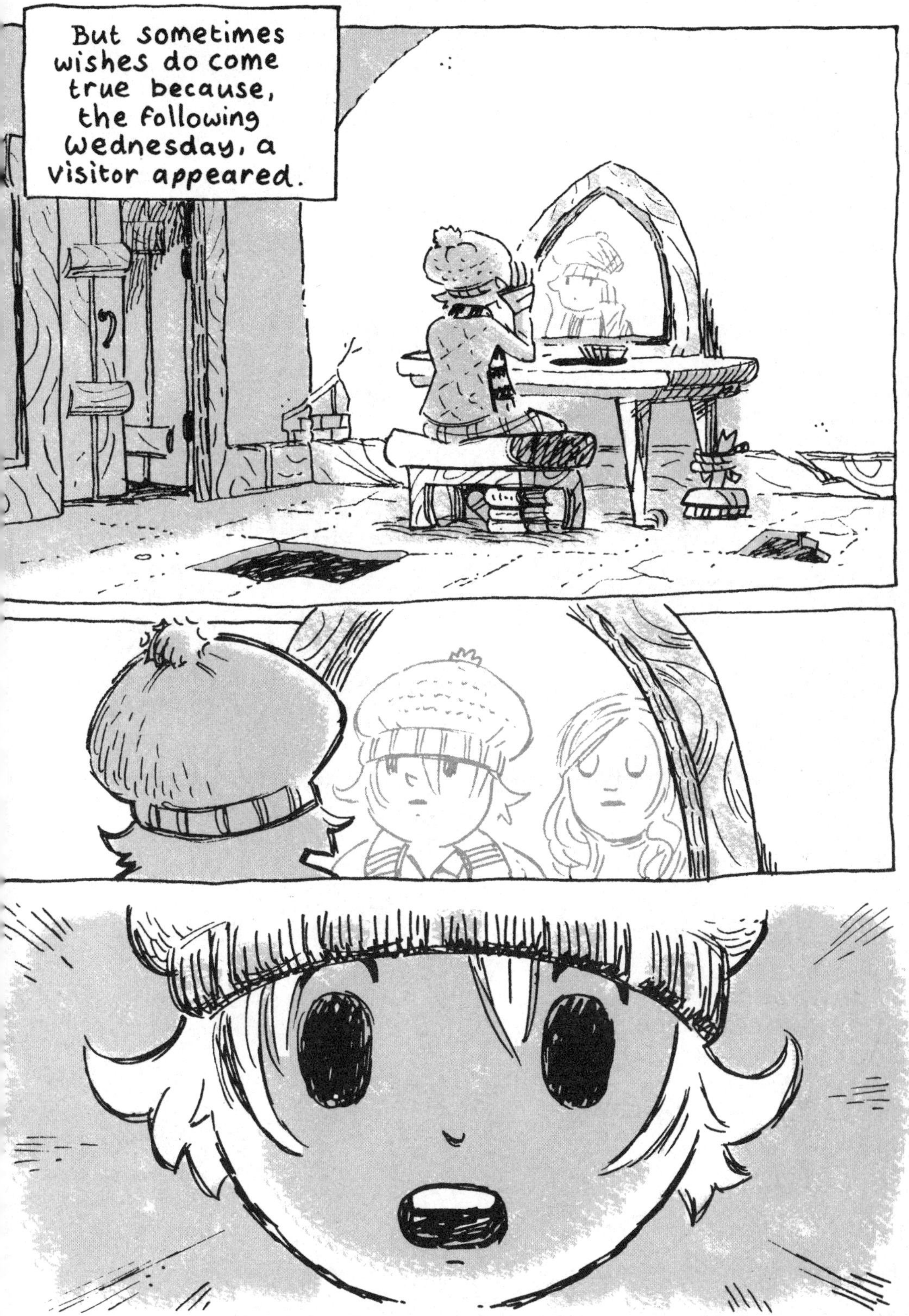
But sometimes wishes do come true because, the following Wednesday, a visitor appeared.

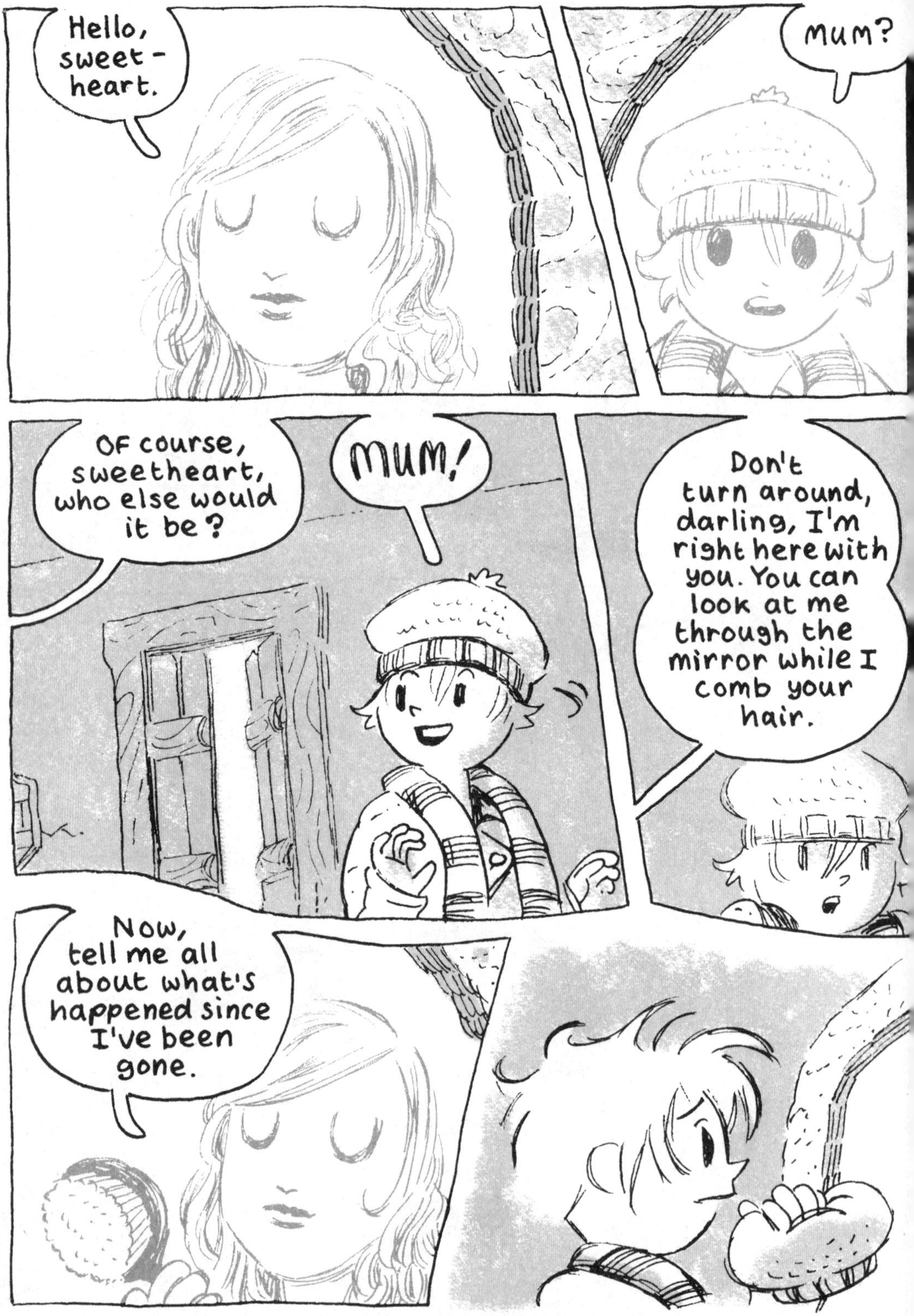

Hello, sweet-heart.
MUM?
Of course, sweetheart, who else would it be?
MUM!
Don't turn around, darling, I'm right here with you. You can look at me through the mirror while I comb your hair.
Now, tell me all about what's happened since I've been gone.

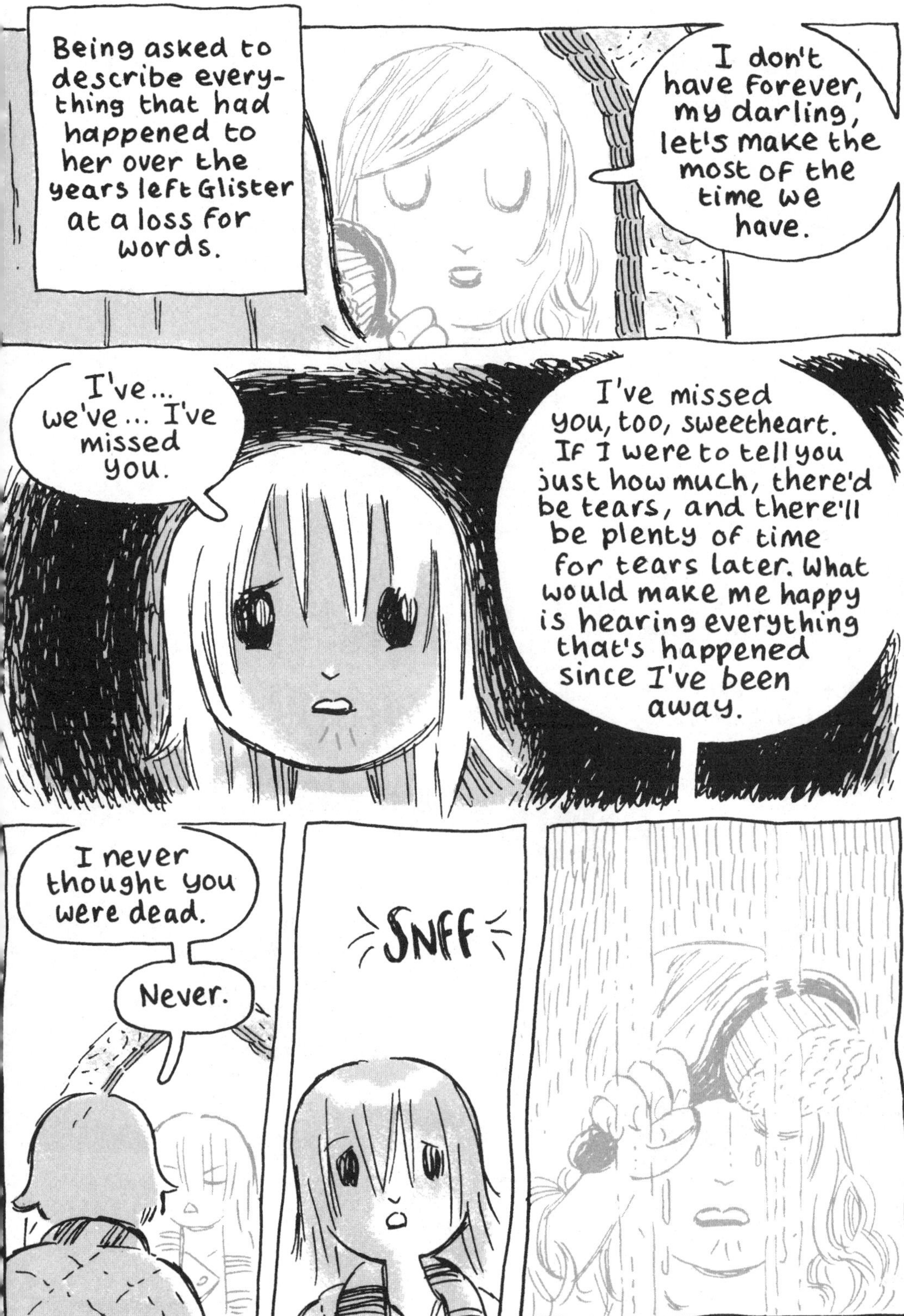
Being asked to describe everything that had happened to her over the years left Glister at a loss for words.
I don't have forever, my darling, let's make the most of the time we have.
I've... we've... I've missed you.
I've missed you, too, sweetheart. If I were to tell you just how much, there'd be tears, and there'll be plenty of time for tears later. What would make me happy is hearing everything that's happened since I've been away.
I never thought you were dead.
Never.
SNFF

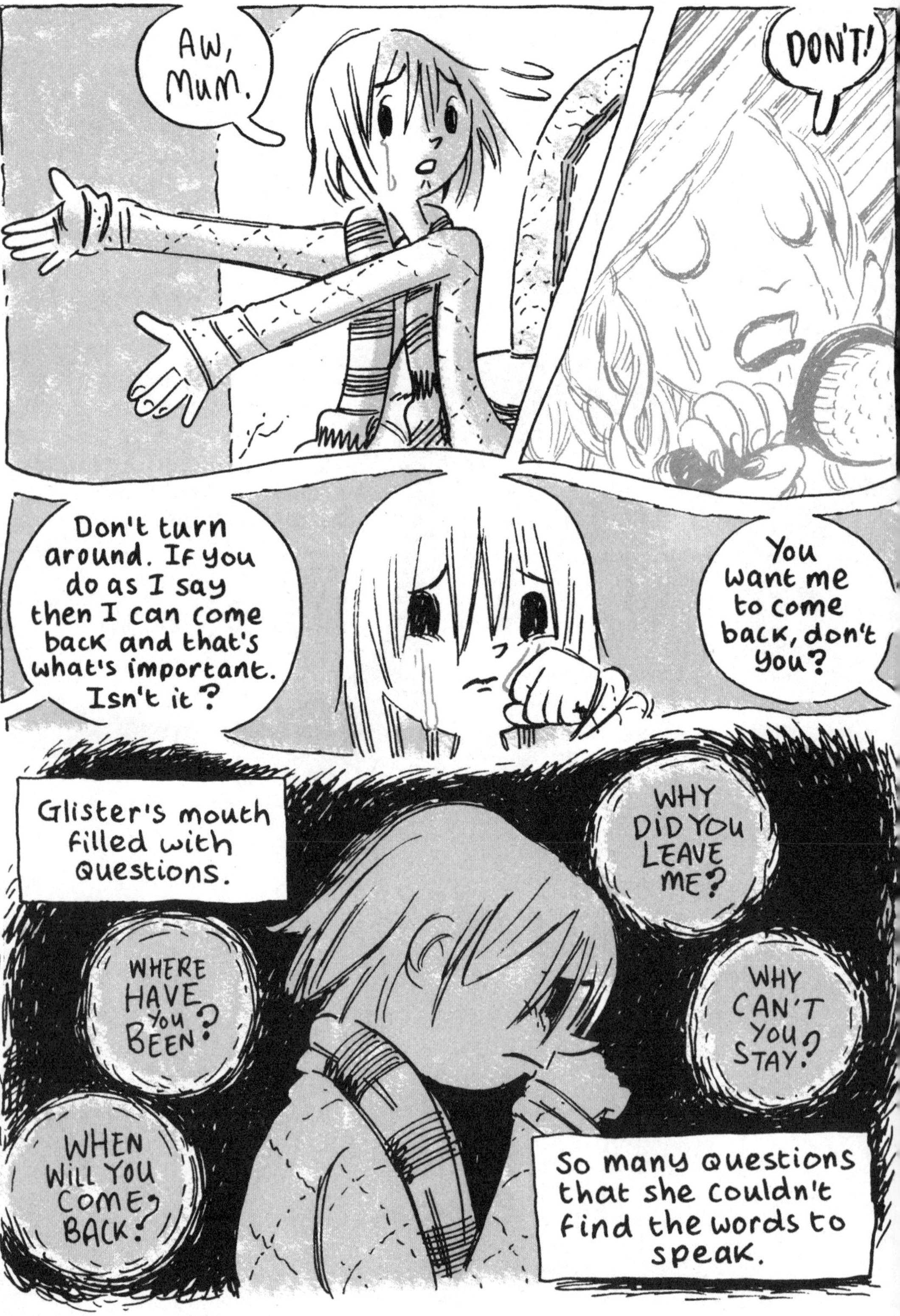
AW, MUM.
DON'T!
Don't turn around. If you do as I say then I can come back and that's what's important. Isn't it?
You want me to come back, don't you?
Glister's mouth filled with questions.
WHY DID YOU LEAVE ME?
WHERE HAVE YOU BEEN?
WHY CAN'T YOU STAY?
WHEN WILL YOU COME BACK?
So many questions that she couldn't find the words to speak.

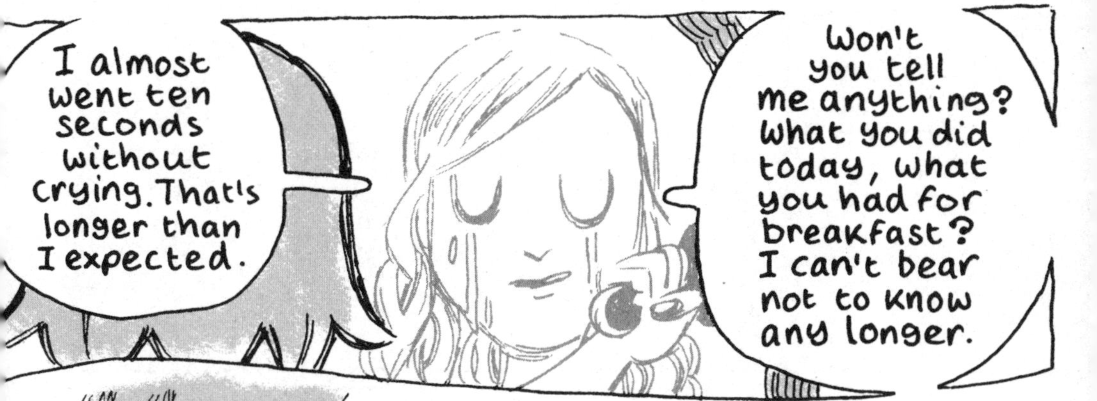
I almost went ten seconds without crying. That's longer than I expected.
Won't you tell me anything? What you did today, what you had for breakfast? I can't bear not to know any longer.

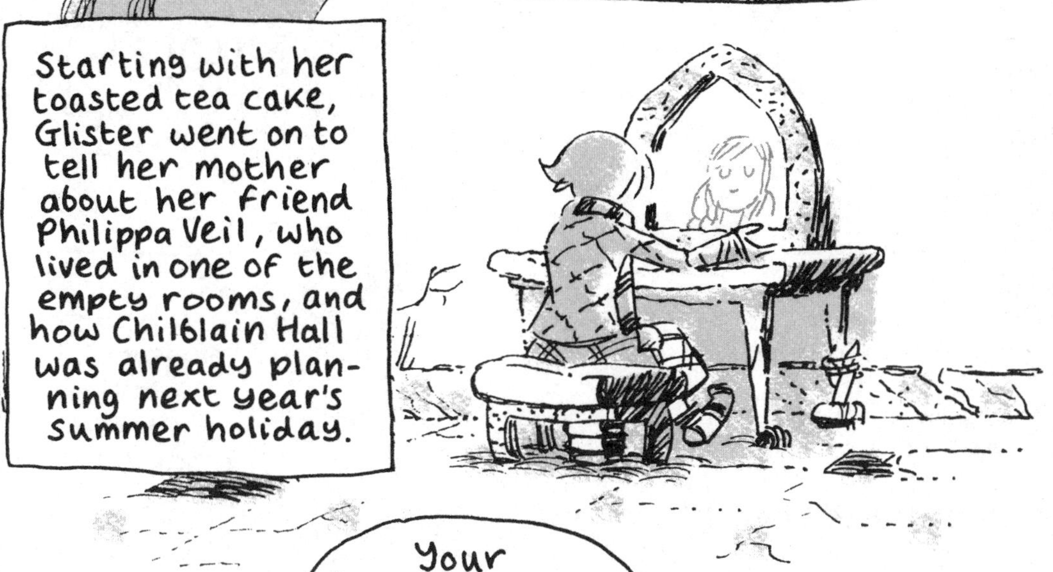
Starting with her toasted tea cake, Glister went on to tell her mother about her friend Philippa Veil, who lived in one of the empty rooms, and how Chilblain Hall was already planning next year's summer holiday.

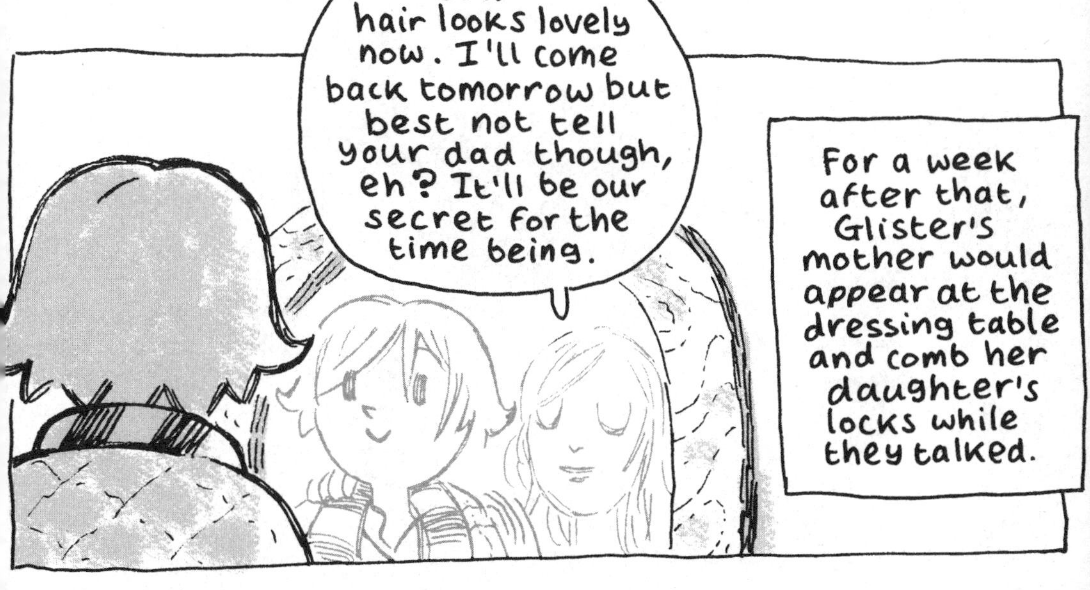
Your hair looks lovely now. I'll come back tomorrow but best not tell your dad though, eh? It'll be our secret for the time being.
For a week after that, Glister's mother would appear at the dressing table and comb her daughter's locks while they talked.

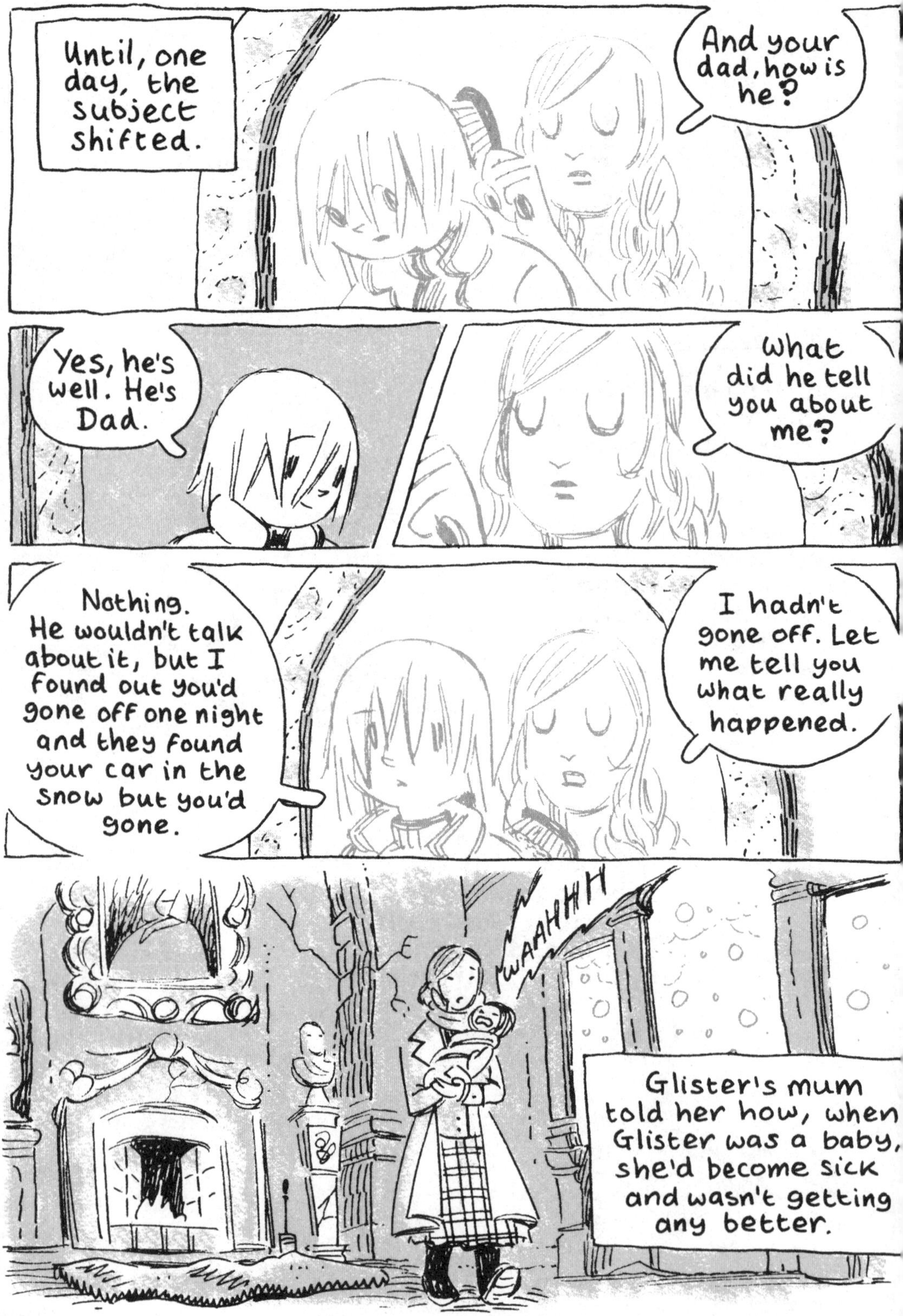

Until, one day, the subject shifted.
And your dad, how is he?
Yes, he's well. He's Dad.
What did he tell you about me?
Nothing. He wouldn't talk about it, but I found out you'd gone off one night and they found your car in the snow but you'd gone.
I hadn't gone off. Let me tell you what really happened.
WAAHHH
Glister's mum told her how, when Glister was a baby, she'd become sick and wasn't getting any better.

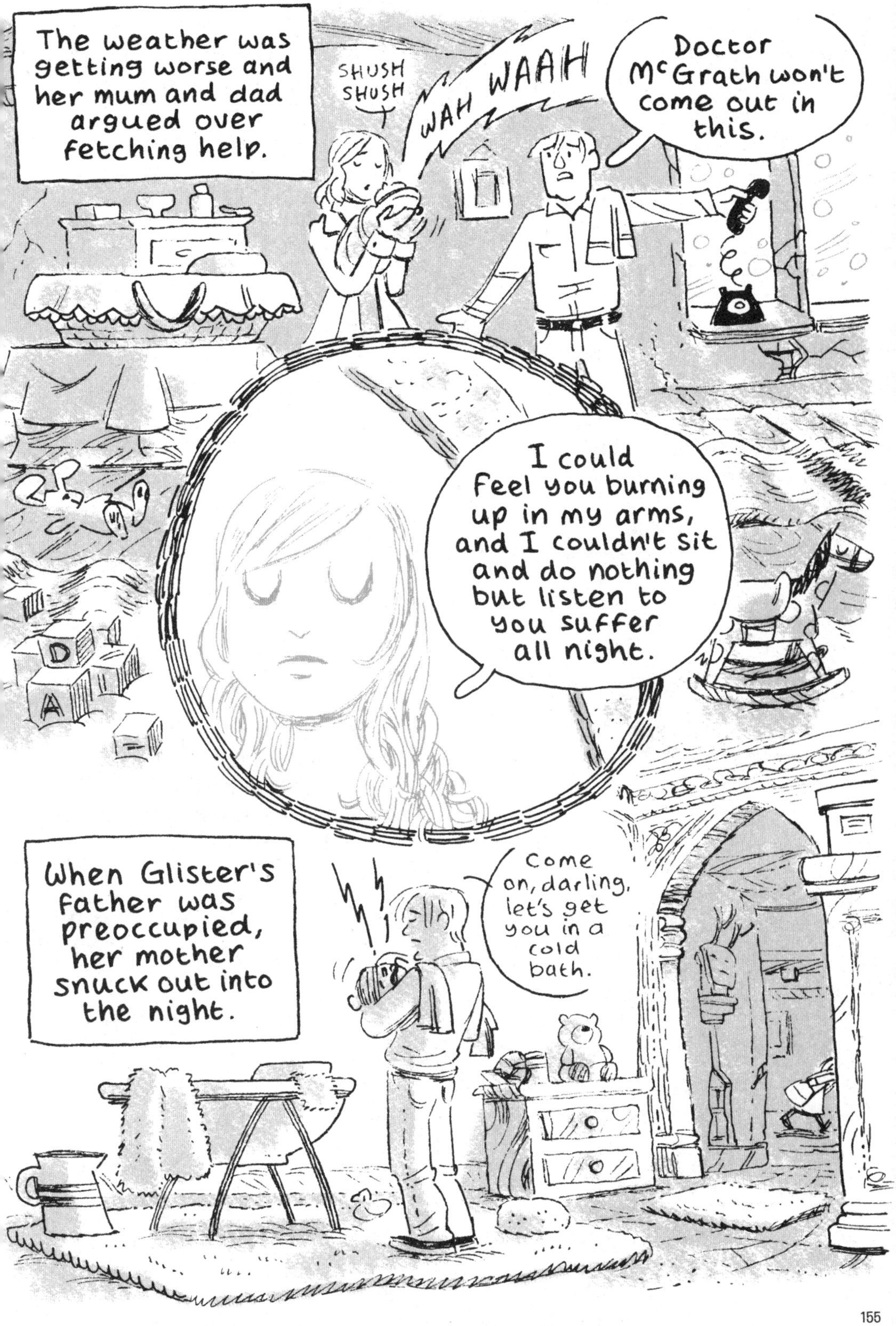

The weather was getting worse and her mum and dad argued over fetching help.
SHUSH SHUSH
WAH WAAH
Doctor McGrath won't come out in this.
I could feel you burning up in my arms, and I couldn't sit and do nothing but listen to you suffer all night.
When Glister's father was preoccupied, her mother snuck out into the night.
Come on, darling, let's get you in a cold bath.

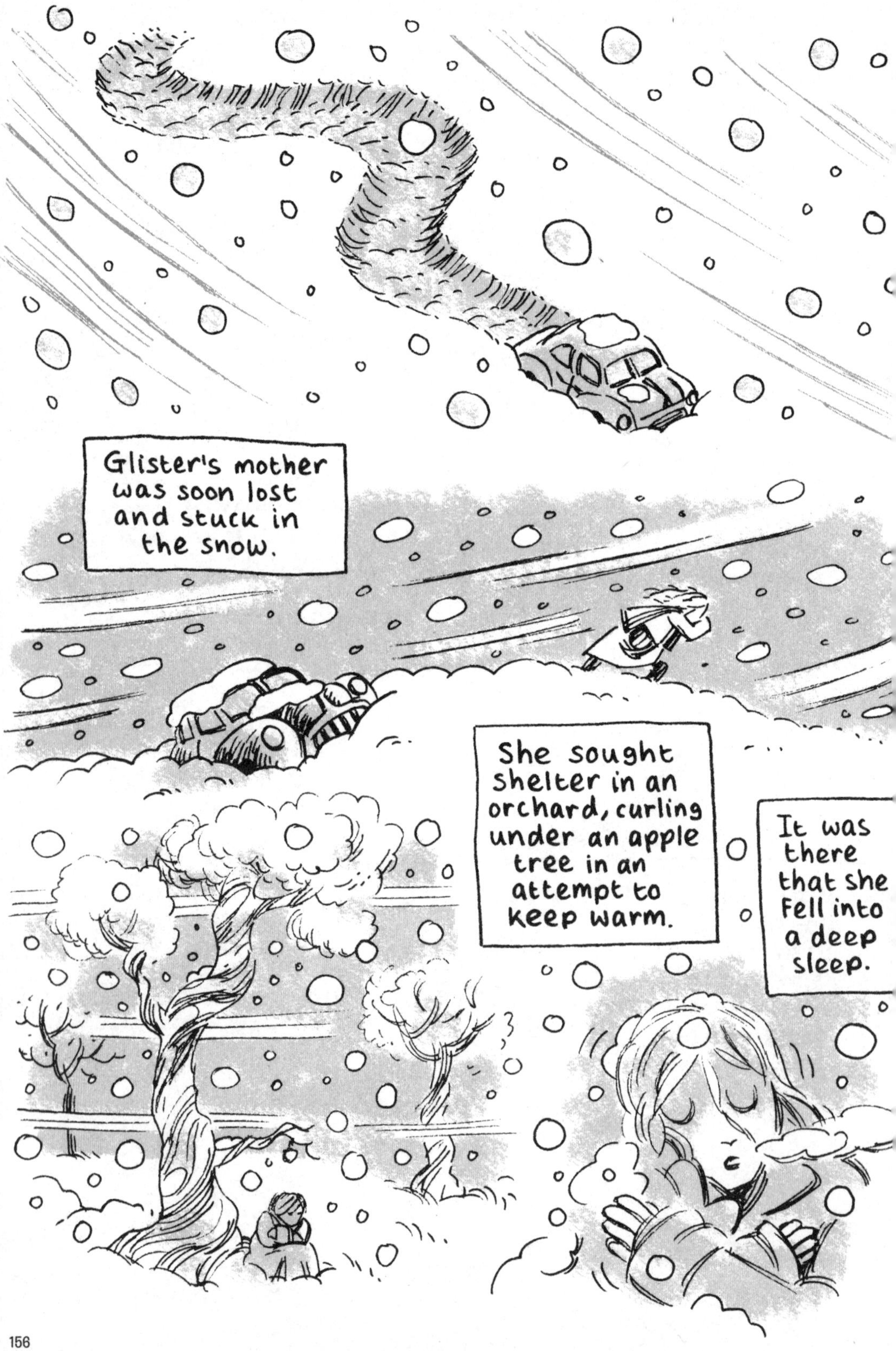
Glister's mother was soon lost and stuck in the snow.
She sought shelter in an orchard, curling under an apple tree in an attempt to keep warm.
It was there that she fell into a deep sleep.

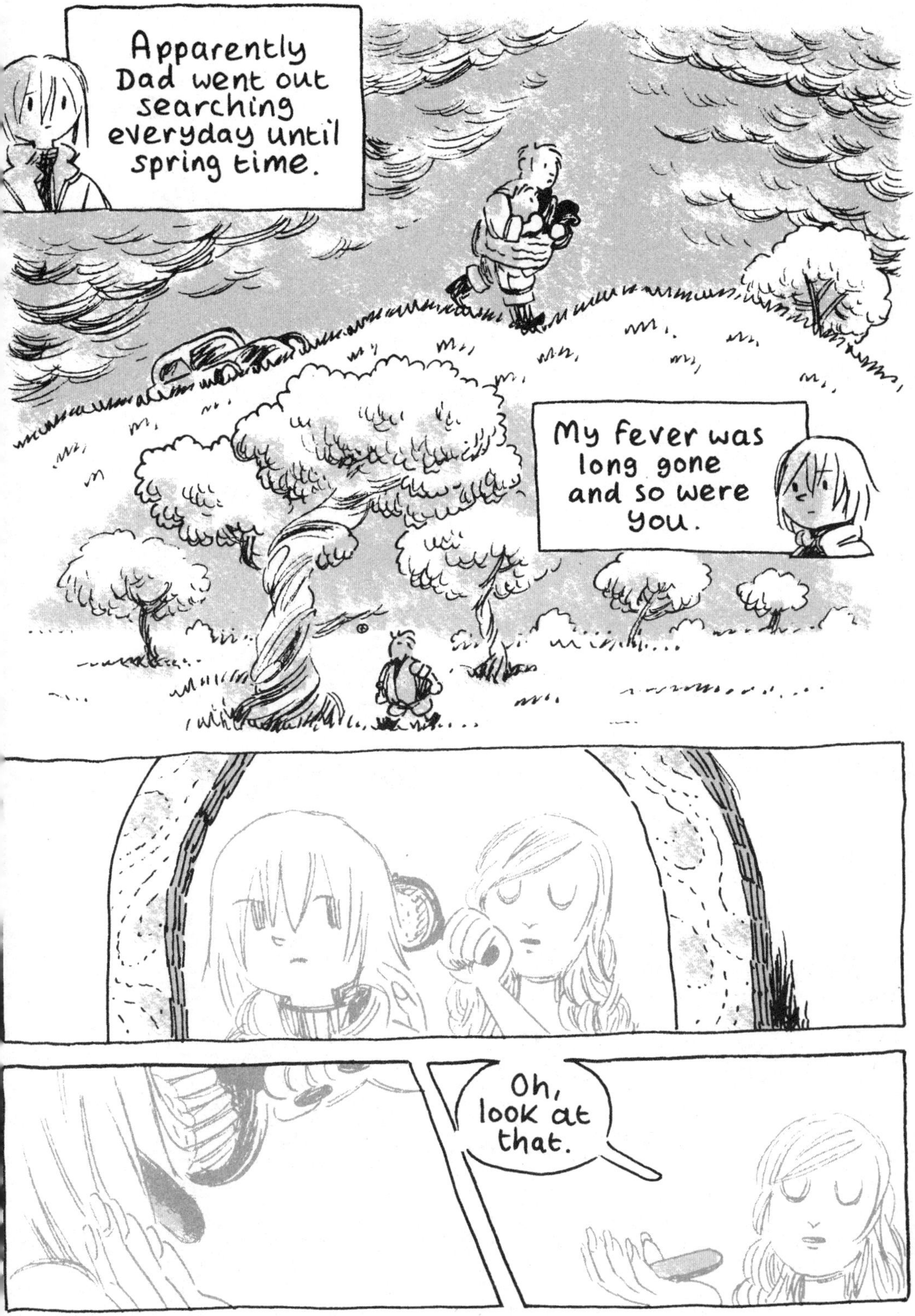
Apparently Dad went out searching everyday until spring time.
My fever was long gone and so were you.
Oh, look at that.

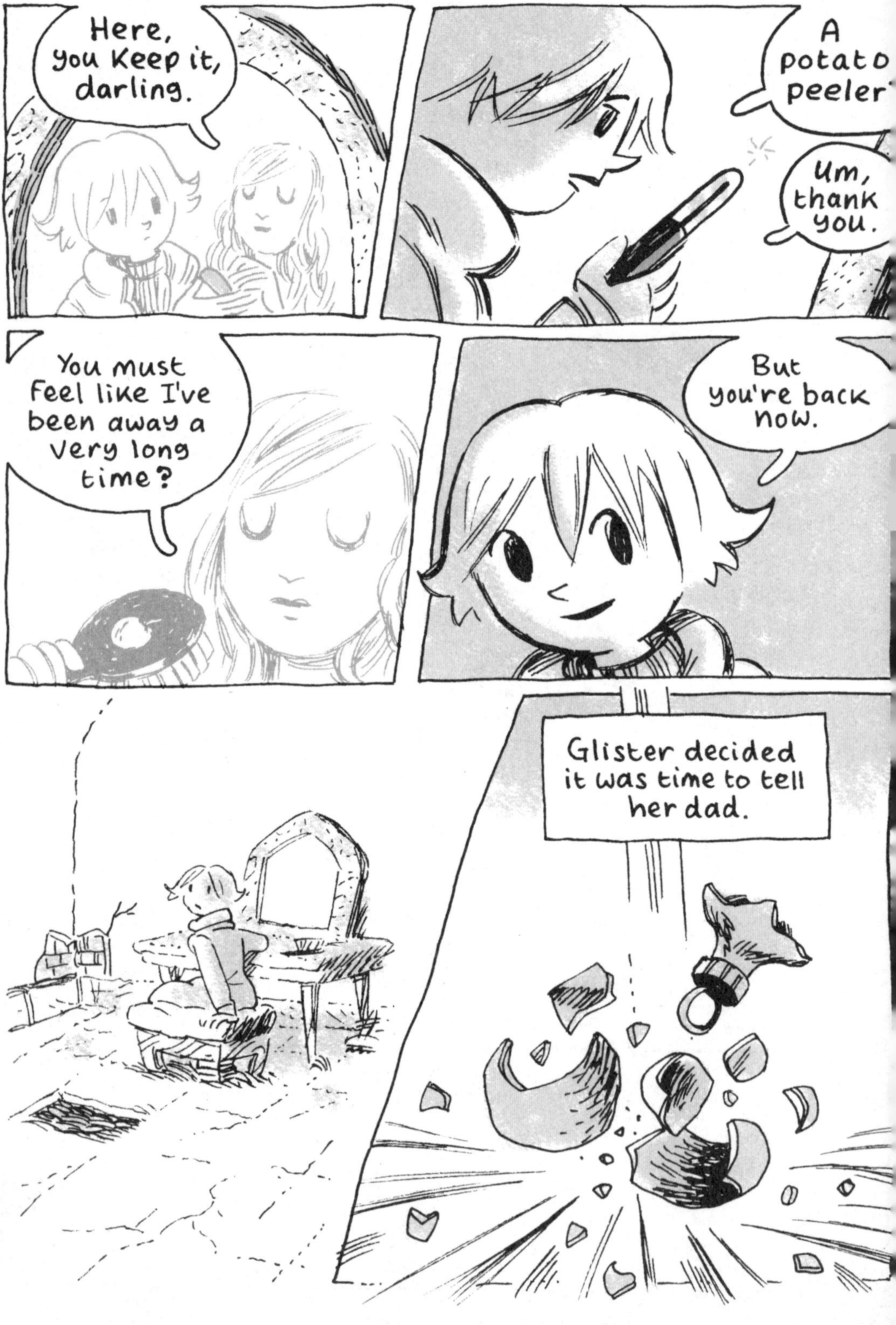
Here, you Keep it, darling.
A potato peeler?
Um, thank you.
You must Feel like I've been away a very long time?
But you're back now.
Glister decided it was time to tell her dad.

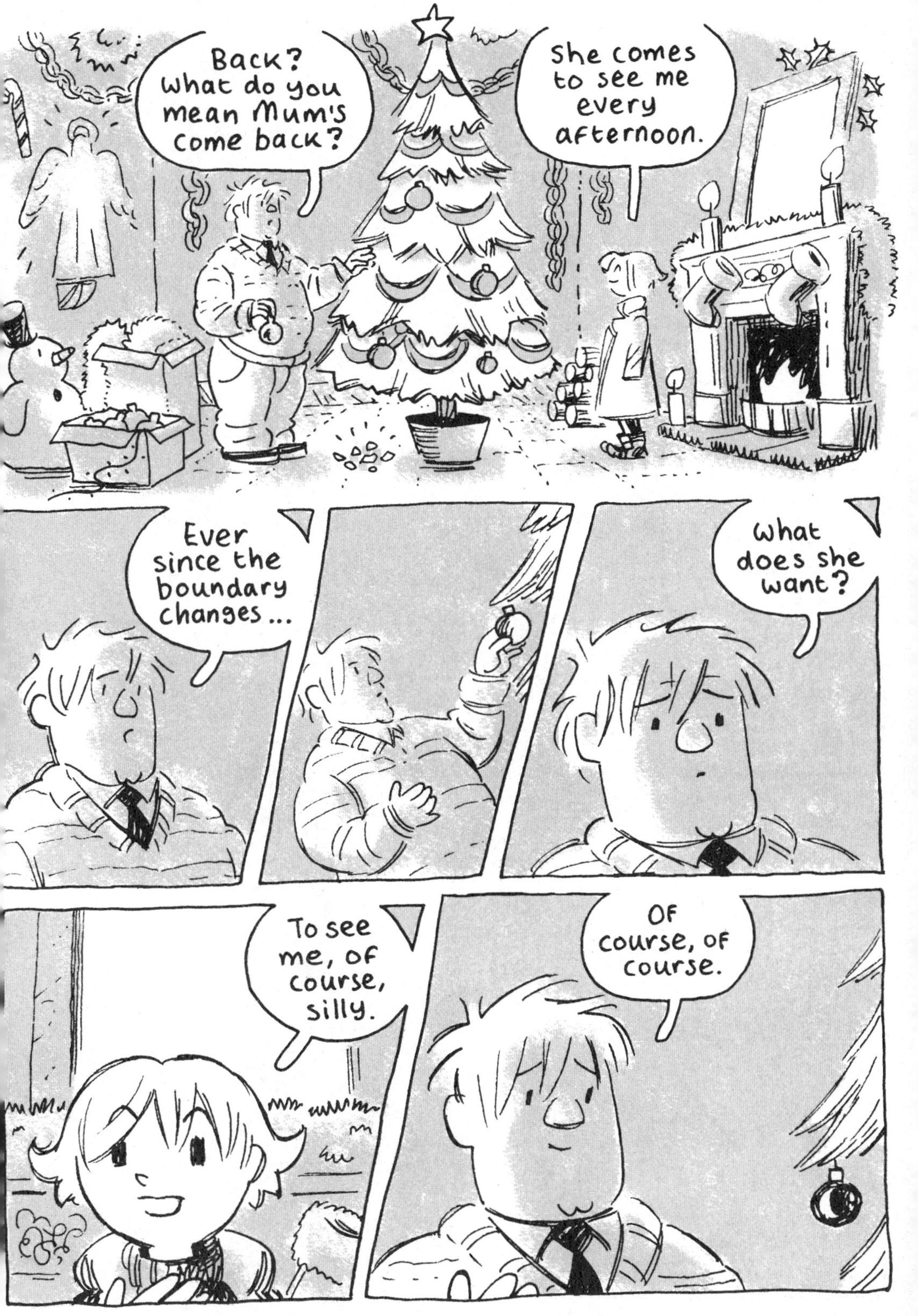
Back? What do you mean Mum's come back?
She comes to see me every afternoon.
Ever since the boundary changes...
What does she want?
To see me, of course, silly.
Of course, of course.

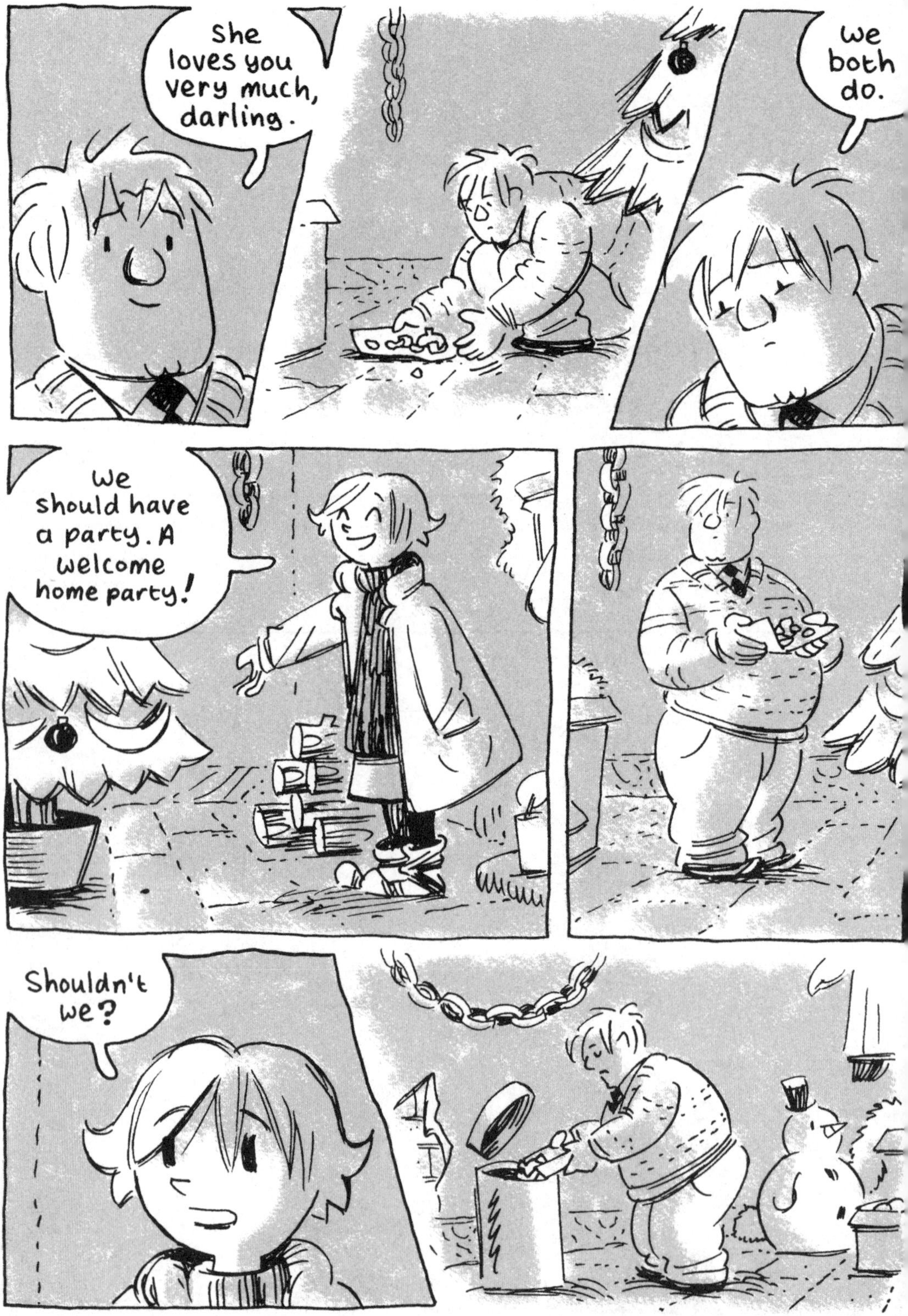
She loves you very much, darling.
We both do.
We should have a party. A welcome home party!
Shouldn't we?

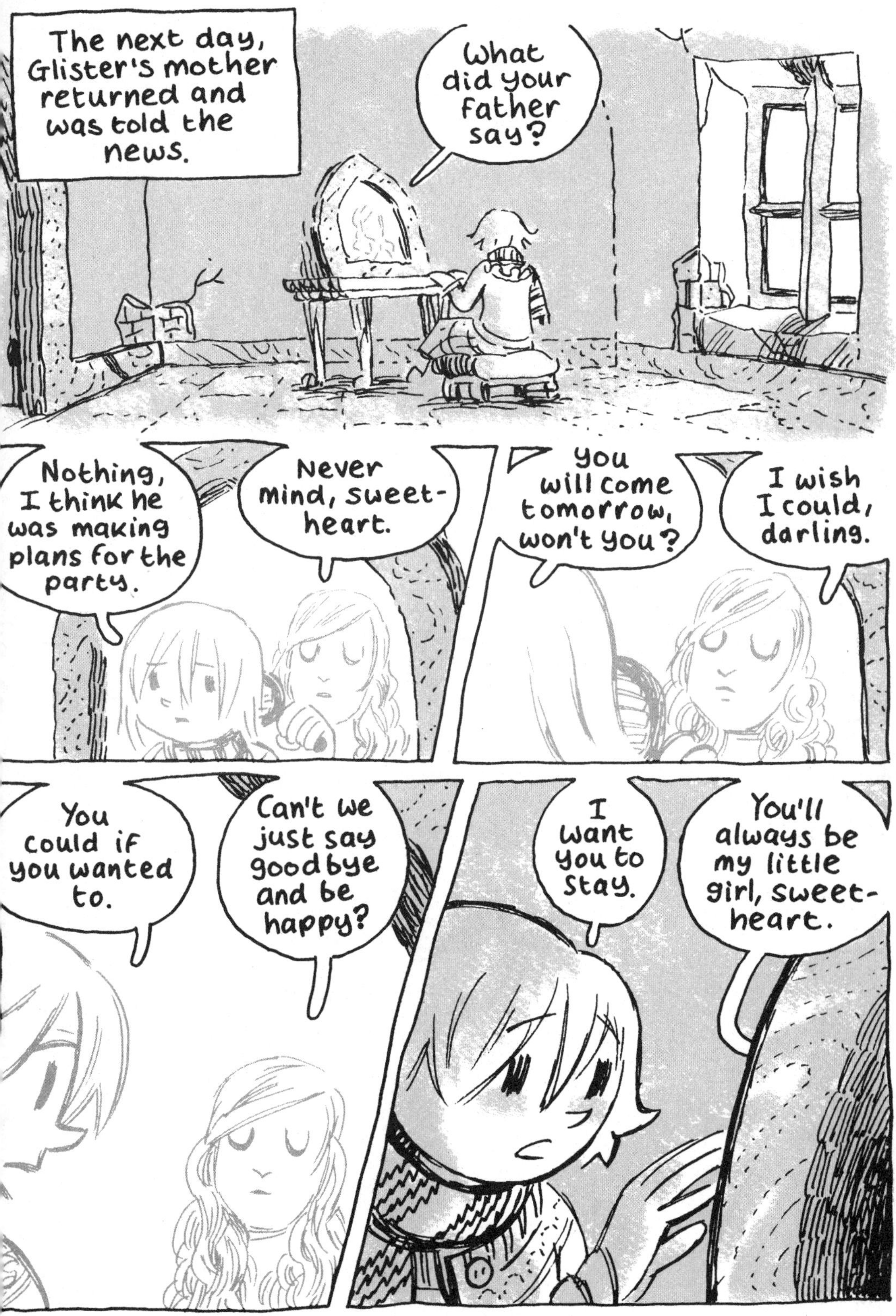

The next day, Glister's mother returned and was told the news.
What did your father say?
Nothing, I think he was making plans for the party.
Never mind, sweet-heart.
You will come tomorrow, won't you?
I wish I could, darling.
You could if you wanted to.
Can't we just say goodbye and be happy?
I want you to stay.
You'll always be my little girl, sweet-heart.

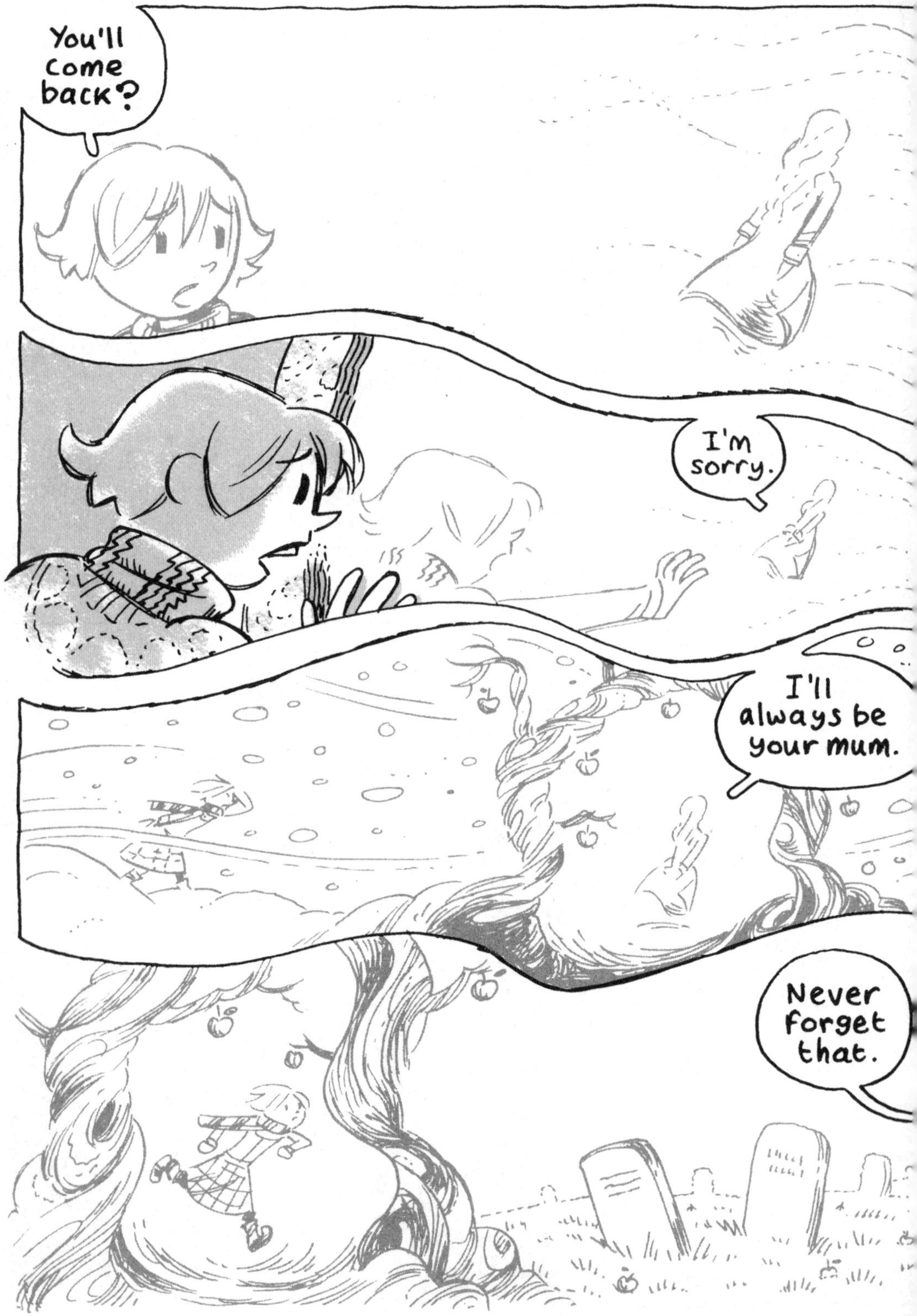
You'll come back?
I'm sorry.
I'll always be your mum.
Never forget that.

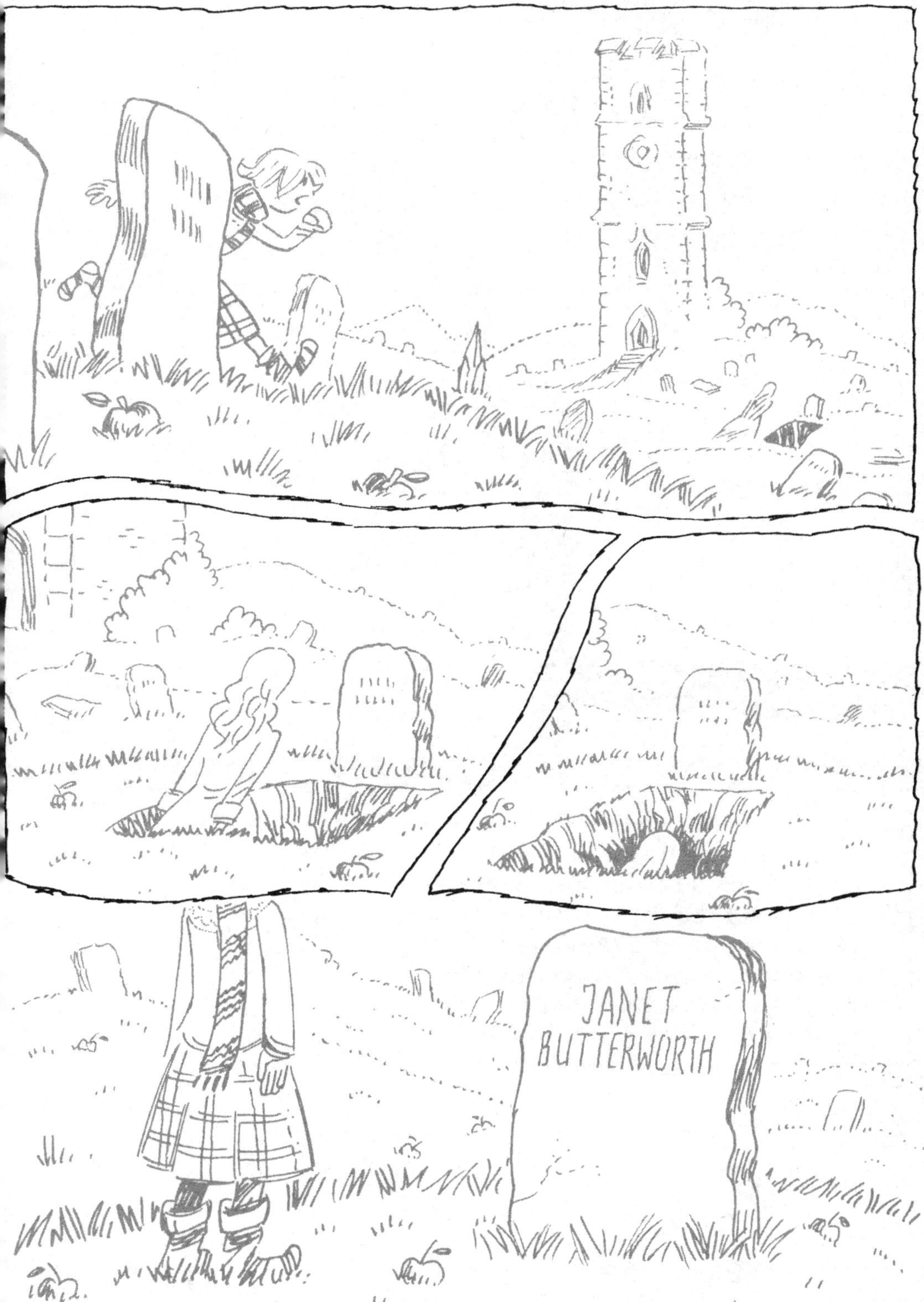
JANET
BUTTERWORTH

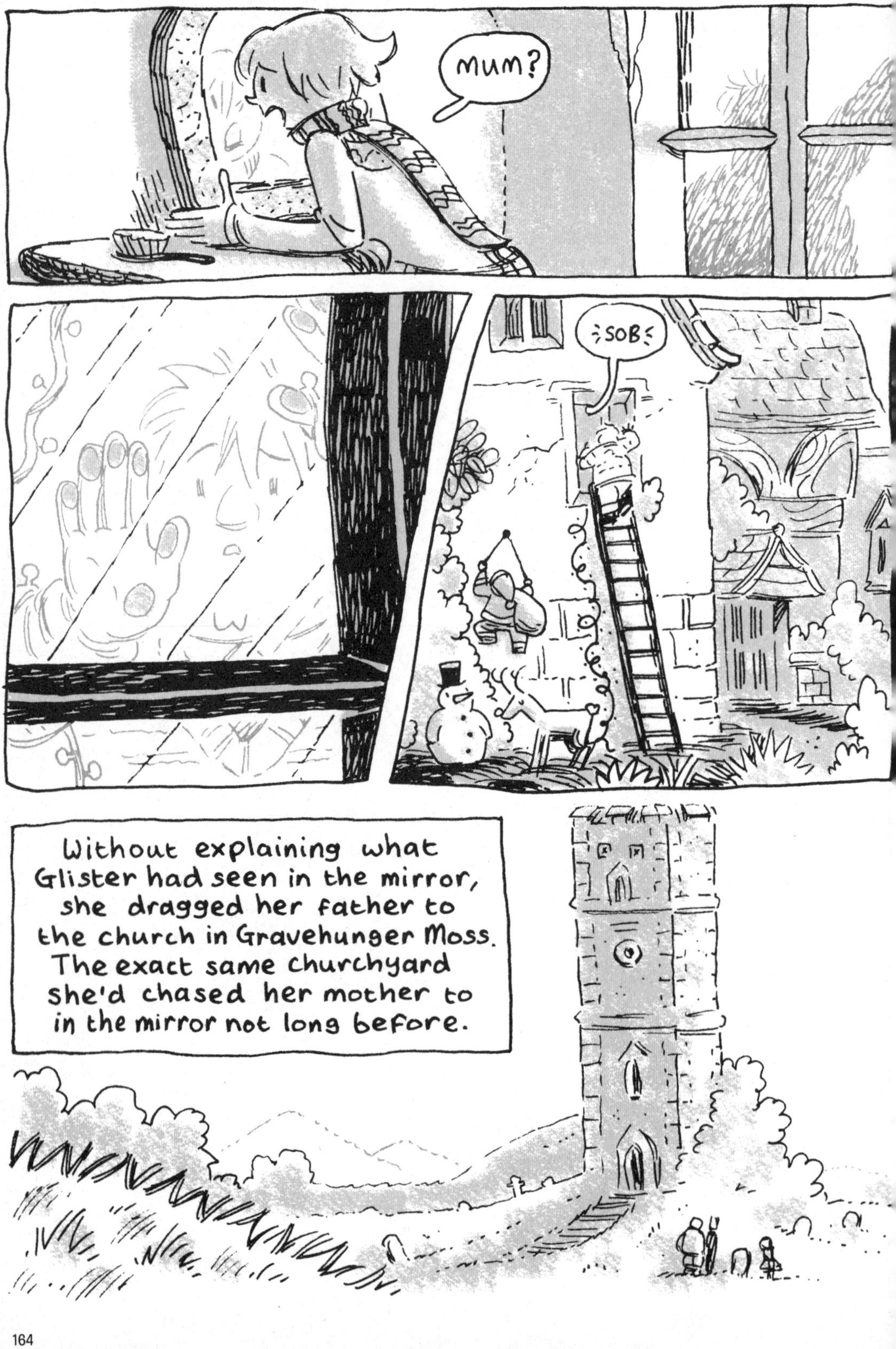
MUM?
SOB
Without explaining what Glister had seen in the mirror, she dragged her father to the church in Gravehunger Moss. The exact same churchyard she'd chased her mother to in the mirror not long before.

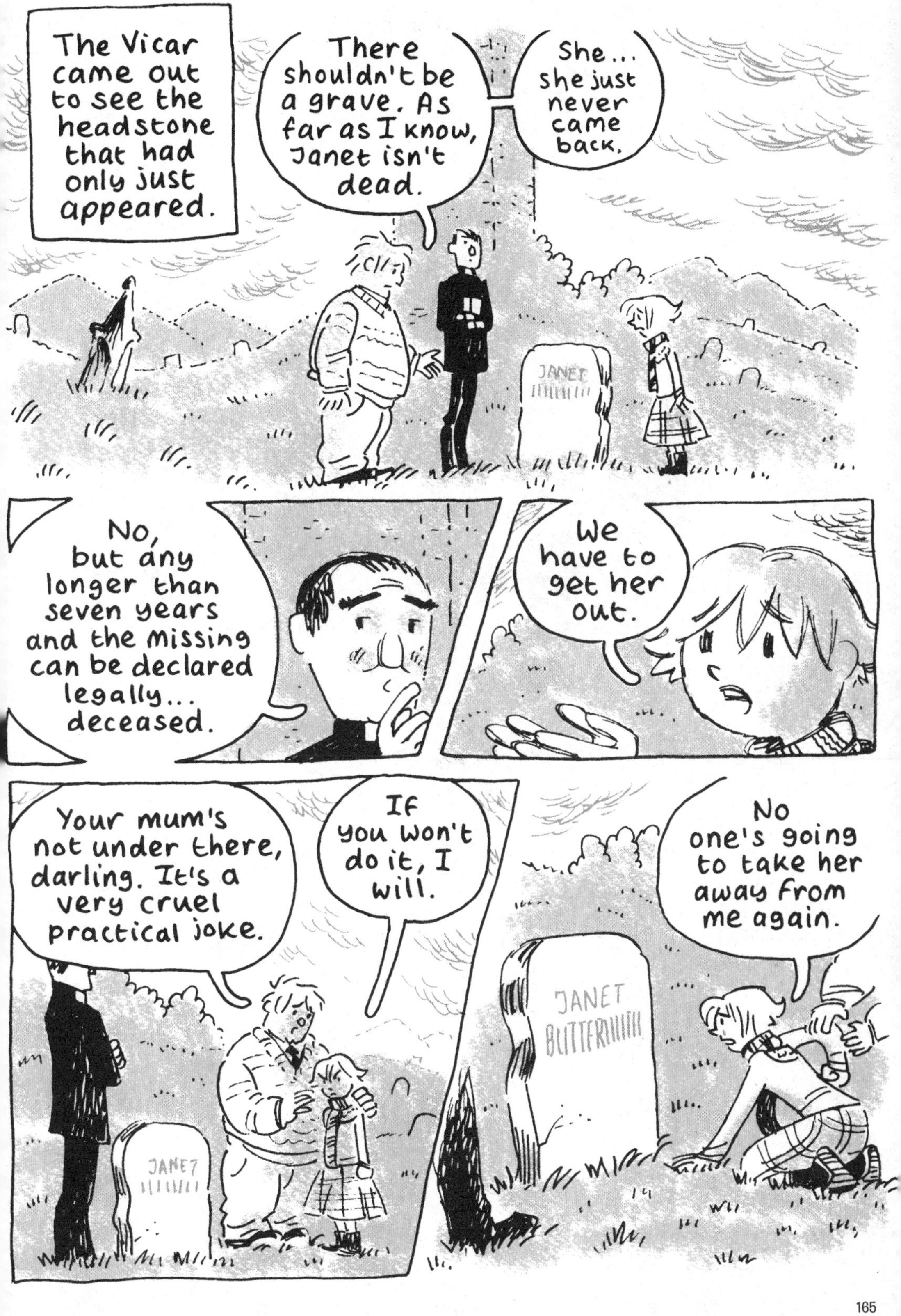
The Vicar came out to see the headstone that had only just appeared.
There shouldn't be a grave. As far as I know, Janet isn't dead.
She... she just never came back.
JANET
No, but any longer than seven years and the missing can be declared legally... deceased.
We have to get her out.
Your mum's not under there, darling. It's a very cruel practical joke.
If you won't do it, I will.
JANET
No one's going to take her away from me again.
JANET
BUTTER

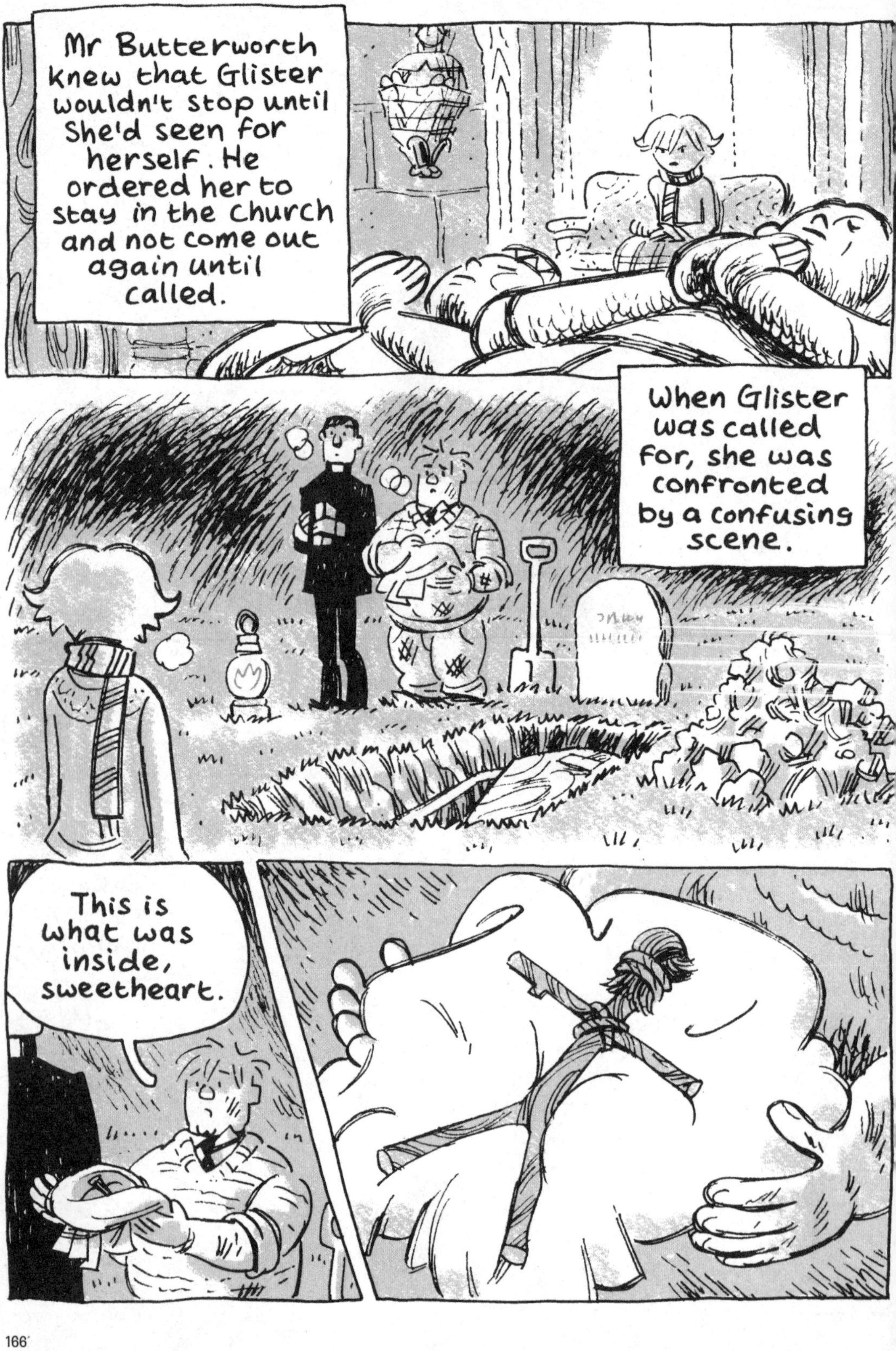
Mr Butterworth knew that Glister wouldn't stop until she'd seen for herself. He ordered her to stay in the church and not come out again until called.
When Glister was called for, she was confronted by a confusing scene.
This is what was inside, sweetheart.

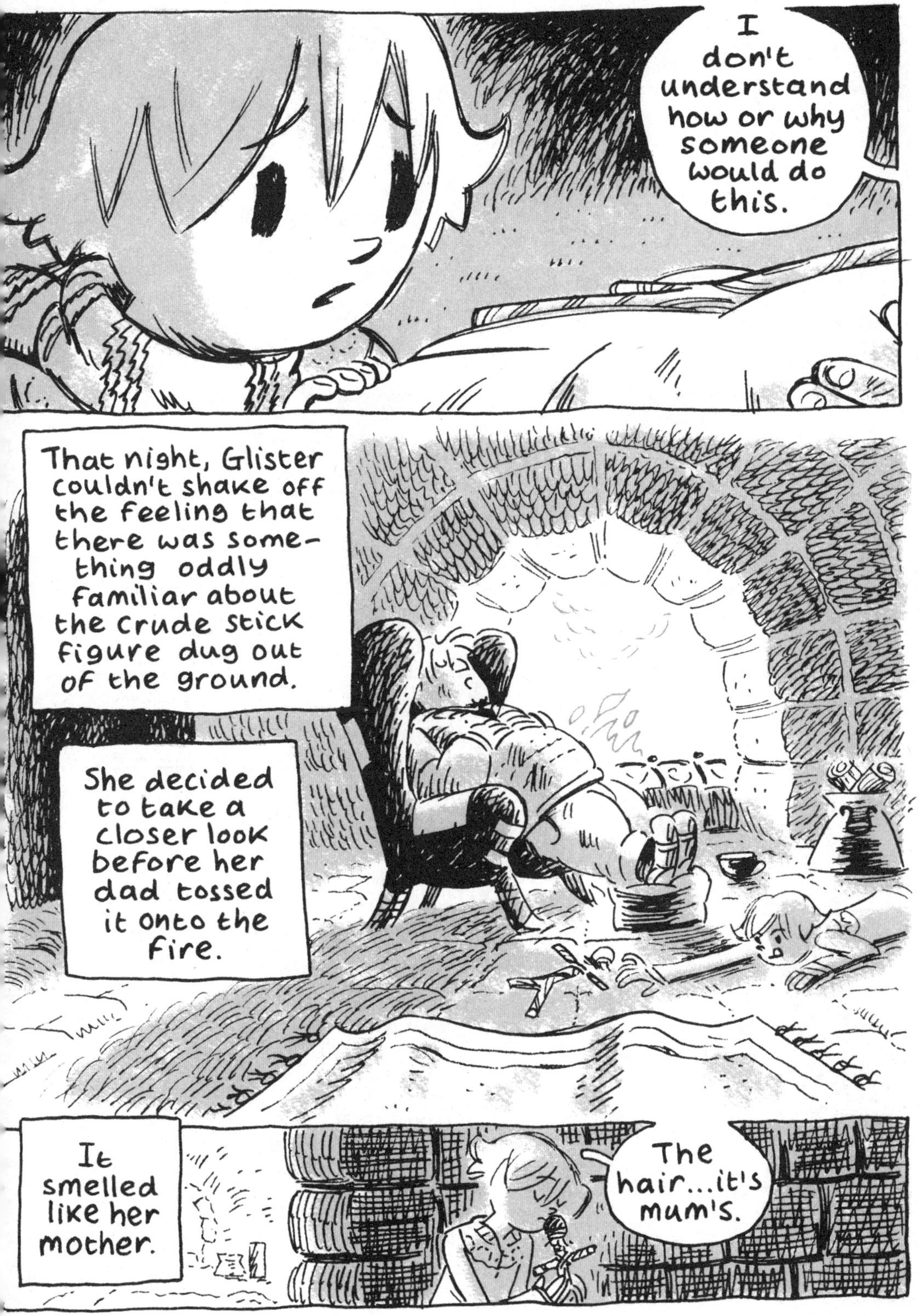

I don't understand how or why someone would do this.
That night, Glister couldn't shake off the feeling that there was something oddly familiar about the crude stick figure dug out of the ground.
She decided to take a closer look before her dad tossed it onto the fire.
It smelled like her mother.
The hair...it's mum's.

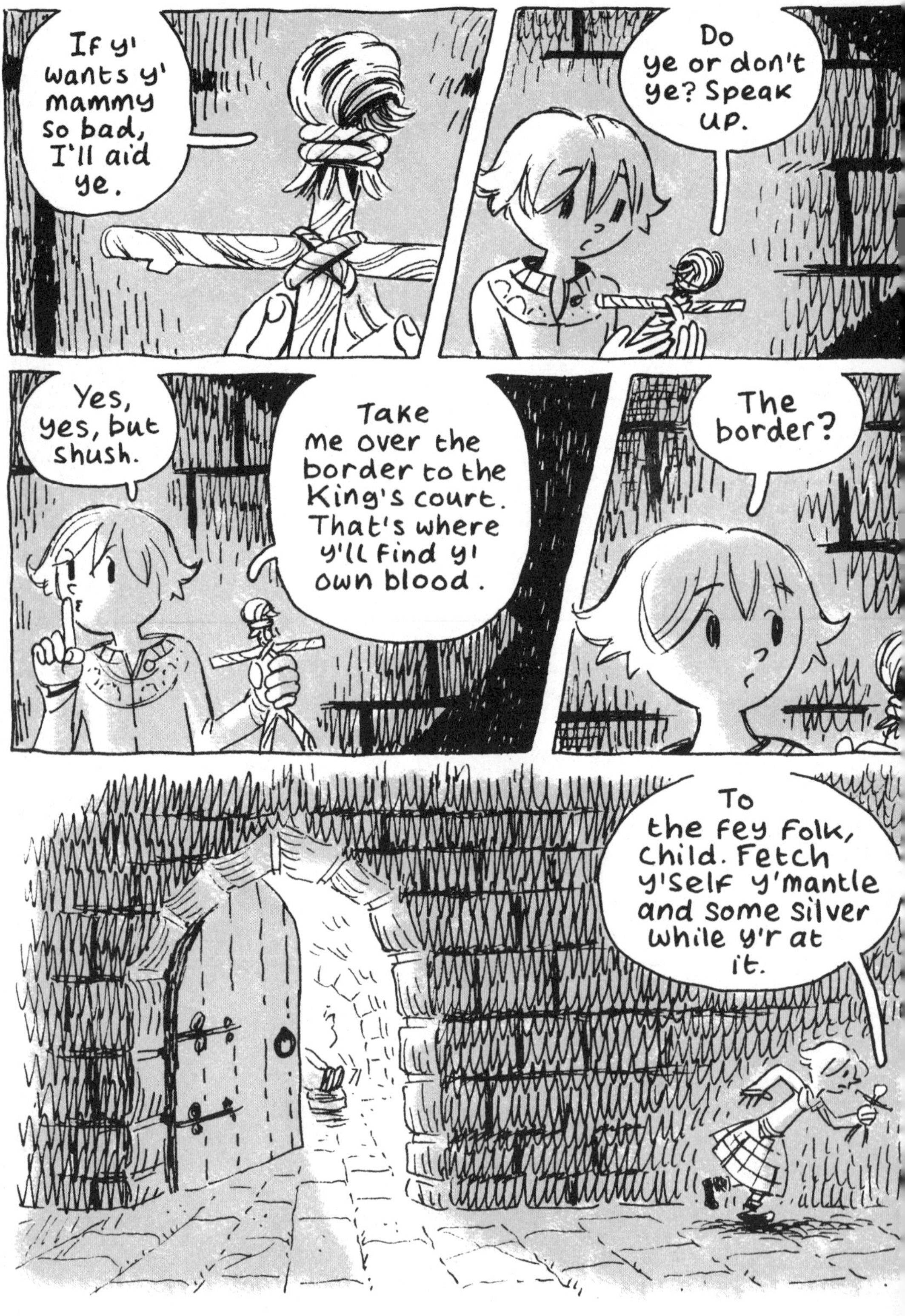
If y' wants y' mammy so bad, I'll aid ye.
Do ye or don't ye? Speak up.
Yes, yes, but shush.
Take me over the border to the King's court. That's where y'll find y' own blood.
The border?
To the fey folk, Child. Fetch y'self y'mantle and some silver while y'r at it.

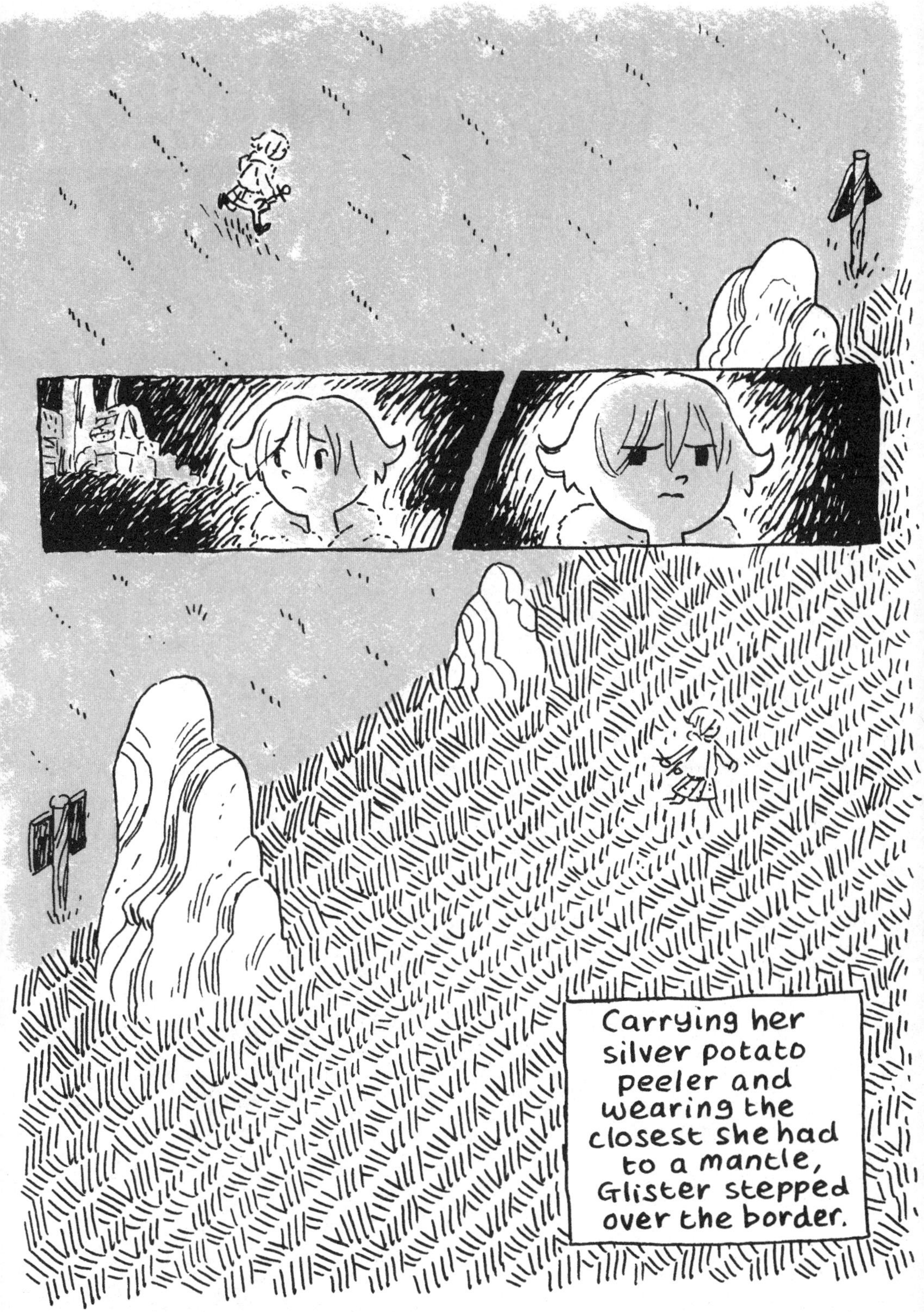
Carrying her silver potato peeler and wearing the closest she had to a mantle, Glister stepped over the border.

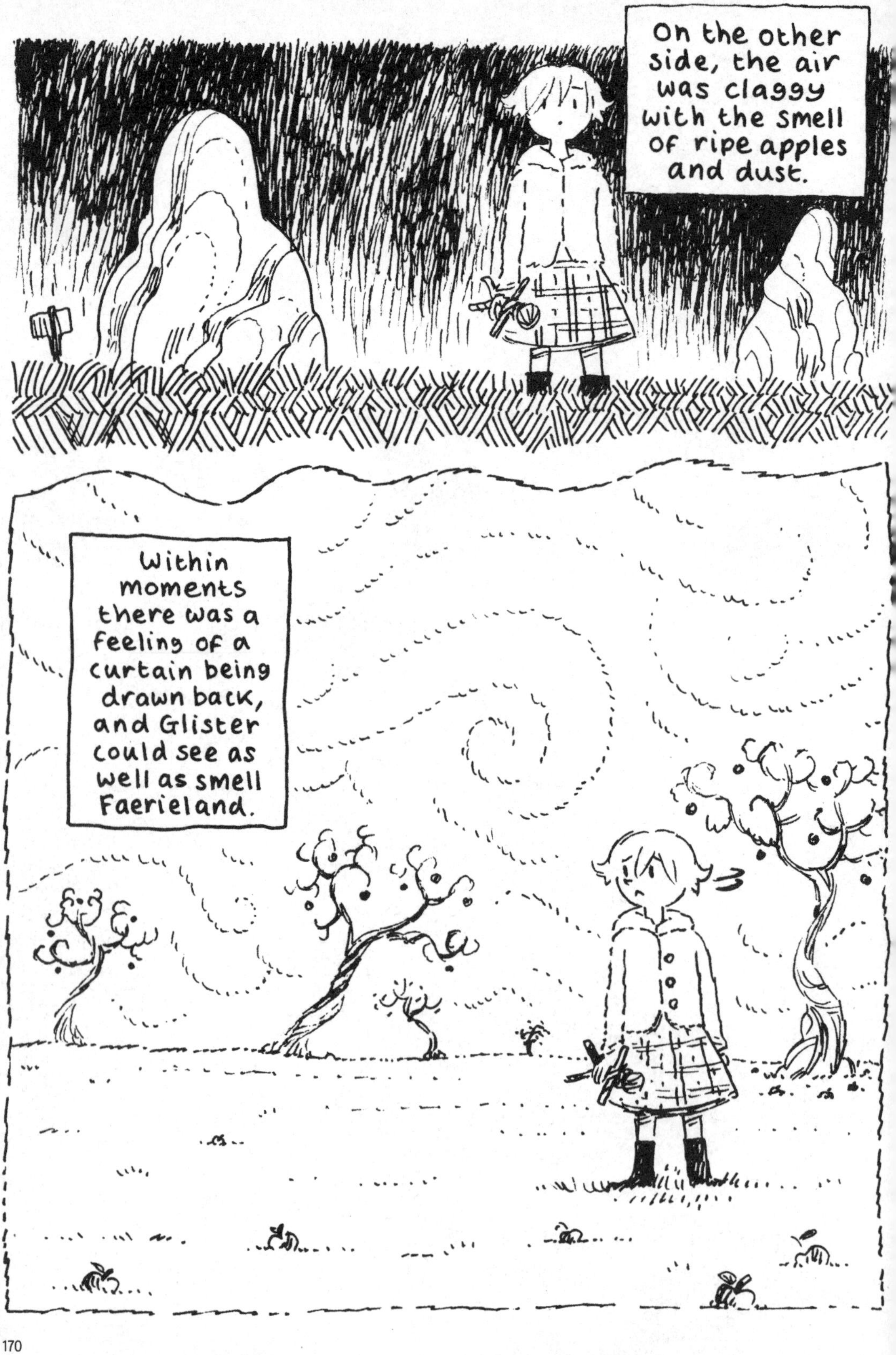
On the other side, the air was claggy with the smell of ripe apples and dust.
Within moments there was a feeling of a curtain being drawn back, and Glister could see as well as smell Faerieland.

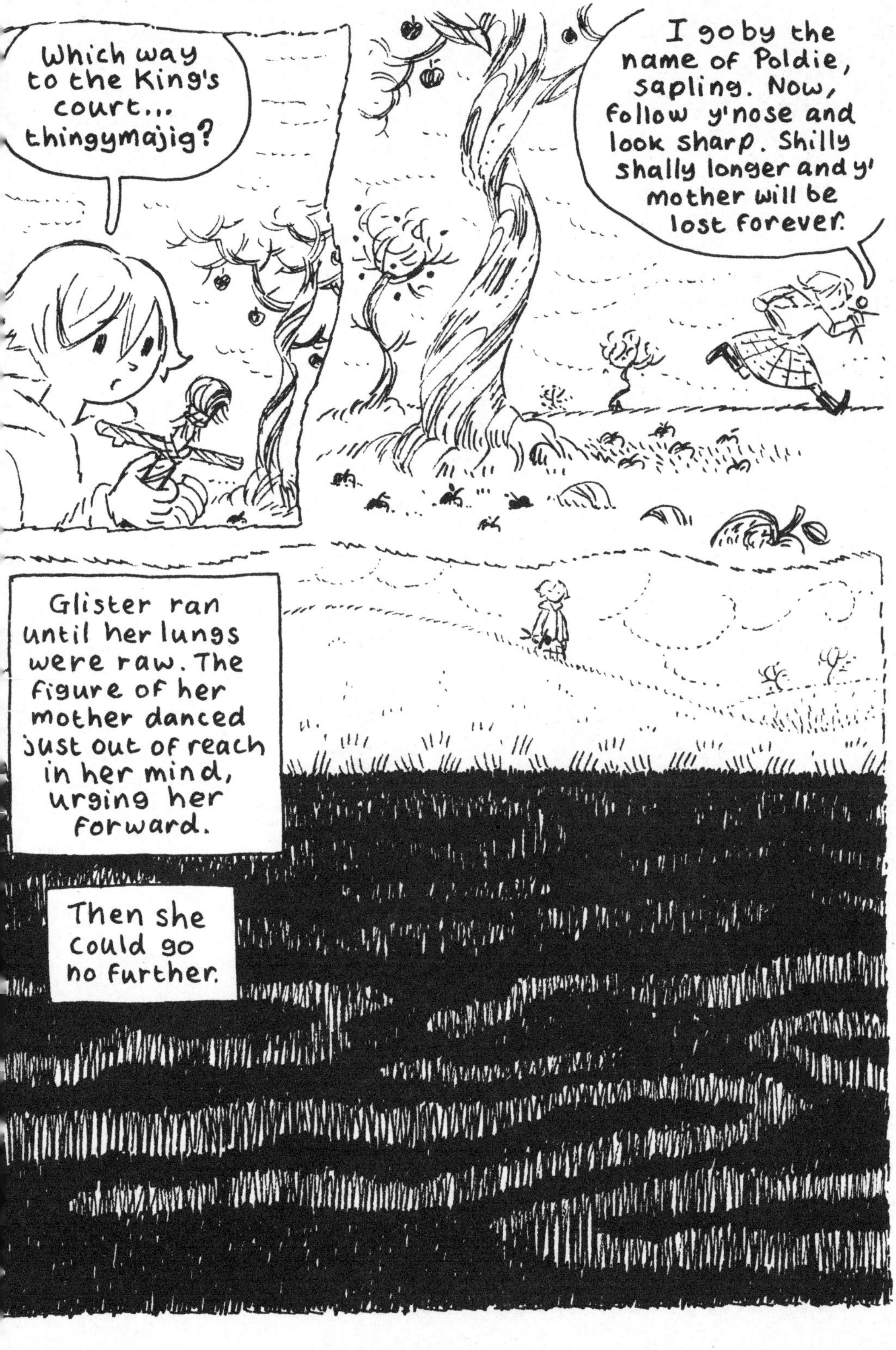
Which way to the King's court... thingymajig?
I go by the name of Poldie, sapling. Now, follow y'nose and look sharp. Shilly shally longer and y' mother will be lost forever.
Glister ran until her lungs were raw. The figure of her mother danced just out of reach in her mind, urging her forward.
Then she could go no further.

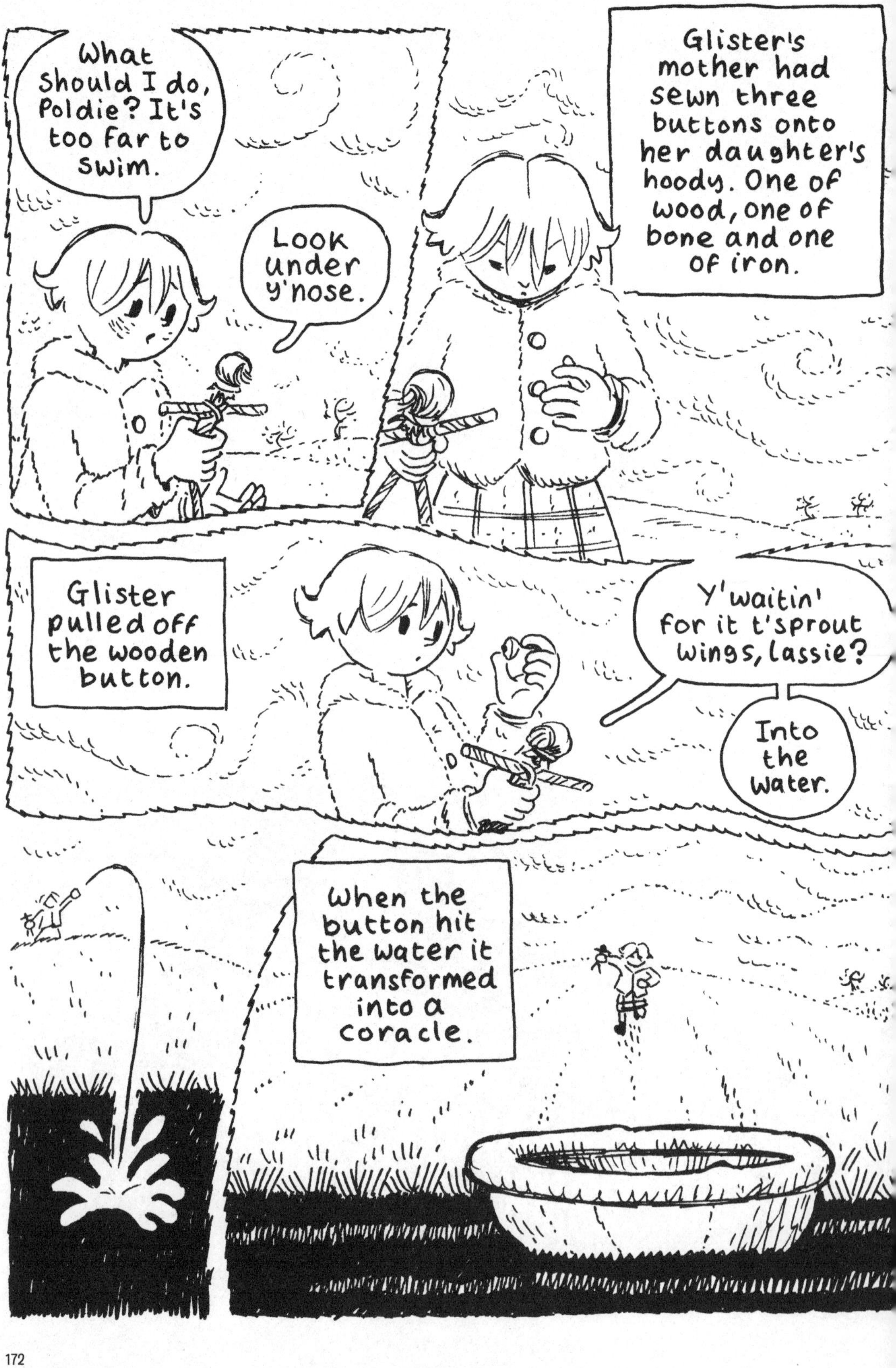

What should I do, Poldie? It's too far to swim.
Look under y'nose.
Glister's mother had sewn three buttons onto her daughter's hoody. One of wood, one of bone and one of iron.
Glister pulled off the wooden button.
Y'waitin' for it t'sprout wings, lassie?
Into the water.
When the button hit the water it transformed into a coracle.

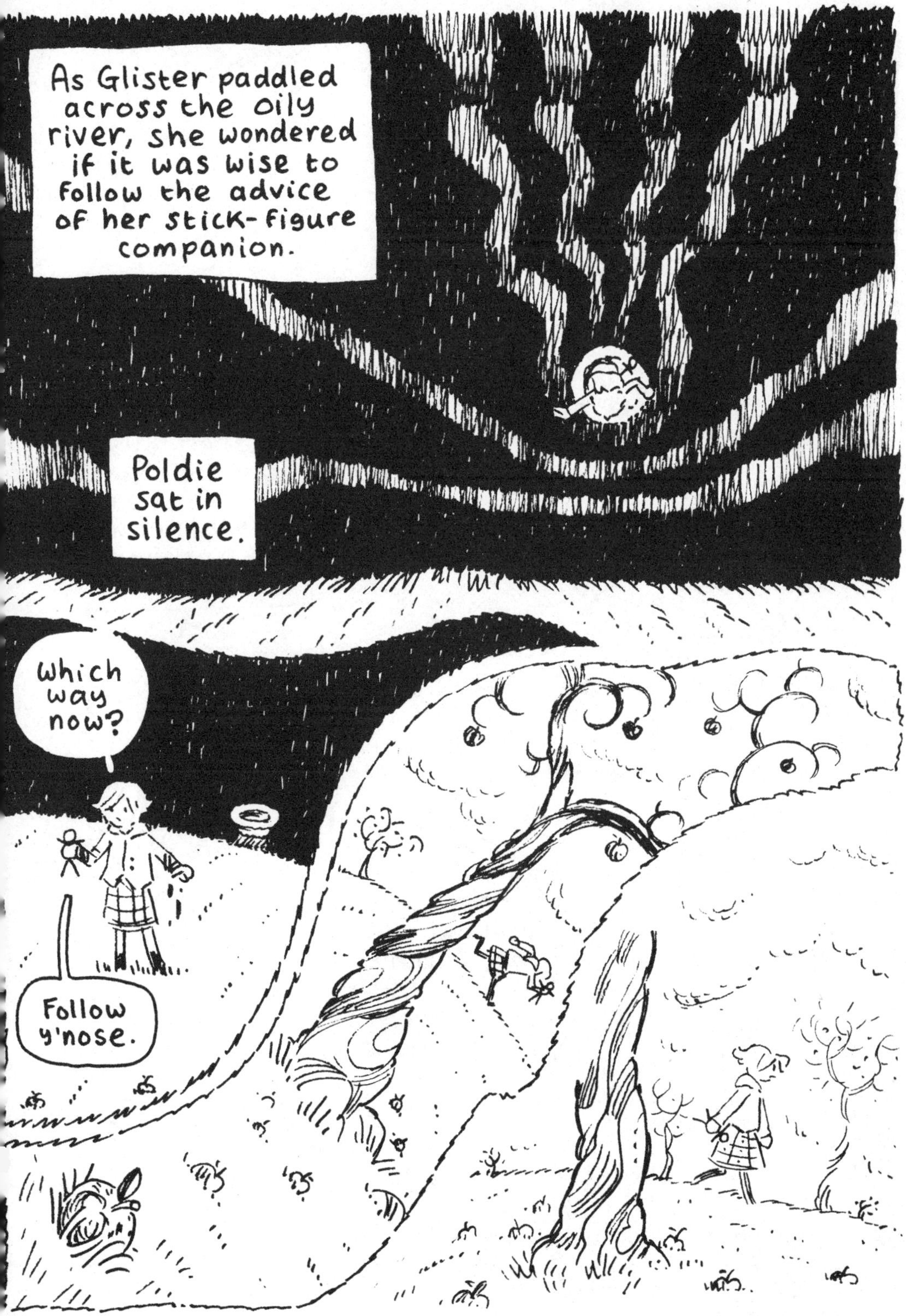

As Glister paddled across the oily river, she wondered if it was wise to follow the advice of her stick-figure companion.
Poldie sat in silence.
Which way now?
Follow y'nose.

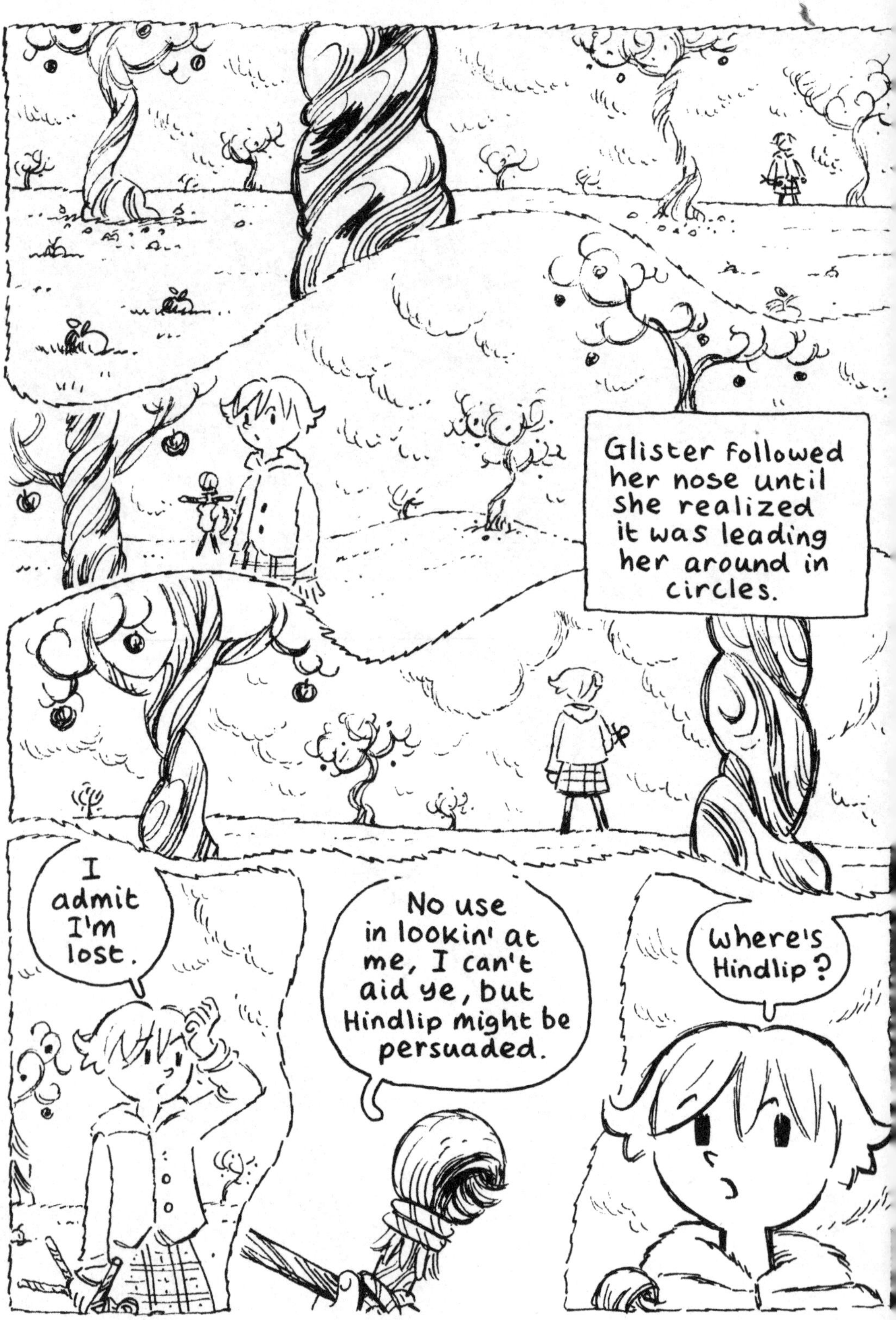
Glister followed her nose until she realized it was leading her around in circles.
I admit I'm lost.
No use in lookin' at me, I can't aid ye, but Hindlip might be persuaded.
Where's Hindlip?

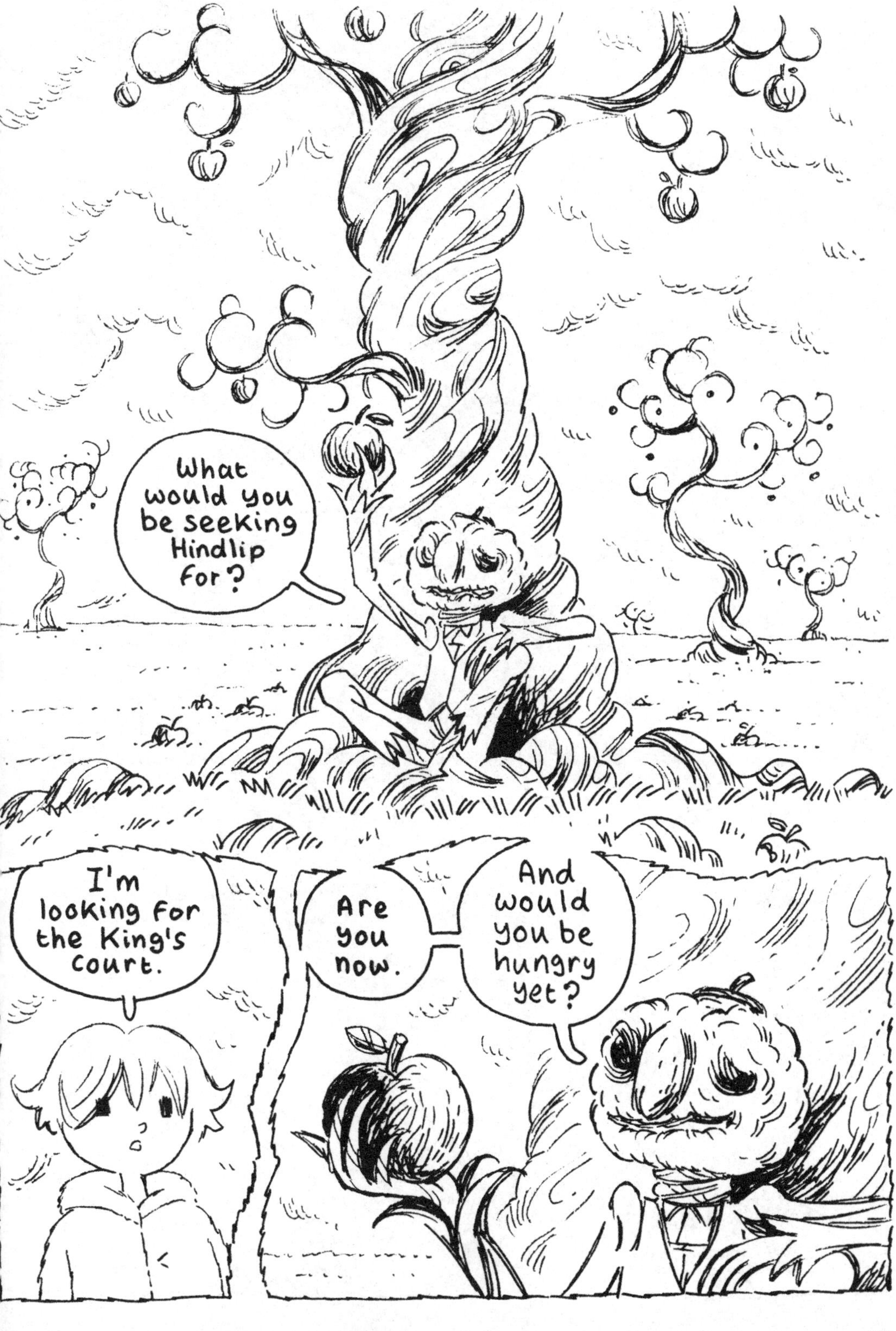
What would you be seeking Hindlip for?
I'm looking for the King's court.
Are you now.
And would you be hungry yet?

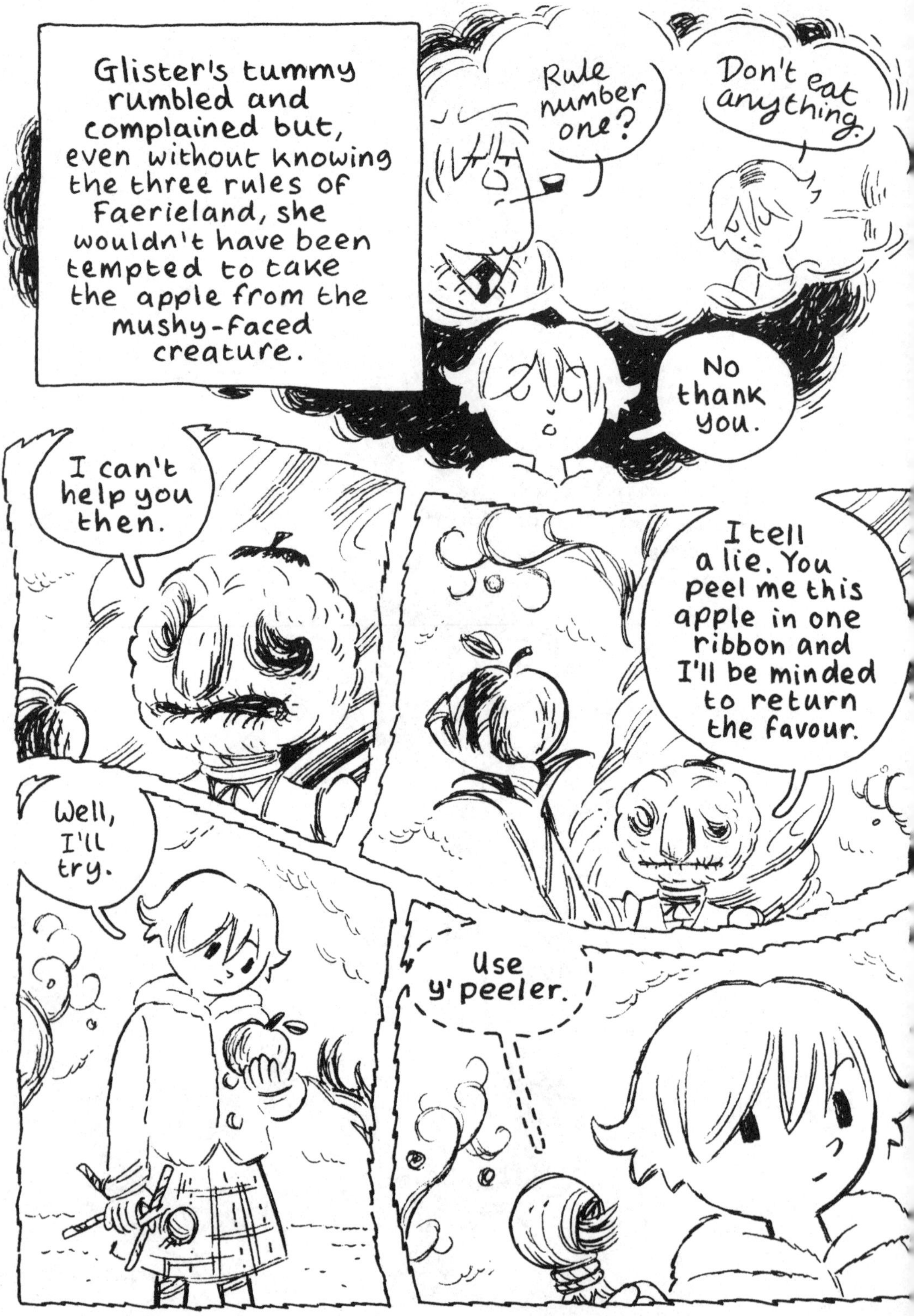
Glister's tummy rumbled and complained but, even without knowing the three rules of Faerieland, she wouldn't have been tempted to take the apple from the mushy-faced creature.
Rule number one?
Don't eat anything.
No thank you.
I can't help you then.
I tell a lie. You peel me this apple in one ribbon and I'll be minded to return the favour.
Well, I'll try.
Use y' peeler.

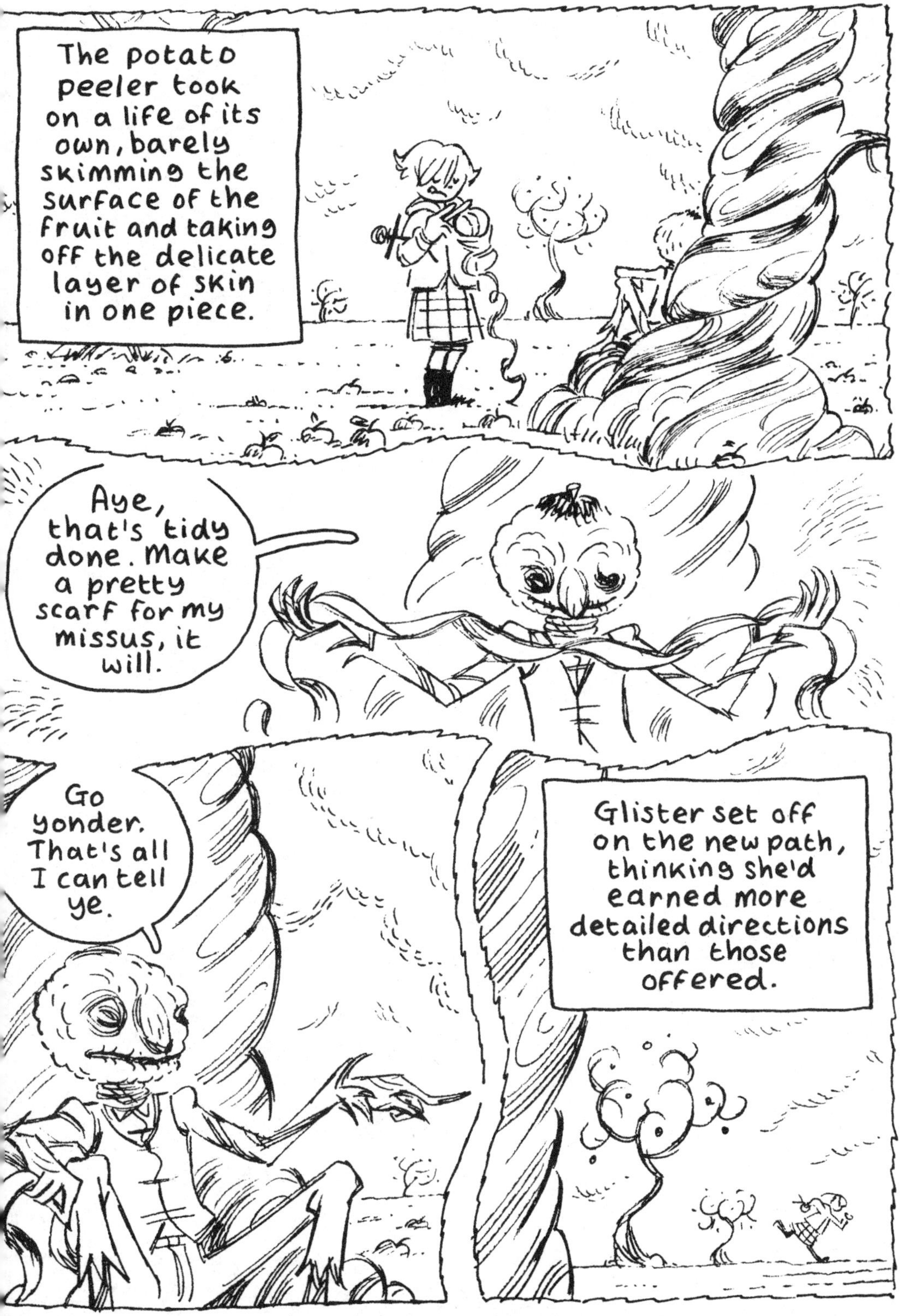
The potato peeler took on a life of its own, barely skimming the surface of the fruit and taking off the delicate layer of skin in one piece.
Aye, that's tidy done. Make a pretty scarf for my missus, it will.
Go yonder. That's all I can tell ye.
Glister set off on the new path, thinking she'd earned more detailed directions than those offered.

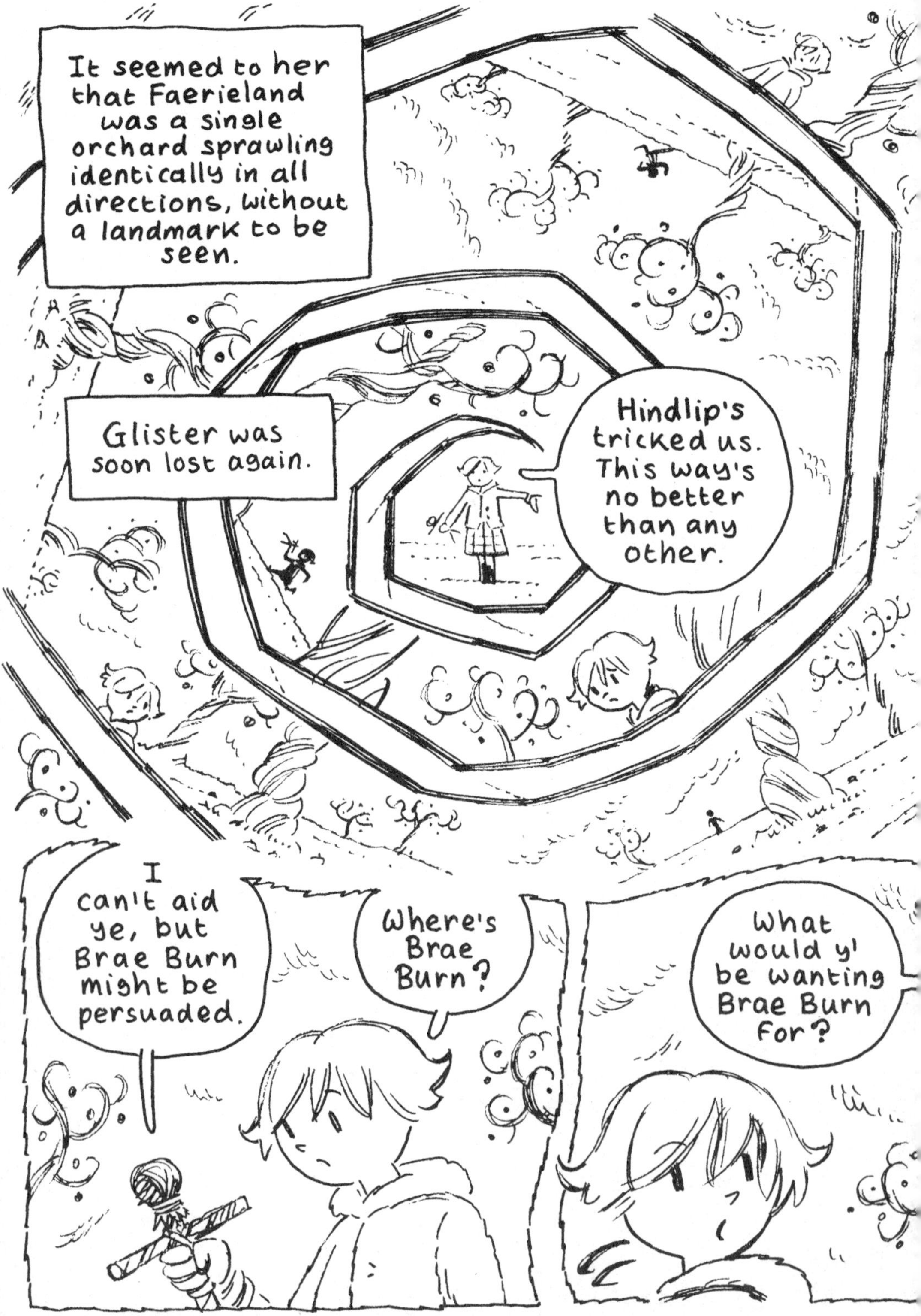

It seemed to her that Faerieland was a single orchard sprawling identically in all directions, without a landmark to be seen.
Glister was soon lost again.
Hindlip's tricked us. This way's no better than any other.
I can't aid ye, but Brae Burn might be persuaded.
Where's Brae Burn?
What would y' be wanting Brae Burn for?

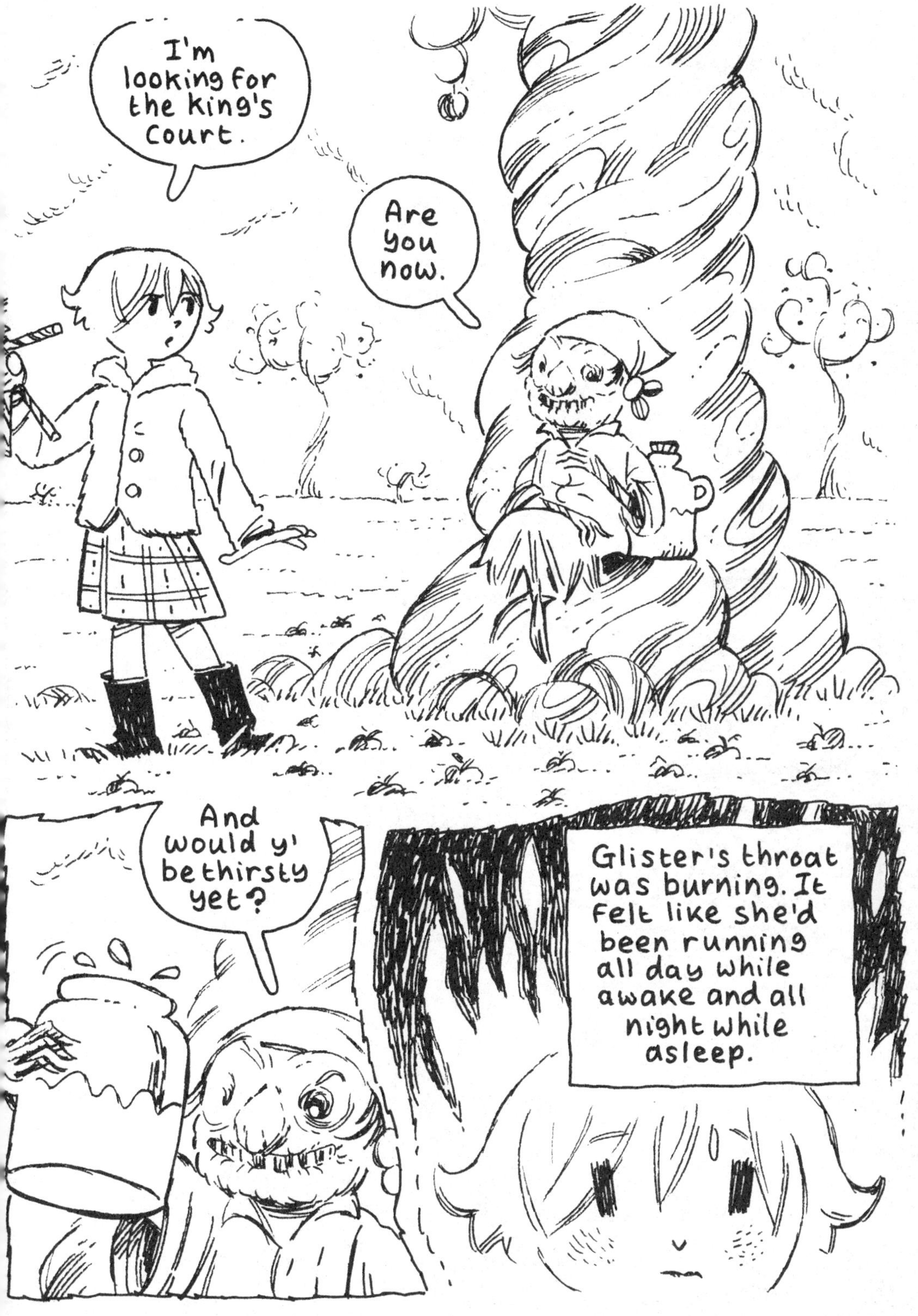
I'm looking for the king's court.
Are you now.
And would y' be thirsty yet?
Glister's throat was burning. It felt like she'd been running all day while awake and all night while asleep.

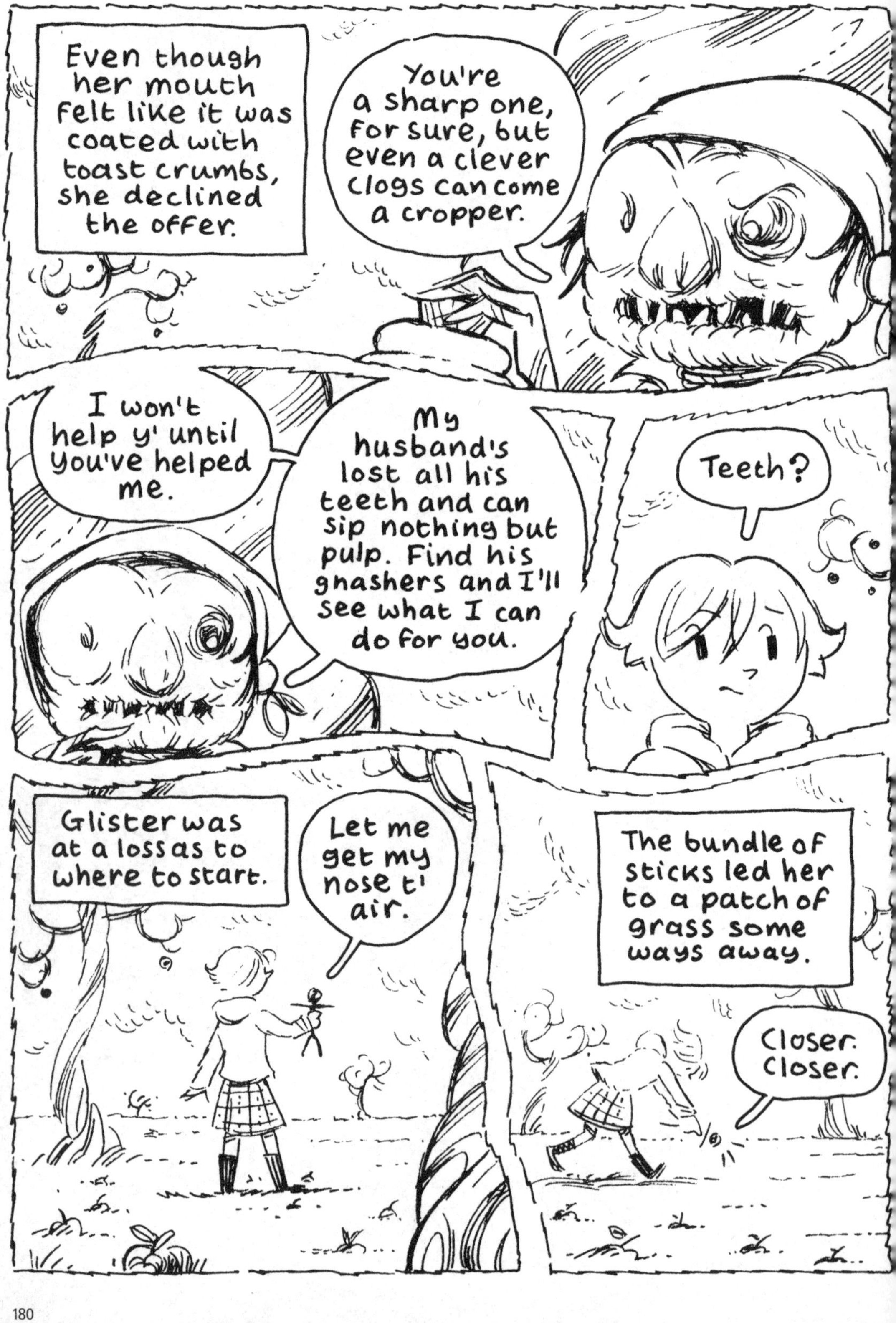
Even though her mouth felt like it was coated with toast crumbs, she declined the offer.
You're a sharp one, for sure, but even a clever clogs can come a cropper.
I won't help y' until you've helped me.
My husband's lost all his teeth and can sip nothing but pulp. Find his gnashers and I'll see what I can do for you.
Teeth?
Glister was at a loss as to where to start.
Let me get my nose t' air.
The bundle of sticks led her to a patch of grass some ways away.
Closer. Closer.

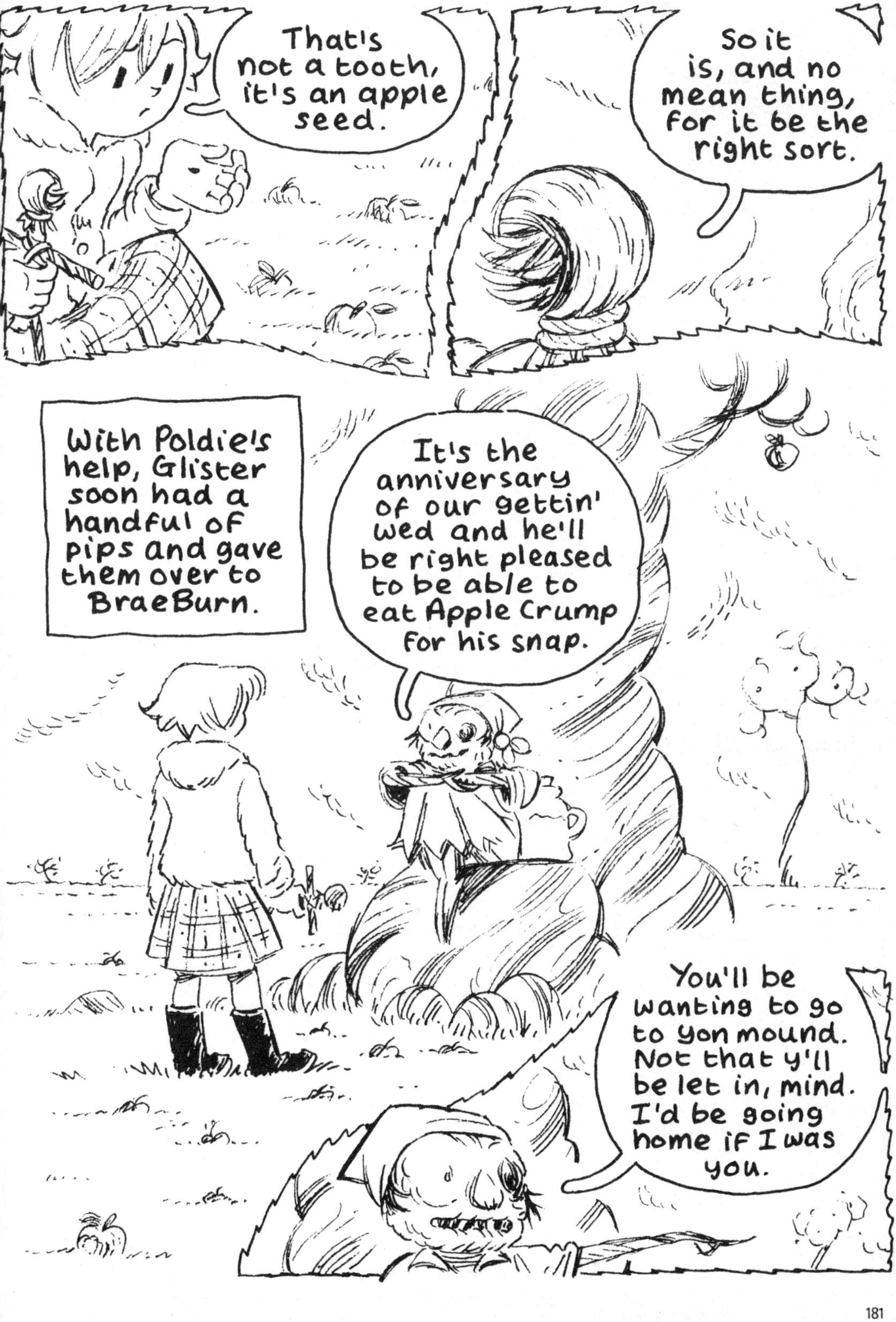
That's not a tooth, it's an apple seed.
So it is, and no mean thing, for it be the right sort.
With Poldie's help, Glister soon had a handful of pips and gave them over to BraeBurn.
It's the anniversary of our gettin' wed and he'll be right pleased to be able to eat Apple Crump for his snap.
You'll be wanting to go to yon mound. Not that y'll be let in, mind. I'd be going home if I was you.

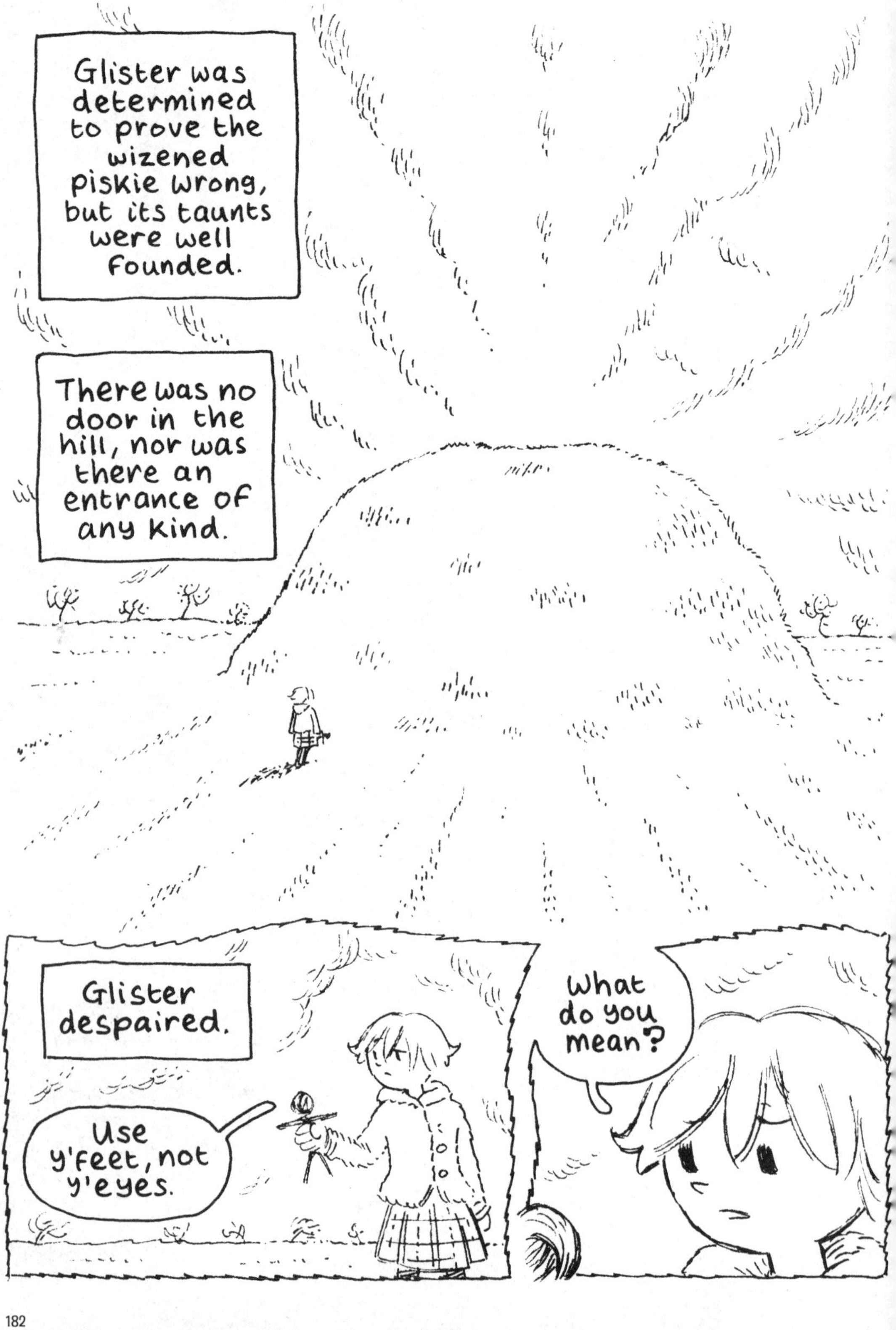
Glister was determined to prove the wizened piskie wrong, but its taunts were well founded.
There was no door in the hill, nor was there an entrance of any kind.
Glister despaired.
Use y'feet, not y'eyes.
What do you mean?

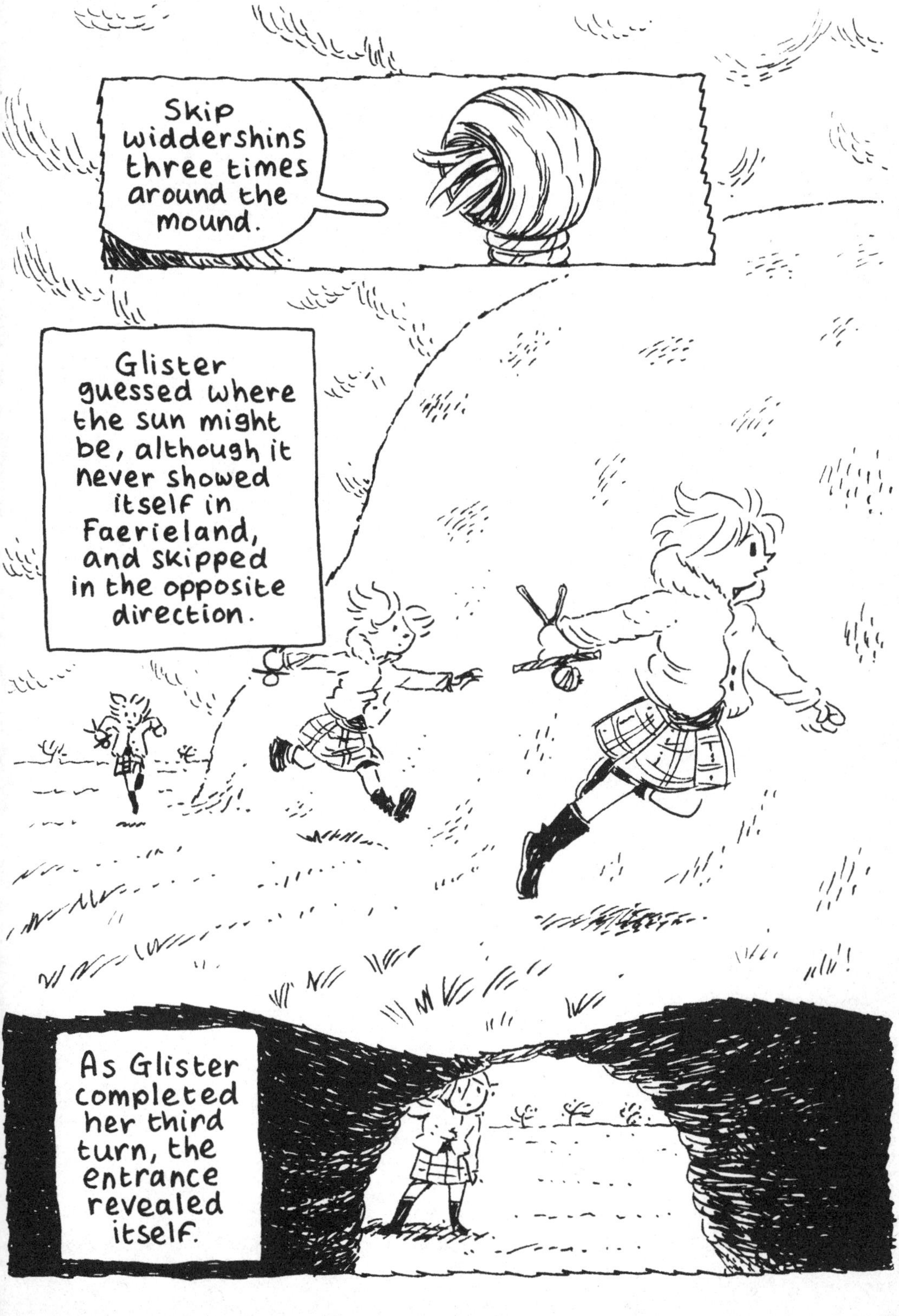
Skip widdershins three times around the mound.
Glister guessed where the sun might be, although it never showed itself in Faerieland, and skipped in the opposite direction.
As Glister completed her third turn, the entrance revealed itself.

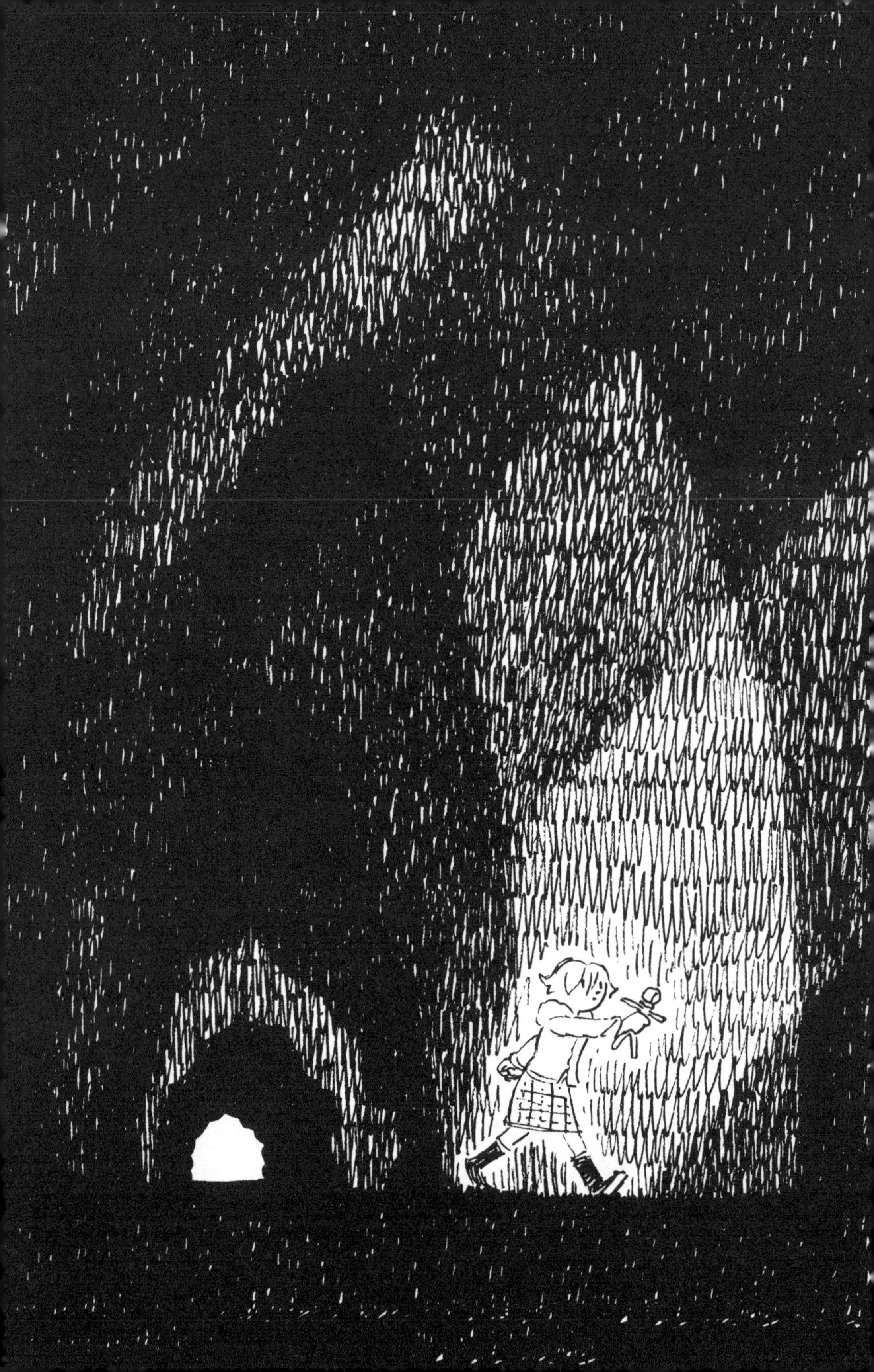

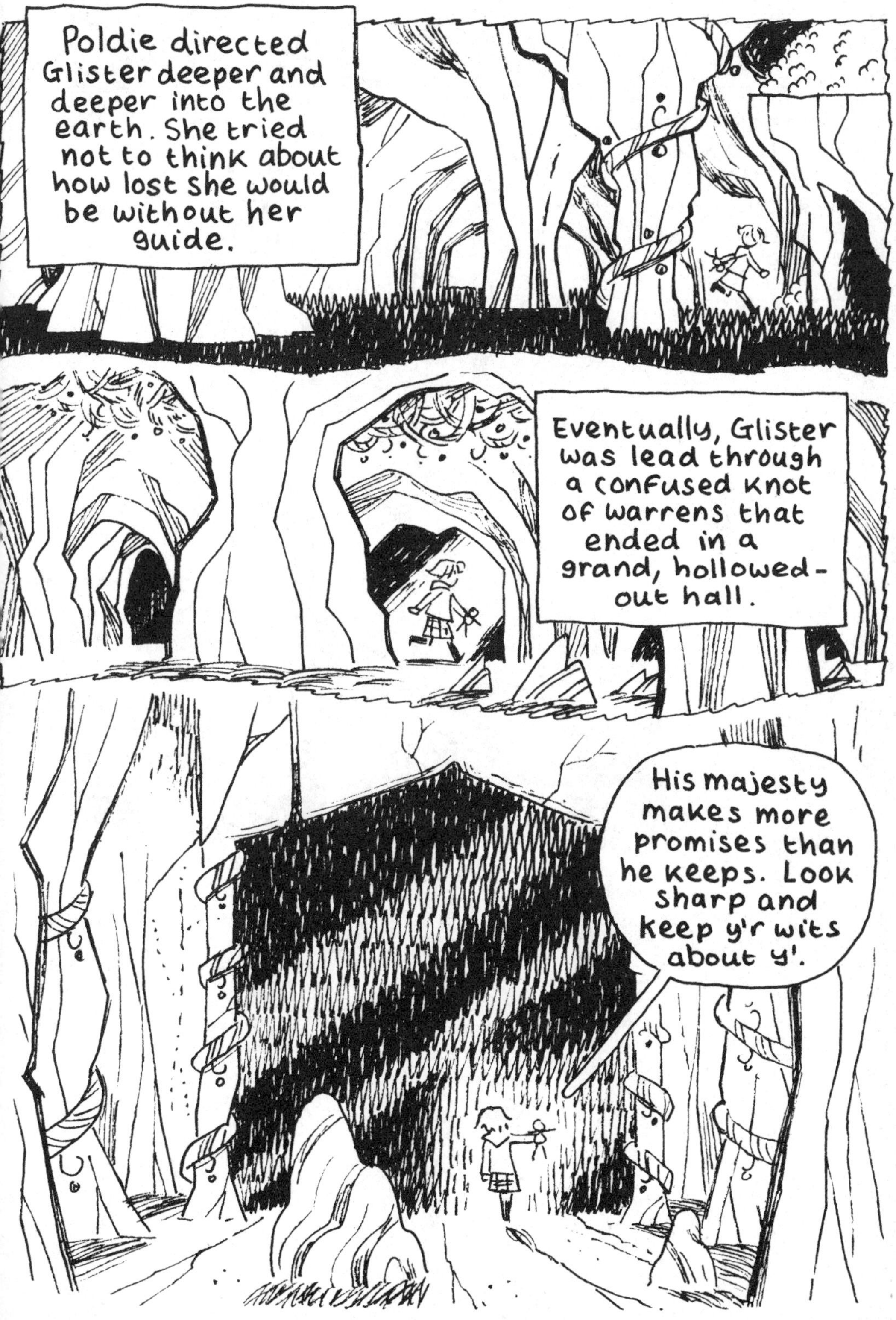
Poldie directed Glister deeper and deeper into the earth. She tried not to think about how lost she would be without her guide.
Eventually, Glister was lead through a confused knot of warrens that ended in a grand, hollowed-out hall.
His majesty makes more promises than he keeps. Look sharp and keep y'r wits about y'.

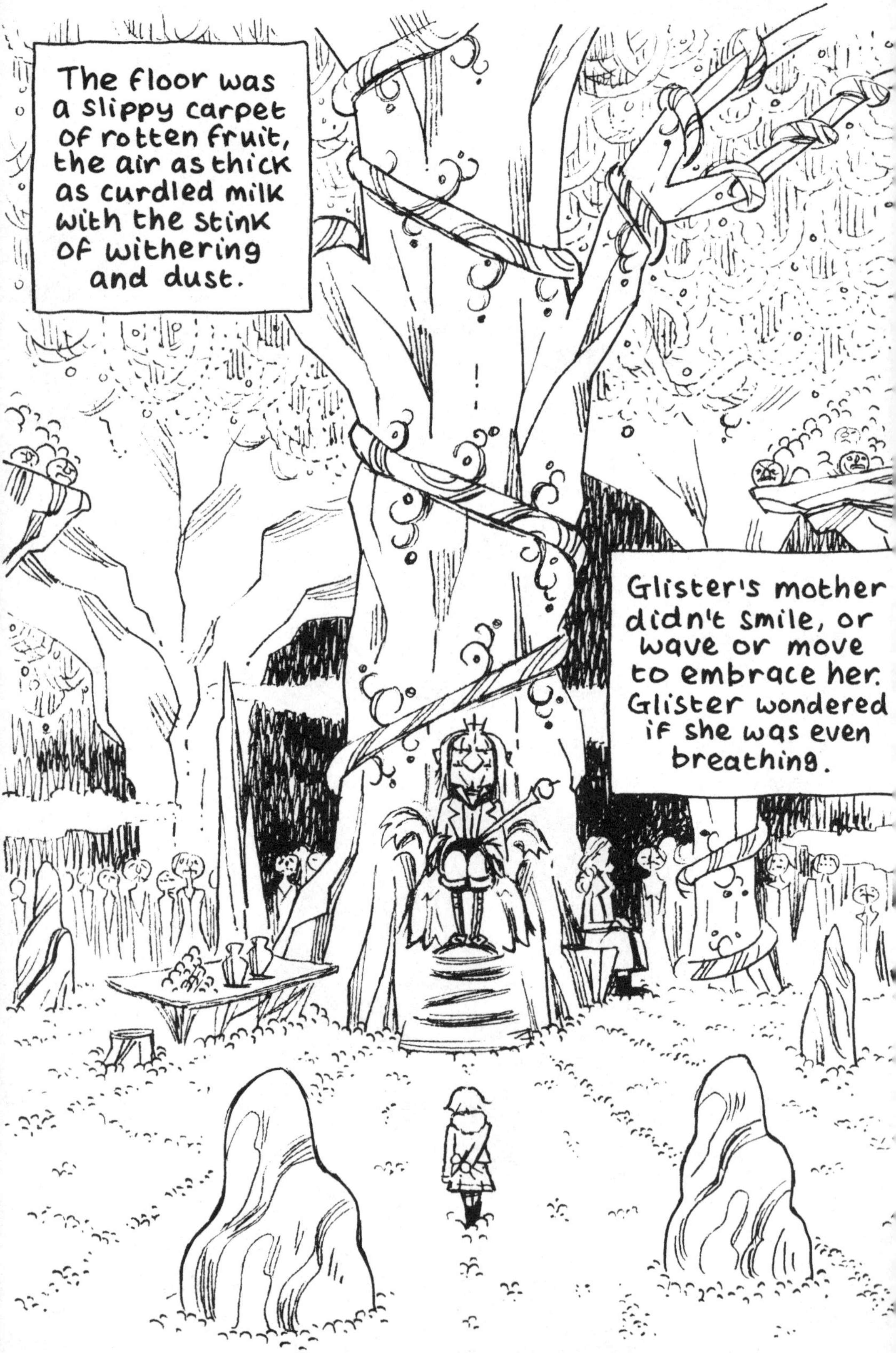
The floor was a slippy carpet of rotten fruit, the air as thick as curdled milk with the stink of withering and dust.
Glister's mother didn't smile, or wave or move to embrace her. Glister wondered if she was even breathing.

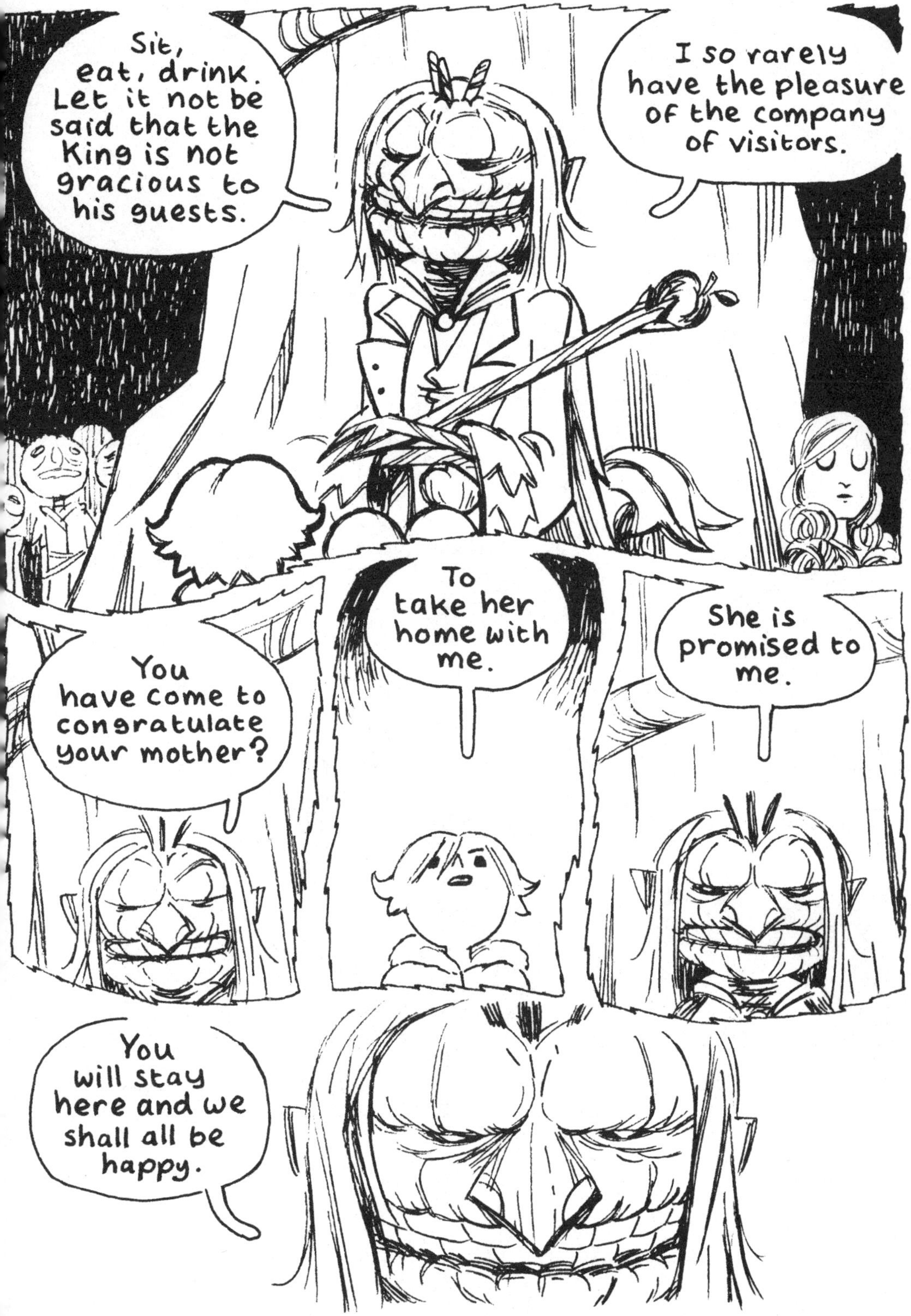
Sit, eat, drink. Let it not be said that the King is not gracious to his guests.
I so rarely have the pleasure of the company of visitors.
You have come to congratulate your mother?
To take her home with me.
She is promised to me.
You will stay here and we shall all be happy.

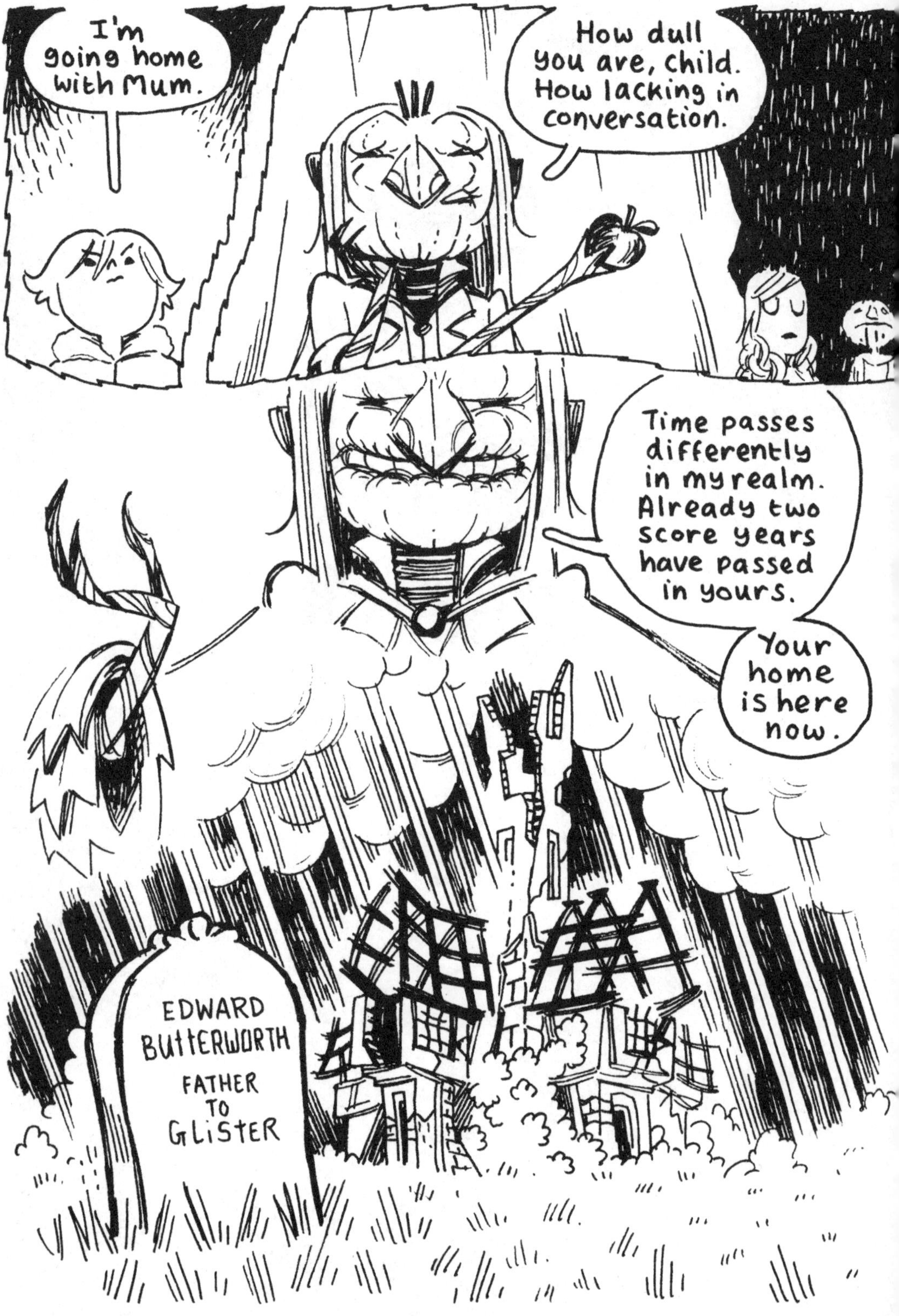
I'm going home with Mum.
How dull you are, child. How lacking in conversation.
Time passes differently in my realm. Already two score years have passed in yours.
Your home is here now.
EDWARD BUTTERWORTH
FATHER TO GLISTER

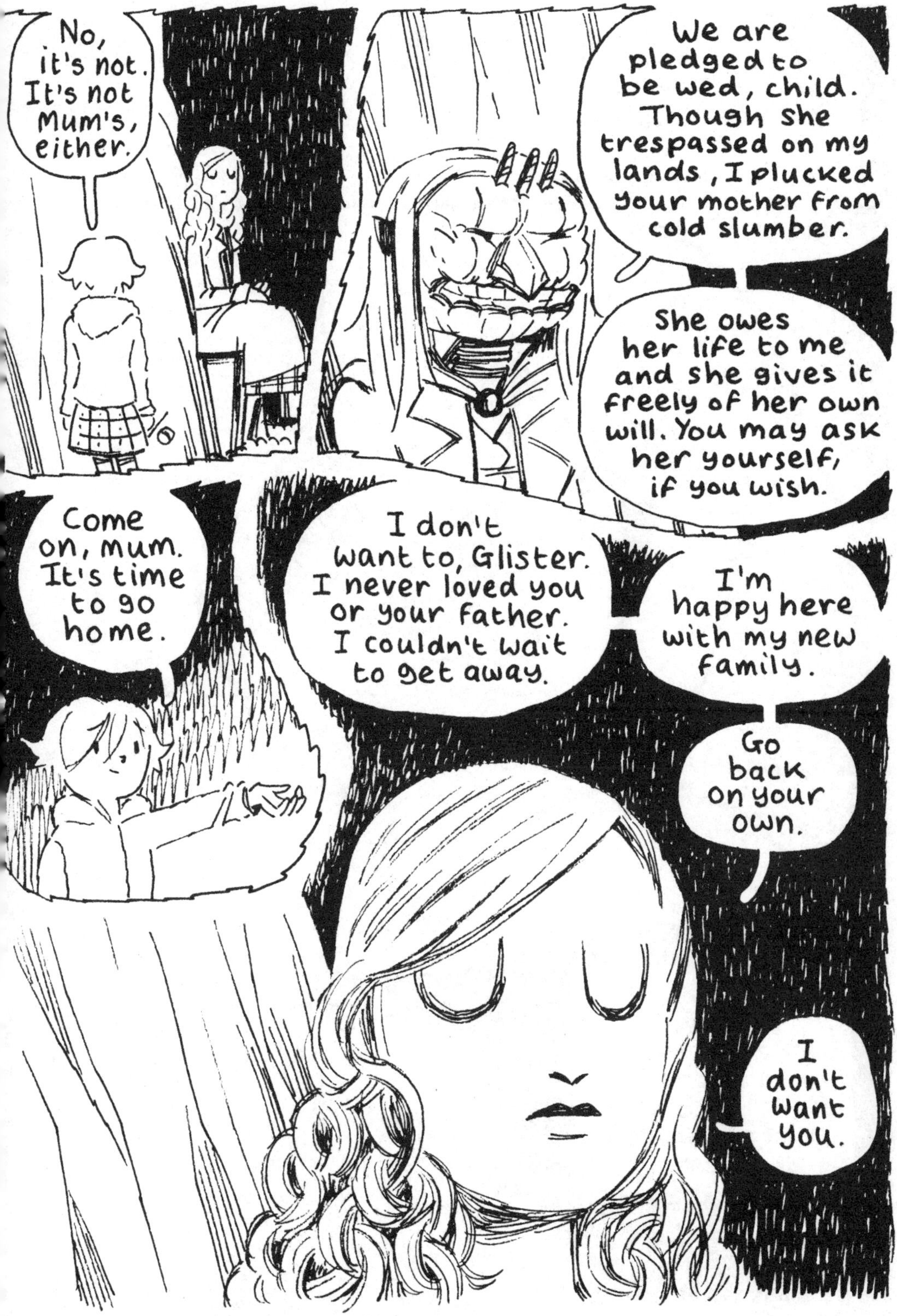
No, it's not. It's not Mum's, either.
We are pledged to be wed, child. Though she trespassed on my lands, I plucked your mother from cold slumber.
She owes her life to me and she gives it freely of her own will. You may ask her yourself, if you wish.
Come on, mum. It's time to go home.
I don't want to, Glister. I never loved you or your father. I couldn't wait to get away.
I'm happy here with my new family.
Go back on your own.
I don't want you.

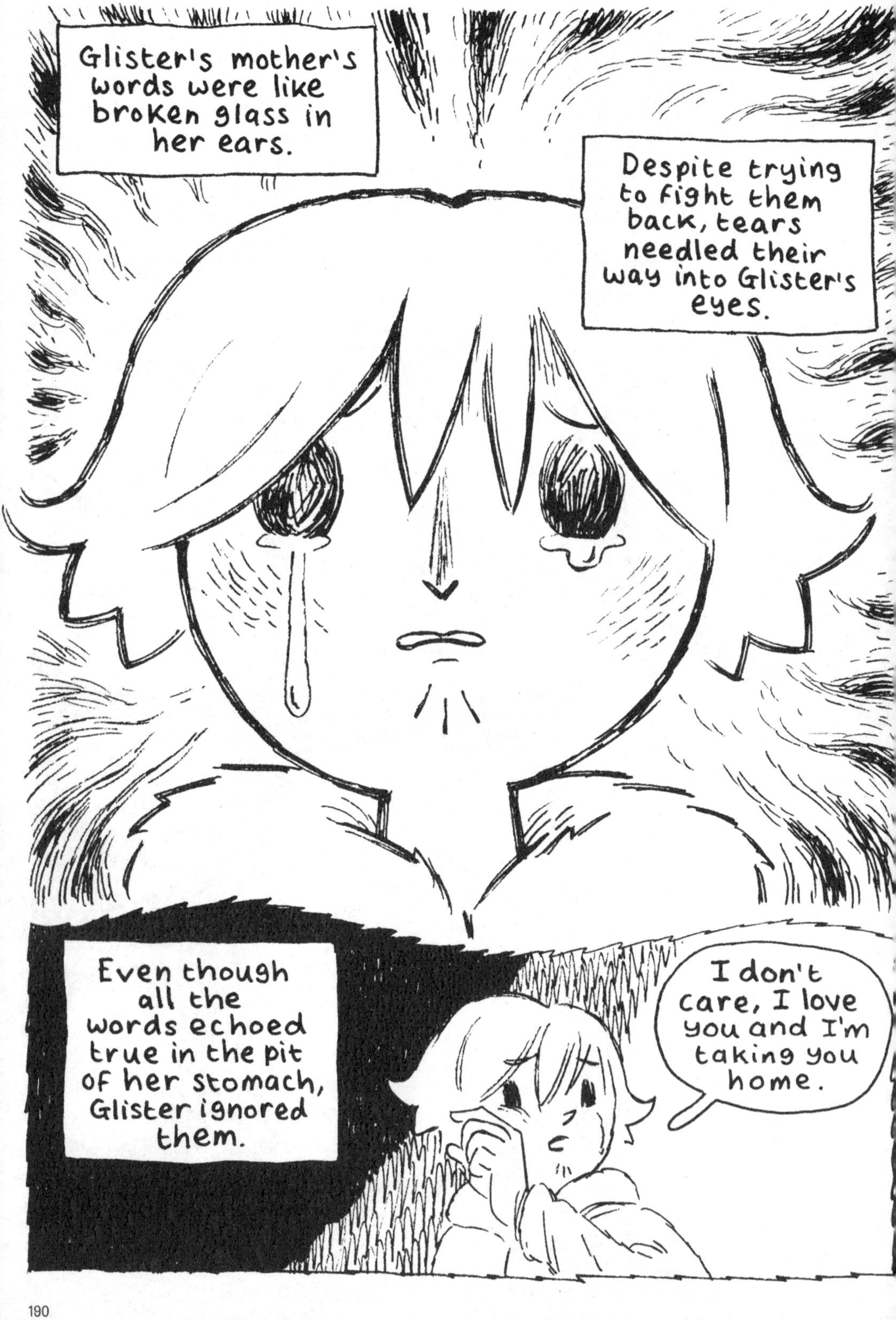
Glister's mother's words were like broken glass in her ears.
Despite trying to fight them back, tears needled their way into Glister's eyes.
Even though all the words echoed true in the pit of her stomach, Glister ignored them.
I don't care, I love you and I'm taking you home.

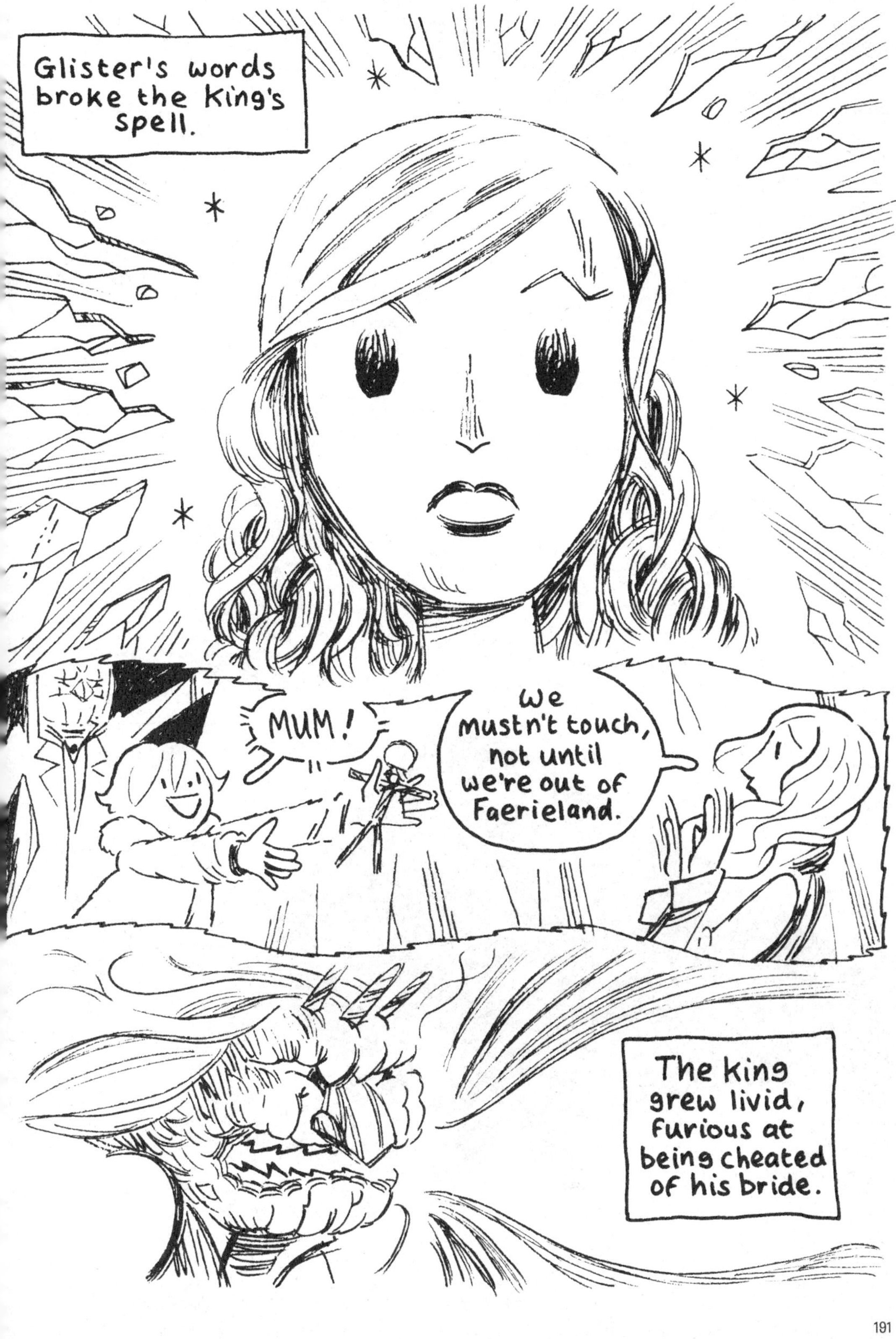

Glister's words broke the King's spell.
MUM!
We mustn't touch, not until we're out of Faerieland.
The king grew livid, furious at being cheated of his bride.

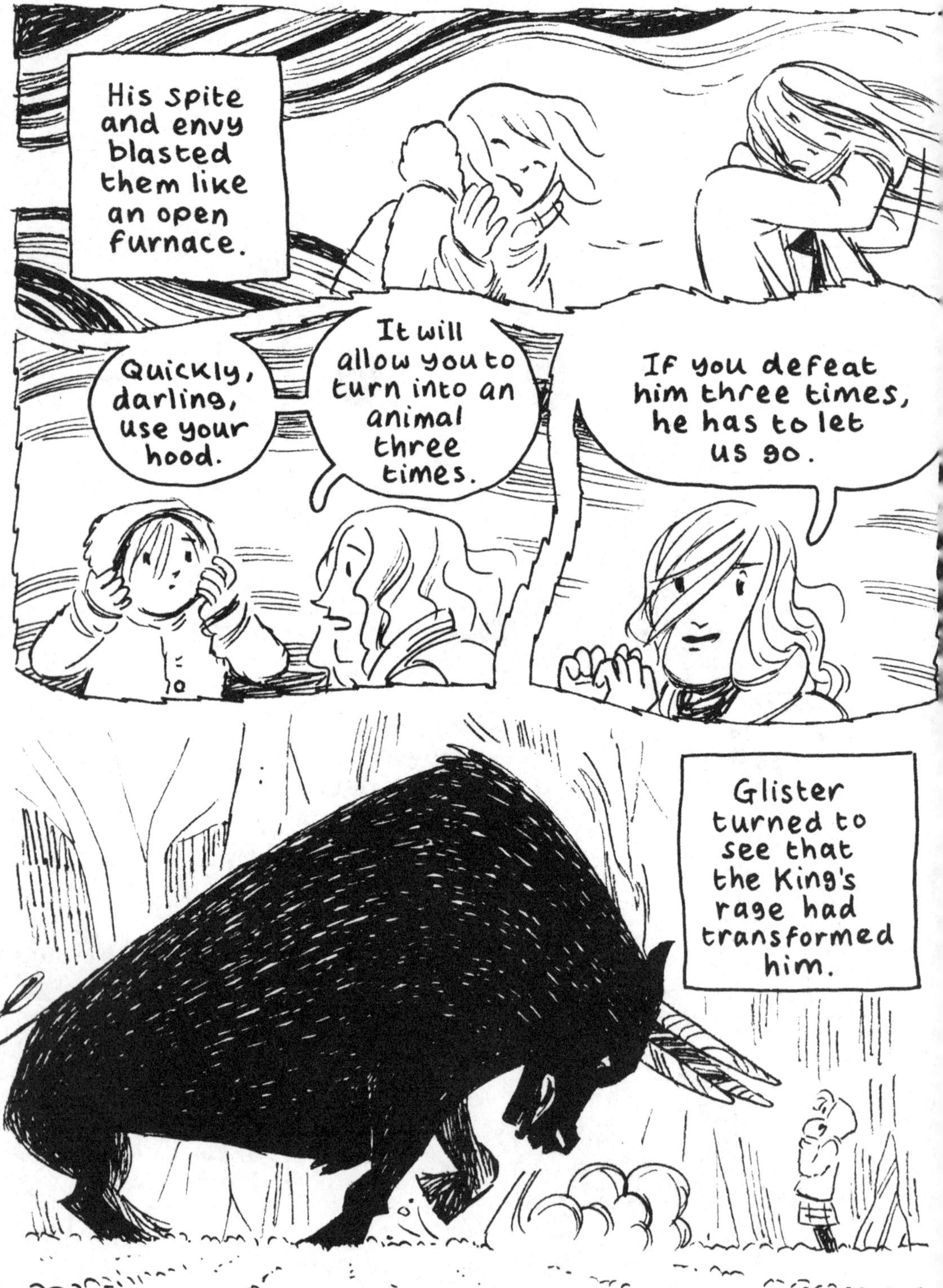
His spite and envy blasted them like an open furnace.
Quickly, darling, use your hood.
It will allow you to turn into an animal three times.
If you defeat him three times, he has to let us go.
Glister turned to see that the King's rage had transformed him.

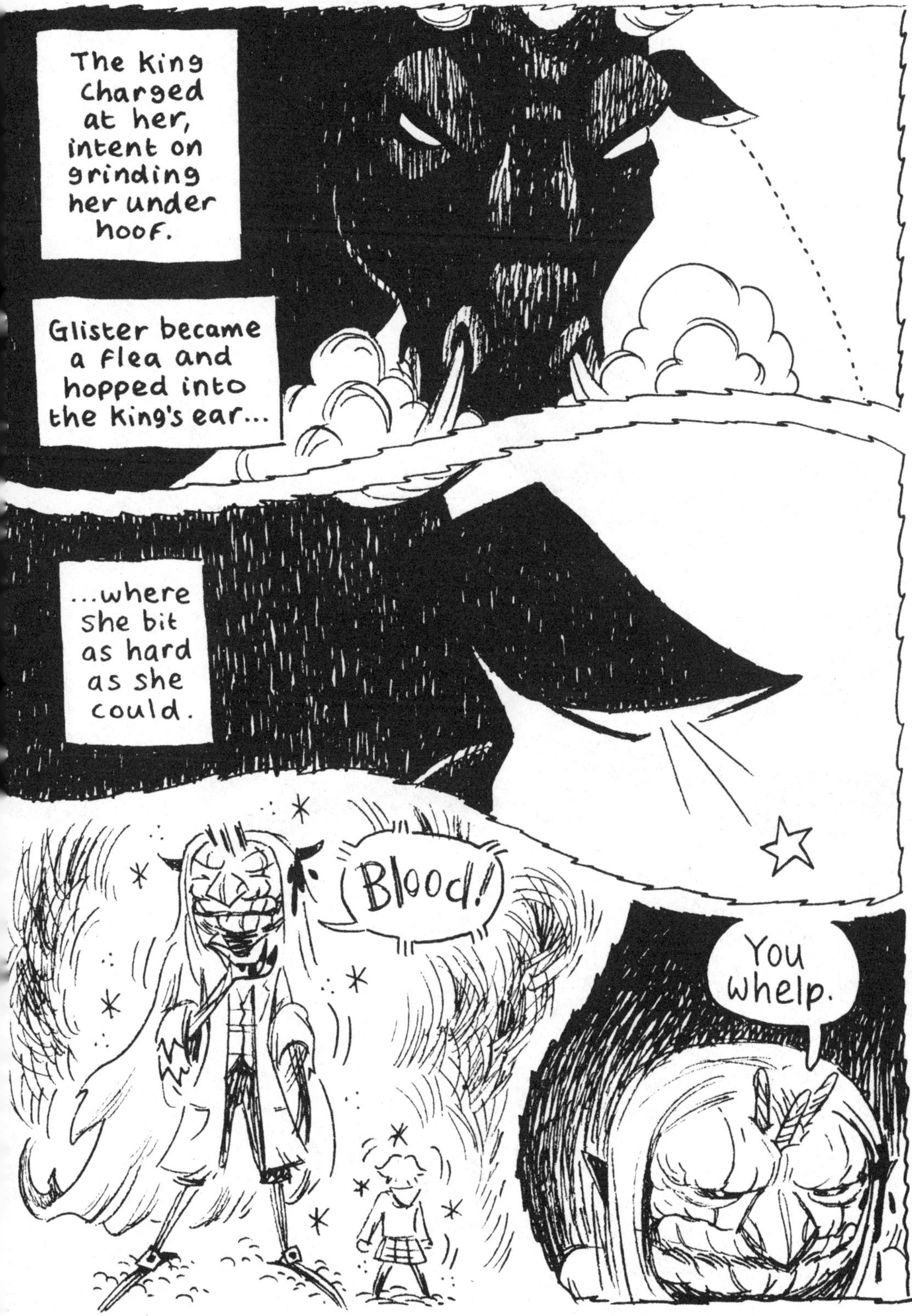

The king charged at her, intent on grinding her under hoof.
Glister became a flea and hopped into the king's ear...
...where she bit as hard as she could.
Blood!
You whelp.

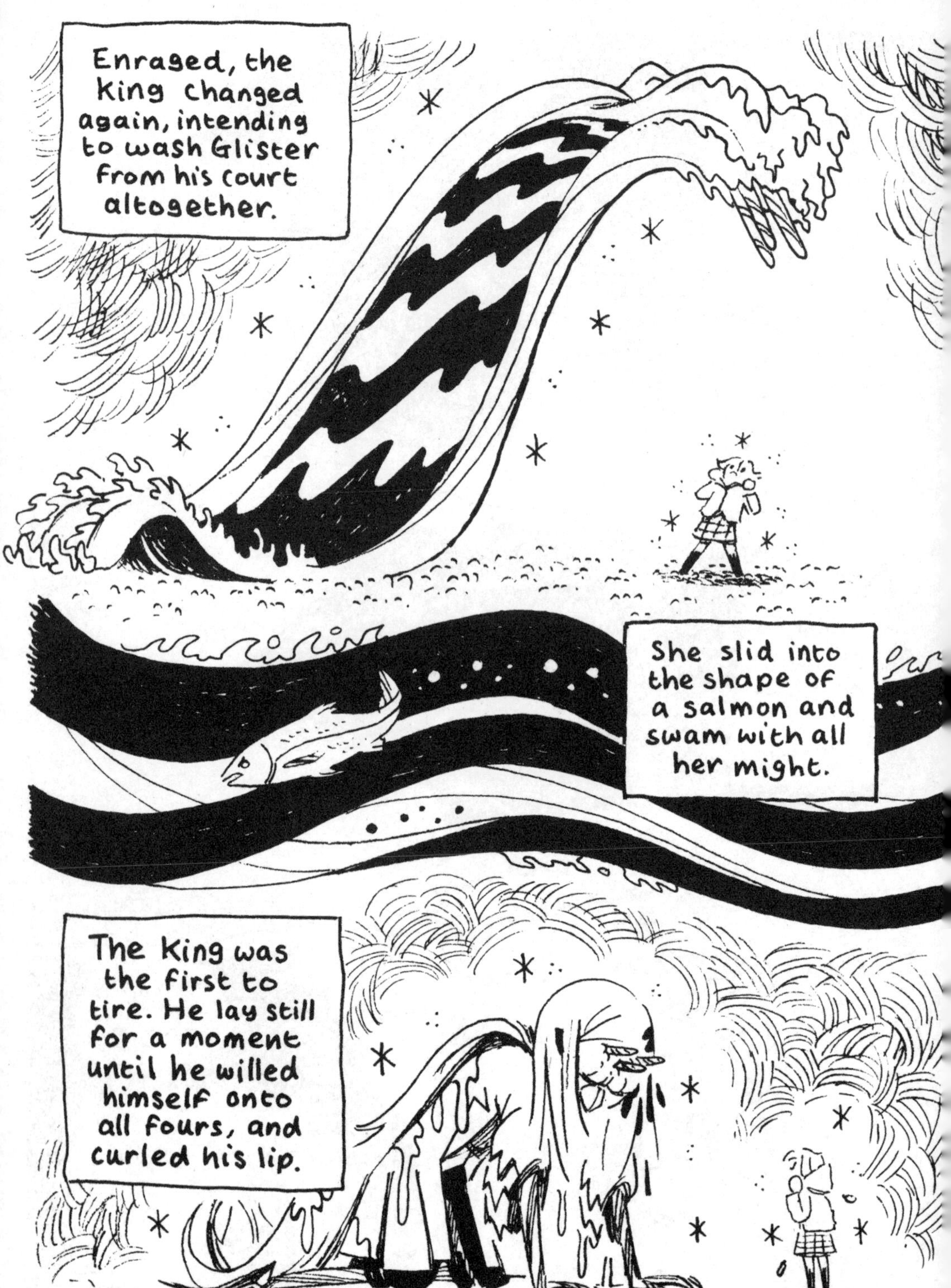
Enraged, the King changed again, intending to wash Glister from his court altogether.
She slid into the shape of a salmon and swam with all her might.
The King was the first to tire. He lay still for a moment until he willed himself onto all fours, and curled his lip.

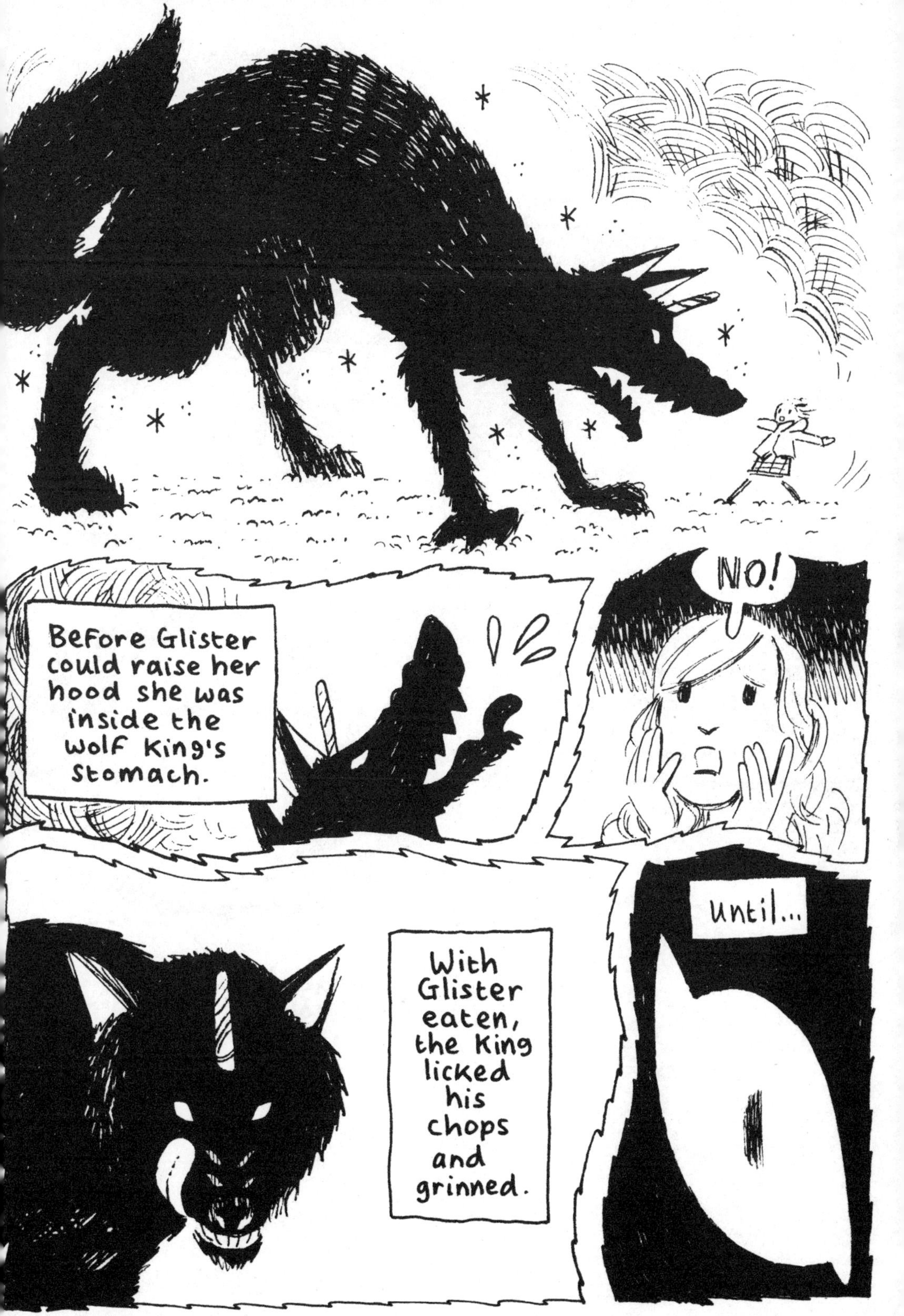
Before Glister could raise her hood she was inside the wolf King's stomach.
NO!
With Glister eaten, the King licked his chops and grinned.
until...

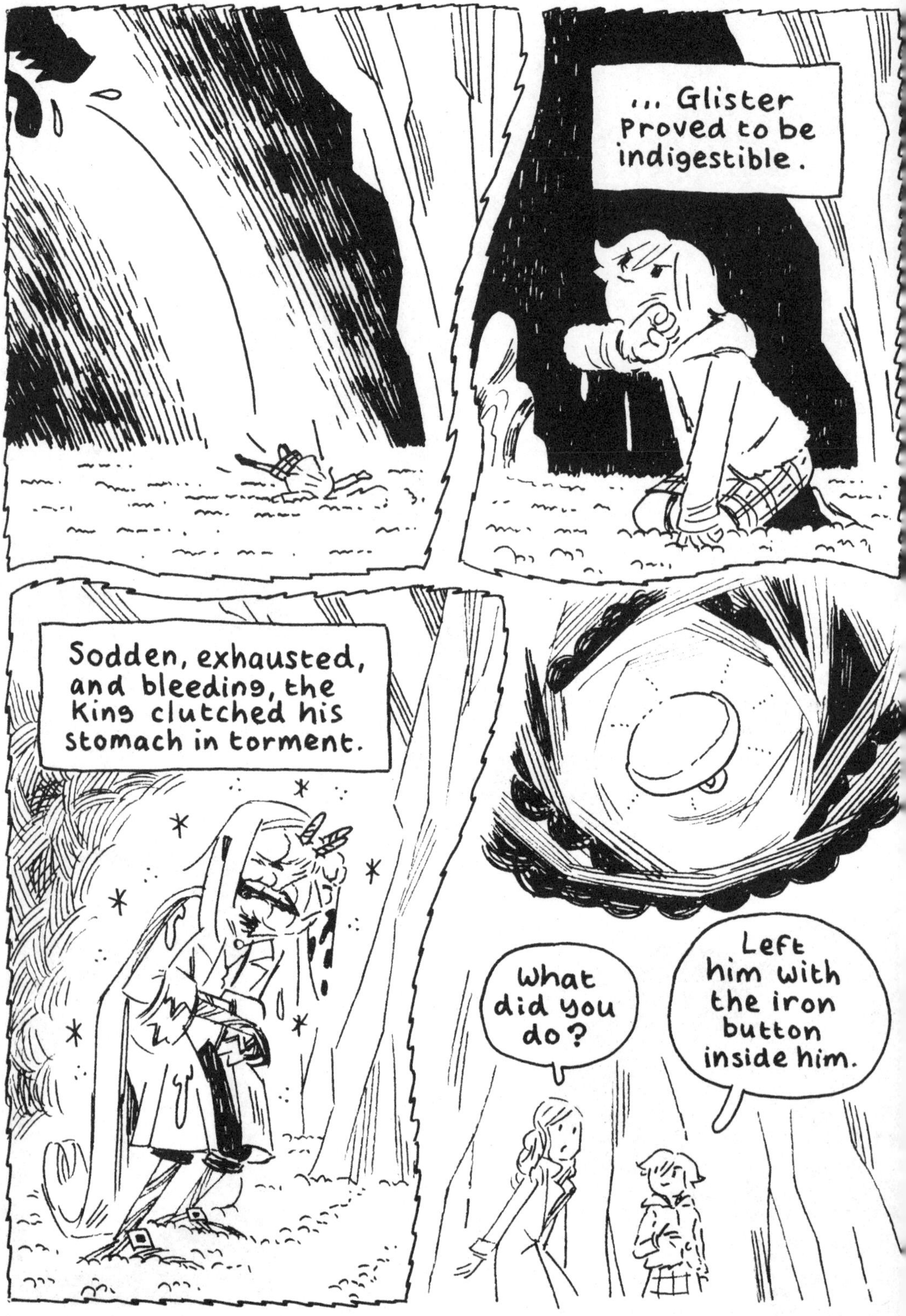
... Glister Proved to be indigestible.
Sodden, exhausted, and bleeding, the King clutched his stomach in torment.
What did you do?
Left him with the iron button inside him.

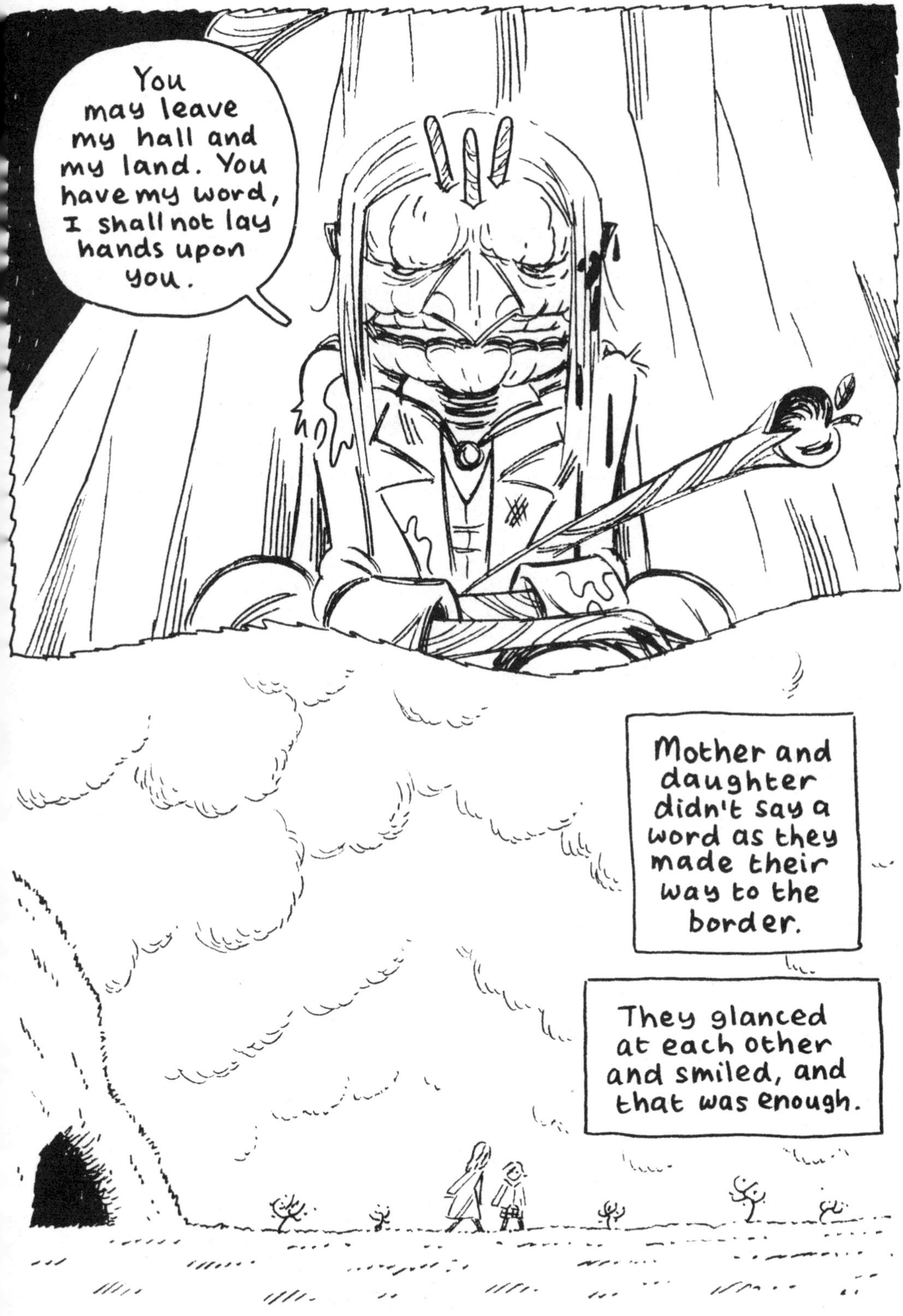
You may leave my hall and my land. You have my word, I shall not lay hands upon you.
Mother and daughter didn't say a word as they made their way to the border.
They glanced at each other and smiled, and that was enough.

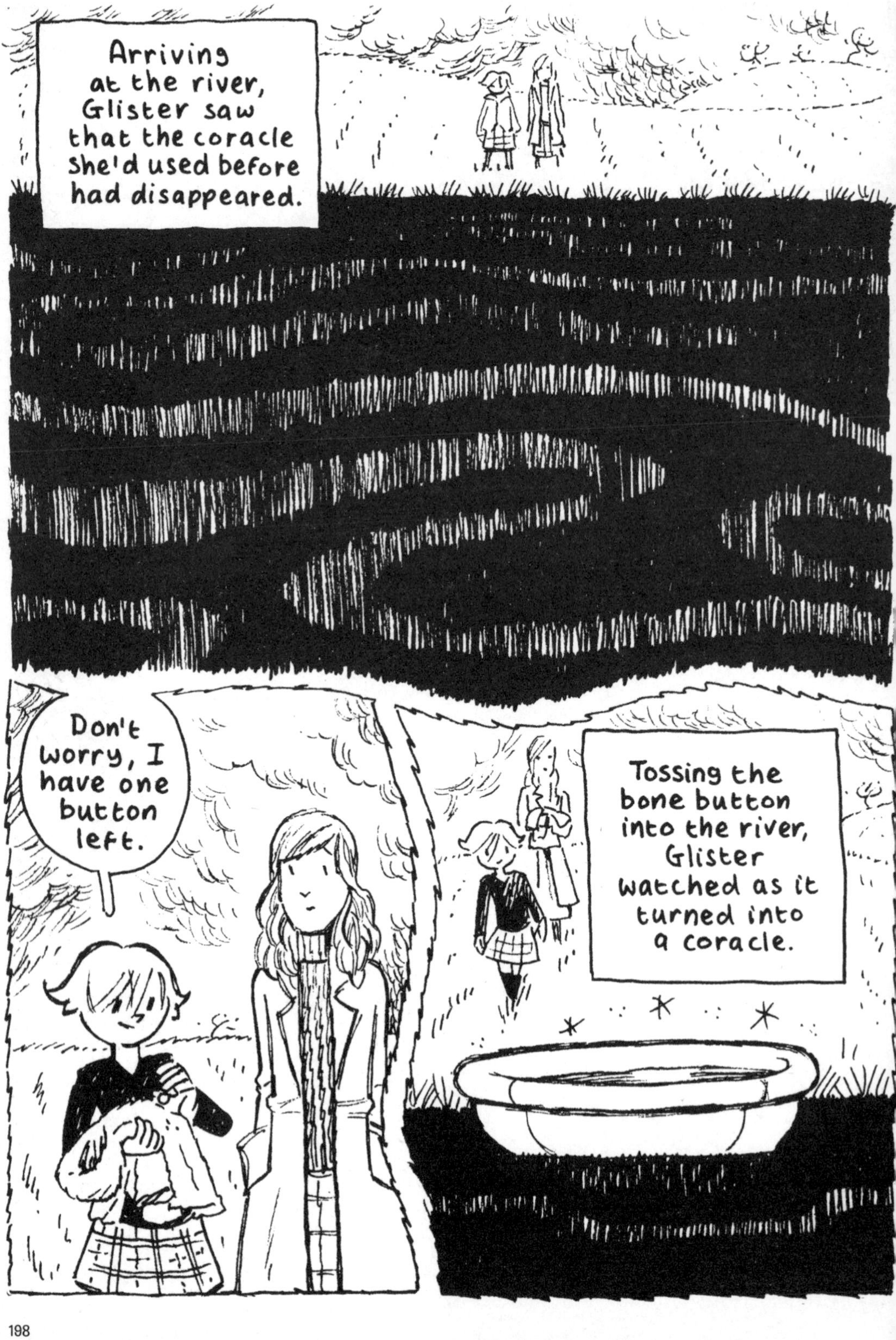
Arriving at the river, Glister saw that the coracle she'd used before had disappeared.
Don't worry, I have one button left.
Tossing the bone button into the river, Glister watched as it turned into a coracle.

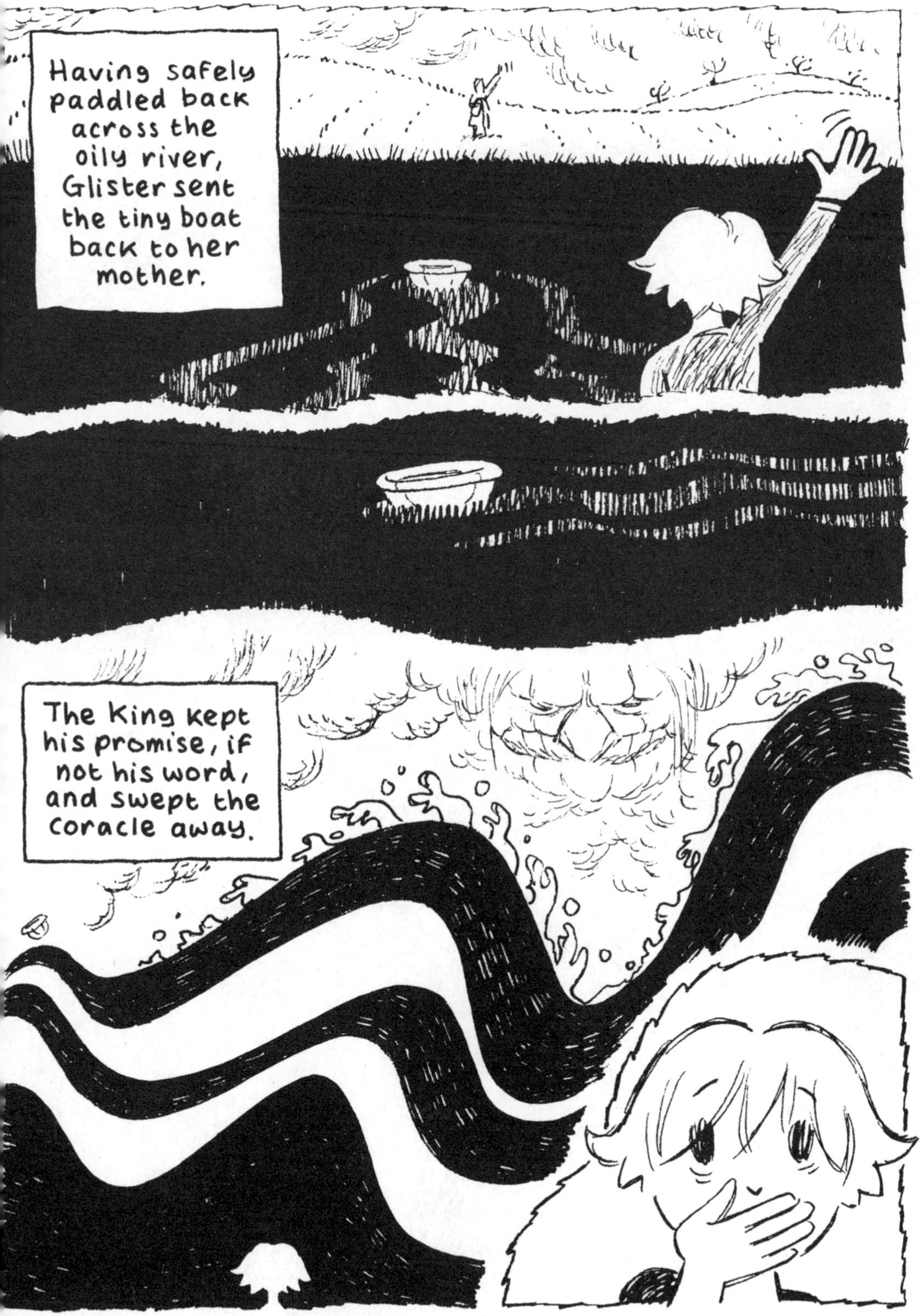
Having safely paddled back across the oily river, Glister sent the tiny boat back to her mother.
The King kept his promise, if not his word, and swept the coracle away.

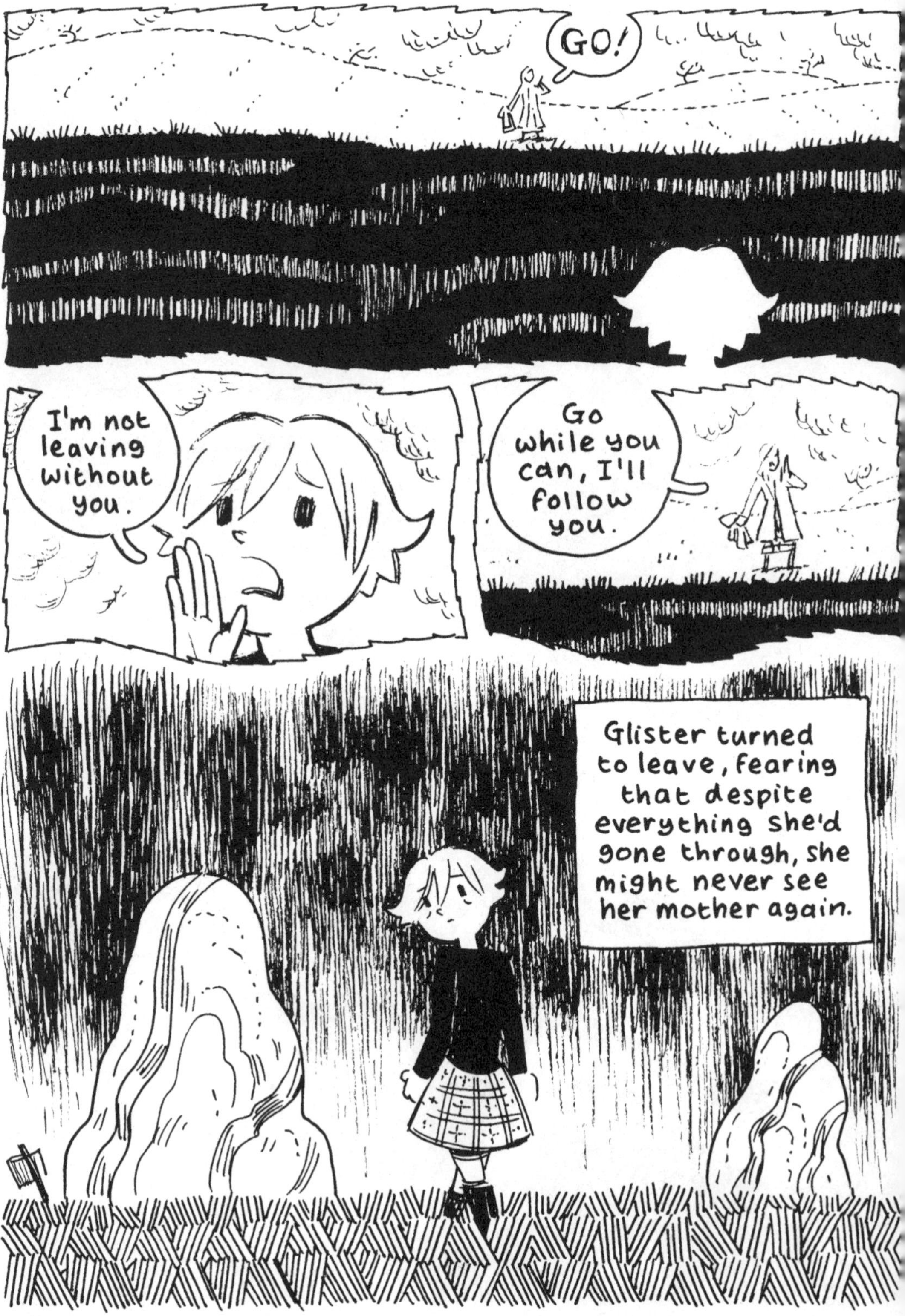
GO!
I'm not leaving without you.
Go while you can, I'll follow you.
Glister turned to leave, fearing that despite everything she'd gone through, she might never see her mother again.

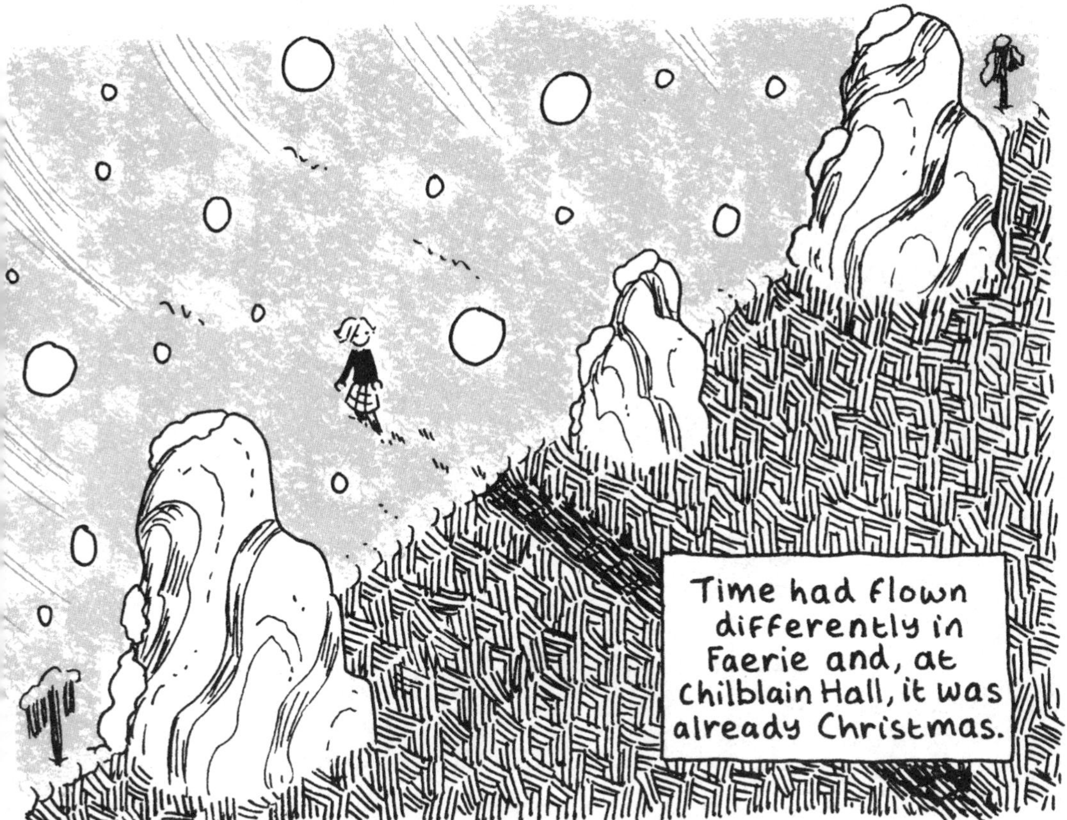
Time had flown differently in Faerie and, at Chilblain Hall, it was already Christmas.

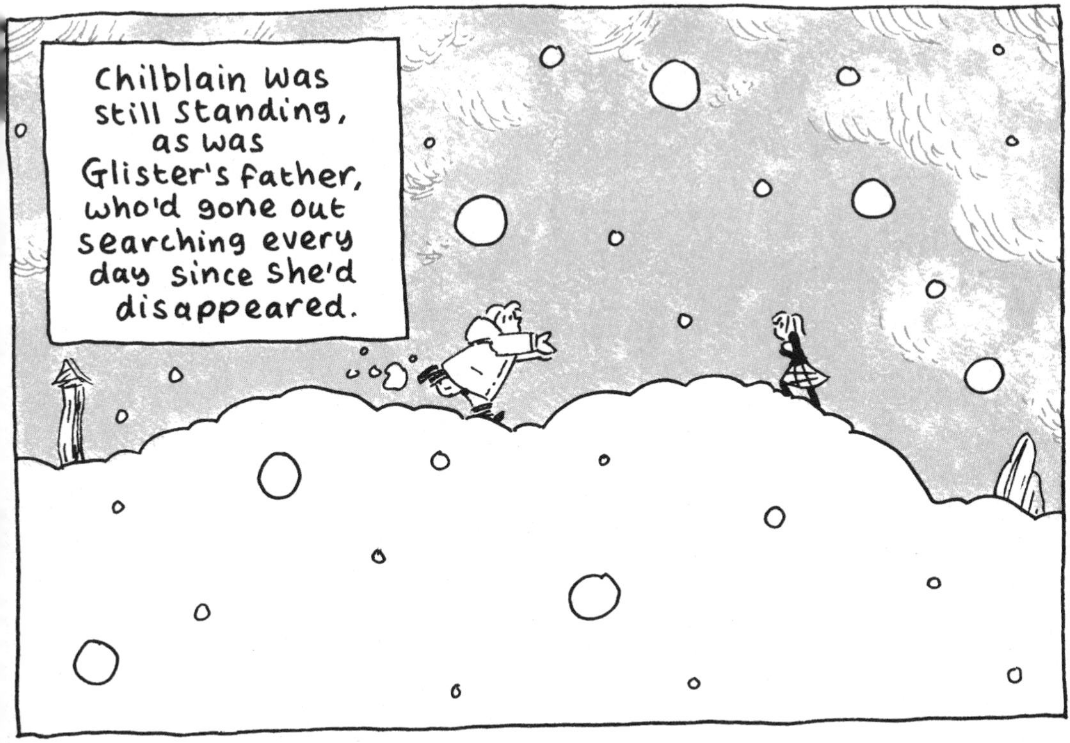
Chilblain was still standing, as was Glister's father, who'd gone out searching every day since she'd disappeared.

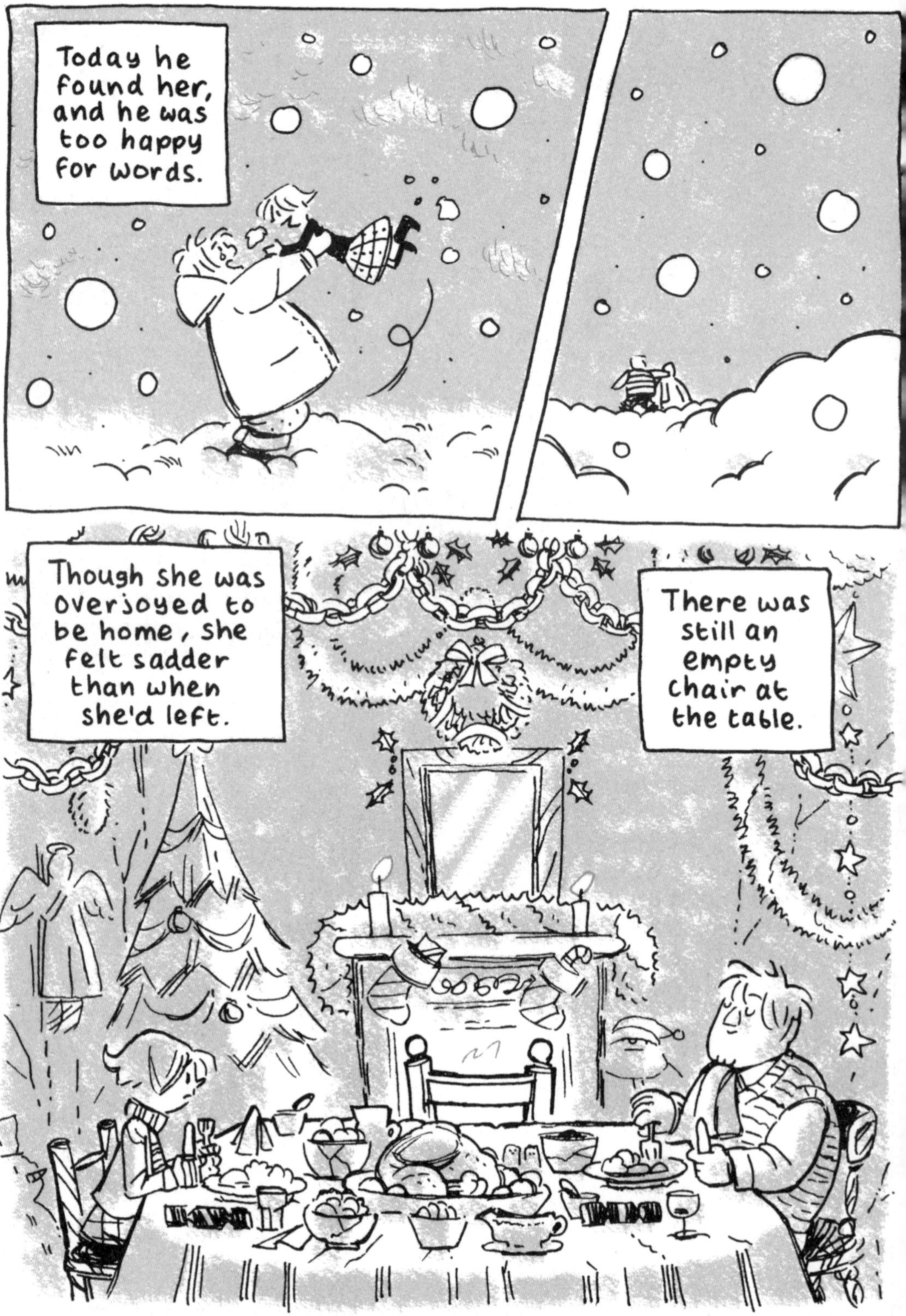
Today he found her, and he was too happy for words.
Though she was overjoyed to be home, she felt sadder than when she'd left.
There was still an empty chair at the table.

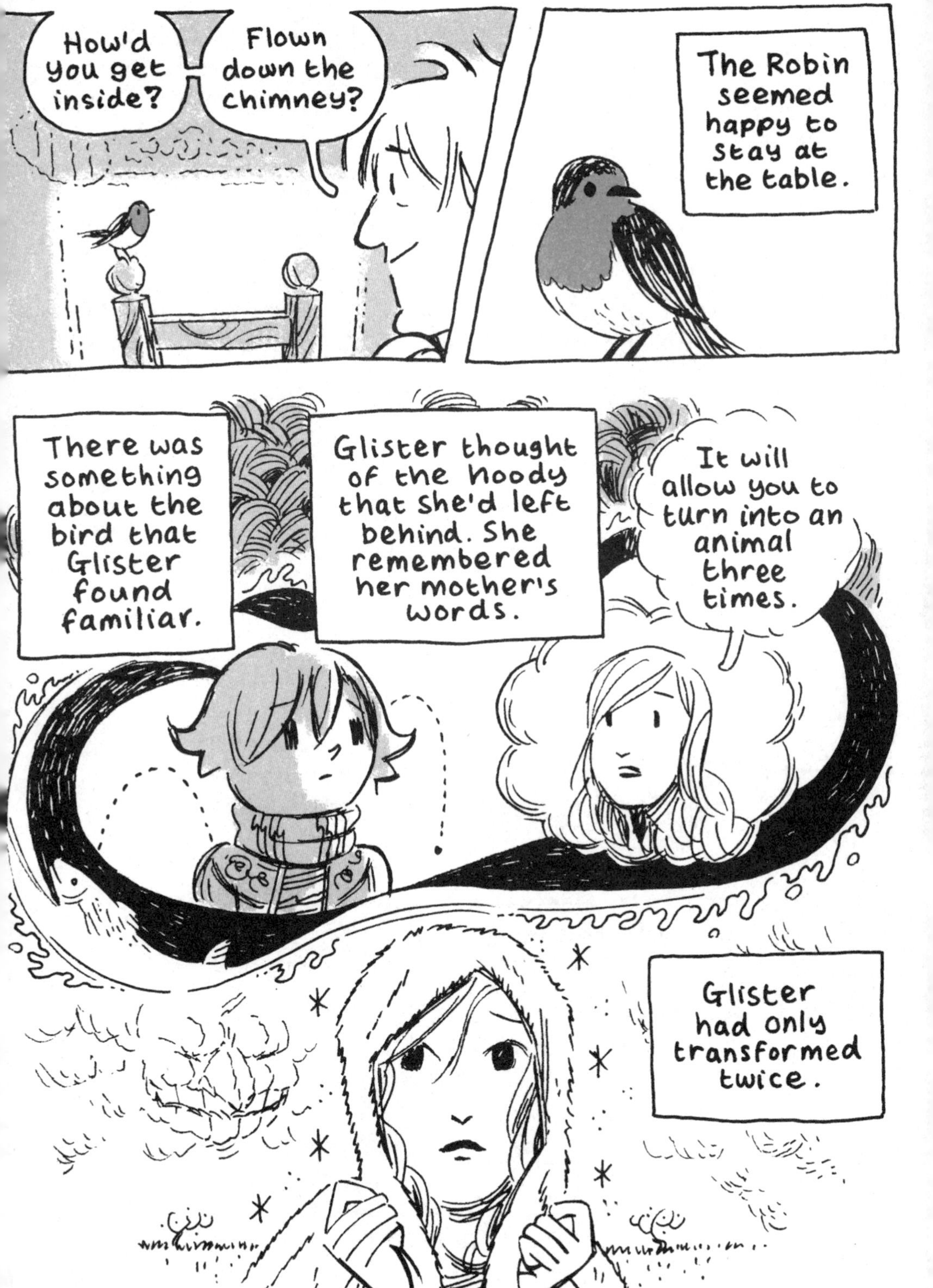
How'd you get inside?
Flown down the chimney?
The Robin seemed happy to stay at the table.
There was something about the bird that Glister found familiar.
Glister thought of the hoody that she'd left behind. She remembered her mother's words.
It will allow you to turn into an animal three times.
Glister had only transformed twice.

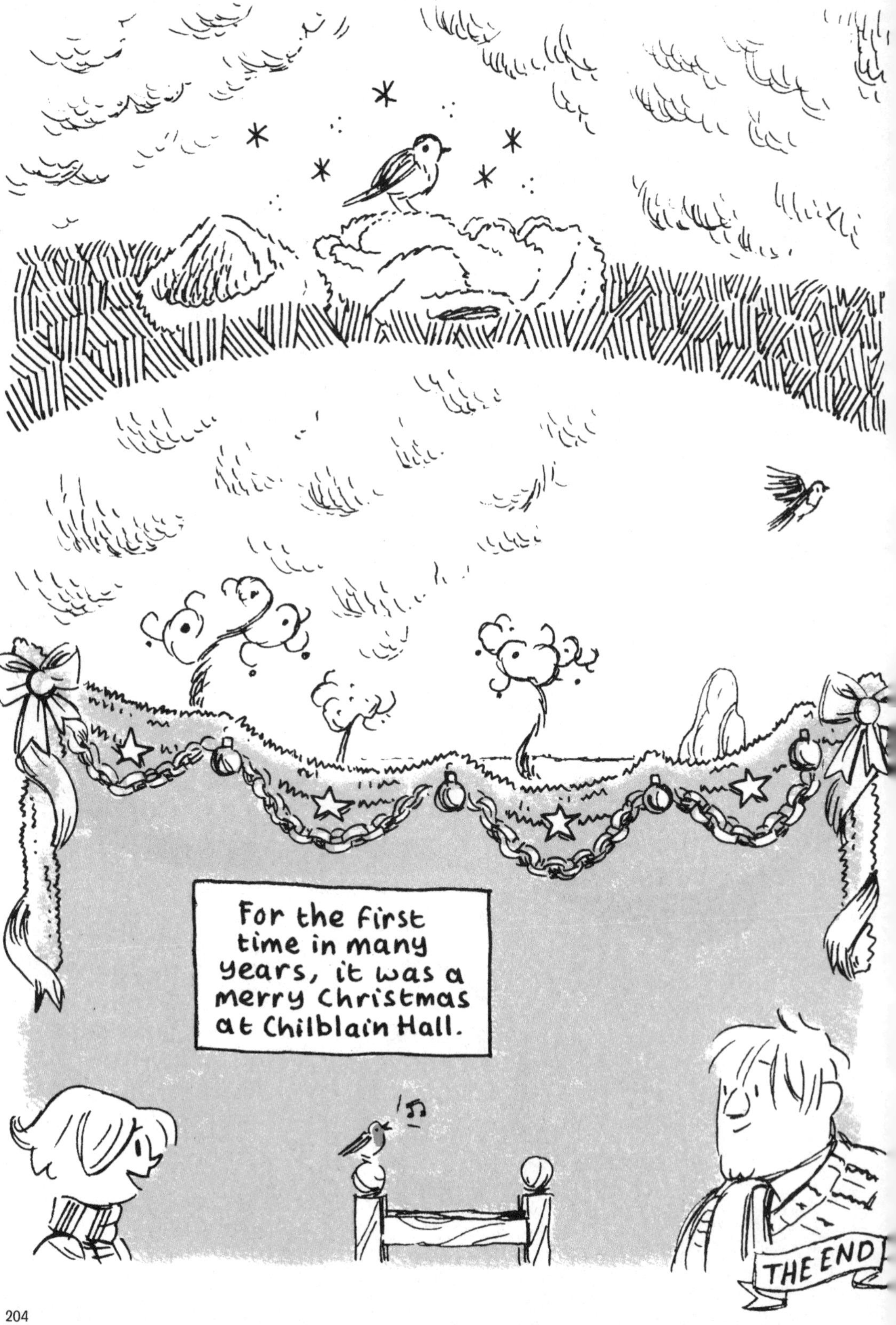
For the first time in many years, it was a merry Christmas at Chilblain Hall.
THE END

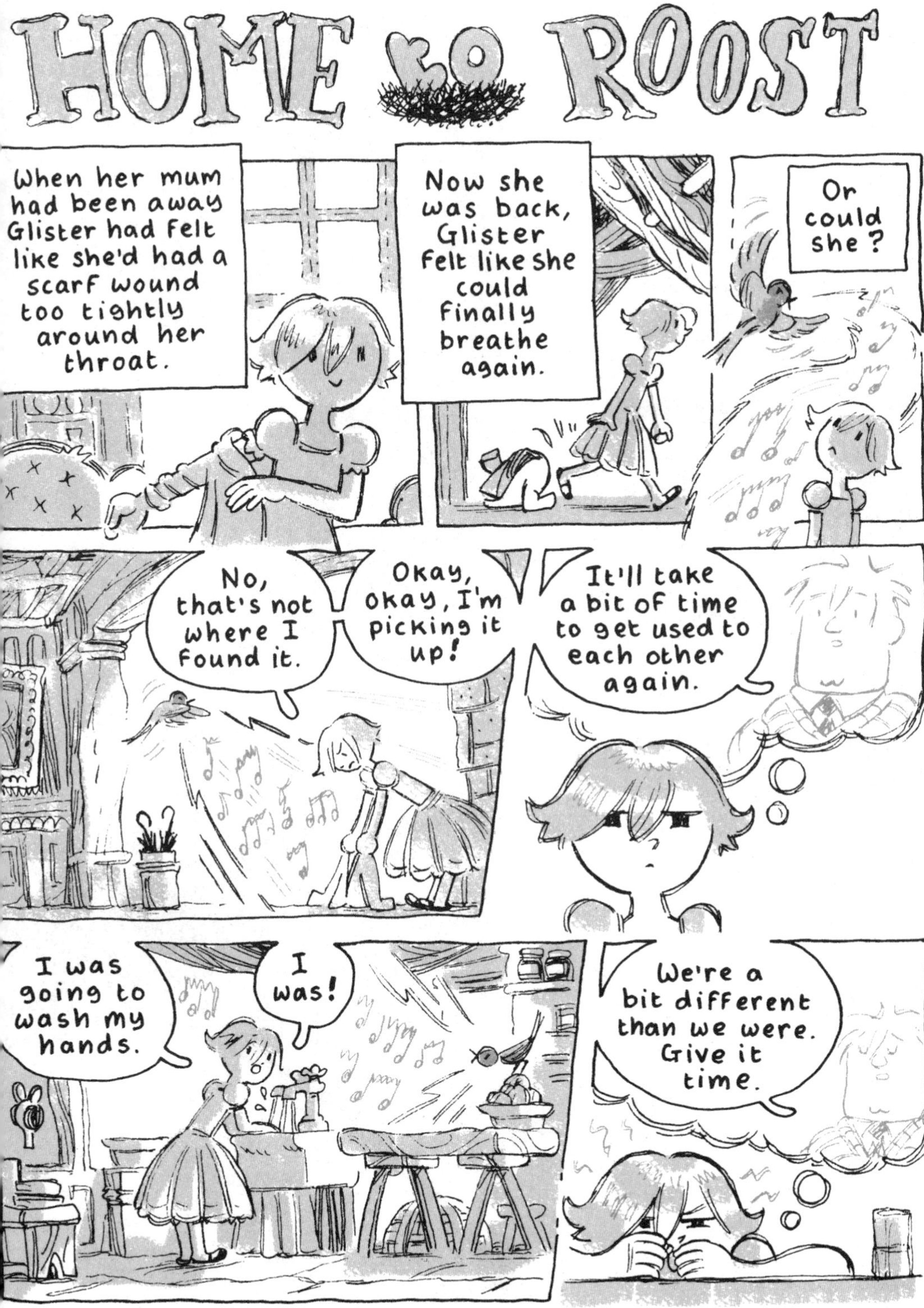
HOME to ROOST
When her mum had been away Glister had felt like she'd had a scarf wound too tightly around her throat.
Now she was back, Glister felt like she could finally breathe again.
Or could she?
No, that's not where I found it.
Okay, okay, I'm picking it up!
It'll take a bit of time to get used to each other again.
I was going to wash my hands.
I was!
We're a bit different than we were. Give it time.

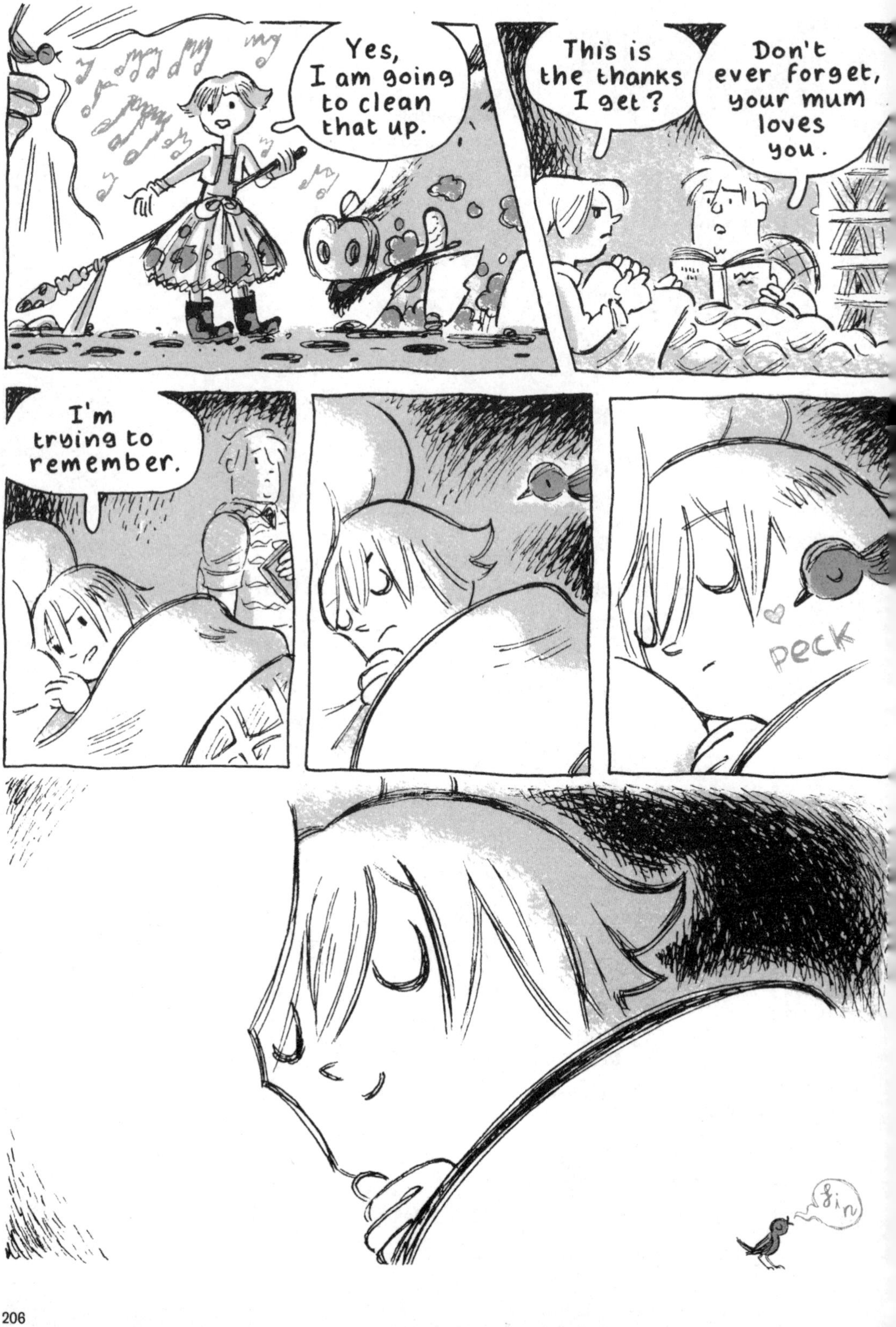
Yes, I am going to clean that up.
This is the thanks I get?
Don't ever forget, your mum loves you.
I'm trying to remember.
peck
fin

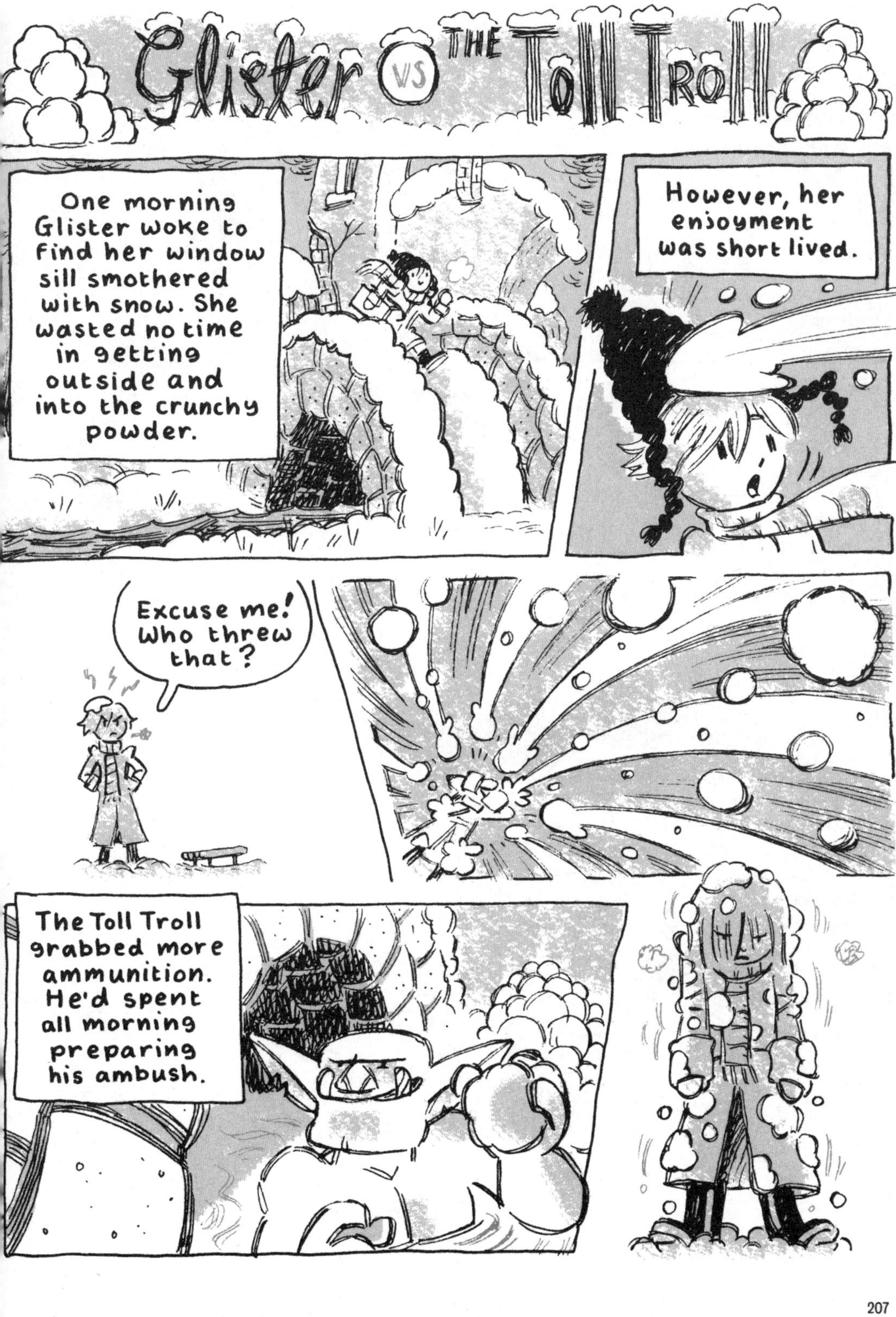
Glister vs The Toll Troll
One morning Glister woke to find her window sill smothered with snow. She wasted no time in getting outside and into the crunchy powder.
However, her enjoyment was short lived.
Excuse me! Who threw that?
The Toll Troll grabbed more ammunition. He'd spent all morning preparing his ambush.

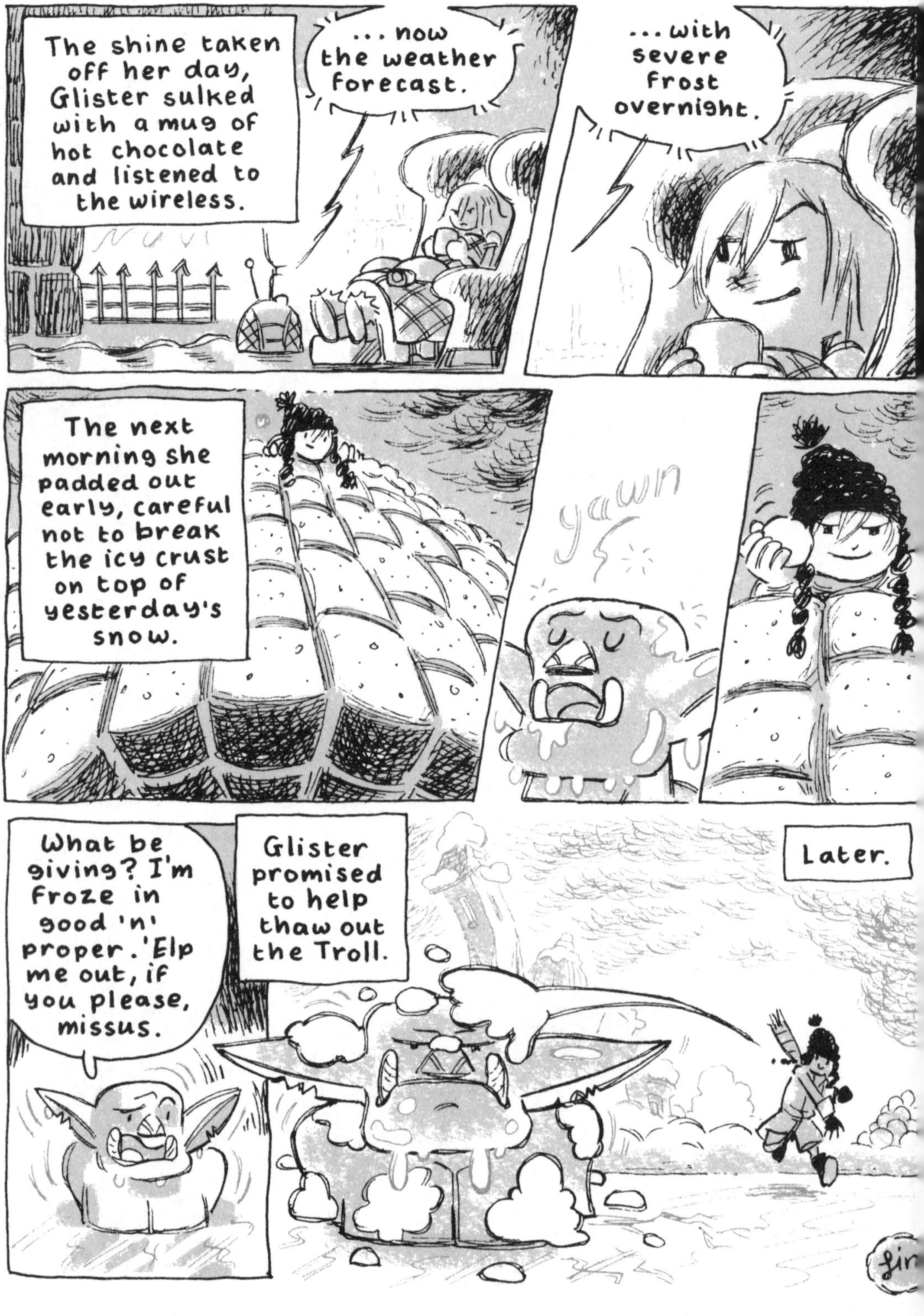

The shine taken off her day, Glister sulked with a mug of hot chocolate and listened to the wireless.
...now the weather forecast.
...with severe frost overnight.
The next morning she padded out early, careful not to break the icy crust on top of yesterday's snow.
yawn
What be giving? I'm froze in good 'n' proper. 'Elp me out, if you please, missus.
Glister promised to help thaw out the Troll.
Later.

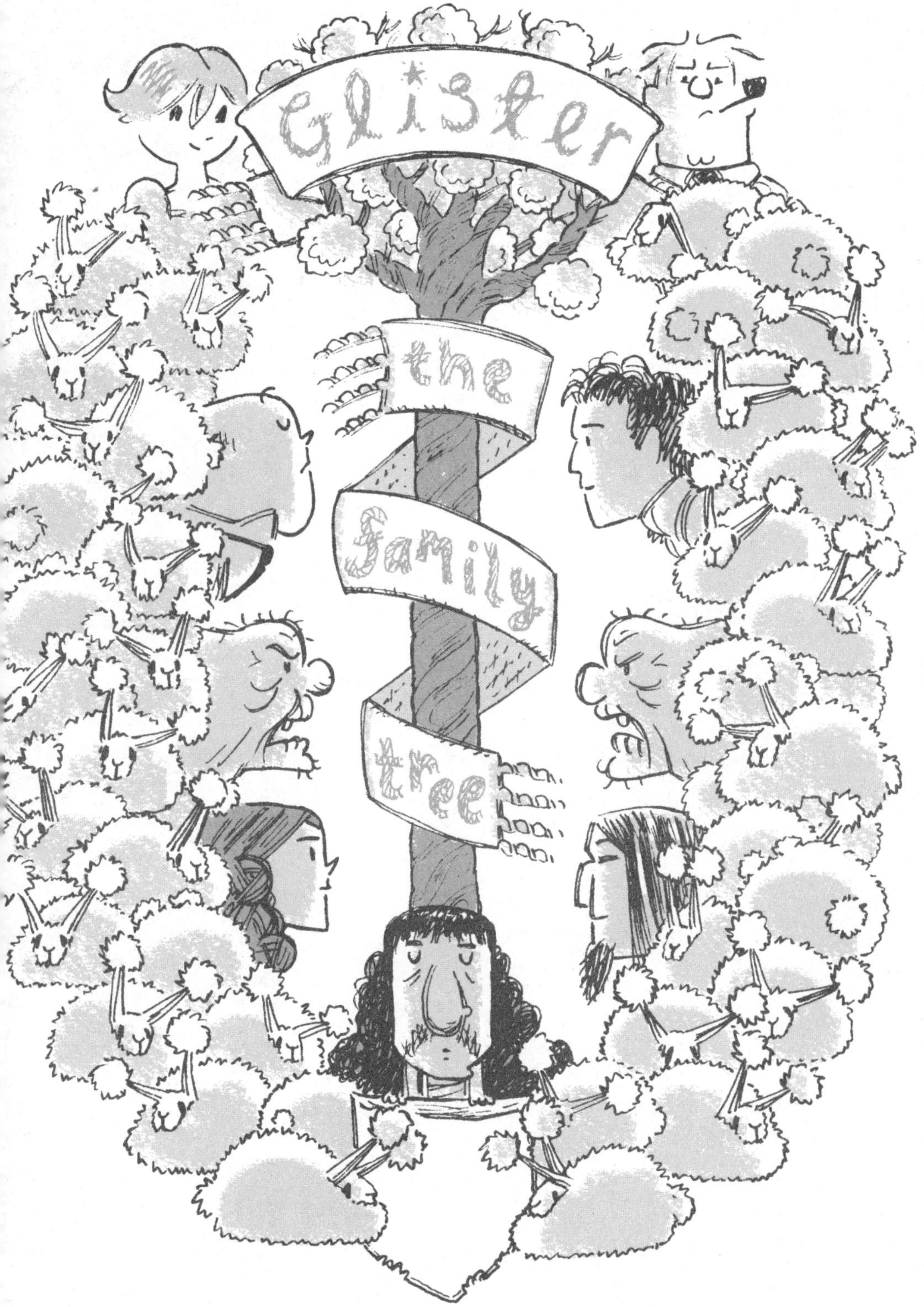
Glister
the family tree

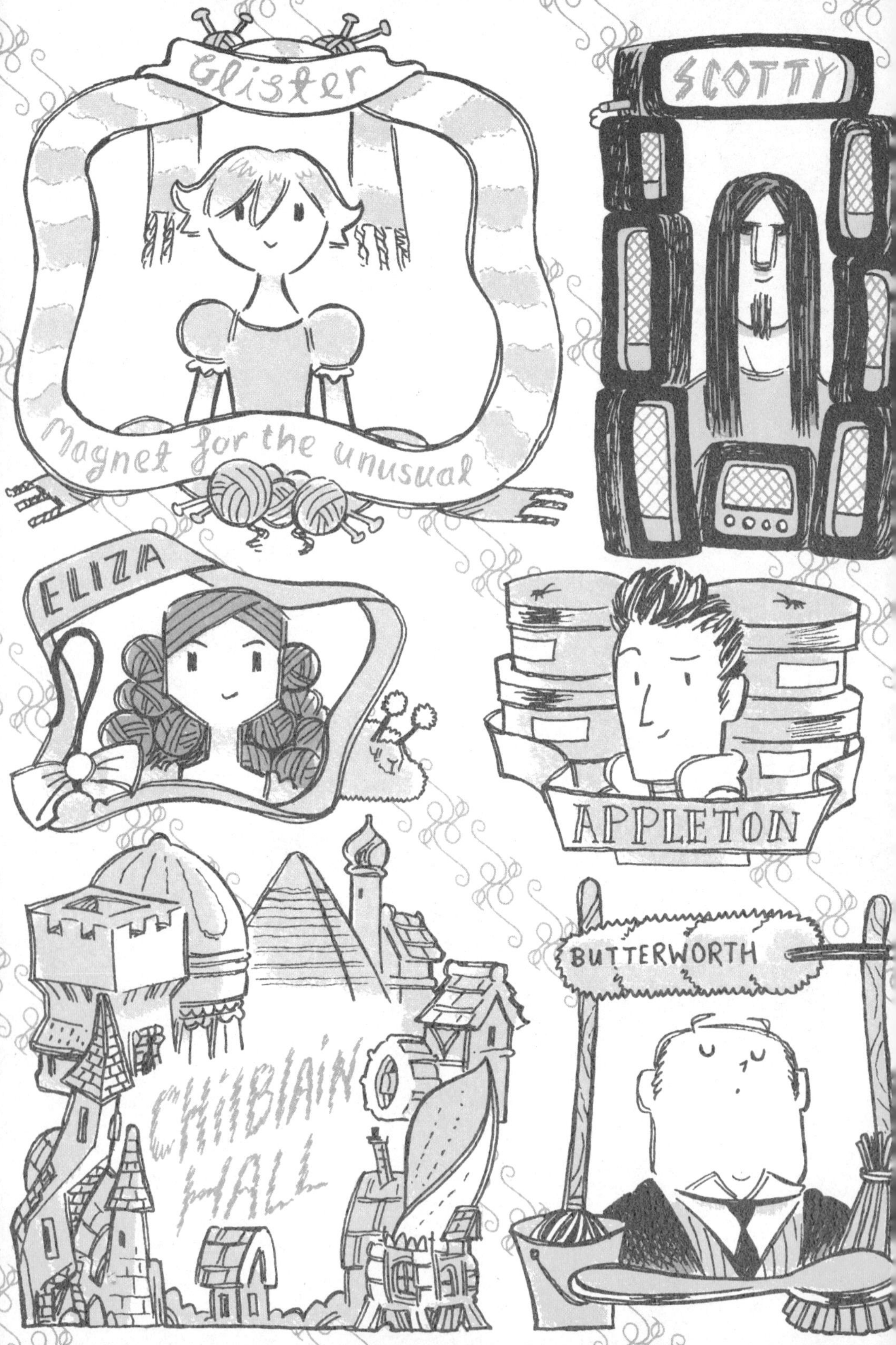
Glister
Magnet for the unusual
SCOTTY
ELIZA
APPLETON
CHILBLAIN HALL
BUTTERWORTH

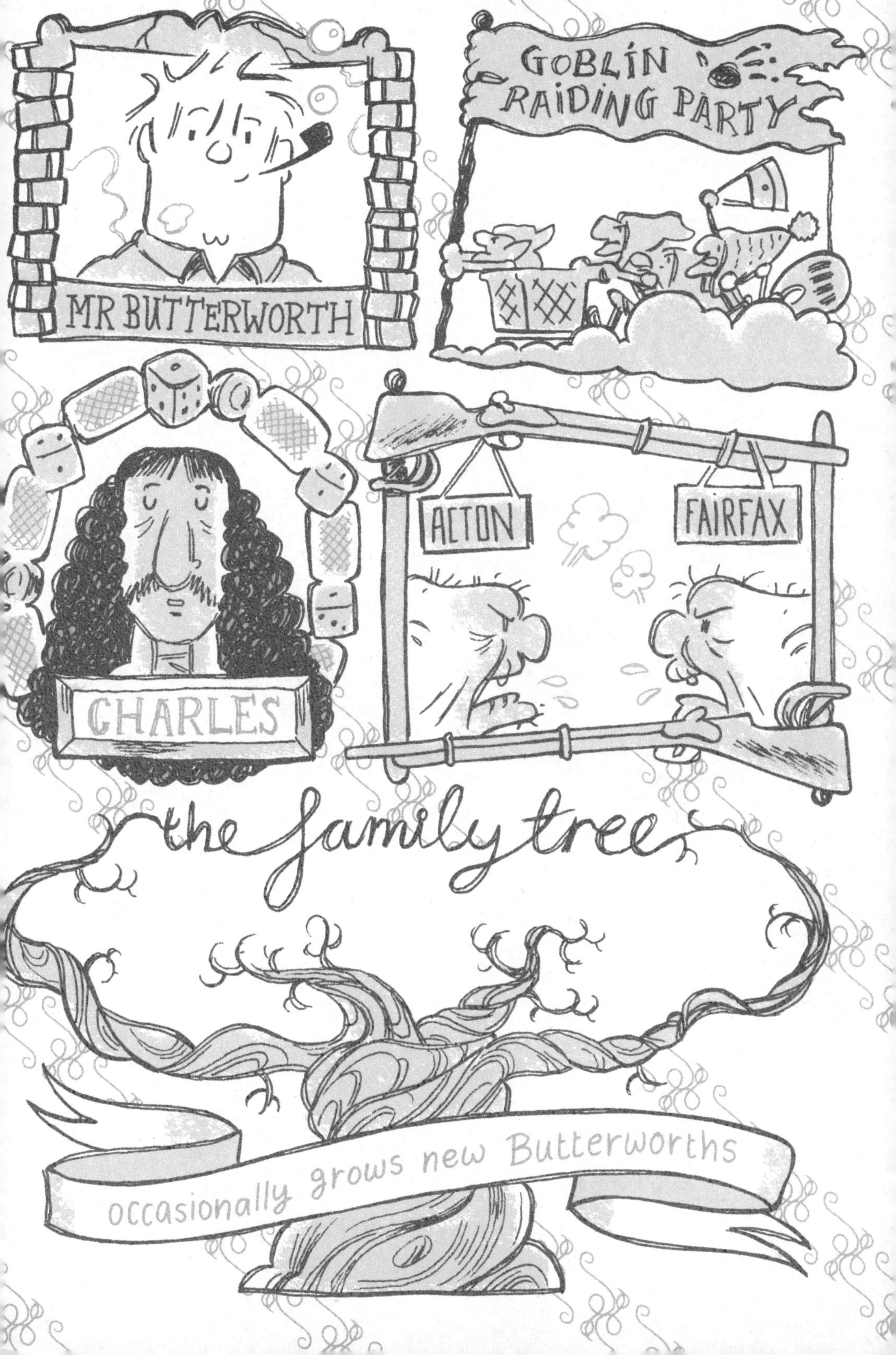
MR BUTTERWORTH
GOBLIN RAIDING PARTY
CHARLES
ACTON
FAIRFAX
the family tree
occasionally grows new Butterworths

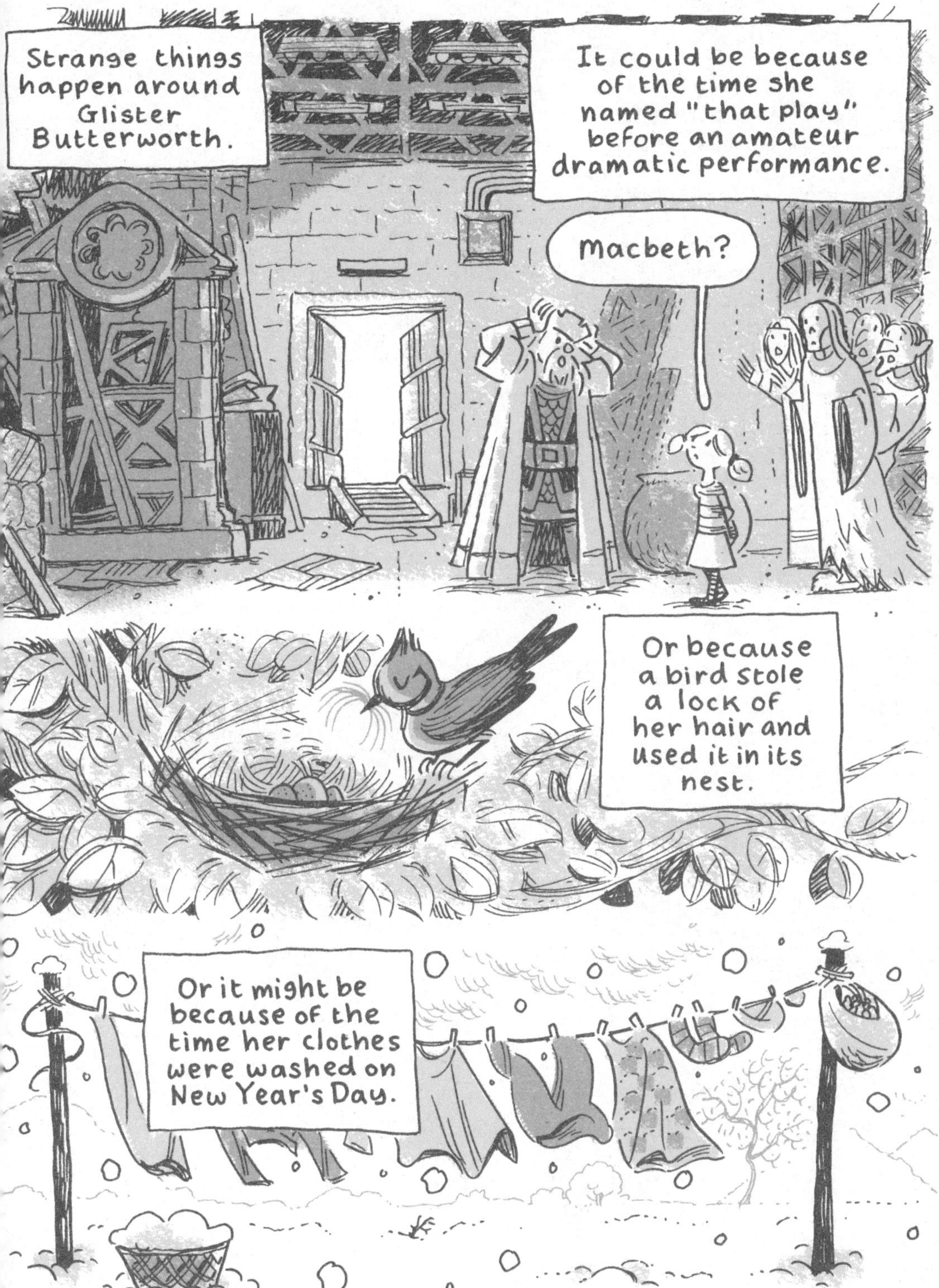
Strange things happen around Glister Butterworth.
It could be because of the time she named "that play" before an amateur dramatic performance.
Macbeth?
Or because a bird stole a lock of her hair and used it in its nest.
Or it might be because of the time her clothes were washed on New Year's Day.

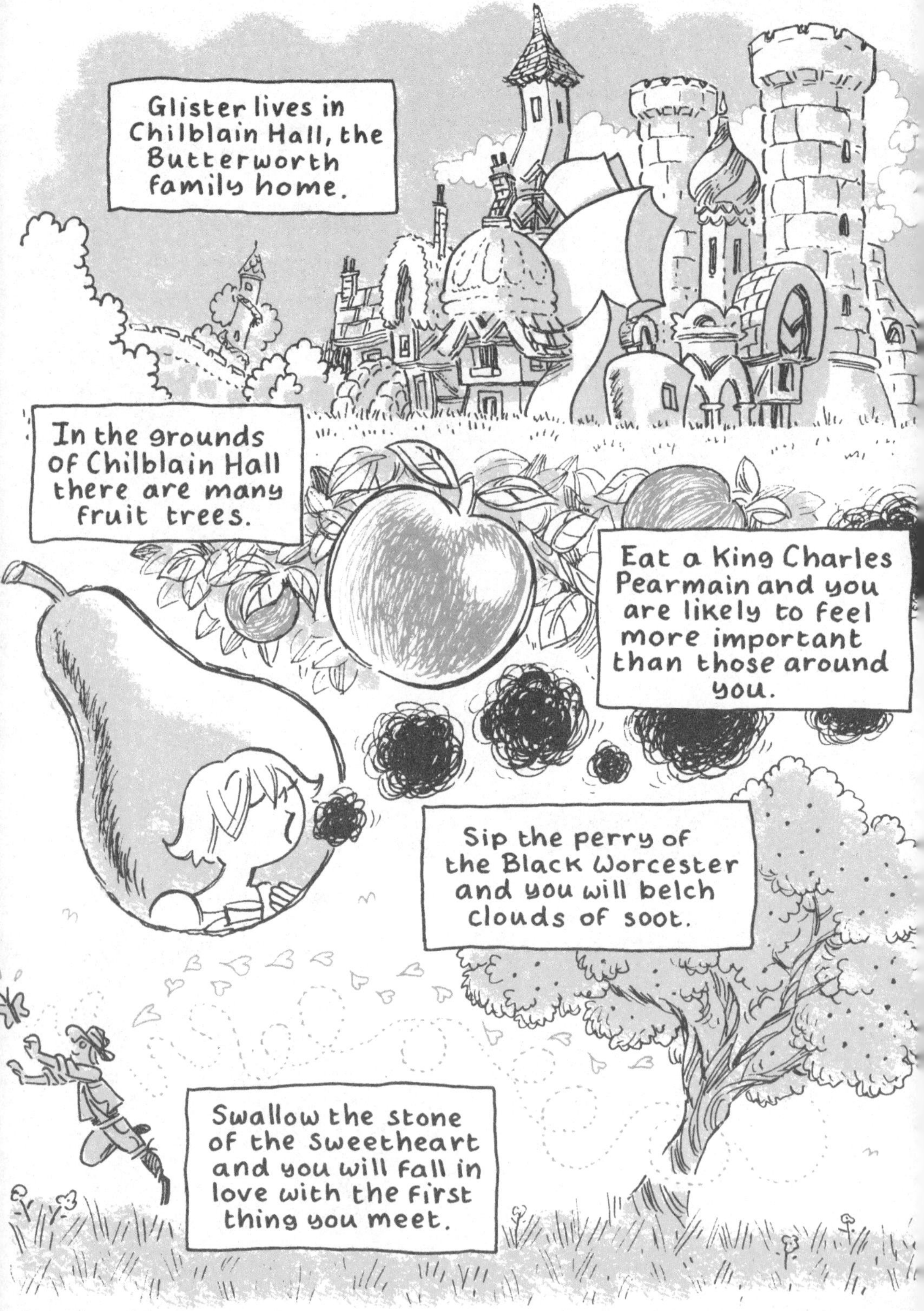
Glister lives in Chilblain Hall, the Butterworth family home.
In the grounds of Chilblain Hall there are many fruit trees.
Eat a King Charles Pearmain and you are likely to feel more important than those around you.
Sip the perry of the Black Worcester and you will belch clouds of soot.
Swallow the stone of the Sweetheart and you will fall in love with the first thing you meet.

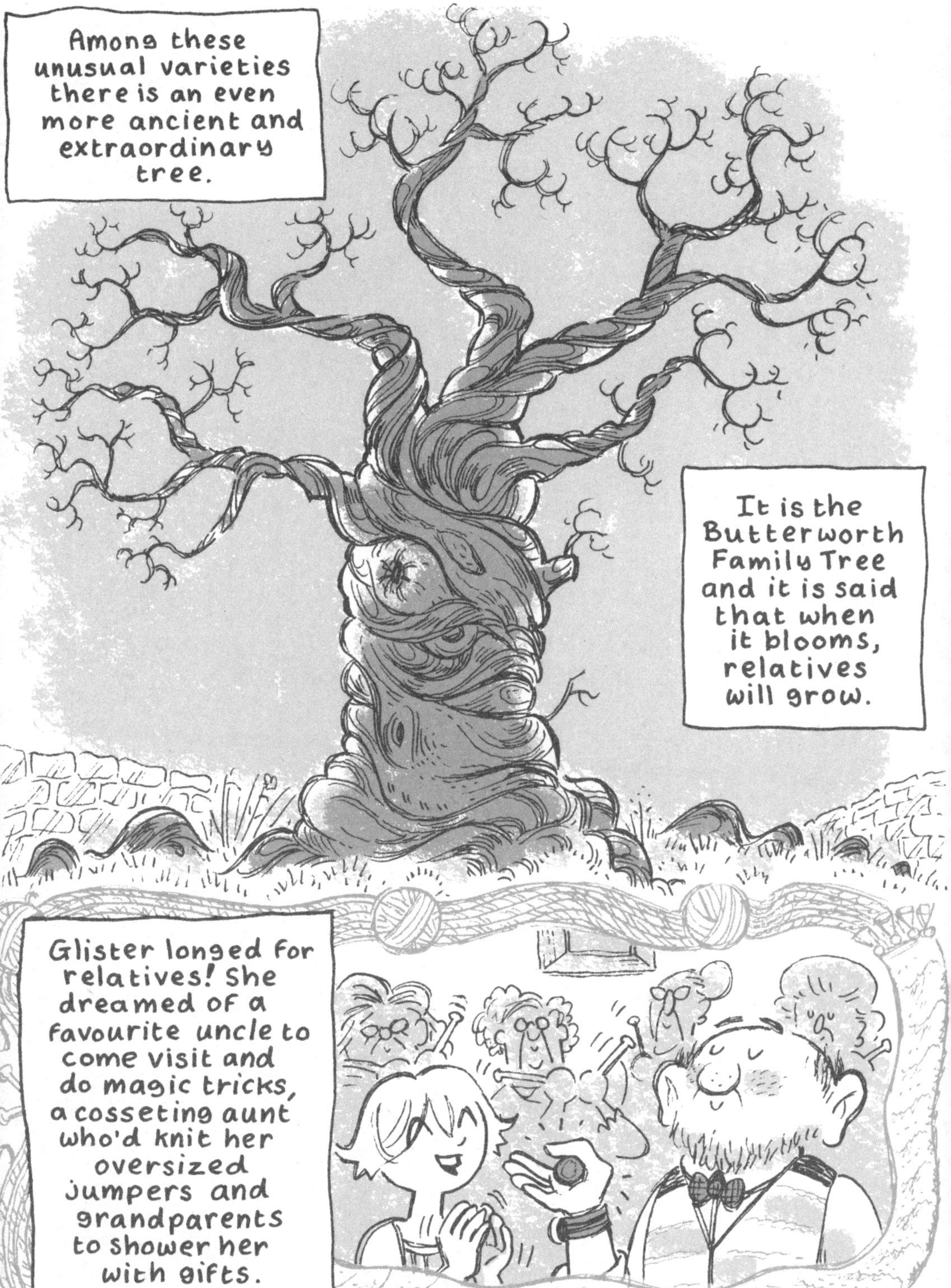
Among these unusual varieties there is an even more ancient and extraordinary tree.
It is the Butterworth Family Tree and it is said that when it blooms, relatives will grow.
Glister longed for relatives! She dreamed of a favourite uncle to come visit and do magic tricks, a cosseting aunt who'd knit her oversized jumpers and grandparents to shower her with gifts.

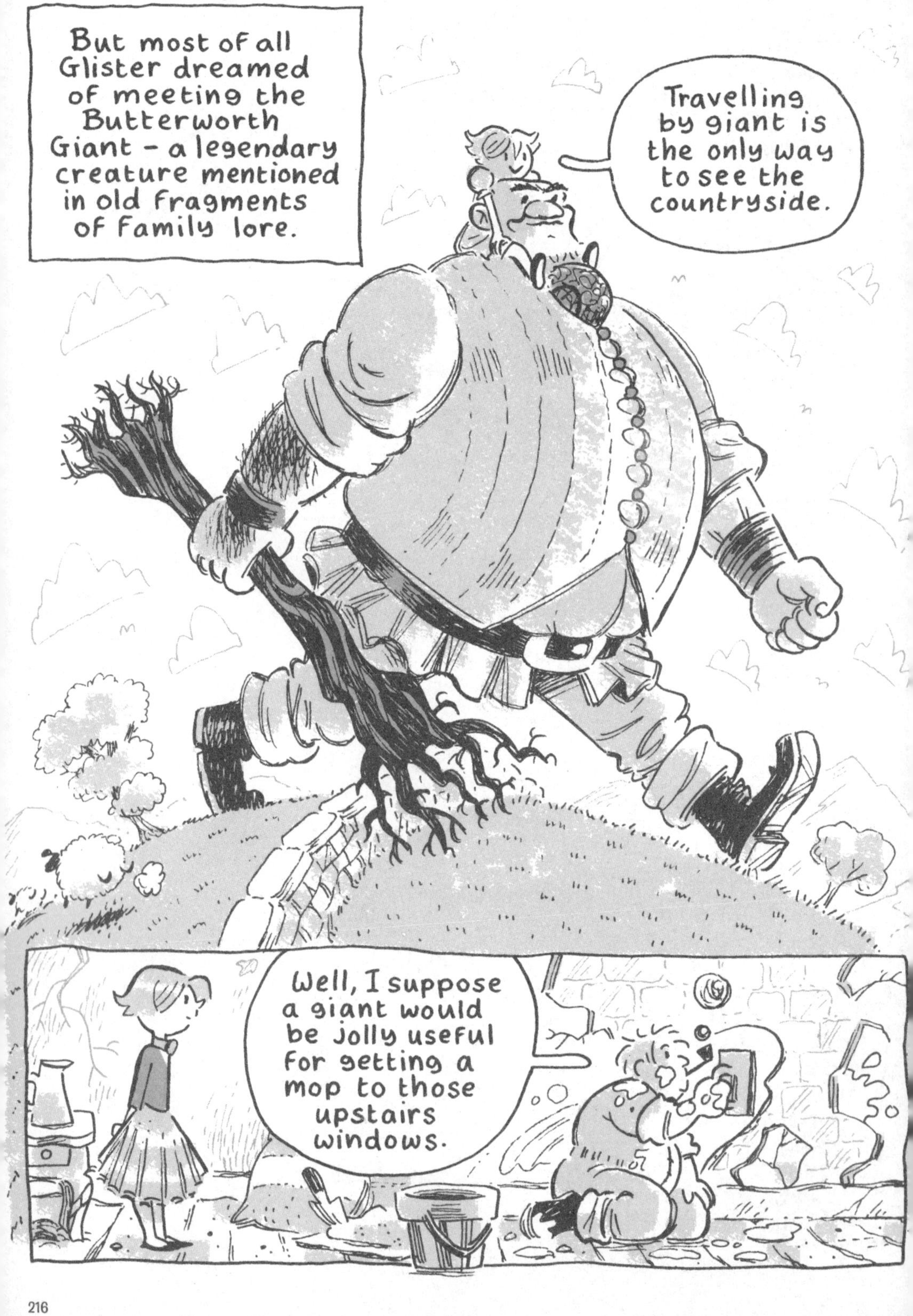

But most of all Glister dreamed of meeting the Butterworth Giant - a legendary creature mentioned in old fragments of family lore.
Travelling by giant is the only way to see the countryside.
Well, I suppose a giant would be jolly useful for getting a mop to those upstairs windows.

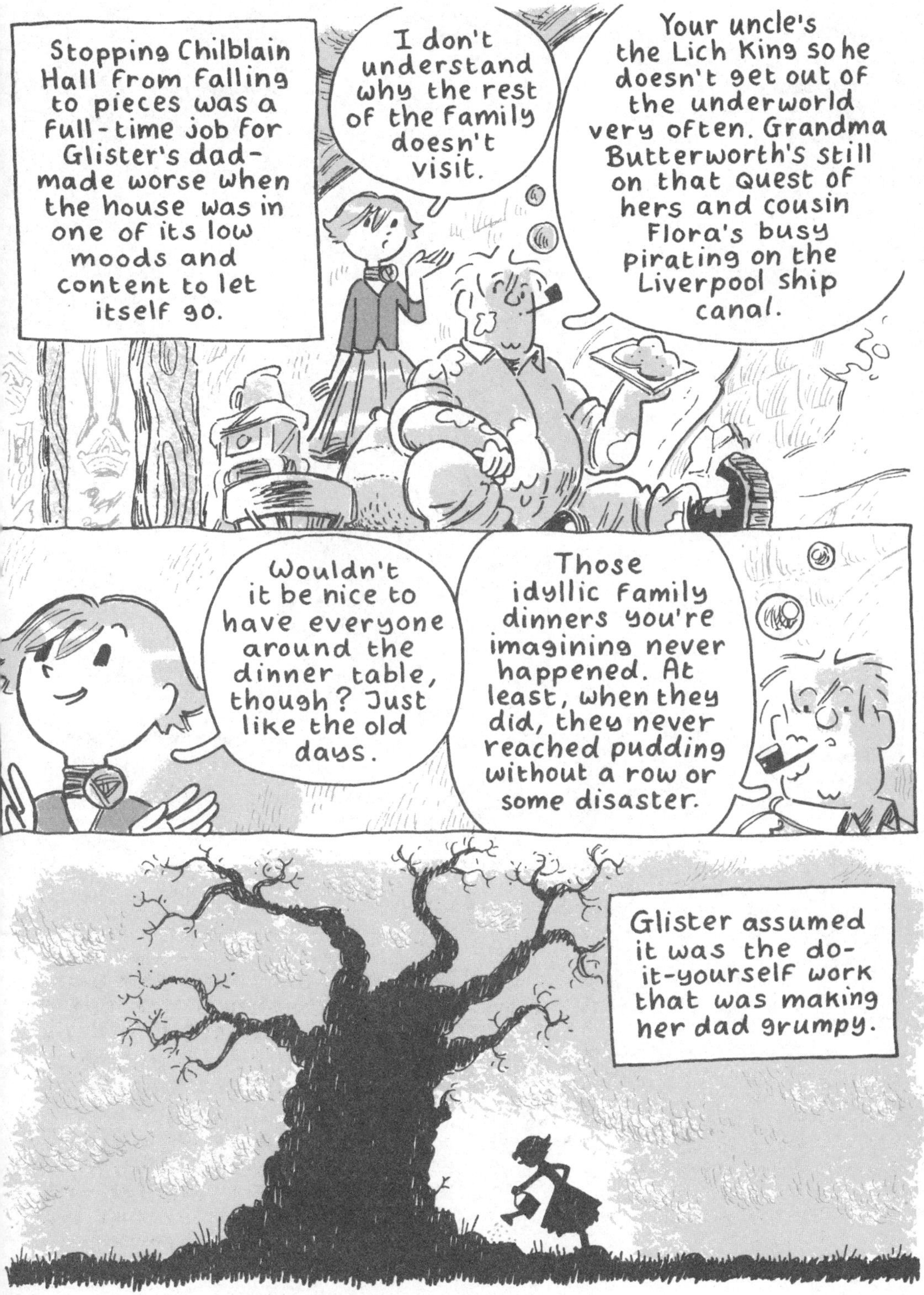
Stopping Chilblain Hall from falling to pieces was a full-time job for Glister's dad-made worse when the house was in one of its low moods and content to let itself go.
I don't understand why the rest of the family doesn't visit.
Your uncle's the Lich King so he doesn't get out of the underworld very often. Grandma Butterworth's still on that Quest of hers and cousin Flora's busy pirating on the Liverpool ship canal.
Wouldn't it be nice to have everyone around the dinner table, though? Just like the old days.
Those idyllic family dinners you're imagining never happened. At least, when they did, they never reached pudding without a row or some disaster.
Glister assumed it was the do-it-yourself work that was making her dad grumpy.

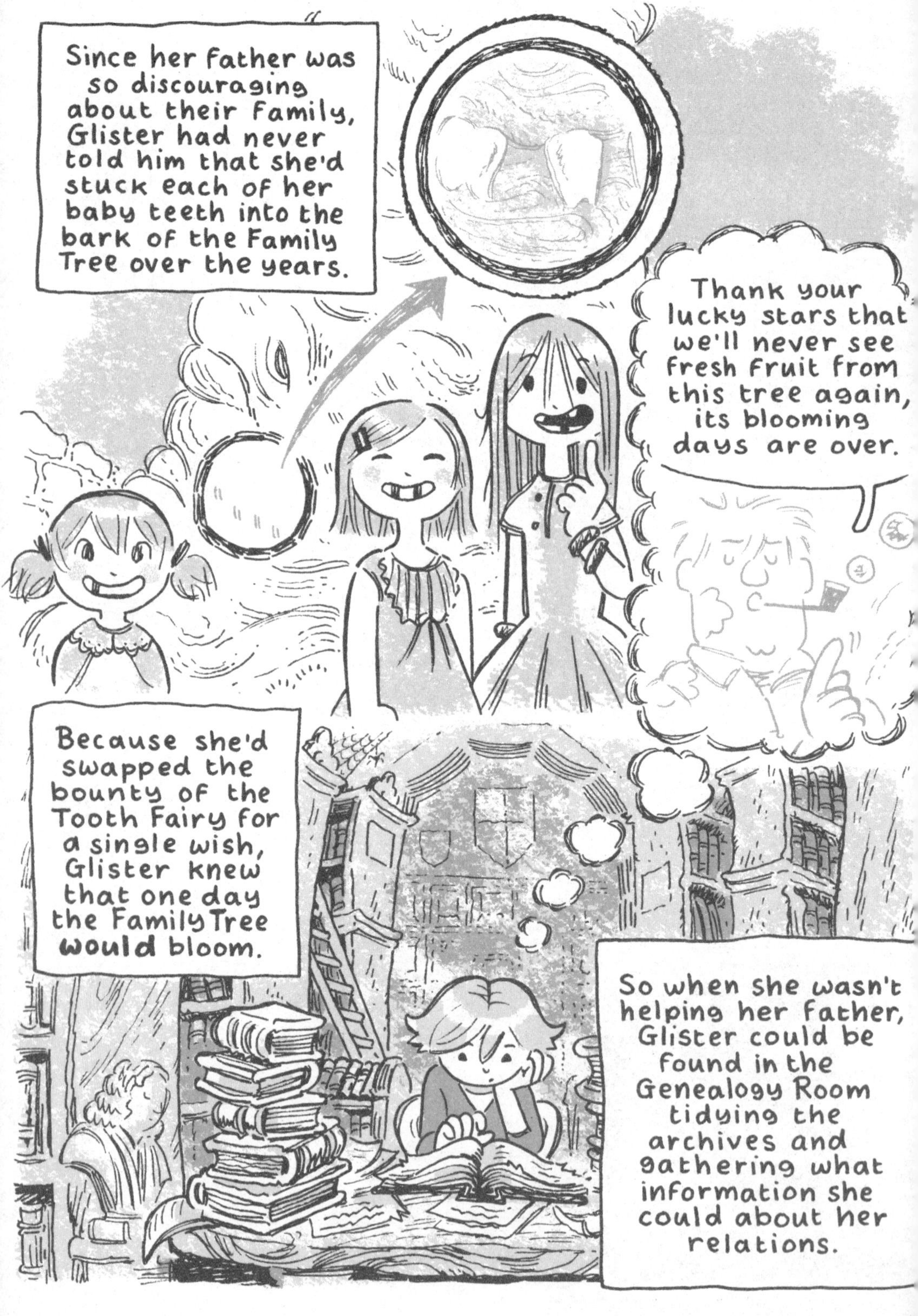
Since her father was so discouraging about their family, Glister had never told him that she'd stuck each of her baby teeth into the bark of the Family Tree over the years.
Thank your lucky stars that we'll never see fresh fruit from this tree again, its blooming days are over.
Because she'd swapped the bounty of the Tooth Fairy for a single wish, Glister knew that one day the Family Tree **would** bloom.
So when she wasn't helping her father, Glister could be found in the Genealogy Room tidying the archives and gathering what information she could about her relations.

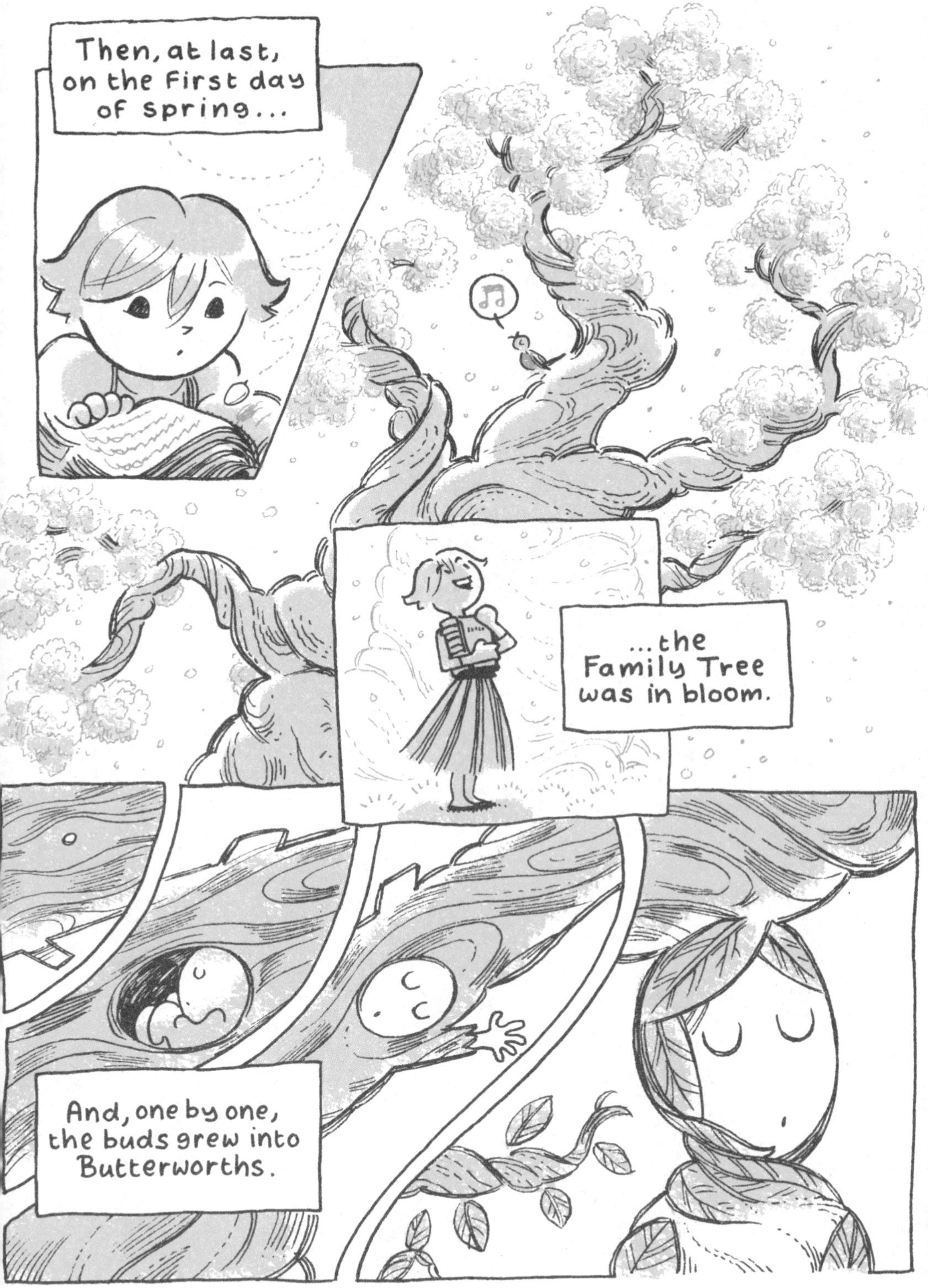
Then, at last, on the first day of spring...
...the Family Tree was in bloom.
And, one by one, the buds grew into Butterworths.

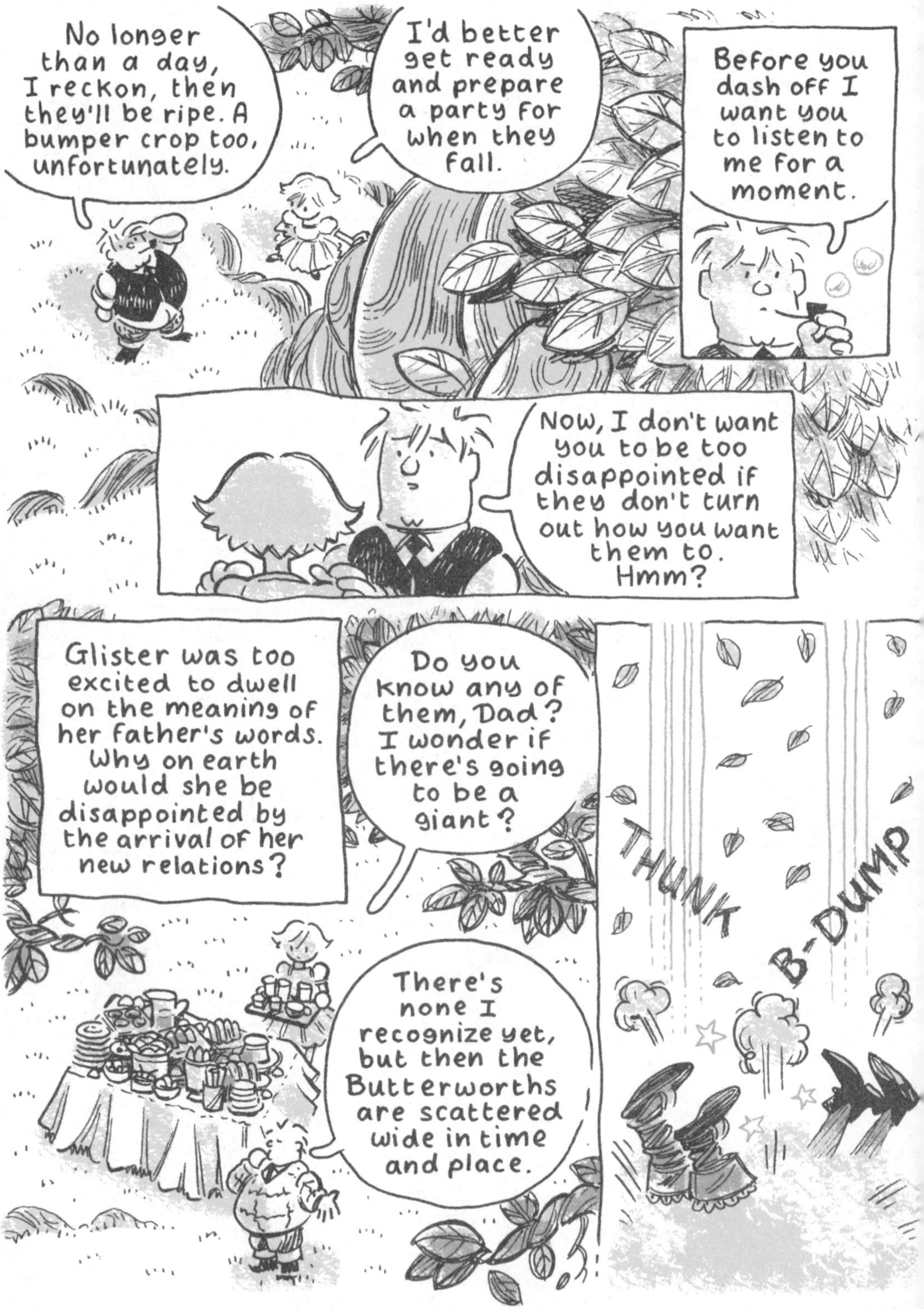
No longer than a day, I reckon, then they'll be ripe. A bumper crop too, unfortunately.
I'd better get ready and prepare a party for when they fall.
Before you dash off I want you to listen to me for a moment.
Now, I don't want you to be too disappointed if they don't turn out how you want them to. Hmm?
Glister was too excited to dwell on the meaning of her father's words. Why on earth would she be disappointed by the arrival of her new relations?
Do you know any of them, Dad? I wonder if there's going to be a giant?
There's none I recognize yet, but then the Butterworths are scattered wide in time and place.
THUNK
B-DUMP

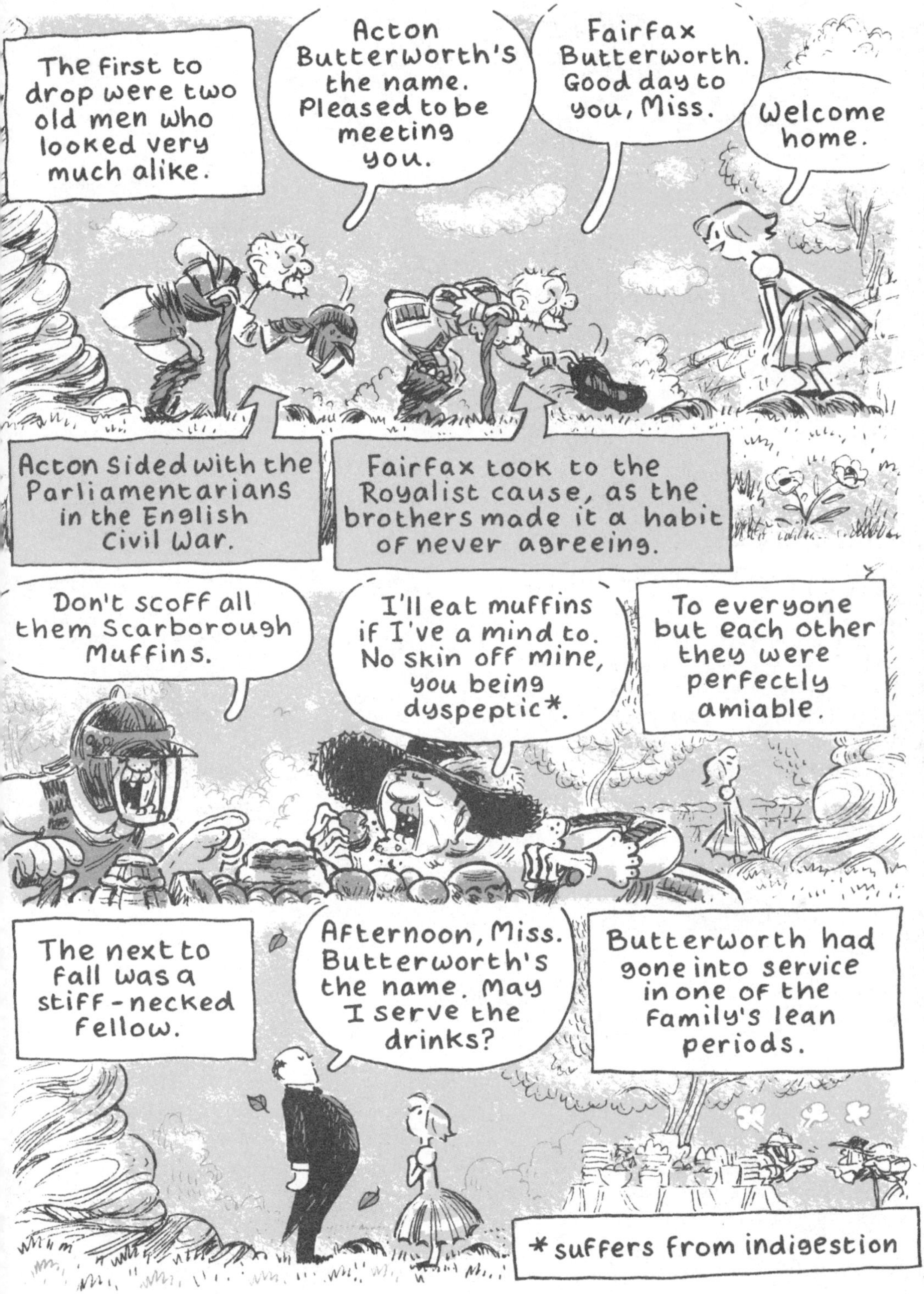

The first to drop were two old men who looked very much alike.
Acton Butterworth's the name. Pleased to be meeting you.
Fairfax Butterworth. Good day to you, Miss.
Welcome home.
Acton sided with the Parliamentarians in the English Civil War.
Fairfax took to the Royalist cause, as the brothers made it a habit of never agreeing.
Don't scoff all them Scarborough Muffins.
I'll eat muffins if I've a mind to. No skin off mine, you being dyspeptic*.
To everyone but each other they were perfectly amiable.
The next to fall was a stiff-necked fellow.
Afternoon, Miss. Butterworth's the name. May I serve the drinks?
Butterworth had gone into service in one of the family's lean periods.
* suffers from indigestion

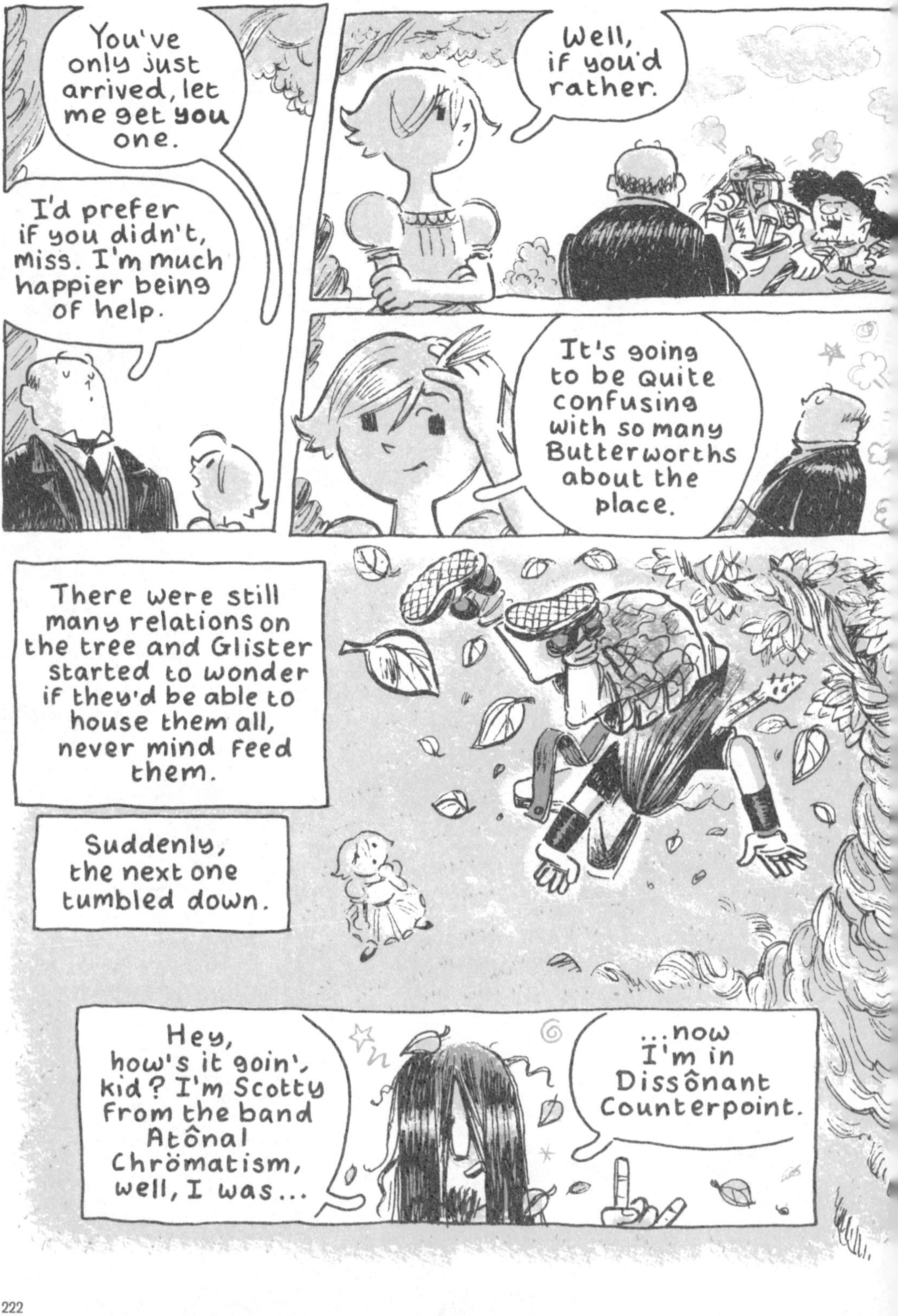
You've only just arrived, let me get you one.
I'd prefer if you didn't, miss. I'm much happier being of help.
Well, if you'd rather.
It's going to be quite confusing with so many Butterworths about the place.
There were still many relations on the tree and Glister started to wonder if they'd be able to house them all, never mind feed them.
Suddenly, the next one tumbled down.
Hey, how's it goin', kid? I'm Scotty from the band Atônal Chrömatism, well, I was...
...now I'm in Dissônant Counterpoint.

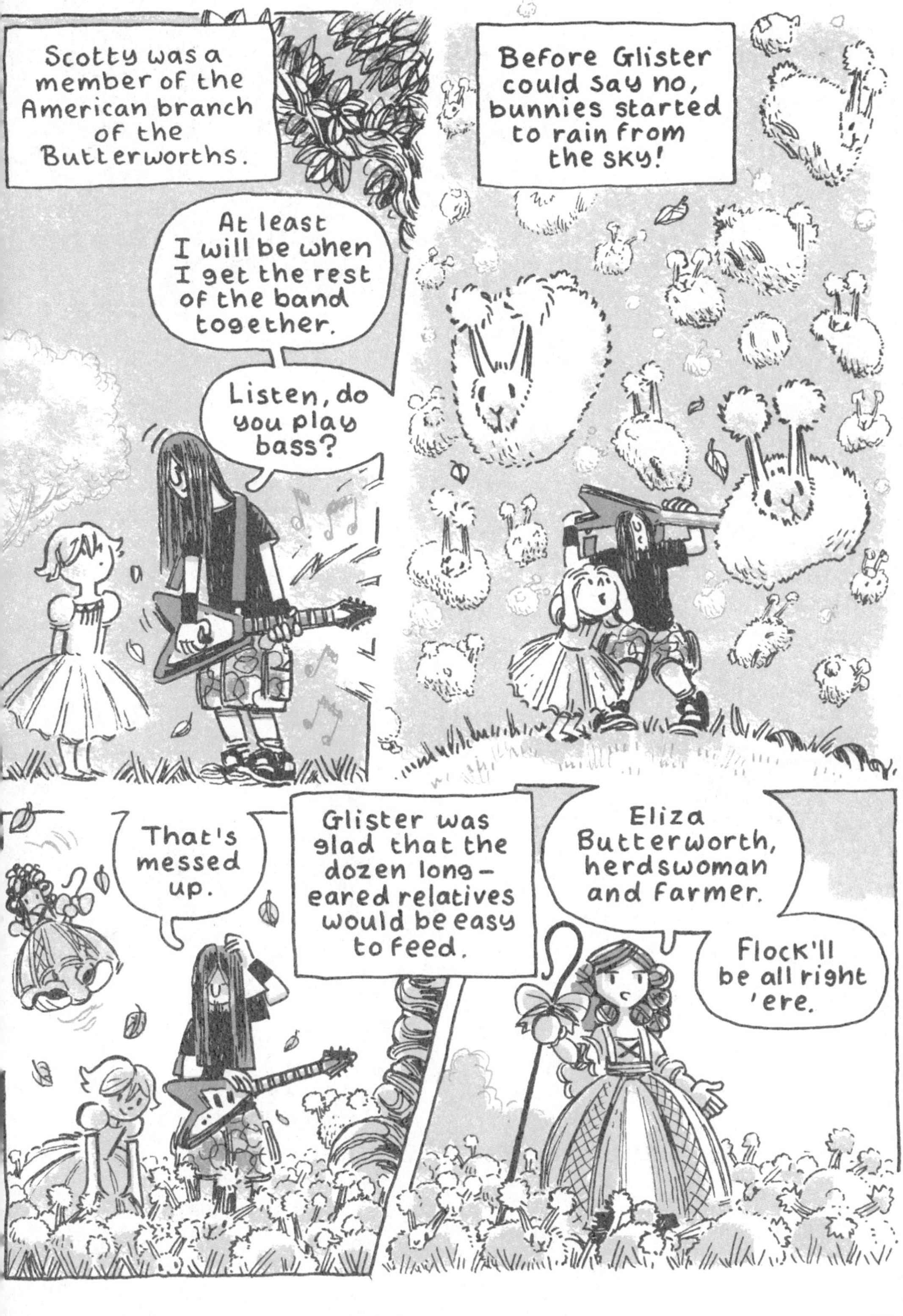

Scotty was a member of the American branch of the Butterworths.
At least I will be when I get the rest of the band together.
Listen, do you play bass?
Before Glister could say no, bunnies started to rain from the sky!
That's messed up.
Glister was glad that the dozen long-eared relatives would be easy to feed.
Eliza Butterworth, herdswoman and farmer.
Flock'll be all right 'ere.

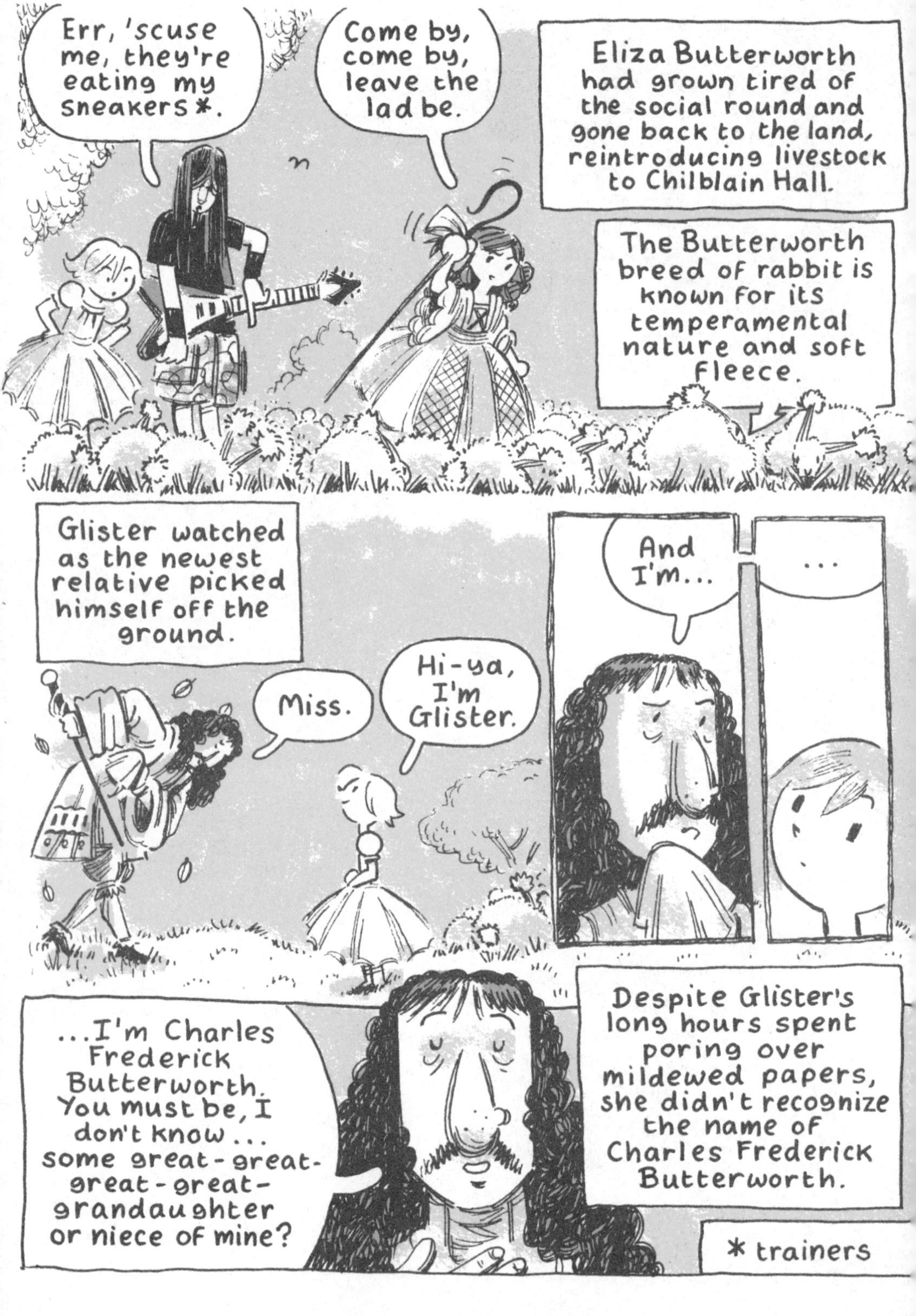
Err, 'scuse me, they're eating my sneakers*.
Come by, come by, leave the lad be.
Eliza Butterworth had grown tired of the social round and gone back to the land, reintroducing livestock to Chilblain Hall.
The Butterworth breed of rabbit is known for its temperamental nature and soft fleece.
Glister watched as the newest relative picked himself off the ground.
Miss.
Hi-ya, I'm Glister.
And I'm...
...
...I'm Charles Frederick Butterworth. You must be, I don't know... some great-great-great-great-grandaughter or niece of mine?
Despite Glister's long hours spent poring over mildewed papers, she didn't recognize the name of Charles Frederick Butterworth.
* trainers

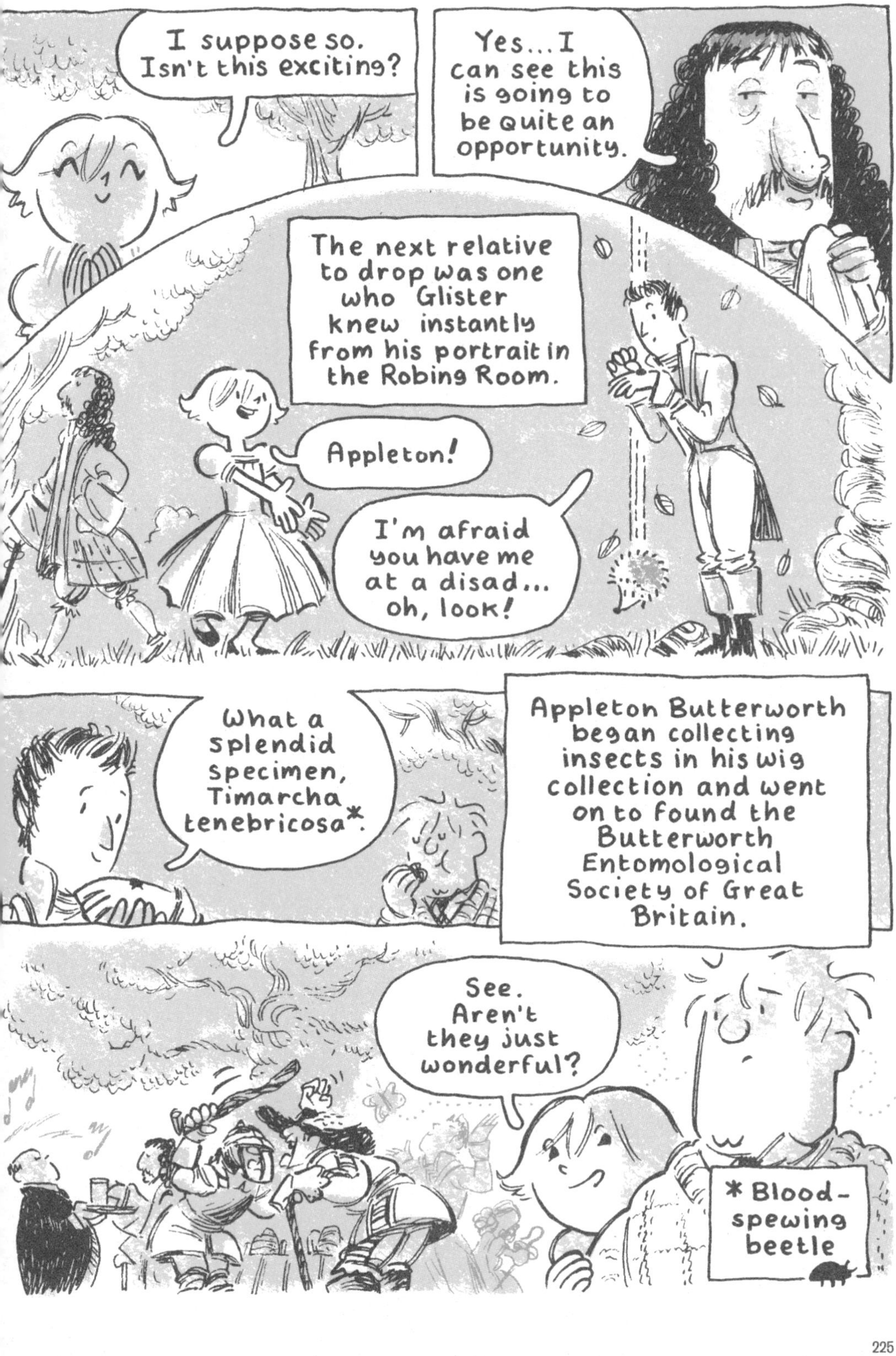
I suppose so. Isn't this exciting?
Yes... I can see this is going to be quite an opportunity.
The next relative to drop was one who Glister knew instantly from his portrait in the Robing Room.
Appleton!
I'm afraid you have me at a disad... oh, look!
What a splendid specimen, Timarcha tenebricosa*.
Appleton Butterworth began collecting insects in his wig collection and went on to found the Butterworth Entomological Society of Great Britain.
See. Aren't they just wonderful?
* Blood-spewing beetle

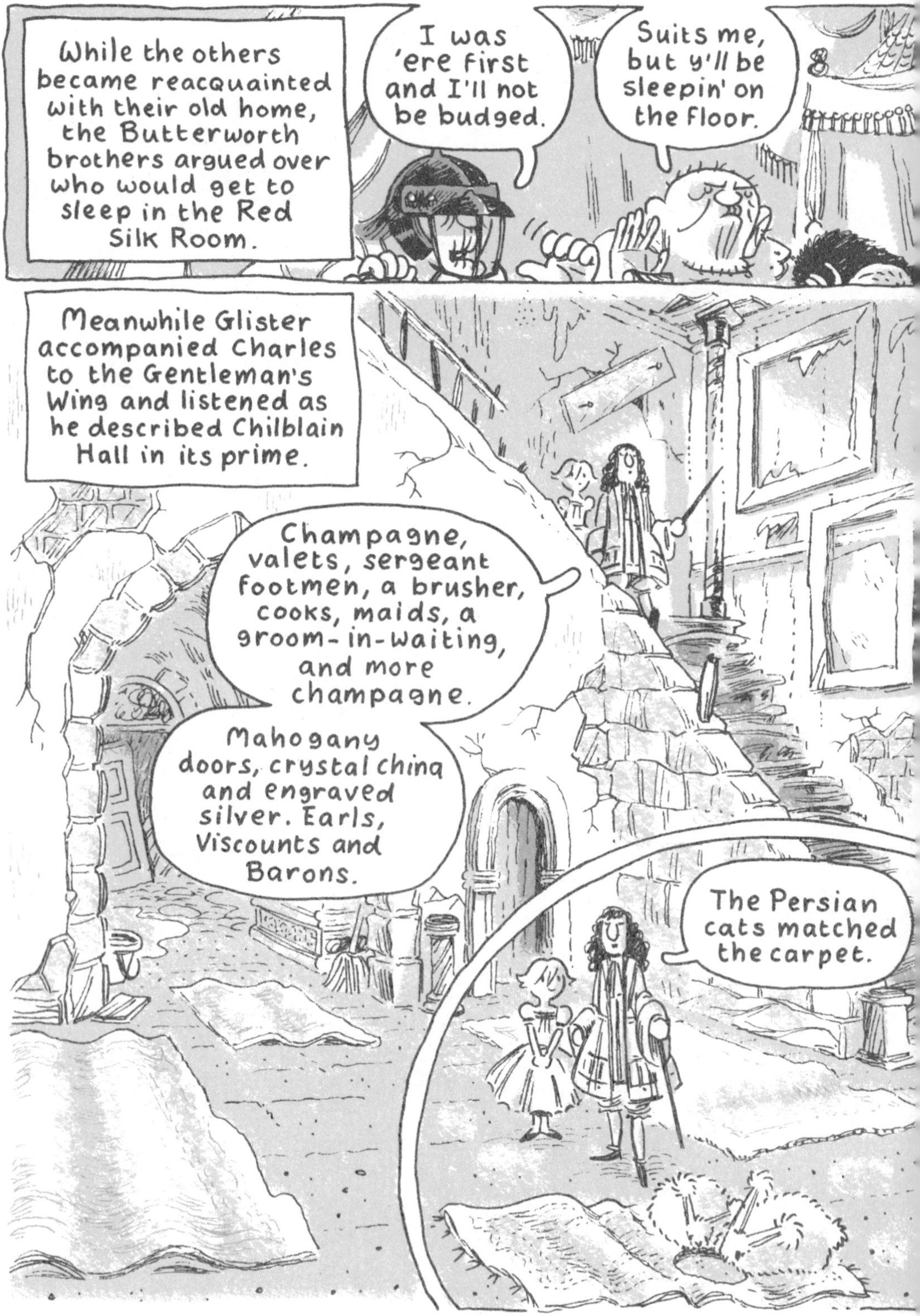
While the others became reacquainted with their old home, the Butterworth brothers argued over who would get to sleep in the Red Silk Room.
I was 'ere first and I'll not be budged.
Suits me, but y'll be sleepin' on the floor.
Meanwhile Glister accompanied Charles to the Gentleman's Wing and listened as he described Chilblain Hall in its prime.
Champagne, valets, sergeant footmen, a brusher, cooks, maids, a groom-in-waiting, and more champagne.
Mahogany doors, crystal china and engraved silver. Earls, Viscounts and Barons.
The Persian cats matched the carpet.

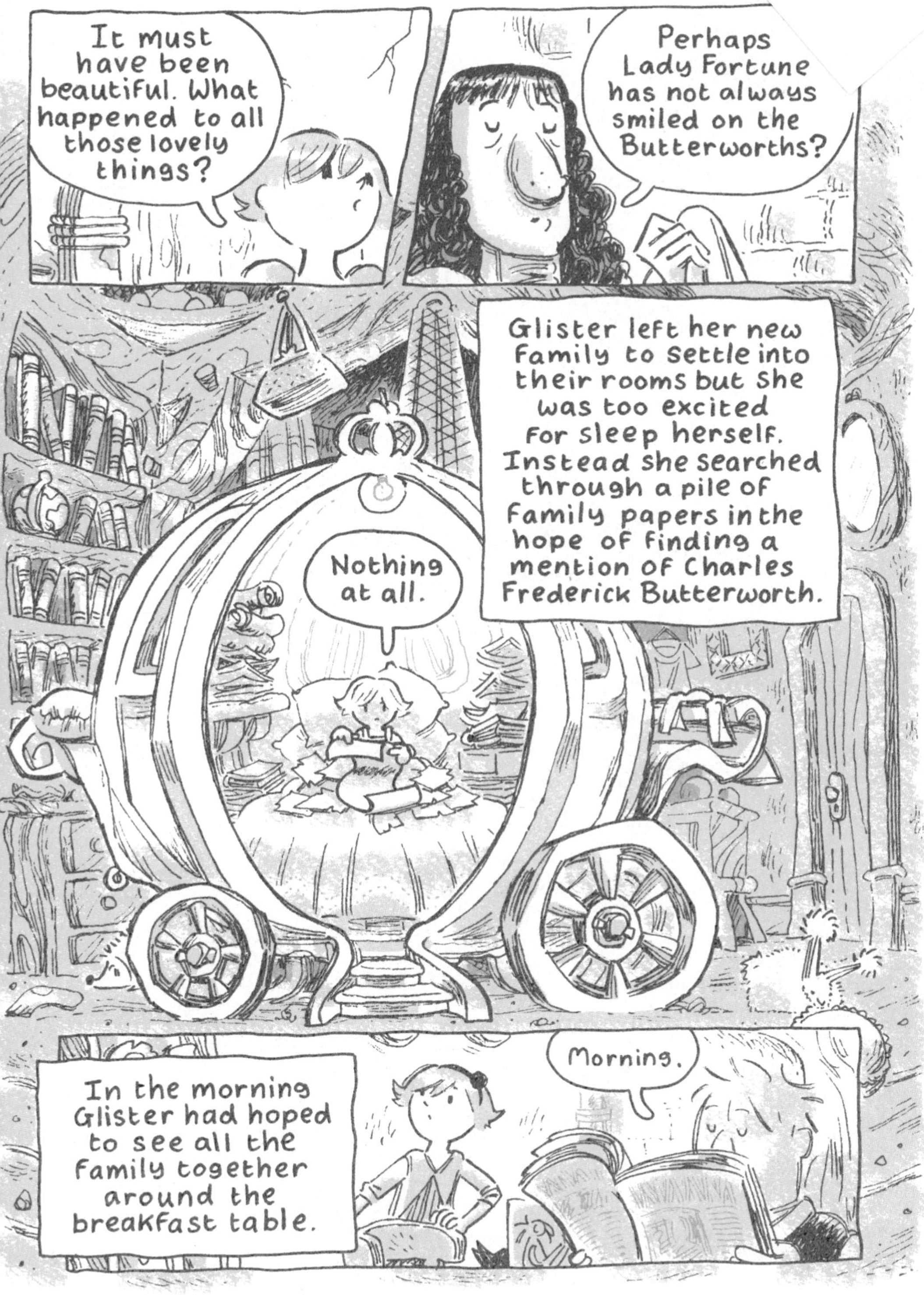
It must have been beautiful. What happened to all those lovely things?
Perhaps Lady Fortune has not always smiled on the Butterworths?
Glister left her new family to settle into their rooms but she was too excited for sleep herself. Instead she searched through a pile of family papers in the hope of finding a mention of Charles Frederick Butterworth.
Nothing at all.
In the morning Glister had hoped to see all the family together around the breakfast table.
Morning.

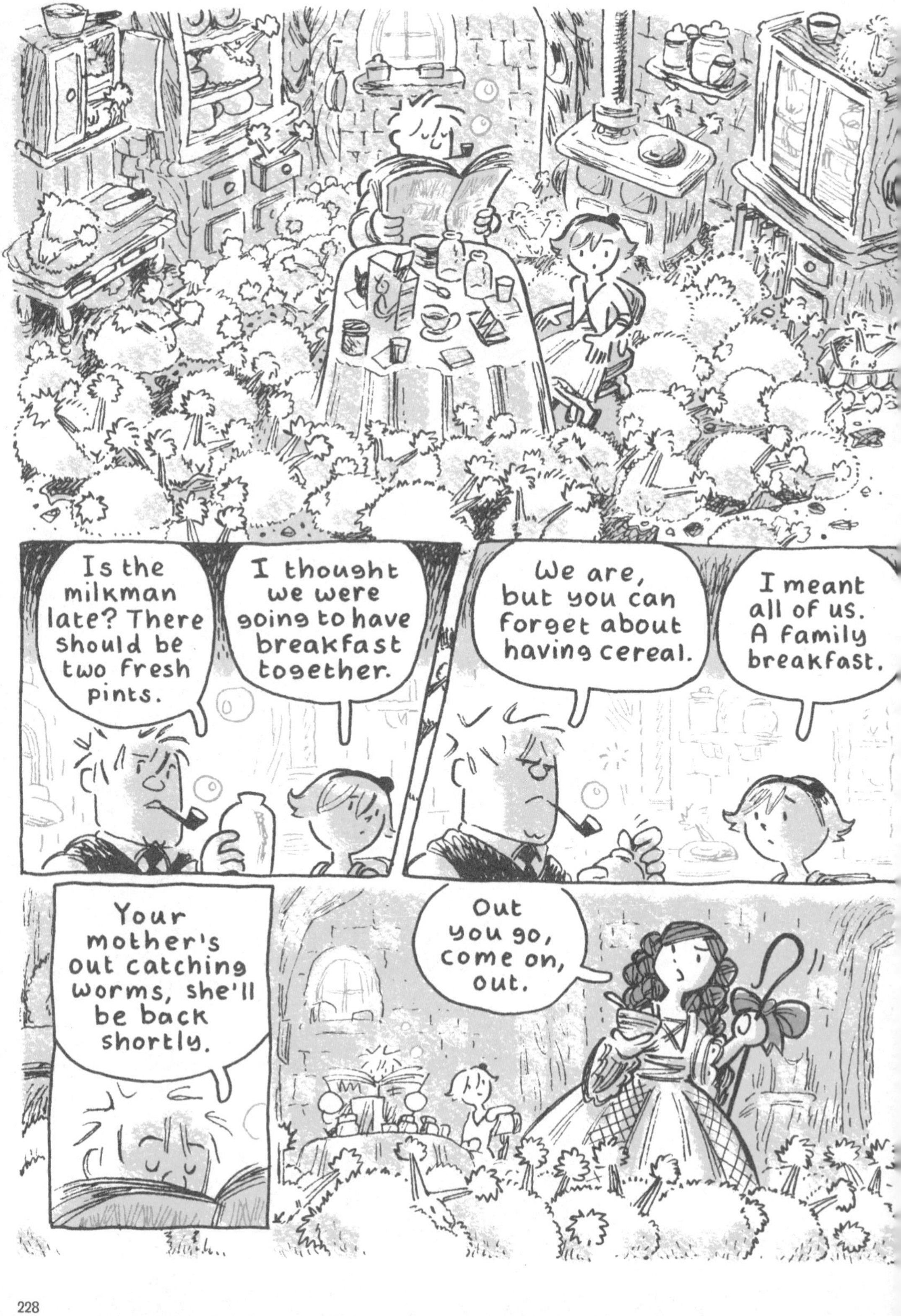

Is the milkman late? There should be two fresh pints.
I thought we were going to have breakfast together.
We are, but you can forget about having cereal.
I meant all of us. A family breakfast.
Your mother's out catching worms, she'll be back shortly.
Out you go, come on, out.

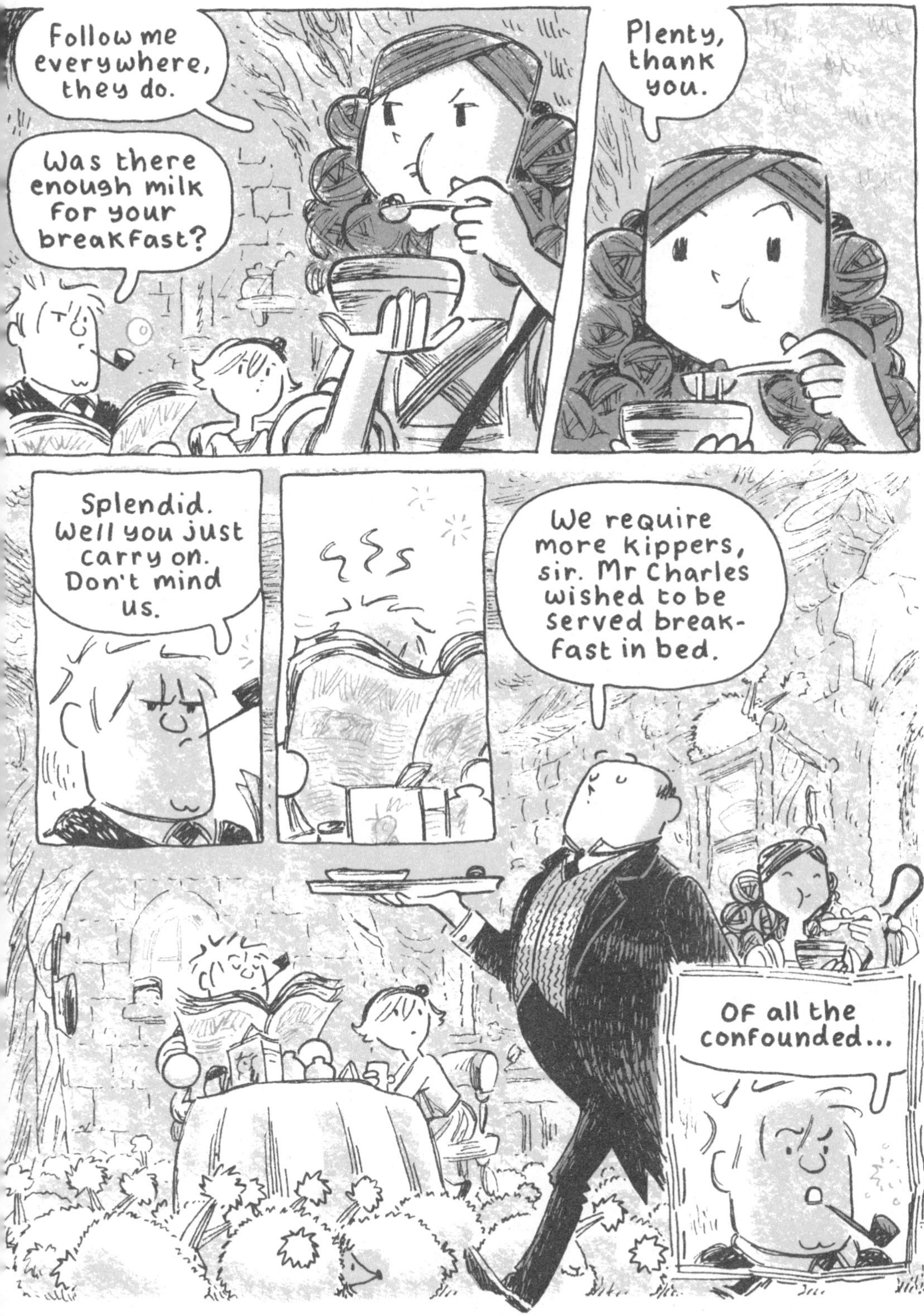
Follow me everywhere, they do.
Was there enough milk for your breakfast?
Plenty, thank you.
Splendid. Well you just carry on. Don't mind us.
We require more kippers, sir. Mr Charles wished to be served breakfast in bed.
Of all the confounded...

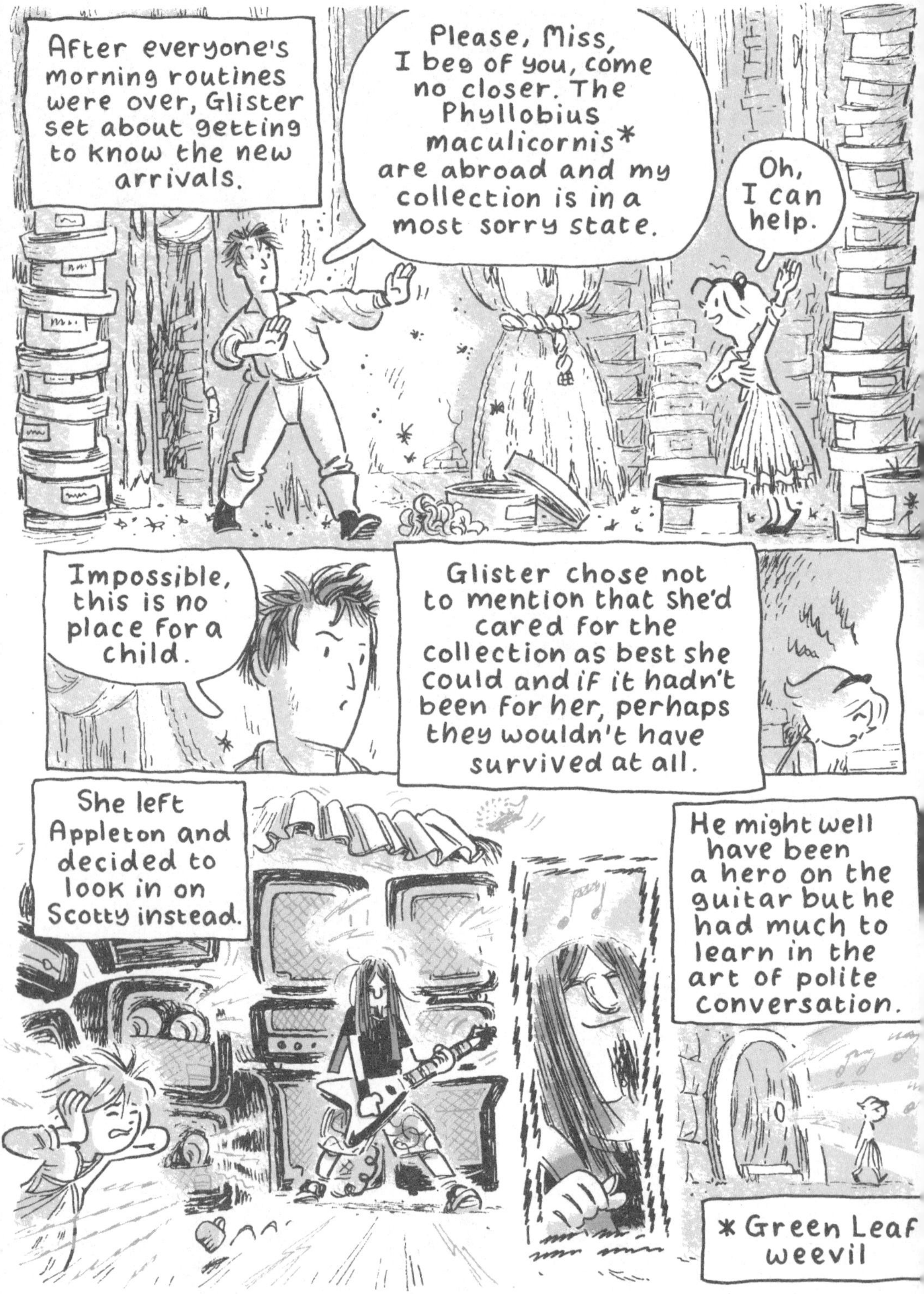
After everyone's morning routines were over, Glister set about getting to know the new arrivals.
Please, Miss, I beg of you, come no closer. The Phyllobius maculicornis* are abroad and my collection is in a most sorry state.
Oh, I can help.
Impossible, this is no place for a child.
Glister chose not to mention that she'd cared for the collection as best she could and if it hadn't been for her, perhaps they wouldn't have survived at all.
She left Appleton and decided to look in on Scotty instead.
He might well have been a hero on the guitar but he had much to learn in the art of polite conversation.
* Green Leaf weevil

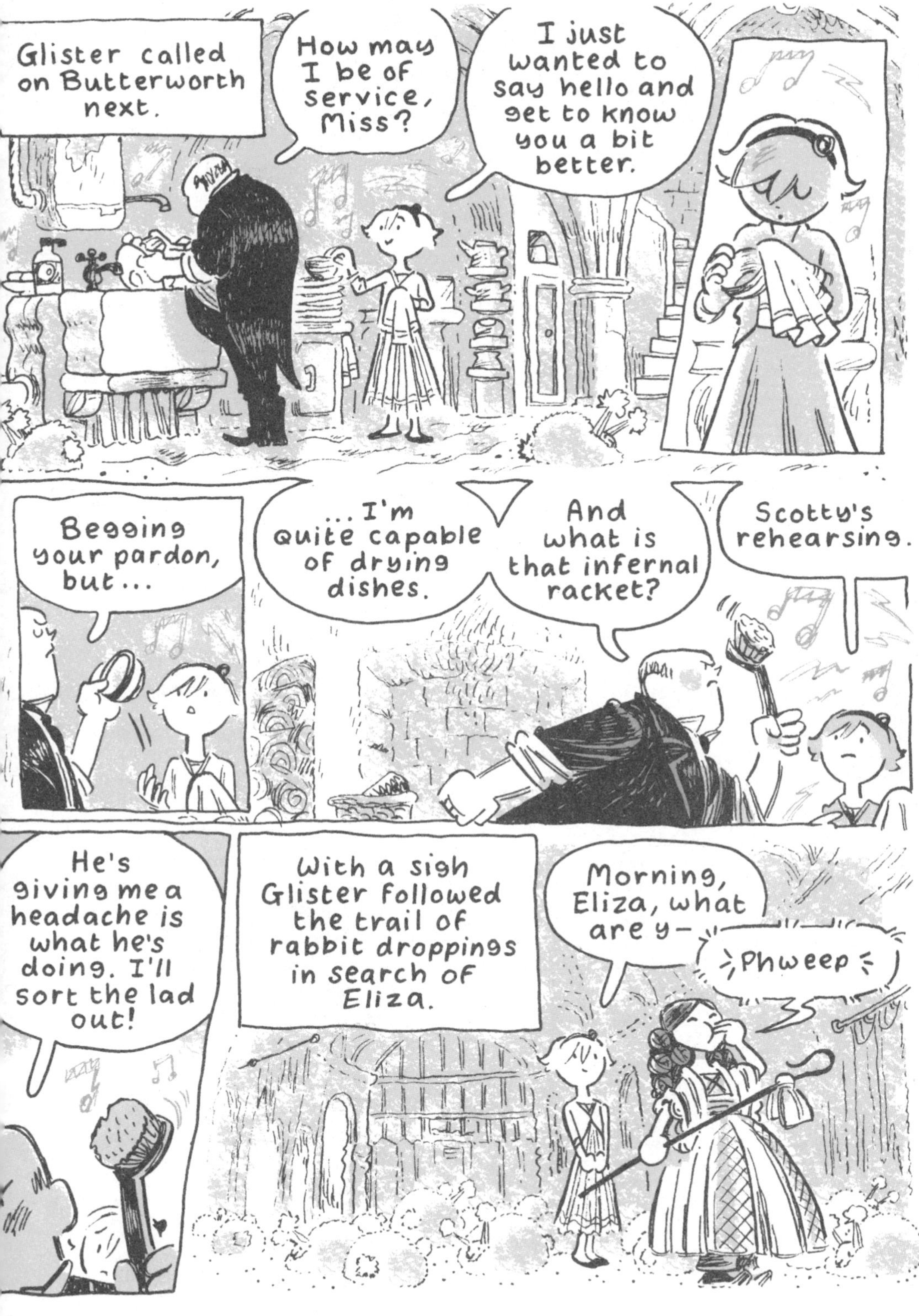
Glister called on Butterworth next.
How may I be of service, Miss?
I just wanted to say hello and get to know you a bit better.
Begging your pardon, but...
...I'm quite capable of drying dishes.
And what is that infernal racket?
Scotty's rehearsing.
He's giving me a headache is what he's doing. I'll sort the lad out!
With a sigh Glister followed the trail of rabbit droppings in search of Eliza.
Morning, Eliza, what are y–
Phweep

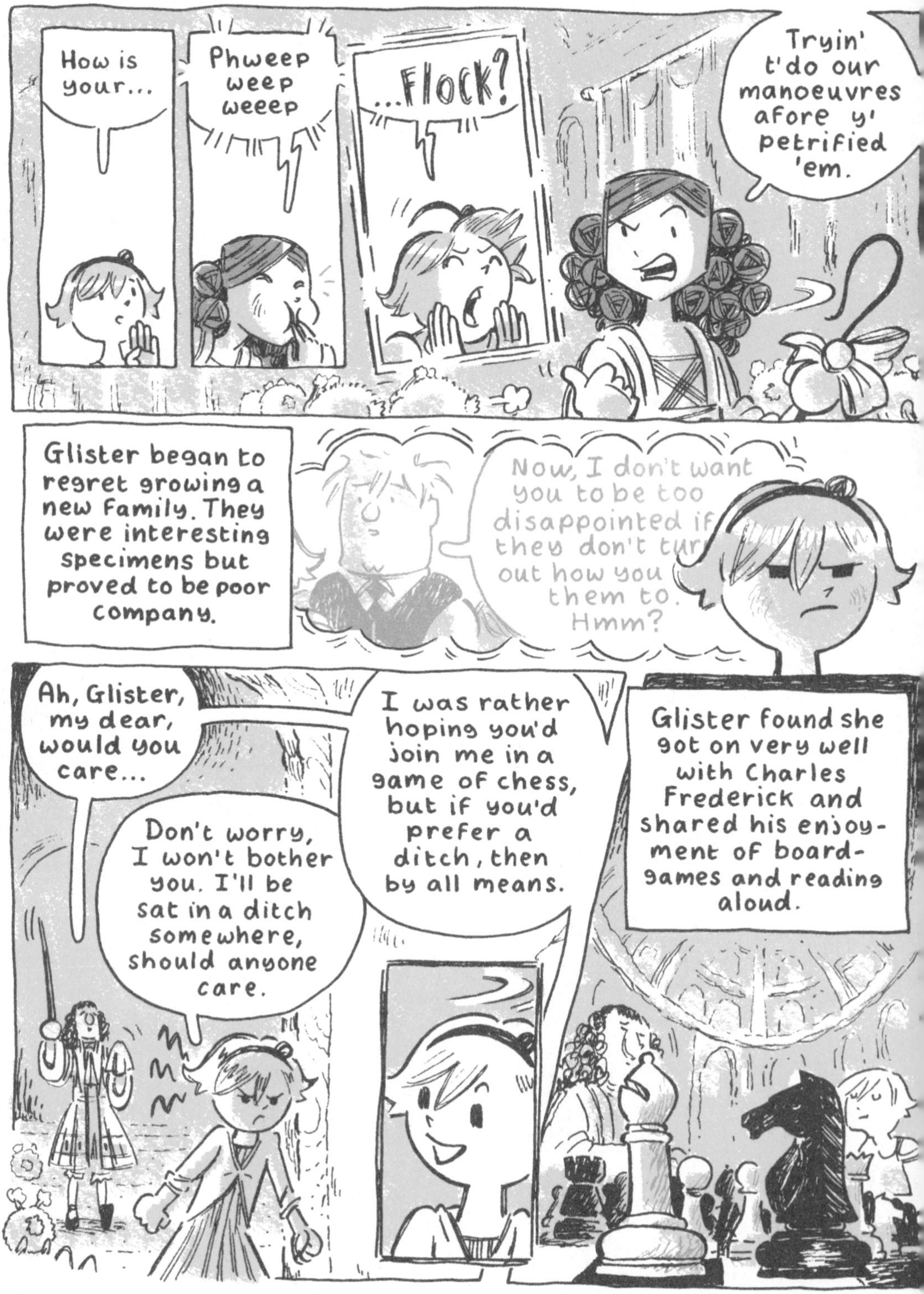
How is your...
Phweep weep weeep
...FLOCK?
Tryin' t'do our manoeuvres afore y' petrified 'em.
Glister began to regret growing a new family. They were interesting specimens but proved to be poor company.
Now, I don't want you to be too disappointed if they don't turn out how you want them to. Hmm?
Ah, Glister, my dear, would you care...
Don't worry, I won't bother you. I'll be sat in a ditch somewhere, should anyone care.
I was rather hoping you'd join me in a game of chess, but if you'd prefer a ditch, then by all means.
Glister found she got on very well with Charles Frederick and shared his enjoyment of board-games and reading aloud.

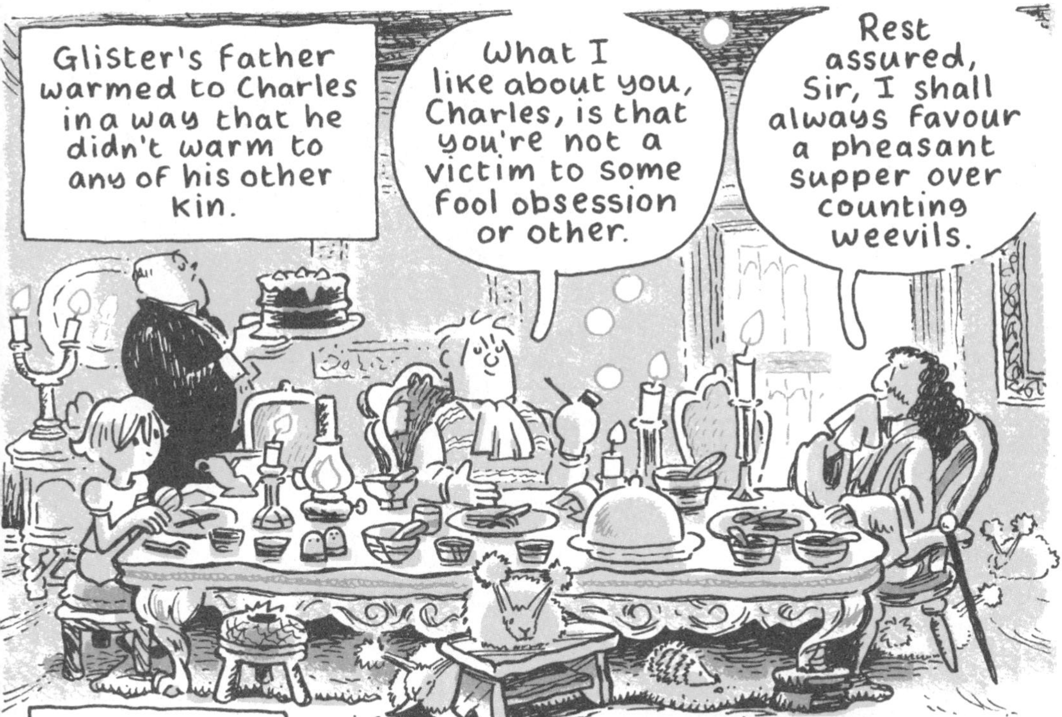
Glister's father warmed to Charles in a way that he didn't warm to any of his other kin.
What I like about you, Charles, is that you're not a victim to some fool obsession or other.
Rest assured, Sir, I shall always favour a pheasant supper over counting weevils.
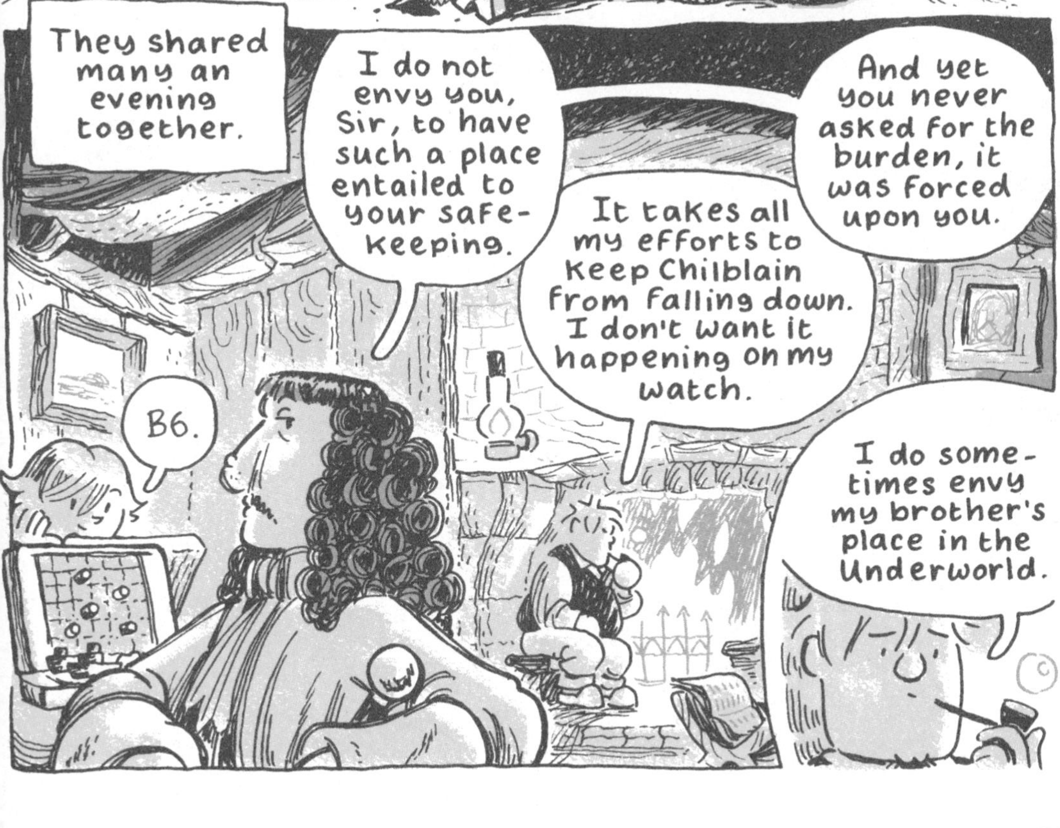
They shared many an evening together.
I do not envy you, Sir, to have such a place entailed to your safe-keeping.
And yet you never asked for the burden, it was forced upon you.
It takes all my efforts to keep Chilblain from falling down. I don't want it happening on my watch.
B6.
I do sometimes envy my brother's place in the Underworld.

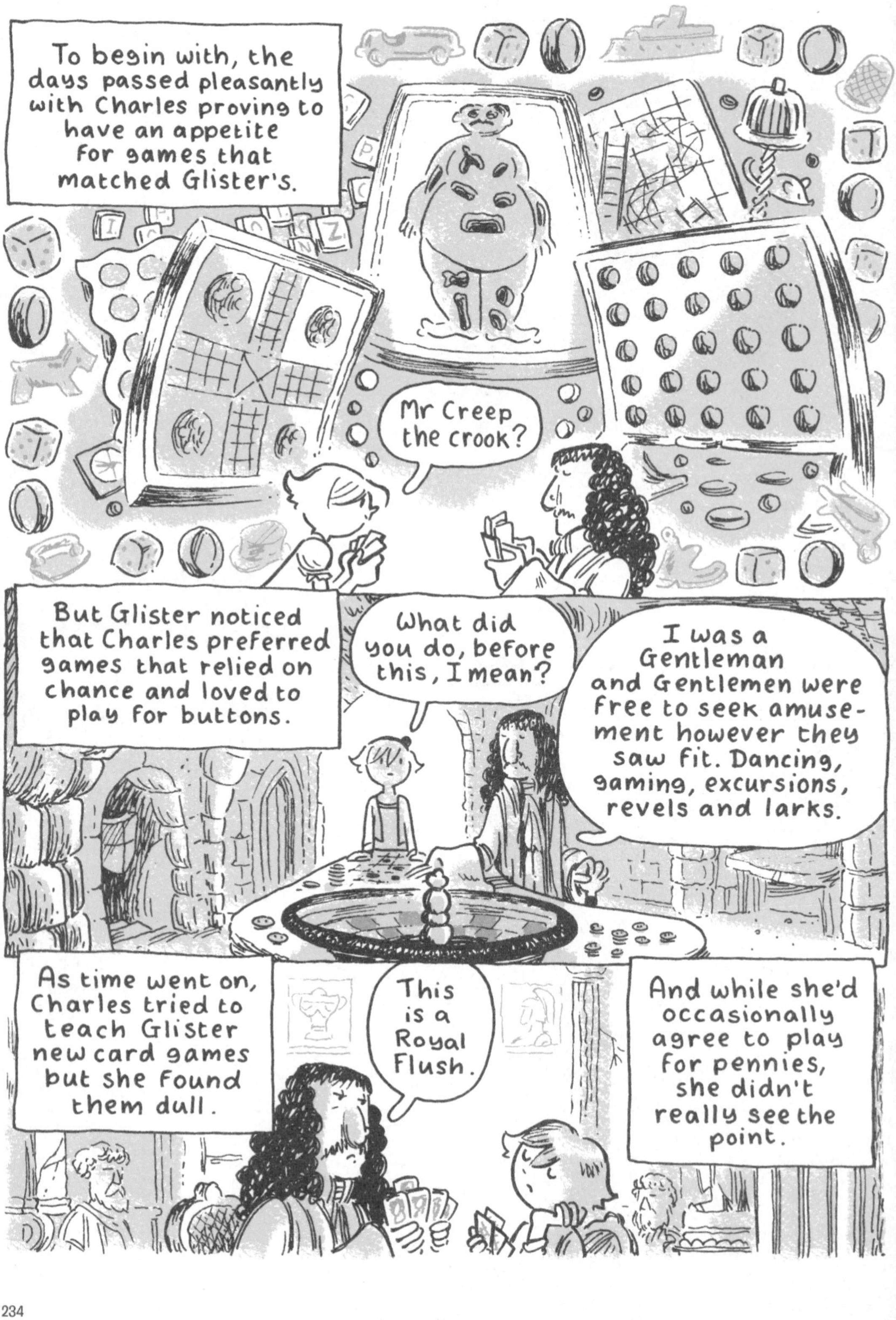

To begin with, the days passed pleasantly with Charles proving to have an appetite for games that matched Glister's.
Mr Creep the crook?
But Glister noticed that Charles preferred games that relied on chance and loved to play for buttons.
What did you do, before this, I mean?
I was a Gentleman and Gentlemen were free to seek amusement however they saw fit. Dancing, gaming, excursions, revels and larks.
As time went on, Charles tried to teach Glister new card games but she found them dull.
This is a Royal Flush.
And while she'd occasionally agree to play for pennies, she didn't really see the point.

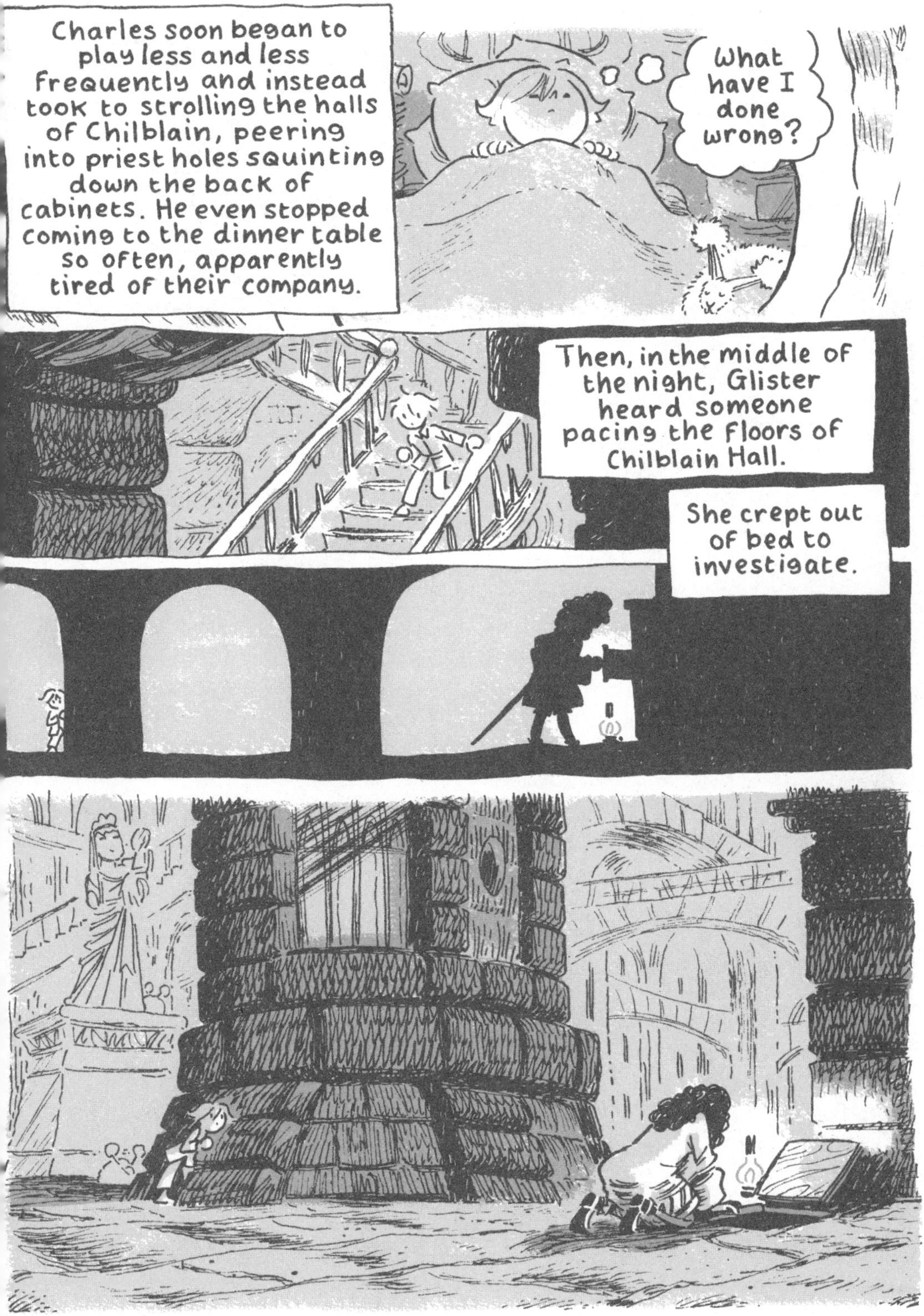
Charles soon began to play less and less frequently and instead took to strolling the halls of Chilblain, peering into priest holes squinting down the back of cabinets. He even stopped coming to the dinner table so often, apparently tired of their company.
What have I done wrong?
Then, in the middle of the night, Glister heard someone pacing the floors of Chilblain Hall.
She crept out of bed to investigate.

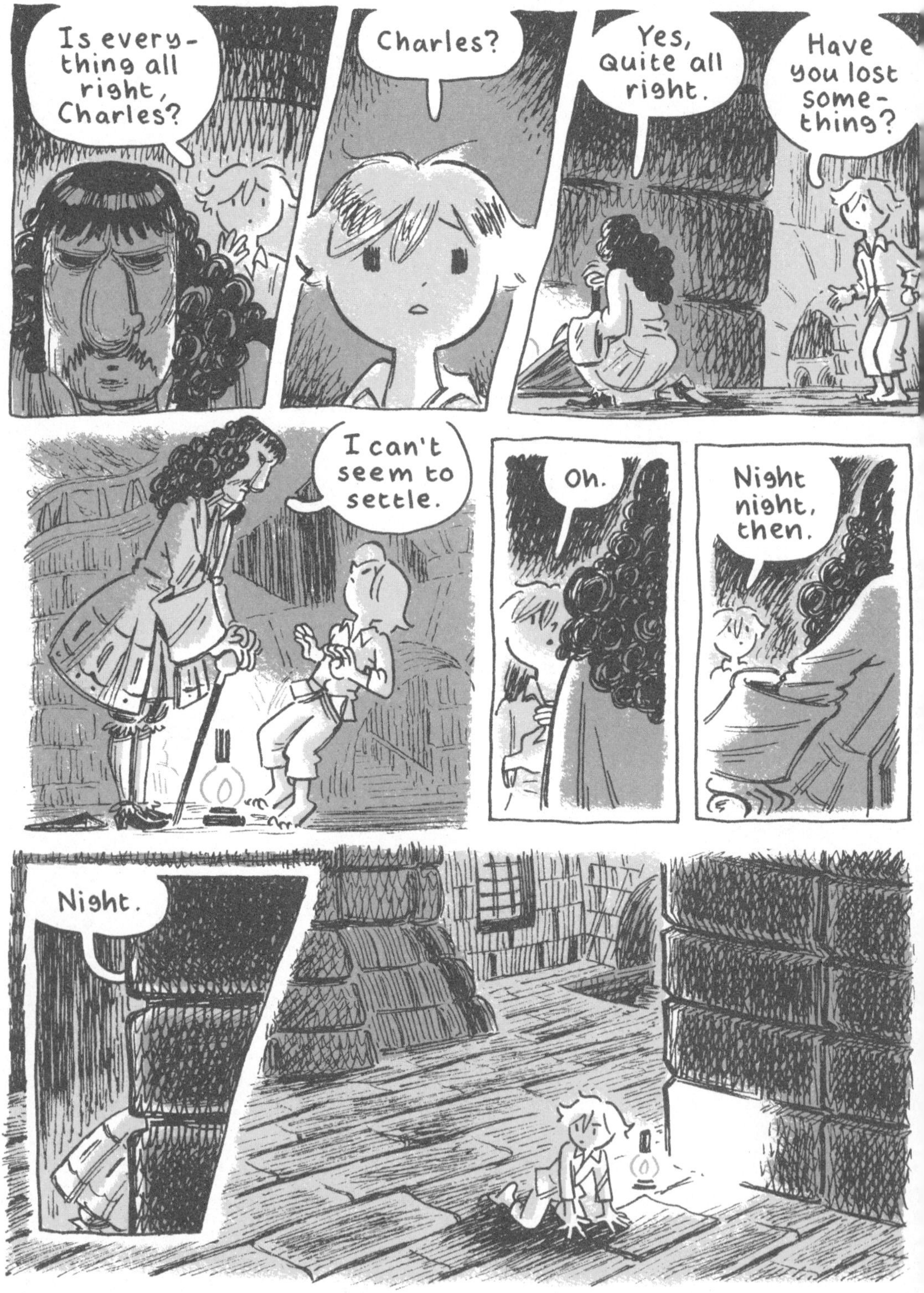

Is every-thing all right, Charles?
Charles?
Yes, Quite all right.
Have you lost some-thing?
I can't seem to settle.
Oh.
Night night, then.
Night.

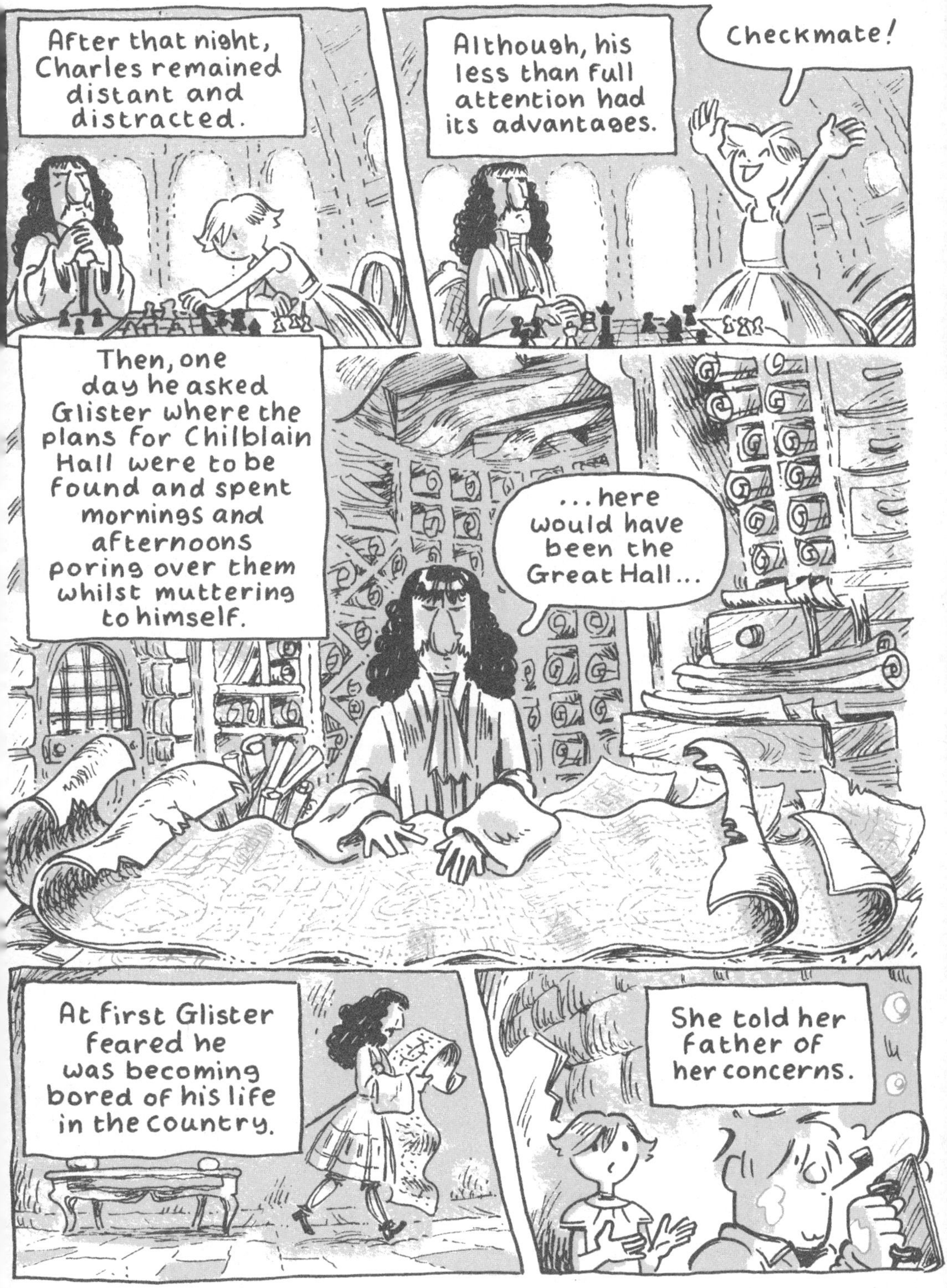
After that night, Charles remained distant and distracted.
Although, his less than full attention had its advantages.
Checkmate!
Then, one day he asked Glister where the plans for Chilblain Hall were to be found and spent mornings and afternoons poring over them whilst muttering to himself.
...here would have been the Great Hall...
At first Glister feared he was becoming bored of his life in the country.
She told her father of her concerns.

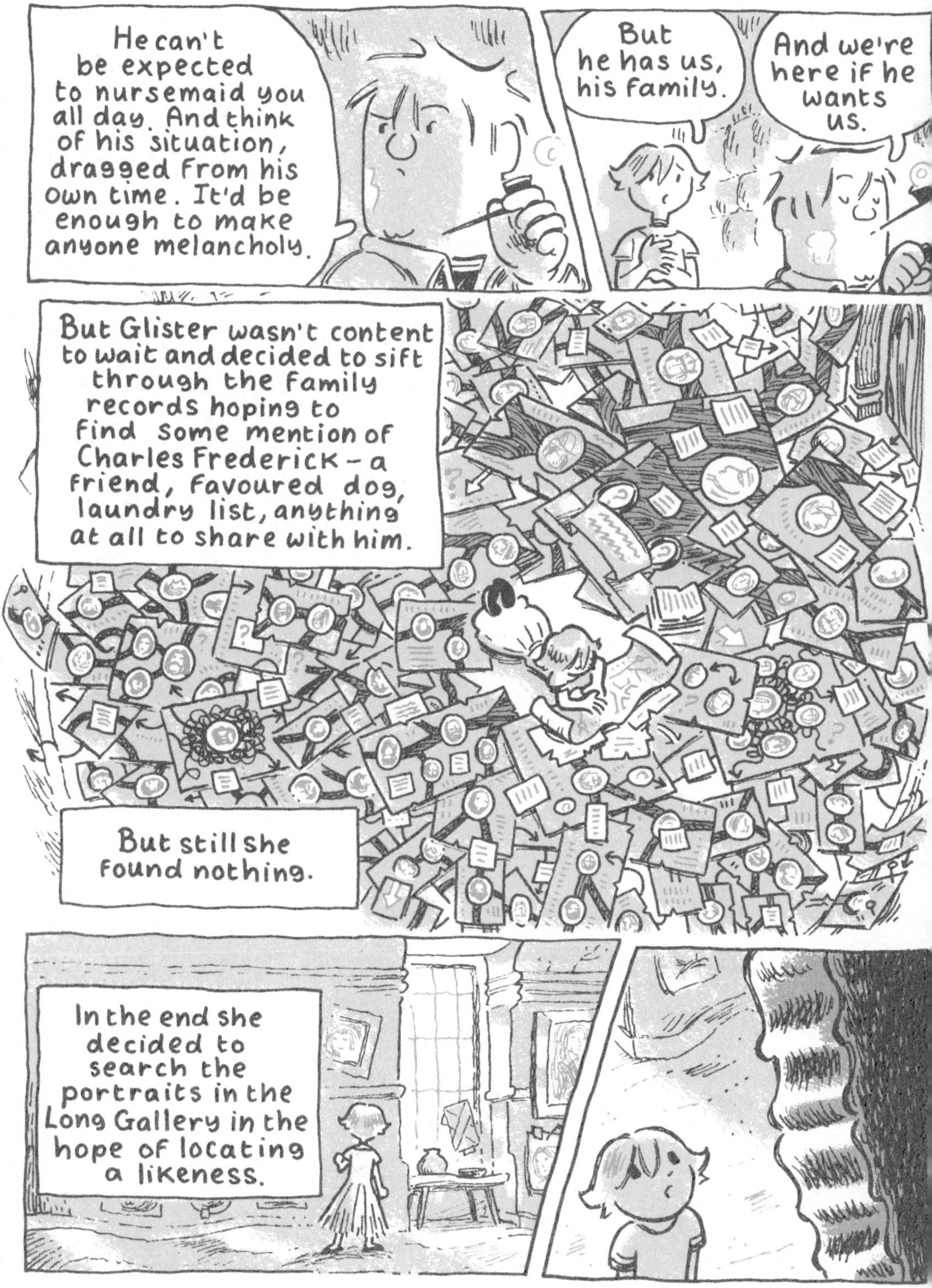
He can't be expected to nursemaid you all day. And think of his situation, dragged from his own time. It'd be enough to make anyone melancholy.
But he has us, his family.
And we're here if he wants us.
But Glister wasn't content to wait and decided to sift through the family records hoping to find some mention of Charles Frederick – a friend, favoured dog, laundry list, anything at all to share with him.
But still she found nothing.
In the end she decided to search the portraits in the Long Gallery in the hope of locating a likeness.

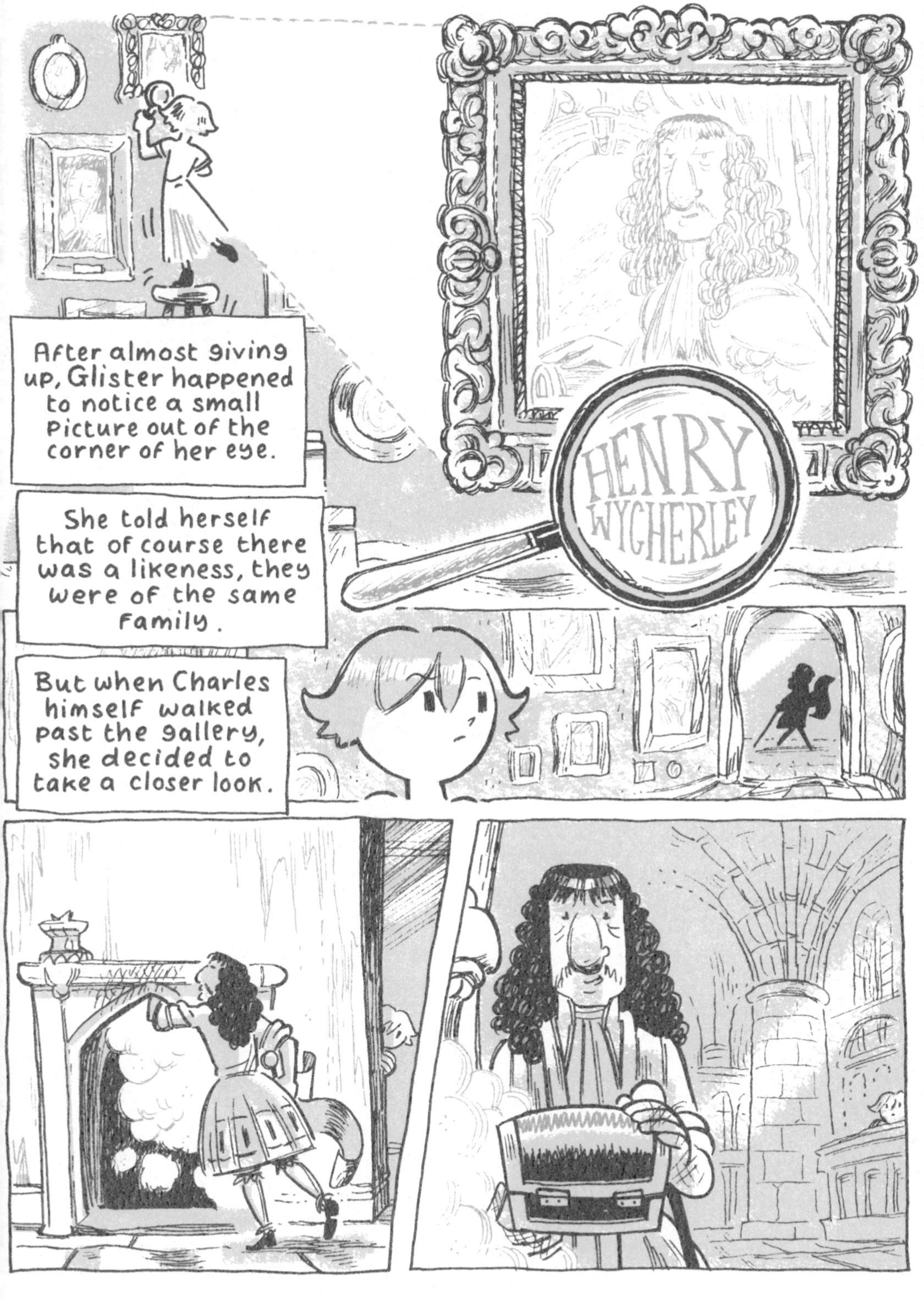
After almost giving up, Glister happened to notice a small picture out of the corner of her eye.
HENRY WYCHERLEY
She told herself that of course there was a likeness, they were of the same family.
But when Charles himself walked past the gallery, she decided to take a closer look.

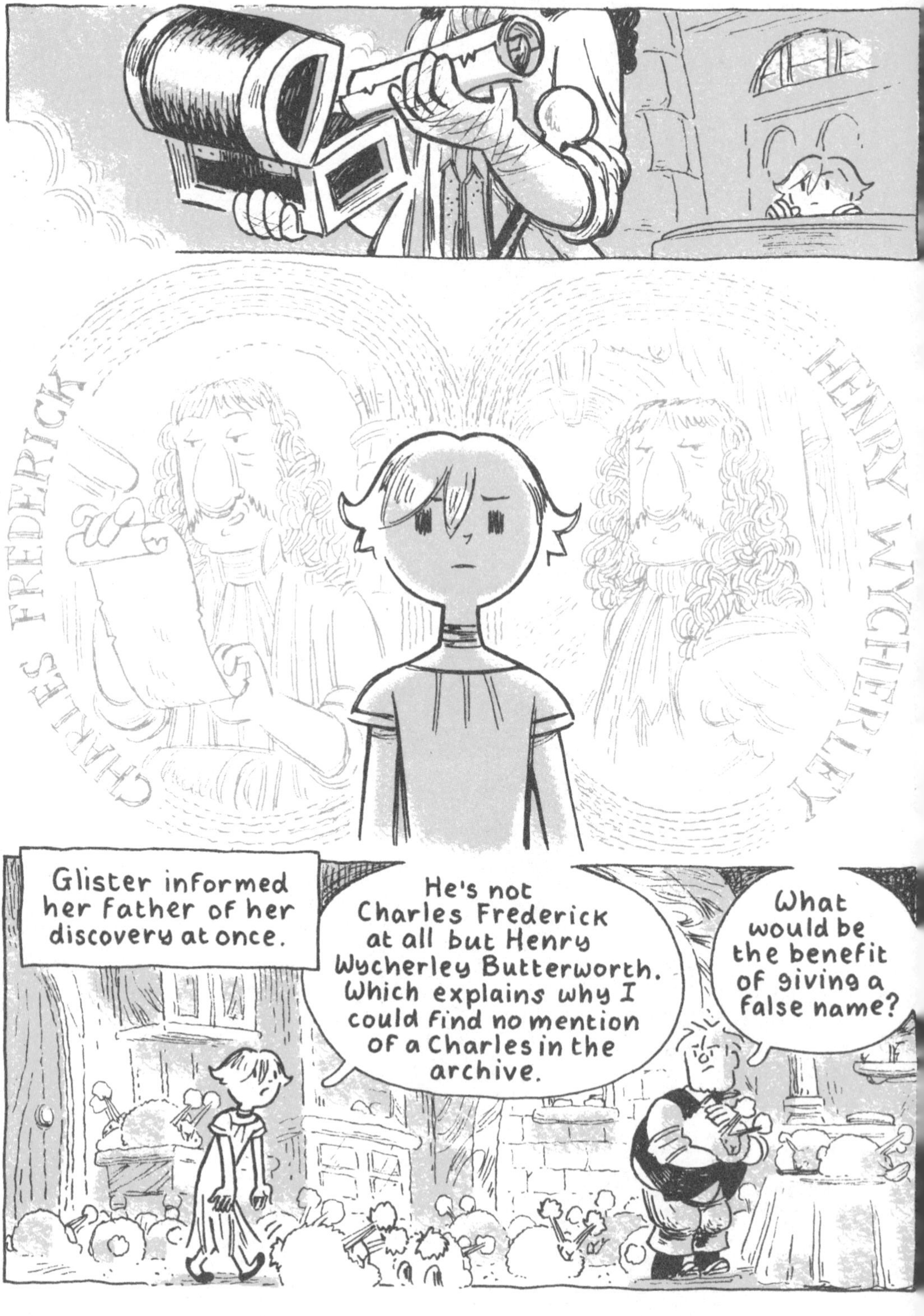
CHARLES FREDERICK
HENRY WYCHERLEY
Glister informed her father of her discovery at once.
He's not Charles Frederick at all but Henry Wycherley Butterworth. Which explains why I could find no mention of a Charles in the archive.
What would be the benefit of giving a false name?

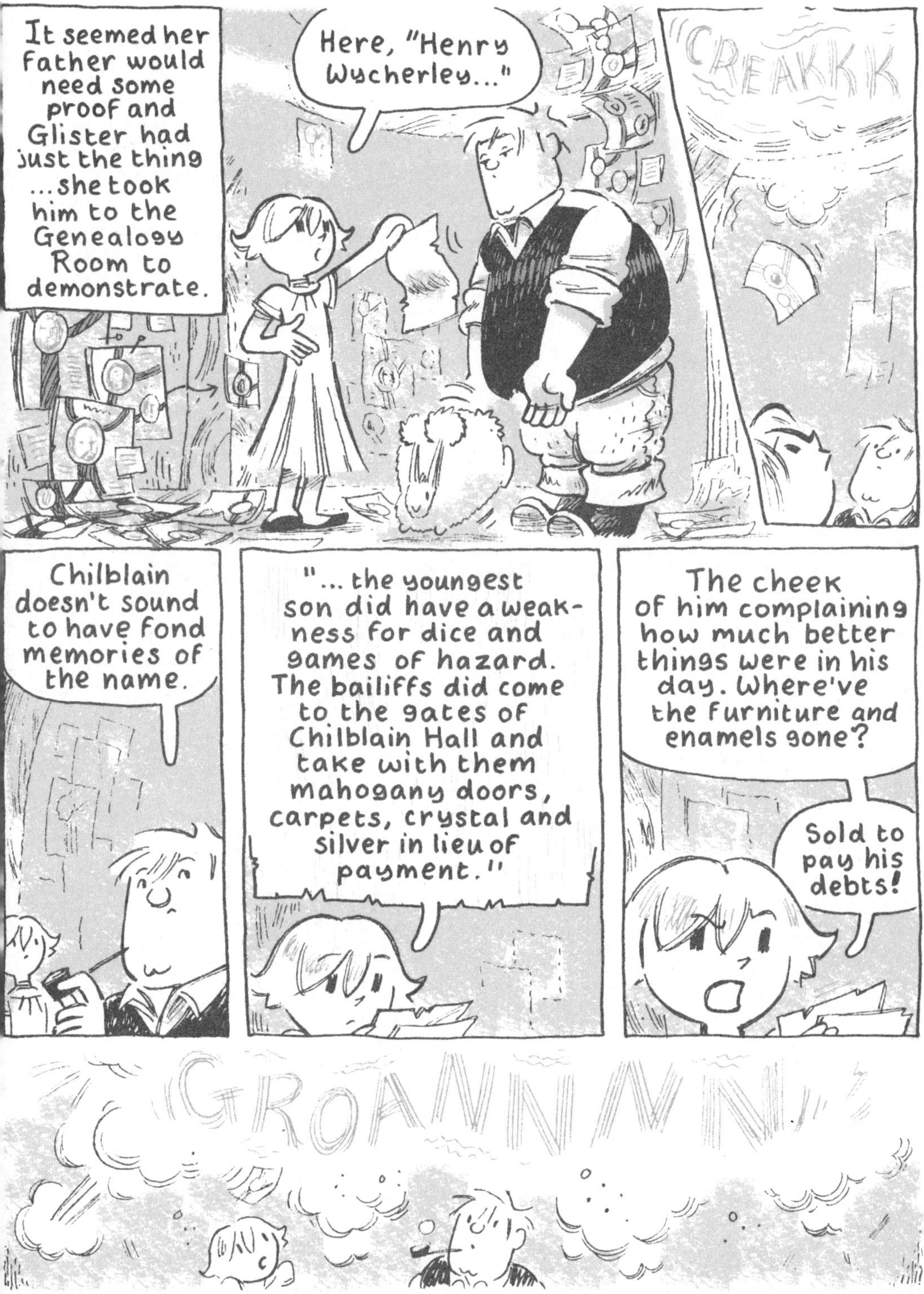
It seemed her father would need some proof and Glister had just the thing ...she took him to the Genealogy Room to demonstrate.
Here, "Henry Wycherley..."
CREAKKK
Chilblain doesn't sound to have fond memories of the name.
"... the youngest son did have a weakness for dice and games of hazard. The bailiffs did come to the gates of Chilblain Hall and take with them mahogany doors, carpets, crystal and silver in lieu of payment."
The cheek of him complaining how much better things were in his day. Where've the furniture and enamels gone?
Sold to pay his debts!
GROANNNN

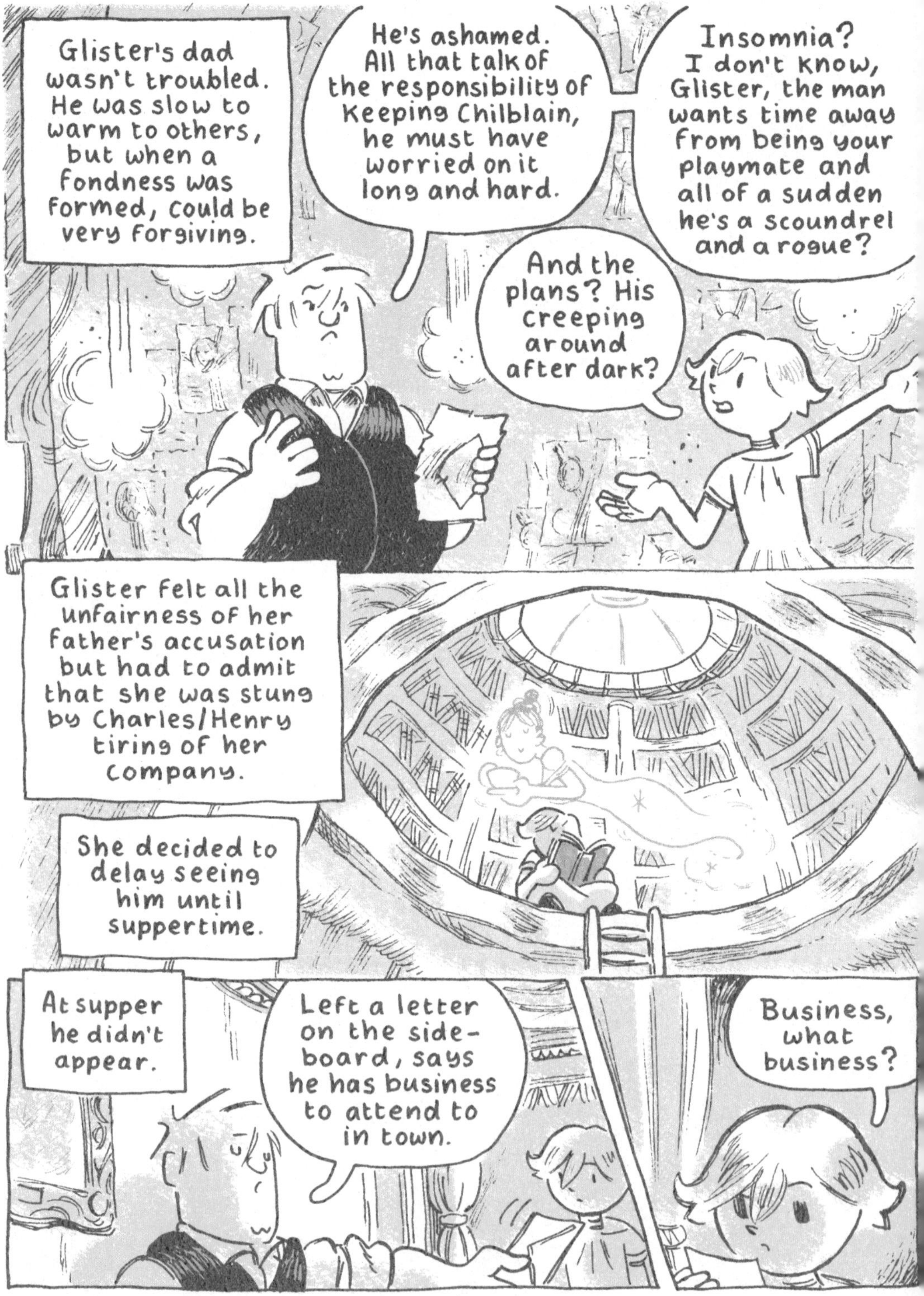
Glister's dad wasn't troubled. He was slow to warm to others, but when a fondness was formed, could be very forgiving.
He's ashamed. All that talk of the responsibility of keeping Chilblain, he must have worried on it long and hard.
Insomnia? I don't know, Glister, the man wants time away from being your playmate and all of a sudden he's a scoundrel and a rogue?
And the plans? His creeping around after dark?
Glister felt all the unfairness of her father's accusation but had to admit that she was stung by Charles/Henry tiring of her company.
She decided to delay seeing him until suppertime.
At supper he didn't appear.
Left a letter on the side-board, says he has business to attend to in town.
Business, what business?

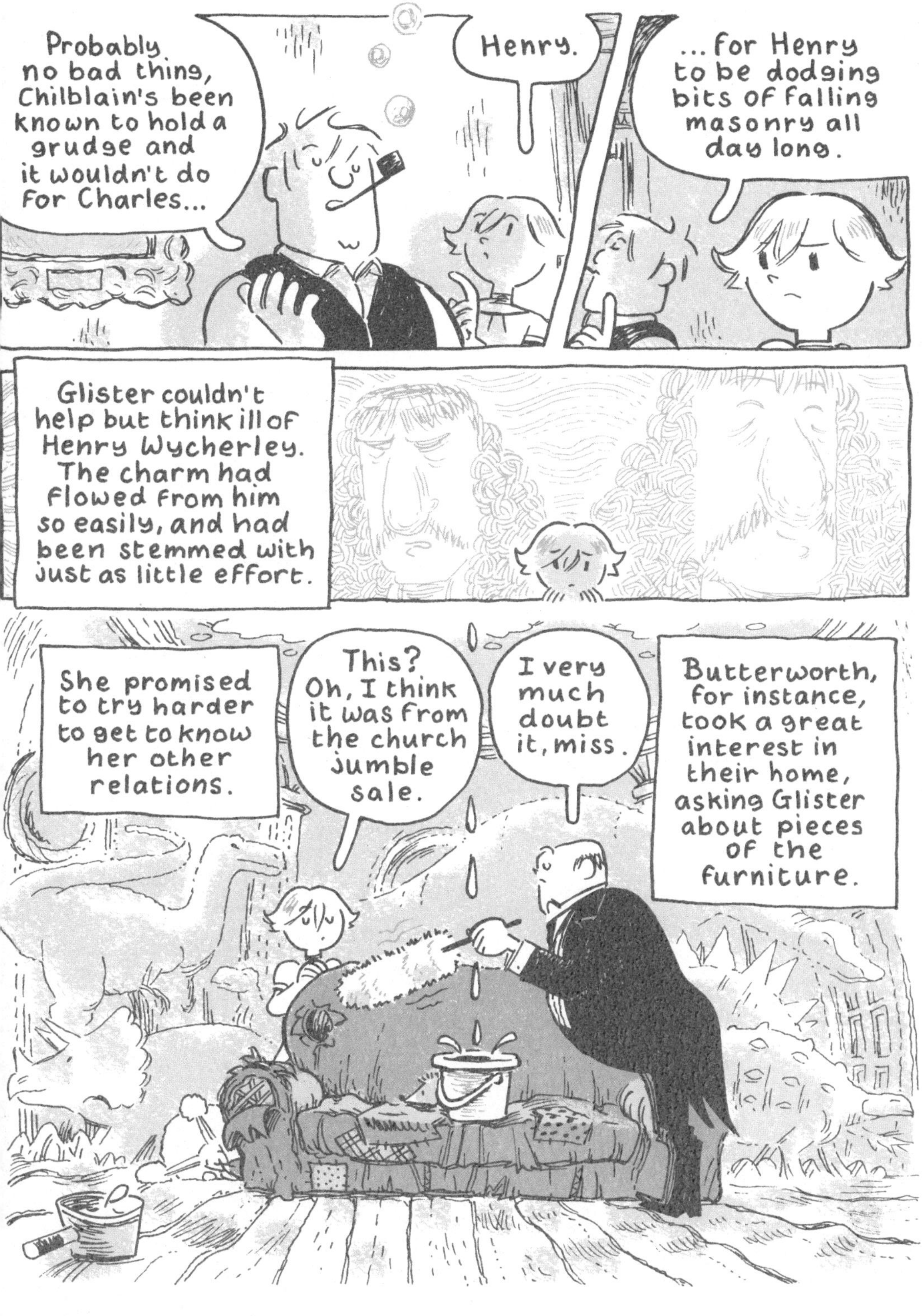

Probably no bad thing, Chilblain's been known to hold a grudge and it wouldn't do for Charles...
Henry.
... for Henry to be dodging bits of falling masonry all day long.
Glister couldn't help but think ill of Henry Wycherley. The charm had flowed from him so easily, and had been stemmed with just as little effort.
She promised to try harder to get to know her other relations.
Butterworth, for instance, took a great interest in their home, asking Glister about pieces of the furniture.
This? Oh, I think it was from the church jumble sale.
I very much doubt it, miss.

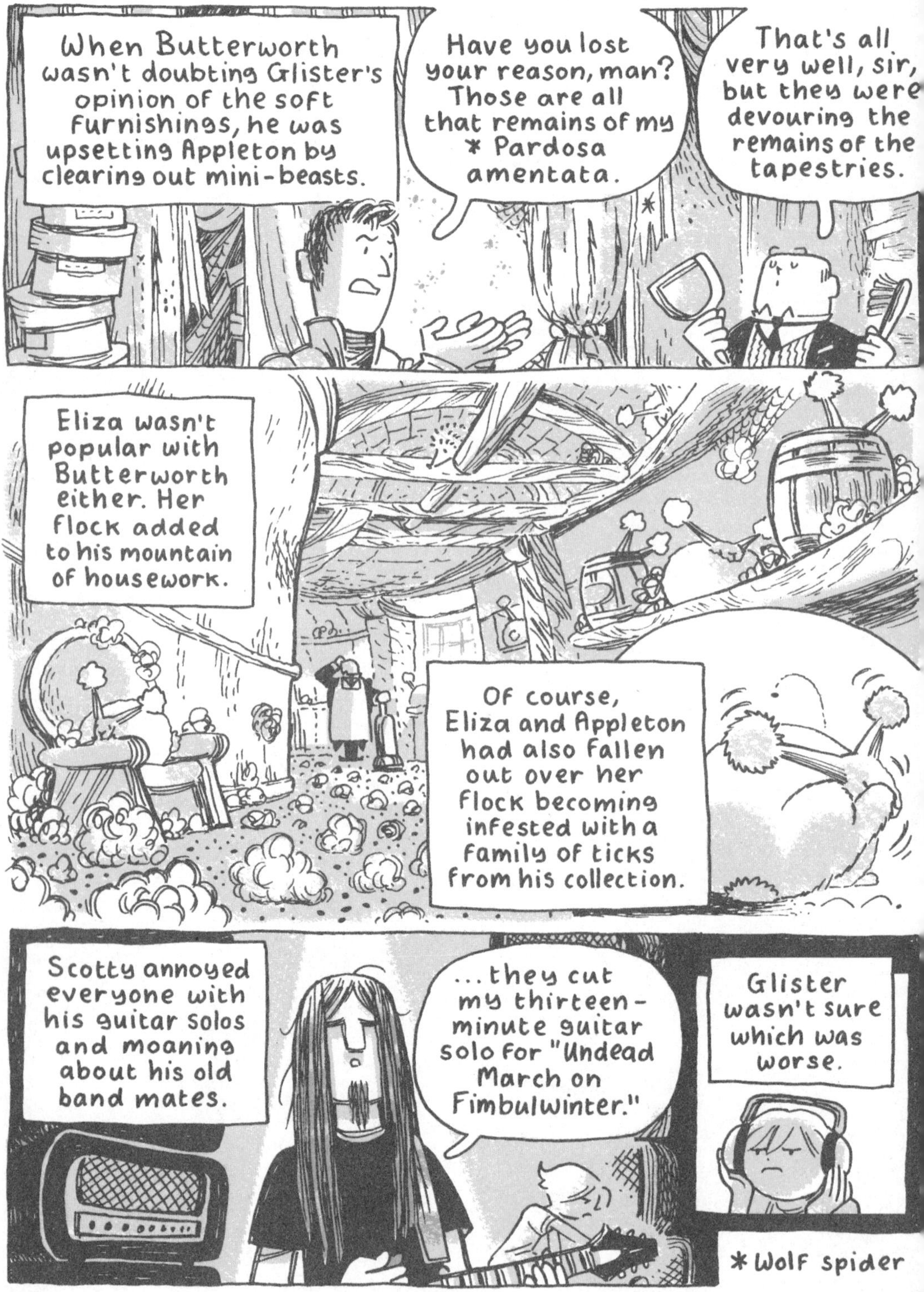
When Butterworth wasn't doubting Glister's opinion of the soft furnishings, he was upsetting Appleton by clearing out mini-beasts.
Have you lost your reason, man? Those are all that remains of my * Pardosa amentata.
That's all very well, sir, but they were devouring the remains of the tapestries.
Eliza wasn't popular with Butterworth either. Her flock added to his mountain of housework.
Of course, Eliza and Appleton had also fallen out over her flock becoming infested with a family of ticks from his collection.
Scotty annoyed everyone with his guitar solos and moaning about his old band mates.
...they cut my thirteen-minute guitar solo for "Undead March on Fimbulwinter."
Glister wasn't sure which was worse.
* Wolf spider

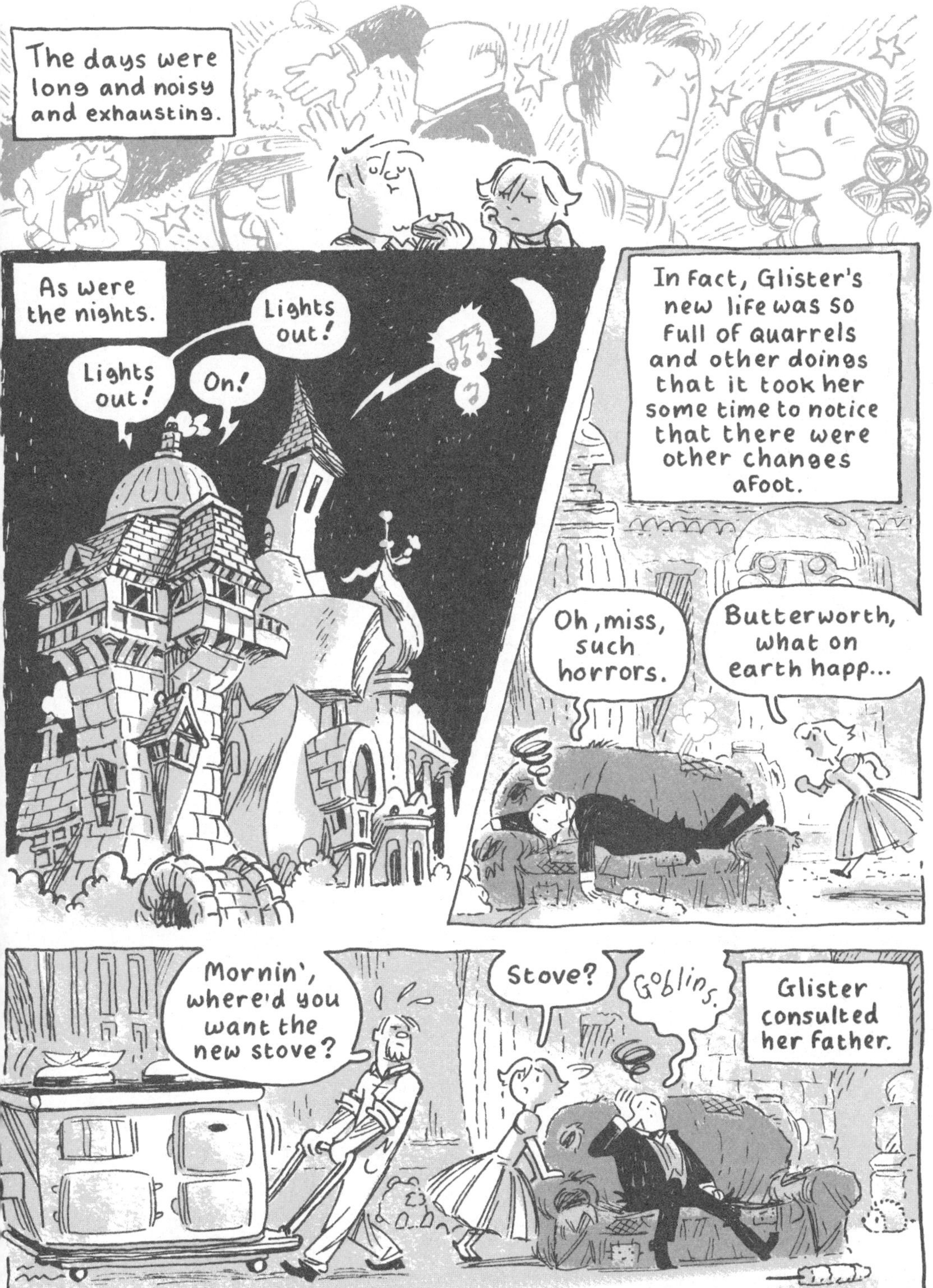
The days were long and noisy and exhausting.
As were the nights.
Lights out!
On!
Lights out!
In fact, Glister's new life was so full of quarrels and other doings that it took her some time to notice that there were other changes afoot.
Oh, miss, such horrors.
Butterworth, what on earth happ...
Mornin', where'd you want the new stove?
Stove?
Goblins.
Glister consulted her father.

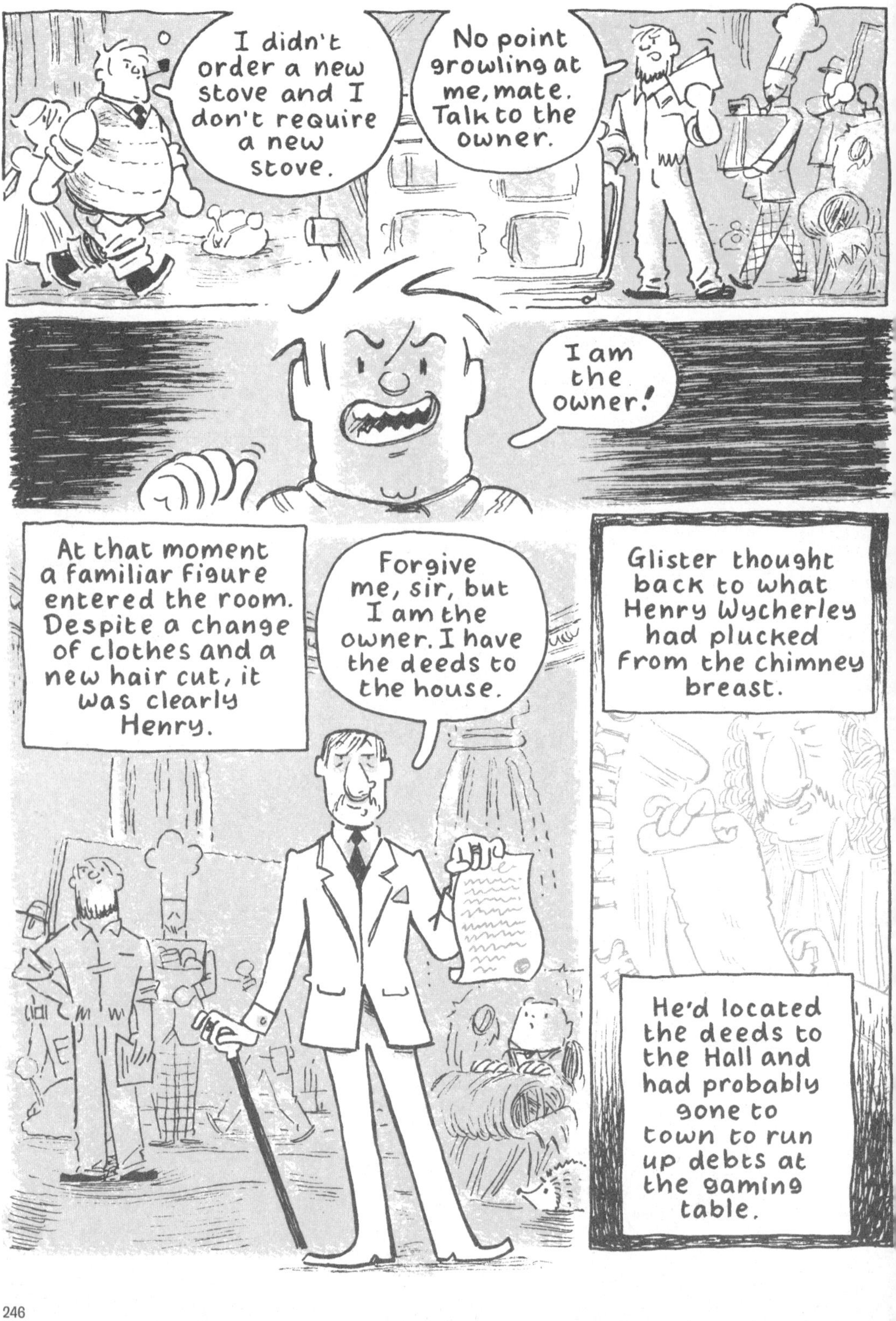
I didn't order a new stove and I don't require a new stove.
No point growling at me, mate. Talk to the owner.
I am the owner!
At that moment a familiar figure entered the room. Despite a change of clothes and a new hair cut, it was clearly Henry.
Forgive me, sir, but I am the owner. I have the deeds to the house.
Glister thought back to what Henry Wycherley had plucked from the chimney breast.
He'd located the deeds to the Hall and had probably gone to town to run up debts at the gaming table.

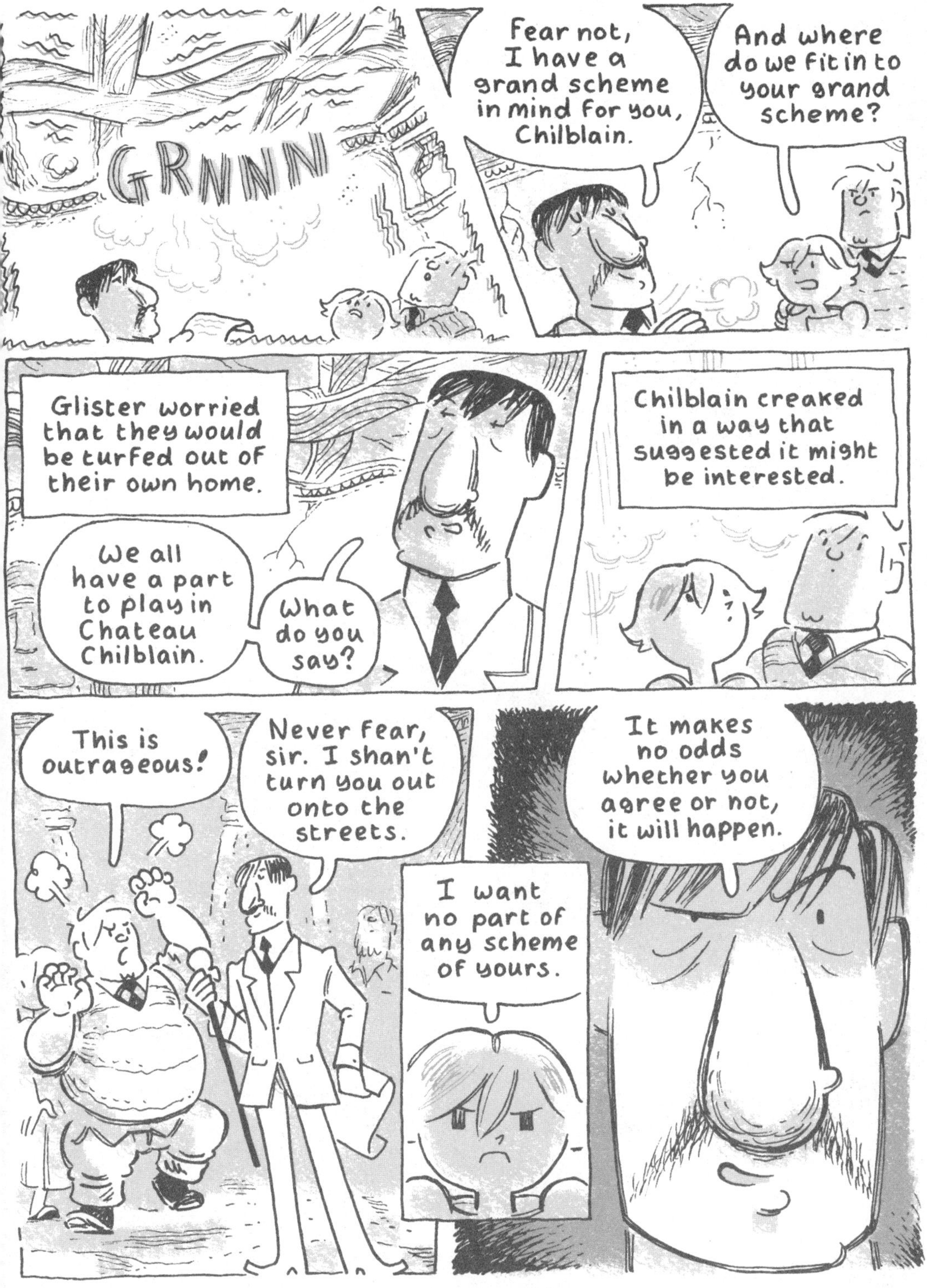
GRNNN
Fear not, I have a grand scheme in mind for you, Chilblain.
And where do we fit in to your grand scheme?
Glister worried that they would be turfed out of their own home.
We all have a part to play in Chateau Chilblain.
What do you say?
Chilblain creaked in a way that suggested it might be interested.
This is outrageous!
Never fear, sir. I shan't turn you out onto the streets.
I want no part of any scheme of yours.
It makes no odds whether you agree or not, it will happen.

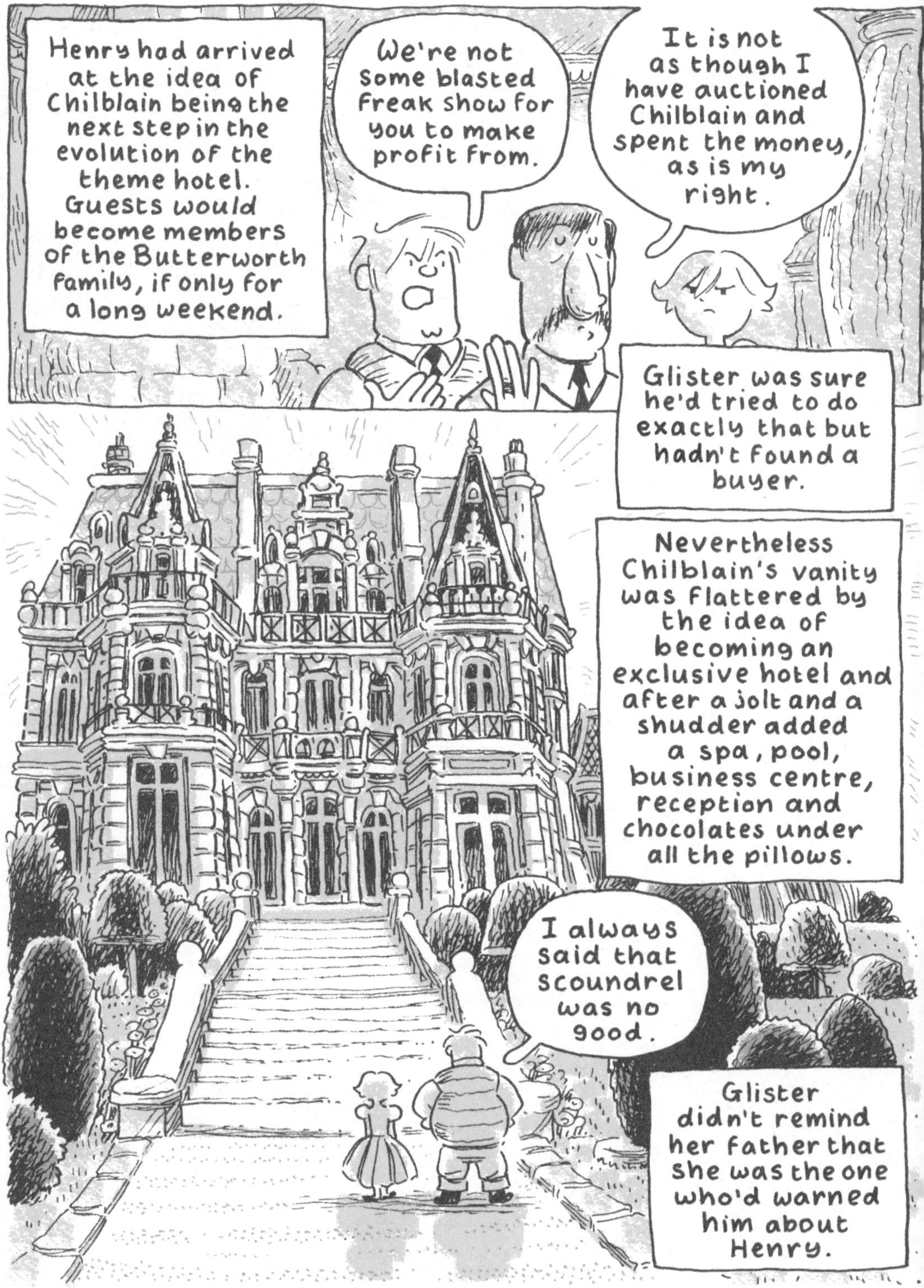

Henry had arrived at the idea of Chilblain being the next step in the evolution of the theme hotel. Guests would become members of the Butterworth family, if only for a long weekend.
We're not some blasted freak show for you to make profit from.
It is not as though I have auctioned Chilblain and spent the money, as is my right.
Glister was sure he'd tried to do exactly that but hadn't found a buyer.
Nevertheless Chilblain's vanity was flattered by the idea of becoming an exclusive hotel and after a jolt and a shudder added a spa, pool, business centre, reception and chocolates under all the pillows.
I always said that scoundrel was no good.
Glister didn't remind her father that she was the one who'd warned him about Henry.

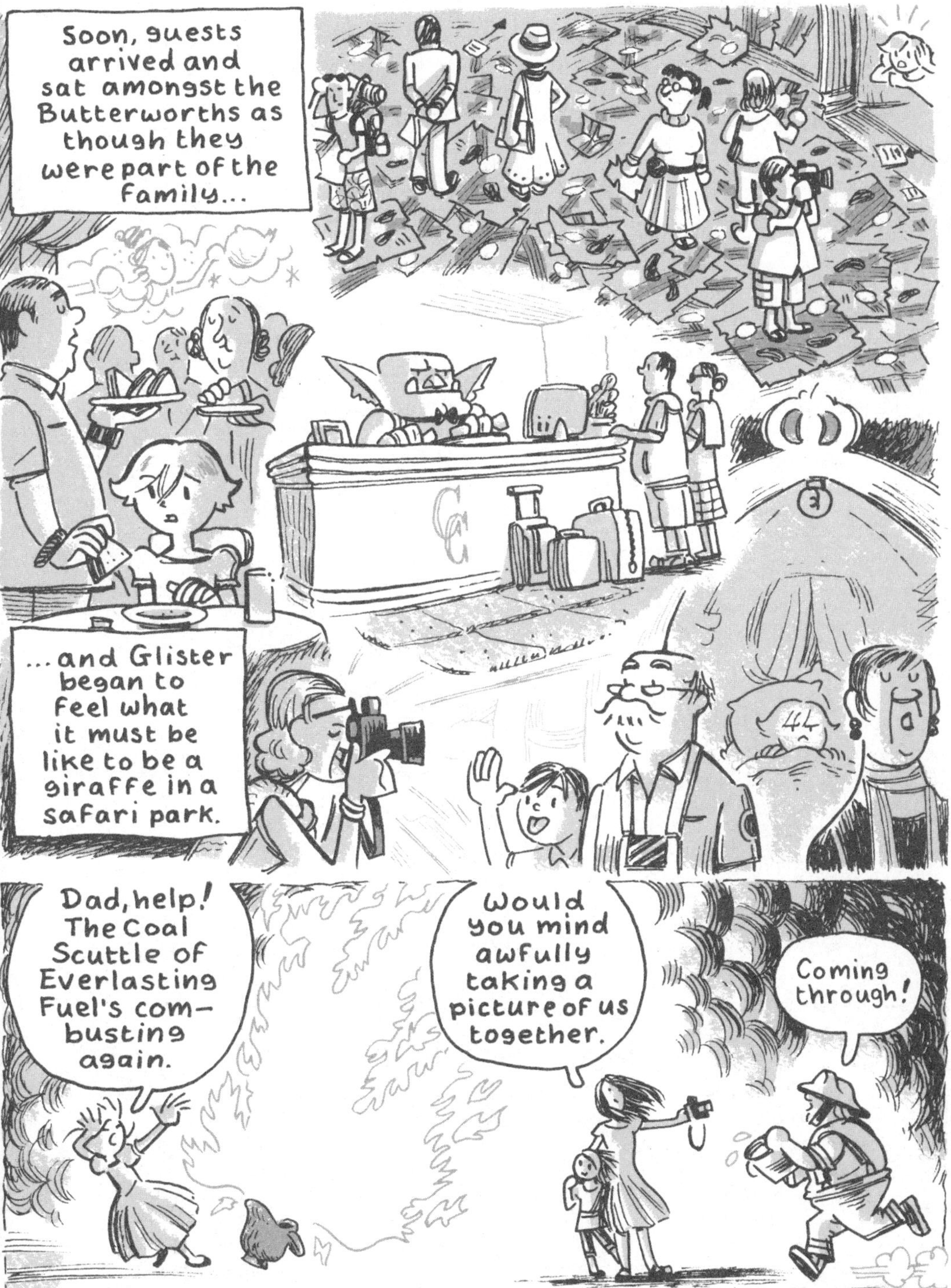
Soon, guests arrived and sat amongst the Butterworths as though they were part of the family...
CC
...and Glister began to feel what it must be like to be a giraffe in a safari park.
Dad, help! The Coal Scuttle of Everlasting Fuel's com-busting again.
Would you mind awfully taking a picture of us together.
Coming through!

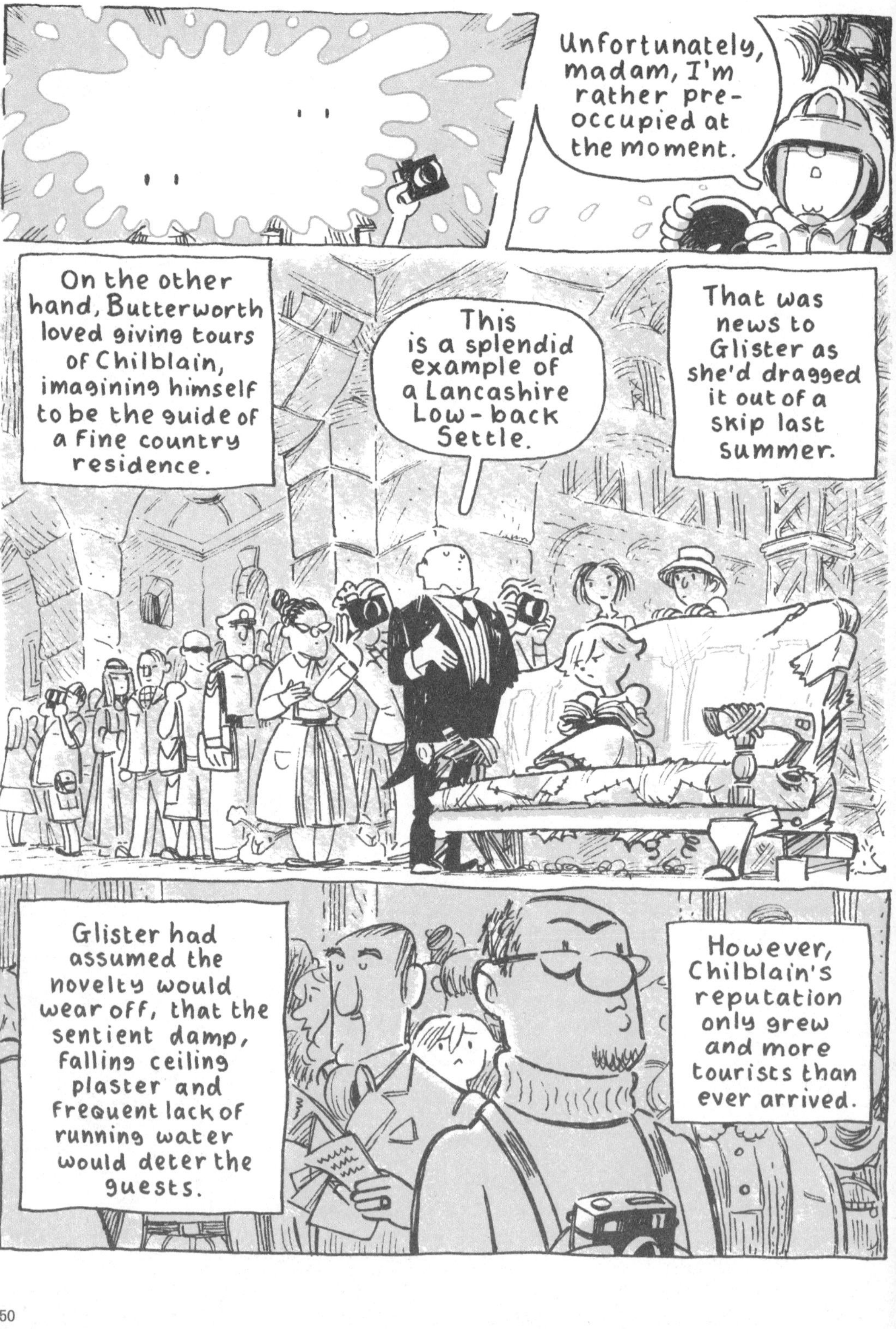
Unfortunately, madam, I'm rather pre-occupied at the moment.
On the other hand, Butterworth loved giving tours of Chilblain, imagining himself to be the guide of a fine country residence.
This is a splendid example of a Lancashire Low-back Settle.
That was news to Glister as she'd dragged it out of a skip last summer.
Glister had assumed the novelty would wear off, that the sentient damp, falling ceiling plaster and frequent lack of running water would deter the guests.
However, Chilblain's reputation only grew and more tourists than ever arrived.

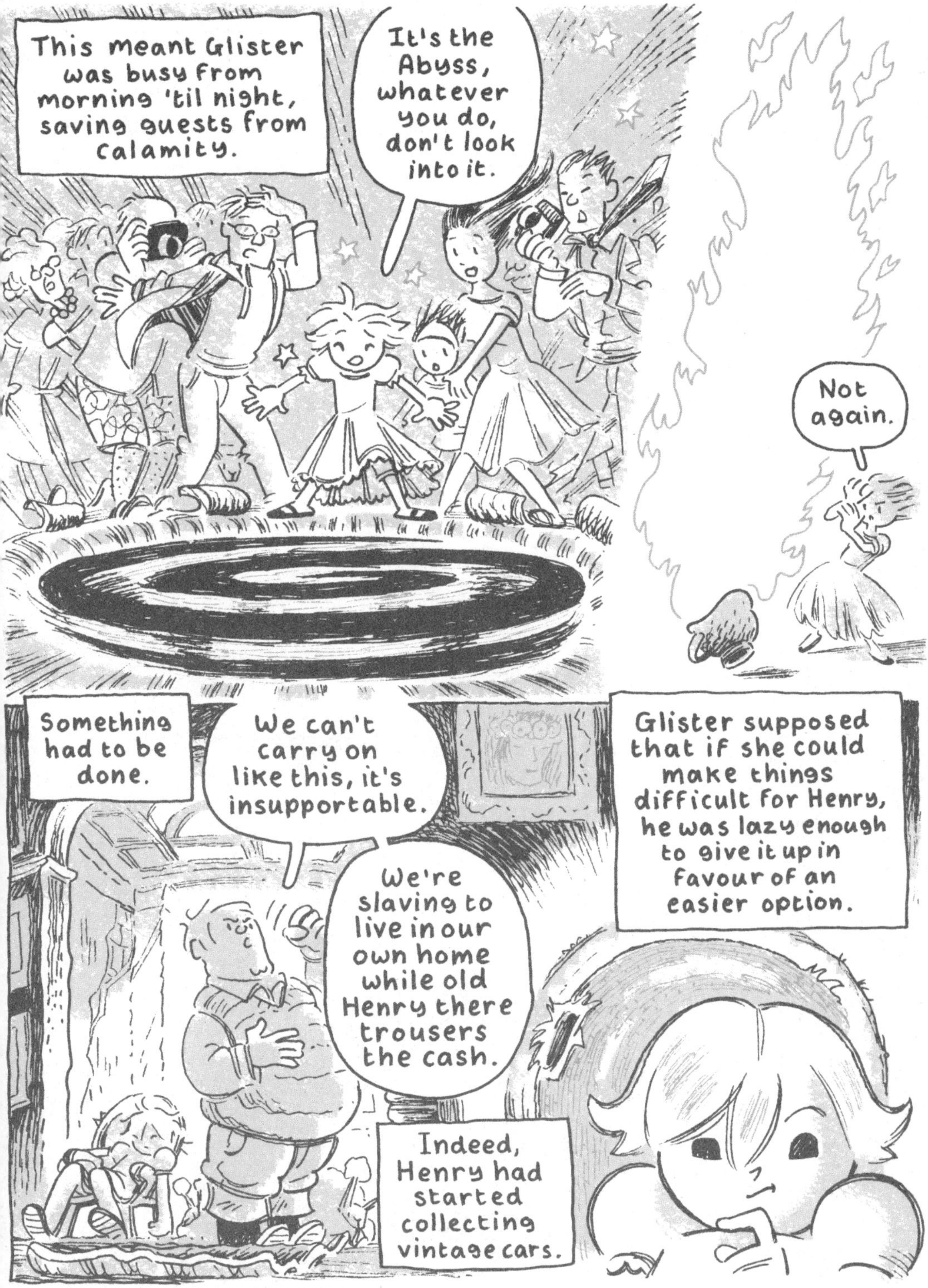
This meant Glister was busy from morning 'til night, saving guests from calamity.
It's the Abyss, whatever you do, don't look into it.
Not again.
Something had to be done.
We can't carry on like this, it's insupportable.
We're slaving to live in our own home while old Henry there trousers the cash.
Glister supposed that if she could make things difficult for Henry, he was lazy enough to give it up in favour of an easier option.
Indeed, Henry had started collecting vintage cars.

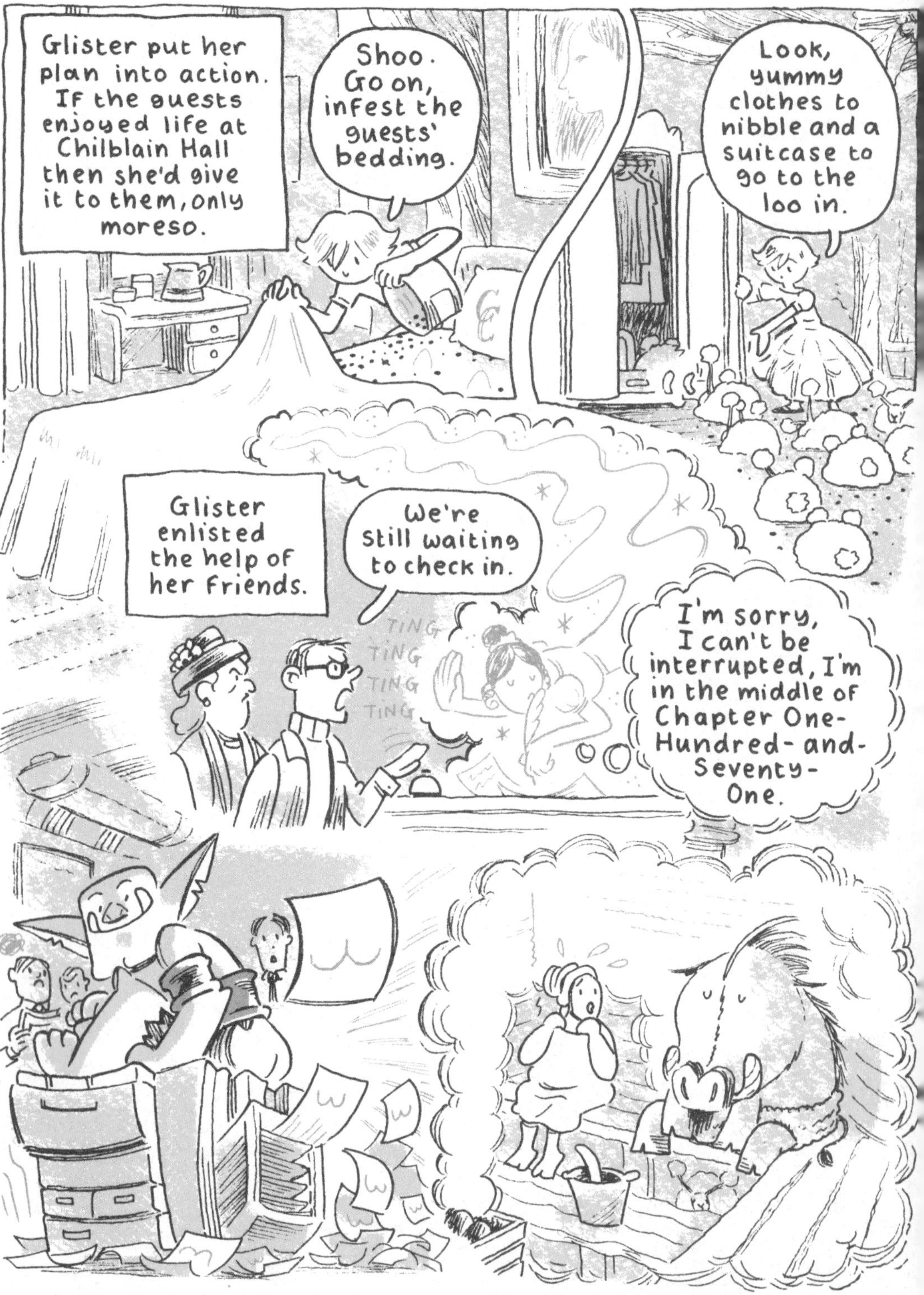

Glister put her plan into action. If the guests enjoyed life at Chilblain Hall then she'd give it to them, only moreso.
Shoo. Go on, infest the guests' bedding.
Look, yummy clothes to nibble and a suitcase to go to the loo in.
Glister enlisted the help of her friends.
We're still waiting to check in.
TING TING TING TING
I'm sorry, I can't be interrupted, I'm in the middle of Chapter One-Hundred-and-Seventy-One.

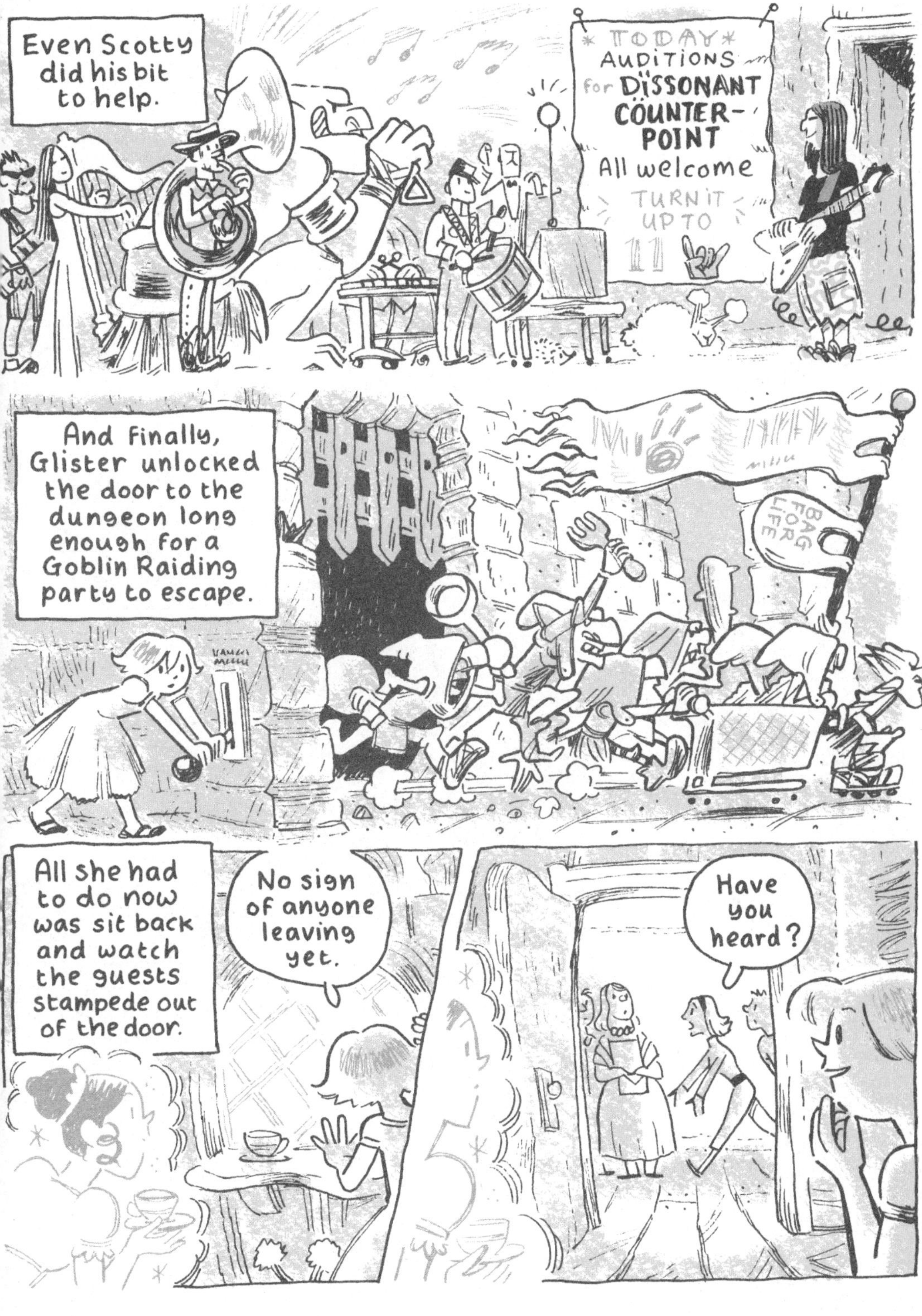

Even Scotty did his bit to help.
TODAY AUDITIONS for DISSONANT COUNTER-POINT All welcome TURN IT UP TO 11
And finally, Glister unlocked the door to the dungeon long enough for a Goblin Raiding party to escape.
BAG FOR LIFE
All she had to do now was sit back and watch the guests stampede out of the door.
No sign of anyone leaving yet.
Have you heard?

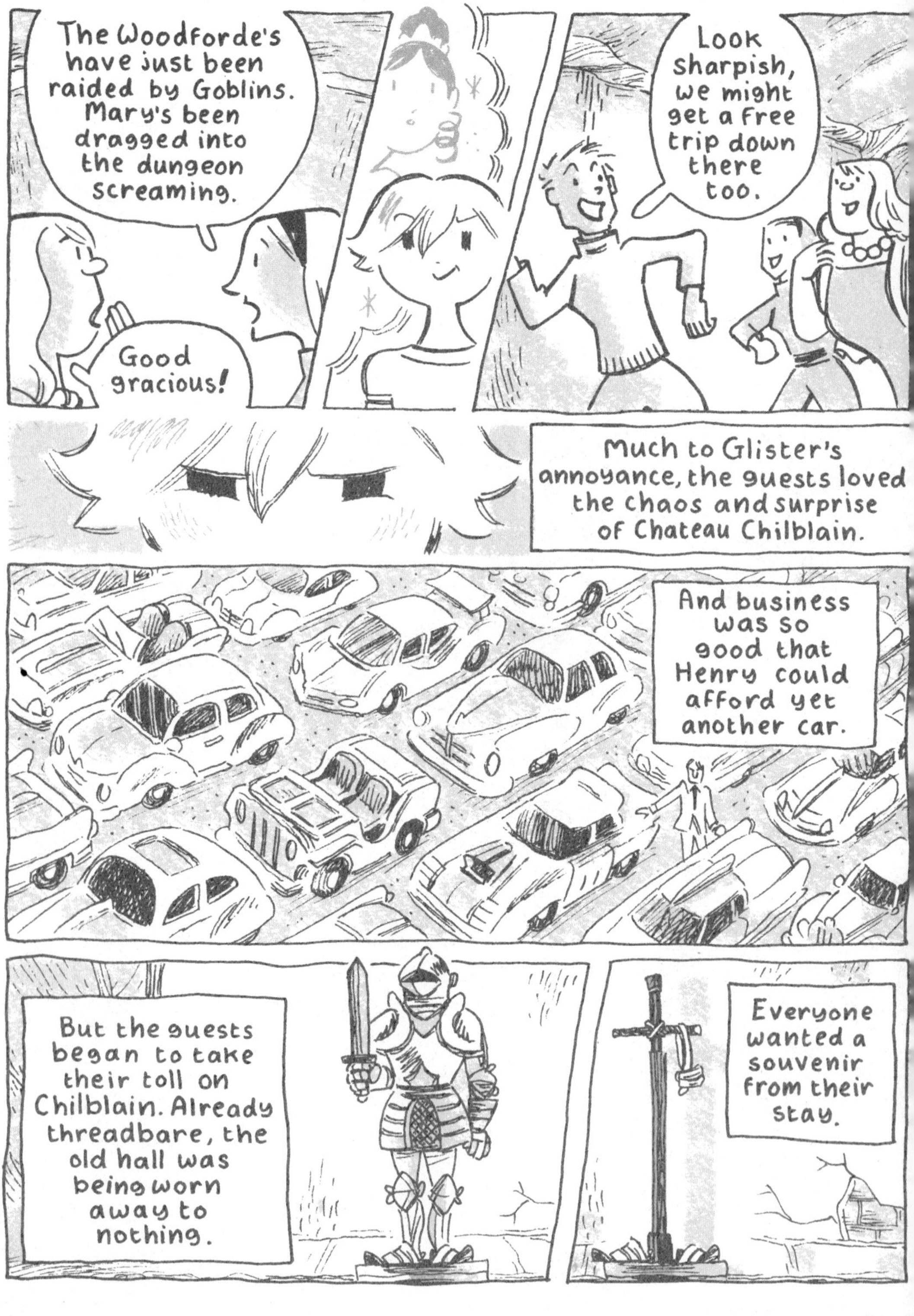

The Woodforde's have just been raided by Goblins. Mary's been dragged into the dungeon screaming.
Good gracious!
Look sharpish, we might get a free trip down there too.
Much to Glister's annoyance, the guests loved the chaos and surprise of Chateau Chilblain.
And business was so good that Henry could afford yet another car.
But the guests began to take their toll on Chilblain. Already threadbare, the old hall was being worn away to nothing.
Everyone wanted a souvenir from their stay.

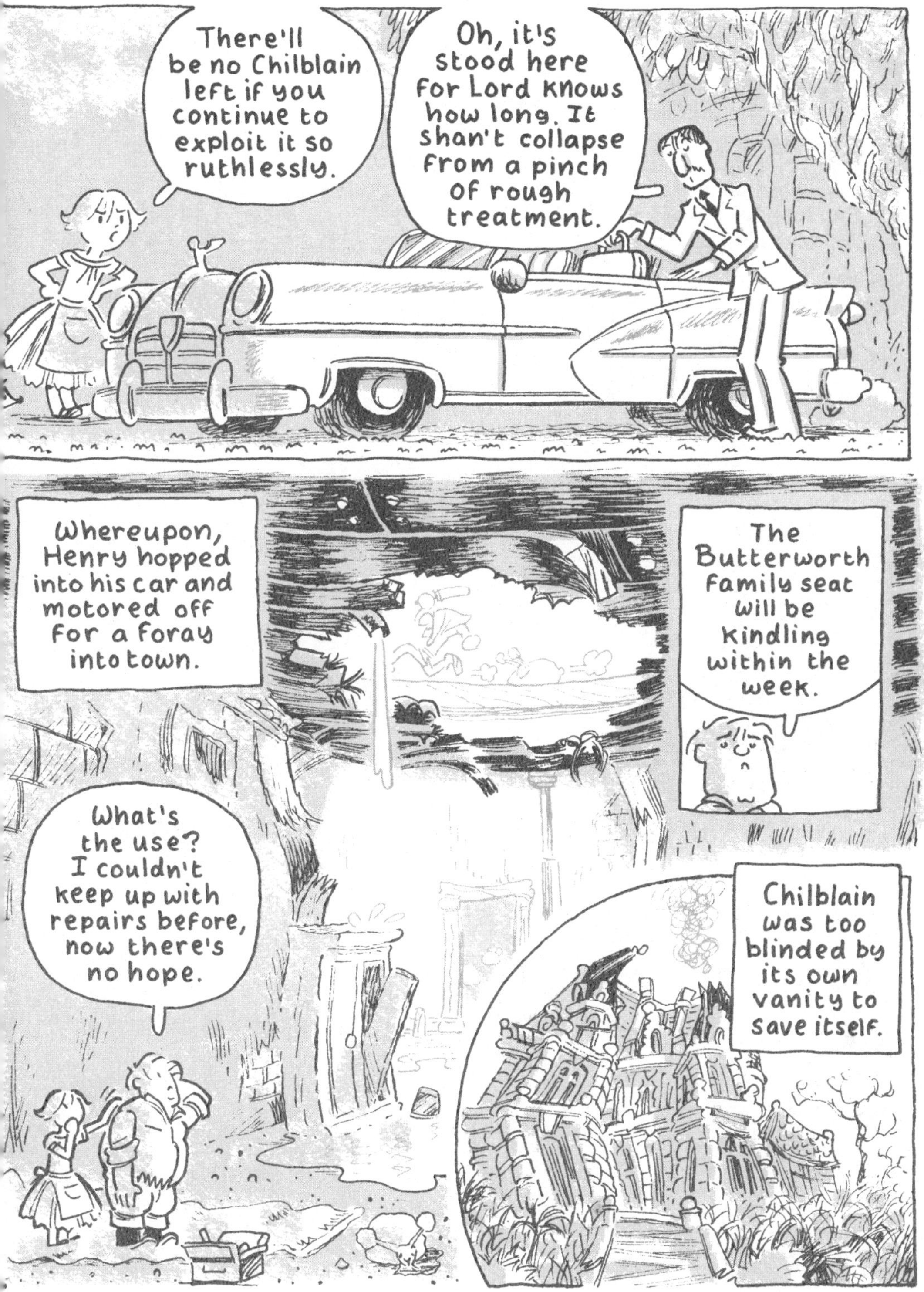

There'll be no Chilblain left if you continue to exploit it so ruthlessly.
Oh, it's stood here for Lord knows how long. It shan't collapse from a pinch of rough treatment.
Whereupon, Henry hopped into his car and motored off for a foray into town.
The Butterworth family seat will be kindling within the week.
What's the use? I couldn't keep up with repairs before, now there's no hope.
Chilblain was too blinded by its own vanity to save itself.

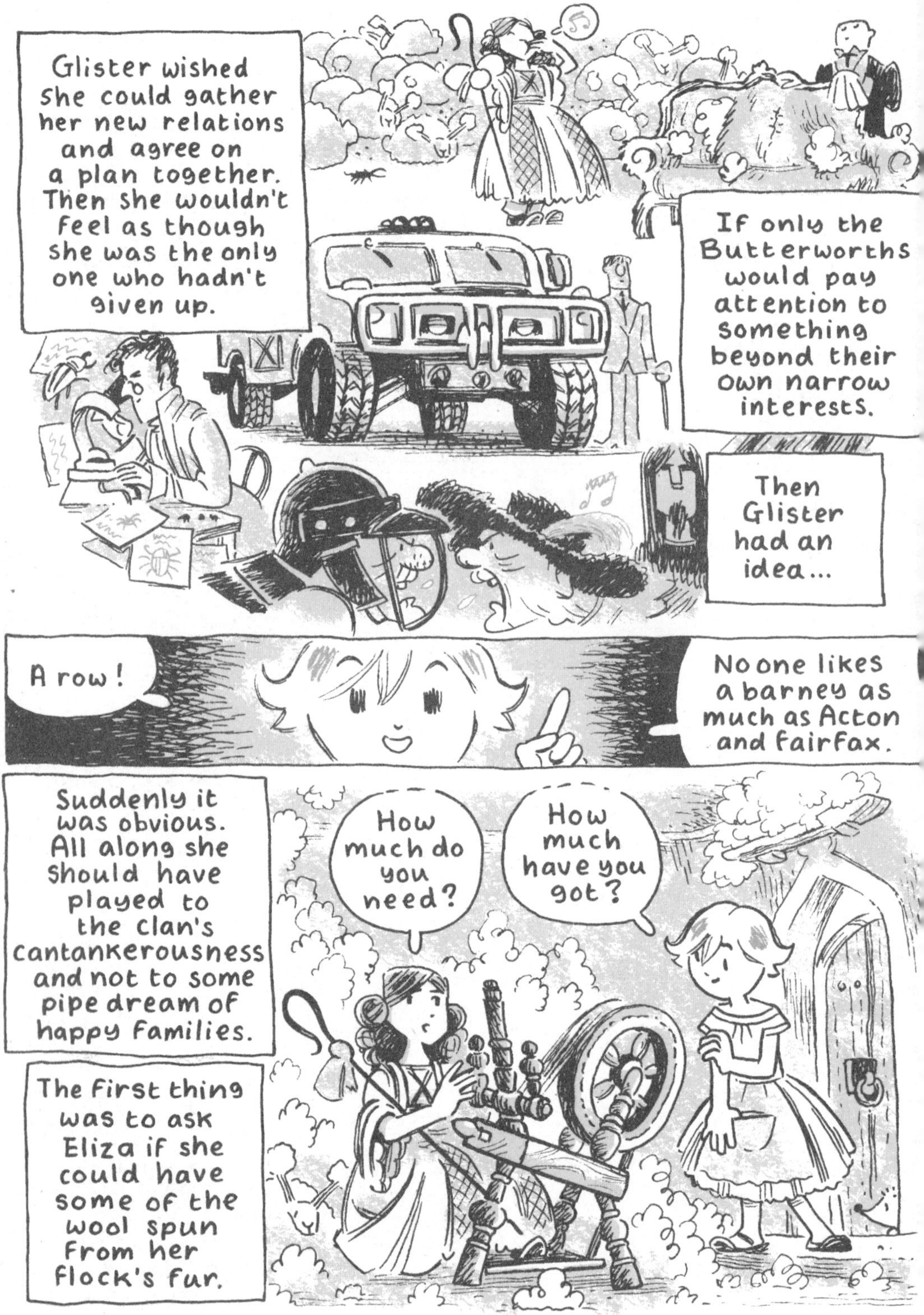
Glister wished she could gather her new relations and agree on a plan together. Then she wouldn't feel as though she was the only one who hadn't given up.
If only the Butterworths would pay attention to something beyond their own narrow interests.
Then Glister had an idea...
A row!
No one likes a barney as much as Acton and Fairfax.
Suddenly it was obvious. All along she should have played to the clan's cantankerousness and not to some pipe dream of happy families.
The first thing was to ask Eliza if she could have some of the wool spun from her flock's fur.
How much do you need?
How much have you got?

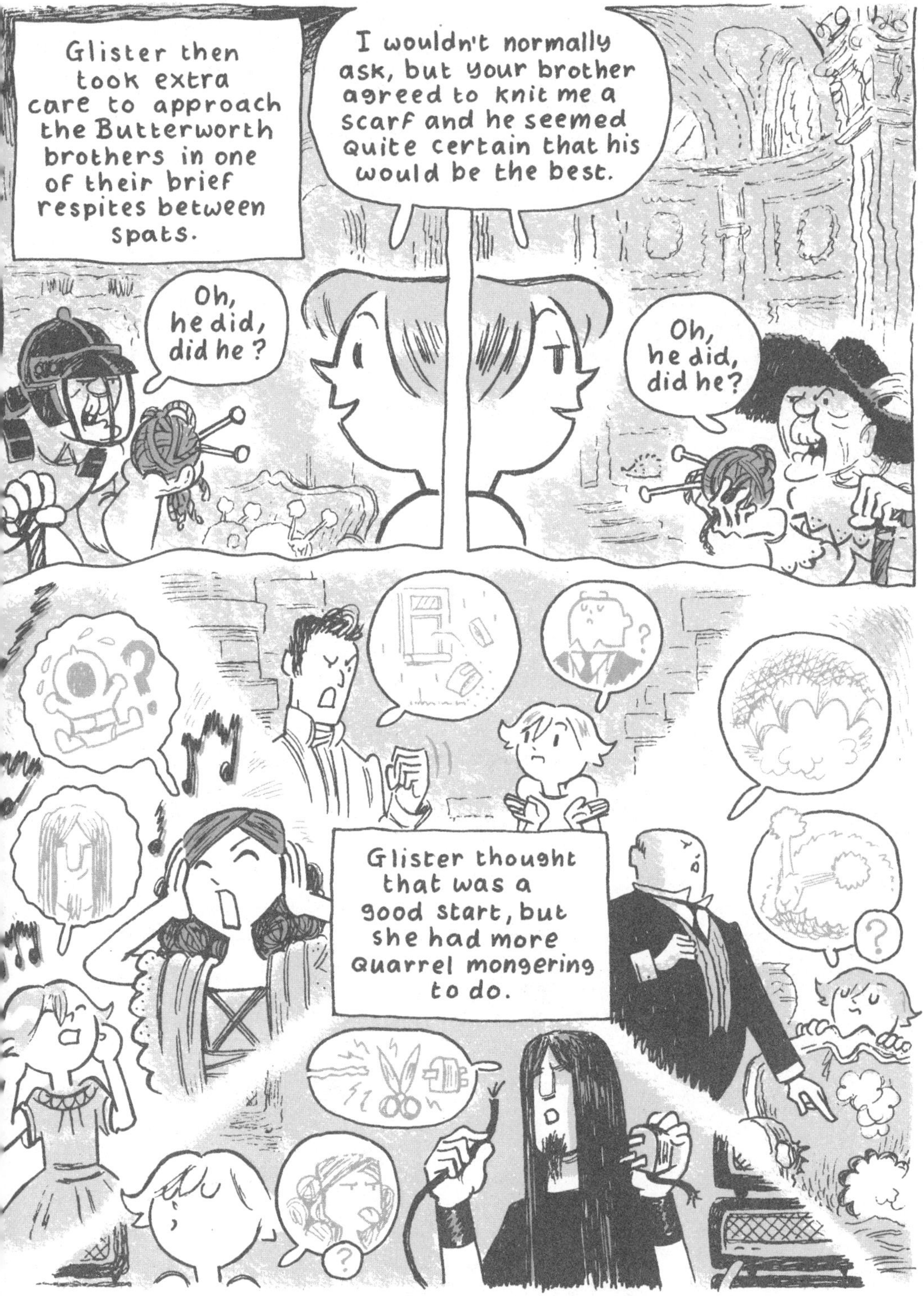

Glister then took extra care to approach the Butterworth brothers in one of their brief respites between spats.
I wouldn't normally ask, but your brother agreed to knit me a scarf and he seemed quite certain that his would be the best.
Oh, he did, did he?
Oh, he did, did he?
Glister thought that was a good start, but she had more quarrel mongering to do.

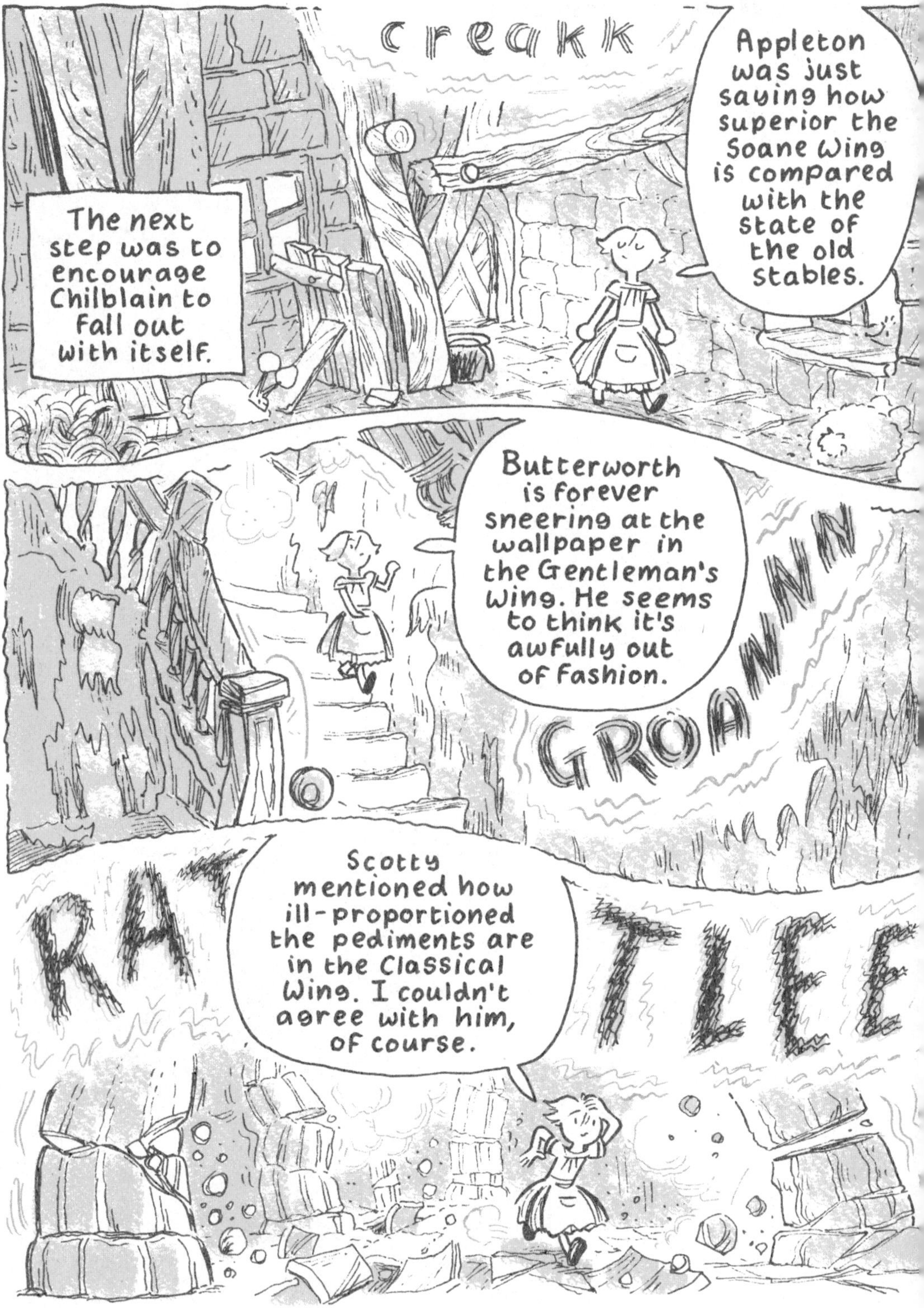
creakk
Appleton was just saying how superior the Soane Wing is compared with the state of the old stables.
The next step was to encourage Chilblain to fall out with itself.
Butterworth is forever sneering at the wallpaper in the Gentleman's Wing. He seems to think it's awfully out of fashion.
GROANNN
RATTLEE
Scotty mentioned how ill-proportioned the pediments are in the Classical Wing. I couldn't agree with him, of course.

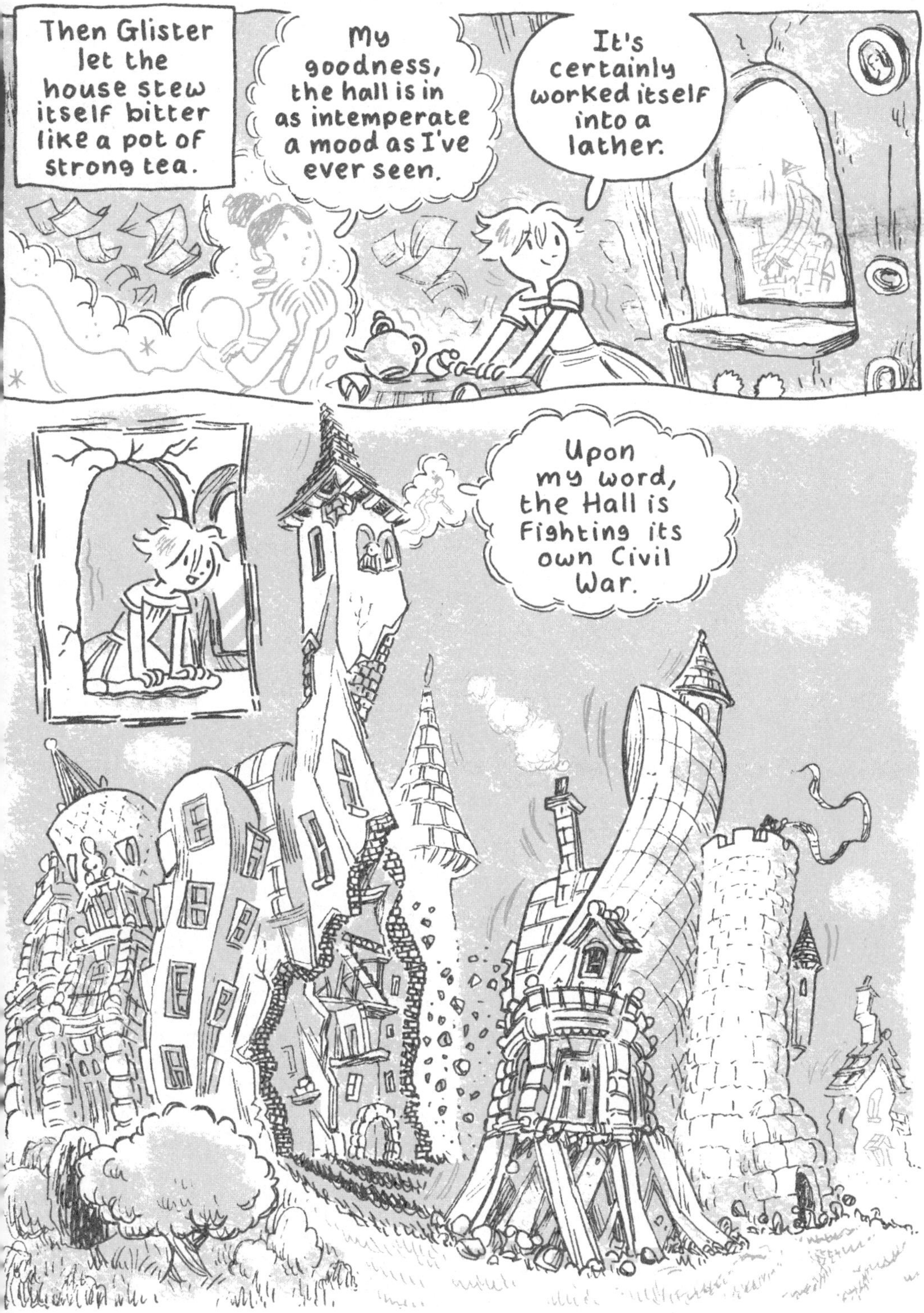
Then Glister let the house stew itself bitter like a pot of strong tea.
My goodness, the hall is in as intemperate a mood as I've ever seen.
It's certainly worked itself into a lather.
Upon my word, the Hall is fighting its own Civil War.

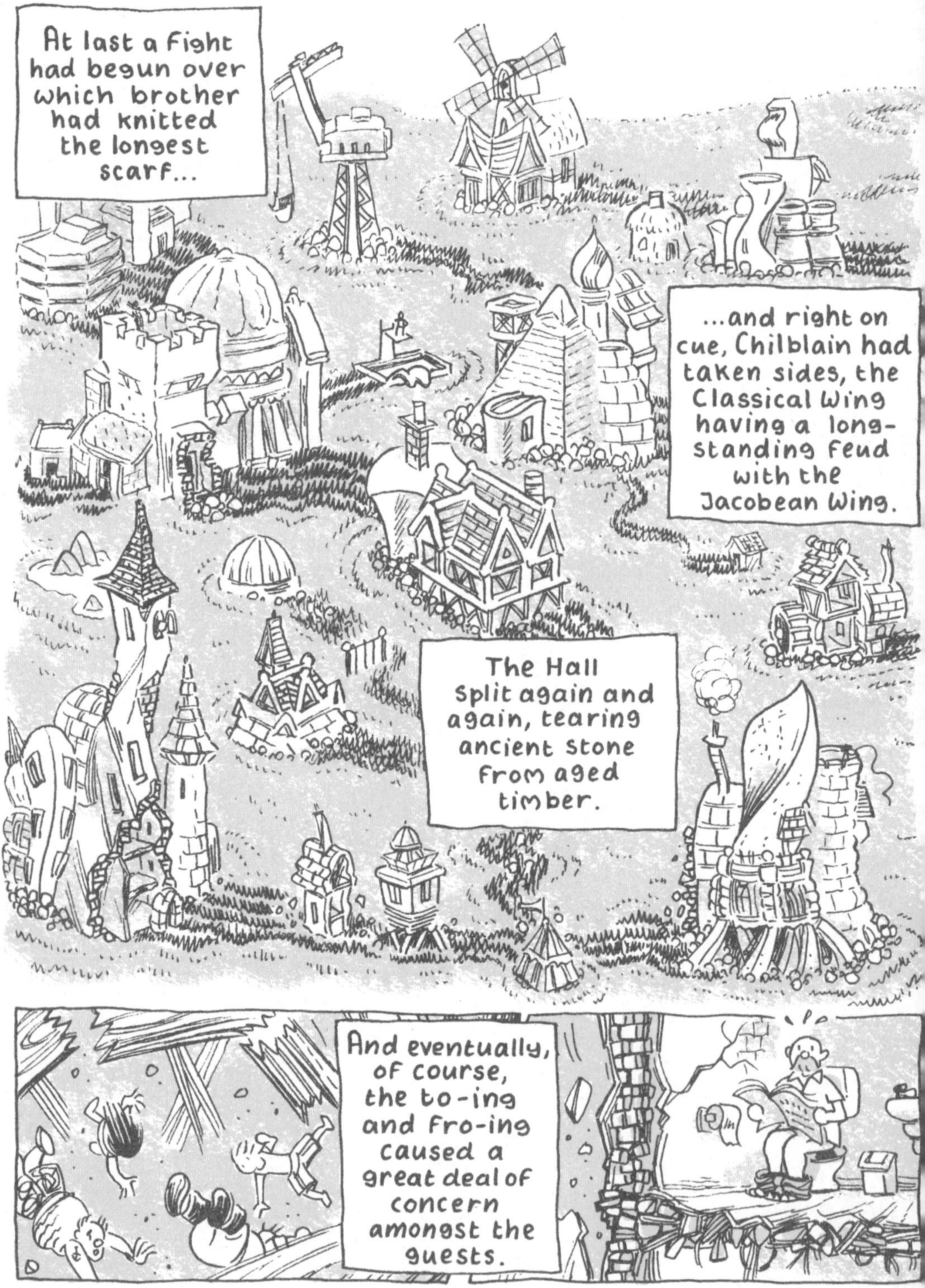
At last a fight had begun over which brother had knitted the longest scarf...
...and right on cue, Chilblain had taken sides, the Classical Wing having a long-standing feud with the Jacobean Wing.
The Hall split again and again, tearing ancient stone from aged timber.
And eventually, of course, the to-ing and fro-ing caused a great deal of concern amongst the guests.

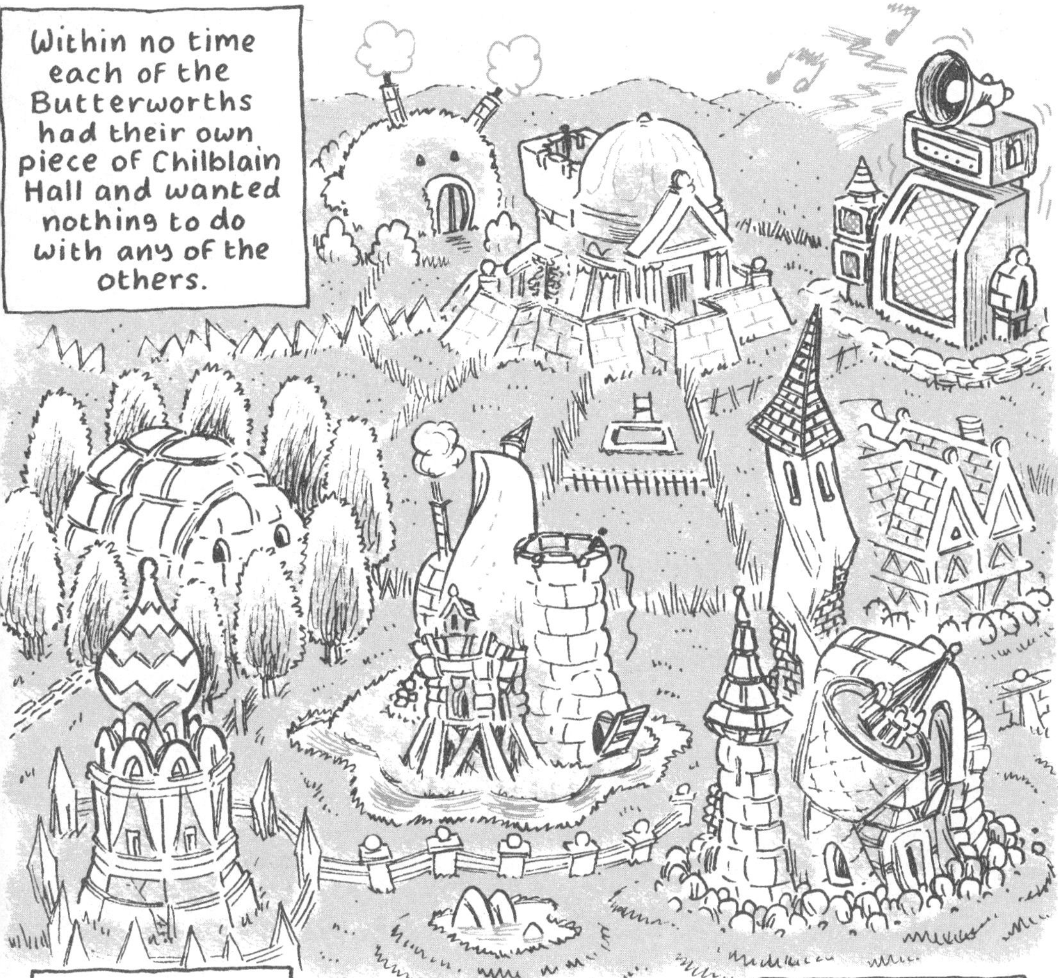

Within no time each of the Butterworths had their own piece of Chilblain Hall and wanted nothing to do with any of the others.

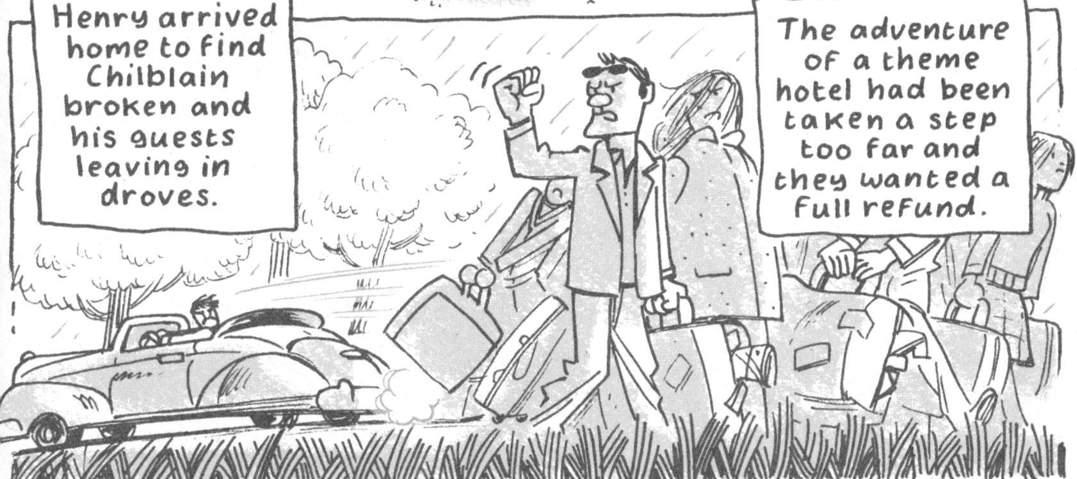

Henry arrived home to find Chilblain broken and his guests leaving in droves.
The adventure of a theme hotel had been taken a step too far and they wanted a full refund.

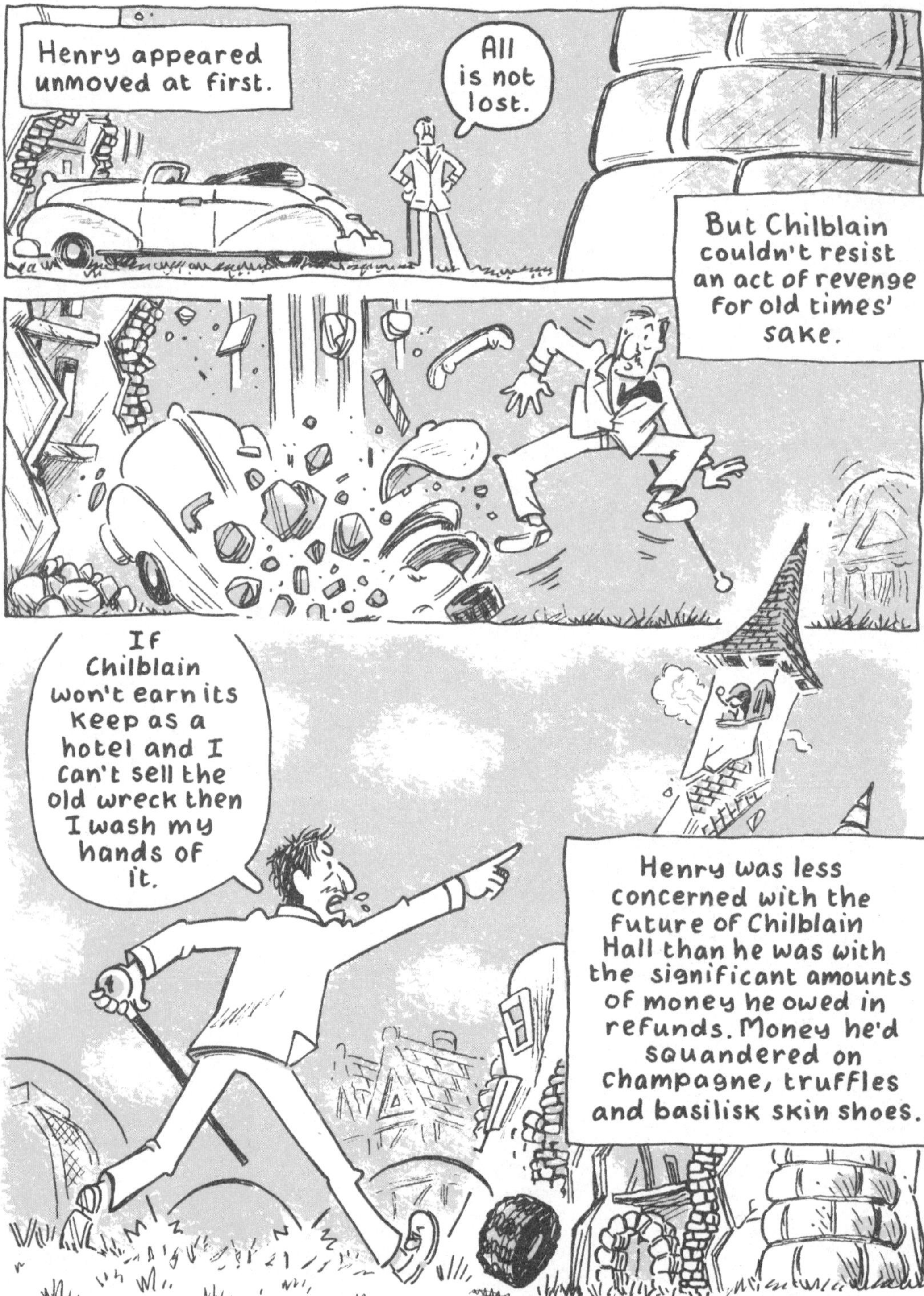
Henry appeared unmoved at first.
All is not lost.
But Chilblain couldn't resist an act of revenge for old times' sake.
If Chilblain won't earn its keep as a hotel and I can't sell the old wreck then I wash my hands of it.
Henry was less concerned with the future of Chilblain Hall than he was with the significant amounts of money he owed in refunds. Money he'd squandered on champagne, truffles and basilisk skin shoes.

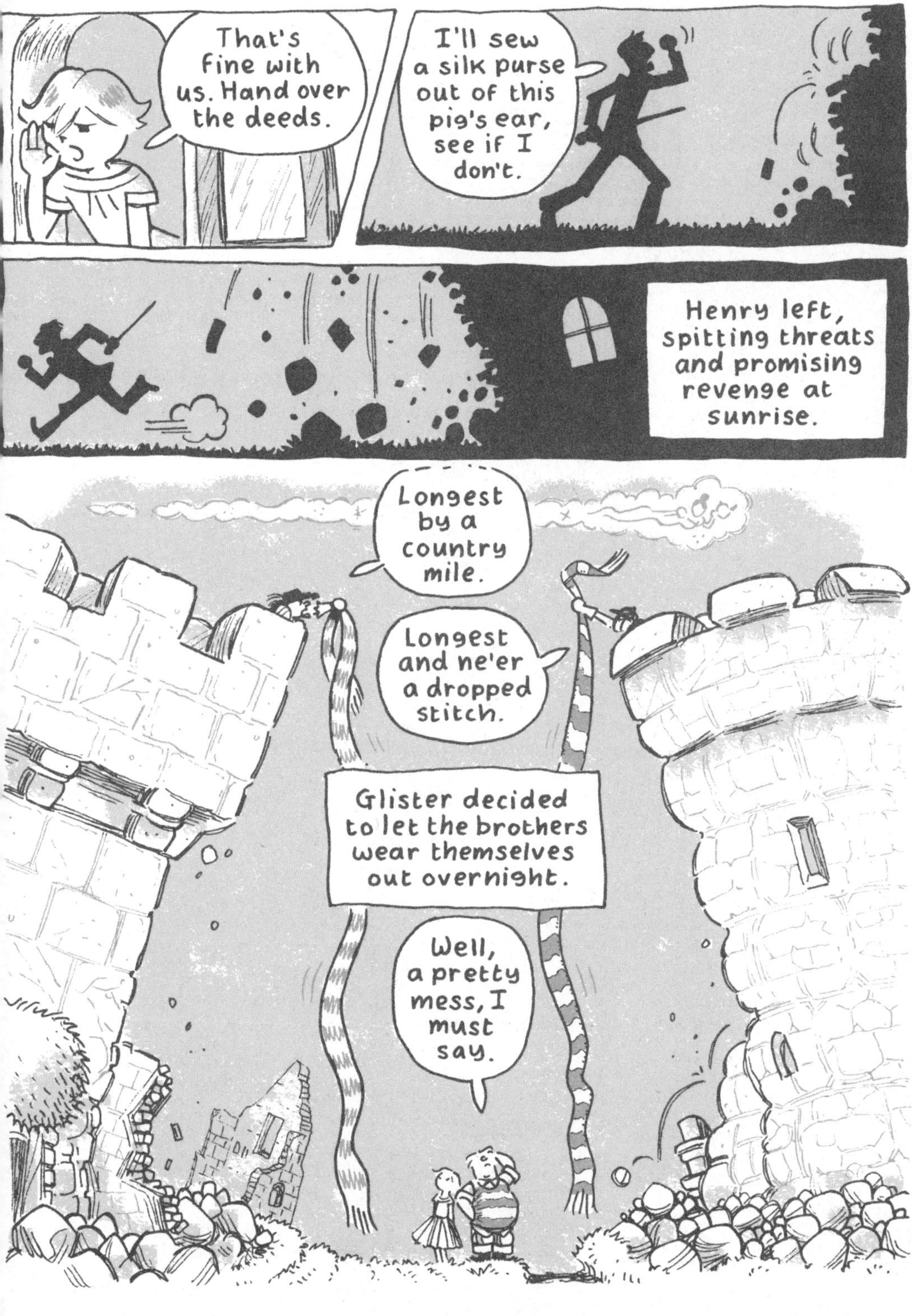

That's fine with us. Hand over the deeds.
I'll sew a silk purse out of this pig's ear, see if I don't.
Henry left, spitting threats and promising revenge at sunrise.
Longest by a country mile.
Longest and ne'er a dropped stitch.
Glister decided to let the brothers wear themselves out overnight.
Well, a pretty mess, I must say.

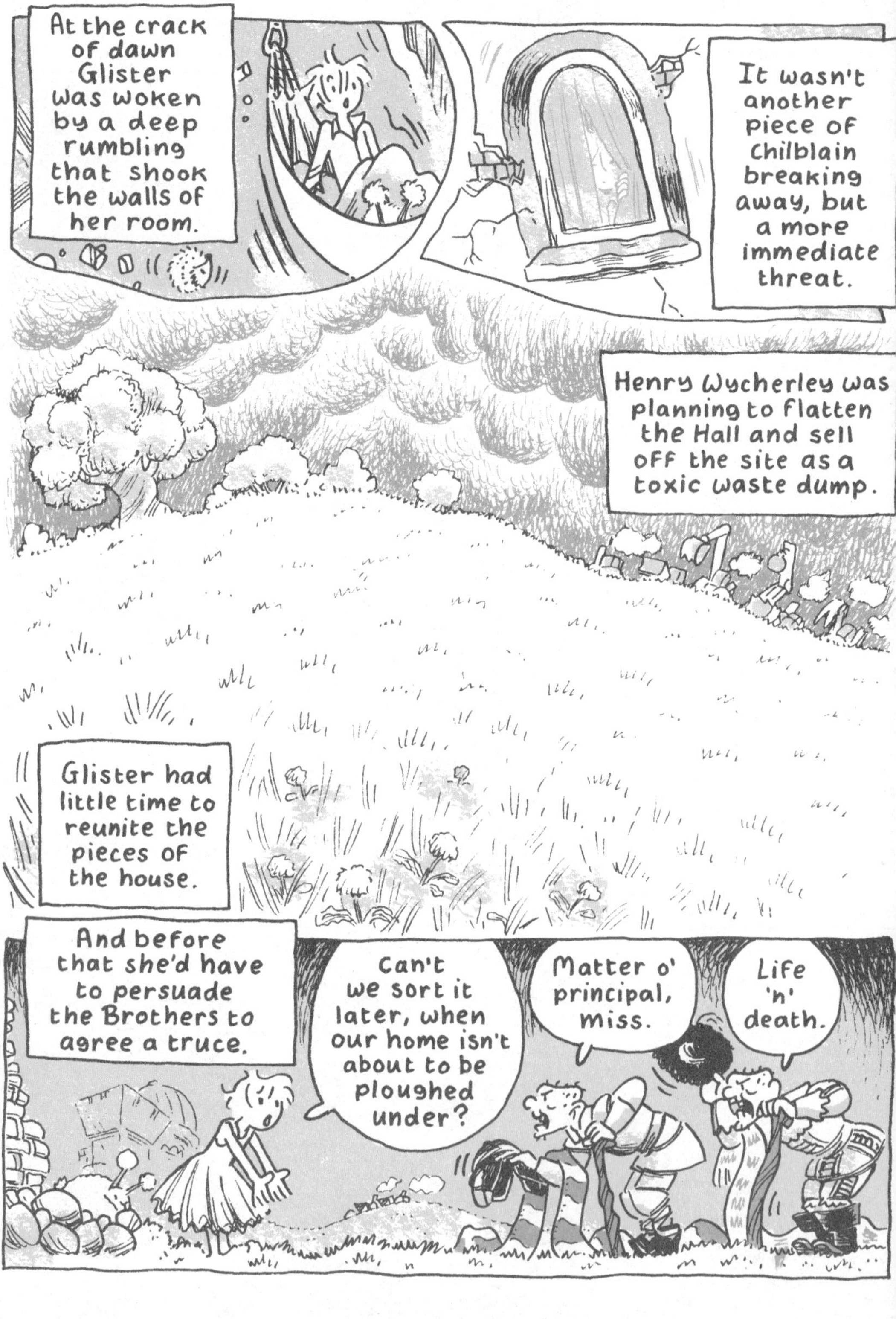
At the crack of dawn Glister was woken by a deep rumbling that shook the walls of her room.
It wasn't another piece of Chilblain breaking away, but a more immediate threat.
Henry Wycherley was planning to flatten the Hall and sell off the site as a toxic waste dump.
Glister had little time to reunite the pieces of the house.
And before that she'd have to persuade the Brothers to agree a truce.
Can't we sort it later, when our home isn't about to be ploughed under?
Matter o' principal, miss.
Life 'n' death.

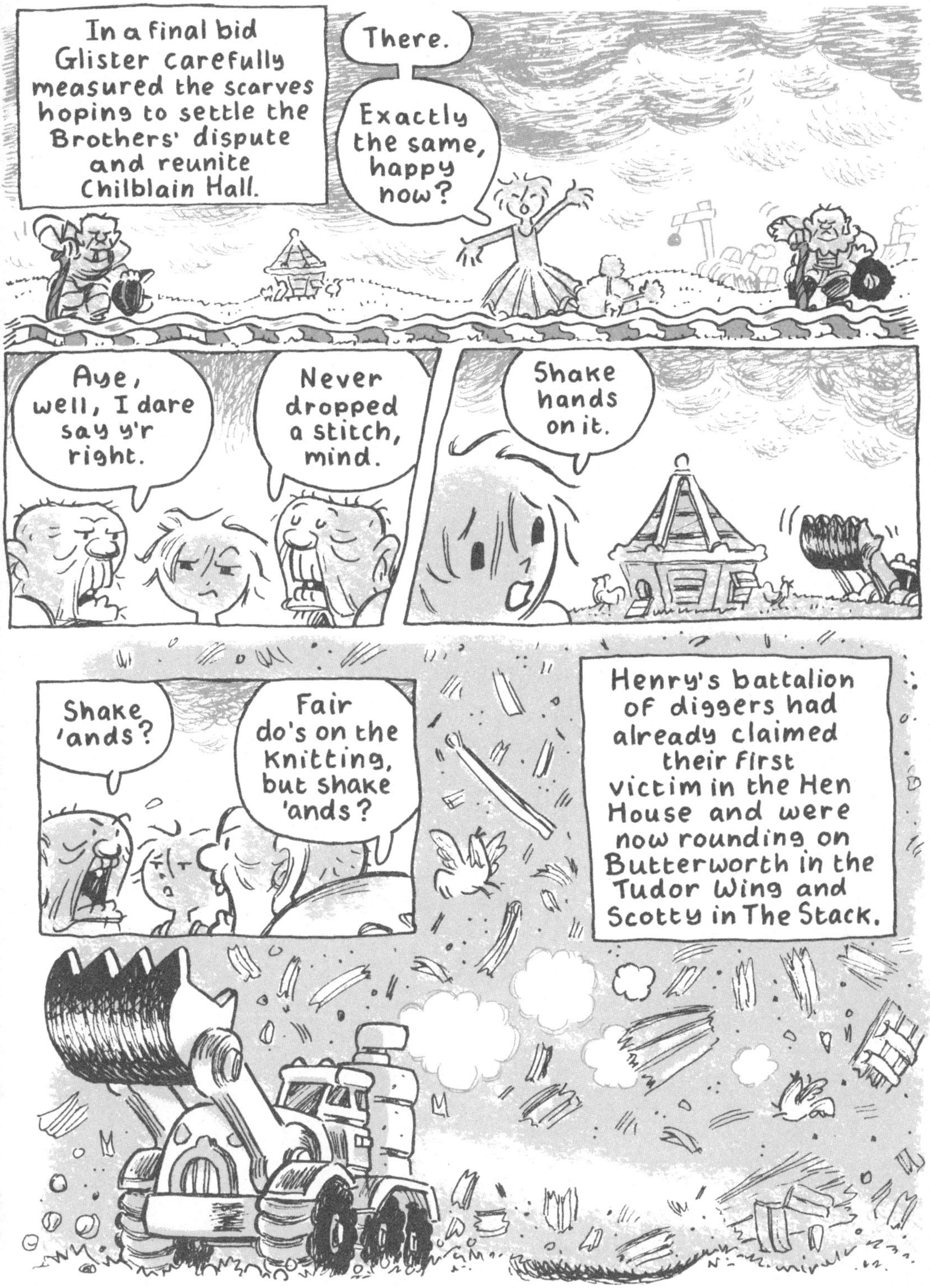
In a final bid Glister carefully measured the scarves hoping to settle the Brothers' dispute and reunite Chilblain Hall.
There.
Exactly the same, happy now?
Aye, well, I dare say y'r right.
Never dropped a stitch, mind.
Shake hands on it.
Shake 'ands?
Fair do's on the knitting, but shake 'ands?
Henry's battalion of diggers had already claimed their first victim in the Hen House and were now rounding on Butterworth in the Tudor Wing and Scotty in The Stack.

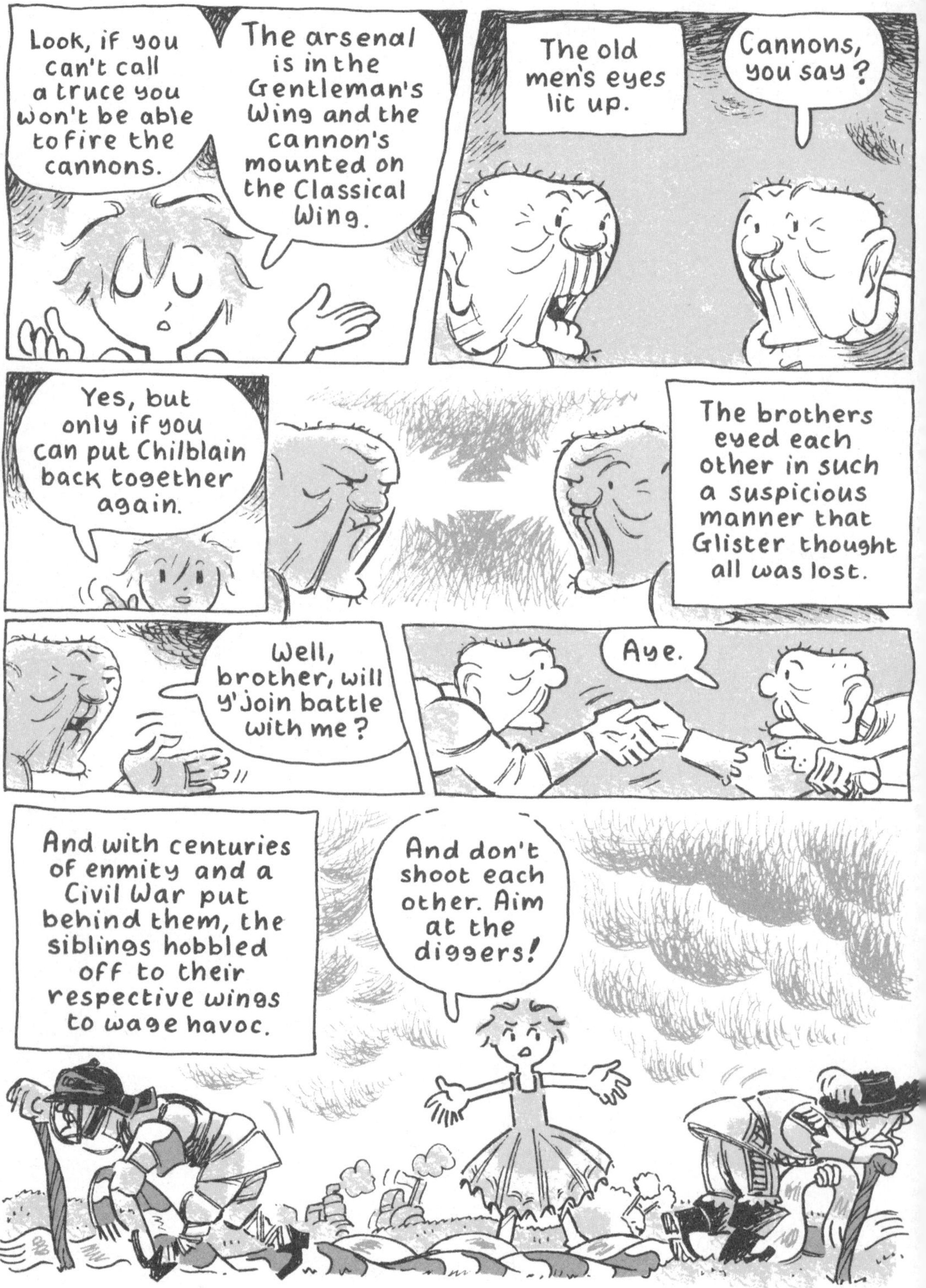
Look, if you can't call a truce you won't be able to fire the cannons.
The arsenal is in the Gentleman's Wing and the cannon's mounted on the Classical Wing.
The old men's eyes lit up.
Cannons, you say?
Yes, but only if you can put Chilblain back together again.
The brothers eyed each other in such a suspicious manner that Glister thought all was lost.
Well, brother, will y'join battle with me?
Aye.
And with centuries of enmity and a Civil War put behind them, the siblings hobbled off to their respective wings to wage havoc.
And don't shoot each other. Aim at the diggers!

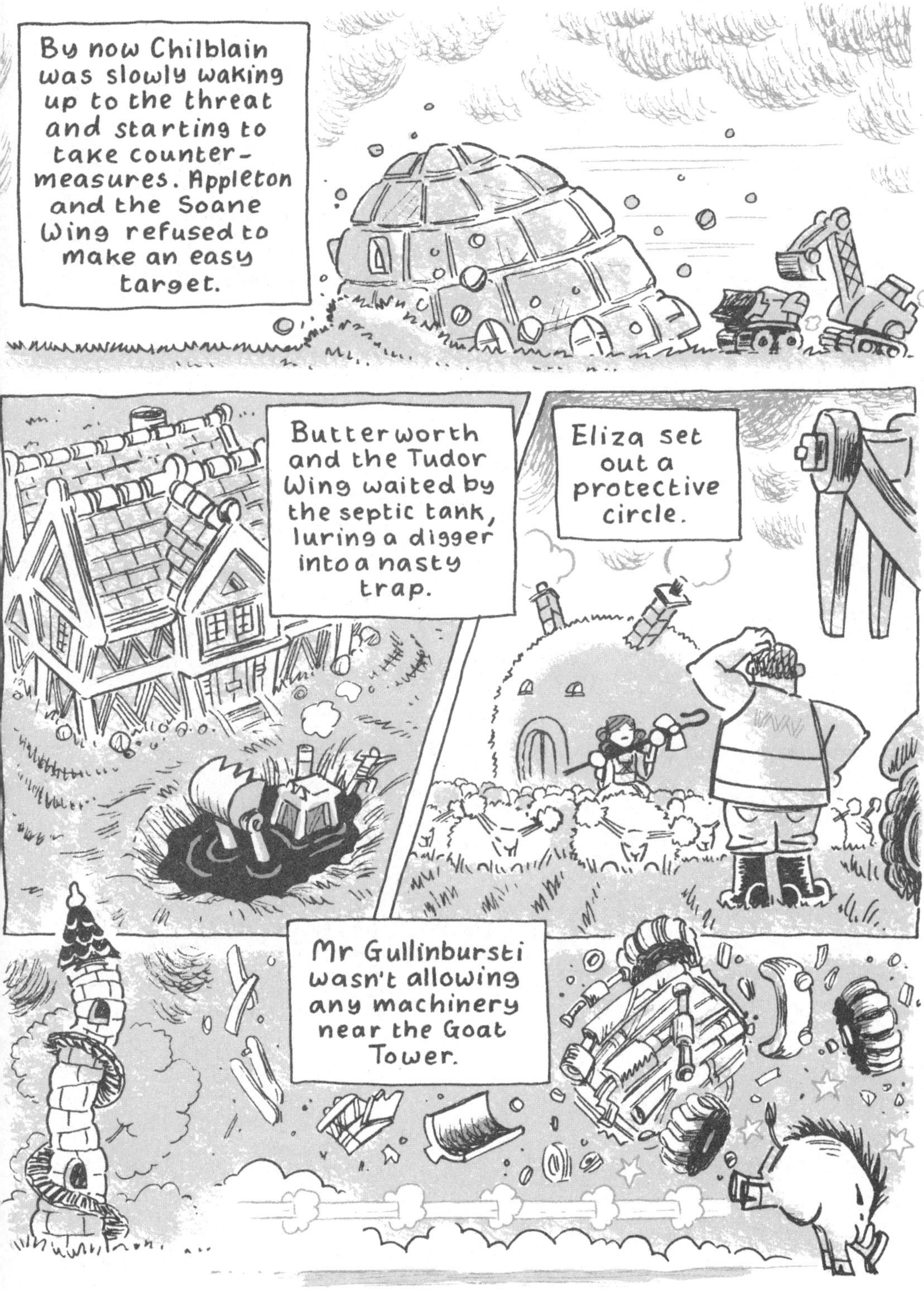
By now Chilblain was slowly waking up to the threat and starting to take counter-measures. Appleton and the Soane Wing refused to make an easy target.
Butterworth and the Tudor Wing waited by the septic tank, luring a digger into a nasty trap.
Eliza set out a protective circle.
Mr Gullinbursti wasn't allowing any machinery near the Goat Tower.

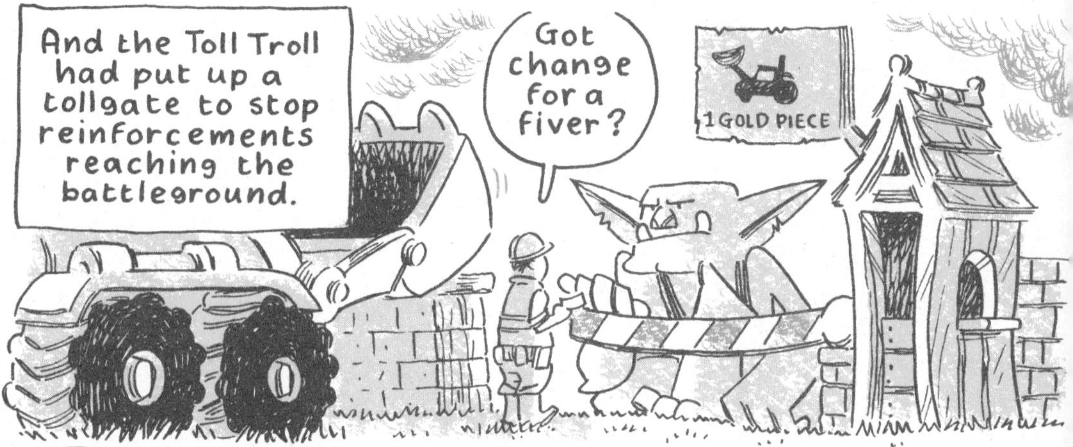
And the Toll Troll had put up a tollgate to stop reinforcements reaching the battleground.
Got change for a fiver?
1 GOLD PIECE

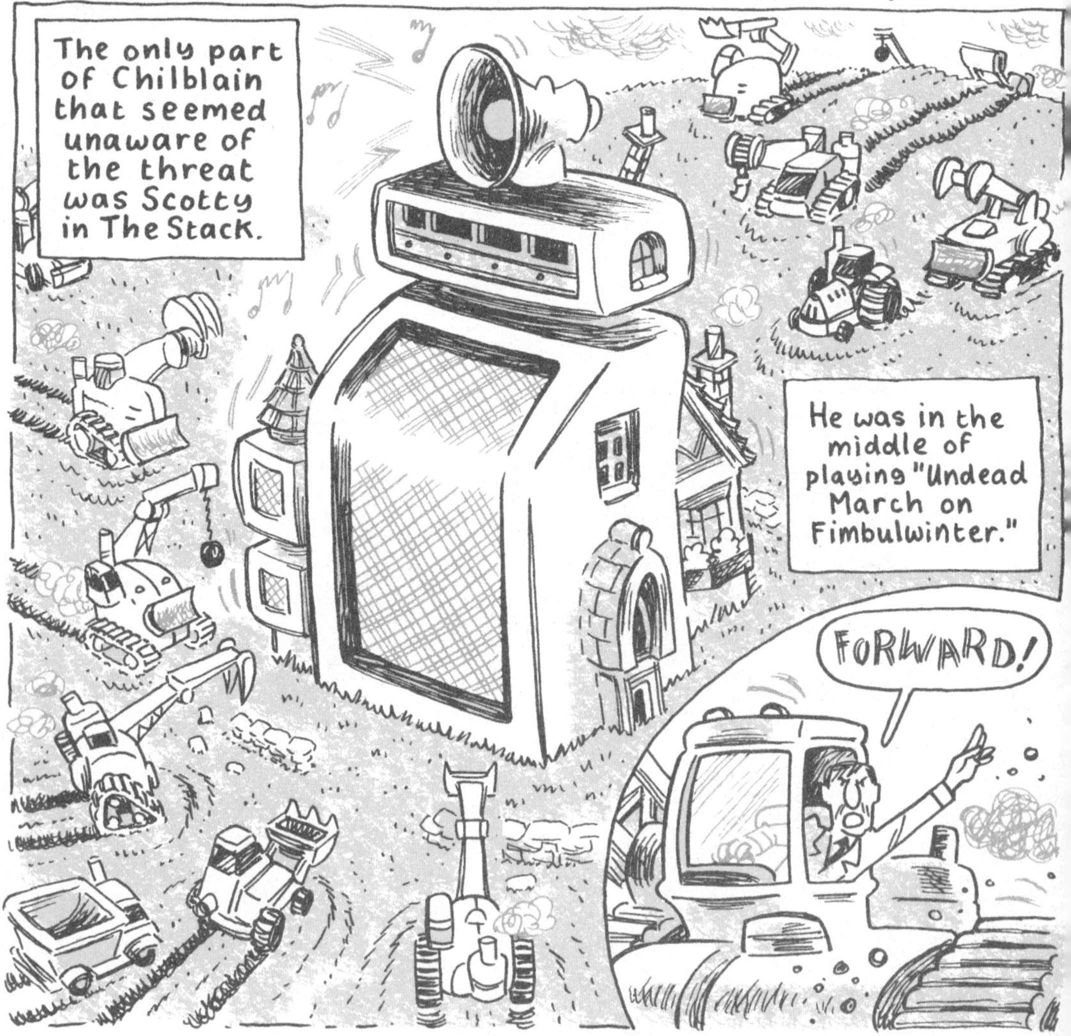
The only part of Chilblain that seemed unaware of the threat was Scotty in The Stack.
He was in the middle of playing "Undead March on Fimbulwinter."
FORWARD!

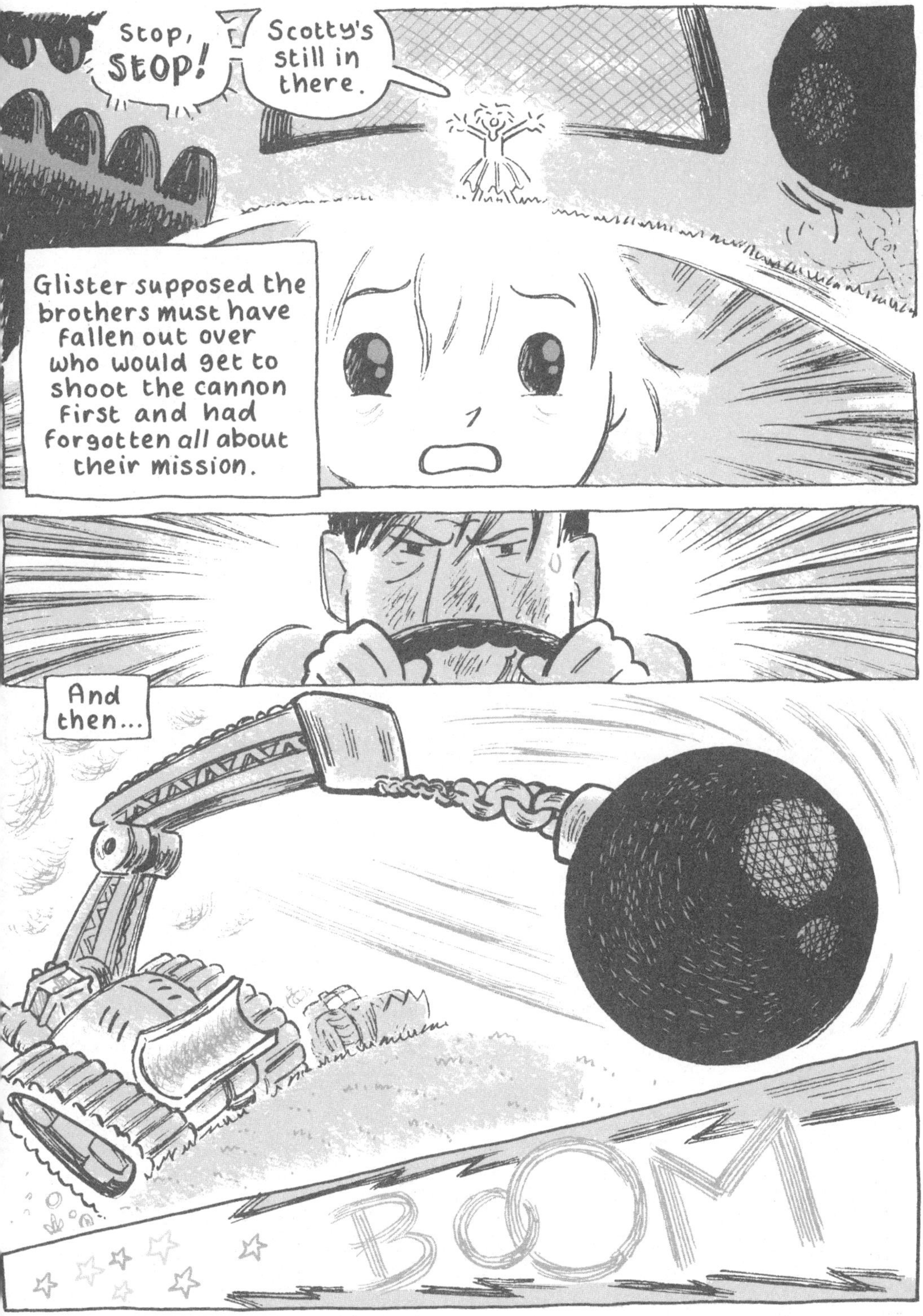
Stop, STOP!
Scotty's still in there.
Glister supposed the brothers must have fallen out over who would get to shoot the cannon first and had forgotten *all* about their mission.
And then...
BOOM

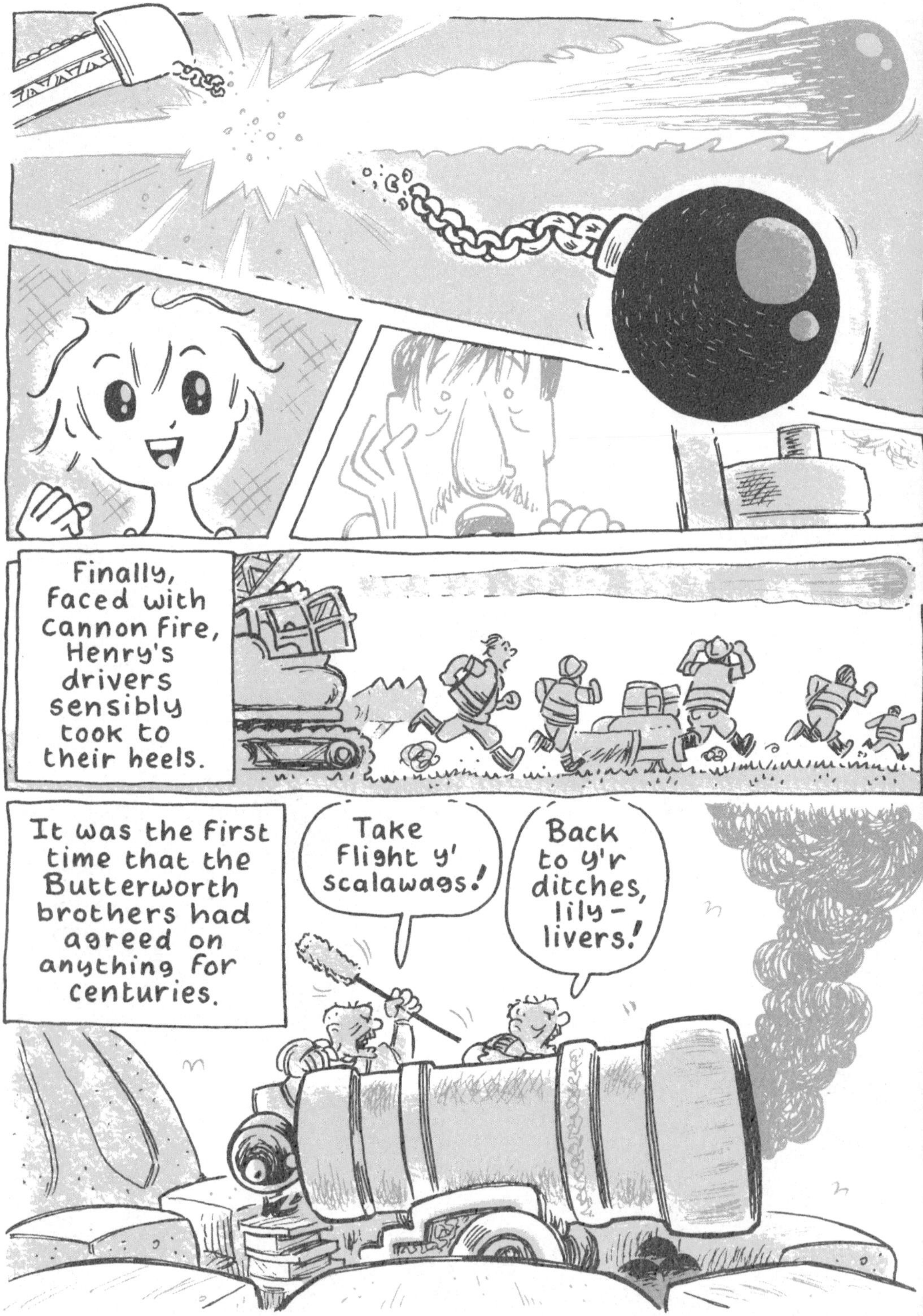
Finally, faced with cannon fire, Henry's drivers sensibly took to their heels.
It was the first time that the Butterworth brothers had agreed on anything for centuries.
Take flight y' scalawags!
Back to y'r ditches, lily-livers!

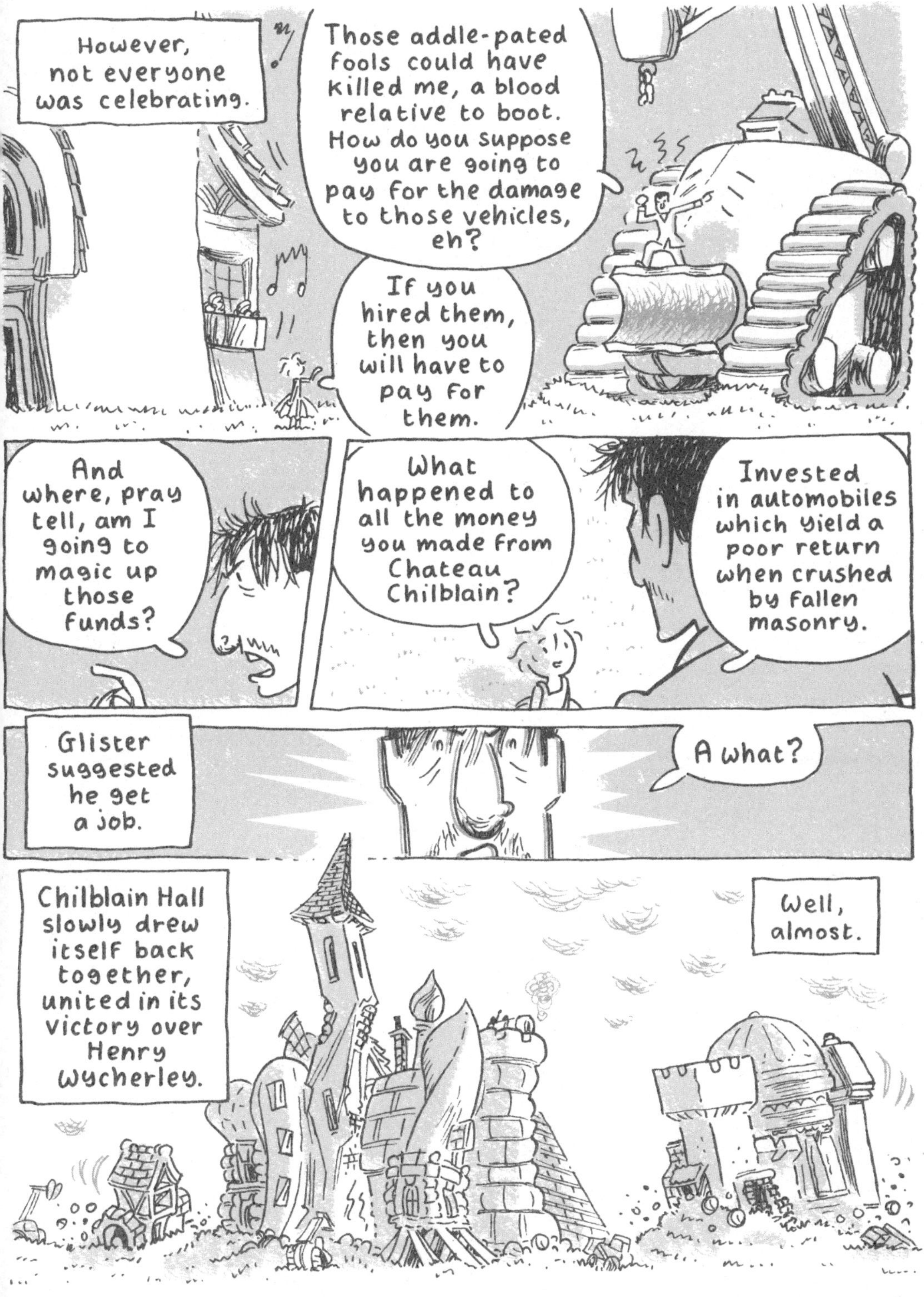

However, not everyone was celebrating.
Those addle-pated fools could have killed me, a blood relative to boot. How do you suppose you are going to pay for the damage to those vehicles, eh?
If you hired them, then you will have to pay for them.
And where, pray tell, am I going to magic up those funds?
What happened to all the money you made from Chateau Chilblain?
Invested in automobiles which yield a poor return when crushed by fallen masonry.
Glister suggested he get a job.
A what?
Chilblain Hall slowly drew itself back together, united in its victory over Henry Wycherley.
Well, almost.

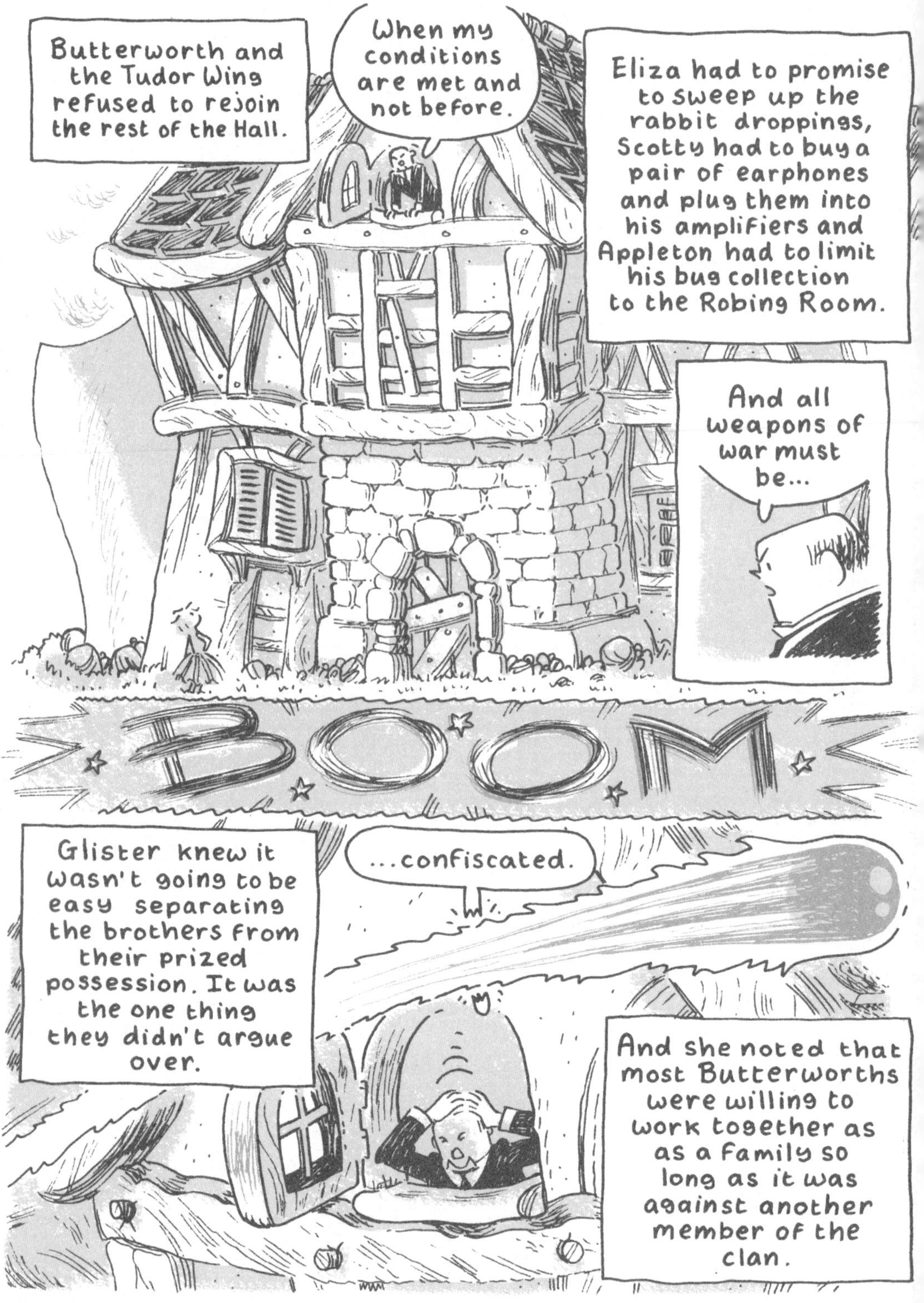
Butterworth and the Tudor Wing refused to rejoin the rest of the Hall.
When my conditions are met and not before.
Eliza had to promise to sweep up the rabbit droppings, Scotty had to buy a pair of earphones and plug them into his amplifiers and Appleton had to limit his bug collection to the Robing Room.
And all weapons of war must be...
BOOM
Glister knew it wasn't going to be easy separating the brothers from their prized possession. It was the one thing they didn't argue over.
...confiscated.
And she noted that most Butterworths were willing to work together as as a family so long as it was against another member of the clan.

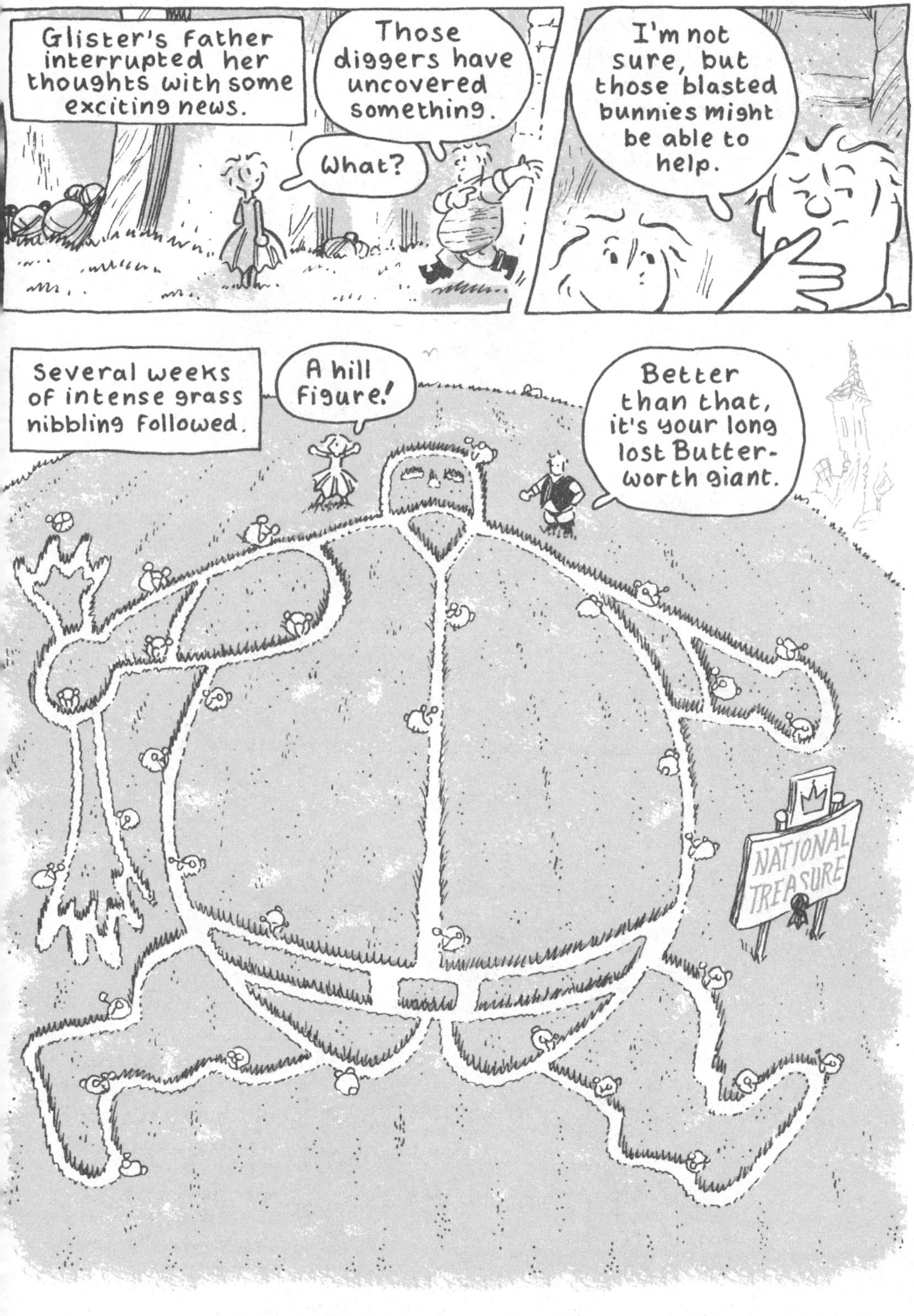
Glister's father interrupted her thoughts with some exciting news.
Those diggers have uncovered something.
What?
I'm not sure, but those blasted bunnies might be able to help.
Several weeks of intense grass nibbling followed.
A hill figure!
Better than that, it's your long lost Butter-worth giant.
NATIONAL TREASURE

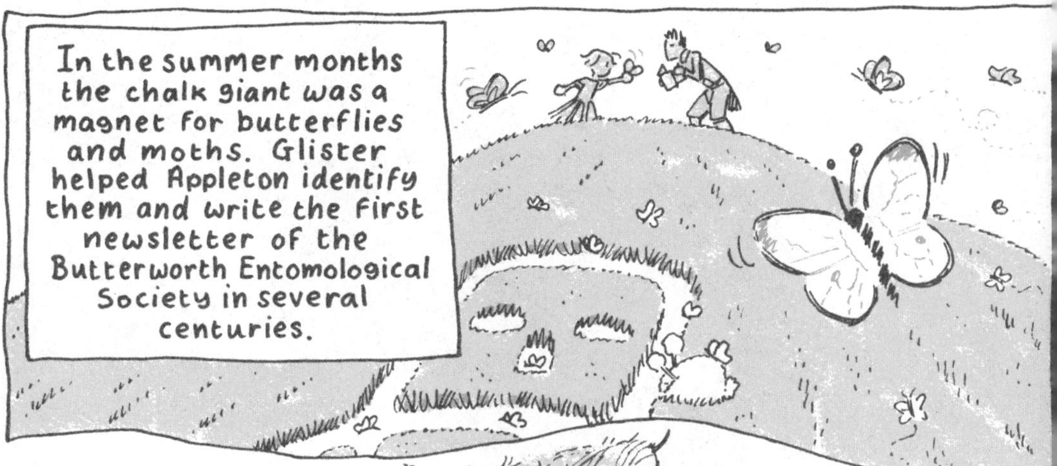
In the summer months the chalk giant was a magnet for butterflies and moths. Glister helped Appleton identify them and write the first newsletter of the Butterworth Entomological Society in several centuries.

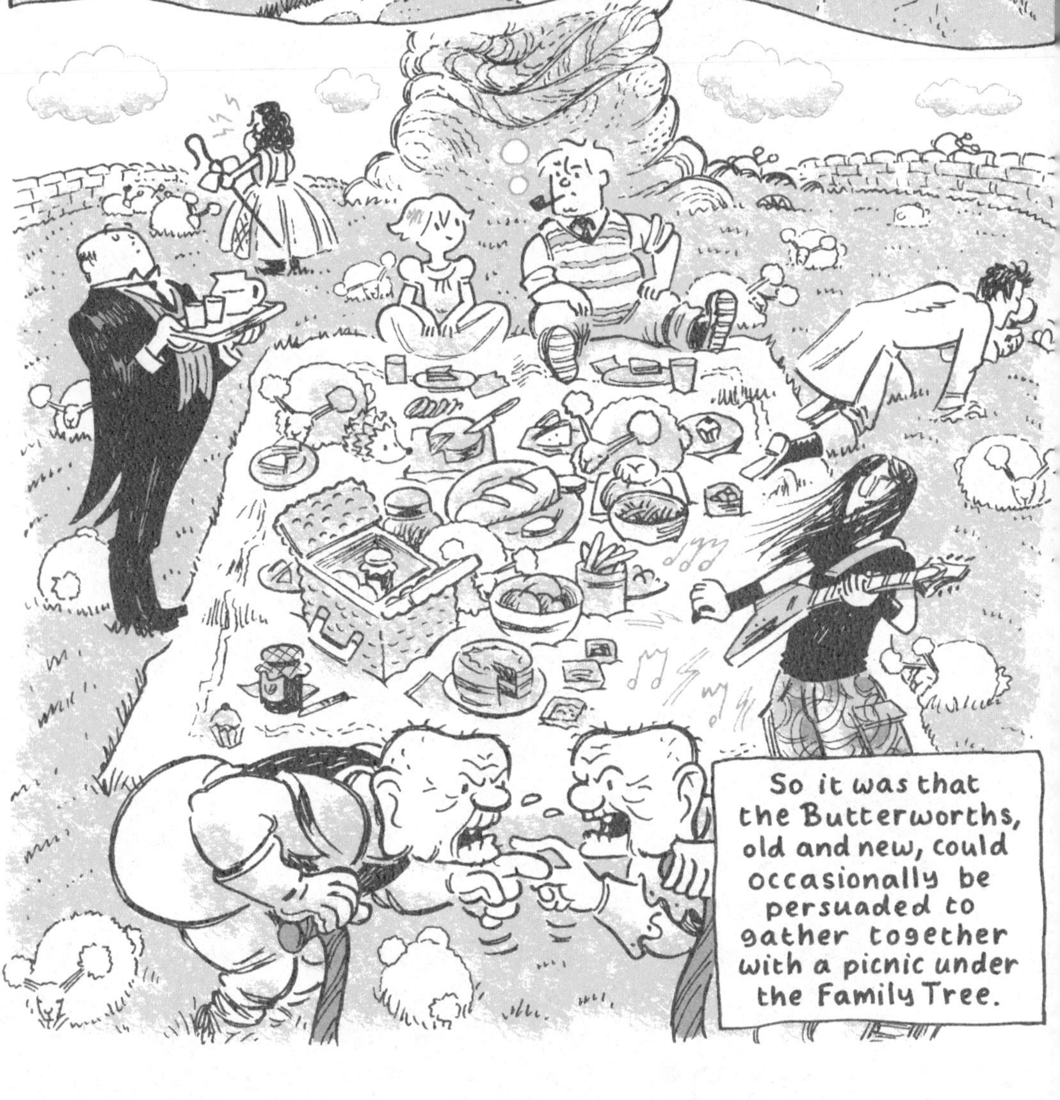
So it was that the Butterworths, old and new, could occasionally be persuaded to gather together with a picnic under the Family Tree.

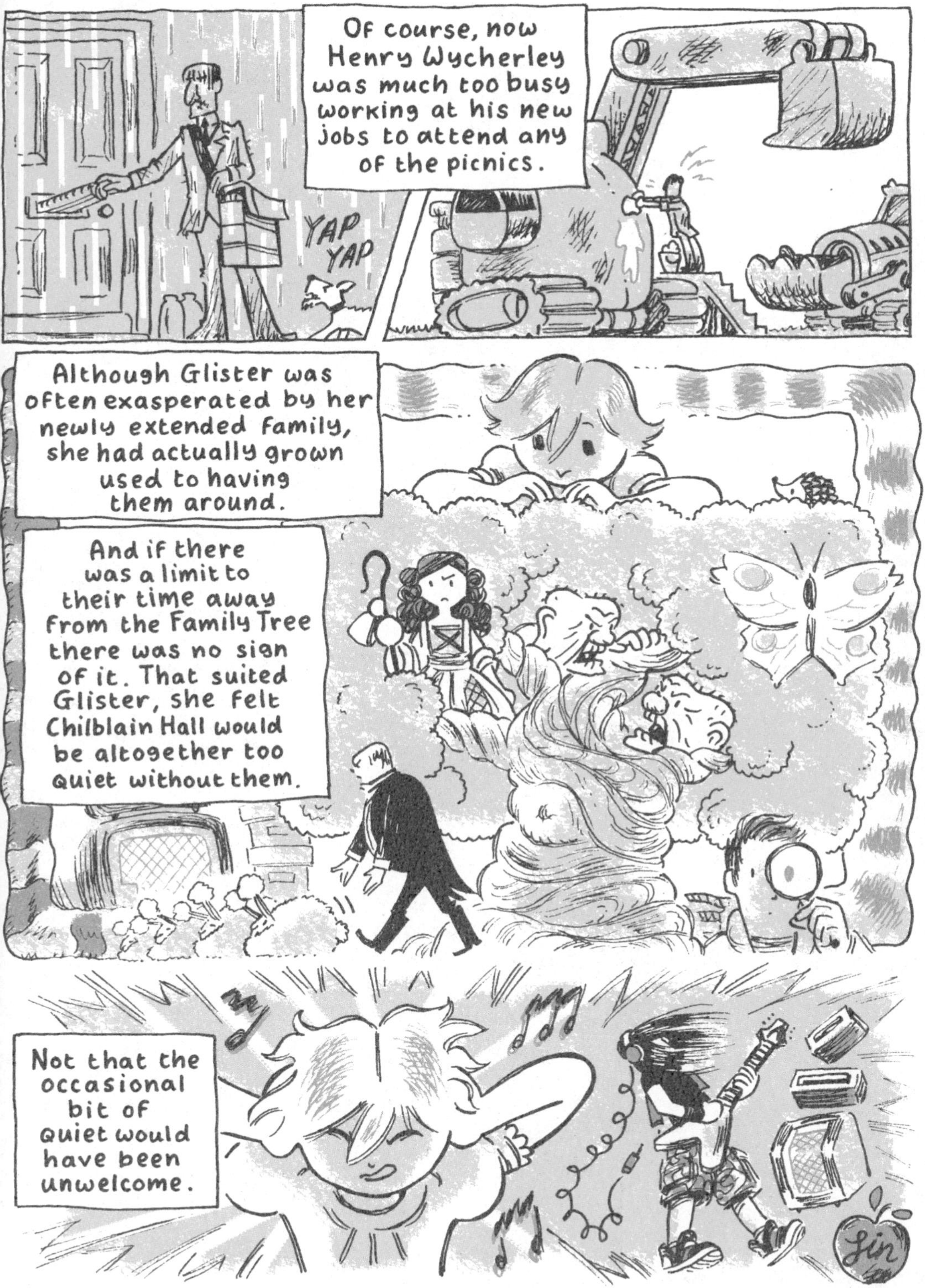
Of course, now Henry Wycherley was much too busy working at his new jobs to attend any of the picnics.
YAP YAP
Although Glister was often exasperated by her newly extended family, she had actually grown used to having them around.
And if there was a limit to their time away from the Family Tree there was no sign of it. That suited Glister, she felt Chilblain Hall would be altogether too quiet without them.
Not that the occasional bit of quiet would have been unwelcome.

Glister: THE HOUSE COAT

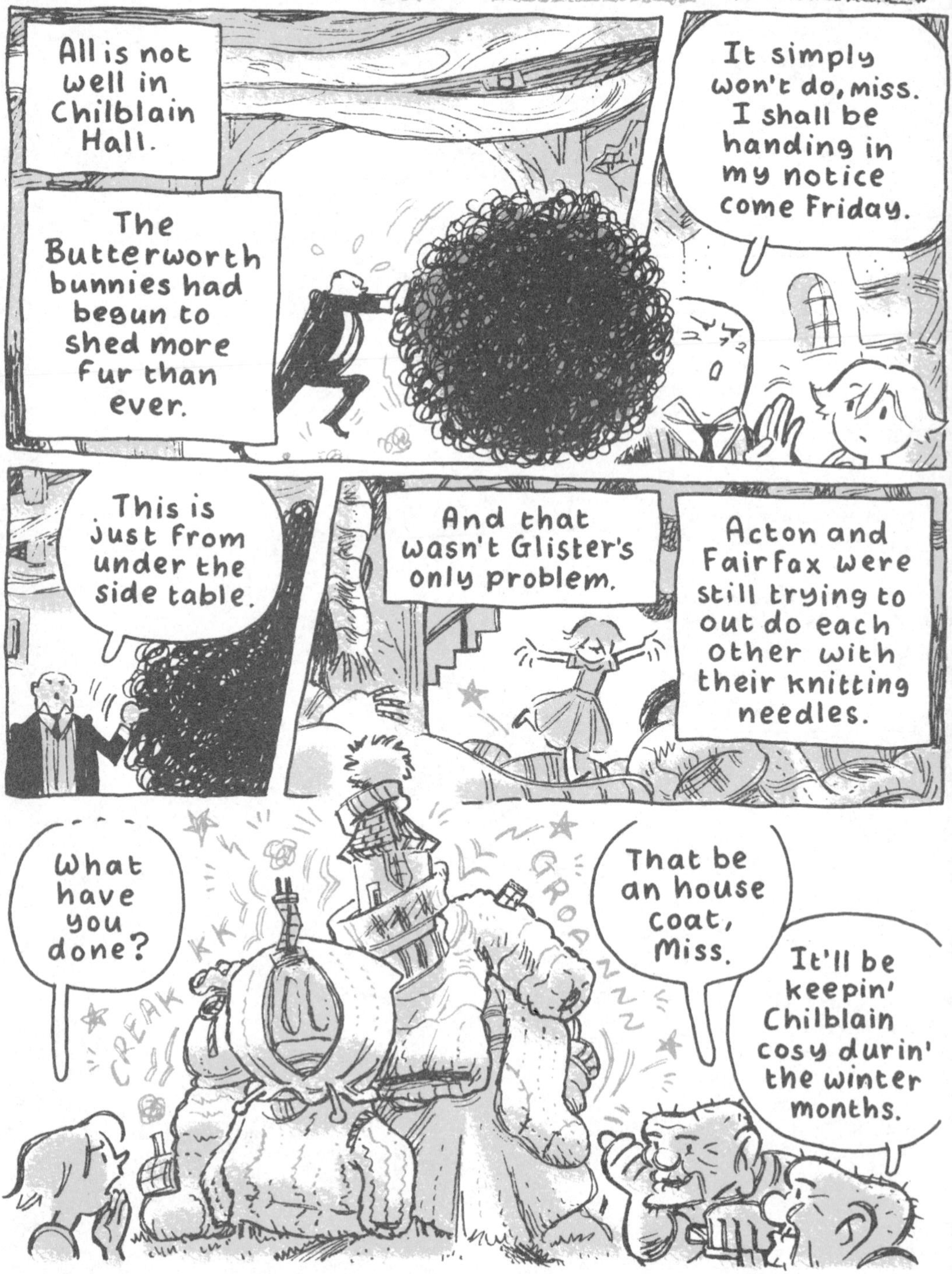
All is not well in Chilblain Hall.
The Butterworth bunnies had begun to shed more fur than ever.
It simply won't do, miss. I shall be handing in my notice come Friday.
This is just from under the side table.
And that wasn't Glister's only problem.
Acton and Fairfax were still trying to out do each other with their knitting needles.
What have you done?
CREAKKK
GROANNZZ
That be an house coat, Miss.
It'll be keepin' Chilblain cosy durin' the winter months.

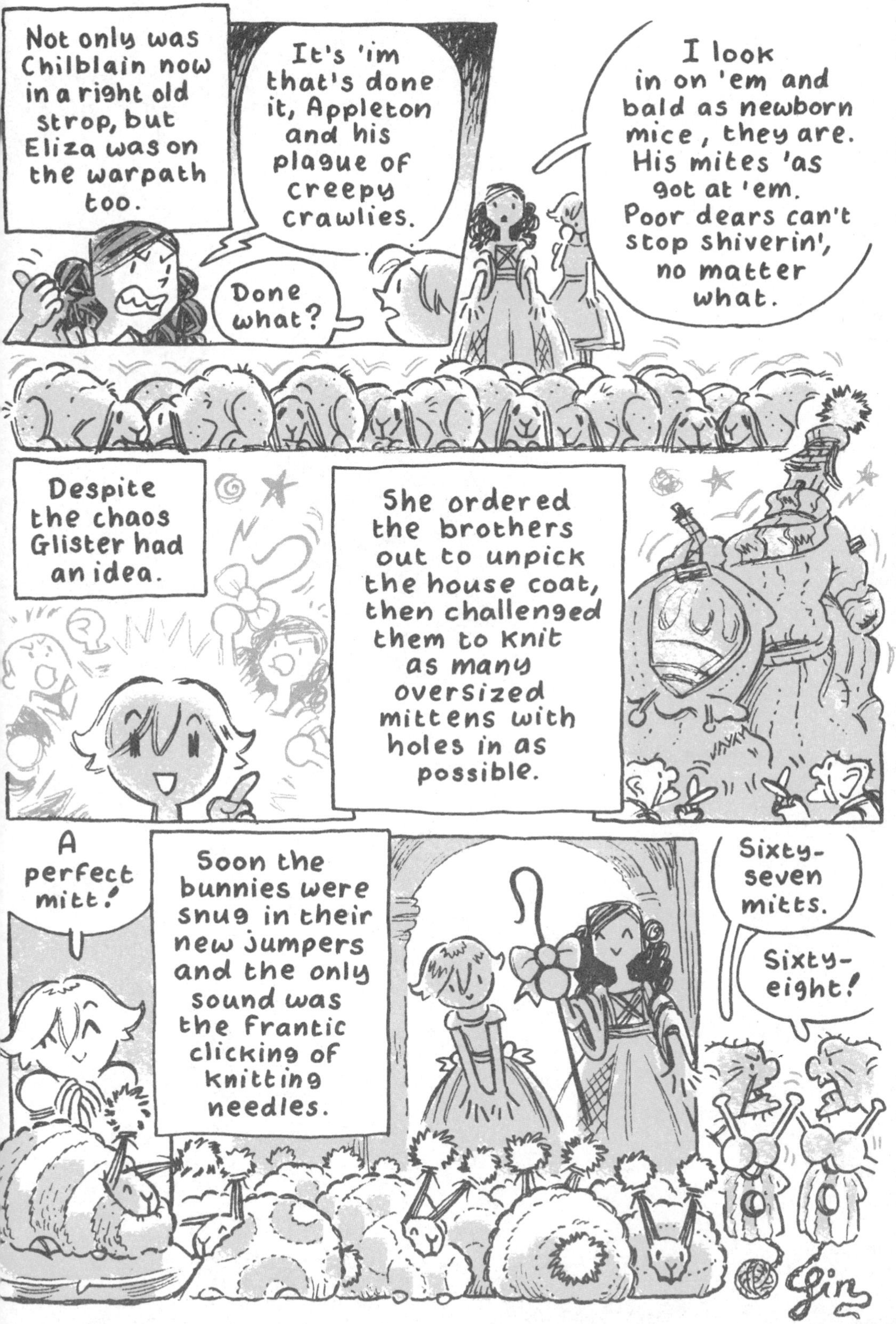
Not only was Chilblain now in a right old strop, but Eliza was on the warpath too.
It's 'im that's done it, Appleton and his plague of creepy crawlies.
Done what?
I look in on 'em and bald as newborn mice, they are. His mites 'as got at 'em. Poor dears can't stop shiverin', no matter what.
Despite the chaos Glister had an idea.
She ordered the brothers out to unpick the house coat, then challenged them to knit as many oversized mittens with holes in as possible.
A perfect mitt!
Soon the bunnies were snug in their new jumpers and the only sound was the frantic clicking of knitting needles.
Sixty-seven mitts.
Sixty-eight!
Gin

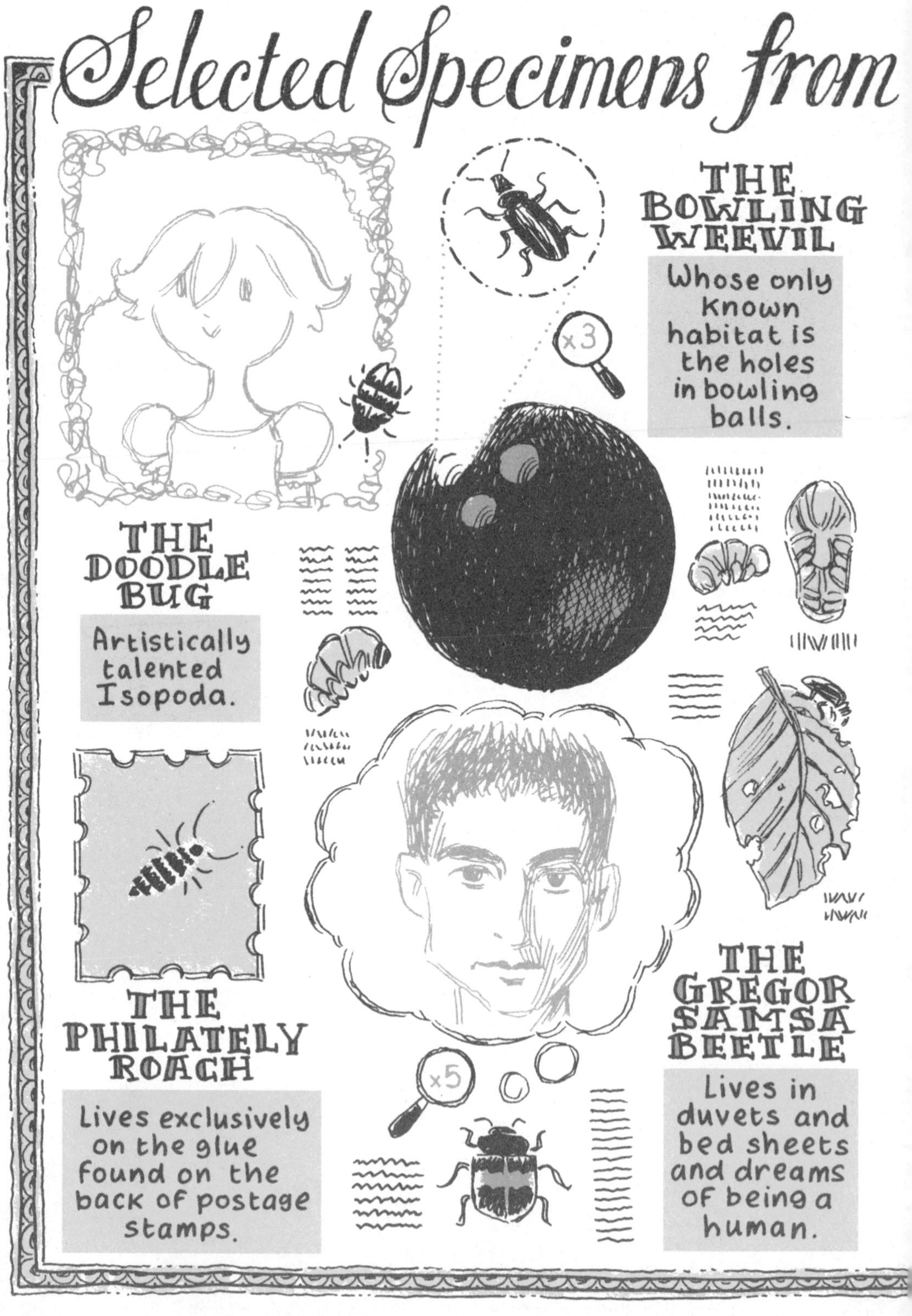
Selected Specimens from
THE BOWLING WEEVIL
Whose only known habitat is the holes in bowling balls.
x3
THE DOODLE BUG
Artistically talented Isopoda.
THE PHILATELY ROACH
Lives exclusively on the glue found on the back of postage stamps.
x5
THE GREGOR SAMSA BEETLE
Lives in duvets and bed sheets and dreams of being a human.

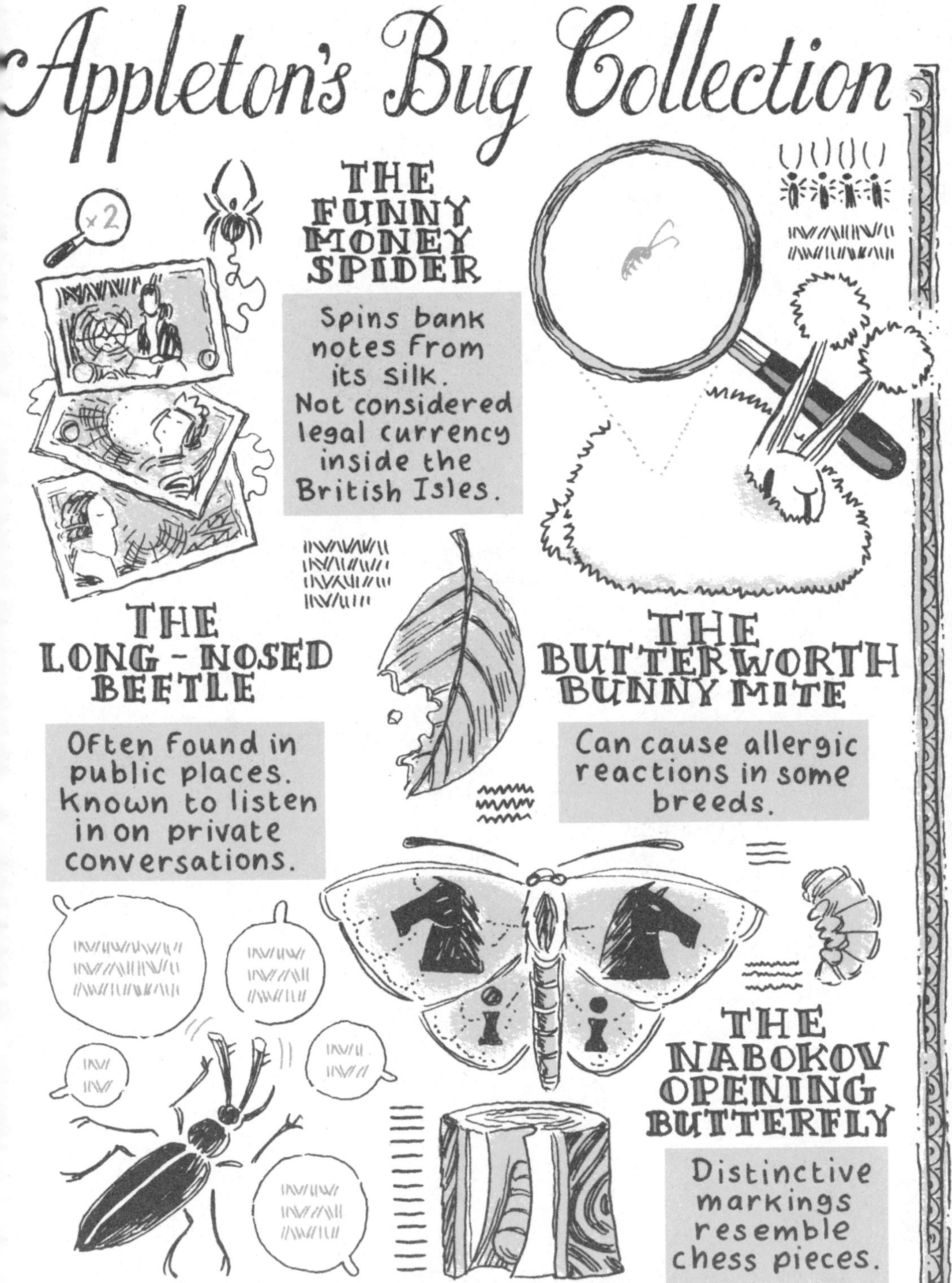
Appleton's Bug Collection
x2
THE FUNNY MONEY SPIDER
Spins bank notes from its silk. Not considered legal currency inside the British Isles.
THE LONG-NOSED BEETLE
Often found in public places. Known to listen in on private conversations.
THE BUTTERWORTH BUNNY MITE
Can cause allergic reactions in some breeds.
THE NABOKOV OPENING BUTTERFLY
Distinctive markings resemble chess pieces.

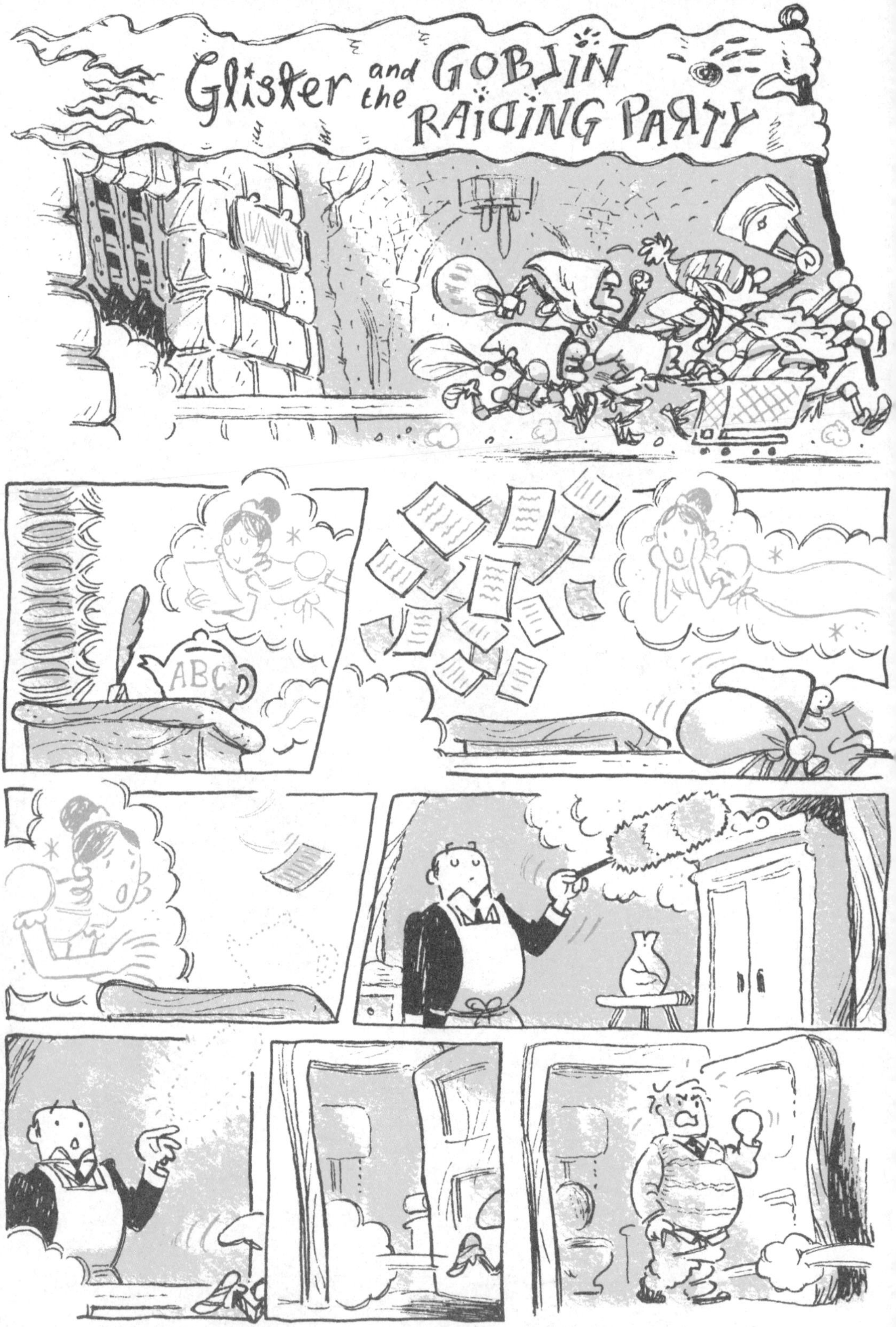
Glister and the GOBLIN RAIDING PARTY
ABC

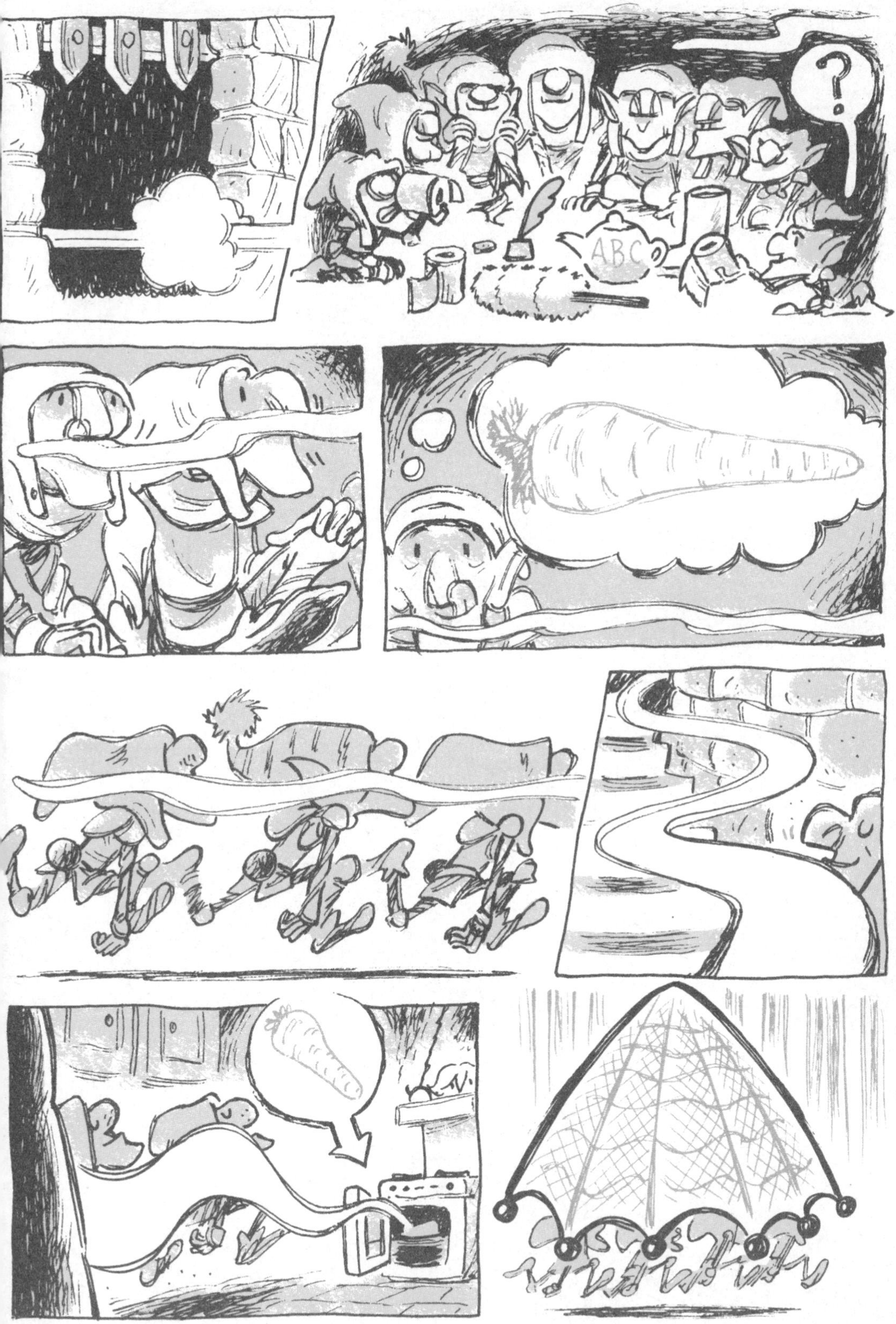
?
ABC

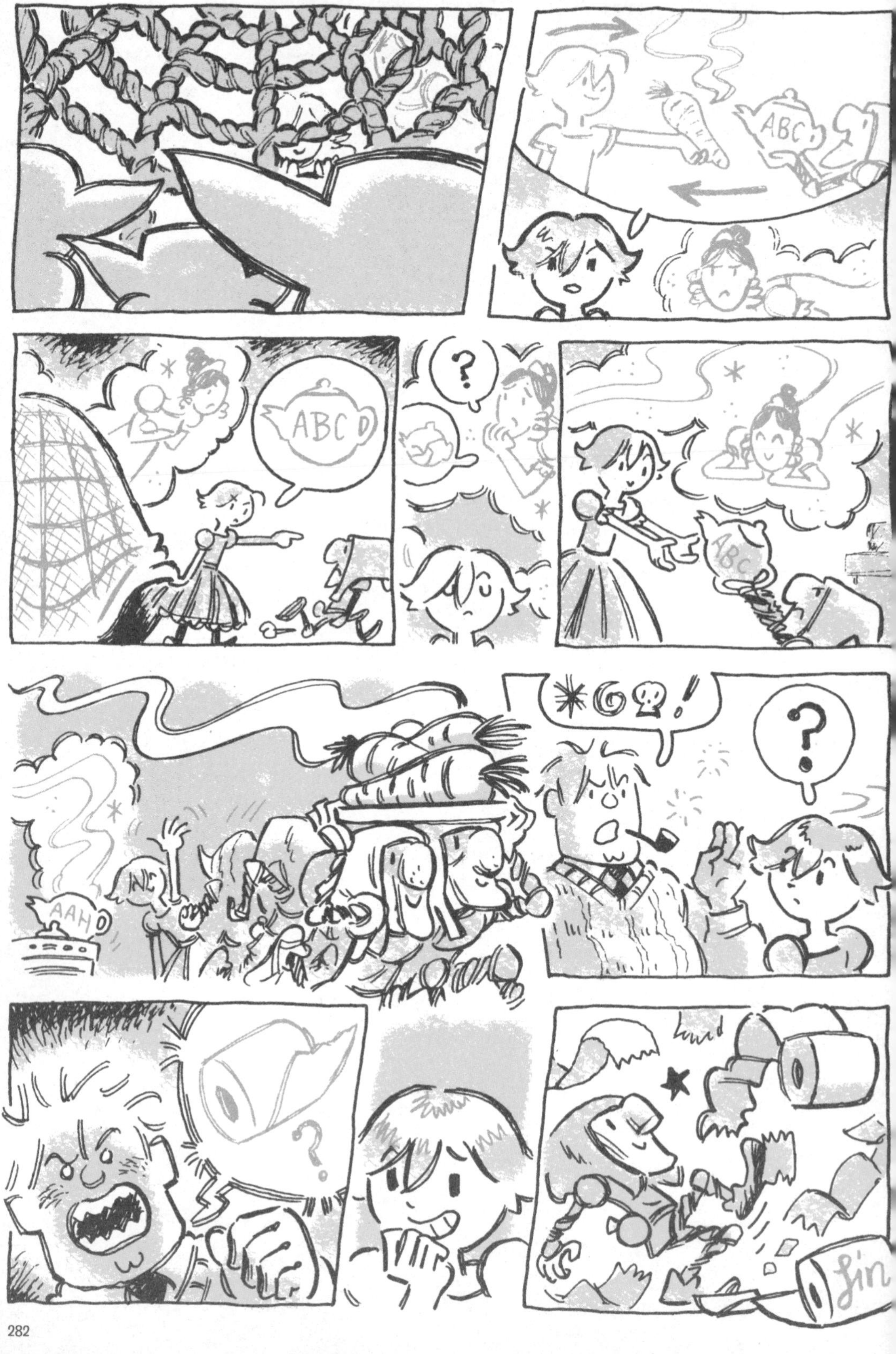
ABC
ABC D
?
ABC
?
AAH
?

Chilblain Hall and the Sunday Painters

One day, not so long ago, there was much excitement at Chilblain Hall. Laurence Sunday had chosen the ancient pile to be the subject of a painting master class. Laurence was a very popular watercolorist, a favorite with the ladies of a certain age who were known as his Sunday Painters.

On a perfect day for painting, blue skies above only a smattering of fluffy white clouds, Laurence Sunday made his grand entrance–to the delight of his cooing and adoring fans.

The charming and unflappable painter had the crowd's full attention as he expertly sketched Chilblain Hall. He briefly turned his back on Chilblain to address the ladies.

"One must delight in the details–take the crooked tower, for instance," Laurence suggested.

Chilblain instantly became self-conscious about its crooked tower, and when Laurence turned back, he was shocked to see the tower was now straight. Confused but determined, he began applying the first washes of color.

"Pay particular attention to the composition," Laurence instructed.

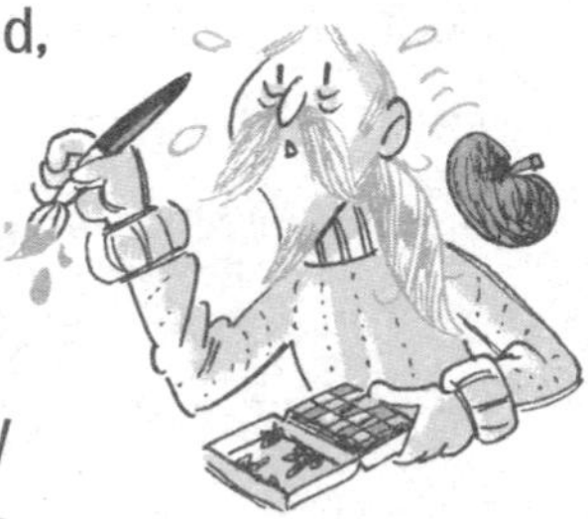

The sun dipped behind a small cloud, leaving Chilblain in the shade. The hall shuffled itself over to be back in the light. When Laurence glanced up from his work, Chilblain was partly obscured from his view by a tree. The painter's eyes grew wide in surprise. He sipped from his painting water by mistake, mopped his brow, and hurriedly explained how darker colors could be used to cover mistakes. He quickly daubed a tree into the foreground of his painting.

By now the cloud that had obscured Chilblain had passed over, but another one was threatening to come between the hall and the sun. Chilblain scooted back to its original position. When Laurence looked up again, there was no longer a tree between him and the old building. Beginning to lose his cool, he stood up and angrily addressed the crowd.

"Is this some form of juvenile prank?" he demanded, reddening in the face.

Recovering himself, Laurence sat back at his easel, intending to quickly finish the picture and enjoy a long lie-down. Chilblain could stand it no longer. Itching with curiosity, it hopped forward to get a look at the painting. Laurence frowned at the long shadow that was suddenly cast over his work. He looked up slowly and saw the tower of Chilblain Hall leaning at a dangerous angle, almost on top of him. Laurence jumped out of his seat in shock, knocking his water, pigments, and brushes all over himself and his painting. The painter and his followers scrambled away in panic, leaving the remains of the painting behind for Chilblain Hall to admire.

ACTIVITIES

Grab your closest adult and have them help you with Glister's fun activities and crafts!

GLISTER BISCUITS

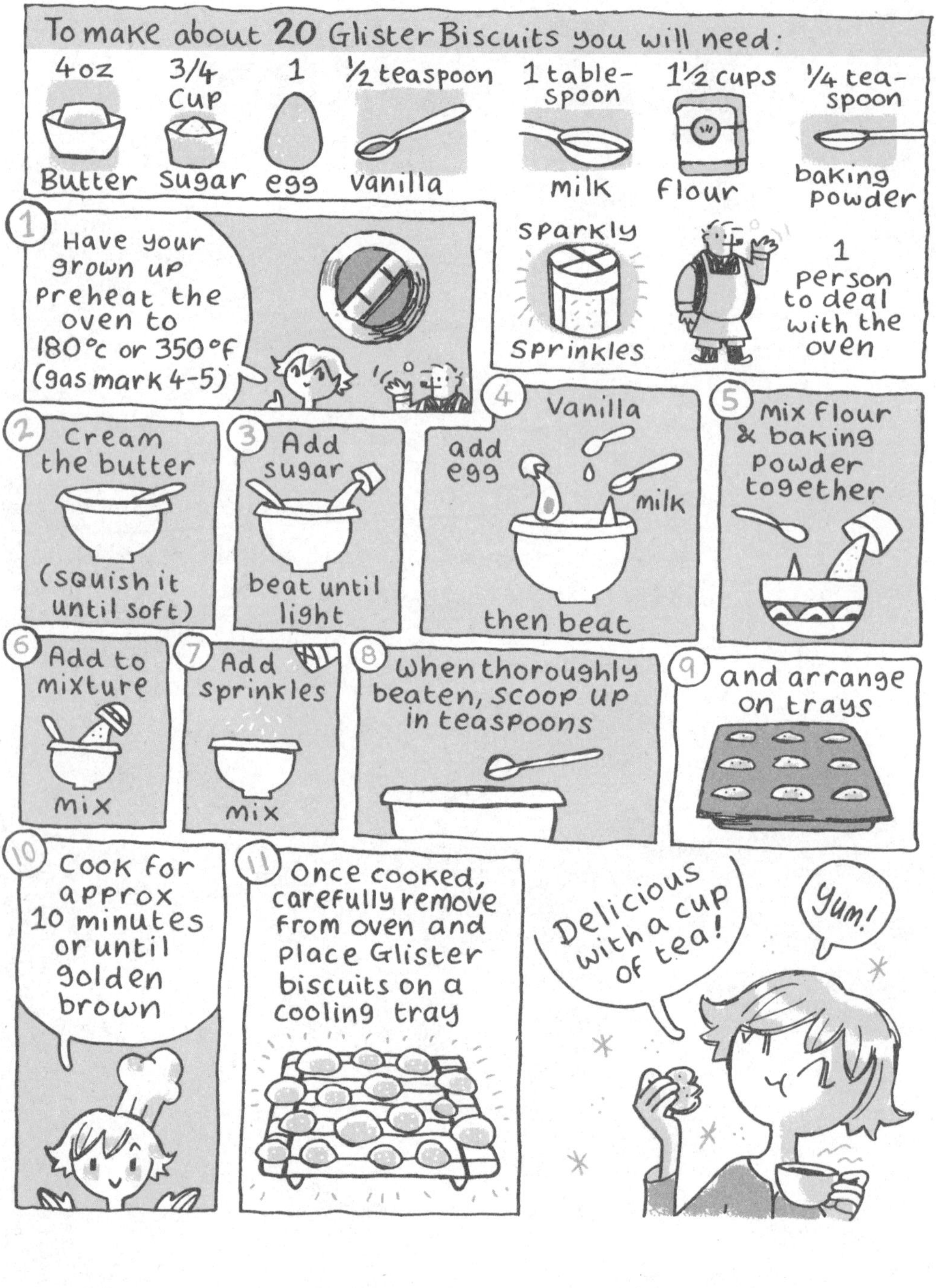

To make about 20 Glister Biscuits you will need:
4oz Butter
3/4 Cup Sugar
1 egg
½ teaspoon vanilla
1 tablespoon milk
1½ cups flour
1/4 teaspoon baking powder
sparkly sprinkles
1 person to deal with the oven
1 Have your grown up preheat the oven to 180°c or 350°f (gas mark 4-5)
2 Cream the butter (squish it until soft)
3 Add sugar beat until light
4 Vanilla add egg milk then beat
5 Mix flour & baking powder together
6 Add to mixture mix
7 Add sprinkles mix
8 When thoroughly beaten, scoop up in teaspoons
9 and arrange on trays
10 Cook for approx 10 minutes or until golden brown
11 Once cooked, carefully remove from oven and place Glister biscuits on a cooling tray
Delicious with a cup of tea!
Yum!

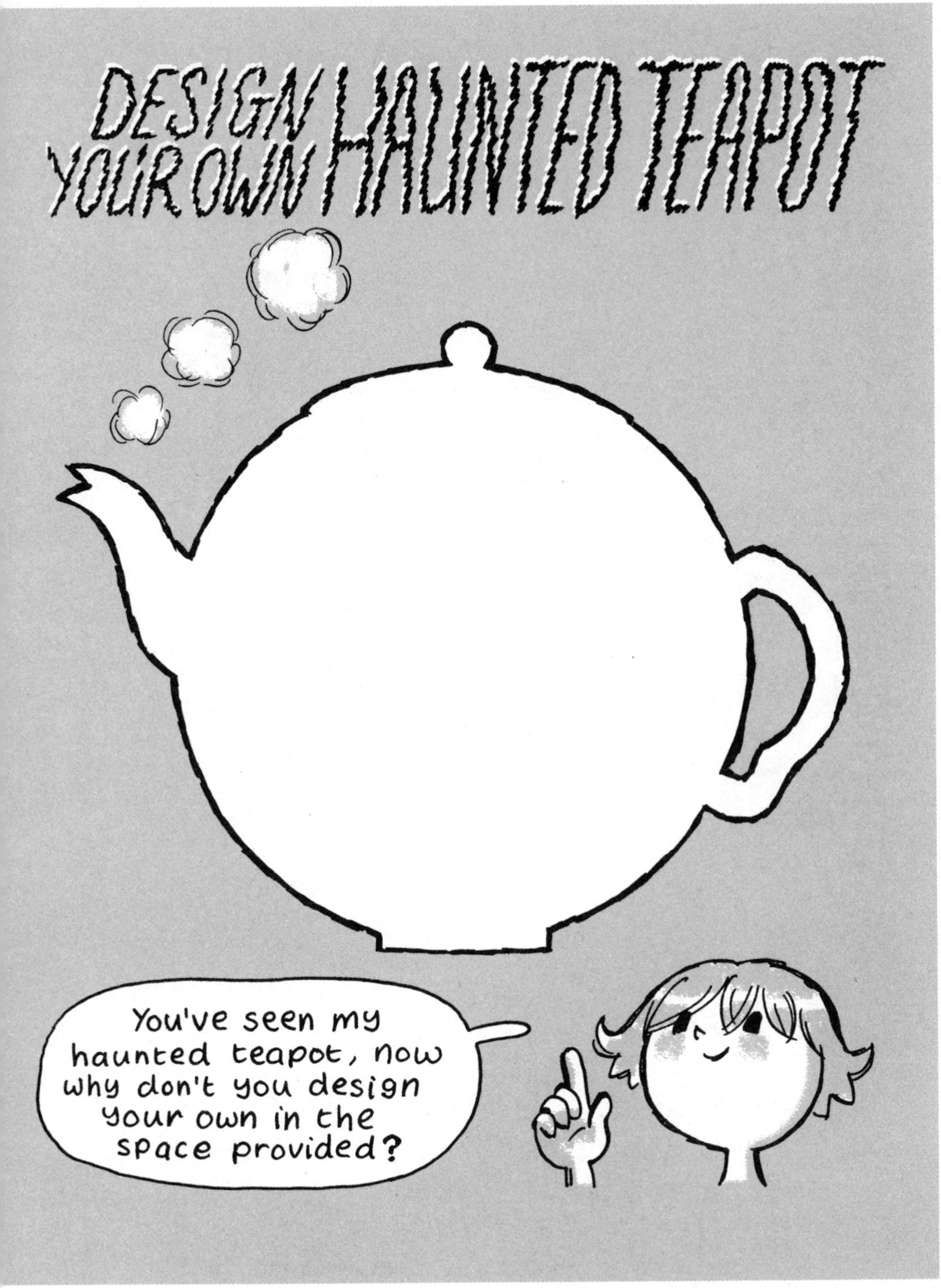
DESIGN YOUR OWN HAUNTED TEAPOT
You've seen my haunted teapot, now why don't you design your own in the space provided?

Glister: THE HAUNTED TEAPOT
*******WORDSEARCH*******

```
I V J E L M P P X D B
N G G L I S T E R T O
K H W J Q U L R M P O
B A T M A L B E R T K
A U Z H E H J H A D L
R N C H I L B L A I N
R T I W T G H O S T D
O E T E A P O T S H R
W D S N C R P L G T O
B U T T E R W O R T H
V O P W I L K E S Q J
```

GLISTER

BUTTERWORTH

BOOK

ALBERT

CHILBLAIN

INKBARROW

GHOST

WILKES

TEAPOT

HAUNTED

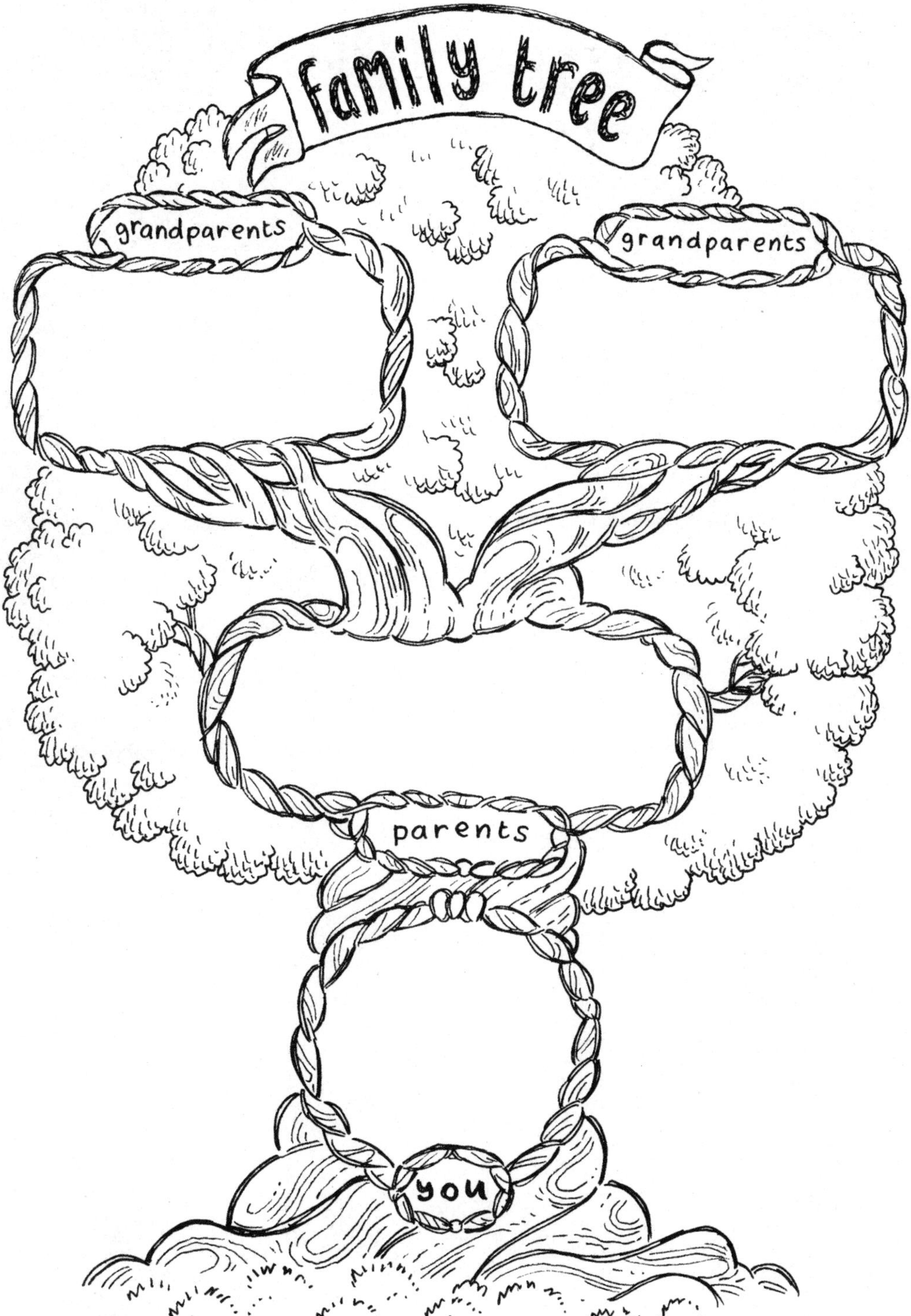
family tree
grandparents
grandparents
parents
you

Glister TIC TAC TOE

The Toll Troll has taken over Chilblain Hall.
Get three in a row to win it back.

1. Print onto card
2. Cut out pieces
3. Choose a side
4. Get 3 in a row to win

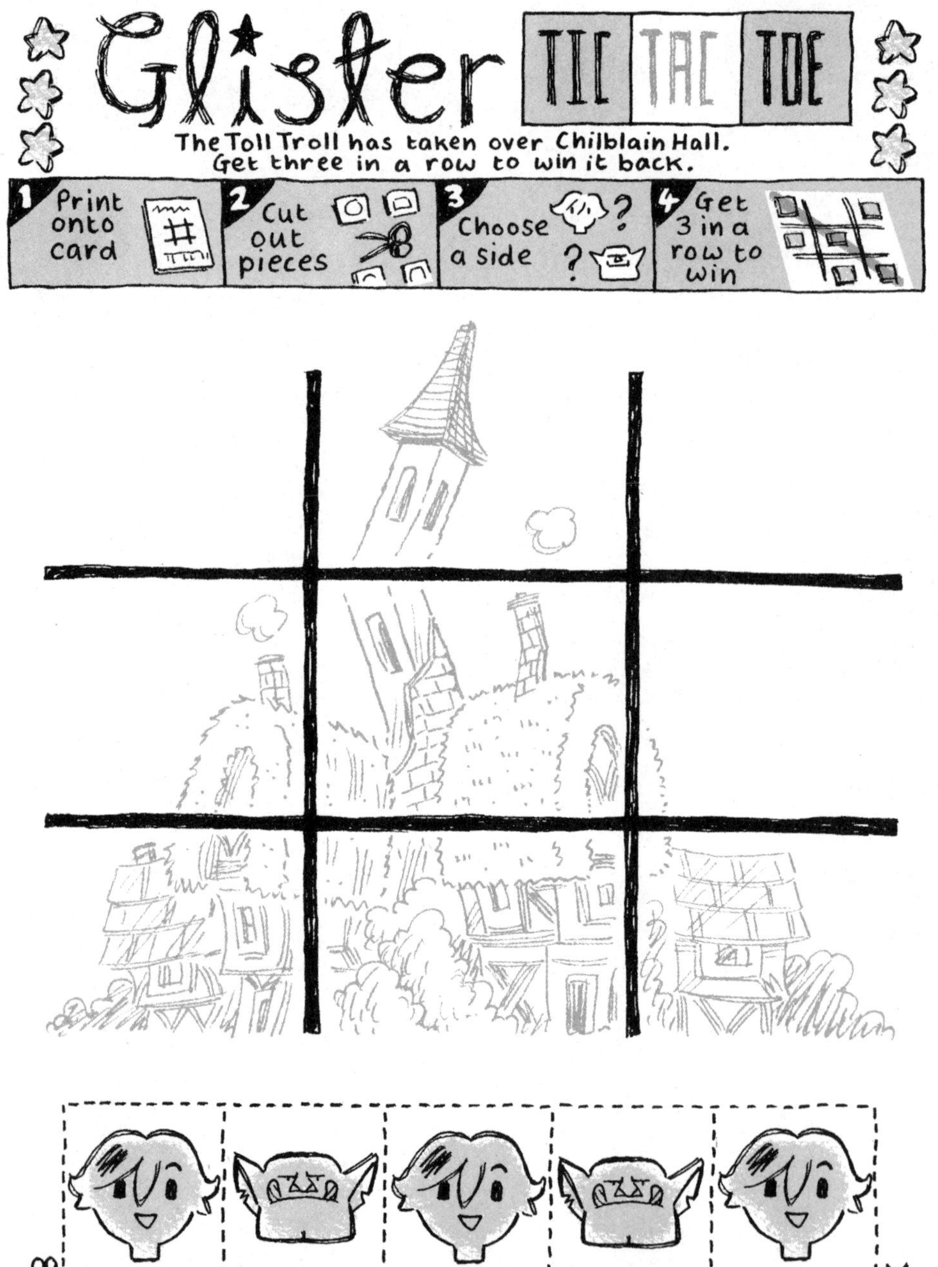

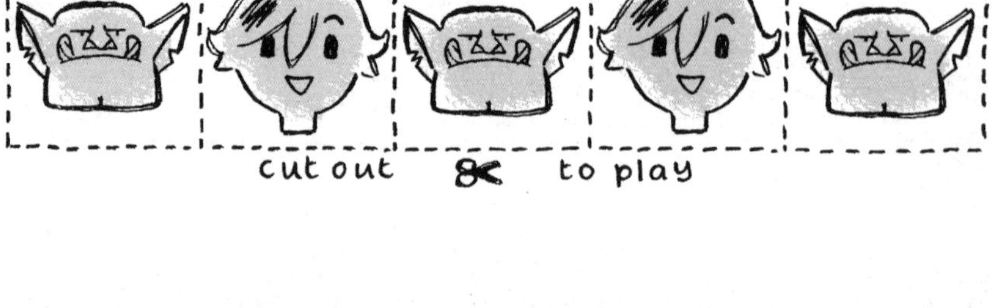

cut out ✂ to play

Glister Skittles

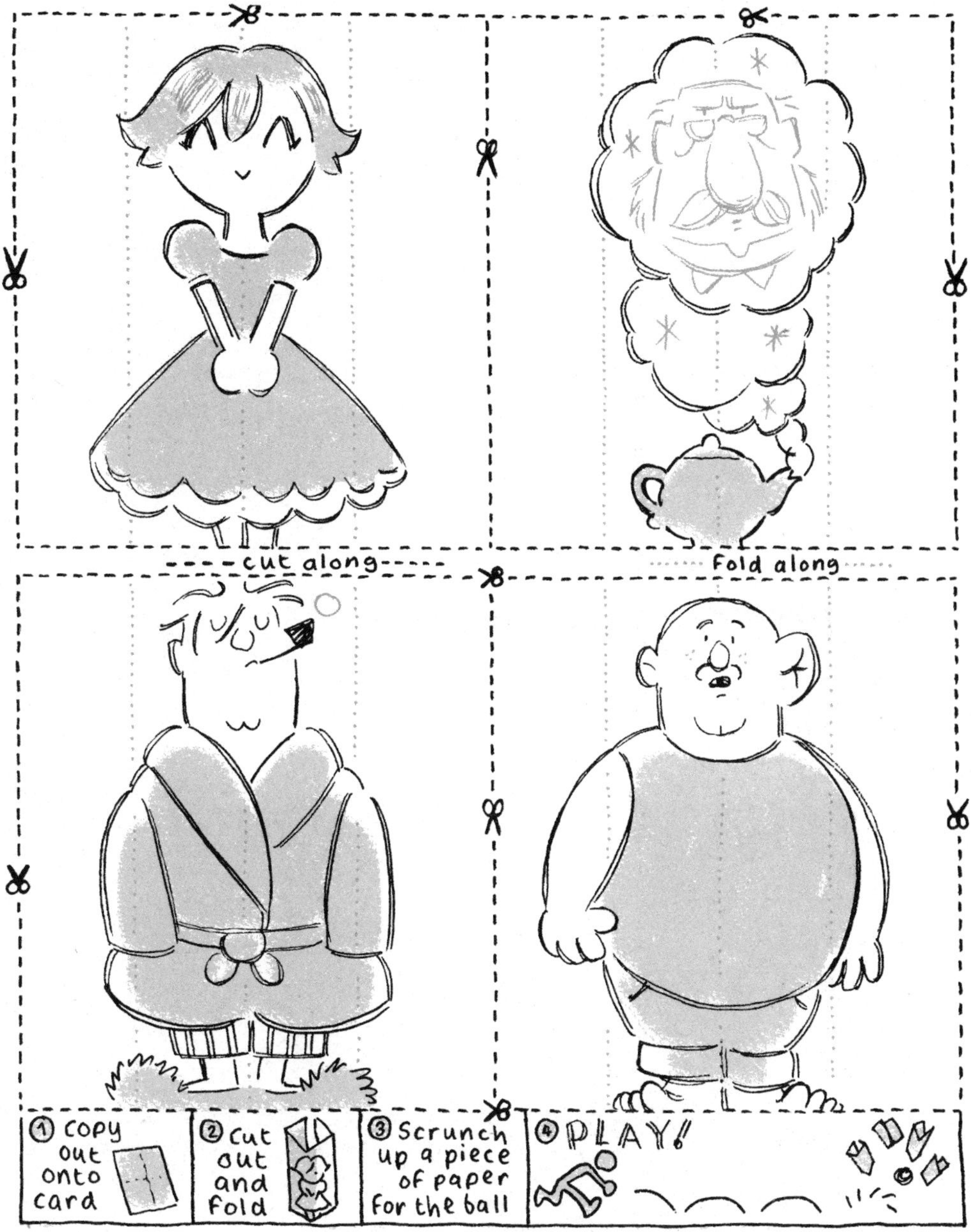
cut along
Fold along
① copy out onto card
② Cut out and Fold
③ Scrunch up a piece of paper for the ball
④ PLAY!

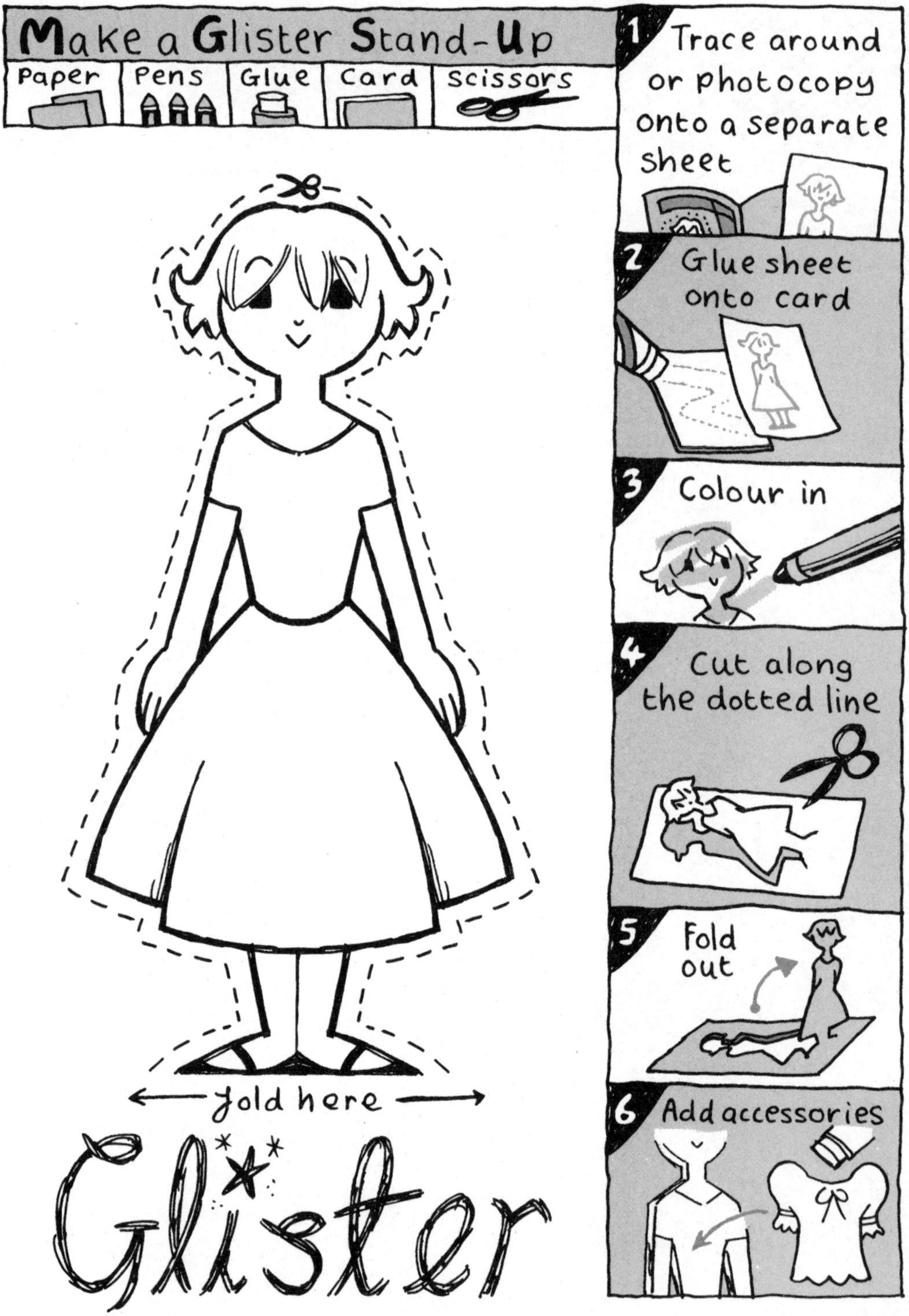

Make a Glister Stand-Up
Paper
Pens
Glue
Card
Scissors
1 Trace around or photocopy onto a separate sheet
2 Glue sheet onto card
3 Colour in
4 Cut along the dotted line
5 Fold out
6 Add accessories
fold here
Glister

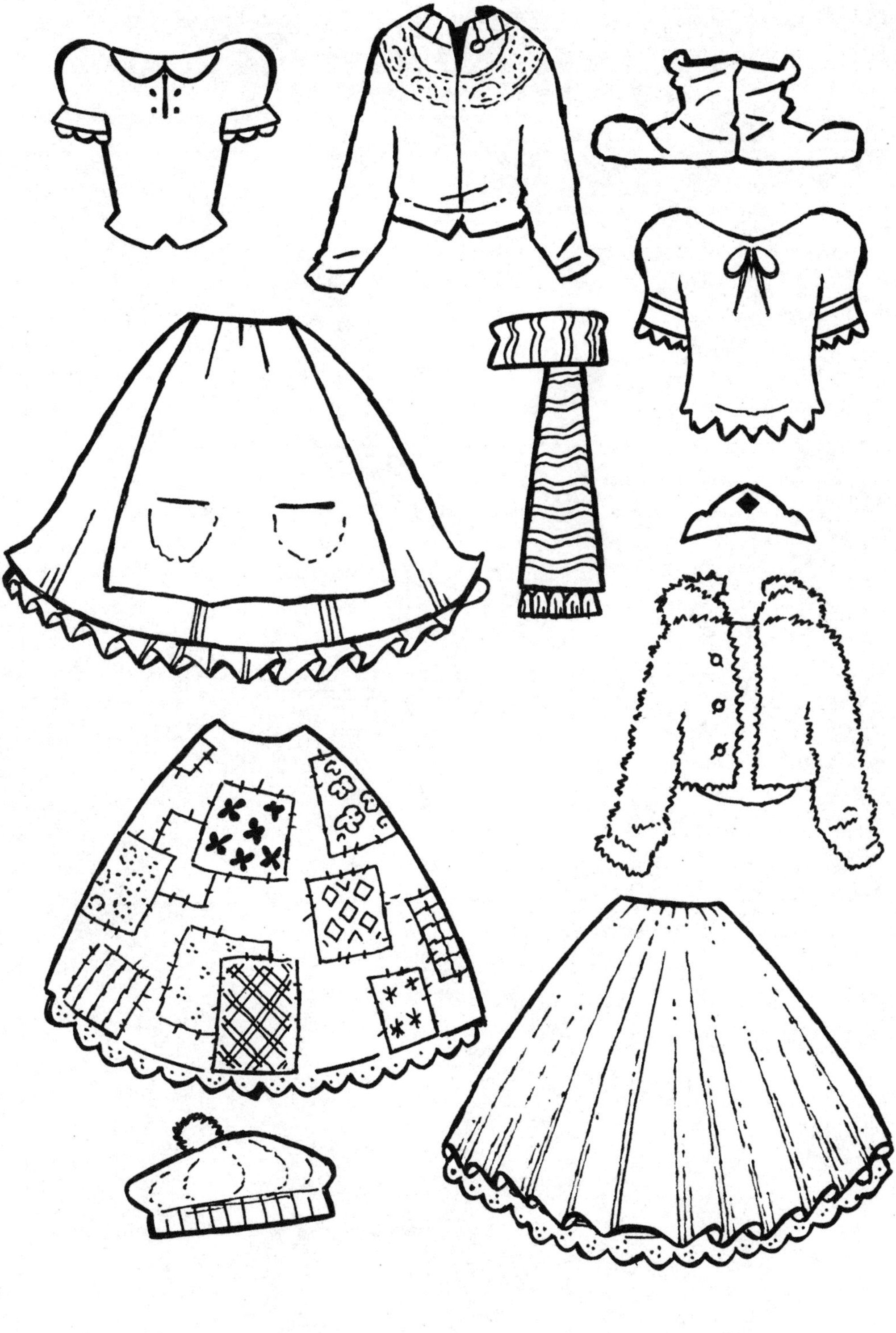

GLISTER FLICKERS

paper	pens	glue	card	scissors

1 Trace around the flicker or photocopy onto a separate sheet of paper

2 Glue sheet onto card

3 Colour in!

4 Cut along the dotted lines

5 Fold down the arms & legs making sure they are of equal length

HOW TO PLAY

1 PLAYER 1 flick into air

2 Score according to how the figure lands

3 PLAYER 2's turn to flick

4 First player to score a total of 200 points wins.

SCORING

5 pts BACK

10 pts FRONT

15 pts HEAD STAND

25 pts SIDE STAND

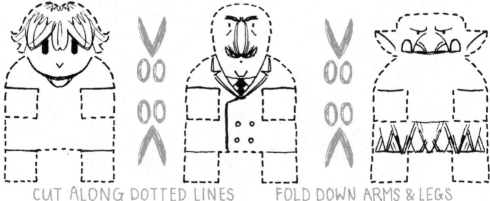

CUT ALONG DOTTED LINES   FOLD DOWN ARMS & LEGS

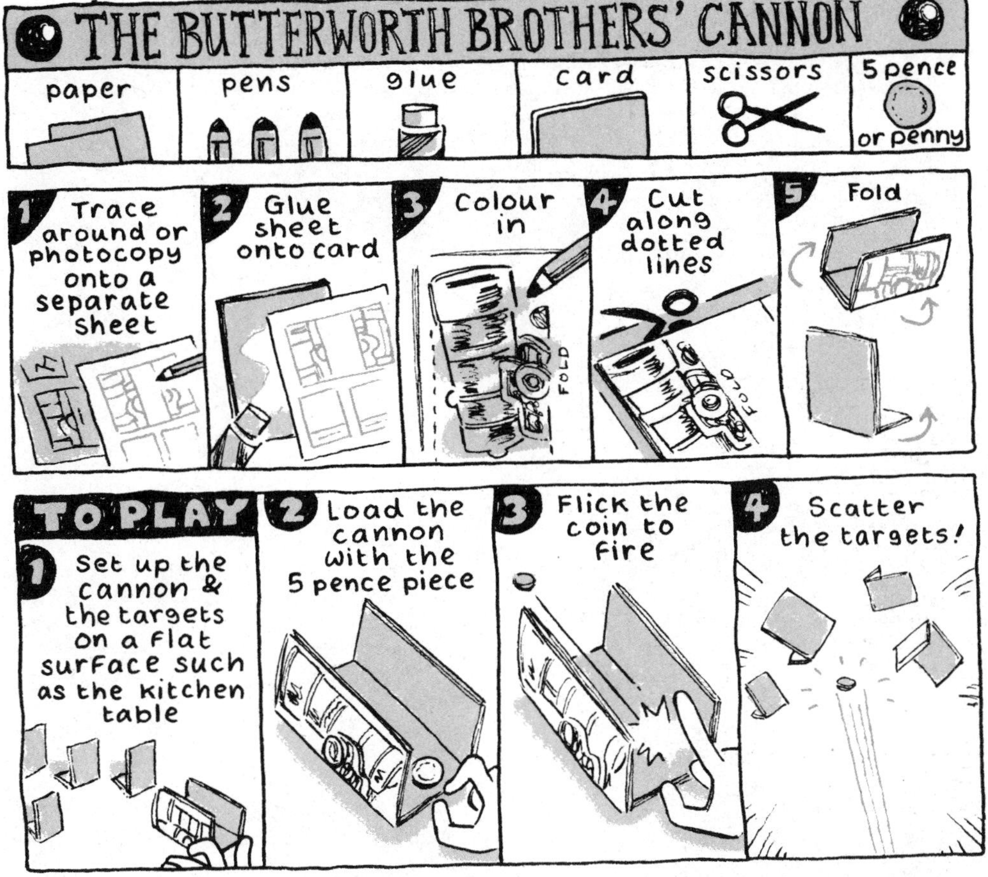
THE BUTTERWORTH BROTHERS' CANNON
paper
pens
glue
card
scissors
5 pence or penny
1 Trace around or photocopy onto a separate sheet
2 Glue sheet onto card
3 Colour in
FOLD
4 Cut along dotted lines
FOLD
5 Fold
TO PLAY
1 Set up the cannon & the targets on a flat surface such as the kitchen table
2 Load the cannon with the 5 pence piece
3 Flick the coin to fire
4 Scatter the targets!

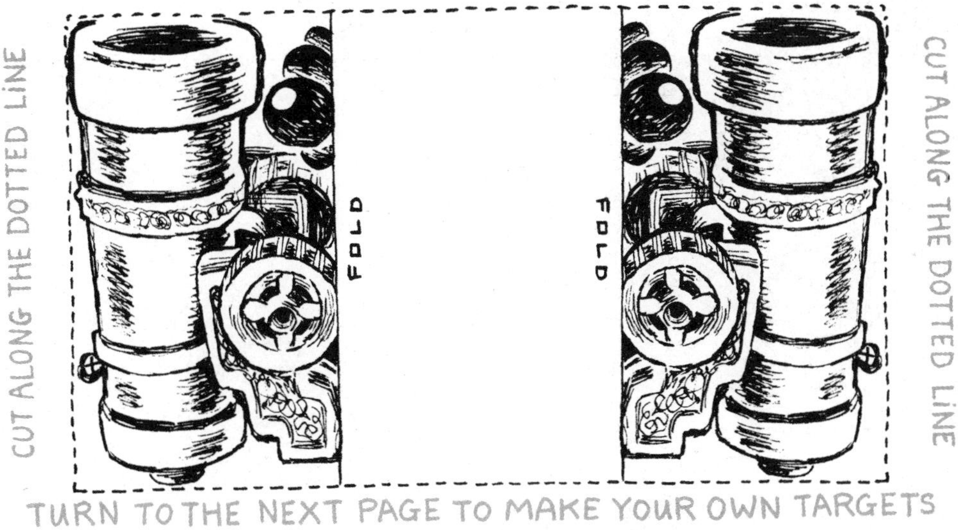
CUT ALONG THE DOTTED LINE
FOLD
FOLD
CUT ALONG THE DOTTED LINE

TURN TO THE NEXT PAGE TO MAKE YOUR OWN TARGETS

CUT OUT, FOLD AND STAND THE TARGETS. TRY AND KNOCK THEM OVER USING THE CANNON

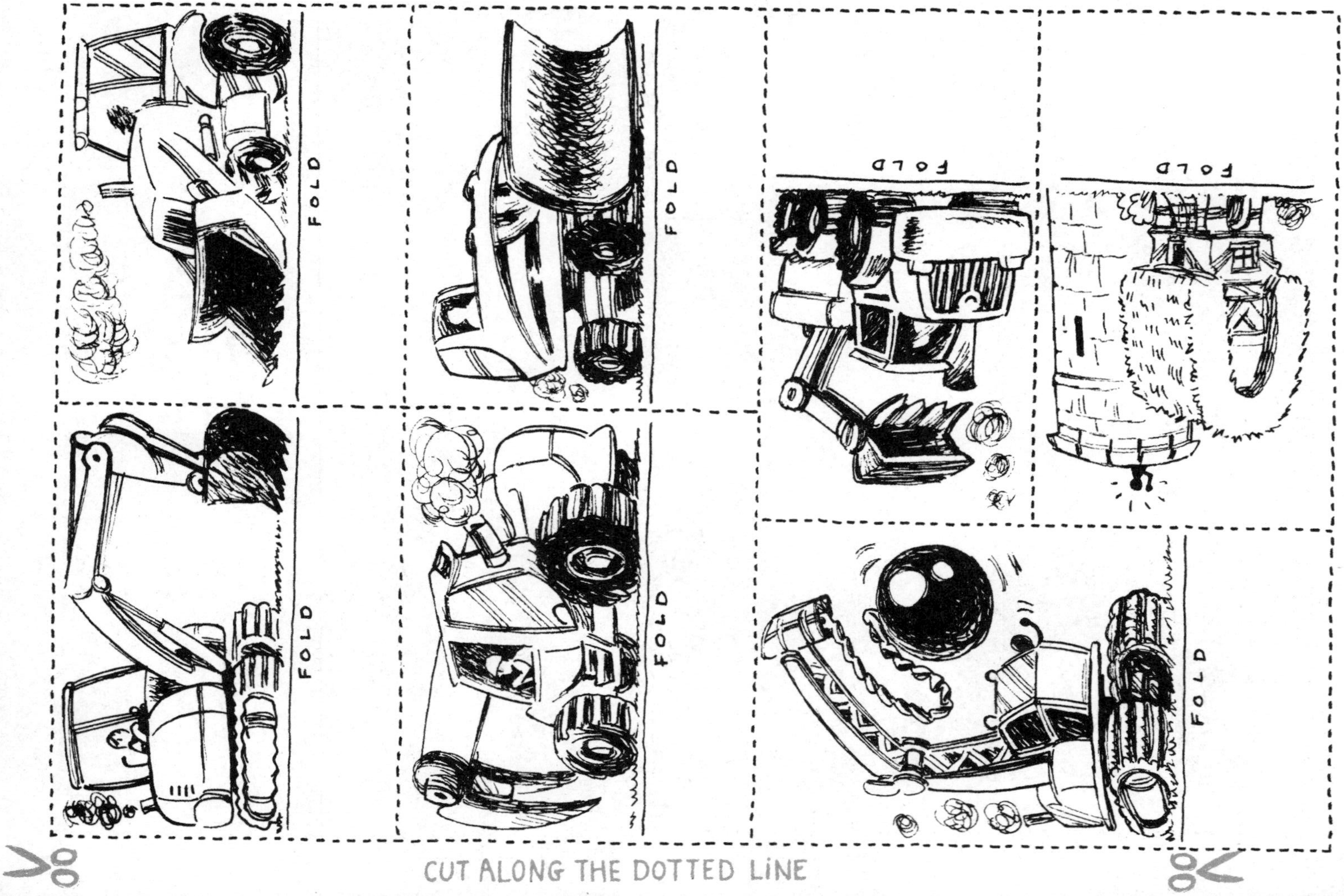
FOLD
FOLD
FOLD
FOLD
FOLD
FOLD
FOLD

CUT ALONG THE DOTTED LINE

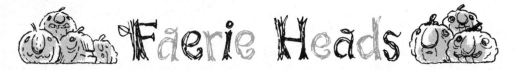

Faerie Heads

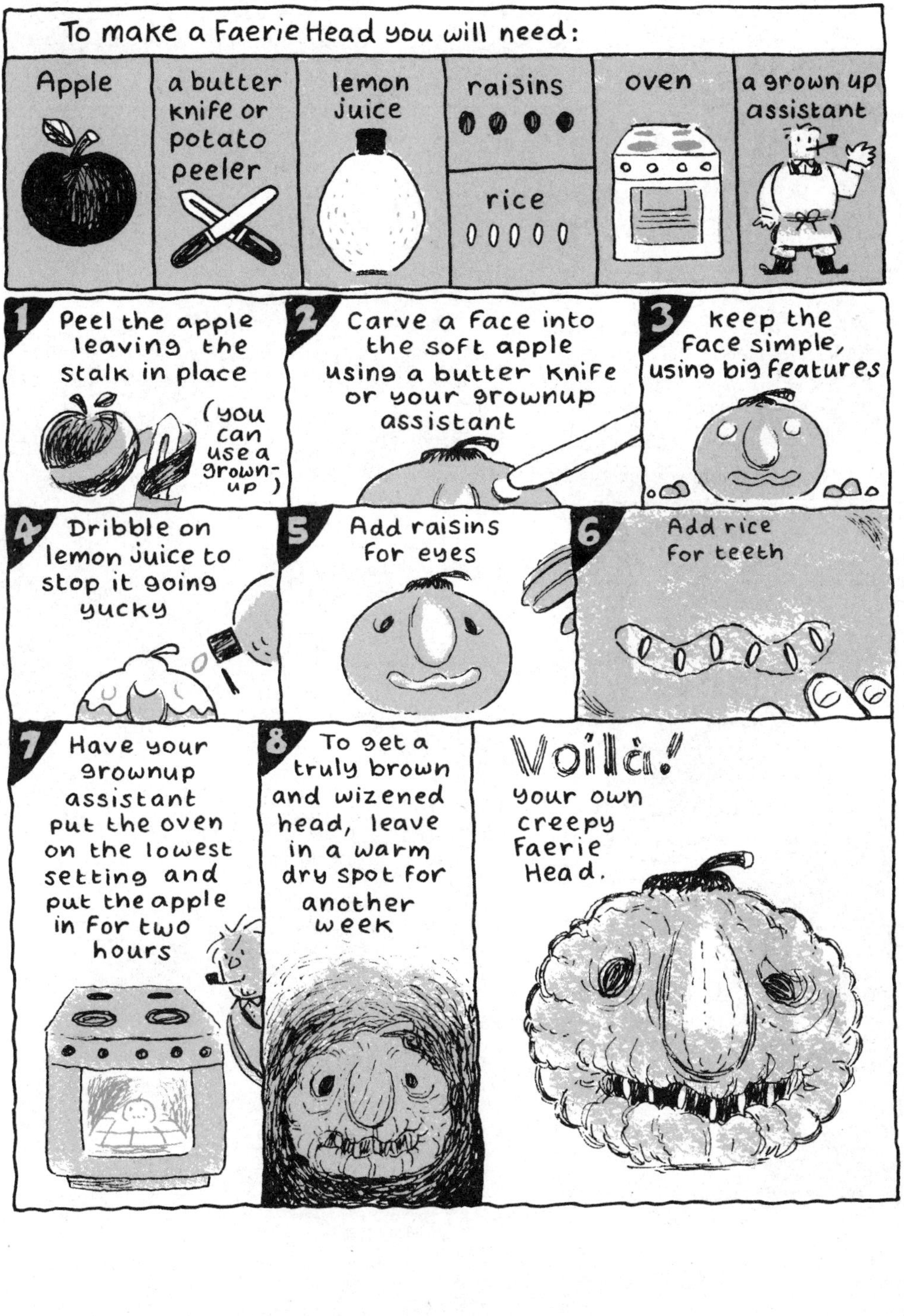

To make a Faerie Head you will need:
Apple
a butter knife or potato peeler
lemon juice
raisins
rice
oven
a grown up assistant
1 Peel the apple leaving the stalk in place
(you can use a grown-up)
2 Carve a face into the soft apple using a butter knife or your grownup assistant
3 keep the face simple, using big features
4 Dribble on lemon juice to stop it going yucky
5 Add raisins for eyes
6 Add rice for teeth
7 Have your grownup assistant put the oven on the lowest setting and put the apple in for two hours
8 To get a truly brown and wizened head, leave in a warm dry spot for another week
Voilà!
your own creepy Faerie Head.

Glister's GUIDE to ILLUSTRATION

1 DRAW, DRAW & DRAW SOME MORE

Get used to carrying a small sketchbook or notebook with you. Then you'll always have somewhere to scribble down ideas before you forget them, make notes, doodle and sketch.

Be prepared

2 Read, read & read some more

Illustration is telling stories with pictures. The words and images work together to bring a story to life. While writing or reading a book, poem or story try and imagine what kind of pictures would go with the words. When you have an idea make a note of it in your sketchbook.

3 Use some of your own writing or borrow a book from the library

Pick out scenes or images from the writing and make your own illustrations to go with it. If you're using a book from the library then pick one that doesn't have any pictures. That way the illustrations won't get in the way of your own ideas.

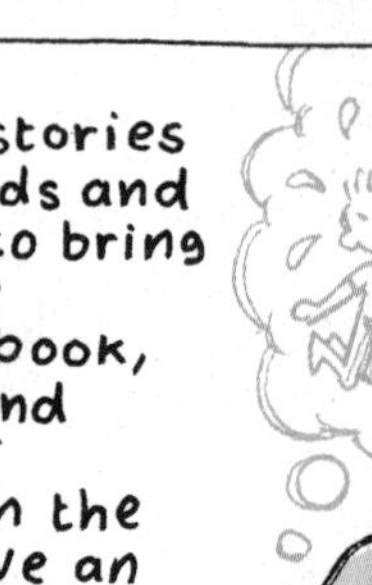

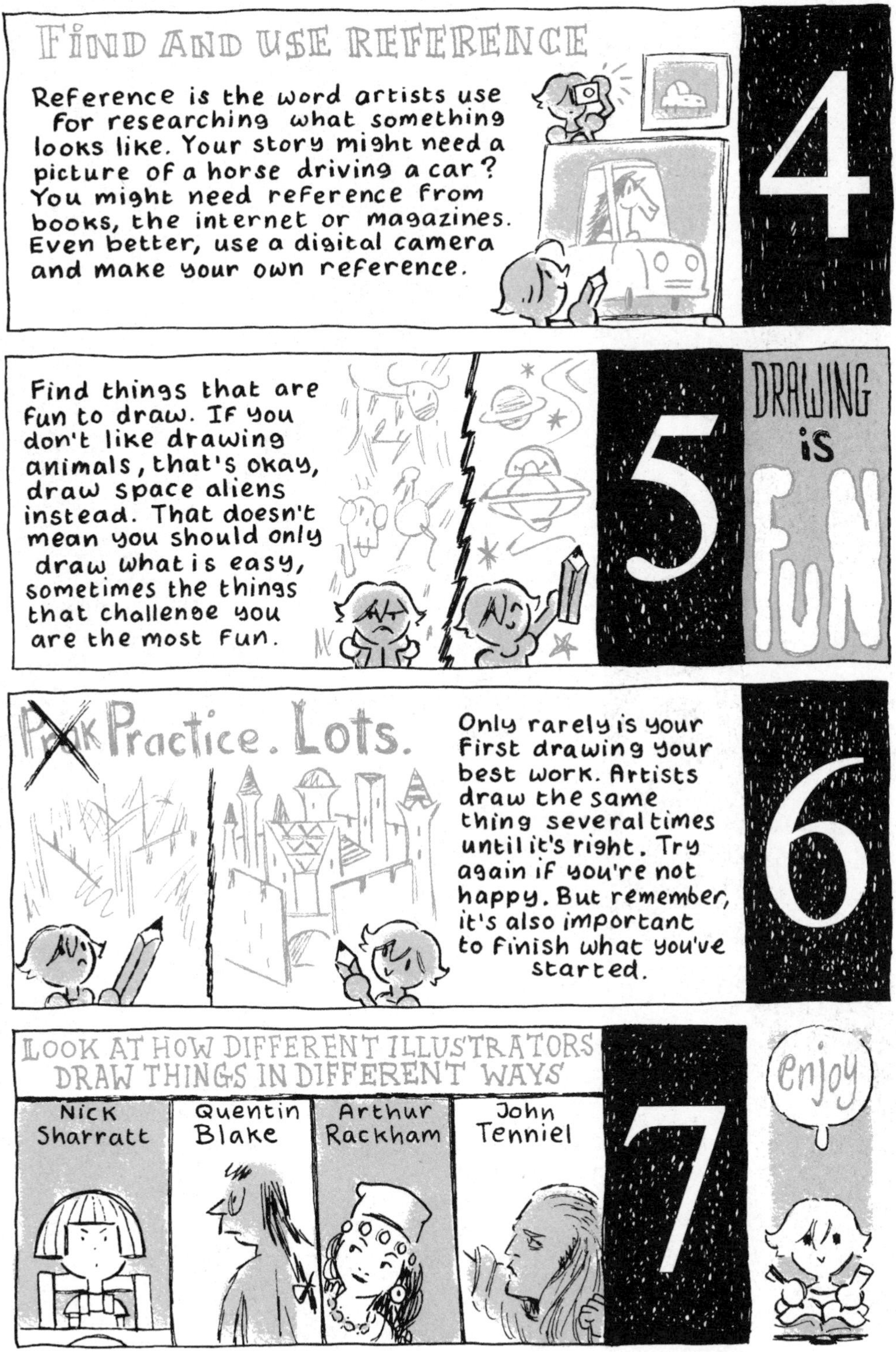
FIND AND USE REFERENCE
Reference is the word artists use for researching what something looks like. Your story might need a picture of a horse driving a car? You might need reference from books, the internet or magazines. Even better, use a digital camera and make your own reference.
4
Find things that are fun to draw. If you don't like drawing animals, that's okay, draw space aliens instead. That doesn't mean you should only draw what is easy, sometimes the things that challenge you are the most fun.
5
DRAWING is FUN
Prak Practice. Lots.
Only rarely is your first drawing your best work. Artists draw the same thing several times until it's right. Try again if you're not happy. But remember, it's also important to finish what you've started.
6
LOOK AT HOW DIFFERENT ILLUSTRATORS DRAW THINGS IN DIFFERENT WAYS
Nick Sharratt
Quentin Blake
Arthur Rackham
John Tenniel
7
enjoy

With special thanks to
ERIC STEPHENSON and **LIZZIE SITTON**

Andi Watson is a British cartoonist, writer, and illustrator who has been nominated for two Eisners, a Harvey, and a British Comic Award. He lives in Worcester with his wife and daughter.

MORE TITLES FOR YOUNGER READERS!

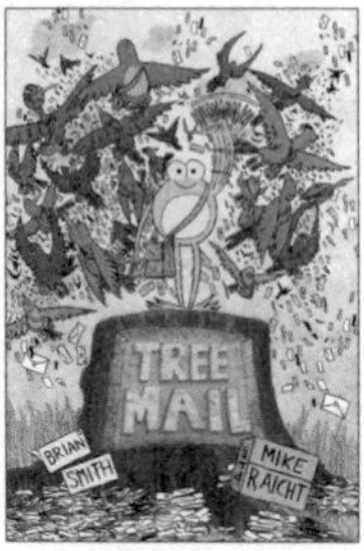
TREE MAIL
BRIAN SMITH
MIKE RAICHT

TREE MAIL
MIKE RAICHT, BRIAN SMITH
Rudy–a determined frog–hopes to overcome the odds and land his dream job delivering mail to the other animals on Popomoko Island! Rudy always hops forward, no matter what obstacle seems to be in the way of his dreams!

Grade level: 3–7 $12.99 ISBN 978-1-50670-096-0

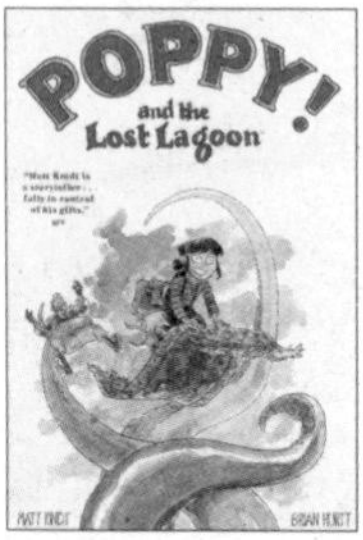
POPPY!
and the
Lost Lagoon
MATT KINDT
BRIAN HURTT

POPPY! AND THE LOST LAGOON
MATT KINDT, BRIAN HURTT
At the age of ten, Poppy Pepperton is the greatest explorer since her grandfather Pappy! When a shrunken mummy head speaks, adventure calls Poppy and her sidekick/guardian, Colt Winchester, across the globe in search of an exotic fish–along the way discovering clues to what happened to Pappy all those years ago!

Grade level: 3–7 $14.99 ISBN 978-1-61655-943-4

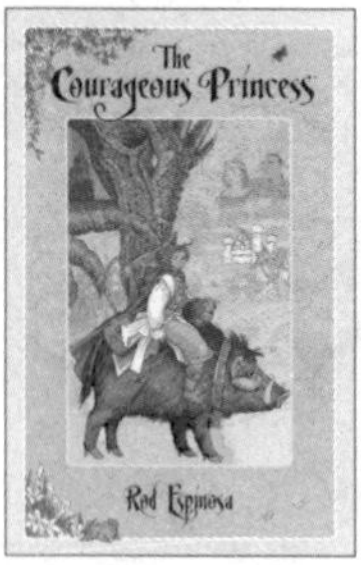
The
Courageous Princess
Rod Espinosa

THE COURAGEOUS PRINCESS
ROD ESPINOSA
Once upon a time, a greedy dragon kidnapped a beloved princess . . . But if you think she just waited around for some charming prince to rescue her, then you're in for a surprise! Princess Mabelrose has enough brains and bravery to fend for herself!

Grade level: 3–7 $19.99 each
Volume 1: Beyond the Hundred Kingdoms
ISBN 978-1-61655-722-5
Volume 2: The Unremembered Lands
ISBN 978-1-61655-723-2
Volume 3: The Dragon Queen
ISBN 978-1-61655-724-9

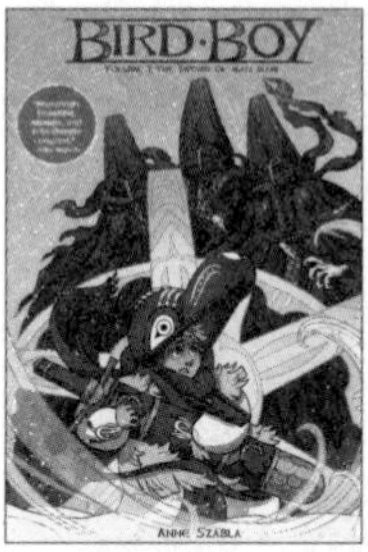
BIRD·BOY
ANNE SZABLA

BIRD BOY
ANNE SZABLA
Bali, a ten-year-old boy, is desperate to prove his worth to his northern tribe despite his small stature. Banned from the ceremony that would make him an adult in the eyes of his people, he takes matters into his own hands. To prove that he is capable of taking care of himself, he sets out into the forbidden forest and stumbles upon a legendary weapon. Bali fights his way across a dangerous land of gods, men, and beasts to keep the sword of Mali Mani, the savior of the sun, from the hands of the terrifying Rooks.

Grade level: 4–7 $9.99 each
Volume 1: The Sword of Mali Mani ISBN 978-1-61655-930-4
Volume 2: The Liminal Wood ISBN 978-1-61655-968-7

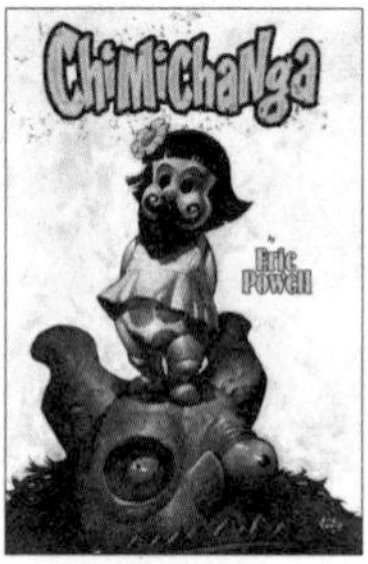
ChiMiChanga
Eric Powell

CHIMICHANGA
ERIC POWELL
When Wrinkle's Traveling Circus's adorable little bearded girl trades a lock of her magic beard hair for a witch's strange egg, she stumbles upon what could be the saving grace for her ailing freak show–the savory-named beast Chimichanga!

Grade level: 5–8 $14.99 each
Volume 1 ISBN 978-1-59582-755-5
Volume 2: The Sorrow of the World's Worst Face!
ISBN 978-1-61655-902-1

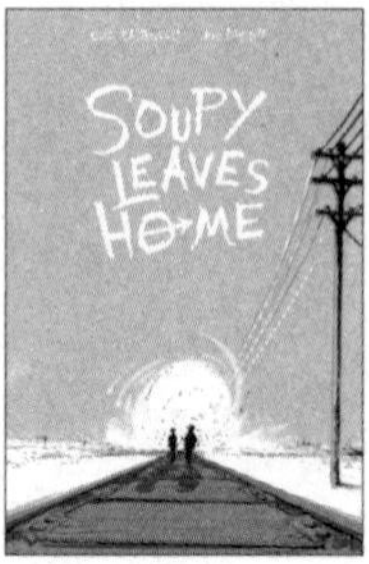
SOUPY
LEAVES
HOME

SOUPY LEAVES HOME
CECIL CASTELLUCCI, JOSE PIMIENTA
Two misfits with no place to call home take a train-hopping journey from the cold heartbreak of their eastern homes to the sunny promise of California in this Depression-era coming-of-age tale.

Grade level: 5–8 $14.99
ISBN 978-1-61655-431-6

DarkHorse.com
AVAILABLE AT YOUR LOCAL COMICS SHOP OR BOOKSTORE. TO FIND A COMICS SHOP IN YOUR AREA, CALL 1-888-266-4226.
For more information or to order direct: On the web: DarkHorse.com Email: mailorder@darkhorse.com
Phone: 1-800-862-0052 Mon.-Fri. 9 AM to 5 PM Pacific Time